# Amazons

## of

## Bluebelle Valley:

### Giantess Collector's Edition

### All Episodes, 1-20

by

## R.B. Greenfield

*All Original Cover Art Included without Titles*

<u>Amazons of Bluebelle Valley: Collector's Edition, All Episodes 1-20</u> presents all of the nineteen-episode series plus the bonus Episode "Amazons in the Burbs", complete in one big volume.  In the specific erotic romantic fantasy genre of amazon mini-giantess and small man, <u>Amazons of Bluebelle Valley</u> stands as a grand and unique achievement.   The hallmarks you can rely on: very well-written, an insightful humorous voice, great characters you will love, and inventive plots loaded with gobs of extreme love-making.   That is why ABBV will appeal to a wide audience and makes a great adult gift.  Be warned: ABBV is an explicit celebration of the dominant Goddess; a joyous ode to voluptuous, tall, gorgeous, and sexy women in the extreme.  All the cover art is presented for your enjoyment without the distracting titles.  Of course this Collector's Edition must be a physically large book, a reminder of how small you are.

Be 21 years old (if not 31) to read the sexually explicit content that permeates these super sexy, XXX-rated, and adult-only adventure stories. This is the Hero's Journey as never seen before, looking up at sexually impossible odds.  Each of the Episodes fulfills the promise to be dependably engaging, heartfelt, clever, humorous, and of course sexually perilous for our unlikely little protagonist, Richie Greenfield. We cast aside all that unhealthy shame, relax and laugh, and rejoice in this particular sexual fantasy and proclivity.  Step into the extraordinary life of our little avatar, our champion, doing his best to be a true man as he lives with, works for, loves under, and is munificently smothered by the Amazons and Giantesses of Bluebelle Valley.

*"The style is exceptionally easy to read.  Each bodacious romp in the juicy fantasy land moves along like a fun amusement park ride. The characters are ultimately open and generous and therefore their world, while edgy and sexually dangerous, seems kind and oddly sweet.  The paradox is that so much outrageous crushing sex could be so uplifting."  J.E. – San Francisco*


Let me be clear about something right from the beginning: I may be too thin and way too short, puny by every standard, and I might even be imaginary.  But I am a 21 year old man.  Every situation I describe in the fictional world of Bluebelle Valley, no matter how dire it may seem; I am there by my own choice and free will.  And by God, you won't find children in any of my stories.

*Richie Greenfield, Bluebelle Valley*

*"Hi there, dear little reader.  And welcome dear fans of Spiritually Uplifting Erotic Crush.  It's just little ol' me, Daisy checking in.  I hope you enjoy all these Episodes of Amazons of Bluebelle Valley in the good fun as R.B. intended.  And hey, doll, if you really like Richie's well-written, funny, good-hearted, and sexy stories about us, go ahead and kindly post us a nice review.  Keep me satisfied, now sweetie; because I do play rough if I get cranky.  Oh, R.B. wanted me to ask you to look for his other great stories under the series titles "Amazon Absorption", "Mini Giantess Proclivities", "Bluebelle Giantess Fancies", and more to come.  R.B. would tell you himself, but he's kind of… ah, yes… oooh – in a tight spot right now, with his busy schedule.  Love you to death,*

Daisy Strickland, Bluebelle Valley

# I.    Giantess Pollination Crew

Hot Midwest humidity blustered in from the open passenger window. Katydid electric screams dropped pitch like little late afternoon sirens as we sped down two-lane country Highway 19.  I could hear the summer sounds and gratefully feel the breeze, but of course I couldn't see any of it around Bethany's broad lower back. Her huge posterior obliterating the rest of my little body as her heavy ass overflowed the bucket seat – and me.

I resisted the temptation to kiss her sugary, salty skin as she leaned back pressing against my lips.  I resisted, because I knew that kiss was what she wanted, that it meant me breaking down and helping her to win this game they played every day on the commute back to town.  Hey, I resisted because I want to win, too; especially when there's money at stake!

In wafted the nicely distracting scent of fresh cut alfalfa, then the unmistakable sweet-sweat smell of tasseling corn, all mixing with the heady aroma of Bethany's shampoo or conditioner, I never knew which it was in a woman's hair.  Her cascades of straw-colored tresses swirled in the wind, around my head, across my face.

A car whizzed past the other way with a rough-buzz on the rural road.  Oh, I seriously doubt those in that blur of a vehicle noticed my trauma: a 4'2" skinny little man under the crushing ass of a 7'6" amazon.  Bethany leaned back again with purpose, overwhelming against my face not even half way up her smooth, tan back. And so, I admit it, maybe I did kiss her, just a little bit, right then.

And oh my God the weight of this woman!  Of course I'd been daydreaming about Bethany taking her turn on me on the ride back to town.  I mean, she was such a big beauty, the tallest of the gals on the crew.  I'd certainly fantasied about this moment, this event, this thirty minutes of dream-come-true under her gorgeous wide ass.  But the reality of her squish, the severe heaviness of her bare legs and half-exposed butt cheeks pressing onto my thin legs, over my lap so much than I could feel the entirety of my thinness rather munched over and up into her buns – my eyes closed to mere slits as I began to completely surrender to her crushing dominance.

Her ass totally sealed me into the bucket seat.  When she leaned back, again and more persistent this time, not one speck of my body could be seen.  I licked at her back now, beyond kissing, getting feverish with a desire to lick her pussy, pretending my mouth was there instead.  And I could feel my hard-on throbbing faster and faster with my accelerating heart-beat.  I would not last much longer – but I had to, somehow, to have any chance at earnings from the betting.

"Oh Bethany," I mouthed onto her lower back, wanting so badly to slip down just a little further and press my face into her big perfect ass crack. "Please, please smother me with your ass forever…" It began to feel so hot under her, sweaty now, and so crushed and helpless.

Small as I was, the amazons always knew when I was responding.  My little "Volunteer", free enough in my loose shorts, would predictably betray my desire for these voluptuous giantesses.  Yes, they always knew and would skillfully pounce on my sexual reaction.

Bethany was hell bent to break Cecilia's record from last week.  It took Cecilia less than 13 minutes to "Stage One" me.  That's what they called it each day when I came the first time, on the ride home – on the contest home.  At 60 miles per hour it took 35 minutes to get back to town.  But Bethany wasn't driving the van.  She was driving me down into sexual submission, measured to the nearest second on how long before I came.  For my part, I resisted best I could for my long-shot chance to earn at their betting pool of "bonus money".  Kind of like wagers the twelve of them against each other and me and my ability (or lack thereof) to resist their amorous attacks, I suppose is what it was.  Sometimes I actually would win little bits of the pot.

Intermittent-unpredictable-rewards: they say that's the most addictive.  Based on that, I suppose I was hooked on this game.  More than that though, I was born a stubborn little cuss.  Excuse me, not "stubborn"; let's call me persistent, more of a never-say-die-guy.  And, well, let's face it; maybe I resented their game a little bit.  You think?  Who knows, really, it's enough to make a man feel conflicted and a bit confused, as you can imagine.

Bethany, however, proceeded without the least bit of confusion as she squeezed and pressured me, bouncing just a little.  "Oh my goodness," My inner voice is always commenting.  "She really is quite talented."  Other stupid thoughts also enter my head, like, "I think I love her." "I want to be owned by her." "I want to be inside her."

I imagined her huge tits flopping around as she bounced on me again and again.  Like many of the gals on the crew, Bethany liked to wear her work shirt knotted in the front, up and under her massive breasts.  With the three top buttons undone, her cleavage all but completely hung out of her red-checkered blouse.  That pulled-out, knotted styling was also why Bethany's lower back was so ideally exposed to me now.

Bethany rocked side-to-side on me, the motion bringing me down into the seat, slouching under her even more – me taking the opportunity to reach under her buns with my arms and get trapped under her more thoroughly. The massive smooth musculature and overly ample tan flesh of her huge ass responded aggressively to the submissive gesture I'd made by inserting my arms under her.  She pounded on me now, not lifting completely off, but definitely humping, my skinny arms mere twigs pretending to lift her up each time she slightly rose up before exerting new levels of smash and squish onto my tiny insignificance. And fresh thoughts came to me: "Bethany is my master." "I want to serve her every wish." "If I kiss her well enough, with enough passion, could she, just maybe, fall in love with me?"

Let's pretend those thoughts are wishes.  That way maybe I'll have some wishes come true.   Like my wish for true love.  For a woman who could look past my tiny size and see that I wasn't a boy, but a man with actual grown-up emotions and mature desires.  Are you convinced?  Nah, I didn't think so.  But it could be true, couldn't it?  Maybe that could happen for a little stick-man like myself.  Little dreamer, is more like it.  True love…  Ha!  Like that's possible with these dominating bitches…

And there's another thing didn't help at all, I could not get the thought of the Sanderling sisters out of my head.  Yesterday they had actually creamed the record time.  Problem was: they cheated.  You see, it was Sandy's turn.  And she started out well and fair enough.  Her sexy 415 pounds were getting me going nicely.  She had a particular fast butt vibration move that should at least warrant a trademark, if not an actual patent, as a potential cum removing technique.  But after only five minutes in, sister Silvia pounced on us from the seat right behind, piling on her extra 414 pounds.  That was breaking the rules big time!

The twin's 829 pounds scrunched my meagerness.  Silvia's super sexy ass stacked onto Sandy's perfect firm posterior annihilated my resistance in no time flat.  And I do mean "flat"!  Sandy and Silvia, oh Lord: imagine the sexiest brunette movie star you've ever seen, now triple her size while expanding the magnitude of her knockers even more.  Then double that heavenly vision into twins.  Shrink yourself down to my tiny size.  Then have these two beautiful amazons ass-smash you in wild sexual vigor.

Oh they had it planned all along, for sure.  Right down to the in-unison coordinated pounding they gave me.  I came in my pants some two minutes ahead of the previous record.  But atypically, only half way home, the van pulled over and stopped.  The Sanderling sisters, scintillating sirens of smother and smash, were summarily ousted from the van.  The rest of the somewhat angry, but mostly laughing, crew told them they'd have to walk the rest of the way home.  They shut the door and left the dazzling duo standing on the gravel by the highway.

But were they sorry?  Not in the least.  I looked at them in the side view mirror laughing and hip-bumping and giving each other high and low fives.  We weren't even up to half speed when I saw a pickup truck stop to give them a ride.  Poor son of a bitch; those sisters weren't anywhere near done celebrating.  Giving the Sanderlings a ride home – what a joke.  I could already see his parked truck bouncing back and forth.  It had made me kind of wished it was me giving them the "ride" home.  I hope he survived, lucky fucker.

Problem was, if you'll pardon the rhyme: all this reflection was adding to my erection.


What was Cecilia's record exactly? Twelve minutes 38 seconds from passenger-door-shut, 4:35p last Wednesday in the parking lot at the Synsonto Ag Research Office.  They talked about it this afternoon, "the Stage One record", as they piled into the large van.  And that was only maybe a mere seven minutes ago?

Bethany sat on me impossibly heavy, the tallest but not the biggest gal on the crew; that was Debbie of course.  Holy cow, big Bethany seemed to have a way of making herself even heavier – good God, was she pulling on the base of the seat? Outweighed by perhaps 350 pounds, I think she just added maybe 150 pounds more of pressure. I could hardly move.  My breathing came at her option.  It depending on whether she leaned back or not.  And leaning heavily into me was something she did with a calculated irregularity, to keep me unsure.

My God Bethany smells good.  I can't help it as my lips part to kiss her again. I'd sunk low enough now, at the very top of the separation of her buns.  She responded quickly by grabbing my wrists, pulling my arms out, up, and fully extended around her, stretching my arms to their limit, and forcing my hands to push up under her huge breasts…

In my mind I can see the hugeness of breasts clearly as she stands with the corn pollination crew.  The farm manager loves these seven foot plus amazons.  They are as tall as the corn plants and can easily reach to the tassels, the male flowers, and thus carry out the pollinations.  They are twice as fast at the job as the old normal-sized crews.  Jeez, I wonder if it's handling male flowers all day that makes them so horny.  Oh, the small pleasures I find in secretly making fun of them.

Yes, I can see Bethany standing there, fresh in the morning light, stretching her arms back, limbering up for the day's work.  Her farmer-girl's blouse knotted in front above and exposing her firm abs.  That same blouse strained to its limit by her massive breasts.  She leans over to stretch her hamstrings, her cleavage is toward me.  I gawk at that heavenly place.  My entire head could disappear into that soft chasm.  But ladies always know when you're looking, don't they?  Even at fifty yards away Bethany glances up and catches my eye.  She smiles and makes a little pucker, as if to blow a kiss.

I looked away, down at my skinny legs and dusty tennys.  Can you imagine?  Twenty-one years old and only 4'2".  I know I said that already.  Excuse me for living; I'm a little obsessive about it.  But I'm not a dwarf.  Let's be clear here.  I'm just really short, and for good reason I'll tell you about sometime, and I'm really thin: a mere 70 pounds.  Thin is healthy right – that's what I keep telling myself.

"Very, very cute, in a boyish kind of way."  I think is what Sylvia said the day I met the Amazon Crew, as they were nick-named.

"Just darling," was Janet's description.

"He's an absolute doll", Vicky lilted overly dramatic like an old-time southern belle as she scooped me up into an embrace.  My feet dangled at Vicky's mid-thigh height, "I think I'm in love."  She laughed as she continued the hug, my face pressed against her neck.  Then she brought me up to her face and gave me a big wet kiss on the lips.  All the other eleven amazons laughed at that.

It was a weird moment, though, because something changed in Vicky's expression as our eyes met right then.  I don't know what it was; I just knew she looked exceptionally beautiful to me, my vision kind of hazy around the edges, and I could see she had some similar feelings.

Vicky let me oh-so-slowly slide down, past her neck, against the side of a huge breast, her exposed waist, ending with my toes touching the ground as my face rested against the soft cotton front of her shorts.  She turned, bumping me back with her huge wide ass-cheeks that were just visible at the bottom of her micro-cutoffs.

Smacked me right at eye level, she did.  And I was taken aback by such, such… rudeness.  My word, I said to myself, trying to not admit to my deeper self, that I kind of liked it.  Yet was it rudeness?  As all the gals turned toward the fields, Vicky glanced back to flash me a stunning smile that I could only categorize as affectionate.

I stood breathless that first day on the job, trembling, as Vicky and the rest of the forest of beauties took playful, skipping strides to their day's work in the corn crossing blocks.  Trying to recover from the social shock of it all, I scanned around for the Secretary Pool Office Building.  That's where I was supposed to report in for my first day as office assistant.

Ah, there's the building, across the from this gravel road, with its own paved parking lot.  In there I suppose I'd find my new boss, one Miss Strickland.  Thank God I got to work in a civilized office.  And not out in the fields with those, those – savages, I recalled now looking back as the Amazon Crew grew more distant.  I only had to commute to and from work with those bullies….

Bethany was positively bouncing now.  Her breasts flopped heavily down on my hands.  There was an opening and squeezing, opening, squeezing, of her buttocks that seemed to pull me inside her.  I could feel the surrender mounting in my body.

"Nine minutes 46 seconds." Coleen announced from two rows back in the van. Bethany responded, pumping me harder, more rapidly…

I made myself think of something else, but nothing was helpful.

I thought of the boring office work I did all day.  Then I pictured the towering secretaries standing by the water cooler.  These were women trained up and, for the most part, promoted out of the amazon pollination crew.  The only difference was they were a couple years older, like maybe 24, definitely a little taller and even more so in their high heels.  They dressed quite stylish in their tight-fitting business skirts and smart-looking tops.

The Secretaries had taken their time, basically seeming to ignore me for the first couple of weeks.  I recall feeling fairly secure and safe in that office before finally one-day the sort of accidental but still obviously overt molestations began.  But didn't I want that?  Hadn't I been dreaming about?

Then the thought of giantess Miss Strickland would freeze me in my emotional tracks.  She was so ridiculously tall and massive, shaking the office floor with the heavy click of her heels.  Oh the doom of her impossibly wide ass seemed to suck away my breath and all hope as she walked by, eyeing down at me with stern disapproval.  No it didn't help my current situation under Bethany for me to think about my work day.

"Ten minutes, 33 seconds."  Bethany plundered me now with butt drops in the front seat.  She was desperate and determined to set a new record.  I was being knocked senseless by her vigor and violence.  She owned me and I loved it.  Think of something else, something else…

Shortly after we reached town I would be the first to be dropped off.  Most of the Amazon Crew lived in the same dorm-style house and the rest, like me, who arrived for the summer later were just overflow, and placed with nearby families around the fancy, edge-of-town neighborhood of Bluebelle Valley Estates.

There was still more than twenty minutes remaining in the ride to town, in the van, at Bethany's mercy….  Twenty minutes; that's like an eternity under the ass of this huge amazon.  I thought of getting out of the car, sticky with my own cum, shamed, weak, dominated once again into complete submission.  Wobbling up to the house…

Then what?  The family that housed me was no reprieve – I mean not-family, because the parents were somewhere in Europe for the summer, what I mean is The Triplets.  Yes, The Triplets were home from graduate school, or was it the recording studios, for the summer.  And boy, were they huge, horny and aggressive – and strange.  What about me could possibly be so attractive to these women, especially large women?  It made no sense to me.  They said I smelled irresistible, that I was so cute, so innocent, like a snuggly little boy toy.  Blessing or curse; you be the judge.

Anyway, these Triplet sisters had been on the Amazon Crew in past summers, and knew I was fair game.  And games they loved to play, every night, and I don't mean Monopoly – unless by that we are talking about someone owning nothing and being at the complete mercy of your landlord.  No it didn't help to think about getting back home.

"Eleven minutes, 38 seconds.  Only a minute left, Bethany."  The pounding went ballistic and insane for 15 more seconds.  Then abruptly Bethany let go of my wrists and lifted herself off me.  Had she given up?  Ha-ha, I win!  Finally, I get good bonus money from their bets.

Not a chance.  Bethany jerked down her cutoffs and panties, exposing her gigantic butt right before my face.  Then she grabbed my legs right above my knees, her hands entirely circling my skinny thighs.  Suddenly I was on the move, yanked down, my back on the seat.  Her gapping ass loomed above my face.  I cringed at that smothering doom.  Then wham, she planted her luscious wonder on my face.

Among all the other feelings that came with that crushing overwhelm, also came relief at the ever surprising freshness of the aroma.  But they'd all had that magical quality, every time they had ass-smashed my face.  I simply relaxed into the sweet surrender of it all.  Bethany grabbed my hard cock and my balls right through my tented shorts, and gave me a firm and relentless squeeze.  I was rapidly running out of air, fully and completely owned by her delicious heavy ass.  And I was turned on out of my mind.  I kissed like a madman, my face way up into her horrendous ass-smash.  I bucked and came like crazy.

Through her body I heard Bethany's screams of delight.  In the background I heard butt-muffled squeals from the other amazons.  Apparently it was a new record.  Bethany pussy-squirmed down on me for another minute.  She alternated between spreading and relaxing, then tensing and finishing off the vestiges or her orgasm, and what little more cum I had to offer.  Bethany lifted slightly.  I gasped for air as she tugged me out and let me crumple to the floor well.

"Twelve minute 18 seconds" I heard.  "A new record!" several laughed and all cheered.

I just groaned and groveled at Bethany's feet.  She was barefoot.  "Why don't you kiss my feet the rest of the way home," her question was really more of a command under the circumstances.

But I wasn't in the mood.  "Why don't you kiss your own feet?"  I mumbled back; grumpy because her breaking a record meant no money for me today – and I could really use it since they had me on paltry intern wages at my job, excuse me, "work experience."

Bethany didn't care, disregarded my insolence, instead celebrating her winnings, and glad-handing with the rest of the crew.

"Aren't you going for the other record?" it was Fat Debbie, by far the heaviest young woman on the crew.

The "other record" was the most times a gal could get me to come in the trip back to town.  That stood at four times, thanks to creative persistence by Jessica three weeks earlier.

"Nah, I don't think so." Bethany sighed in post orgasm satisfaction, "Little Richie shot his wad pretty good, didn't you pal?" She nudged me with her foot. I moaned listless. She continued, "I don't think he's got anything left, do ya'?" She pulled me up between her moist thighs; her shorts were still down so I was looking right at her sexy bush. She eyed me, "Don't tell me you are interested."

That got some more hardy laughs. She let me go and I collapsed again. "No ladies," Bethany boasted, "One record in one day is enough. Maybe on my next rotation, in a couple of weeks. I've got some ideas I've been saving just special for our little lover boy."

The girls moved on in their dialog, thankfully ignoring me for the rest of the drive. When we reached my driveway Bethany hauled me up and devoured my face for a full minute of kisses, that sort of felt like I was being eaten by the victorious conqueror. When she released me and rolled me out on my driveway, I was fully hard again. "Look at that!" she pointed at me curled on the pavement. "He does want it again."

"Of course he does," chimed in MaryEllen.

"He *always* does," smiled Vicky, as she gave me a friendly wink. And they were all laughing as the big van backed out.

"See you tomorrow, sweetie." Fat Debbie called out lovingly, and I believe she meant it kindly. It was her turn tomorrow.

After a few minutes I pushed myself up and stumbled toward the house – and toward the mysterious and certainly kinky games the Triplets had in store for me tonight.

# II. The Towering Triplets

The Triplets wouldn't be home for two hours.  Two hours of glorious freedom in the Johansen's beautiful home before the giantess Trio of Terror arrived.  Don't get me wrong, I mean they were friends of the family and all that.  And I'd seen The Triplets like every third year or so when I was growing up – make that every year on Christmas cards.  So how could I be ungrateful when the parents were so generous with me, to let me stay for free in their master suite while they were gone to Europe for the summer.  No, I certainly couldn't complain about the digs.

My problem stemmed from fear, I suppose, because The Triplets were scary big and I, well, as you know, pathetically small.  Which is okay in and of itself, except we lived together for the summer, and they weren't exactly good at boundaries, as in observing my personal space.  At least I wasn't lonely – wow; now that was a lame rationalization….

At first I nicknamed them (for self-dialog only – not to say to their faces, mind you) The Trinity of Terror, because of the divergent games these 8'6" 620 pound perfect bounteous beauties wanted to play every evening.  I think it might be hard to develop some sympathy here.  After all, they didn't look like terrorist, quite the opposite actually.  Did I make their magnificence clear yet?  Each perfect face has the same bright intelligent expression of energetic mastery.  Their skin is paler than most with just the hint of the unavoidable Midwest summer tan.  Their ivory platinum hair is full, long, and wavy.  Their faces are ideally oval, exquisite with elegant character, penetrating gray-blues eyes, lovely wide mouths with full lips that automatically beckoned with temptation.

Oh, and their bodies were to die for – not literally, I hope.  Long, super strong legs, ideally proportioned but thicker than you would think given how sleek they looked from, let's say, across the room.  But up close the stoutness of the legs was very evident to me, looking at those grand thighs at eye level.  And only a slight angle of a glance up from that, their huge asses just slayed me with their ever impending wide, firm doom.

I couldn't tarry long at the perfect sexy curve of their waists, because I would have to move on up to gawk at their huge, heavy, breasts.  Owned I was, by their magnificent tits, each one far more than enough to smother me into the most willing of groveling slaves.  Damn, I was getting hard just thinking about them.

And there was more to it, more than my feeble brain could process into cohesive hypothesis.  I knew somehow, but did not understand, that there was something going on way over my head.  Hey, no pun intended – give me a break, will you?  It was rumored the Triplets had super IQs.  So, no surprise I couldn't reason out what their real 'game' was.  All I had was my intuition, not exactly warning me, just sayin' it was like it wasn't just for their fun; more like I was being tested – probed, if you will.

I ran a bath, and enjoyed the tub's second story grand-view window of the park-like setting of the Johansen's back yard.  In good old Midwest style the back yards of these mansions had no fences, so it was hard to know where one estate stopped and the next one started.  It doesn't sound very secure, does it?  But don't worry, they are quite secure.  Everything about Bluebelle Valley Estates was well under control.

Let me confess something, and I'm sure I'm not alone in this discovery: I've found a bath is the perfect place for sexual fantasies.  I hate making a mess, but I had to allow for the water spilling out of the tub by gallons as the first of the three huge 620 pound Triplet sisters joined me in the bath.  "Sorry" I said to the other two, "You'll just have to wait your turn because your sister's ass is so big there's no more room in the tub…" I didn't get to finish my imaginary sentence because of the massive ass that covered by face and plunges me underneath the warm sudsy water.  In my fantasy I could breathe underwater and enjoy her overpowering smothering facesit for minutes or even hours if necessary, loving being lost at the bottom of the tub, pinned out of site under her huge hot ass.  I struggled mightily but could not move nor escape – only succumb as she squeezed and adjusted her devouring ass down on me, opening in to engulf my face as I pleasured myself while mouthing servitude up into her munching pussy…

Let me double-digress for just a minute here.  Maybe because everything sexual has always been so extreme for me, at least in my own mind, but I have to let you in on something.  I have figured something out that can save you a lot of grief in this life.  Ready?  Here it is: you can't do anything about your deepest desires.  So don't fight it.

Take your desires and put them in one bucket.  Take your behaviors and put them in another.  The place you have choice in the behavior bucket.  It's that simple.  Be creative, sane, and live up to your personal ethical standards in your behavior bucket.

Let's take a simple example.  Let's say some guy marries a brunette because she is awesome and they are in love.  But this guy really has a thing for blondes, and while he is, more or less, able to conduct himself through daily life, he's frustrated in that his desire for sex-with-a-blonde is not being met.  Can he tell himself: I don't have this desire?  Nope, doesn't work.  Should he call himself a sinner and flog himself for these desires – doesn't make the desires go away.  But what if he went to this hopefully still loving wife and said, "Hey honey, I have this desire to have sex with a blonde.  I don't know what to do and I'm feeling bad with the un-met desire."

Now she might say.  "Tough shit, live with it."  Which might be possible for our friend to do, but unhappily so.  However, presumably this hypothetical couple is in love.  I mean they're married, for criminy sakes, in the biggest mutual commitment of their lives.  So I'm imagining she might say, "I could try out a blonde wig some evening."  Or even more awesome, "I've been thinking about bleaching my hair anyway.  Would you prefer more of a platinum white or maybe a strawberry blonde?"

And the guy's like.  "You are so amazing.  Can I do something for you – like all the dishes every day from now on?"  And she's like, "Oh, that won't be necessary, but I would like a little more oral sex.  Especially I'd like to tie you up first and mount your face and own you…"

Oh crap, here I am, trying to give you a good example, and then my own frigging fantasies got in the way.  Sorry.  But you got the main idea, right?  Desires just are.  The choice lies with behaviors.  And what if you're having trouble with choosing good behaviors?  Well, I'm thinking there's got to be plenty of places to get help for those who get off their dead asses and look.

As I fought in my fantasy to escape from being drowned under bubble bath by enormous luscious butt, I thought about the Johansen estate resting securely in the large gated community that had essentially become Bluebelle Bend….  No, I confess, I lied a bit just then.  Actually, I wasn't really leaving my fantasy to think about stupid Bluebelle Bend. I'm just forcing myself to be responsible for a moment so I can tell you about what the heck happened to the poor town.

Okay, so the original village, while still quaint if you like ghost towns, had been abandoned by the wealth sequestered behind the gates and the walls Bluebelle Valley Estates.  That's right: the company had originally paid for the whole development, some one hundred and fifty unique and hand-crafted mansions.  A key feature in most of the large manors was the minimum 20-foot ceilings throughout.  And God, I hope that proves high enough.

"Come on woman, let me breathe." the day-dream progressed….

My dad was a VP of Synsonto Corp so I knew quite a bit about how it all came about.  The law suits of twenty years ago.  Some blamed the water.  Some blamed the air.  They all blamed Synsonto's Agriculture Research Station to the east and the experiments they had been running for years on the farms and soils around Bluebelle Valley.  The exact cause was lost in legal obscurity.  But whatever was in that biologic enhancement or plant growth hormone or genetically modified soil amendment or combination or whatever it was, it affected girls and boys oppositely.  The girls grew into towering, enhanced, practically superhuman amazon giantesses.

… just like the vast woman that had turned around in the tub and now sat on me backwards, pumping my face with vigor and purpose.…

… And the little boys pretty much stayed little boys.  Or more typically, once the problem had been identified, the boys were shipped out at a young age to matriculate at boarding schools and then never came back.

My fantasy woman now sat on me frontwards again, hauling me up and into the perfect position for some serious sudsy tit-whipping…

… Except me, of course.  Early in her marriage my mother had almost died of the toxic aspects of Bluebelle Valley contaminated ground water.  The story they told me: they had to move out of there almost overnight.  Her life-saving brilliant, but also absent-minded, Synsonto doctors back East didn't find out until three weeks into the aggressive cures that my mother was already pregnant with, guess who, yours truly.  The toxic syndrome along with the chemo-treatments administered to my mother's altered body hit me hard.

So here I am at almost 22, only 4'2" and skinny as a rail.  Where was I going to fit in?  Come on, you tell me.  That's right, nowhere.  Oh yeah, grade-school, high school, college – lots of fun, oh yeah, just loads and loads of shits and giggles.  But that's another story…

The old angst of my youth had dissolved my fantasy without resolution.  Instead, I made myself forget about it, release it, just relaxed.  Ahhhh… the warm water felt good to my smashed and aching body.  But I was young.  In a couple of hours I would be recovered from Bethany's tough crush-ass treatment of me, and be OK again.  I better be OK before the Trio of Gamesters gets home.…

You think I'm kidding; well I'm not.  Get this!  One evening last week they wanted to play Twister, of all things.  Only it wasn't exactly Twister because the mat was much larger, and the circles where you place your feet and hands were a little further apart.  Instead of the little finger-flip spin dial they had some kind of app that would voice out the next move every time one of them called out "Squish."  Oh, and, it wasn't only feet and hands on the colored dots but could be any body part like: elbow, knee, face, ear, tongue, ass….  Sometimes the app's mechanical, fake-sultry voice would call out very specific moves like: "Left knee, Sweetheart, on Richie's mid-back." or "Right butt-cheek on poor Richie's head."  I mean, that's a seriously rigged game, wouldn't you say?

Every move I'd become more entwined under their impossibly long and sturdy legs, wound up in their wicked arms, pressed between their abs and butts, gradually obliterated in the middle of a giant knot of succulent woman flesh, until it all collapsed on me in a heap.

Right there in that luscious dog-pile of woman the Triplets seemed to somehow suspend time.  How could that much chaos not move at all?  Then I felt them kind of entering my body in a sensory sort of way, very hard to describe.  It would have been boo-ku creepy, except there was a positive aspect to it, this inspection – like some kind of alien abduction sequence, except, what – like beyond their curiosity it was also for my own good?  I don't know…

The Triplets – I had no idea whose big smothering butt was on my back for those thirty minutes they took to unwind the Twister-like game, requesting the app to call out the reverse sequence of moves, to step-by-step undo the pile we were in – and I was under.  I hadn't a clue whose crushing ass pinned me desperate for air, because the frigging beautiful Triplets were absolutely identical, as near as I could tell….  Ahhh, but for now, just relax.  I added a few drops of Tangerine Mist essential oil and, of course, more bubble bath.  I just loved, loved playing with lots of heaped up suds.

Every evening with the Triplets brought a new kinkiness.  And two nights ago, holy buckets, that had to be the weirdest of all time.  After the usual line-up and panty-pussy greeting in the foyer they declared: "Tonight, we want to play Dairy."

Oh my goodness, I think to myself.  A game of "Dairy", while sounding innocent enough, just can't be a good thing with the Triplets.  I mean I'm not actually recalling a "Dairy" game, but at best it sounds pretty juvenile, and at worst – I don't want to think about it.  There's no way this will be anything like that little shake-out-to-funky positions game Tip-the-Cows we used to play as kids.

After that long, uncomfortable pause while I went through all that consternation considering what "play Dairy" might mean, some response on my part was required.

"I don't know that one, girls.  Is that like Shoot and Ladders?"  Can they tell I'm being sarcastic?

"Shoots…" tithers one.

"… and ladders…" trills another.

"Oh, we don't think so." The third shakes her finger "no-no" at me.  And then they all laugh; a bedeviling, beatific frolic of mirth, so surround-sound seductive it just makes me feel weak with desire.

"Richie, could you be a dear and pretty please come up to your room in, say, fifteen minutes?"  A command never sounded so gentle.

My room, meaning the master suit I had for the summer while their parents were in Europe?  That's something new, really odd.  But I answer them in some expected affirmative. "It would be my pleasure".  Because if I said "no" I'm not sure what would happen – I never have said "no" yet.

They all three bent way down, their faces inches from mine on three sides. Their lips parted, as if kisses were forming.  Instead their voices came from deep inside, penetrating me with their magical harmonizing and wilting my dwindling resolve to resist this odd game, "Mooooooo."  The vibrations dissolved me.  "Mooooooo, little farmer Richie."  Then each took a turn with flirtatious sass. "Your cows have finally come home, darling."  "It is time to be of service to your herd or they might become utterly uppity." "Yes, yes, poor tiny farmer Richie, you better tend to your bossy cow-cows now and to their complete satisfaction."  And with that they turned and paraded out of the room, shaking the floor as their sum total 1860 pounds marched in unison.

I found that I had fallen to my hands and knees.  I started crawling toward the stairs, toward my gigantic bedroom, the absent parent's master suite of grand proportions.  This was a first, going to a bedroom – "yes, a room with a bed."  What was I even muttering; it seemed my IQ had been cut by half.  What did the weird mooing Triplets mean?  Given how tough the evening sessions had been so far, graduating to some new level of exploitation seemed worse than a bad idea.  With so much trepidation weighing on me, the stairs seemed neigh on insurmountable.   Oh for sure, it might take me the full fifteen to get up there.  Really, not a thing had happened yet, but I felt quite feeble and overwhelmed already.

Still crawling, I finally achieved my bedroom door.  Cracked slightly, light slanted through into my dark hallway.  I made myself stand; I didn't think they wanted Farmer Richie to come in on all fours.

I paused, reviewing my life you could say.  I listened to mooing starting up, insistent on the other side of the door.  They sensed I was standing there, and they protested the delay, mooing louder now.  I'm sorry to say the review of my life came up kind of short on success and joy.  What the heck, might as well go in the room, even if this is the end.

Now, just to warn you: there are those who claim that sometimes I am not politically correct.  I know, I know, hard to believe, but it has happened.  I once described this bizarre upcoming scene to an intelligent woman of normal stature.  Her 5'9" 165 pound frame, reasonable by most standards, still proved far too much for me to handle.  And though we had met when she accidentally sat on me – claimed she didn't see me in the seat in the dark theater – I thought it rather rude and odd that she simply continued to sit on me through the rest of the movie and would not get up.  Heaven forbid that I would respond in protest, make a disturbance, and cause the few others attending to miss the enjoyment of the show.

She simply squirmed around on me the dark, eventually her insistent squish causing me to cum, only a little bit, but more than once.  Bless her heart, though, because she did share her popcorn.  Once the lights came the sexy buxom brunette kept me pinned until all the other patrons had exited.  I doubt many knew I was under her at all, what with her rather comprehensive covering of my lap, and my head only perhaps to her mid-back and covered by her cascading locks.

By way of amends for causing me to completely miss the movie, she offered to buy me a cup of tea at the coffee shop across the street.  Already impressed with her aggressive sexual proclivity, and now in the light, seeing that she was indeed strikingly attractive, how could I say no?

She queried about my obvious proclivity to sit passively in the theater while being so dominated under her ass.  Straightforward to a fault, she put it this way: "How is it that you are such a wimp?"

I explained that I didn't mind so much, as I'd prefer a real ass-smash any day to light-flashing forms of entertainment limited to two dimensions.  And though I answered politely, I confess I found myself a bit annoyed by the tenor of her question.  Maybe that's why I decided to tell her about that peculiar outrageous night the Triplets wanted to play Dairy.

So when I described to her what I am about to tell you, she claimed that such a story was offensive and traumatically degrading to women.  As I expected she might, she got all bitchy on my ass and told me off in an impressive rattle of eloquence.  This sexy stack of big tits and curves and beckoning sizzle of emotions had the nerve to suggest I objectified women.  Can you believe her audacity?  Here I was, merely the messenger.  I'm telling you it was the Glorious Triplets who came up with all this kinky stuff.  I mean, I could have been very happy with a quiet evening of checkers or bridge – since we did have a foursome.  You believe me, don't you?

Anyway, oh my God, when I entered the bedroom, the beautiful Triplets occupied positions nearby on all fours, wearing only their sexy panties and bras.  They paused from their impatient milling around to give me that soft but expectant bovine stare.  Yes, there in the open space of the vast room, as advertised, the Triplets pretended to be three cows.  And at 620 pounds each they were indeed some half the weight of full grown Holsteins.  The room had all the furniture shoved to the edges as if to create… a barnyard?  How bizarre they could be.  And how weird was I to be intrigued – no, make that eager – to tend my herd.

Their silky panties, each a different violet pastel, served to highlight the enormity of their massive asses.  The bras strained mightily to hold in their huge "utters".  The beautiful bovines looked over at me and started mooing more adamantly.  I knew I was supposed to do something, and do something right away.  There came an impatient desperation in their moos.  This herd was definitely a bit agitated.

I walked up to the nearest heifer.  Even on all fours her head, when lifted was as high as mine.  This cow commanded, "Milk me."

Well, the bra had to come off.  That much was clear.  I reached to the middle of her wide back, and wrestled with her bra hooks.  It was very tight.  And I was still feeling weak. "Mooo!" She insisted.  I kept fighting the hooks, got one.  Now the other cows crowded over.  I got another hook free.  A second cow was nudging me with her huge ass.  It was hard to stay upright.  Finally I got the third hook and bent over pulling the bra forward and down to her hands.   That brought my face even with her huge hanging breasts.  I reached over and started trying to "milk" her with my tiny hands.  It made no sense, my little hands on the side of this huge, basketball sized breast.  Suddenly she swung around, knocking me over with those huge breasts.

"Not like that" she said as she mooooved over me.  "Like this, Farmer Richie" and she lowered her huge breast onto my face, her nipple into my open aghast mouth.  "Suck!" she commanded "Suck like your life depends on it!"

I sucked and sucked hard, fighting for breath around her massiveness descending on me.  There are a lot of mysteries about these amazons I'll probably never understand.  But milk started to flow.  It tasted so sweet, I can't describe it.  It was like… like a taste from the Goddess from a previous life.  It wasn't a lot of milk; just enough to make me crazy with desire.  The flow slowed.  I had to have the other breast.  And this cow was happy to oblige, pinning my face with her other boob.

When her second breast slowed I wrestled my way out, strangely newly energized. I unhinged the bras off the other two cows and sucked each of their breasts the same way.  They seem satisfied.  Then I stretched out on my back, satiated.  I figured I might be done.  I was wrong about that.

All three beautiful amazons positioned themselves over me.  Was this some kind of impending doom?  I didn't care.  I was actually feeling weirdly grateful… worshipful?  Maybe they would finally kill me tonight.  One of them straddled her great panty-clad ass above my head.  Another one over my thin little midsection.  And I couldn't see, but I could certainly feel the third doing what – pulling off my shorts, her hand then her mouth taking my erectness.  The first two then slowly, slowly descended with the huge asses closer and closer, fresh laundried panties just beginning to settle onto my face, the gentlest first touch before her heaviness would smother me.

They all suddenly paused in unison, essentially motionless and absolutely quiet. Fine, whatever; my desires were out of control.  I brought my face up and attacked the hot pussy panties.  I kissed her everywhere I could reach with my lips.  All around her covered crotch, then over to her smooth thighs, left and right and left and right… then back to the somewhat damper panties.  I kept trying to move her panties to the side with my lips and tongue.  But I would have to give up and launch into more desperate kissing.

Why wouldn't she just lower in on me, smash me and smother me? The perfect woman on my middle had no problem squishing her big ass on me and quite thoroughly it seemed.  And the third still hand her hand firmly on my cock, even though her arm must have been pinned under the back of her sister's ass.

I was going to cum almost immediately.  Then they suddenly released, and they all stood towering above me.  What just happened?  I was confused.  Again they weren't moving at all; I mean statue-like frozen.  Were they receiving a message from the Mother Ship?  It was the strangest feeling in the room, like reality was being altered.

I felt emotionally destabilized by it, and therefore, afraid.  Were they going to just stomp me to death?  I stared at the huge long legs rising up, up… to three gigantic asses….  Was it going to be one massive triple butt drop from that great height?  Certainly that would do it.  Surely this was how my life would end very soon.  And I was strangely OK with that.

But instead they reached down, picked me up.  "We are not cows," they said, almost mechanically.  OK before it was weird, kinky, but I kind of understood it.  But now they were acting downright spooky.

The Triplets sat me on my bed.  Then they proceeded to move all the furniture exactly back to where it had been before.  That included two of them effortlessly lifting the ginormous bed, with little ol' me on it, and placing it where it belonged.

Standing before me, three in a row at the foot of my bed, and looking strangely formal for women dressed in just panties, they had these three things to say, one-by-one:

"We are stopping this game so that we do not hurt you." (Wow, that's damn civil of you.)

"We thank you for your kind participation." (What the hell?  A thank you?  And "kind participation", are you kidding me?)

And finally, "If you need more milk, you know where to find us?" (Holy shit, what the heck was I supposed to do with that?  I mean, hadn't I just escaped certain smothering death?)

Then the three identical, beyond-gorgeous, but alien-weird amazons left-faced and walked out of my room single file.

That was two evenings ago.  Now, if you don't mind, I'm dying to tell you about yesterday.  In some important respects, it was probably even stranger.

Out of the blue, for something completely different, the Triplets had challenged me to track and field Olympics.  They donned sexy and silky pink running shorts and some sort of matching hopelessly overwhelmed sports bras.  Just looking at them limbering up and getting ready unfairly ruined my concentration.

Out in the park-sized back yard they proceeded to cream me at every event.  It would be me against one of the sisters while the other two were "officials".  On your mark, get set, go!  In the hundred meter dash I think I got maybe one-third the way before my competitor had already crossed the finish line.

Then they handed me a big iron shot-put ball.  First of all my 70-pound sack of bones could barely lift it.  As I sought to spin with it, you know, to give it the toss, I lost my balance and maybe it dropped away from me the distance of my body – which, at 4'2" isn't saying much.  One of them sent her shot-put somewhere into the next county – I don't know really, it disappeared over some trees.

Event after event I hadn't a prayer.  What were they trying to prove?  After several drubbings it began to feel quite shaming.  Finally, post three ridiculous rounds of Greco wrestling – yes they each wanted a shot at me on that one – I'd had enough.  Slammed by legs, smashed by breasts, and now finally pinned with my face under an armpit, when that last one released me I jumped up, ticked off.  My temper flared red-hot and I had some fairly fowl words on the tip of my tongue.  They sat on the grass in a kind of semi-circle, looking at me most intently; penetrating intelligent eyes, overly-interested in my reaction it seemed.  Right then, just before I blew my top though, I got an idea.

"All right, enough already!  How about we try something I'm good at?  I challenge you to a chin-up contest."

They leaned together, ignoring me for a second.  That gave me a chance to study their silky red tops, huge breasts barely contained within, pressing together as they sat huddled.  Oh boy, that nest they formed looked so inviting.  After whispering for a minute, they faced me again, excited by my challenge.

"OK, Richie.  You're on."  They stood and started jogging across the wide lawn.  "Come on.  There's a tree back here with branches at the right height."  In another two minutes we arrived under a grand old maple, massive tall, glorious and green, loving the wet Midwest summer.

Finally, this had to be my event.  Little mister wiry; ha, I could do like thirty, maybe forty chin-ups, easy.  I knew the sisters were super strong, but at over 600 pounds each, no way they could come close to what I could do.

"I'll go first."  What a strange feeling to have, confidence.  "Lift me up to that branch, please."  I saw a good horizontal one, sturdy, but small enough to get my hands around.  After a quick hoist I started popping up the numbers.  "One, two, three, four…"  I counted out loud as I racked up ten, then twenty, then starting to feel it a bit decided to stop with, "twenty-nine, thirty."  Just to show off I could have done more, I then pulled myself up to sit on the branch.  After a moment of lording my proven prowess over them I called out. "Ok, catch me."  I jumped off into strong hands that sat me gently on the ground.

The impressive tree also had a big branch some fourteen feet up they could just hop up to reach.  You wouldn't expect anyone their size could do two chin-ups.  But the strength of these amazons never failed to impress, as the first sister did ten comfortably, then straining managed two more.  "Twelve."  She exhaled, spent, as she dropped off the branch.

"Yes!" I thought to myself.  I've got them now.  No way sister number two or three could do much better.  And in fact, they each topped out at exactly twelve.  I won, and not only that, it had been very entertaining to watch them pumping up and down.  I had even moved closer, almost underneath, for a fair inspecting look at the allure of the tension in their bodies.

"Finally I beat you at something."  I couldn't help gloating.

"No, we won."  Came a matter-of-fact response.

"What do you mean?  I did thirty.  You only did twelve."

"Yes you did thirty and that is very good, excellent, in fact, very impressive.  But *we* did thirty-six.  So we won."

Now I was hopping mad.  "You don't get to add your scores together.  Every contest so far was one-on-one.  You're trying to cheat."

"Let us quote your exact words, Richie, you said: 'I challenge you to a chin-up contest.'  The word 'you' is a plural, so that means all three of us."

"No way."  I wasn't having it.  "'You' can also be singular."  I knew that much about pronouns.  "That would be like adding high-jump scores together to say you jumped three times higher than humanly possible!"

"OK," They suggested, "Let's put it to a vote.  All those who think that the pronoun 'you' is plural in this case raise your hands."  Three hands went very high.  "Those opposed?" One hand went up and not very high at all.  "Looks like, by vote, we interpret 'you' as plural."

The logic kind of made my head ache.  "Listen, I don't see how 'you' can be a plural 'you' for adding your scores together, then be singular 'you-s' when it comes to getting three votes.  Sorry, not happening.  You three only get one vote on the matter of adding your scores together." I stepped forward toward them, chin up, chest puffed out as much as possible as I looked up at them standing twice my height before me.

They eyed me in good humor, but not so rude as to laugh. Then they huddled once again; more whispering. The huddle broke. "OK Richie, we get only one vote. Let's do the voting again."

"All right." I nodded. At least it would be a draw. Then maybe we could do the contest over. This time I would do forty chin-ups if I had to, and beat their damned combined score.

They took the couple steps forward to stand by me, arranging themselves around and over me on three sides. Then alarmingly the sister behind me dropped down on my body, falling over me, and flattening me to the grass. She sat up and pinned me on my back. Her big butt centered right on my shorts and on my immediately hard Volunteer. Her inner thighs spread out just slightly to cover my sides, shoulders, and arms.

One of the two standing sisters called for another vote. "All right, all those who think that the pronoun 'you' is plural in this case raise your hands." Again three hands went up. "We count that as one vote in favor. Now, all those opposed raise your hands." Of course I couldn't budge my arms in the least. "That's it then, the vote stands…"

"Bull shit!" I hollered from my pinned position. "Not fair. I can't move my arms."

"So you abstain, then."

"No, fuck no!" I protested. "Since I cannot more my arms, I demand we have a verbal vote."

"No problem. If you are feeling handicapped we can do it once more. All those who think that the pronoun 'you' is plural in this case say 'aye'." There was a chorus of three ayes. But before asking about those opposed, the big ass that had my torso pinned suddenly hopped forward and planted heavily on my face. Instant blackout: my face probably several feet from any light or sound. I knew a vote must be taking place. So I tired desperately to wiggle free, shouting my vote up into the crotch on my face. Even the slightest movement of her bulk was completely impossible for me. And for all my shouting all I got was a mouth full of sweet silky shorts.

She sat on me a long time until all my protests had subsided.  And that took quite a while because I was white-hot mad at the unfair treatment, probably almost hysterical at first.  When I finally gave up, completely subdued, she waited a little longer to make sure, then got off me.

The daylight blinded me.  Then, as my eyes adjusted, I saw all Triplets sitting over me, studying me intently, like I was some kind of vastly interesting experiment.

"Well," I queried calmly.  "How did the vote turn out?  I think I missed it."

"Oh, we won, 1-0.  So that means we won the chin-up contest."

"That's interesting."  I commented as dryly as possible. "Say, I wonder if one of you would be kind enough to lift me up to my branch again.  I want to do a few more chin-ups.  Apparently I need to practice."

After a gentle lift to the branch I did a few chin-ups, then hauled up and sat on the branch, looking down at them where they stood.

"I guess..." Staying very casual, "… you figure you can beat me at any physical contest."

They nodded. "Yes, most likely."

"Well then you won't mind one more contest and I get to pick it."

"Sure Richie, what do you have in mind?"

"What I have in mind is double or nothing on the entire Olympics we've been conducting.  You win; then I lose double on everything.  I win, then nothing counts at all."  I figured they couldn't resist the challenge.

Again they huddled briefly. Then: "OK Richie.  You're on."

"Here's the physical contest this time.  Whoever can climb highest in this tree wins." And with that I took off like a new-world monkey, up the tree faster than that cartoon-squirrel on caffeine.  I could tell they were in the tree right away by hearing the branches groaning beneath me.  I also knew they would cheat again if they caught me – probably sit on me in some crotch of branches while the others got a tiny bit higher, enough to claim victory.

But when it comes to climbing I'm truly blessed with ability: so light, agile, but with relative man-strength for my size.  Too soon I was out of reach, into the finer branches, higher and higher into the canopy, and far beyond where their bulks would allow.  Oh they got creatively high, spreading over many branches to achieve it.  But I was long gone from their reaches, waving in the summer breezes up where the butterflies find sunlight, looking out from on-high over the tree lines.

"Well, what do you say, girls?"  I called down through the canopy.  "Give up?"

After a minute, I think with more whispers, they called back, all three.  "Yes Richie.  You win.  Come down to us.  Claim us, Richie the Victorious.

How bizarre.  What were they talking about, I wondered?  I shouted down from the top of the tree.  "What are you saying?"

"Come claim us as your prize… for this clever conquest…"  The Triplets sang to me, their harmonies so alluring, irresistible. "… we willingly submit to be your servants, your slaves for the rest of the afternoon and evening."

Holy shit, I thought to myself.  What am I going to do with that offer?  I monkeyed back down the tree, swinging and sailing past the branches.  Rapidly approaching my lower chin-up branch I saw they were already back on the grass.  I hollered out as I flew past that last branch. "First command then: catch me!

Two of the sisters caught me fireman style, only instead of interlocked arms they used interlocked breasts.  I couldn't have had a softer landing.  They knelt coordinated with my momentum, and by a final flourish and twist I stuck the landing on the grass.

"You're saying I'm the Master?"

Since I couldn't tell them apart and they looked and were dressed the same it didn't matter who answered. "As you wish, we are commanded."

"In that case, lie down right here on the grass, on your backs."  As they did so, I continued. "Close your eyes, relax, and take nice deep breaths."  I stalled, needed a minute to figure this out.

What a glorious sight they presented, a triumph of splendor, perfectly beautiful, oh so generously proportioned, and not really wearing much clothing at all – just the thin, silky pink track shorts and matching sports bras.

"Are you relaxing?"

"Yes Master."  Their sudden abdication of authority, while kind of disconcerting, was also pretty funny, I thought.

"I must confess," I mused as I strolled around them. "I am thoroughly enjoying this view, looking at whatever I want, as you keep your eyes closed."

"Is there anything we can do to show you more?"

"Oh, that won't be necessary just yet."  I remained kind of stuck marveling at how their breasts seemed to defy gravity, so huge, yet not seeming to lose their shape at all.  I mean, shouldn't they be somewhat flattened out, at least more than a tiny bit?

I sighed, thinking about all the possibilities for the evening.  What would have them do? I found myself opening up, as they just lie there, relatively vulnerable, and not observing me for a change. "You know, and you may find this hard to believe, I haven't been very successful with the ladies."

"What ladies, Richie?"

"Basically any ladies.  And by 'not very successful' I mean no success.  Think about it.  If you're a normal young lady, do you want a 4'2" skinny little dude asking you to the prom?  Or even on any kind of date?"

"I don't know, Richie, all men are short and small to us."

"So it doesn't it bother you to date shorter men?"

"We've never been on a date."

"Whoa, hold it right there.  Are you telling me the three most beautiful women in the world have never been on a date?  I find that hard to believe."

"Most beautiful you say – really?"

"Without a doubt."

"Well thank you then.  Our problem is we can see into hearts and know honesty perhaps too well.  We've never found anyone suitable or therefore interesting enough."

It stung me to hear that.  It seemed almost better to go blindly into love, projecting what you want, hoping the other person could measure up to some semblance of your dreams.  It worked well in my fantasies anyway – of course that's all I had.  Real love?  I'm the last guy to ask about that.  Didn't seem likely I'd ever know that.

But these thoughts did give me an idea about what I wanted to do this evening. "OK ladies.  I know what I want."

"Yes Richie.  Shall we take our clothes off now?  Want to make love right here on the grass?"

"Nope, I have something else in mind.  If I'm in charge I declare: no more games or fooling around this evening.  Instead, let me ask you, isn't there a nice country club out here somewhere?"

"Yes, right here in the Estates, a couple of miles.  There's the Wildflower Bar and Grill.  Or for more formal there's The Oak Grove restaurant."

"The Oak Grove – that sounds perfect.  Tonight there will be no odd Twister games, no crushing pony rides, no bobbing-for-Richie in the hot tub, no steam-roller destruction derby, no smother-the-piano-teacher fantasies, no pretend rat-maze experiments to escape from your legs, no smashing Farmer Richie, and definitely no more Olympic events.  Tonight we go on a date.  That's what I want.  I've been saving my money, really thanks to generous free rent, so let me take my meager earnings and buy you a fancy dinner.  Do you except my offer?"

"You're the boss, Richie.  And it does sound rather nice."  They were still lying on the grass, but now they wore precious, rather satisfied, smiles on those beautiful faces.

"All righty then.  There's a little more to my instructions here.  Get dressed fancy, comfortable, but snazzy.  And I know how you like to wear matching outfits.  But not tonight. I want you each to have your own style; wear something completely different.  Got it?  So, how long do you need to get ready?"

"Give us an hour.  And, Richie, we'll make the reservation.  Is that all, can we get up now?"

"Sure.  Go, go."  I recall watching them for five minutes as they crossed the broad lawn that led eventually past the Olympic-sized pool then wide patios and outdoor entertainment areas and to the grand house.  I could hear them laughing, or more like giggling, as they went.  They kind of danced and playfully punched at each other, skipping along all the way into the house.  Happy girls they were, and… that had made me smile yesterday.  And it made me smile again now. I turned off the water – my bath had sudsed-up to the brim.

I kept on musing as I floated in a white cloud of bubbles.  Man, that was fun last night.  And wow did they look extraordinary, like they could read my mind.  For starters they each had worn high heels.  I just love the way that accentuates the leg muscles.  And their dress stylings ideally showed plenty of leg.

"Miss Socialite" wore a peacock pleated dress, so colorful, deeply plunging at the cleavage, her platinum hair wound and held by some pink-patterned chop-sticky things into a sophisticated asymmetrical weave that finally cascaded off to the right.

"Miss Country-gal" donned a bright yellow sleeveless dress with black poke-a-dots, her big shelf of All-American breasts fifty percent displayed from the top, and her hair braided into long farm-girl pigtails.

"Miss Trouble" tortured black fish-net stockings, cheap with holes here and there as they disappeared up into a tight military-gray skirt, her blouse the matching gray but with wavery red sashes, her hair teased organized-wild, and she looked like maybe she should be caged.  I asked for some variety, and by God I had gotten it.

The Club House had to cater to amazons as well as people of normal size.  I thought it pretty awesome that we didn't even get more than one or two double-takes as the four of us walked into the dining room, then over and two steps up to our spacious reserved table with a view of the golf course.  Naturally they had the proper seating for those huge amazon butts.  They also had a nice chair design that allowed me to find a good height at the table without any fuss.  Yeah, we ordered, and it was expensive.  Thank goodness, as I recalled my concern from last night, I had been oh so grateful that the Triplets did not want any of the Club's expensive wine.  I had gotten more than a little concerned, hoping I was actually going to have enough cash after all.

The food came steaming hot and savory.  Each of us had a great meal, good conversation.  I learned a lot about their hugely successful music business.  At one point I asked them if they would sing a song for everyone.  Sure, it was my night.  The little combo that had set up to entertain us was more than happy to play some background for the famous Triplet Trio.

From the first harmonious note the Triplets quieted all conversations and even the movement of the servers.  Their song mesmerized, relaxed us all, took us on a journey far away to a beautiful place, dare I say a view of Nirvana. Their magic music could have lasted three minutes; it could have been an hour.  They tapered their harmony down to a final single note, so beautiful and soft there was not a dry eye in the restaurant.

No one wanted to applaud as it seemed too harsh a sound to follow them.  It was more like you wanted to blow them kisses of gratitude.  The mood in the restaurant had been great; now everyone felt downright superb, royal if you will.  I know I felt like a king as the three celebrities came back to the table, smiling at me like I'd been freshly served as desert.

The combo started up and they sounded good.  For sure they, too, like everyone else in the room, had to feel extra inspired.  I winked at my dates.  "Anybody care to dance?"

"Absolutely." It was Miss Trouble.  As we took the dance floor she signaled the combo to step it up.  They blasted out a surprisingly good rendition of some old fashioned rock and roll.  All I could do is watch in amazement as Miss Trouble cleared the floor with a dance exposition like none have ever seen.  She went wild, athletic, such awesome moves of fast rhythmic juxtaposition of hips and legs and shoulders and arms all while spinning, a rapid dance full of quick sexy poses.  I shuffled my feet a little bit to qualify to stay out there.  But all any of us could do was gawk in amazement that such a huge woman could have such agile, quick and coordinated moves, and then stand applauding when she finished.

I barely sat down again, somewhat exhausted from just watching Miss Trouble, when I heard a little country sing-song from Miss Country-gal.  "My turn, partner."

If I was a spectator before, I was anything but that as Miss Country-gal taught me a lesson in country swing I could not have imagined possible.  Once she started with me, my feet never hit the floor for the entire dance.  She swung me, tossed me, passed me through her legs and around her back, twirled me over her head like a baton, had me ride her hips the bucked me off to swing me through those legs again, my hair all but brushing the floor at thirty miles an hour.  This continued like perfect choreography for five minutes.  At the end she held me up cheek-to-cheek, nodding and smiling to the applause.

Miss Socialite took me by the hand all the way up to the leader of the combo.  She suggested a classic slow fox trot.  As the music started she gestured to the crowd to join us on the dance floor.  So there in the midst of all the other couples, we danced.  For the most part I did my best to lead, but it was silly, mostly wedged between her gorgeous legs as I was.  Conversation?  That proved impractical, my face buried in pleated peacock at her crotch.  I tried to look up to her, but her face was totally hidden from view by enormous breasts swaying back and forth to our dancing.

They lowered the lights to very dim for the romantic song.  Miss Socialite took that opportunity to lift her dress over my head and snuggle my face into the confluence of her upper legs, her panties soft down on my forehead.  I guess she was leading now.  I noticed the music getting fainter.  We seemed to be in another room; I think maybe an adjoining dining room not needed on a Wednesday night.

Miss Socialite backed me up against a wall and pressed her panties against my face.  There she ground against me, still keeping the beat of the music.  Now her naked thighs pinned my shoulders and arms against the wall as well.  I kissed at her through the sweet scented cotton.  Certainly this sister had all the same moves and athleticism just demonstrated by the other two sisters.  But she focused all the strength and coordination into her skillful gyrations onto my face and body.  This would undoubtedly make me cum and soon.  She seemed to sense that and pressed more.

Then the music stopped, and so did she.  She stepped back, and I slid out from under her dress.  Miss Socialite squatted all the way down to my height and looked me intently in the eye, waiting to see my response.

"Well," I confessed. "That was a lovely dance.  Thank you.  But we don't want to be unfair to your sisters, do we?"

She smiled and shook her head in agreement; like I had just passed another test, but said. "It's up to you Richie?  You say the word, we'll make love right here in this room."

"Lovely, to be sure.  But hadn't we better get back?"  You'd think I got offers like that every day.  Not to get too grandiose, but that might have been the best offer that ever existed for any man all time.  So, even though my knees buckled as my body sort of spasmed with desire, I attest that those were indeed the humble words that somehow found their way out my mouth.

"Okie-doe."  Sounding unconvinced she nevertheless shot me a coy look and popped back up.  Like a love-sick zombie, I followed her ass back to the table, hoping I was well hidden enough behind her that no one could see the tent in my pants.

At the end of the meal, as I sat a bit mortified looking at the bill, the Country Club's restaurant manager came to our table.  The dapper middle-aged man was all smiles as he thanked the Triplets for gracing his establishment with the gift of their presence and especially the song they had performed.  He went on about how important were their songs and recordings.  He especially complemented some of their singing chants, I guess that's what they were, that dealt with all kinds of health conditions.  Anyway, finally the guy gets around to talking about his wife's depression; and damned if he didn't claim that the Triplet's music had cured his wife, gotten her off meds, and that she was truly happy for the first time in decades.

I could tell he was about to leave, and being the cad that I am and not knowing that in such a fancy place I should talk about the tab with my waiter not the manager, I touched the fellow's arm to get his attention.

"Yes sir?" He responded with professional courtesy.

I held up the bill about to ask about one of the appetizer charges, calculating if I could get that knocked off the bill my little wad of cash might just cover it.

"Ah."  He took the bill from me before I could speak.  "Let's see now.  How about, the honor is completely mine."  And he tore the bill into half and half again to let it flutter to the floor.  He smiled graciously then abruptly took his leave.

"Well, I guess that's that then."  Said Miss Socialite, regal sophisticate, her pleated peacocks swirling as she stood.

"Good move," Laughed Miss Trouble, the sexy military tramp, as she stood and leaned into her sister.

"Wow, Richie" Miss Country-gal sounded amazed, "talk about getting lucky on a date.  What you going to do with all that money you saved?"  The farm girl spun as she stood, her yellow poke-a-dot dress fanning out sufficiently to give me a nice look up her legs all the way to the sunny thong she wore underneath.

Ah yes, I knocked some suds around.  Last night was the best…

Finally, as that evening drew to a close, I stood at the entrance to their super grand bedroom.  It was only some thirty feet at the opposite end of the upstairs hallway from where I stayed in the absent parent's master suite.  I had walked them to their bedroom door and stopped right there even though they clearly invited me in with flirtatious encouragement.  No, the perfect ending to that first date was most appropriately a good-night kiss – or was it three kisses.  Singular or plural; shall we put it to a vote?

***

I drained the bath and rinsed the bubbles off me with the water wand.  Better get a little food.  Maybe microwave a TV dinner.  I had to eat.  I'd only been in Bluebelle Valley and working at the Synsonto station for a month, and already I'd lost five pounds from my brutal schedule of amazon antics.  Ha, five pounds of cum, probably.  Really funny.  I had almost no fat, so it must have been five pounds of my meager muscles.  Five pounds, no big deal you say?  Well it is when you start at 75 pounds.  Yeah, I better eat *and* digest it before the Triplets get home....

My breath quickens with adrenaline when I hear the Triplet's car pull up.  I choke down the bite of turkey and cranberry sauce I'm chewing on and wash it the rest of the way down with a quick swig of apple juice.  Better get out to the Living Room where I am supposed to greet them each evening.

I can already feel it, feel them, like they are probing the house with telepathy to locate me.  Last night, my "night in charge", boy-oh-boy, that feeling is definitely long gone.  I can't help but wonder, let's say feel extremely apprehensive, about what's in store for tonight.  Oh my lord, the front door is opening.  I honestly don't know from night to night if I will survive.

"Hello?"  They call out in three-part angelic harmony.  "Anybody home?"  They know damn well I'm quivering with fear in the living room where I have been instructed to meet them each day.  And here they are now, before me: three identical giantesses dressed and posed exactly the same.

"Ah Richie" they sing lovingly to me, "we missed you today.  But we will have fun tonight."  The beauty of their voices melts me.  It is astounding how their vibration penetrates and subdues.  They are so stunning.  I look up at their faces, to be undone by their perfection.  They sway a bit from side to side in unison, towering and voluptuous, form-fitting pale green pullovers stretch to cover huge jiggling breasts as they continue to shift their pose.  All the time they are eyeing me, not quite licking their lips.  I try not to think about what craven game is in store tonight.  Their matching green skirts are short, only covering the tops of six necessarily sturdy but beautifully tapered thighs.  They are wearing light-gray sheer nylons that I trace down with my eyes.  Their thick muscular caves are crazy sexy.

"Give us the little kisses now."  They purr and pucker, kind of joking, batting their eyes at me.  "Come on, baby" They sound so... so gentle and flirtatious, like it is all loving fun.  But I know clearly what is expected and it is expected right now.  I walk quickly to the first set of legs before me.  I duck my head under the skirt, press my face up into her panties, and kiss her sweet-smelling pussy as best I can through the cotton.  "Mmmmm" they all moan in harmony, each of course, feeling what the other feels.  I do that greeting two more times, and they sigh, satisfied for now.

"OK Richie, tonight's the night."  Said the first, and goes skipping off.

"Please meet us in our bedroom in, shall we say, thirty minutes."  Adds the second, and goes bounding off after the first.

"And Richie…" The third bends down, her face less than three inches from mine, her sweet breath like a life-force of perfect health.  She brings her lips to graze against mine, while her striking intelligent eyes look down at mine.  When she speaks again her lips are touching mine and most other places on my face as well.  "… remember to keep leading with your heart.  Don't be late, Sweetie."  She swooped up to full height, slowly stepping forward and completely over me, pausing a moment, timed perfectly with my predictable look up, at her panties, and then her magnificent wide and flawless ass departing for the stairs.  I fell over backwards as I tried to follow her exodus without interruption.

Twenty minutes later, The Triplet's tall and wide bedroom door stood shut.  I knocked.  The door opened to a dark room, definitely warmer, more humid than the rest of the house.  I entered the shadowy tropical environ.  And the door shut solid, maybe too permanent a closure, behind me.  Right then I expected to be snatched and taken off for whatever this sinister game might be.

As my eyes adjusted I could make out that the array of tall windows that made up the western wall were fully open.  The shear window coverings trailed out in the wind like softly flapping dimentors too anchored to the wall to fly around the room haunting me.

Outside an intermittent light show of heat lightening, blasted away silently, perhaps one hundred miles away.  The explosions of far off electricity back lit thunderheads and cast hues over Bluebelle Valley from orange to deep red.  As that distant battle raged on its occasional flashes through the tall windows animated anything in the cavernous bedroom that could boast three dimensions.

There they were, revealed in a split second of reddish light, the Towering Triplets sitting on their grand bed at the three points of a ceremonial equilateral triangle. Ten steps in the dark and I reached the edge of the bed.  Another flash of crimson and I could see they were all three already looking right at me, and in fact, right into my eyes.  Darkness reigned again.  Now unseen once more, before me on a bed serving as throne sat three terrible Queens of the Night, completely nude, and beautiful beyond endurance.

With some significant effort I climbed up onto the high bed, using what purchase I could find with the silk sheets, gaining the surface and rolling to my stomach. Somewhere in my upbringing I got that one should not walk on a bed – I guess even a world-record bed this size.  So I crawled toward the Triplet Triangle of glorious doom.  Another briefest waft of light proved I had come quite close.  I saw it all in that flash: the Triplets now sat in a lotus-type yoga pose, eyes closed, perfect posture, their generous bounty displayed by that fraction of photons, more than sufficiently seared into my mind.

I knew the clear pathway in, found it, and entered their triangle.  I didn't know which one to face, so, I suppose democratically, I just lie down, face up, waiting.  Breathe. Whenever I talk to God, which is not so often as it might benefit me, the first thing God always, always tells me to do is Breathe.  And every time, without fail, I find comfort.

Breathe.  It was no different, even now, at the ceremony of my undoing.  And strangely, but doubt it if you wish, the energy that I felt coming from the three Goddesses harmonized perfectly with that of God of my prayers.  Breathe.  And with that breath I could see them now, the faintest of blue light glowing from every cell of their skin.  Breathe.  And as I took in a deep breath of wonderment, I saw they too breathed in unison with each other and most phenomenally, in synchronicity with me.

And now they sang, a wordless song, old it was, before the time of words, channeled up from the womb of the Earth itself.  More ancient than any forest, older perhaps than the mountain stone, so far back there was no time it seemed.  For at the beginning of time is no time, only The Song.  They sang, I wept.  Inside that song I could not have doubt or fears.  And cleansed throughout I was… Breathe.

Three splendid and exquisite hands came to me from the Goddesses, to touch my cheek, to feel and understand the mystery of my tears.  Those tears absorbed, those fingers glowed brighter, then hands, arms and all three bodies bright and flaming blue light like lit cocktail Sambucas.  I looked down at my own body and could see my arms and legs with the same little dancing blue flames.  But I had to see all of myself, so I quickly slipped off my shirt and shorts to become the fourth nude person on the bed.

I laughed. I couldn't help. I'd never experienced anything so magical and delightful. I looked up and they all three grinned down at me, white teeth in blue lips, also beginning to giggle a little bit. I brought up my hand like a wizard's gesture, blew my breath across the final twist of wrist, and cool blue flame shot out from me like a little dragon. That comedy brought forth a chorus of laughs. Fine and appropriately the ceremony ended now in mirth.

The Triplets tumbled away from me and off the bed at once. At first all three shut the windows. The shears dropped, ghosts quieted. Candles were being lit, all shapes and sizes, and not in any even kind of equal distribution. In fact not all flamed yellow, notably many blue, greens, reds, and a few purple in color. And some seemed to occasionally snap and sparkle. The room took on a festive quality. One of the sisters turned on some mindful but cheery enough instrumental music, guitar and harp perhaps.

Now they returned to the bed, surrounding me in a star-shaped hexagon of outstretched legs, foot touching foot. Okay… so here we are, nicely visible in all our nude glory… I think maybe I began to feel a tiny bit inadequate for the moment. I mean they sat completely nude, with legs apart, and socially I have to say the situation was beyond me. Yes the cool ceremony lingered with me, but, come on man, the physical reality shifted and impinged. Awkward, there existed no place to look without a shitload of sexual charge. And it certainly wasn't going to be me to break the ice.

I didn't have to: "We intend to make love to you in our bed, exactly the way you would like it." Then finally it must have looked like I was about to speak. Each woman put an index finger to her lips, "Shhhh. We already know exactly what you want."

Moving forward and onto me, flattening me out on my back, they proved very quickly that they did know exactly what I wanted. One straddled and descended on my cock. Another gently mounted my face and slowly pressed my head deep into the mattress. The third, I think must have sat on the lap of the first, because it got really, really deliciously heavy down there. Yes, I was being loved into obliteration; that was exactly what I wanted and exactly what they administered to me.

And they sang. They sang deep into my soul as I felt myself building toward climax. Thank goodness for Bethany earlier today or I would have cum already. They knew just when to let me breathe, and just when to pound down with more pressure.

I could feel them building as well.  All three at once; that was the goal.  "No," a message was coming into my head from them, "All four at once."  The singing became more glorious, more penetrating, and their rhythm increased in perfect synchrony with each other, and with me.  Building, building, pounding, crushing me down, deep into the bed and up into their bodies.  I felt I was being absorbed.

I soared past the point of no return, but I held back best I could… for them.  Then it was time, no stopping.  And they met my orgasm and tripled it with their own 1860 pound explosion of love -- wild harmonious siren screams of love and release.  Up they lifted, just briefly for me to catch one breath, then down again, writhing, building even more, for another and yet another more intense orgasm.  It made me cum again, even though I must have been spent.  Then up again for my briefest breath.  Then down again, heavier and unbelievably more vigorous that I thought possible to endure.

They reacted to my third orgasm, clamping tighter, pressing more, and it held, held vibrating my body in a vicious shaking pressure, on and on, tighter into horrendous clamping tremors – then, after being thoroughly re-shaped by their squeezing shuttering legs, pussies, and asses, and held beyond all fortitude… finally, then, the pressure started to subside. They relaxed, mushing me down under their pure loving heaviness, taking their time for all the echoes of pleasure to play out completely.  Then after several more minutes of hot wet blackness under them they lifted off my face and climbed off my receding spent cock.

Two of them arranged to either side of me, breasts beautifully at my eye level.  The third lay down on top of me, kissing my mouth now, insistent hungry kisses, making sure I knew… they loved me.  That became the new and clear message now: they loved me, and I don't mean just a little bit. I could hear the message inside my head, almost like it was being spoken.  "We love you.  We want you.  We choose you."

I was not sure at the moment how much of my thoughts they could read.  So I tried not to think about how scary their love was to me.  So I thought about actually how much I loved what had just happened.  I had been perfectly and completely owned by love and sex.  That, I had to admit was quite beyond very nice.  The Triplets proved that they were, in fact, capable of perfection.

"OK" I said at last into her smothering kiss.  She rose up and smiled down.  She placed her hands on either side of my shoulders, powered her butt up off me, raised her legs straight up and into a classic-form handstand, then continued to arch over backward, twisting 180 at her torso, her feet softly touching the bed opposite sides of where they started and to either side above my head, the rest of her body followed, until she was all the way back down, sitting on the bed with her upper thighs to either side of my head.  Very impressive athleticism.

She pulled me up enough until my arms rested on the tops of her thighs, my back against the warmth of her crotch; my head leaned back against her abs, looking up as the terrific breasts canopied majestically above my face.  The two other sisters propped themselves up on the sides, their ample breasts spilling over sister's thighs and pinning my arms, nipples nudging the sides of my face, inviting me to partake if I desired.

Tempted I was, and soon it seemed I would "partake".  But I was curious, "So this 'love' you are talking about.  It isn't part of some game.  I mean it doesn't seem like it.  But I have to know.  Because I feel like I'm being asked to invest my heart here a little bit, I mean maybe a lot."

"We are quite sincere." They sang to my heart softly and very clearly, "We finally realized it completely and with certain clarity yesterday.  It had been evolving, certainly, over the last weeks.  But yesterday we passed the threshold.  And suddenly we just knew.  We are in love… with you."

"Wow." I said, still trying to catch up with my sudden good fortune.  I mean certainly good fortune compared to thinking maybe I would be cravenly smothered to death. I wondered, "Did you read my mind?"

"We won't do that unless it is some kind of emergency.  But we did read your feelings, your trueness, your virtue, your good-heartedness.  We already find you physically irresistible.  You didn't know that, did you?  You're just so darn handsome and sweet smelling.  We had never been attracted to a man before.  We are perhaps too sensitive to their energies.  The men we have met are always so quick with their darker energy.  At first we resented you too, and especially for that desire you elicited in us.  Yes, at first we wanted to hurt you."

"Like in the first week when you pinned me on the pool steps and all three sat on me.  I nearly drowned."

"We also had a fantasy to practice mouth-to-mouth on you.  We recall you like that part quite a bit."

"Sure.  But from now on can we skip the water-boarding and go right to the month-to-mouth part?"

They laughed at that, and then resumed serious again. "Even still this week we harbored some thoughts that were unkind, Farmer Richie" they teased.  Then they each looked quite sincere again, "But something finally shifted.  And now we are clear about how we feel.  We choose you.  Do you choose us?"

"This is still sudden for me."  It was a heavy decision, so to speak.  But these gals and their singing, they would be impossible to resist if they were given the go ahead to put the pressure on, both physical and emotional.  "Could I have a little time, a couple of days, to think about it?  I want to be fair and truthful with you."

"Yes, we understand."  Their faces continued to look kind yet also impassive and unreadable.  Then there was a hopeful solicitous look, "Do you still want to play our evening games?"

I'd never expected this could be a choice.  Actually I didn't need a couple of days to think about that. "Honestly.  Yes I do.  You gals are incredibly fun – scary as hell, but fun."  They laughed at that; I continued. "But maybe, once in a while, I might need a night off."

"Then we are dating." They declared.  It was in that moment that I realized for all their skills, intelligence, sophistication, dominance, acumen… how completely naïve they were.  I was their first boyfriend.  And at a very basic level they were just three young women "in love" for the first time.  Not that I was all that experienced in relationship either.  But I knew these sisters had not yet felt the pang of lost love, the heartache and longing it can bring nor the insanity of jealously.  And I shivered at that last thought, for if angry enough I was quite sure they could inflict damage and pain and torture far worse than death.

"Are you cold?" They said to my shiver, apparently not reading my thoughts.  Not waiting for an answer, the legs that were beside my head raised up further down to cover my legs, both covering them and pulling them slightly apart to either side.  It was then that we all noticed at once that my little volunteer kind of had his "hand half up".

"Well," they said, "Let's see what we can do about this little development.  You are going to need your strength.  Have you noticed our milk sustains you, has given you special endurances?"  The amazon to my left leaned her breast over, finding my mouth with her nipple.  Come to think of it that had to be how I had just survived the sex we'd had. Though I sucked weakly now, that magic elixir flowed no problem and I could kind of feel the energy in it.  They had actually started re-forming me to be able to endure their love-making.  That astounded me.

Just as I was having these thoughts I heard her say, "There's much more to this milk we provide than you have dreamed possible.  Yes, you will be more than amazed before we are half way through."

I felt the sister to the right leave her position.  Of course I couldn't see anything with the huge breast smothering my face.  But I felt my cock being handled, then licked and sucked and licked and squeezed and teased and sucked and sucked…

They started singing to me again, telling me wordless things as their voices entered my head, as if I were in a dream.  I was so relaxed, feeling so unbelievably good, like I'd found the center of the universe inside a giant goddess of love.

I learned a lot as they sang to me, nursed me, blew me, owned me with their loving.  Now they sang in worded stories and I learned they were being studied quite intensely at the Synsonto Institute.  Their skills and special talents were deemed super extraordinary, and the extent of their potentials was yet unknown.  For example their intelligence was telepathically combinable, and it was off the IQ charts.  The scientists didn't know how to properly test it.  They revealed a prediction they were likely to live to be at least 250 years old.  Oh, and their milk would likely do the same for me if I drank it daily.  Yes I was amazed and could tell we were nowhere near "half way through."

They clarified something I thought I already had detected: they were still growing.  But maybe that was a bit more typical.  It seemed most of the Amazons of Bluebelle Valley kept growing until they were at least thirty years old.

I think maybe I came again.  I was so lost in their love, so mesmerized by their signing, so overcome to the point of having no boundaries remaining; I could hardly notice my own orgasm.  I didn't know whose body smashed me again now, their juices flowing over me, lost in the deliciousness of pussy pressing down… again… and again…

The last thing I recall before sleep finally overtook me, or if I just passed out, I'm not sure which, I lie there calculating an inventory in my head about the Triplets and me… let's see: three voluptuous athletic Goddesses of womanly perfection and exquisite beauty, intelligent beyond current measure, ultra-wealthy because they routinely cure people by the thousands by just expressing their magnificence and understanding through their songs, likely to live extraordinary long lives, and inviting me to do the same by partaking of the magic elixir in their milk that tastes beyond heavenly, expressing certainty of their love for me, and inviting me to be their boyfriend – that about sums it up, doesn't it?  Oops, and I almost forgot, the sex was pretty good, too.  And my best response, in essence, is: "I'll think about it"? Man-oh-man, Richie, what an odd duck you are…

I must have slept soundly because the next thing I noticed was: the sound of the showers running full blast, a feint morning light coming through the sheets that shrouded me, and the dependable lonely greeting of the mourning dove.

# III. Smothering Secretary Pool

Maybe it was the glow of me new love for the Triplets clouding my senses, but it took me a while to notice that the feel in the office had changed. Did I see an actual welcoming smile on Miss Peterson's face? Yes, definitely that's something different.

And look at cute little Miss Rasmussen. Did she actually wink at me as I walked past her office door?

Pause. Hang on a second. Something is way off today. I've got to explain something to you. Actually I need to: double pause. Let's backtrack a bit more, or nothing will make sense.

First of all, "little" Miss Rasmussen wasn't that little, unless you think at 7'11" 492 pound woman is small. I mean, that puts her some seventy pounds heavier and five inches taller than Big Bethany of the pollination crew. In fact, of the eight secretaries in the pool only Miss Rasmussen and Miss Mansfield were less than 500 pounds, and not by much. But size is all relative, isn't it? So while those two beauties would dominate the Pollination Crew for size, in this office they did not even make par.

In fact the largest of the secretaries, Miss Monroe, stood at 8'4" and 588 pounds. How did I know these numbers? Well, they talked about it every day. It seemed a big matter of pride. And since it appeared they were all still growing, they were always checking in about it. Of course, they could care less if I heard. For them I barely existed.

So at 588 pounds Miss Monroe squished her big office chair at only maybe 30 pounds less that one of the Triplets. The other thing that I thought was totally awesome about Miss Monroe: she was absolutely drop-dead gorgeous. And I mean stupefying good-looking: big wavy ginger hair, huge wide firm ass, bra-busting breasts, and a super-sexy movie-star face with little those beauty marks for accents. And best of all, she knew it, parading around the office with her big classy chassis and expression of casual supremacy. Instant, instant hard-on I tell you.

None of this counts with respect, and I mean a hell of a lot of fearful respect, to Miss Strickland, the big gigantic boss whom we seldom saw from behind her massive closed door at the end of the hallway. Apparently she must have been completely off the premises today.  Otherwise, the bubbly mood would not be possible – nope, not at all.

OK, so that was pause number one, this relative size thing.  Pause number two had to do with the jovial ambiance that seemed to be pervading that office today.  I looked in the break room.  And Miss Jorgenson and Miss Klingbell actually took a second to look my way and give me little good-morning waves, each with the fingering tweetle-dees on her free non-coffee-mugged hand.  What gives?

You see, these eight secretaries I serviced frightened the heck out of me.  They kept me on an adrenaline fight-or-flight edge all the time.  And the fight scenario was not remotely reasonable.  For weeks they had treated me like I wasn't even there, like I didn't exist, until they needed something.  There was no "Good morning, Richie" or "How are you today my good fellow".  More likely they would walk right through me or over me if I didn't watch myself and get out of the way.

What's the big deal you say?  Well you get knocked over in the hallway by a 500 pound woman and tell me how you like it.  Yea, how about you step over here and be the avatar for a while.  Let's put a couple of these 500 pounders on you and see how tough you are.   I'm sorry; that wasn't fair.  Let's give you a little time to think about.  But let me know when you're ready to step in here because there are some days I could, quite frankly, use a break.

So I had to be on the alert all the time.  The first time it happened, like my second day of work, it was Miss Taylor.  She came out her office door and ran right into me; sent me sprawling back to the other side of the hallway, against the wall, where I slid down into an angular little heap.  As I looked up for a helping hand or an "excuse me" Miss Taylor's strides had taken her well on down the hallway.  That's the day I found out I was the invisible man.  When I kept that in mind, treated the situation like they were all blind when it came to me, then I had a lot less problems.

Still there was the surprise attack routine.  OK, like the game is you can't see me.  But then don't go purposefully backing into me, butt-pinning me against the cabinets in the break room, or making a point to sit right on me like they didn't notice I was already in the chair.

Another favorite: a Secretary might ask me into her office to do some bullshit task like empty her garbage, then pretend to forget I was there and maybe knock me over onto the carpet or into couch.  What's that supposed to be about?  It couldn't be harassment if she can make a case she never saw me – a case I figure would seem reasonable given my miniscule size.

At least the Pollination Crew conducted business above board.  They made it clear what was what, and the 'what' was me being pumped every afternoon on the way home with them trying to break sex records – good betting, gamesmanship we all understood.  And definitely I was noticed, I mean really noticed in terms of how my body reacted.  But this office treatment, well, it was kind of screwy.

And yet, for all my complaining, I liked it.  Yes, I confess, I liked it.  It excited me, never knowing when some big butt might capture me out of the blue.  And damn the secretaries looked fine: huge, sexy, well-dress, sophisticated, and luscious.  Oh man, what a gig I have to admit.

When it came to giantess Miss Strickland herself, I'd have to say she presented beyond aloof, acted a bit hostile most of the time.  She definitely would notice me and look down at me from her extreme fifteen foot height, and I wished she wouldn't – too intimidating.  No, she hadn't said anything mean to me, and never came close to bumping or touching me at all, only glared, seemingly annoyed, or… something else was wrong, maybe… I couldn't put my finger on it.

For the rest of the ladies, I would come into existence for them when they needed something, some grunt work done – like take out the shreddings or go get some reams of paper or bring me a decaf latte from the truck in the parking lot.  Smartly dressed, pampered and paid well, I figured they were all stuck up and hadn't a clue how to be relational to me.

But there was, without a doubt, a very different feel to the office this morning.   My goodness, was that another smile, this time from Miss Monroe?  Oh wow, that's a moment to treasure.  Of all the daydreams in the Secretary Pool, Miss Monroe took the prize going away!  And now it appeared this dream-come-true was walking directly toward me.  I loved the look of her tight-fitting skirt, smooth sheer stockings, and her totally unnecessary high heels. It seemed like I was about to get my first assignment for the day, "Richie, will you please come to my office."

Yes, they each had a private office, fully outfitted with wide walnut veneer desk, matching built in walnut bookshelves, good second story view window of the research plots and tree-lined Bluebelle River in the distance, exotic indoor plants under contracted care, and a generous sitting area including a big leather couch.

As I ran along behind, trying to keep up with Miss Monroe's long strides, I took advantage of my relative position to study her big sexy ass, muscles and great mass shifting clearly underneath the tight forest green of her short skirt.  Sorry to say it so blatantly; but that sexy physicality, so literally in my face, was all could think about.  After all it wiggled in front of me right at my eye level; so it was reasonable to look straight ahead and notice, wasn't it?  That wouldn't be leering or anything, now would it?

Who was I kidding?  I wasn't just projecting all this excitement.  Oh yes, Miss Monroe definitely had a more noticeable teasing sway today in her ample ass as she paraded before me down the hallway.  Was there a new policy maybe?  "Be nice to poor, tiny Richie."  I'd be the last to know.  Whatever it was, I had to like it.

You might be asking: "What about your new girlfriends, the Triplets?"  And thinking I'm the worst new boyfriend ever.  I can only say to you that I probably do love the Triplets.  How could I not?  But recall, I said I need a little time to think about the relationship(s).  I mean I'm supposed to get along with my office workers, aren't I?  Maybe I could somehow get promoted.  That would be cool – finally something to write home about.

Miss Monroe's big strong butt: tick-tock, tick-tock, back and forth it swung to the sharp and heavy click of her heels.  "Close your mouth, Richie", I had to tell myself, don't gape like cad.  Problem was, the more I experienced these big asses up close and oh so personal, the more I wanted them.

Tick---tock; Miss Monroe was slowing down.  And me running, I had to put the brakes on to keep from crashing into her, my face stopping just and half-inch from where the tightly taught material of her skirt met the perfection of upper thighs begging to be kissed.  She looked around and then down "Oh there you are.  Please come in."

I followed her into her office.  She shut the door behind us – and locked it?

"Well, she looked down at me.  I need your special skills, if you can be so kind."  Miss Monroe was being downright sweet toward me.  It was unnerving.

A little dumbstruck: "What special skills?"  I mean really, what could I do that was special?

"It's back here behind my desk."  She led me over, near the wall.  Down there."  She pointed at the floor, "I dropped my favorite pin."

I looked down but didn't see a damn thing except her sizable feet in her sexy high heels, her well-turned ankles, terrific calves, leading to particularly lovely, sturdy legs, ascending…

"No, down here." She must have noticed I was getting distracted. "Down in the vent. I dropped it down in the vent and my hand is too big to reach in. I thought maybe you could retrieve it for me?" her shy shrug was precious.

"Oh, of course." How could I decline? I got down on my hands and knees and started tugging at the vent cover. It was a struggle, actually, like maybe the darn thing had never been moved since it was installed. Next I knew she was on her hands and knees as well; right over me, looking around my skinny shoulders.

"Let me help with that." She reached down, leaning in a bit, her breasts resting on my back. My arms strained to stay locked and not buckle. "There." She easily palmed the cover loose, and set it aside. But she did not rise back up, still leaving me under the pressure of her heavy bosom. I could feel her breathing quicken slightly. Breathing faster from the light effort on her part to remove the vent cover? Not likely. Was she, ah… maybe a little bit excited?

I dropped down to my stomach on the floor and peered down into the venting. "Do you have a flashlight?" I requested.

She stood, took a couple of steps over to her desk, then back, dropped all the way down on the floor to lie next to me, and I have to say just a little bit on me. I mean only her left breast and arm on my back, the curve of her neck over and on my head – really, not more than 150 pounds of her on me – but like twice my weight. Her long lustrous light auburn hair cascaded all around past the sides of my face and over my shoulders, and enveloped me in her perfume that must go by the brand name "Crazy Desires."

"Here ya go." She handed me the small flashlight.

Fortunately I was in the right spot to search into the vent, because I actually couldn't move with just that much of her on me. The flashlight was plenty bright. And sure enough, there was her pen about 14" down where the venting elbowed at 90 degrees. I stretched down, and fished it out. I managed to turn my head enough to say to her very close face as I handed her the pen. "Here you go, Miss Monroe."

I was just noticing that the pen was maybe too thick to have actually "fallen" through the vent slats when Miss Monroe responded. "Oh, my hero." And she gave a nice wet kiss on the cheek.

"Wow!" I remarked as she raised a bit. I rolled onto my back, still trying to be polite. "Jeez, Miss Monroe, that was a nice reward."

She held her ground above me. "Did you like that little kiss?"

"Sure, I mean, we all need to get along well here in the office, don't we."  I really didn't know what to say.

Her eyes gleamed as she abruptly lowered back down, "If you like that you're going to love this!"  And she planted a kiss square on the lips.  The kiss grew and grew, spreading over my mouth, chin and cheeks as she opened her mouth wide, her tongue working me over.  It was a little hard to breathe with her upper lip pressing against my nostrils.  No, actually it was very difficult to breathe at all with her huge body covering my skinny bones and pressing on the hard floor.  She broke off the kiss and actually began licking my face, like she was a little girl having fun devouring her ice cream.

But my back hurt against the floor and a little involuntary "Ouch," escaped my lips.

Immediately she was up and off me, "Oh, I'm so, so sorry.  I was hurting you?"

"No, I'm OK.  It is just the floor is kind of hard…"

But she was mortified by her behavior, "Oh, can you forgive me.  That was so unprofessional."  She walked over and sat down on the leather couch.  I noticed how the cushions yielded deeply, bending high to either side of her bottom because she had seated herself right on the middle crack.  Her upper legs angled up at maybe 45 degrees, they were so long.  Of course that outrageously exposed her panties, which were really the merest threads of a shear thong.

Miss Monroe seemed to have more regrets. "I don't know what came over me.  Please don't tell Miss Strickland.  I'll lose my job.  And, oh, I am so sorry Richie."  Loved the sympathetic way she said my name.  That's what had been missing these last several weeks, especially from the Pollination Crew as well, an apology.

"Oh, that's OK, Miss Monroe.  I know you didn't mean any harm.  Of course I won't tell Miss Strickland.  You have my word on that."  I never shut up soon enough.  I found myself adding, "And, you know it wasn't all bad.  You are quite a kisser."

"Well," she smiled, "Thank you for that. Maybe we could just pretend like that didn't happen and get on with our work."

"Sure Miss Monroe.  You bet."  I started toward the door.

"Actually, there is a little more work we could do right here, that is, if you can still trust me."  It seemed she really didn't want me to leave.

"Yeah, I guess so, Miss Monroe." I stopped mid-stride. "You're the boss and I do want to make you happy."

"Oh you are so forgiving Richie." Her smile was dazzling, irresistible really. She patted the bent cushion next to her.

I got the message and dutifully went over and sat by her. But the tilted cushion caught me off balance, and I slid clumsily right down into her. I righted myself, sort of. Yet I was wedged between the cushion forcing me down and her right butt cheek.

"Well," she shrugged, "It looks like you have forgiven me."

I wanted to say, "Well actually your big heavy ass is creating an Event Horizon on this couch, and I couldn't get off this couch any more than light can escape a Black Hole." But I've learned it is a good idea to keep a giantess is a good mood if possible. "Of course, Miss Monroe, I think you are terrific."

"Well, then." She seemed quite satisfied and happy now. "Now that you've recued my pen, maybe we can get on with the next assignment." She wiggled in position a little. I slid under her ass just a little bit. She seemed not to notice.

Stupid me, I could not leave this nagging thought alone. "You know, Miss Monroe, the bore of your pen is too wide for the slats of the vent cover. So was wondering just how the pen got down there, because it could not have just fallen through the slats."

"What are you saying, Richie?" There was a very slight sternness to her tenor that I maybe should have heeded.

"I'm thinking maybe someone put it there."

"Are you saying that I took the vent cover off and put my own pen down in the vent? That for some reason I put that pen there on purpose? And that reason was to lure you in here under false pretenses, and then take advantage of you? Is that what you are accusing me of?" Yep, the tone was getting a little threatening now.

"Miss Monroe, I'm just saying, it doesn't make sense. Of course I'm not as smart as you. So I was wondering, that's all." I was trying to back pedal, but it was still lame.

"So your story, what you are not saying, is that I put the pen in the vent, put the cover back on firmly, went and asked for your help, knew your weakness would require my help to remove the vent, at which time I could take advantage of your inferior position below me on the floor, lean down on you, pin you, pretend to be grateful, then stoop so low as to molest you right here in this professional workplace office?  Is that your theory, Richie, sexual harassment in the office place?"  She sounded furious, her face red with anger, her expression indignant.

"Well, I, ah… er…" I shrugged, "I mean, you know, it's just that… and so… well.. I thought that, ah, with you being…I mean who you are…"  Talk about a fail.

Miss Monroe burst out laughing.  She tried to hold it in with the back of her hand; I guess not to make too much noise that would escape to the hall way.  But that made her laugh more.  I thought she was going to fall off the couch.  She could hardly catch her breath.

At first I was in shock at her reaction, then relieved and kind of laughed a bit along with her.  Then it hit me.  It was all a big joke to her.  I stood, my feelings were really hurt by this.  "I think I'll leave now."

Before I could take one stride she grabbed me with both hands and hauled me back to her.  I stood between her slightly spread legs, her face staring right down into mine. "You are right, of course.  I did do all the manipulation.  But it is no joke.  I mean it is kind of funny."  She seemed to glance at her watch.  "But I'm not joking about my desires.  I might be a little ashamed of my behavior.  But I just can't help it any longer.  I want you.  Actually, I want you now."

I could see she was waiting for any positive response from me.  I stared into her big beautiful unblinking eyes as long as I could.  Then I looked down – that didn't help as all I could notice was her beckoning cleavage, all mine, for the simplest nod of acquiescence.  She waited.  I continued to melt.  She tilted her head just bit, her smile coy, knowing, knowing the effect she had on me.  I looked up to her again.  She tilted her head once more, eyebrows raised, mouth parted, tongue just visible, a reminder of her luscious aggressive kissing.  I must have smiled a little.  Because her smile spread wide and triumphant in response.  Still she waited for me to say it.

Finally I succumbed, "Oh what the heck…"

With that she said, "Yes!"  She grabbed the lower hem of her sweater, whipped it up and over my head, pulling me in to nestle in that cleavage I so desired.  Oh sweet lord, I could not have imagined the vigor pent up in one Miss Monroe.

I'm not sure, but I think she stood and ran around the office, celebrating what fun she was going to have.  Her bra was like her thong, shear and almost not there.  I was bounced around, knocked almost senseless by her wild breasts and passion

unleashed.  Wham!  I was slammed down under her, I think back on the couch.
Then it really got really crazy as she went to work on me.

Her clothes came flying off.  My shirt and shorts went sailing across the room.  She
road me out of control, not knowing where to start, what she wanted next.  And of
course this crazy lover wanted it all at once.  So first it was "Kissmekissmekissme."
But her mouth and my mouth were not enough for her.  Suddenly it was,
"kissmybreastkissmybreast."  Then boom her pussy was on me, smothering my
face and I had no idea what she was saying, probably "Eatme-eatme-eatme!"  Then
back to kissing.  She held me upside down and sucked my cock.  Then, before I
could come, she threw me on the couch and prowled over me, growling like a
panther.  Then she was on me again, tip-whipping me dizzy.  Then pausing to make
me suck.  The up again and on me with her vast butt.  Oh my word she demanded
that I lick that beautiful ass, her amazing magically delectable sweet-smelling ass,
as she wriggled on down, spreading her butt cheeks on my face.

After nearly suffocating me, she squeezed her cheeks tight, literally lifted me off the
couch face first buried in her ass.  She paraded around the room, me dangling limp
behind her.  Then she squatted over the couch, and I felt as if I had been pooped
out.  Sorry that's kind of gross.  Then it was her pussy again on my face; this time
for a long time.  I guess she was deciding she liked that best.  I think maybe I did
too because it was really, really sweet and I loved the feeling of being owned like
that.  For my part I was vigorous with my tongue and lips and sucking and nosing
and chin – my entire face was in there and all parts were busy.

Yes finally she settled down for a good long session of oral sex.  We got into a
rhythm and she even remembered to let me breathe on a regular basis.  Oh yeah, I
was starting to like Miss Monroe quite a bit.  And I respected her learning curve.
See, I think maybe I was with a virgin.  Actually she still was a virgin at this point,
because we had not done it yet.

She figured out she could easily play with my cock while she rode my face.  So on
and on we went, who knows how long.  It occurred to me someone might wonder
where I was.  But there was nothing I could do.  I was being obliterated by pussy
and ass.  My puny arms barely reached to the sides of her butt, my hands just
barely free, flopping around out there at the end of invisible limp wrists.  It did not
seem like I was going to report for further duty anytime soon.

Her first orgasm was kind of small, just a spasm really.  I don't think she actually
knew what it was.  But like I said, steep learning curve with Miss Monroe.  She
latched onto that feeling and rode my face in very specific ways to milk the

sensations in her key spots.  I did my darnest to respond as well.  You might say I did my *job* well.

When the explosions came they were fierce.  Oh did that woman want me inside her!  We needed to shift to fucking, but she didn't get that yet.  Her body demanded it.  But all that occurred to her was to fuck my face.  There was no way I could let her know.  Perhaps she would figure that out eventually as well.  Orgasm after orgasm after orgasm, each one grander.  And still her body would not fully release.  I don't even know what was going on with my cock she had squeezed it so much and for so long.  My entire world was the opening wet pussy that clamped onto my face and seemed intent on forcing my head up inside her.

Finally the light went on somewhere upstairs.  I watched her wonderful pussy ascend off my bruised, swollen, and dripping wet face.  Don't get me wrong; I'm not complaining about the memorable face ride. Then down she plunged onto my cock, still holding its own, what a soldier.  The muscular control Miss Monroe demonstrated astounded me.  She had opened her pussy to take in my entire face, and now she closed almost too tightly around my little cock.  Such a tight squeeze.  Such heavy pressure.  Such extraordinary gorgeousness I viewed in the up past her narrow spread of the legs that pinned my shoulders, past the her swinging swollen full and massive breasts, to see her grinning with satisfaction and knowing dominance.  I knew I would cum within a minute.  Miss Monroe came even quicker as her body had been waiting for this for some two hours of vigorous foreplay.  And my-oh-my, Miss Monroe, the culmination was indeed glorious.

Some ten minutes later Miss Monroe still sat on me.  The orgasms and after-orgasms were long gone.  I wondered if Miss Monroe knew it was over.  She looked at her watch – again.  Finally I said, "You know, we can stop any time.  I don't think there's anything else that's going to happen right now."  Post sex, her heaviness on me was starting to feel a bit tough.

"Oh that's OK.  I like it."  She said it but she sounded unconvincingly bored.  Then her cell phone rang and she reached over and nabbed it off the floor.  "Valerie."  Wow, I didn't know her first name. I always called her Miss Monroe. "Yes.  You're ready?  OK. Good."  She tapped off and sat the phone aside.  Then to me, "Aren't you getting bored with this?"

God, I thought she'd never ask.  "Well, if you're done, I suppose I could stop too."

"Good" She kind of jumped up off me. "Go an in and clean yourself up, why don't cha'." She indicated the door to her private bathroom. Yes, each of the secretaries had one.

"Sure." I ambled across the room, kind of stretching my back a bit as I went.

"Hey, Richie." Meet me in the break room after, will ya'? There's something not working right in there."

"You bet." I think she left the office as I entered the bathroom. I washed off, thinking about the delicious turn my office job had taken. Miss Monroe, wow, I hope she "lost" something else down her vents real soon.

Out in the hallway all was quiet. No one seemed to be in any of the offices. Maybe they all went out to lunch. What time was it anyway? Well. No matter. I was still on assignment with Miss Monroe and that was fine with me. I wondered if I could be more familiar with her now, or would I become invisible again. Just as I pondered that disturbing note I rounded the doorway into the lunch room.

"SURPRIZE!!!"

What the heck…

"HAPPY BIRTHDAY RICHIE!" Shouted out eight tall smiling beauties.

Dumfounded into a mute state, I just stared at them. And that made them laugh like crazy. Now waiting for me to recover they began the song. "Happy Birthday to you, Happy…" From behind the chorus, Miss Petersen and Miss Appleton produced a cake, carrying it to the forefront, twenty-two bright candles and the message "Happy Birthday Richie!" with a small script at the bottom: "Love, your Big Babe Bosses".

Honest to God I couldn't help but let a tear or two escape. This was the nicest thing ever, and it was such a complete shock. You got to understand the last birthday party I'd had, sixth grade, ended up a complete failure – as in nobody came. I had tried to tell my mother I didn't have any friends. So she figured to solve the problem by inviting my whole class. But that's just the easiest out in the entire world for everyone to skip it. So all that showed was my sister and some of her somewhat sympathetic friends. What really killed me though was the look on my dad's face; he'd come home early from work to be supportive of his scrawny, disappointing son. Underneath his propped up smile I could see the mixture of anger, disappointment, and embarrassment. That was the last birthday party for me in that household. And at college I just kept quiet about it.

I looked up from my thoughts.  The secretaries were all looking at me concerned, quiet.  Finally I found some words, and the genuine smile they deserved.  "Wow – I mean, thank you."  I looked at the flaming cake.  It was really a work of art with an icing landscape of Bluebelle Valley green hills and colorful spring wild flowers.

"Make a wish, Richie."  Yep, the wax dripped liberally down the red candles.  If time meant anything, it meant the fleeting life of a short, skinny candle.  With sympathy, and a really great wish, I rescued all twenty-two candles from the flames.

The raucous cheer went up and some calls of: "What did you wish for, Richie?"

"Well," My goodness I felt warm to the center of my heart.  "You know, I'd have to say any wish I might have here in the office – well, you've already exceeded it."  I caught Miss Monroe's eye and growled out best I could, "Especially with one Miss Monroe's stalling technique while you set up this party.  And holy cow, look at these decorations!"  The room had all kinds of balloons and streamers and glitter.  Even so, it couldn't have taken the entire two hours of delay that Miss Monroe crushed onto me.

Miss Monroe saw me calculating.  "It was the cake, Richie.  They got the order wrong and the girls had to order another one after I'd already called you to my office. I was only supposed to stall you for like fifteen minutes, silly."

"With the pen in the vent gag."  I got it.

"But when I didn't get the call, well, I had to sort of improvise, press on now, didn't I? You're not thinking of complaining are you?"  She took a half-step toward me, threatening in a fun-loving big-ass way.

"Hell no."  I assured her.  "Talk about a fantasy birthday gift coming true.

"That's what I figured."  Miss Monroe purred.  All the gals laughed.  Miss Monroe continued, "Now that I know you better, I can promise you there's a lot more where that came from."

Good God Miss Monroe, that's a distracting thought.  But I couldn't help thinking: they were one day off though.  My birthday was the day before.

Right on cue Miss Klingbell seemed to anticipate.  "Sorry we missed your actual birthday by a day.  Of course we knew from your application records it was yesterday.  We just had to wait a day until you-know-who [meaning Miss Strickland] was out of the office."  She'd said it like Miss Strickland was some kind of evil wizard.  To me, the severe giantess was even scarier.

"And today," Miss Jorgenson piped in, "Miss Strickland is at the Synsonto Research and Medical labs all day for her quarterly examinations."  I felt like we should all pause in prayer and cross ourselves on that news.

"Meanwhile," Miss Appleton beamed her winning smile, "Let's get on with this party!"

"You mean there's more?"  I felt very happy and satisfied already.

"Oh Richie…" Miss Monroe took two steps forward, reached down, and picked me up.  "I do love a humble man."  She stood me on the main break room table, next to my charming birthday cake.  All eight secretaries gathered around the table, their attractive faces not much above my eye level.

I looked around at them as they all smiled at me, I have to say with far more affinity than I ever expected from them.  I thought about the cake, that wasn't it time to cut it up and eat it.  Standing next to it and looking around at these, perhaps lunch-time hungry, women, I began to feel a bit like a food item myself, on the lunch table and all.

"So," I offered a bit cautiously, "What's next?"

"Well, typically one would have a few birthday party games."  Miss Taylor suggested with an edge of intrigue.

"We made up some just special for you," Miss Mansfield almost giggled. "Want to give them a try?"

Of course I could not disappoint.  "Sure.  Sounds like fun."

"More than fun, Richie," Miss Rasmussen encouraged.  "It's games, prizes, and birthday presents all rolled into one."

"Come on," Said Miss Mansfield, "Let's get this table out of the way."  Miss Mansfield and Miss Peterson picked up the table with me on it and carried it to the corner of the room.  Three of the other secretaries bent over and rolled out a lovely thick area-carpet to cover most of the break room floor.  Miss Peterson picked me up, carried me to the center, and had me sit down.  All eight secretaries sat around me in a circle.

So for the first game I'm blindfolded.  Remember Pin-the-Tail-on-the-Donkey?  I suppose you could say they created a version of that.  Only instead of a tail to pin on the donkey, I was supposed to blind-man my way around the room, lips puckered and kissing the air until my lips found a target.  They called the game "Bull's Eye".  And "Bull's Eye" is what they all shouted when my lips landed on the soft target of Miss Klingbell's big exposed left bun. "Kiss it again!" Someone shouted.  As I did I felt a small piece of rolled up paper placed into my hand.

I recalled I had heard some rustling while I was being blindfolded then spun around for disorientation.  Turns out those swishing noises were eight secretaries taking their clothes off.  And now I realized they struck poses around me in some loose circle and waited for my lips to run into… "Bull's Eye" they all shouted again, my face unmistakably buried in deep soft cleavage.  After several required kisses another piece of paper forced into my hand.

The next Bull's Eye I'd landed right up into a nice juicy pussy.  I had to pause and lick that a while to the enthusiastic cheers of the ladies.  This time maybe three pieces of paper got shoved into hand.  Were they giving me money?

I could actually recognize the delightful smell of Miss Monroe as I approached the next target.  I sensed some slight movement, maybe she cheated a bit to get me to "Bull's Eye" the loudest cheer yet as my face entered deep into Miss Monroe's exquisite ass.  She squeezed me in tight and sat right down on me, smashing me onto the rug they had rolled out.  Oh Miss Monroe, such a beautiful ass, I kissed up into it.  She shifted back enough to go from the ass smother to a perfect pussy smother.  I started in licking like crazy.  Miss Monroe, let me be your pussy slave forever…

Right when I felt things could not get any better, I felt my shorts being gently but quickly removed.  Then as ideal as could possibly be in that moment, a luscious heavy pussy engulfed my very erect Volunteer.  The big ass covered all my lower body and pumped down on me hard. One, two, three…  I felt about to cum… four… for sure about to blow… five, and then up and off, just in time for me to pull back.

Miss Monroe lifts up just enough for me to grab a gulp of air.  Oh bless her merciful ass.  In that moment amidst laughing I hear, "Your turn Rachael."  And down comes Miss Monroe's pussy again.  And on my cock descends a slightly heavier woman, with a very nice squeeze.  Again, one, two, three, four, five vigorous pumps and off just in the nick of time.

Up lifts dear Miss Monroe, more laughs and "… OK Lorraine…" Down smashes Miss Monroe, and I can tell she is working up a lather.  And on comes Lorraine (Miss Appleton?) significantly heavier than the last secretary.  One, two, three, four, five, and off without a split-second to spare.

Miss Monroe lets me breathe again.  Even though I do breathe, I'm so crazed and excited I can't stop licking up into her, her delicious juices starting to flow over me.  The laugher is more excited, and someone is calling for Francine.  Miss Monroe plunges down, working it right away, doing all she can for the five-count.  Francine is smarter, taking her time to make each pump last too long, wiggling and gyrating on me at the bottom of each smash.  One… two…. three… for sure I would have cum by now except, well, now, I didn't want to yet.  I wanted to make it all the way through… what, all seven, that is, minus Miss Monroe who I hoped would never leave my face… four… five… and pressing down extra-long, then off.

Breathe around the drenching by Miss Monroe. Squeals of laughter and protest at Francine's antics.  Oh to be a thousand years old and have a birthday like this every year.  They cheered as the heavier yet Lorna climbed on.  Of course she had witnessed Francine's tactics.  Lorna did all those and added her own special squirming.  Miss Monroe's clinching on my face told me she tried to hold off too, like me, hanging on for the climax that had to be coming soon.  …and Five.  Lorna climbed off before I had time to fully appreciate just how wonderful it felt to have her on me.

Miss Monroe lifted, my face still squeezed into her pussy.  I had to pull back, slide out to get a breath.  And already, whoever was next, had climbed on, slid down, and proceeded to smash me more than the previous amazon.  This anonymous queen had an up and down vibration that made each count more like ten pumps.  Obviously the rules were loose.  I wasn't complaining.  Even if I tried I doubt Miss Monroe's pussy would have put up with any protest from me.

Time to breathe again.  I suppose air was necessary, but my sentiment was more of "please don't take this pussy away".  I heard applause of approval for "Good job, Kathy."  Then I heard what I'd been waiting for. "Take him home Donna."

I knew already that Donna, was Miss Klingbell, only second to Miss Monroe in stature.  And she crushed onto me good and hefty.  But this time there seemed to be no counts.  Miss Klingbell quite simply came to destroy me.  And now so did Miss Monroe.  For some reason I pictured them above me kissing each other, Miss Monroe nicely backward on my face, Miss Klingbell frontward on my middle.

Then the real birthday punishment began.  A secretary evidently climbed onto Miss Klingbell's lap.  Then another onto Miss Monroe's.  Then another on each and finally one more on each.  The one ton of woman forced my head completely inside of Miss Monroe right as she exploded with a phenomenal orgasm; lifting all three women above her, and then all four of them crashing with smothering finality.  Only, the finale seemed to have several encores of quadruple butt smashes.

Down below, only slightly behind in sequence, Miss Klingbell led her fearsome foursome with an orgasm that must have been building for years.  That ton of woman turned my body into a wasteland of pussy devastation.  I came and came and came, and Donna's great and heavily-augmented authority took it all and smashed it back on me one hundred fold.

It was a two-ton titanic twat termination.  When the 500 pounders finally rolled off me one by one, the last to leave was Miss Monroe.  I gasped for breath, curling into a fetal position.  Did I survive, or was I about to die now?  My goodness that felt so good. I felt a hot breath in my ear, my face being licked, then a voice I recognized, dear Miss Monroe.  "Oh Richie, my ass, my pussy wants you more, right now.  I just want so much to smash you up into me.  I want to take you home and put you in my bed and smother you all night long and all day and all night forever."  Then louder she said.  "Pull me back, ladies.  I want to sit on him right now.  I am craving him so much!  To smother him!  Save him from me!"  And she planted her big ass on me again.  But I was in a bad sideways position.  She would have ruined me except four ladies held her up while Miss Taylor slid me out from under her.

But then Miss Taylor had caught the butt smashing fever.  She mounted me saying.  "Oh I have to smash him now.  Sorry Richie, I can't help.  My ass must own you.  Others pulled Miss Taylor off me.  Then they in turn succumbed to the hysteria.  They climbed on me.  And soon there was no one left to rescue me.  They all fought to get their asses and pussies on me.  The only thing saving me temporarily was the bedlam of their disorganization.  One thing for sure: I descended to the bottom of a pile that condensed onto me and they all pressed in and on.

All the sudden, with my life in the balance of suffocation, I felt the pile grow lighter and lighter and lighter, like great bodies were being tossed aside to find me.   As my head emerged from the blackness of smothering ass I heard a booming. "What the hell are you doing?"  And there stood giantess Miss Strickland, holding up a 500 pound plus secretary in each hand like trying to decide which watermelon was heavier.  She looked at me with horror.  "Can you walk?"

I nodded, yes.

"Then get the hell out of this room!"  Miss Strickland commanded.

I stood, looking over at Miss Rasmussen and Miss Jorgenson in a heap at the wall to the right.  Miss Taylor and Miss Mansfield seemed to be rubbed aching body parts as they struggled to stand at the left wall.  Miss Monroe sat up, but looking dizzy only a few feet away.  Her eyes focused on me, calm and maybe sane again; "I'm sorry" she mouthed.  Miss Strickland kind of growled at her, a warning to make sure she stood down.  As I made the door Miss Strickland ordered me.  "Wait in the front lobby."

Out near the front door I noticed it must be getting near quitting time.  Pickup trucks lifted low dusk plumes as they rolled in slowly from the field.  Crews gathered, work and data being summarized for the day.  Soon the Amazon Pollination Crew, my carpool crush-buddies would come striding in from the corn research plots.

My face hurt a little bit; my back felt kind of bent but okay.  I wiggled my finger and toes: all working.  Miss Peterson appeared with my shorts and shirt, kind of bowing apology as she handed then to me.  I dressed.

Shortly after, the rest of the secretaries came out, followed by Miss Strickland.  Each apologized for the overly aggressive behavior.  Miss Klingbell, after apologizing and at the same time wishing me a happy birthday, grabbed my hand and put a wad of bills in it.  "Here's $185, your prize money from playing Bull's Eye.  Too bad we didn't get to all the other games.  You could have made a lot of money, birthday boy."  Miss Klingbell backed up, smiling a bit sheepish.  I looked down at the nice amount of cash in my hand that I almost didn't live to spend.

At last it came to Miss Monroe's turn who said with great solemn conviction, "I'm sorry we got carried away Richie.  We promise will never do anything like that again, where we lose control of ourselves.  Meanwhile, I hope you did like your surprise birthday, I mean until we all went too crazy over you."  Then taking a chance with the stern Miss Strickland watching, she leaned in close to my ear and whispered.  "I do really love you."

Miss Strickland clapped her hands and told the secretaries that was it for the day.  They understood and cleared out, back to their offices to gather their things to go home.  Miss Strickland took two steps to close the fifteen feet between us.  She made no effort to kneel or bend over to me, instead talking down from her overwhelming fifteen foot height.  "Are you sure you are okay?

"Yes, I'll be fine." I tried to look up to meet her eyes. But I got kind of stuck looking at her impossibly huge breasts not at all hidden by her thick blouse. I think she noticed that and disapproved. So instead I looked straight ahead, basically at the lower part of her huge strong thighs, just above her knees.

"Good. Then if you know what's good for you you'll head on home before these gals come back out, and maybe offer you a ride home or something. I know about their frenzy; they need the whole night to calm down. I'm sure none of them had ever experienced it before. But come tomorrow they should be okay. It's an amazon thing. Don't worry, you should be safe though, come tomorrow." I noticed Miss Strickland right leg trembled ever so slightly. Was she nervous; excited? Miss Strickland discerned I hadn't moved yet. "Richie, the hysteria they had, the hormones they released are still in the air. You need to leave. Now!"

Suddenly I got it. Miss Strickland was not immune to the frenzy. If the hormone and temptation combination rose too high, would she too be destabilized. I traced her thighs up, so huge and massive as they entered her skirt. Did she seem to be leaning toward me, over me? Oh my goodness! I finally got her warning.

"OK. Thanks for your help." I opened the office front door and as I stepped out, "Good night then, Miss Strickland."

She reached toward the knob… or was she reaching for me? I closed the door behind me quickly, bounded down the steps, and ran across the parking lot. I'd wait way over by the corn field, for the tall pollination crew to come out. Good plan. Get in the van where I would be safe and sound for my ride home.

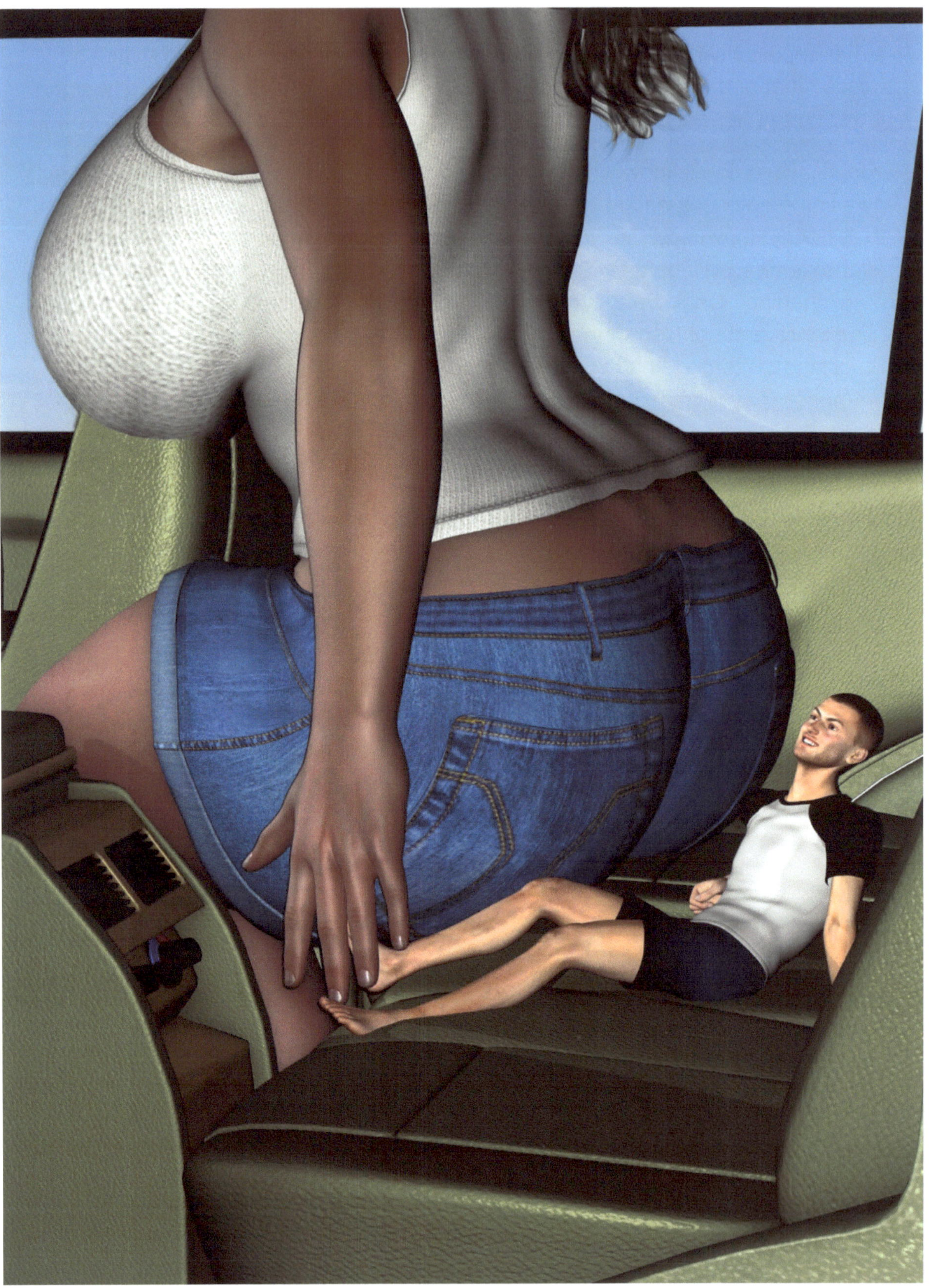

# IV. Saint Debbie Sits

Saint Debbie was an anomaly.  She was a great big giant anomaly that was sitting on me, her ass completely covering my body.  If you looked at the van's second bench seat that was reclined flat to a small bed, you would have thought she was sitting there alone – like she usually did on the commute back to town.  But no, she was not alone.  She was with me, correction on me, correction smothering me, correction virtually devouring me with her ass.

You might think I was suffering, perhaps finally meeting my doom crushed under the butt of an 835 pound woman.  Actually, quite the opposite, crushed yes, suffering no.  So forget about me for a minute.  Don't worry.  We'll get back to my peculiar circumstance in just a minute.  To explain, you need to understand about Saint Debbie.

And the first thing you need to know about Saint Debbie: she is probably the nicest person one could ever meet.  So get this.  It's Debbie's turn to "ride me home", right, you know, the daily cumming contest on the commute back to town.  Call it forty minute of bliss or forty minutes of torture – it was both.  So this Thursday afternoon, it's Saint Debbie's turn.

Debbie speaks in the sweetest high little voice, quite incongruous with her immense size, "OK Richie, so you know I guess it is my turn today at the contest.  I was wondering if would be okay with you if I sat on top of you on the way home?"

Here we are all in the van, actually already leaving the parking lot.  So Debbie's game clock is ticking.  Yet she's still sitting there on the van's bed with me next to her, and she's kindly, patiently negotiating with me.

"Well sure, Deb, I guess." This is the first time any of the Crew had asked permission for anything.  I venture a request. "Maybe be a little gentle?"  Especially after just being attacked by eight amazon secretaries!

"Oh for sure, Richie."  She gave a little shy giggle. "Don't worry about anything.  I promise you will be OK."  Her voice got even higher and smaller.  "Now would it be all right if I sat on you nude?  I would like that a lot and I think it would be more pleasurable for you as well."

"You're the boss." I mean 835 pounds is basically 835 pounds with or without a couple pounds of clothing.  I could not believe how she was letting the time slide by.  We must be two minutes into the ride by now.

"Would you be willing to remove your clothes as well?  I am quite sure you will like it better that way."  She blinked innocently at me.

I felt kind of shy with the other gals curiously watching.  But somehow I trusted Debbie more. "OK" I shrugged.

"Oh goodie!" She seemed really happy about those little requests being met.  She lifted off the bed and pulled off her shorts and panties.  I quickly slipped out of my shirt and shorts. Then she said to me, "Please Richie, go ahead and lie out on the bed comfortably sideways."  She indicated where with a sweep of her thick arm. "And let me know when you are ready."

I stretched my puny body out on the bed.  Above me, quivering when the van shook from the little bumps in the highway, was Debbie's giant, slightly tan butt.  Had she been sunbathing nude somewhere?  Oh, Saint Debbie you naughty girl.  Oddly her butt, while enormous, did not look abnormally fat, it was too smooth, not exactly firm, but not at all flabby either.  She descended just inches from my body.

"OK Richie, are you about ready?  You can go ahead and feel it if you want to."  She offered, still amazingly patient, given the time she seemed to be wasting to be considerate to poor little me.

"I reached up, taking up her offer, touching her ass.  Surprisingly it was not cool like normal fat.  It was decidedly warm, alive, active.  I was inspired, "Actually, Debbie, could I kiss it?"

"Oh Richie, I'd love that.  Please go ahead."

I pressed my face up into her hovering flesh.  It was warm, and immediately relaxing, really just lovely."

"Richie, are you about ready now to get started?"

"Sure" I rested my head back down.

"Here, use this to help you breathe." She actually handed me a sturdy plastic tube.  "Just put your lips around it and breathe.  Also, at any time just wiggle your fingers and I'll rise up to make sure you are OK."

"OK, Debbie." That was damn thoughtful of her.  "Thank you."

"All right now, here we g…." Her ass cut off the rest of the sentence and all was silent.  Except I could hear my own breath through the tube.  I had the brief thought: "She'll never break any records today.  She wasted way too much time.  But, anyway, what a sweetheart…"

So the second thing you need to know about Saint Debbie is, while she might look fat, she totally is not fat.  No, she is a true anomaly, and I mean far, far to the edge of the bell curve, even for these giantesses.  I got to know this quite personally as her ass first covered me, then crushed me, then embraced me, then loved me.  She was incredibly alive, warm, probing me with a thousand, thousand – what were they, receptors?  Like a school of loving fish lived inside her and kept coming up to my body kissing me.  That sounds really weird, I know.  Maybe I was delirious.

And she was hot, not just warm.  I felt I was being gently cooked under her ass.  Not absorbed into her heat.  But loved by her activeness, her high metabolism, her acts of kindness at the cellular level that permeated her body and being and were being pressed and pressured into my body.  It was one of the most irresistible forces imaginable.

I had heard a lot of talk about Saint Debbie's story.  It was a consistently high interest story out at the Station.  Well, because it is so incredible.  Saint Debbie is not fat; she's embryonic.  She's basically a mass of stem cells growing and differentiating at a high rate.  Her metabolism is so high, she's hot.  Of course she must consume enormous amounts of food.  But I have to say, from my vantage point, she is worth every pound of investment.

Yes, Debbie is a 23 year old young woman with all the attendant intelligence and emotions, but she's also kind of a big baby.  They figure she'll mature fully at about 29 years old.  And get this: topping out at an estimated twenty feet tall. I pictured that and came for the first time.

"..K then." I heard Debbie saying as she rose up.  "You OK there sport?  How about a tissue?"  She handed me one.  Like I said, she was very considerate.

"Wow, Saint Debbie."  That super good-looking Vicky admired.  "You wasted all that time and still almost broke Bethany's record."

I cleaned myself up and dabbed a little spot off Debbie's right butt cheek.  I noticed it wasn't very much cum.  In fact, I kind of felt ready to get going again.

"Thank you."  Deb said to me.  Then to Vicky, laughing, good natured, "Oh time's not wasted if it keeps your customer happy."  Then back to me, "Right Richie?"

"Right boss."

"OK then.  Ready to go again?"  Her ass still hovered over me.  "How about this time you turn 90 degrees and we'll see about getting my pussy on your face?"

My God, I almost came when she said that.  "Absolutely, Saint Debbie."  And when I called her a saint I meant it.  She certainly seemed destined to be one of the most extraordinary women the planet has ever known.  I shifted around as suggested.  "I don't think you'll need the breathing tube for this one."  She suggested, and I let it drop to the floor. Saint Debbie lowered her pussy on my face in such a way that I could still barely see out at the hugeness of her thighs, her belly hanging over above, and her great tits a heavy shelf far above also clearly partially visible to me. I think my feet must have just extended beyond her ass on the far side, because they seemed cool.

Perhaps these memoirs should be titled "Summer of Sweet Pussies" or "The Delicious Amazon Pussies of Bluebelle Valley" because I was certainly tasting more than my share.  And I could say that Saint Debbie's was no different.  But, actually, it was different.  It was like every cell in her body had a cinnamon-rose-petal gene for smell and a nectar-of-the-goddess gene for flavor.  I hardly had time to get going, to even appreciate how overwhelmingly delightful she was before I came again."

"Okie-Dokie."  Debbie was rising off me.  She handed me another tissue.

"Good God, Debbie." Now Bethany was impressed. "That hardly took a minute!"

"Could we try that one again?" was my sheepish request. I guess I was feeling like I'd had some kind of premature ejaculation.

"I would certainly love to."  Debbie was so gracious.  "Here we go, then."  She was always so carefully considerate to let me know.

Her pussy settled onto my face again, opening a bit wider now as she relaxed more. Her juices started to flow.  I wanted to be flooded by them, to drink her delicious juices.  And again I responded down below.  I am not exactly sure where my dick was situated, but it was definitely up into some hot crack being squeezed and probed lovingly.  For the first time Debbie pumped me a bit, gently up and down, up and down… and further in… my hard on, deeper insider her… and her wet pussy sliding completely over and tenderly massaging my face… my head. I slurped like crazy. I came again.

"…y, my." Fat Debbie was saying, her pussy kind of trying to clamp onto my face as she lifted up.  For my part I was licking up as much of the sweet essence as I could.  She didn't bother with the tissue this time.  We both knew my deposit was too deep.

"I think someone's going for a record." MaryEllen chimed.  Everyone loved Saint Debbie.  Of course they did.

Stupefied by desire, I lazily blurted the first boundryless dumb comment that came to my head, "My God, Saint Debbie.  I'll bet your shit doesn't even stink."

"Actually," she shrugged modestly, "I don't believe it does.  Would you like to check that out?"

Reflexively, I nodded affirmative.

"Then please flip around 180." She instructed.  I moved into the new position.  Her ass hole loomed above me.  "Now don't be afraid.  Again, I promise you will be OK.  Just so you can tell for sure, do I have your permission to fart on your face?"  She said that with an amazing amount of loving sincerity.

At this point if there was one feeling Saint Debbie elicited above anything else it was Trust, "Yes," I heard myself unbelievably saying, "please do fart on my face."

She dropped her butt down on me.  It wasn't the same cinnamon-rose smell of her pussy.  It was more like I had walked into the best candy store on the planet.  Unbelievable!  And I have to tell you I am kind of squeamish about smells.  But this was extra ordinarily good.

The other great thing about this position was the proximity of my penis just to the outside of her pussy, at the confluence of her great thighs.  While her ass pumped my face I felt her meaty fingers curl around my cock.  Her other hand, I could tell, was busy right nearby, working on her clitoris.  Now, finally, Fat Debbie began to buck up and down in earnest.  This activated her cells even more.  She became hotter and hotter.  Pussy juices flowed over my crotch.  Sweet candy sweat ran off her ass and crack drenching my face, my hair.  She paused briefly, twisted a tiny bit, and then let out a huge fart right into my face.  I stiffened and cringed.  But I was blasted with a sweet zephyr wind from a candy factory.  And that's the honest truth, my friend, candy-ass farts are for real in Bluebelle Valley USA.

Of course I came for the fourth time.  God bless Saint Debbie.  She kept pounding away, a bit out of control, her great body demanding orgasm.  I could feel it building, building and for the first time I was truly afraid of her.  Then wham, she pounded down hard, up she lifted, scooping my face up inside her tightening ass, rising up she bent my body, hands behind my little buns, to jam my cock into her hungry pussy.  We paused at the apex.  Then down and smashing deeper into the van's bed.  My body flattened and my cock popped out of her pussy.  On no!  Then up again, face tucked ever more deeper inside her ass, my cock jammed more vigorously into her pussy, rapidly in and out her hands essentially vibrated my tiny buns back and forth into her all the way up to the apex and all the way down.  Again crushingly she plundered me down, straining the bed, flattening me out of her pussy again.  Faintly I heard her moaning scream of orgasm.  Up, way up again, even higher.  Then we were flying down, I had that roller-coaster feeling of weightlessness, then nothing but massive flattening weight as she smashed me into the bed.  The bed creaked, cracked and yielded, breaking to the van floor.

I came a fifth time – a new record.  She quivered on me for maybe a minute, finishing her orgasm, and draining the last of my cum.  I still licked hungrily at her legs and pussy, hugely satisfied for sure, yet somewhat sad as she pulled away.

The van bounced into my driveway.

The ladies were congratulating Saint Debbie.  We were being involuntarily separated by other bodies, her friends, my goddesses.  I saw Saint Debbie trying to smile at me, lovingly, almost grateful.  I felt so humble to know such a woman.

The giantesses passed my limp body over.  Bad Jackie, by the open door, rolled me unceremoniously onto the driveway saying, "Here," She flicked a wad of bills at me.  "I have no idea why, but Fat Debbie wanted you to have her winnings."  Bad Jackie made a weird, perplexed face at me, then kind of snidely. "Have a good evening, you noodle."  And the van door slid shut as they pulled away, noisy and laughing.

My-oh-my the world suddenly felt cold, even on a warm, humid Midwest afternoon.

But oh my word, I have to say: God bless Saint Debbie!

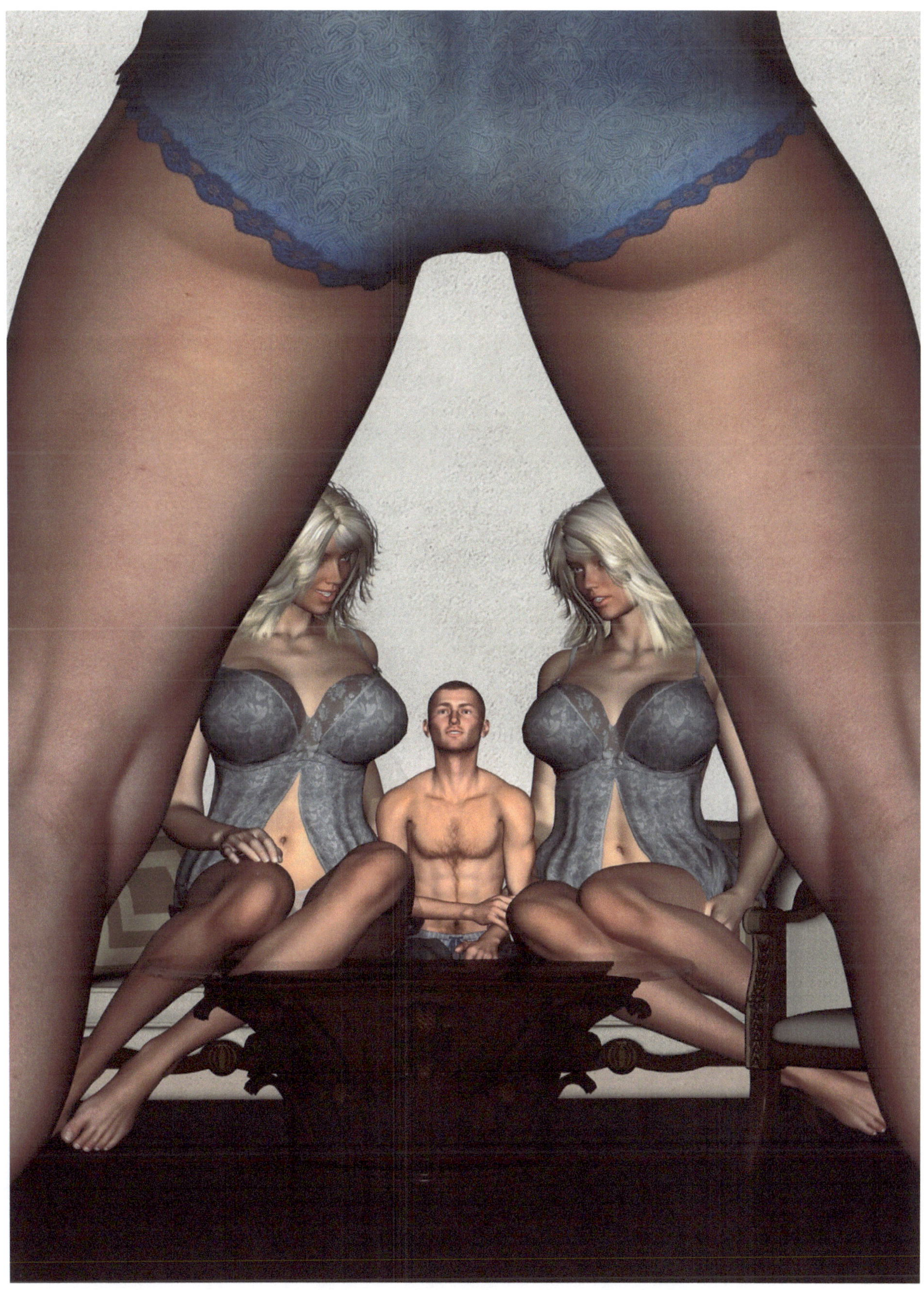

# V. Home Again – Giantess Jiggity Jog

It took me longer to scrape myself off the driveway than it did the day before.  Saint Debbie plum wore me out.  And I felt like I would never need to cum again.

I got mechanical, and that helped.  1. Crawl upstairs.  2. Run a bath.  3. Get in bath.  4. Drown yourself.  No, just kidding.

Soaking felt good.  Buoyancy felt good.  Actually, I was recovering more quickly than I expected.  And I don't think it was the wonder of the Epsom Salts I'd dumped in the bath.  It had to be… could only be – the magic of The Triplets milk.  Mmmm, that sounded kind of good right now.  Yes, I definitely needed a fix of that elixir.

I realized that for the first time, I was truly looking forward to The Triplets coming home.  But hang on… wait a minute, what would my new girlfriends think of all my sexual escapades today?  Better not tell them was my first reaction.  Yes, let's start with secrets the first day of boyfriend-girlfriend – not!  Thankfully, I knew they would know if I was trying to hide something.  Well, then, that makes it simpler, doesn't it?  A new game tonight: I tell them about my day.  Then they get crazy jealous and kill me.  Game over.  I don't know why this made me laugh.

I heard the front door shut.  They were home an hour early, and I was just getting out of the bath.  Panicky, I rushed to get dressed, to get downstairs, to greet them properly, you know, those crotch kisses way they liked it.  My hair was wet; I combed it over with my hands as I ran to get my shorts, which I pulled on while hopping across the bed room.  Bounding down the stairs I realized I was shirtless.  No matter.  I mean, there was no dress code, was there?  I have to admit, I'm a bit sloppy when it comes to rules.

"Well, hi there, ladies."  I wet-feet, stutter-slid into the foyer as they dropped their purses.

They eyed me, amused it seemed, "Rushing to greet us, are you?"  Their questions often weren't questions since the seemed to know so much about what was going on.  "OK then, boy, come on."

Teasing me already.  Well, maybe I would make them wait.  I folded my arms, trying to look at them with mock distain.

"Oh, really," They sang it; folding their arms in reply. "So it's going to be like that." They stepped forward, surrounding me in a triangle of legs. "Still going to make us wait?" They unfolded their arms, putting them around each other's' shoulders, huddled over me. I looked up at the great canopy of breasts way above me, their beautiful faces obscured. They were toying with me and I knew it, and they knew I knew it. Already we were playing a little game; one I would certainly lose shortly. Their irresistible scent surrounded me. I just kept staring up at those breasts. They were too far away. My mouth watered. They waited, sort of, micro-stepping closer to me.

I knew I was hard again. OK, so I lied early. It seemed likely now I would cum again, probably even tonight. Meanwhile I just had to get some access to those breasts. And that was going to require me unlocking the next step in their game – the first step in the evening's festivities.

I sighed, thinking, "Who am I kidding." And I lifted the first skirt, tucked my head under, and pressed my good-evening kiss into her panties.

Their sing-song sarcasm was high soprano. "Oh, my goodness, what a surprise!" I was so owned.

I twisted 120 degrees against their closing thighs, and planted my next greeting.

"Mmmm. When he makes us wait, that makes us hot." They were pouring it on now.

Their thighs were beginning to interlock, and it was very difficult for me to shift the final 120 degrees. In fact, I was a bit contorted, my feet slightly off the ground, now held up in a twist of legs, as I managed my final panty-kiss.

"Ahhh!" They sighed, releasing me to drop, off balance, my butt landing on the foyer floor. With just the tiniest bit of sympathy "Was that so difficult, darling." They walked toward the kitchen, "I'm starving." Said one.

"Aren't you?" a Second called over her shoulder to me.

"Or maybe you're thirsty." Teased the Third, hefting a breast as she skipped around in a three-step circle, dancing to catch up to her sisters.

I hopped up and following them. Yes, definitely I was thirsty.

My job was to set the table. Even doing that was a bit odd, as the oversize table was at neck height to me. But, still, at least I could see what was doing.

I could also enjoy seeing what they were doing.  It was like watching a choreographed ballet in the kitchen as they waltzed around each other, cooking, grabbing this ingredient and that, tossing shakers of spices and oils.  There flew a rainbow of cut veges, caught in the sweeping arc of a hot fry pan.  One circled and ducked under the other's arm, as they traded knife for spatula, and pan for pot.

Remember in The Hobbit movie, when the dwarfs cleaned up Bilbo's kitchen.  It was a little like that, watching them, except they were cooking and cleaning at the same time… and they were, dah, not dwarfs, but beautiful graceful giantesses.  OK, so it was a dumb comparison.  But put yourself in my shoes, and try to think straight.  OK, OK, already, I know I'm not wearing shoes.  Jeez, give me a break…

Dinner was served.  They sat in three normal-looking, albeit overly huge chairs.  "Lucky chairs."  Was I really that horny again already, and actually jealous of chairs?  I climbed a high stool that positioned me well and proper in relation to my plate.

They liked a silent prayer.  Their piles of stir-fry sent steamed toward the high arched ceiling in the brief pause.  Then they deftly attacked their meals with chop sticks.  No way for me.  Give me a fork any day over chop sticks.  I eat like an American Man, I told myself as I studied an asparagus spear on my folk, finally decided it was too long, then cut it into thirds for consumption.  Heck yeah, I nodded my head to myself, a real man.

I looked up; the sisters were studying me, their faces bemused.  I glared at them, my best mean look.  But I could tell they were doing well not to laugh as they cast their eyes upward, eyebrows raised.  I gruffly turned my attention back to my bowl and decided to do battle with a crispy Brussels Sprout.  Oh for sure, I can be a tough guy when the situation requires it.  Dinner hit the spot, but I was still thirsty, and remained a bit tough and grumpy.

Usually only one of the triplets spoke at a time, unless they were more unified for emphasis, or singing and working their special brands of magic.  So one of them says, and to this point it didn't matter which one, "We have a new game tonight, but we're not sure right now that you are going to like it."

"Hold on a minute," I proceeded to get a bit coy in my protest.  "I thought since we *might* be in a relationship, that these games were going to be, you know, mutually consensual.  I'm just saying…"  My tough guy was starting to sound gangster.

"No, you are right, Richie.  Totally consensual, that is as long as we *might* be in a relationship."

I wondered, was that some kind of threat at the end there.  But I did hear agreement also.  "Ok then."  I shrugged, what I imagined was assertive.  "What kind of game we talkin' about?"

"Would you trust us enough to come up to our room in about thirty minutes and just give it a try?  We would like to shower off, get ready, and do our best to please our man."

I noticed they didn't say "little" man.  Hell, what kind of cad would say no to that request.  "Sure, Babes," I was rolling now, almost bossy, I thought a bit smugly, "You go on up and get yourselfs all prim and proper, and I'll be along after a while."  As if to say when I'm damn good and ready.  Yep, wearing my man-pants now.

"Okay, then."  They eyed me like I was a bit strange, which of course I was.

"Shall we get ourselves all 'prim and proper'?" said one, without a doubt mocking me.

"Prim, absolutely" Said a second, flipping her hair with the back of her hand.

"And oh so pro-per." Said the third, batting her eyes, her fingers interlaced under her chin.

They giggled and bounded upstairs.

Honestly, I'd be lucky to be half as smart as The Triplets.  But as I sat on the bottom stair, making myself wait thirty minutes, my little mind was calculating that maybe I actually was in trouble tonight.  And it wasn't even tonight's game that worried me the most.  Somewhere along the line I would have to tell them about the crazy interlude with Miss Monroe and the Secretaries, and worse yet the record-breaking encounter with Saint Debbie that maybe I liked it and her a little too much.

"Richie… Richie…" I entered a beautiful cool forest.  Green, the light yellow-green of early spring, all around… "Richie… dreamer boy…" I heard my name again, being gently called above, from the treetops above the gurgling stream.  "Oh, Richie… Mama wants you…"

I woke.  It was dark, and way too much later.  I had fallen asleep on the carpet at the bottom stair step.  Well, it had been a rough day.

"Richie…" I still heard the voice, the beautiful harmonizing voices from my dream, calling me from the top of the stairwell. "Richie… we are ready. We need you now."

My God look how dark it had gotten. It must be two hours later. "Sorry, sorry. Just a minute; I'll be right up." What happened to the tough guy, I was asking myself. Fuck I have to pee; and I quick-stepped to the downstairs hallway bathroom. A minute and a half later I was marching up the stairs, "Coming!"

I saw the crack of light issuing from their bedroom almost-shut doorway. It reminded me of two nights ago, but in my room. Was there going to be another barnyard full of cows? That was kinky, ultimately awesome, but kinky. I took a deep breath, then nudged the big door open, as manly as I could muster.

No barnyard. No cows. Whew!

All three sisters were sitting on their oversized and especially long couch. Very long it was, but still barely enough room for their three wide asses, as they sat cheek-to-cheek, so-to-speak. Like that rhyme? Distracting with jokes. I must be getting nervous.

Their garb seemed weird to me. Not kinky weird; but a conservative opposite of kinky. Their gorgeous legs they kept tightly crossed. I would have liked to see some cheesecake, but they wore almost old-fashioned paisley-patterned green and gray skirts, loosely fitted, that came well below their knees. Their beige blouses, lovely with frills buttoned up the middle, and right on up to collar their necks. And how odd, I'd never seem them do this before, the hair was done up, braided and twirled into tight buns, right up on top, making their necks look longer and more elegant than ever.

They offered no explanation; just waited for me to cross the room – to approach – what was that I'd heard in my dream? "Mama."

Oh my lord. I stopped dead in front of them. Terrified. I actually pictured myself running from the room. But my feet wouldn't budge. My mouth opened, but mute I was, and no words came out. They did not want my words anyway.

Perfectly prim and proper they were. Just like I'd asked. It would have been impossible to take my eyes off these beauties, off the dreamy look of motherly love in their eyes.

Still silent, the triplet on the left began to slowly unbutton her blouse.  First her neck came into view, skin so soft and promising.  Then unbuttoned more, her burgeoning breast pushed her blouse partially open.  With her left hand she gracefully pulled aside the left side of her blouse, exposing the left bra-covered breast, seemingly bigger now than I remembered it.

I was taking little steps toward her.  Baby steps?  Her look of unconditional love remained unwavering.  With both hands she carefully undid a little latch at the upper end of her bra.  It flapped open wide, exposing her hard nipple and much of her enormous, rounded breast.

My mouth watered as I tugged to climb her skirt.  She deftly helped me onto her lap, sliding me onto my back.  Then she lifted her breast over my head and held it there waiting.  I have to tell you I did not feel very manly any more at that moment.  But I wasn't feeling that bad either.  I was starting to relax.

The Triplets were humming now, softly soothing.   All the craziness that had been my day fell away.  All cares released, my face relaxed, but I was not sleepy.

My entire world was a huge, beautiful, tempting breast that she still held up barely above my face.  It looked so smooth and perfectly formed, and I could sense the warmth there.  Why did she make me wait?  Why didn't she let it smother down upon me?  I could not see her face; so I could not read the intent in her expression.  But I already knew her expression anyway.  It would be that same look of unconditional love.

Then I knew why she waited.  I reached up, my thin arms in meager contrast to her full womanly dominance of me.  It was then that she finally released her breast to descend upon my face, covering me completely with her warmth and love.  I fought with it, shoving rather hard with my puny arms, my little hands kneading into her vast softness.  What seemed like great vigor on my part must have only been a little stimulating massage to her, as she pressured into me more, toward my shoving hands and my head turning back and forth.

I kissed her softness, open mouth and losing control.  I lunged into her with my face, my kisses becoming something more, an involuntary response of my mouth, a kind of open-mouth chewing toward her, my tongue licking rhythmically in synchrony with the mouthing here and there on her breast, wherever I could reach.

Then suddenly I found it, and latched onto her firm nipple. I sucked hungrily, probably as hard as I could. In response her warm love flowed into me. The feeling of satisfaction was heaven.

This was not mere quenching of thirst. This was a tingling throughout my entire body. Yes, it was thirst-quenching liquid, yes it was sustenance, yes it was her love literally flowing into me. And it was much more. I could feel the intelligence and design of it – from all three sisters. This was my formula they had somehow concocted in their extraordinary bodies.

The triplets were giving me a gift, incredibly devised in their bodies, specific to me, to help me, that would alter me cellularly, metabolically, and ultimately physically in ways I would absolutely need to survive. And yet I also knew it was a measured gift; that is, only what I needed and nowhere near all the magic they could bestow.

I could also sense a certain kind of "selfishness" is a strong word for it. There was something in it for them. It was a sustaining of me, for them the reward of a vigorous lover: me. As they continued to sing, and I continued to nurse from breast to breast to breast to breast… more was revealed. "So much milk!" you say in astonishment. But no, not at all. These were not lactating mothers. These were bountiful young women who through their gifts and bizarre kind of intelligence had devised to produce in their bodies and deliver to me in the most loving way a product in just the right amount of volume perfect for me, without a doubt, in every way.

So breast to breast to breast… they sang and revealed to me downloading information to my mind and heart and life changing elixir to my body. I could see in their visions, that I would be stronger for both me and for them. That they could soon love me with more vigor and I would not just crumble into a pile of broken sticks. There was more, much more, but I only knew that as a sensing, as so much of the specifics were not revealed. Perhaps even they did not know exactly how I would evolve.

I finished at the sixth breast. What a happy little camper I was. Then I found myself rolling off a lap and onto the carpet.

They stood above me now, stretching their arms, "Ahh" they sang as they yawned, the purred to me, "That was fun. You feel better, baby?" But is more of a boyfriend "baby" than a baby "baby", if you know what I mean.

I nodded affirmative, certainly smiling.

"Well good, good, good." They said.  They were taking off their cloths now, dropping their blouses and skirts and big nursing bras on me playfully.  The mood had certainly changed rapidly, as they changed from "mothers" back into girlfriends.  They undid their hair from the buns.  But they left the tight white braids, actually very cute.

"Come on" they nudged the pile of clothes with their feet.  "Get out of there.  We need some entertainment.  Let's go downstairs and watch a movie, make some popcorn."

I popped out of the clothes pile like a jack-in-the-box.  They laughed.  Then they took off toward the bedroom door, "Last one downstairs is a rotten egg."

I stumbled after them.  OK, so I'm a rotten egg.  I slowed on the stairs, feeling a little more kingly but no longer the tough guy – who needed him anyway.  Call me a rotten egg any day, but this rotten egg was looking forward in an in-house cozy date with three beautiful towers of perfection, who, by the way, seemed to love this rotten egg.  Ah yes, I was thinking, nearing the bottom step.  Then I remembered, I still have to tell them about my other sexual escapades of my day… darn.

They were wearing just their panties and shear nighties.  And me, shirtless with shorts.  It was going to be warm and comfortable most of this Midwest night.

One of the sisters spread out on the living room carpet and started stretching her hamstrings.  My goodness, what long, strong, and flexible legs!  I don't think I needed a movie.  I think I could watch her for a couple hours.

The other two, who sat side-by-side squishing the poor couch, moved over to make a little gap for me to sit.  Once I was situated, they closed back in gently, the curve of their big legs rising over my skinny bones, and their hips lodging nicely above mine and against my sides.  The magnificent splendor of those breasts I loved more each day; protruded above and in front of the sides of my head, tunneling my vision straight ahead at the amazon who was now arching high in a backward bridge  The tightness of her huge ass astounded me, almost incongruous with that much size.  Slightly above that beautiful display of sexy strength, the movie was beginning on a ninety inch screen.

There was an opening scene from high above a city – New York.  I wondered again why so many movies start 2000 feet above a city, as if it begins with a soul coming in to inhabit a body.  I shrugged, like I usually did when I started to go too deep, and sighed.  I don't think I've seen this romantic comedy the triplets seemed excited about.

"Wait" said the sister on the floor. "I want to make popcorn."

"And ice cream floats."  The other two said at the same time.  It had to be some ritual I wasn't privy to.  They seemed really excited about it.

So that made it kind of extra hard, like I felt I was going to be a real bummer, when I just finally had to say.  "Could we take a minute?  There's something I want to talk about."  Ah shit, I thought to myself.  There's going to be no turning back now.  I no longer thought they would kill me or even hurt me at all.  I was experiencing what men fear most – that they were at risk of hurting someone else; in this case emotionally.  But if honesty made me lose them, made them give up on me, then so be it.

While I was having these thoughts, the two by my side had gotten up and sat with their sister on the floor, each cross-legged.  They had formed a semi-circle and beckoned for me to come sit and complete the circle.  I moved on down and sat there, looking up at each of the expectant faces.  They certainly could tell I was quite serious about something.

As I looked up at them, I tried not to let their ever increasing beauty distract me from what I had to say. "OK, so here's the thing.  Yesterday you told me you would like to be my girlfriends.  And that is the most awesome invitation I've ever gotten, I mean by far."  They smiled a little, but waited for me to continue.  "And I said I needed a little time to consider.  That seemed fair to you, right?"

They nodded agreement, but nothing new so far from me.

"If I'm maybe going to be your boyfriend, well I'm afraid I'm doing a terrible job."  Get on with this Richie. "Just this first day, since we talked last night, I had sex with nine other women."  I looked down, waiting to hear a gasp or moan or some utterance of dismay at me.  Nothing.  I looked up again.  But their expression remained impassive and a bit kindly.  What gives?  I was puzzled. Oh, I thought, they must want details.

"So I had sex with Miss Monroe this morning, right in her office at work.  Then early afternoon all the rest of the secretaries."

"Miss Strickland as well?" The sister in the middle voiced the surprise they each had on their faces.

"No, of course not.  I'd be dead." I shuttered at the thought.

The sister on the left said, "Oh, well. Yes we heard about the surprise party and the fun you had with the secretaries."

The sister on the right added. "I'm afraid Miss Monroe couldn't wait to share about her superlative experience.  From the details we got, it sounds like she had a really good time."

The sister in the middle: "You are quite the little lover, aren't you?"

What was going on; they knew and didn't say anything.  They knew and still played out an extraordinary and generous fantasy with me?  They knew and wanted to pal around, watching a romantic comedy like we're best friends.  I was mystified, and my face showed it.

"What's the matter, Richie, did you do something wrong?"

"Yes, my maybe-girlfriends, I had sex with Miss Monroe and the rest of the secretary pool, and I liked it."  Now I was almost challenging them to react.

"Well, we hope you liked it."

"Valerie (of course they knew Miss Monroe by first name) is a heck of a looker."

Her sister added, "And I just love her ginger hair."

The third comment blew me away: 'I'd fuck her myself if I was a man, but we haven't even tried to work that one out yet."

That made them all laugh for a minute.

"No thanks." One responded, still laughing, "No way I'd want to be a man."

"But it wasn't just sex."  I was now actually arguing, it seemed, for them to be upset with me. "I liked it so much I found myself saying to myself that I wanted to be owned by her, that I loved her."

"Oh Richie…" They sang gently to me now.  "That right there is why you are such a good lover, such a good man, and an important reason why we want you more than ever, even as you say this thing you think should upset us.  When you make love, you really make love, investing the best of yourself.  When you focus your attention on someone, you focus with your heart, lead with you heart."  I actually saw tears forming in their eyes as they sang.  That touched me so deeply I cannot hope to tell you how seen and understood I felt in that moment.

But there was more: "I also made love with Fat Debbie."

They eyed me dryly, one said, "You mean Debra?

I guess they didn't like the "Fat Debbie" moniker.  "OK, Debra, then.  And you are right; I shouldn't have called fat, because she really isn't."

"Yes, of course we heard all about the new record.  It's all anyone can talk about on the Bluebelle Amazon page."

"Bluebelle Amazon page?"  I queried.  I'd never heard of it.

"Of course you wouldn't know.  It's like our secret, local Facepage.  It's a private-group amazon page that you have to have proof of seven foot plus to join."

"Yes, and it's all the rage that Debra got you to cum five times."  She blinked at me, matter of fact.

I felt a bit mortified to think my, call it degradation, was the big local news story.  But I did not feel degraded by Saint Debbie.  I only felt very much respected and loved by her.  Good God, even if she did fart on my face.  I am telling you it was an oxymoron you morons; it really was a sweet fart.  Anyway, I'm stalling.  I still have to fess up about the rest of it how I felt with Saint Debbie.

"I liked the sex with Debra also, maybe even more than with Miss Monroe, which I didn't think would be likely."

"We expect you would."

"We do know you pretty well, Richie."

"Why, that I like getting crushed?"  I felt a bit upset, defensive.  "That I'm just a puny, tiny little man that loves to be smothered under the gigantic asses of the world's largest and most beautiful women?  Is that who you know pretty well?"

"Well there is that…" she seemed to be agreeing with me.

I cut her off, "Let me tell you something else my big beautiful girlfriends.  I very much loved being smothered by 'Debra'.  She is like the nicest person you could every meet, completely respectful, kind of funny, and absolutely good-hearted to the core.  In fact, I think I really love her.  There I said it." I stood defiant, ready, I thought, for whatever upset might come my way.

But I didn't know these sisters near as well as they knew me.  "Of course you love Debra!"  One started.

Another explained. "She is a being of love at the cellular level as well as the soul level.  Just to sit in the room with her is to feel emotionally uplifted."

"And you do really love her; are you sure in what you say about this?"

Now I was really confused and not confused – I guess that means I was confused, I think, "Well, I think I love her.  I would like to see her again.  I'd like to be under her again."  I admitted. "I'm sorry to say this to you, but I'd like to make love with her again."

"Don't be sorry, Richie.  But are you trying to tell us something?

"Richie, you look confused, is there something you want to say about how you feel about us?

"Do you love us, Richie?  Is that why you are so worried?"

My eyes widened in wonder and realization.  "Yes.  Yes, I do love you.  Man do I love you, so much that it kind of scares me.  I think that is why I needed time before, you know, committing to the 'going steady' thing."

I couldn't really tell if they were actually moving toward me or if they just seemed closer by way of intense affinity.  I definitely felt both smitten and afraid of their penetrating love.  "We love you too."  They said it very simply, without singing it.

"Richie, if you are sure about your strong feelings for Debra, you may invite her to come live with us."

Wow, that was a shocker, even my imagination had not dreamed of that one.  I had to think about that; don't want to be hasty here. "Well, I just don't know.  We're still getting to know each other for now.  But, wow… I just don't know."  I couldn't get my pea-sized mind around it.

"You let us know if you want to."

"We would make Debra our sister in a New York minute."

"In a heartbeat," another added for emphasis.

I was dumbfounded.  My worst fear about The Triplet's reaction to my philandering was turned on its head into more bonding with them.  I was in complete awe of such openness, such acceptance, their ability to incorporate circumstance into love.

They seemed to anticipate my thoughts.  There was a harmonious singing aspect to what they said next.  "There is a change coming to this world.  Love is bigger than we ever suspected.  Love's definition must expand as must we."

They were definitely getting closer.  Then then were on me, lifting me to their faces, their lips.  My face was being kissed from three sides.  The talking was evidently over.  They were proving to me that nothing I had done or said detracted whatsoever from their love for me.  Firm, moist kisses, over and over.  I kissed back, finding one set of lips then another.

They began to hum as they kissed, and my worries about all that stuff that had tortured me earlier, fell away.  I felt I was spinning in a vortex of love and kisses.  After I while, I could hardly pucker anymore.  I was just marinating in the bounteousness of their kisses.  Then gradually they slowed, longer kisses, gentler, if possible even more lovingly, lingering with each one.

Finally lips just rested against my face.  I was back on the couch again.  The sisters were piled around and on me in such a tangle that allowed all four of our heads to come and stay together in what seemed like a permanent kiss.  I have no idea how they figured these body knots out.  That telepathy that allowed it was their genius.  It was my job to enjoy and appreciate.  And I did.  My arms and legs disappearing into the tangle, definitely tied up in their flesh, with which of their luscious body parts I could not tell, nor did it matter to me.

Somehow the arrangement allowed me to breathe just fine.  "Well then, is the movie over?"  I joked.

"What movie?" came a dreamy response.

They seemed to be waking up.  I could detect just a little more tension bodies; nothing alarming, just them becoming alert.

"You know, Richie, it is a good thing we started providing you with our milk when we did.  You might have had a hard time surviving today."

"Yes, I wanted ask you."  I was recalling from the mama-game earlier in the evening.  "What was that vision I had of me being more durable?  That's from the milk isn't it?"

They took turns explaining, still leaving us in the intimate jumble of bodies.  Maybe a few minor adjustments on their part, our faces separating just a bit for normal conversation, though I felt I had descend under them a bit more.  But that was OK with me….  I relaxed against the shear of a lacy nightie over a soft breast.

“The milk we have for you is quite a special concoction.  We make it especially for you.”

“It should strengthen you bones, most definitely, and permanently.  That will be good for you your whole life.”

“Thank you.” I said

“It is also changing your metabolism, not faster or slower, but more efficient in certain ways.  We expect you will get to where can swim under water for fifteen minutes at a time, maybe more.  That might also prove useful for certain kinds of entertainment, if you know what I mean.”

“I know exactly what you mean.”  And I did.  “I could have used it today.  At first I had to breathe through a tube that Debra brought along so I could survive under her ginormous ass.”

They laughed.  “We hadn’t heard that part.  Good for Debra to think of that for you.”

“There are other physical alterations that should prove a permanent improvement for you.  We think it more fun for you to discover some for yourself.  And they may take some time to fully develop.”

“Will I get bigger?”  It had been dream for a long time.  But actually I wasn’t so sure that was important to me anymore.  I was getting comfortable with who I was – how weird!

“No, we thought we should consult with you about that one.  It might be possible to make you a little taller and more stout, but at twenty-two, and being a man, we don’t have much science to back that yet.  Also, it tends to be a one-way trip.  Smaller to bigger – some possibilities.  Bigger to smaller – very little known or even ever tried.”

“What about, you know…” I was going to point but couldn’t retrieve my arm.  I wasn’t quite sure where my crotch was anyway “… you know, my little Volunteer.  I realize it can’t be especially ideal for you, with your sizes and everything.”  Talk about a sensitive topic.  Yes, good idea: do talk about a sensitive topic.

"Well.  First of all know that we are very happy. But we anticipated your concern.  If you could be sized there, with your 'Volunteer' as you call it, proportional to our sizes I'm afraid you would be very uncomfortable.  It would be like a third leg."

"And the other thing is, we are still growing.  And if you keep on with your flings with these other women…" I heard her teasing in that statement, but also their permission. (Yippie, I guess?)  "Who knows what "ideal size" you might need to be down there for women of various sizes."

"So we came up with a plan in the second category of changes in your body."

"What second category?"  I questioned

"Essentially non-permanent changes.  Changes that mostly depend on a continued supply of our milk, at least for now.  Call these "experiments".  If you like it, we can keep supplying it."

"So we came up with one for your Volunteer you and your sexual partners might enjoy; I know we will."

"What, big during sex, and not at other times?"

"No, a completely different tactic.  You have to understand women.  We have given you a kind of Sparkle.  Just introduced it today.  It should be operational by tomorrow."

"Operational?"

"Right, Richie, sorry.  We are spending too much time with scientists at Synsonto. Sometimes we start to talk like them."

"It is kind of a little vibration and very, very slightly electrically charged releasing when you get hard.  The more excited you get, the more it releases, crescendo-ing bigtime, kind of geometrically spiking with your release, your ejaculation."

"Holy shit, you got to be kidding me."

"No, we're not kidding.  We are crazy looking forward to it – tomorrow.  Not that we're complaining at all today.  But you know, more fun is more fun, right?"

"You are way too good to me."  I was truly feeling like a champ now.

"Well, it is definitely experimental.  Remember that."

"And it won't make you feel any different.  Remember that also."

"Hold on, girly-girls." I had a correction. "Now you have to understand men.  The more pleasure I can give you, the better I will feel, definitely.  This might be a better gift to a man than it is to a woman."

"That's the experiment we want to run on you – tomorrow."  They said it together, right away.  Their use of that little preposition "on" was not lost to my imagination.

"So," One of them grabbed a handful of my hair firmly. "Are you still feeling guilty about fooling around with other women?  Like you ought to be punished?"

"No, not any more.  I actually feel marvelously accepted.  You amaze me.  I feel blessed."  Again I just don't when to shut up… continuing with less confidence.  "But maybe I should be punished a little bit anyway."

"That's what we figured."  She released my hair.  I felt myself descending down through the pile, around arms, under weighty breasts, turning over, sliding through a tight crook of bent leg and twisting through another, darker, heavier, squeezed by thigh, then hip, finally completely under and pressed down into the couch by ass and more ass and more huge ass.  This was punishment?  Then how do I commit more crimes?

I suppose their bouncing would have looked gentle from across the room.  But underneath, that was not exactly the case.  Their skillful buns moved my body around, positioning me just-so for a pump or two of pussy on face, a nice grind of sex for a few ups-and-downs, then cycling me on, ass-passing me around until every intimate part of them had had several turns on overwhelming every intimate part of me.

This had to be the most helpless I'd felt yet.  Here I was, hidden away in this vast estate, nobody to know what was happening to me, being ground, squished, and smothered every which way at the complete mercy of three glorious goddesses.

After some thirty minutes the gentle vigor slowed and slowed, and they became even heavier and heavier until finally all activity ceased – dead weight.  And soon I would be dead meat if they actually went to sleep piled on me like this.

At last there came a little movement, then dim light as they untangled themselves off me.  They yawned and stretched as they stood up.  Me? – I was still trying to distinguish myself from the sofa cushions.  Something had occurred to me while so thoroughly under them, kind of out of the blue, something I thought I needed to know and long overdue.  "You know, I don't even know you names."

"No, you don't." was their rather flat reply offering me nothing.   They were so drowsy.  They hadn't had a two hour nap like I'd had.

They stood above, so frustratingly identical, "I have to know.  There must be some way to tell you apart.  How do I do it?"

They smiled, identically, "You can figure it out, if you work at it." And they left it as the challenge, stepping back from the couch, obviously preparing to leave.

"Hey, what about the movie?" I teased, like I really wanted to see "When Bertha Met Billy" or whatever it was.

"How about tomorrow night?" They yawned again, migrating toward the doorway, toward the stairs.

"Oh, sure." I feigned enthusiasm.  "Good night then."

"Aren't you coming with us?"  They meant it, but necessarily kept on ambulating out the room, toward their beds upstairs.

"Really?" I called out.

"Yes, Richie." They sing-songed, dreary, down the stairwell.

"OK, then, save me a spot.  I'll be up in a while."

# VI. Midnight at the Amazon Oasis

There's a magic place on a woman's body that too often goes overlooked.  Lying down behind her, I was staring up at it now.   It's the perfect confluence of the lowest part of her broad back meeting the very first indentation that was to become the bisecting crack of her mighty ass, on to the thunder of her upper thighs, and other places I loved to be trapped and smothered under.

I had taken me more than half an hour to calm down enough, to set aside my fears, return to that place of leading with my heart, and, by God, get my skinny little ass upstairs.  You've heard of "losing yourself in love."  Imagine how I felt about the idea of losing myself in 1870+ pounds (yes, they had grown a little bit) of pure loving women.

They call that the "upper limits problem": when things seem just too good, and by experience things usually aren't good, so you don't believe they can be good, so then you make sure they aren't good, and then you can't be disappointed, see?  Sounds like a fun life, doesn't it?  I don't recommend it.

I burrowed into the sheets and looked worshipfully up at that magic spot on her lower back. I could feel the heat emanate onto my face from her warm sound asleep body.  Her nude figure, an art composition of ideal majestic curves, seemed a generous gift to humanity, and at this moment – all mine.

Moonlight from the window wavered in breeze-lifted gauzy shears.  Those shifting soft silver shadows animated the grand silhouette arc of her buttocks, the smooth inward sweep of her waist, giving way to the wicked muscles of her resting arms.  Even asleep, just this one amazon sister effused enough power and dominion to weaken me with submissive desire.  It shivered with delight as I reached up to so gently stroke that lower part her back.  My tiny fingers dithered in careful, modest exploration between her buns.  I felt so excited, so sneaky and awake, and so full of bright little horny ideas of ways I might kiss her ass and be smothered under her.

My thin body paralleled the arc of her right butt cheek, and just that much of her was wider than my entire chest.  The other half of her ample ass loomed entirely above my torso and the rest of my legs as they curved around and out of sight and I imagined under her.

It was in that enchanted moment that I saw the little pattern of tiny moles, barely more than freckles they were, that proved unique to this sister.  These seven little betrayers almost perfectly formed the shape of the Big Dipper.  Eureka!  It had to be a way to tell this sister from the others.  And for the moment it was still only a theory. I had to find proof – proof that would be lying on two maybe-not-so-perfectly-identical bodies, also sound asleep in this very same bed.

I softly placed my lips against middle of the cup of her Big Dipper, as if to steal a stellar sip from a heavenly goddess; she did not react whatsoever.  That caused me to linger and see what other kisses I could get away with.  I kissed lower, between her buns.  Pressing my face into her ass crack, I risked all, kissing more vigorously. Was I crazy?  How might she react to this sneak-attack?  I retreated, kissing my way vertically down to where the vastest width of her ass met the bottom sheet.  I pressed my face into that crevasse, the soft sheet against my right cheek and the crushing mass of her ass dormant over and squishing gently my left cheek.

I prayed she would roll over onto me and simply flatten me under her gargantuan butt. "Come on 'Big Dipper' please make this dream come true.  Don't you know I'll love you forever?"  Nothing, just a sleeping giantess, dominating me without even trying.  Bolder now, I scooting down further, around that curve of her ass, and there it was – her glorious pussy right up there above my face.

Sitting up and turned my head sideways I brought my little lips to kiss her lips that were far bigger than my entire face.  God I was so excited, so extremely hard.  I flitted my tongue and licked her like a timid snake.  She made no moment, no sigh, no sign of any sensation.  Embolden, I licked again, unabashed and with about as much trepidation as you'd expect a beta-puppy happily servicing the alpha-dog. Yes, that's what I was to her, the most subservient of all creatures, and the thought titillated the heck out of me.

But who was she?  I didn't know her name and that bugged me. And "Big Dipper" would never do.  No way would her identical sisters be so exactly identical that they would share that same little constellation on their lower backs.  Damn, I had to find out.  It was my chance to one-up them.  God I wanted to stay and try to entice her sleeping pussy to roll down on me.  But no-no, too invigorated and enthusiastic; now I had a mission.  I slowly rolled away to my back and sat up out from under the sheet.

I turned 180 and there was another magnificent amazon's back, right there, facing me.  Man, what a feast! I scooched over and came to her same lovely and low confluence at the top of her big buns. With her asleep I could my feelings opening, like they just did with her sister.  And the vibe from this woman felt different.  I thought the last sister overwhelmed me with her power.  But in contrast I could see that the first sister was, by comparison, more of a lover.  This gal, though sound asleep, absolutely slayed me.  I really don't know what it was.  I mean, she looked exactly the same.  I had no idea why; maybe some dream she was having.

"Come on Richie, don't melt so easily."  I muttered to myself, shook my head and snuck on down for a closer look at that not-so-secret-anymore place just above her ass.  Low and behold look at this!  Who should I see, as clear as any bright night sky, Orion, like me, also lying on his side, his dotted sword sheathed into the crack of her mighty ass.  This was too easy. Ha!  Two down… and one to go.

I reverse army-crawled to the bottom of the bed and off onto the carpet.  Tip-toeing around, the third sister lay widely sprawled out sleeping on her back.  This position could be a problem to see her lower back.

I stood beside the bed, studying her.  Her breasts were so massive, even in what should be their most flattened position.  They were still nowhere near flat, but two huge mounds both soft and firm, culminating in tempting nipples that were eyeing me back at my own eye level.  Oh I wanted to kiss the one closest, then realized she would probably react, even in her sleep.  Wait a minute.  Ah-ha!  That was the trick now, wasn't it?

I needed to get her to roll to her side and not wake, and especially not fall off the bed either.  I'd have to get back on the bed, to the inside, and get her to roll toward me.  Excited at my genius, I climbed back on from the foot of the bed, between the feet of triplets two and three.  My plan: get on up there and kiss her left breast, the one on the far side, but kiss it on its near side, if you get what I'm saying.  That should make mama to want to move her nipple closer to the kiss.

But the positioning looked to be awkward.  She spread too broad for me to even stand over stably, even with my legs wide as possible.  I would have to crawl onto her, and try to get a gradual response and movement.  Probably, she wouldn't be that pissed off if woken in this manner; kind of like me wanting to make out with her shouldn't invoke too much penalty.  They did invite me to the bed, after all.  I just hoped she didn't wake up with a start, and knock me across the room and out the open second story window!

With my best stealth, I crawled up the spread-V of her legs.  I kissed ever so lightly her soft sweet scented curls. I spidered from between her legs onto her lower abdomen with my chest and arms – zip, nada, no reaction.  Sidling up her torso I glided my head between those huge breasts.  Was I really so insignificant that she didn't notice my weight?  Up and down I moved with her deep full breathing.  I steadied myself and gently planted the first kiss on the near side of her left breast – nothing.  I kissed a little harder – still nothing.  This time I kissed harder and reached up and with two fingers lightly piano-trilled at the nearest edge of her nipple.  This time she responded, turning just a little toward me.

OK, I'd have to do that a bit more.  But now, on a slight slope I found it more difficult to balance.  Fortunately that left breast leaned a bit toward me now.  I applied the same technique again, and it worked the same, with another slight leaning toward the stimulation.  Just one more time should expose he lower back.

Unfortunately, I was losing my position and very slowly sliding down her right breast.  I'd have to act fast.  At the last moment of my purchase, I applied my best technique again.  I slid the rest of the way off her breast as she shifted exactly as predicted.

Yet, and not as predicted – because with that final shift to her side, as I slid to the mattress she also scooched over a body width; sleepily hugging her nearest sister, sandwiching me in between them and under their four massive breasts.  Then the second sister responded in her sleep, rolling over to her other side and shoving herself ass back and up into her sister's embrace.  This locked me completely in tight, now on my back, my upper body and head smashed under one huge breast with another on top of that.  My lower body significantly pinned by prodigious ass meeting warm crotch.  And that's more or less the way I would stay six long hours until morning.

It gave me a lot of time to think.  Sleep.  Wake.  Think.  Oh, and of course, get horny and stay horny.  That's what I was really good at.  I worked my right arm around and found the nipple of her right breast.  I managed to squeeze my left leg up between the two sisters.  (My right leg was completely under "Orion's" big ass.)  I worked that left leg up further and further in until it was pressed against her pussy, right about where I figured her clitoris would be hiding.

So now I was working this third sister's right nipple and snatch.  My left arm was pinned against my side, kind of perfectly positioned.  So with my left hand I grabbed myself.  Naturally, I'm right handed.  But when it comes to this, believe me, I'm ambidextrous.  With my mouth, I licked and kissed the breast pressing my face down.

Yes, this was an entirely workable situation.  Interestingly, it was *both* sisters that started moaning, maybe all three.  I couldn't hear very well noise from the far side of the bed.  But I could hear the little sounds of pleasure reverberating through both the bodies that were on me, sandwiching now a little tighter.  Oh yea, I felt quite clever about what I was up to.

They continued to progress, foreplay in their sleep.  It seemed there was actually nothing that I could do that would wake these amazons. Even if I shouted it would be the merest muffle the way my mouth was covered.  I tried it.   In response she leaned heavier into that vibration.  Not awake by any means, just more stimulated.

They plateaued at a nice level and just kept on going.  I stayed with them, kind of at 80% of max, not at risk of cumming unless some kind of additional vigor was to happen.  It was blissful.  Heavy, crushing, kind of hot, yet blissful.

My mind wandered back to the entire point of my foray.  I realized, dummy, I actually already had all I needed to know to tell the sisters apart.  That is, unless this third one, that was starting to gyrate on me, also had either the Big Dipper or Orion on her lower back as well.  I think I faintly heard a mourning dove's wooing call.  Out there, beyond my world under smothering flesh, dawn was breaking.

The second sister, still asleep but also into rhythmic movement now, turned back toward me.  In the brief opening, I lifted my right leg to lodge it between her upper thighs.  And shortly I was working them both with my legs.  This doubled the response.  They had to wake up soon.

I felt so excited.  I felt warm and getting hot. I wondered what response they were going to have when they found out I'd been stimulating them in their sleep.  Would they be happy, accepting, and loving?  Good.  Would they be angry, offended, and punishing?  Even better.

Suddenly there was an intense increase in crushing weight on me.  The 623 pound Big Dipper sister had piled on.  "What's this, our new alarm cock, I mean clock."  I thought she was pretty funny for first thing in the morning.  Heavy, but funny.  The other two sisters were also awake now, but did not miss a beat, liking waking up well into foreplay already.

"Oh man, let's fuck this little horndog."  Big Dipper was certainly a morning person.  Grinding me vigorously now, they were all obviously morning persons. "Open up sisters, I want what he is about to give up.

The two on me rolled back a little, but kept my legs trapped.  I was now spread eagle.  Big Dipper descend on me, her wet pussy sliding right over my hard on.  Three hard poundings and I was ready to cum.  She pulled back, clenching firmly, just in time to hold me at peak.

"Don't you dare cum until I release you."  Her command and controlled tightness governed my body. "Oh Richie," she continued. "I have to tell you, your Sparkle is working already."  I could see the other two nodding agreement.  I loved that they could all feel the best sensations of each other.

Big Dipper was getting a bit crazy with her vigor.  I think the Sparkle affected her most directly and maybe a little more than the other sisters.  Perhaps my look of proud satisfaction got her ire, but I think it was just her letting go and having overly enthusiastic fun.

"So you think it's funny, do you Richie, that you can drive us wild like this?" The tigress growled at me, still holding me in her cum-stopping clench.  It wasn't in-and-out sex, but locked in her pussy and upper inner legs it was up-and-down sex with my whole body as she bounced and thrashed more and more out of control.  She shouted out. "Somebody please put a jackhammer on that silly smirk of his."

"I'll do it."  And "Our Sister of the Unknown Constellation" released her thighs' vice-grip on my left leg, steamrolled over me, belly momentarily on my face, jammed her hands into the mattress, did a pummel-horse kind of move to swing her legs around and lift up and over me, released her arms, and let her great big juicy cunt plant itself right on my face, her ass crushing the wind form my lungs.  My whole face entered her pussy as it chewed down on me, seemingly wanting to devour my face, and pull it in, then deliver it way up to somewhere like her ovaries.

They pumped me like this for some twenty minutes, vigorous and vibratingly fast.  It seemed I was kind of OK without getting air.  I mean it was a little panicky, but the sex was also maddenly delicious. I didn't care.  The stimulation fried my brain.  Every nerve in my body craved more and more of their delicious squish, their fabulous irresistible bodies that vibrant with sensuous tingle.

Their orgasms were beginning now and accelerating fast.  But the peak was to be much higher than any of us anticipated as they built and built and built.... Thank God they were synchronistic in their pleasures or I might have been torn to pieces.

Even I could feel the Sparkle now.  It made me think of a lit firework, fountaining out pleasure.  Its effusion was evidently driving them crazy.  I felt Big Dipper release me a tiny bit and I knew that was the signal.  I think I barely heard her shouting something like, "All right.  Let's see what you got."  She quivered her great ass on me, shaking the bed with her rapid intensity.  The drenching pussy that engulfed my face did the same.  And God did I cum.

Six hours of foreplay.  And it seemed the Sparkler delivered more like pyrotechnics.  The sisters squealed like banshees, wild harmonizing screams that pitched higher and higher until squeaking out of normal hearing range.  Because I was obliterated I could not hear that dogs started barking a mile away.

Their pounding knocked me senseless.  They were gone, over their limits of control.  I would have to somehow endure their complete unleashed ecstasy now.  And as they wasted me with their freed and unrelenting pussies and mammoth asses, all I could think was that I loved them, I wanted to serve them in any way, and I did indeed, in that circumstance worship them.

If ever women owned a man, it was me in that moment. My surrender to them was a 20 on the 1 to 10 scale.  I would have done any debasing thing they asked.  Thank the Lord that they didn't.

And still my three girlfriends sat on me, little shudders of sensation releasing from them and down into me.  I could tell they were all finished. It was just that it had felt so fucking amazing they didn't want it to be over.  But I guess duty called – time to get the day going.  Finally, after wiggling and smashing their asses on me a few more minutes, just for good measure, they climbed off me.

As Sister Number Three rose from my face I managed a wet and bleary-eye glance at her lower back.  Sure enough, wouldn't you know it, The Southern Cross.  At last, proof positive to differentiate these triplets.  Who says science is easy?  Ha!  That made me laugh, then cough, then groan.  Yes, I was a little bit sore.

"Come on, tough guy. Want me to lick you clean?"  Said Southern Cross.  I'd have to get their real names soon.  But at least now I had leverage.  No girl I knew would want to be called "Orion" or "Southern Cross" for that matter.  And hell, certainly not "Big Dipper."  I laughed out loud at that thought.

They looked at me quizzically, as they went to and from the bathroom and got dressed for their work day.

***

They were busy at breakfast when I stumbled downstairs.  I'd taken a quick shower, and was dressed in my blue shorts and green pullover polo shirt.  Silently, I poured myself some granola and sat, not at the table, but in a big folding chair over by the phone and notes station.  I looked at my dry bowl.  What a dip; I'd forgotten to pour on the milk.

"Don't you want some milk with that?"  It was Orion, and I could tell it was her for sure.  Yes, all the sudden I could tell them apart.

"Sure, that would be great… Orion."

Her eyes went wide, "What did you call me?"

"I called you 'Orion'.  And by the way, your two lovely sisters are 'Southern Cross'."  I indicated by pointing which one with my spoon.  "And 'Big Dipper'." pointing at the third.  Then I folded my arms in satisfaction at the priceless looks of shock on their faces.  "So, you want to tell me your real names, or should we just stick with these."  Oh, had them good.

"I still don't think we should tell him."

"OK. *Southern Cross*," I responded with emphasis.  "That's fine with me."

It was Big Dipper, "I think it is time to let him know.  No big deal anyway.  It was just a game."

"A game I'm winning."  Finally.

It was Orion again, "Sure, we'll tell you.  But let me bring you your milk first."

With that she strode over, hiked up her tight skirt so she could spread her legs, then with magnanimous dominance, straddled me and sat down firmly.  She unbuttoned her blouse, dropped it, took off the black lacy bra, flung it.  Then with one strong right hand, grabbed the back of my head and turned my face to look up through her cleavage at her face and penetrating blue-gray eyes.  "My name is Aria.  A-R-I-A, pronounced Ah-ree-ya.  It means –"

"Song." I interrupted

"Very good."  She bounced a little on me, her big breasts jiggling against my face.  "Now, my little smarty. I have a question for you?  I brought you milk.  How do you want it served?  Left tit first, or right?"

"Ah… er…" was all I got out.

"That's what I thought."  And with that she jammed her left nipple into my gapping mouth.

"So," Aria talked as she sat on me and nursed me.  "You were quite busy sneaking around last night…"

Of course I couldn't answer, so I didn't try.  Their conversation drifted on, about their day ahead, the time they needed to allot at the Synsonto Research labs, their session at the recording studio next Wednesday, their upcoming weekend conference in Montreal.

"Hey," It was Big Dipper.  I didn't know her real name yet, "I've got an idea.  Maybe Debra would like to come stay with Richie this weekend while we're gone.  Keep an eye on him.  Keep him out of trouble."  Did they ever stop teasing me?

"I like it."  Aria broke off that side, and offered me her other nipple.  I wondered if she noticed the hard on I had.  Probably figured no way; or more likely was just ignoring it for now.

I managed to get a word in.  "You mean like babysit me?"

"Oh come on now.  You know you want it."  It was Southern Cross.  "It is the perfect chance for Debra to check it out here, see how she likes it.  See if she can stand you for more than a day."  See what I mean, always teasing.

I had a good comeback, but Aria jammed her other nipple in my mouth, and shut me up for the next five minutes.  She smiled down at me, kind of petting the back of my head.  Undoubtedly the release and the sucking felt good to her.

Big Dipper suggested, "Why don't we leave it up to Richie to invite her if he wants to.  We're saying it is OK with us, totally.  So you decide, Richie."  The other two sisters nodded agreement.

I tried to say something, put it was too muffled.

"What's that you say?" Aria asked, but obviously not seriously as she pushed her breast into me more firmly, shutting me up but good.

I listened to the sisters talk more about their schedule, and it seemed most of their time was at Synsonto, not in the recording studio.  I thought it would have been reversed.

Finally Aria finished, and scooped up her blouse.  But before she stood up, she grabbed my hard no through my pants and said, "Save that one for later, Champ." Of course she knew I was hard for her.

Big Dipper stood over me.  She took off her blouse and bra.  Then she also hiked up her tight skirt.  Looking at the tent in my shorts, she suggested, "Why don't we find a place to put that.  It might be more comfortable for you."  With that, she pulled off her red panties, then reached down and deftly snatched off my shorts.  "Nice one."  She said, referring to my hard on. "Considering…" More teasing – yea, considering the sex we'd had just an hour ago.

When Big Dipper straddled me and positioned onto my lap, my volunteer slid nicely inside her.  It wasn't exactly sex, just a cozy place to be held.  She hefted her big boobs with her hands, raising her eyebrows, tilting her head as if to say, "What's it going to be, left or right."  I gestured to the right with my head, and she was polite enough to comply.

"OK."  She bounced lightly (if that's possible) to get the adjustment below just right.  And the milk started to flow into my sucking mouth.  "Well, my name is Aria."

I broke off, "Oh no!"  The same name… all that effort and gaming for nothing, I thought.  That almost shrunk my hard-on.

God, she laughed at my disappointment.  "No, come on silly, I'm just fucking with you.  You thought we could have the same names?  What kind of parents do you think we have?"

The question was rhetorical, as she had me nursing again.

"My real name is Pavane.  It's Italian for a 16th century kind of stately dance for couples.  You can call me Pavie."  She winked at me.  "Good name, huh, 'cause I am sooo stately and proper."  She gave me a good squeeze.  I felt a little Sparkle start up.  "Ooooh." She said.  "I like that. But be careful boyfriend.  Don't bite off more than you can chew."

Nice names, so far.  But I was thinking about something else.  Something didn't make sense.  At the next nipple changeover I got a quick chance to ask my question: "I had the impression you guys made your living singing.  But it seems like most of your schedule is over at Synsonto Research Labs.  What gives, Babes?"

"Oh God," Said Aria.  "Don't you love it when he calls us 'Babes'?  I wish I'd thought of what your doing, Pavie, because it's feeling awfully good from here."  The Triplets were doing their share sensation transference again.

"Here's the thing," Pavie began explaining, but interrupting herself with little gasps of pleasure.  "We only need about ten to fifteen hours a month to make our recordings.  We don't need to rehearse.  We just need to understand the purpose."

Southern Cross commented. "For example, you've probably heard of our recordings to lower blood pressure.  We've made a fortune off those."

"Or to alieve anxiety…" Aria added.  "You know that's been a big seller."

Then Pavie again, definitely feeling the Sparkle now, "We clear…  ah, ooo… some eight figures a year, each, from our recordings… ooo, baby…"

"We spend some time at the Research Labs because of the amazing things are bodies seem to do."  Aria again. "Lately, it's been a lot of research about the milk we can give."

"They've found it can shrink tumors, regenerate nerve tissue, repair damaged kidneys."  Southern Cross had quite a list of miracles.

"So, you see, Richie" Pavie summarized  "We have plenty of money, and still kind of a lot of responsibility with this medical research."  Right then Pavie finished nursing me, though she hadn't finished down below.  But it wasn't her turn anymore, so she stood up. "You know what else."  She smiled at me; "You're clear on this I hope, that it is estimated we'll live to be at least 250 years old, and that anyone who gets a steady diet of our milk can do the same.  Oh yeah, that's right, *boyfriend*."

Southern Cross stood in, looking down at my aching hard on.  "You know, Pavie, it's a shame you didn't get to finish.  It was such a great idea you had."  Then she continued, "Too bad we can't sit reverse on him and still nurse him.  I think I'd rather fuck him that way."

"Well," Aria offered.  "There is a way…"

And immediately the other two sisters got it.

"Let's get him out of the silly chair!" Exclaimed Pavie.

Southern Cross lifted me up, a big hand under each armpit.  She carried me to the nearest carpet in the downstairs den, and placed me flat out on my back.  As she unbuttoned her blouse and removed her bra, Pavie stood over me, her great ass toward my head.  She sat on my cock, right back in her nicely wet pussy, her ass covering most of my torso and chest.

Then Southern Cross kind of did the cow thing with her breast over my face, only instead of staying on all fours, she leaned down on her elbows, her ass somewhere out of my sight up in the air.  Her nipple entered my mouth, then her breast spread the rest of the way across my face, over my entire head, and onto the carpet on every side of my head except my skinny neck.

It was a very, very nice smothering, as I sucked for five minutes.

Meanwhile, Pavie had the Sparkle going again as she gave me a thorough ass pounding – or you could say cock pounding with her pussy and ass.

I was about to cum when Southern Cross lifted to shift breasts.  "I couldn't tell you sooner, what with your entire head pressed under by breast.  My name is Calliope.  She was the Greek muse of music.  You, my dear love, can call me Callie."  And with that came down her other nipple then smashing breast.

I ruminated to myself in the heavy warmness; so then: a song, a dance, and a muse.  I should have known.  It was silly, but somehow knowing their names made me love them more.  Made me feel like, heaven forbid, I was in a relationship.

The thoughts of love got my Sparkler going even more.  The wildness that built, overtaking Pavie, made her crazy to make me cum.  Maybe it was all the earlier activity, but, excuse me, my response in that department needed just a little more time to build it up.

Callie's milk had been flowing like crazy.  She finished, but instead of standing up, she quickly whipped off her panties and sat her pussy on my face.  Then Aria piled on Callie's lap.  That extra weight stretched Calli's pussy completely over my head.  I was squeezed inside her.

If I had been a little slow before, that was certainly no longer the case.  If I didn't cum soon they'd have to find a straight-jacket for Pavie.  The double-pressure on my face and head was unbelievable, like a birth experience of divine sex.  Meanwhile, Pavie was about to break me in half down below.

That was it.  What seemed like a massive ejaculation erupted from me.  I thrashed, I bucked, I tossed madly about, knocking the love goddesses off me.  Are you kidding, I tried to do all that.  But of course I could not dislodge them one iota.  For all my fight and squirming, they only drove me down more with their colossal smothering crush of my body.

But just because I finished did not mean they were.  Their massive smother kept on for some ten minutes more of uncontrolled thrashing of my body.  Their combined weight pounding me practically beyond consciousness, certainly into a state of crushed delirium.

When they finally got off me, I didn't even know where I was… who I was… for a minute of two.  I was just pussy fodder, a boney little sex tool.  Emotionally I was no more than a puddle of spent weakness that they could use to wash their feet.

I just lie there, breathing long and slow, in and out.  Vaguely I heard them getting their clothes back on, stopping to prim before the foyer mirror.  I heard the jingle of keys, then a harmony. "Bye-bye, little super lover.  Be good, now.  We love you…" The front door shut, and they locked it from the outside.  "Live to be 250, like this?" I thought to myself. "It doesn't seem likely."

# VII. Miss Strickland's Crush

Where was everybody?  The air conditioner had just shut down, and the office creaked in an eerie quite.

I'd missed work yesterday, due to being too thoroughly smothered first thing that morning by my new amazon giantess lovers: Aria, Pavie, and Calli.  You know, the Towering Triplets – in another time they would have been called witches for all their strange powers they loved to exert over and on me.  Ah yes, 8:00 in the morning and already I was thinking about getting on home…  Is that what it was "home"?  Were my three girlfriends becoming more than just girlfriends, more than lovers?

Miss Monroe's office: empty.  I sat in her big chair, gave it a twirl.  As I spun around I recalled how she had devastated me here in this office, the sweet taste of her ginger pussy, then her special form of "dick-take-tion".  Ha!  I spun out of the chair and trotted out her door.

Back in the hallway: still way too quiet.

Office after office: nobody.  Where were these big-ass secretaries?  Suddenly I missed them.  I missed… their scent filling the office air, the swish of their scissoring nylons as they wiggled by in their smart, tight skirts, and the way they often had pretended to ignore me as insignificantly small.…  Then I had to smile recalling the surprise birthday party… and then I couldn't help a frown recalling the sexual frenzy that almost killed me.…  Gosh, I was definitely horny; unbelievable after the phenomenal events of last night.  No, actually anything less would be unbelievable.

In Miss Johansen's office I sniffed the cushions of her big leather couch for the scent of her.  Not detectable there – but her chair, yes, I think definitely, and I kissed the spot where I knew her cunt would rest all day.  I was getting a little bit hard.  What a fuckin' weirdo!

In Miss Rasmussen's office I stood with my hand up on her copy machine.  I pretended she was standing behind me, hovering over me, impatient to use the machine, too.  But I took my time, like driving slow in the fast lane, making her wait.  That made her angry in my fantasy… she pressed her legs against my back.  "Hurry up," I made her say, "Or I might have to squeeze you with my legs."  But then she didn't wait at all, stepping over me, my head sliding up under her skirt.  Yes, I definitely liked that scenario a lot…

Not a single office was occupied.

At the end of the hallway uncharacteristically Miss Strickland's door stood open. I'd never seen it. I peaked in. Wow, palatial in scale; I mean huge – for an office. Again nobody there. Well then, let's have a look around, shall we?

By the door a candy dish. I took a couple of mints and popped them in my mouth. Pretty good; kind of buttery the way I liked it. There was plenty of open space in the middle, covered by a beautifully detailed and thick Persian carpet. It was nice and squishy, cushioning underneath no doubt. I strode over, climbed up and sat on her giantess-sized beige leather couch. Firm but deep. I guess it would do. Lying on the couch I looked up at the very high ceiling. It was actually painted with replica classic artwork and fresco. Wow, that was not expected in a work office. But, Miss Strickland had been here a long, long… long time. It made sense; she had to personalize it over the years.

The scenes painted out on the ceiling were arresting, vibrant, mostly al fresco green-and-flowery or darker-and-forested settings. Women hunted with bows and arrows. Little cherubs at the feet of picnicking ladies, a tall queen laughing at the antics of a troop of dwarfish jokers… OK, I'm not always a quick study, but I was starting to see the amazon theme here.

"Well then…" I got up and sashayed flamboyant and goofy-gay over to Miss Strickland's desk. I hauled myself up into her huge chair. "Too hard" I thought, then laughed when I realized, "Goodness gracious, I'm Goldilocks." I still chuckled as I slid out of the chair, my feet finally touching the floor.

I stood at the neck-high desk, thinking about drawing a silly picture on her stick-um pad, something a little obscene maybe. I looked over at her computer screen; at the tube pattern that lazily bounced off the screen edges, changing color and diameter as it went through its progressions. The screen crackled faintly as it went dark. Timed-out. Oh shit! Miss Strickland was in the building and had been at this computer, what, not more than ten minutes ago – or five?

I heard a door shut. The break room. Crap, I hadn't checked in there. Damn. Heavy, heavy steps clumped down the hallway, coming this way.

She was going to be pissed. That was her biggest rule – nobody was allowed in her office. That's why she always kept her door locked and shut. Except when – what – everybody else had the day off. That must have been the fucking memo I missed yesterday.

Oh shit, shit.  I panicked.  Those heavy steps were getting too close, three more and she'd be at the doorway.  Her massive dark walnut desk was paneled in the front wasn't it?  I hope yes, as I dove down into the chair well.  It was.  I hid.  She entered.  And firmly shut and locked the door.

I heard her sip noisily as one does – with hot coffee, tea? "Hummp" she harrumphed at some stray thought.  Then passed gas.  Oh, Miss Strickland, how rude.  But then again, it was her office, and she knew she was alone.

Heavy steps and she was around the desk.  I looked out at her black nylon massive legs, and I mean colossal. Her calves were so extremely muscular.  They had to be, as the foundation to cart around her tonnage.

Yes, tonnage.  You see, Miss Strickland at some fifteen feet tall, was, who knows, maybe more than 2,500 pounds.  Now you get it, don't you?  Why I was shivering in my shorts, cowered under her desk.

She rolled up her chair and sat down affording me the deep, dark grand-canyon view up her skirt.  I put my hand over my mouth not to gasp at the sight.  She scooted her chair in further, spreading her legs for comfort.  Oh thank God, she stopped just short of running into me.  And oh my Lord, what a view up those gargantuan inner thighs, to a triangle of deep blue panties way, way in there.  Horny already, now I was big-time hard, and at the same time mortified at the thought how merciless those legs could be to my little body.

Think Richie.  But I was trapped.  Maybe I should just come out now.  Take my medicine, so to speak, and get it over with.  The longer I stayed here looking up her skirt, the more pissed off she's bound to be.  But she will know, of course, that I already looked up her skirt, already broke the rule and entered her office.  I felt a little shell-shocked, like a soldier staring out at a battle scene and knowing, "I might die here today."  That, I felt, was my reality.  "I might die here today.

Miss Strickland could snap my neck in two seconds.  And, sorry, but this is how my sick mind works, especially when I'm freaked out: she could kill me, eat me in one sitting without a shred of me remaining, and then go home and shit me out, down her toilet to get rid of the evidence.  I'd like to see that CSI episode on television – that is, starring someone else!

No, sit tight.  I can smell the coffee it now.  She slurped at it again.  She'll have to go to the bathroom eventually.  Heck, she farted a little while ago; maybe she'll have to do that, too.  Good.  More time then to make my escape.

God, what a dolt!  What was I thinking sneaking into Strickland's office?  Fuck.

She scratched her leg a bit above her right knee.  Goodness, look at those red painted nails, beautiful, sexy, but sharp and the size of bear claws.  A big but dainty bracelet jangled as she withdrew her hand.  But her knee still itched, so she scratched it a bit more vigorously.  That seemed to do the job.

She shifted her feet about and I tiptoe-danced around the movement.  Then she settled down again for a long time.

She didn't seem to be working on her keyboard.  But I could hear a kind of scratching right above me – like she was working on something right on top of the desk surface.  Drawing or sketching, with pencils?

I just kept on staring up her legs to those panties.  I was mesmerized by the thought of her grand pussy, her monumental ass.  I don't think I could really imagine it properly.  I was kind of on tilt.  I needed someone to hit my reset button so I could think straight.

Come on, Richie; keep your wits about you.

Now the entire desk was shaking.  There was a familiar squeaking sound right above me.  I know this one: erasing, and a lot of it.  It seems like she'd had about a 50% change of heart about the concept she was drawing.

There came a soft, raspy sound.  She was dusting the erasure curls off her paper with her hand.  Yes, I could see them now, a not quite floaty cascade over the front edge of her desk.  Plenty landed on her legs, which she proceeded to flip off forward with both hands.  And, oh boy, into my face.

I felt it building quickly: a sneeze, and likely a whopper.  I blinked, held my nose and twisted it to cut the sneeze off.  But that doesn't work so well, does it?  It only delayed momentarily, allowing it to insistently build up more.  And "KERCHEW!" How could such loud sound come out of such a small body.

The 400 pound desk went flying off and across the room.  No, you idiot, not from my sneeze.  But from Miss Strickland's shocked reaction and tremendous strength. The desk tumbled to a stop, unfortunately blocking the door.

"Do you have a tissue?" Sheepishly, I tried to make a joke; I'm sure my face a blinking twist of grin and dismay.

Miss Strickland stood to her full 15'7" height, (OK add the heels and call it an even 16'). But I didn't hear any laughter coming down from the heavens. No what I heard was a deep reverberating growl; "What the fuck are you doing there!"

"Well, I came into work and nobody was here so…"

"So, what! You thought, let's sneak into Miss Strickland's office, and hide under her desk." And she seemed to finally be realizing what I saw. "… while I'm sitting there?" Oh, she was way beyond indignant now.

I am a terrible liar and should never even try it. But anyway, "Oh, I'm so sorry, Miss Strickland. I wasn't like looking up your legs. And I didn't see any blue panties or anything." What a fuckin' fail.

"Oh, you nasty, nasty little man. Go over there," She pointed. "…and sit right down on the couch." She seemed to want to put a little distance between us. Maybe she was afraid of what she might do to me. I know I was.

I scurried over, hauled up to the middle of that same beige couch again. At sat dutifully, on my hands, looked back her as innocently as I could, and kept my mouth shut. She hadn't twisted my head off yet. Maybe, just maybe, I would survive.

I studied the giantess as she studied me. So big, sturdy and solid in every aspect. Atop, her wide mane of black hair thickly framed a rather striking face with wide-set green eyes under dark eyebrows. Her generous scarlet lips and full mouth drew my eye, really quite desirable. Innumerable thick wavy locks cascaded from her mane across her broad shoulders. Those great shoulders and her back had to be quite strong to hold up the biggest pair of tits I could have imagined, each breast probably more than the weight of my body. Though she tried best she could to conceal them in her conservative dress, there was no hiding those mammaries – no way.

Miss Strickland had a well-defined waist that set off her extremely ample goddess curves. But she was also necessarily thickened through the middle. There was just too much strength needed for support and foundation for her titanic frame above. Her prodigious butt was so wide, so record-breaking in every aspect; it was unnerving just to behold it. The colossal legs matched the ass for proportion, so sturdy with muscle you could almost lose perspective on how toweringly long they were.

I clinched my jaw tight because my teeth wanted to start chattering – with fear. Fight or flight, they say. How about: moronic and catatonic? I could think of no strategy at this point or place to flee.

She took one step toward me.  "So you saw my panties, did you?"

That was her take-away message from what I said.  Well.  OK then.  "Yes, very lovely.  Very lovely indeed, Miss Strickland."

She took one more step toward me. "Of course, you know, you must be punished for: number one, sneaking into my office without my permission, and number two, for your nasty little violation of my privacy under my desk.  What was you plan; just stand in there all morning, ogling my crotch?"

"Well, I figured, what with you drinking coffee, you might eventually, you know, need a potty break.  I reckoned I'd leave then."

"Oh you reckoned', did you?  Just sneak out like nothing ever happened?"  She was still indignant, but not near as growly.

I nodded that she understood my plan.  Of course, I didn't know when to shut up, "Or maybe you'd need even longer in the bathroom, and I would have been like: I never even came to work."

Her eyes widened, a bit mortified, realizing what I had heard – you know – her fart. "Oh great," She said.  "So you heard that too."

"Well, Miss Strickland, that doesn't mean anything.  I mean, it is your office and everything."  What, like I'm forgiving her now.  Shut up, Richie…

"What would be suitable punishment?"  I realized she really did not know what she wanted to do with me… to me.

I raised my hand.

"Yes?" Like an impatient teacher.

"How about, instead of "punishment" I could do amends.  You know, try to make it right.  That way, you know, we're both better off."

"How about…" She eyed me dryly.  "We do a little bit of each."  She walked over and stood right above me, her legs a bit apart.  "Maybe we can start with the amends.  I'll figure out the punishment as we go along."  But the colossus just stood there over me, and I felt like my bones were turning to putty.  Can you believe it; I almost looked up her skirt again right then?

I suppose you know, that sometimes, on rare occasions, pools of secretaries have been known to gossip?  So at break times, as I'd weave around the legs of the secretary forest, trying to get my meager share of the pastries or maybe a little cup of tea, I heard things.  Things all too often about Miss Strickland, who never, never took her break with the rest of us.

Probably I should have checked these "facts" with my new girlfriends, Aria, Pavie, and Calli.  But I always seemed otherly occupied performing my boyfriend duties under the contortions of sex they kept dreaming up.

Anyway, this is what I've heard about Miss Strickland that I believe might likely be true.  Rumor says she's approximately 44 years old.  Studying her face in her office today, I'd say that face could have passed for 35 for even 30.  But I'm no expert.  Anyway, the math does support an age more like 44.

Then one day in the break room, Miss Johansen leaned her ass against me, backing me into a corner, and pressed my face there for the full fifteen minutes of break while she chatted with Miss Taylor.  I caught a few snatches, so to speak, of the conversation.  They were saying that Miss Strickland was the first of their kind – I'm saying the first of the Amazons of Bluebelle Valley.  Until her, nobody around Bluebelle Bend had been affected.  They didn't know yet about any of the chemical contaminations, or that the whole affair would trace back to Synsonto.  I didn't hear all of it that day because Miss Johansen is one of the people that talks with her body, very expressive, I guess, but her ass kept shifting this way and that, tightening, jiggling when she laughed, which was frequent – you get the idea.

Anyway I did hear that she had already been working at the research farm, had been growing like crazy from a young age, and had soared past eight feet tall by the time she was only eighteen, when they finally discovered aspects of the contamination in the soils and water supplies in the area.  So, as part of that first settlement she got promised a good job with Synsonto, for life.  They moved her from the pollination crew to the office staff, and started getting her properly trained.

What that gossip didn't cover was the poor girl's misery.  Imagine being the first, the only "Amazon of Bluebelle Valley", the interviews, the hated publicity, the stares, the rejection, the missed young adulthood… the loneliness.

Another day in the break room a while back I'm sitting there at lunch, peacefully chewing on my sandwich.  Up comes Miss Klingbell, pulls my chair out like it was empty, and plops her big tight ass on me like I'm invisible.

"Excuse me." I say.  But she just leans back to shut me up.  Then I hear some really juicy gossip about Miss Strickland.

"Well," Says Miss Petersen. "They say she had an affair with an executive at the company when she was young.  It was a married man, still with the company today, I tell you.  They say, a bigwig now, back East at Headquarters, all very hush, hush."

"You know what I heard about that."  Miss Klingbell, wiggled on me, loving the titbit she had – the gossip, not me!  "I heard his wife made him leave Bluebelle Bend.  A daughter of one of the original owners, she was.  He stood to lose everything.  And…"  She whispered.  "They say the he and Miss Strickland were in love."

The five who were listening laughed loud at this, then it was all: "Shhh, Shhh."

Still they whispered, "Imagine Miss Strickland in love with a normal sized man."  They snickered again.

"Oh, come on," One said. "She was much smaller back then when that happened.  Probably not even nine feet tall yet."

"But she was much taller, some say more than eleven feet, when she got married five years after that."

"I heard he was a football player from Green Bay."

"I heard he was a basketball player from Florida."

"No, no."  It was Miss Petersen again.  "I looked up the newspaper articles.  He was a musician from St. Paul.  And get this, only five foot nine inches tall.  According to the court records, he died only four months into the marriage.  Suffocated to death!"

Miss Klingbell laughed and bounced on me without a mercy, finally acknowledging me.  "Like I might just do to little Richie here."

They all giggled at that.

Then our historian Miss Petersen continued.  "Get this, for reals.  There was an investigation and everything.  The DA didn't file any charges, but the dead husband's family filed a civil case for Wrongful Death.  They dragged Miss Strickland through the courts for months.  But in the end, the attorneys from Synsonto prevailed, of course.  It was her, for sure, everyone knew it, but someone the jury thought it could have been an accident."

"Wow," I'd said to myself at the time. "Poor Miss Strickland."

But now, recalling this gossip and looking up at my giantess boss, I was saying to myself, "Poor Miss Strickland's husband."

"Well." Miss Strickland had come to some conclusion." I think I've decided on what I want for the first amends. Your sneaking around and surprising me like you did has caused me to get a little tense."

I thought: "Oh we don't want her to be tense."

"So you," Was it possible for someone of her size to sound even slightly coy? "You get to give me a back rub."

She sat all the way down to the Persian in front of me. Even that gentle movement caused a significant air disturbance in the room. Then she slipped off her high heels. But she stopped there. I guess we didn't know each other that well yet. For my part, however, I did know her a little better and could not get that image of her blue panties out of my mind.

Miss Strickland stretched out on her stomach. Then said over her shoulder to me. "OK, get busy."

I slipped off the couch, walked four steps past her impossible legs, two more steps past the great mound of her ass, then two more steps between the space of her huge muscular left arm and alongside her upper back. The surface of her back rose close to my waist height, thanks in no small part to the huge tits under her chest. I reached out and down just a little and began to rub firmly.

"Have you started yet?" She moaned.

I mean I knew she could feel it. "Your clothing is really thick, Miss Strickland." But I didn't say: "Because you are always trying, in vain, to hide you mammoth mammaries."

"Well if you insist." She sat up. Just sitting she was three feet taller than me. After a full minute of buttons and hooks, her heavy blouse finally came off, her immense breasts mostly revealed for their great size but not quite unleashed as they strained against blue fabric of the poor bra. They were bouncing just up from in front of my face. "Better?" I heard her say. Yes, she was definitely getting coy.

I looked up at her face, unable to speak, nodding that "yes" it was better.

"Good." She heaved herself back around and plunged down again. This time her massive breasts squeezed outward quite visibly – the near one bulging against my legs.

I began again. Her skin was smooth and soft. And she smelled good. Not overpowering, just surprisingly wholesome. I was doing my best; actually kind of enjoying it and certainly the view.

But she was complaining again. "This isn't working for me. It's feels like mice playing cards. Get up on me and get some force behind it." Man she was bossy. But then, she was the boss.

I pulled off my tennys and my socks and set them aside. Standing, I grabbed her thick bra strap, swung my leg up, and rolled onto her back.

"Try standing, walking." She ordered.

I got up and started pacing around on her back. I could tell it still wasn't doing it. I dug my heel in between a couple of her ribs.

"Ahhh." That got a response. "Good."

I continued with that for a quite a while, working systematically and symmetrically, rib by rib and side to side. I could feel her with my feet, her muscles relaxing, unwinding. She was definitely a tight woman. But she also was a woman that responded well to touch, at least this kind of touch.

I called down to her. "My goodness, Miss Strickland, you're so tight. When was the last time you had a massage?"

She sighed, her voice far more relaxed than I'd ever heard it. "Oh I don't know, maybe twenty years…"

That right there was heart-breaking. I didn't know what to say.

But I did feel inspired by that lack of human contact. I wanted to make this a damn good massage. She sighed, pleasure. And apparently I was off to a good start.

I looked around at her back. Her skin was beautiful, olive, soft, and supple, with cute little moles here and there. Her shade darker skin color was complimented well by her long black curls that still covered her outer shoulders and upper arms and spread out several feet to either side on the carpet. "Wow," I thought. "That – is –a –beautiful – image."

She wiggled just slightly form side-to-side as if to suggest with her body, "Get going again."

I progressed now, to baby steps down her spine, stepping in just the right spots on either side of each vertebra.  I continued right over the bra strap, ignoring it being in the way – for now.  She moaned with pleasure at each backbone.  I think my small feet were getting to the in-between spaces kind of perfectly.

The progression led me to the top of her skirt, of course.  I stood there, marching in place as I decided what to do about that thick material.  I still had three or four more vertebrae to go.  I knew how it felt.  When you massage down someone's spine, you have to finish.  Or it's kind of like when someone turns off a song on the radio before it hits the final chord.  You still want to sing it to end, to its proper major chord, singing sometimes even louder, maybe even with some irritation.

Miss Strickland reached down on both sides, hooked her thumbs into the fabric belt of her skirt, and shimmied her clothing south about a foot.  I could see that place on a woman, on this woman, that I love so much, the lowest, lowest part of her back – honestly that's not what it is really – it's the beginning of the ass that I like so much.  And I could just see Miss Strickland's ass crack rising before me and lost into the folds of her skirt and vastness beyond.

I continued on down with my baby steps until the very last tail bone.  At this point I wanted to drop down, push my face into her and kiss the beginning of her divided buns.  But I behaved, turning around, baby steps back up seemed like a good idea.  However, I wondered right then how she would have reacted if I had, you know, kissed her like I wanted….

As I got to her neck, I dropped down to my knees to continue on up.  My boney knees dug in nicely to her relaxed neck that was wide enough to accommodate me still working either side without slipping off.  I did not stop at the top of her neck, instead continuing on through the attachment points up the back of her head.  Her pleasured sigh, right beneath me now, let me know it was feeling very good.

Finishing there, I dropped a body slam over to her right shoulder blade, digging in my elbow, working my way down and then back across.  It was harder work, now, like a combination of body-planks and sideways push-ups.  Plus I was speeding up, a faster rhythm and vigor was required.  I'm not a perfectionist, but I do like to get it right.  And poor Miss Strickland; no massage for twenty years?  She deserved the best I could offer.

It took me a while and a lot of work, but I finally finished her shoulders and upper back.  It was worth it, as I could feel her appreciation.  My desires wanted to head south again, probably figure a way to crawl under her skirt and have a field day on that ass that was kind of dominating me from afar.  But what really demanded my higher attention was an odd inspiration I had.

I sat down on her uppermost back, dangling my legs over the tops of her shoulders, either side of her neck.  Reaching down, I grabbed two handfuls of those luscious black curls, and tugged on them.

"Oh, yeah," She let out a big exhale. "Harder."

 My intuition was right.  Some people love to have their hair pulled.  And Miss Strickland was one of them.  I tugged harder.  She moaned more pleasure.  I pulled as hard as I could, trying to test her limits.  She responded, "Oh, that's good Richie.  Ooooo…"

Bringing my legs back up, I placed my feet against the base of her skull.  I wound my arms through big swaths of her hair, symmetrically on either side.  And using the firm purchase I had with my feet tugged with all my might.

"Oh my-oh-my, that is…" But I cut her off with another hard pull.

I grabbed two other swaths, wound my arms through again, and pulled on those reigns. "Getty up!" I thought, pleased with this success.  I rode her this way, working through as much of her mane as I could possibly reach.  But it was exhausting, like working out on a rowing machine.  To reach further I stood, continuing the rhythmic pulling for as long as I could.  And finally I just collapsed on her upper back, falling with my face against the back of her neck. I could feel her against my cheek.  She was melted.

"Wow," she slurred in a tranquil low voice. "You are a very, very talented young man…"

I was also feeling very, very emotional.  There was so much sadness that came out of her body, tapped in all those places I'd been releasing.  It was very intense for me to feel that pain she'd stored.  As I lie against her neck, my eyes closed, feeling my breathing slow and stabilize, my heart ached for her.

"Miss Strickland," I spoke ever so gently, her ear was within a whisper of my mouth.

"Yes, Richie?"  Almost timid with softness, there was a lot of long lost little girl in her voice.

I felt a hot tear form in my left eye, right by her neck.  It welled then fell, maybe half an inch.  But I could tell she felt it.

"Miss Strickland," I said again.  This time she was completely silent, still, vulnerable.  I continued with what I had to say, my lips brushing her neck as I spoke. "I'm sorry.  I am so sorry for what happened to you, your stolen youth, your isolation, the meanness of people and the press," It just poured out of me. "…the projections from others you had to endure, to be so big, yet not really be seen, to have loved and lost so bitterly.  Oh Miss Strickland, you break my heart."

She was so, so still beneath me, not breathing.  Then there was a little catch, a quick inhale, a tiny spasm of an exhale, then harder, harder.  She was weeping, silent but for the rush of breath. Crying harder, she was bucked me around with her sobs.  She needed to sit up.  I rolled off.

She sat up, her great chest heaving as she wept, twenty years of loneness and I don't know what else.  But it was a lot of grief, and profound.  She kept a roll of paper towels on the end-table by her couch.  She ripped off a square, blew her nose, and tossed it with minimal accuracy at her trash can by where the desk used to be.

I looked on, with a mix of feelings: some concern, more sympathy, quite a bit of respect, and much more affinity than I ever expected to have for her.

Finally her sobs subsided.  She took in a big shuttering breath, magnificent to see really, if I had been in a sexual mode.  As I looked up at her face, she turned to meet my eyes.

There was the most beautiful expression on her face and in her penetrating green eyes.  I was seeing right into her soul, and her mine.  "Thank you Richie.  That means so much to me, what you said, more than you can know."  She paused, just looking at me, with kindness, probably with gratitude, and there was something else: something deeply heartfelt in her expression, at the corners of her eyes something from long ago; at the parting of her lips as they turned into a smile so genuine, it could only come from a centered spirit.

"There's something I have to tell you Richie.  Something important.  Lie down on your back.  I want to be closer to you when I say this."

I did as she requested, her face now some nine feet up from me, as she sat up on her haunches.  She reached around behind her back. "I hope you don't mind, but I'm going to give you a little gift before we continue.  I know you've been dying to see these."  My God, she was undoing her bra.  "And I hate this bra, it's so damn confining.  The massage made that obvious.  Get ready, these haven't been seen by any man for more than fifteen years.  Never, really, since they've gotten to this size."

Unlatched, the bra sprang away, the massive piece of blue elastic fluttering like great wounded, oxygen-starved eagle past my head.  I cannot describe for you those breasts from that moment.  Because, for my part, I kept my eyes transfixed hers, not wanting to lose the connection, for in that instant that bond was more important to me than my desires.  And she kept her eyes on mine as well, smiling a little more, knowingly, and somewhat impressed with my resolve and perhaps character.  After all, in spite of her long time of relationship dormancy, this was a mature woman towering over me, experienced at life, and with some capacity of understanding that, who knows, might even match her physical size.  That depth in her was something I certainly wanted to explore further.

She came down toward me now, not allowing anything to break the locked bond of our eyes.  I felt a huge warm breast settling across my lower body and leg.  She relaxed on her side beside me, right elbow on the floor, her right hand supporting her head as she leaned her face over mine.  The weight of her left breast now rested down on the other one that was already pressing me – very, very heavy and soft and quite divine.

"This is what I must tell you."  Her wide full mouth was not a foot from my face, her breath fresh and minty – like the butter-mints in the bowl, I thought.  Black curls of hair, almost heavy in their bounty fell over my face.  She carefully brushed them aside with her left hand, surprisingly delicate.  I noticed again how large and beautiful were her fingernails, gleaming red before my eyes, long and sharp as they barely grazed across my cheek and forehead, casting the black curls aside with a final flip.

I looked at her mouth, half open, about to speak again.  But she seemed to pause, while I searched inside with my eyes to see a glimpse of her teeth, her tongue.  Catching myself in this little revere of distraction, I brought my vision back to her eyes.  They were very intense now, up close like this.

"My first love," though she spoke softly her voice was quite penetrating being proximate like this. "…was at this very station.  I was barely eighteen, and I was so smitten, infatuated I guess.  But no matter, the love was real enough.  He was much older than me, of course, thirty-two, a bright young executive with Synsonto.  Brilliant, handsome, and ambitious he was. And, unfortunately for me, married.  Actually a newlywed, no children yet." She paused to study me for moment, drinking me into her intense green eyes.

This was interesting to me, of course.  And I was looking forward to the unfolding of her version, as I'd heard nothing but rumors up until now.  But honestly, situated as we were on the carpet, pressed under those goddess breasts, her beauty hovering over me, her increasingly delicious smell… well.  She could be telling me the story of Chicken Little and I would have been fascinated... and oh, the potentials of the wide sensuous mouth and full lips…

"Ah-er-um," She was clearing her throat.  I had gotten distracted again.  But she was patient, relaxed with me now, and seemed to have an intrinsic understanding of the male.  Her eyes were still quite bright, and there was a little more humor in her lilt. "Shall we continue?"

I let her know I'd been listening. "Yea, so he was married…"

"Yes he was.  And I was naive.  He said he would leave her to be with me and I believed him.  I thought my beauty and power reigned supreme.  Though barely more than half my current height back then, I was still the tallest woman in North America.  I was the first of my kind; of the new 'Amazon Nation of Bluebelle Valley'."  She was a bit sarcastic.  "Statuesque in the extreme, I was, too beautiful, and intimidating.  I knew that I made men weak, and thought of myself as irresistible.  But there is a force in this world that has more sway, and that force is money – money and power."

She paused, studying me again, searching my face, my eyes, my soul.  I couldn't tell what she was looking for.

She continued. "His wife's family was a major stock holder at Synsonto.  As he explained it to me, if he divorced her, left her for me, he would get nothing.  Not only that, he'd be out of the company and likely black-balled in the industry, virtually un-hirable.   More than that, his wife had pleaded with him, he said, professed her love.  She claimed it wasn't fair, that he was under my spell, that there was something strange and dangerous about me.  Yes, it was a sad and confused man who, though he still claimed to love me deeply, said he would be moving back East, leaving this Station that very hour, not even risking a kiss good-bye."

Again she paused, almost waiting for me to, what, say something?  "Well the dirty rat, I say.  The marriage was new.  No children to consider.  He could have claimed he'd made a mistake.  I mean, what kind of fool would ever leave such a gracious heart as yours."

"Careful what you say, Richie."  There were tears in her eyes again, not falling, just welling.  "That 'dirty rat' was your father."

She saw the look of shock on my face, but tried to help me, explaining further.  "That's why your sympathy, your sorrow, and your acceptance of me earlier were so dearly profound to me."  She paused, because that statement was so important.  Then she continued.  "And think no evil of your father, please.  He has become a better man.  He has helped me as he could along the way.  After my husband died, it was your father that rallied Synsonto to give me all the legal aid in my court defense.  Without your father's help, I would probably be in prison serving a life sentence for murder."

"Good God, Miss Strickland, I had no idea."

"Of course you didn't.  Your father and I have stayed in touch by email and letters.  Even you mother has forgiven me, and I her, and that means a lot to me."

"Wow."  I said, dumbfounded.

"In fact, it was your parents who sent you to work for me this summer.  They said you lacked discipline and direction, and also, what with your size, that first high school and even college had been very hard, disappointing for you."

"Man, that's kind of harsh to hear."  I squirmed a little under her, but had no desire to pull away.  It was just embarrassing, that's all.

"Just think," Her smile was a little too turned up.  "If things had been just a slight bit different, I could have been your mother."

"Oh, I wish you hadn't said that."  Now I really was embarrassed.

"Are you turning red?"  She was not quite laughing at me.

"It's just that you're so damn heavy." I shot back.

"No," She said.  "That's not what's got your goat."  Now she did chuckle a bit.  "You just don't like the idea of being pinned here, by your mother.  Lucky for you, I'm not your mother." Then suddenly she seemed a somewhat melancholy. "I'm nobody's mother…" She actually looked away for the first time.

"Miss Strickland, are you all right?"

She sighed heavily (and I mean heavily), and turned back to face me, eyes still bright for me, though she looked sad again. "It's just that it was so hard after I lost my husband."

"What happened?" I was really curious about this.

"It was three years after your folks had moved away. I had this music group I really liked, called "Itasca Breakdown." They were getting popular up north in the Twin Cities. I contacted, not the lead singer, but their songwriter and keyboard player, Rollie Giles. Back and forth by email, we fell in love, though we had never met. Boy was he shocked when came to visit me at my home in Bluebelle Bend. I was 10'11' by then. Poor Rollie, he was only 5'9".'

She reflected on that day a moment. A silly smile crossed her face. I thought that really must have been some shocker for Rollie. She blinked, focused into me again and continued. "Size difference didn't matter to us. We were in love. Got married that very weekend. Four days later he was back down with his stuff and moved into my house."

She looked very gloomy now. "We had only been married four months when it happened. He didn't die in a fight with me or from sex or anything that people tried to blame on me. It was just stupid what happened. He had apparently simply wanted to kiss me while I slept. I rolled over and smothered him in my sleep."

I added. "And you amazons are practically impossible to wake up once you are sound asleep."

She nodded, glad I understood that already. "That wasn't commonly known back then. Thanks to your father, Synsonto stepped in right away. Got it ruled an accident on the initial police report. But Rollie's family, who barely knew me at all, sued me in civil court for unlawful death. It was just awful."

"And you never fell in love again?"

"Are you kidding? Look at me!" She brought her face close to mine. "I'm the size of a troll."

Trolls need love, too." I tried to lighten the mood.

She did laugh one smirk-worth, and then backed off, resigned. "Anyway, I couldn't risk it again.  No more smothered lovers for me…"

"And?" I sensed there was more.

"And no motherhood, either."  She became quite still now.

There it was, I thought.  The core grief: she wanted to have a baby.  Of course she did; that's what she wanted all along, even from when she first met my father.

"You could still have a child.  There's lots of ways…"

"No, even if I could get pregnant somehow, it's too risky now.  I'm 44 years old."

"Hang on a second."  It always drove me crazy when people lived their lives on self-depreciating false assumptions.  "Who says?  Have you asked a doctor?"

"I never go to a regular doctors any more, only my contractually required check-ups with the scientists at Synsonto.  I just go get studied, measured, tallied for the record books.  I kind of have to; it's actually in my job description."

"Hey, I hear they're not so bad at the Synsonto labs.  Anyway, so you are telling me you don't really know.  Aren't you supposed to be living to 200 or something?  You at 44, well that's probably like being 21 for a regular person.  I'll bet you could get pregnant and carry a baby to term no problem."

Her expression looked kind of dazed.  Evidently she had been keeping all this to herself, talking to nobody, getting no medical examinations about it or even opinions.  Sad thoughts in a vacuum: that actually is the best formula for personal disaster.  She needed encouragement.

"Look, Miss Strickland.  You are beautiful. Still very young, plenty young enough, in fact, it seems that you could totally have a baby.  A little while ago I pulled about every hair on your lovely head, and guess what, pure jet black, not a hint of gray in any one of them.  And not at the roots either."  I was on a roll.  "And furthermore, the most obvious thing in the world is that you have so much to give, such a sensitive, caring heart… Oh my God, Miss Strickland, don't give up on love.  It is too important.  And you, well, you are too precious for that sad fate."

I could see a new spark in her eye already, intense almost to the point of predatory, still very sweet, but there was a kind of purring deep inside the woman. "Where could I ever hope to find a lover to help me on this quest?"  She sounded so forlorn; but was she?  She leaned closer again. "Someone who understands my needs, appreciates my broken heart and can heal it." She was coming around kind of bucking up well, "…who is not afraid of a woman my size, maybe even would prefer it." She flashed those green eyes at me. "It has advantages, you know – extraordinary possibilities, especially for someone loving, appreciative, properly devoted, and acquiescent."

Why was she making to case to me?  Then it dawned on me: she's talking *about* me.

She continued.  "Know anybody like that, Richie?  Someone understanding and compassionate, kind of like you are?  Someone who could understand me deeply, see the real me, get me, like nobody ever has.  Know any ideal candidates like that, Richie?"  Her lips were so close to mine.  Her breath quickening onto me, humid and hot, sweet and intoxicating, huskie. "Yes. Richie. That's the spirit."  She could see my wheels turning, my fantasies unfolding.

"You're looking for a volunteer." I said.  She was making herself *abundantly* clear to me.

She only batted her eyes in response, waiting expectantly.  At this point it was truly up to me: yes or no.  Crudely putting it, as I often would in the privacy of my own mind, she needed me for a stud service.  Well, that should take care of the "amends", I kind of joked to myself – but there might be no small measure of punishment involved as well – undoubtedly there would be.  And it would end up being much more than just stud service, with a heart like hers – and like mine.… Yet the truth was, I was very moved by her story, by her deep feelings, for her desire to actually be a mother and have that special love, and right now by the passion in those eyes before me… for these reasons, I'd like to think above all else, I said "Yes, Miss Strickland.  I'll do it."  And, yes, BTW, OMG, what a body!

She smiled, so happy, like someone freed from a 20-year prison sentence.  She leaned toward me, excited, celebratory.

But I stopped her advance with, "Miss Strickland, I have to tell you up front, that I am already in a relationship."

"That's OK, no problem.  Anyway, I've been seeing the gossip about you and The Triplets on the Bluebelle Amazon Page." She said, nonchalant.  "So technically, then, we're just really, really good friends, with er… benefits, right?  And besides," She winked. "This will go a long way toward clearing away those amends you owe your boss."

"*And* the 'punishment'." I insisted.

"Well then, you'll have to promise never to look up my skirt ever again."

"Sorry, *boss*, but I don't think I can do that.

"Good." She had a satisfied smile.  "Then you'll have to promise you *will* look up my skirt again. You'll have to return to the scene of the crime and properly apologize." She pretended to be a bit pouty.  "All that sneaking and peaking," She scolded. "Kiss and make it better, that's the proper path to forgiveness."

"If you say so, Miss Strickland.  You do strike a hard bargain.  Very hard, I might add."  I sighed, giving in.  "So that's it then.  If I must, I must."

"Oh believe me, my kind and dear little man, you 'must'." And she leaned in again, planting the softest of kisses on my lips.   I admit, I definitely did kiss her back.

"Ah, Miss Strickland." I felt the sweet surrender.

"You, can call me Daisy."  And so the amends began.  My first thought being: "Really?... Daisy?" She lowered her wide mouth surrounding my lips.  Slowly, as her kiss spread across my face, she rolled over fully onto me with her breasts and upper body.  Thank goodness the Persian carpet was so plush, as I was being steamrolled into it.  So much crushing weight pressed onto me.  Would she flatten me into two dimensions or worse yet, into another chalk outline? I guess only time would tell.

Right now I was enjoying myself too much to worry about it, as I was being devoured by a kiss of epic proportions, of butter-mint perfection.  Daisy's oh so generous lips encircled my cheeks, and chin, and up along my forehead.  Her sucking, for now, was gentle; nothing but loving.  I kissed at the edges of her tongue as its tip rasped tenderly across my closed eyes.

As I felt her tongue tasting me, I did not see how this particular activity was going to exactly lead to her getting pregnant.  But I didn't care.  Could she even tell if I was smiling; because a silly old cynical rule of thumb had crossed my mind: "No good deed goes unpunished."

# VIII. Angst under the Amazon Unfortunates

Lots of people say they hate long good-byes.  But then, they've probably never been the good-bye-subject of three 8'6" 625-pound adoring superstar giantess triplets.

In the second hour now of that long good-bye I'd forgotten even what room of the house we were in – hell, what planet I was on!  Of course I couldn't see a damn thing, what with my head so far up Callie's ass.  You have to understand that, my big, big girlfriends were in that early relation phase when now it's suddenly okay to have sex and, holy bejeesus, did the flood gates open.  And there was nothing I could do about it except take it like a man as best I could.

You know by now that I can be a squeamish little fellow when it comes to body smells.  But the whimsy of Mother Nature with had gifted these Amazons in many wonderful ways.  One of these gifts, and I considered it a gift to me really, was: every part of their body I could possibly encounter, up close and face-smashing personally, smelled as magically sweet as a bouquet of wild flowers, and I mean no problem.  Magic or simply superior chemistry, I don't know.  Even on a hot summer sweaty day they never varied below neutral.  At the upper extreme, Saint Debbie's perfumed ass was downright addictive.  And I must say Aria, Pavie, and Callie, were not far behind, excuse the pun, and getting more delightful every day.

I can tell you right now, as I squirmed like a trapped little rat under Pavie's more-than-ample posterior, I worshiped her confectionery ass with uninhibited enthusiasm.  Oh yeah, what a sweetheart – she pumped me to get busy, and I knew that meant she wanted some more tongue now, excuse me, I mean *right* now.

Still, if it was all on my dime, I'd probably rather be eating their super sweet pussies.  But that's the thing with these sisters, the one constant was change, creative sexual change.  Well, except that whatever the new game was, they would always be on me one way or another, smashing me into sensual oblivion, and more all the time as they grew a little bit bigger and heavier each day.  "Squish the Boyfriend Early and Often", just as Callie was as this moment, that seemed to be the motto.

What was so cool: the Sparkle worked just as well in their asses as it did in their pussies.  This wonderful discovery was no mere accident, but rather a sounded tested scientific hypothesis.  A hypothesis they had now proven.  The Sparkle they biochemically nurtured into my hard-ons and cum, it worked orgasmic miracles for them, pussy or ass – and either way, it worked wonders for me too.

At first the mouth-in-butt, that made no sense from the Sparkle standpoint.  Neither did the mouth-in-pussy, Sparkle-wise that is. Oh, but be patient my friend, that was destined to change.  Hell, look at me now, being kind of picky about.  The truth was they loved both; I loved both.  So in the course of a day, with three of them, I got plenty, you'd have to say more than my fair share, of each.  I knew damn well, for example, when this huge ass finally lifted off me, a fresh one, could be pussy this time, would slam down on me faster than I could say, "That's OK, I don't really need to breathe."  Which was kind of true these days, for up to almost fifteen minutes, thanks to the changes that had happened to my body.

Right on cue, Callie lifted off, and hungrily pounced down to my waiting cock that had already started to Sparkle a bit. Yes, even before she got there.  Aria planted her pussy on my face, the perfect after breakfast capper post breast milk.  But after only two minutes she shifted over to offer me her big ass – one of those offers you can't refuse.  A minute later it was her pussy again, then her ass again.  For heaven's sake, make up your mind girl!

Fuck it.  Callie had me anyway.  I unleashed another big one.  The third time I'd cummed that morning.

The Triplets scampered around on me, uncharacteristically agitated, being more than a little bit frantic with their sex today.  Vigor, I always expected that, at least before it was all over.  But usually they liked to take their time, build it up more, play a little bit, you know, be relational about it.

But today they were leaving.  Maybe within the hour, if my internal clock still had any gears working that weren't smashed yet.  And they would be gone three whole days.  Since we started this four way relationship… though it was really kind of two-way because they often acted as one mind in three bodies… and one might think it was even kind of one-way given the way they dominated me, that is basically they fucking owned my body for their daily pleasures...  But you just have to take my word on this, no matter how it looked physically: it wasn't one-way at all.  I felt I was getting way more than I was giving.  Think about it – the health benefits of their milk; that alone was a hell of a gift to me….

Yes, today they would be gone-girls shortly, and they were desperately trying to store up enough sex for three days. Three days-worth in two hours: not possible. But they certainly were giving it the college try.

Oh the Triplets were taking care of me, too.  Of course they were.  They were the best girlfriends ever, bar none!  First thing that morning they had nursed me thoroughly so I would be tanked up properly on their, for lack of a better word, "treatments."  Then all this sex – yeah, that had to be ending soon.  Because I knew that they planned to unload their milk into me again and comprehensively, one more time before they took off for the airport.

Callie finished down below, and Aria rolled off my face.  A quick two breaths, and now Callie lowered her full breast onto my face, nipple insert, I began to happily suck.  Ah, sex was over for now – err, not.  Pavie needed one last Sparkle up her ass, and rode me now, coaxing my little volunteer to stand up for one more mission.  "Reporting to duty." He seemed to salute.

"Good job!"  I heard Pavie's appreciation. "I'm impressed."  And also in a hurry.  Once she had that beginning of a hard on, she switched over to let her talented pussy did the rest, lifting me up into her, squeezing me harder, to be harder.  Indeed, in a hurry, she vibrated her great weight on me, faster than a little dog can scratch its ear.  Oh man, pressed nursing while getting fucked like this – that had to be my favorite.  Each gave me a last turn at each breast.  I felt tit-satiated, completely.

As always, they left me utterly spent, and I could only lay there, a wet mess, while they tidied themselves up.  Seeing them priming and smoothing out their tight professional skirts and blouses, dressed up smartly for travel – it made me want them again already.  I got up, only a little bit wobbly (but I must have been getting in some kind of shape for this heavy sex) and tried to look suitably hang-dog.

"Ohhhh," came their overly-sympathetic response by the open front door. "Poor baby.  Are you going to miss us?"

I nodded, mouth downturned, playing my part, but eyes smiling.

"Bye-bye now."  They blew me kisses, no time for real ones, the limo was already loaded and waiting. "And remember, Richie, you be nice to Debra."

"Of course." I waved bye to my girlfriends, to my sustenance, and to those sweet, sweet majestic asses.

Door shut, I sighed and I thought the day.  My-oh-my, what a warm and beautiful morning!  No way could I go to work yet, feeling this spent.  Maybe I would sunbathe out by the pool a while, nude and natural, the way I liked it.  Yes definitely, a little bit of sunshine and relaxing out in nature sounded perfect.

In ten minutes I stood out by the pool's edge.  Just jump in?  It would feel good.  But my girl friends' juices were still on me.  Maybe keeping that lather would prevent me from missing them too much.  Nah, I thought that over again.  It was already getting a little crusty in the morning sun.  I let myself keel over into the water.

The Triplets were right about my physical progression.  I could swim back and forth forty laps, under water, without a breath.  It was extra refreshing to stay down there that long.

Back out beside the pool I arranged my lounge chair just so; getting the back angle perfect was so critical for comfort.  Then I stretched out for a nice long snooze.  That frantic sex session this morning plum wore me out.  Then all that extra milk, oh I felt so sleepy all of the sudden.

Saint Debbie.  I better rest up before she came over this evening.  I thought she was tough to endure before.  But now… she'd gone through yet another growth cycle.  She eats and eats, bulks up extremely plump but not fat.  Then she grows like eighteen inches in a really short time.  Differentiating and getting her figure back with all that new height.  Actually looks damn good!  But then, she keeps on eating and starts bulking out again.  Right now she was in the bulked out phase, Fat Debbie big time.  If she was 835 pounds before, she must be pushing close to 1,200 by now.

No wonder her shit don't stink.  She probably doesn't have any; turns all the food into more body mass with no waste.  Is that even possible?  Hey, I'm not dumb, I just never cared about science that much.

"Fat, fat Debbie…" I yawned, closed my eyes and drifted.  I imagined Saint Debbie floating around in the pool, all buoyed up by the water.  I kind of pictured her as that future giantess that was her destiny, wherein they would have to fill the pool again after she got out.  Probably I had a really silly smile on my face as I went to sleep.

***

I must have slept in that lounge chair for a long time because when I awoke, even with my eyes still shut, I could tell it was already getting dark.  It was peaceful for a second, then I suddenly realized, shit, Saint Debbie could be over here any minute. I jumped up, ran into a brick wall, and fell back down by my chair.

"What the f…" I looked up at a deeply tanned, long, long pair of shapely and very thick muscular legs that ended in sexy deep purple bikini bottom stretched tight over a massive sexy ass bent toward me.  It wasn't evening yet.  No, it was the sun eclipsed by this ginormous big beautiful butt over me.

"Oh, I'm sorry Richie." It was Amanda the pool girl, working a pool sweep. Of course she wasn't a girl; she must some thirty years old.  But that's what everyone called them, her and Brandy, the "pool girls."  She continued, I guess apologetic, more than a hint of a southern drawl.  "I thought you was sound asleep.  Say 'Hi" Brandy."

I peered around Amanda's calves.  Super sexy Brandy twiddled her fingers hello from the middle of the deep end, so tall, her upper torso and bright pink-patterned bikini top still dry out of the water.  I waved back as Brandy plucked a leaf that floated by her.

Amanda didn't stop to help me up.  I don't think it occurred to her.  She just kept working that long-handled net, her extraordinary big in-shape posterior waving around in counter-balance to her sweeping motions, some six or seven feet above me.

Amanda wasn't exactly ignoring me though.  "Got yourself a day off, Richie?"  A southern accent like Amanda's was not that unusual up here, given that Synsonto hired people from all over the USA, well, and the world, these days.  Of course, Amanda didn't work at Synsonto, never did, never would, but most likely her parents did – that is, at one time.  Now she probably just practiced her drawl for effect, and reinforced it with crappy radio and probably bad attitude.  Terrific ass up there above me though, no denying that; but right off, I didn't like her much.

Brandy chimed in, kind of dancing with her upper body, bouncing her phenomenal big breasts, singing some country song I'd never heard. "Working down on the farm, on the farm, yeah, yeah, on the farm-farm…"

"I got a late start.  So I decided to take the day off.  Things were getting too intense at work, anyway.  Just needing to sort a few things out."  I must have been hung over from the nap because I was kind sharing with them like I actually knew them which, really, I didn't.  "Hey, either of you gals know the time…"

Brandy looked at her watch-less wrist.  "Off hand; can't tell." An old joke, she kind of hee-hawed when she laughed.  It was a little embarrassing.

"Pushin' noon, maybe" Amanda looked up at the high sun.  "But what do I know?"
Speaking with more of a slight bit of an edge now.  She answered herself: "Nothin'.
No, us pool gals don't know much about nothin' at all. Don't even know the time of
day.  We're out here just'a 'sorting things out' best we can, right Brandy?"  Amanda
mimicking me a bit, her sarcasm was border-line rude, and bitter, I thought.

"Yep, that's us, Amanda, just doing the best we can.  Only trying to keep our little ol'
asses out of trouble."  Brandy still danced out there in the deep end.

"No sir, Mr. Richie, we sure can't afford no trouble…"  Amanda kind of looked back
at the house, studied it for a second with squinted eyes.  Looking for, what, the
Triplets?  Anyway she sure didn't see them.  In her next step, as she worked her
way on by, her back foot "accidentally" kicked my lounge chair, tipping it over
toward where I still sat on the concrete.  "Oh sorry, Mr. Richie.  Do you mind?" What,
I was supposed to pick the chair up?  "I got to keep working this sweep."

Yes, she did expect me to right the chair.  And yes, I minded.  It had kind of grazed
my shoulder a bit when she backed it over.  Don't get me wrong.  I'm not getting all
country-club on you.  You got to admit, though, that this massive tall pool girl
Amanda was being kind of insolent.

Brandy waded over toward me. Leaning down, she shelved her huge micro-bikinied,
nipples-barely-covered breasts over the edge of the pool right in front of me.  She
kind of chewed at her lip, tilted her head to fling her red curls, obvious and flirtatious,
but probably plenty effective with the guys she and Amanda undoubtedly hunted
down at the bars on the stretch of Highway 33 from Weaverton to Blackwing. "Don't
pay her no never-mind."  Brandy whispered loudly behind the back of her hand,
knowing Amanda could hear her.  "She's always a little bit pissed off."  Brandy
winked at me, licking her lips absentmindedly.

It was a tough shake for these no-talent amazons.  No eight, or seven, or six, and
sometimes not even four-figure wages for them.  No fancy career with Synsonto or
fun-and-games at the Research Labs.  No college entrance exams.  No good pace
in the world really.  Could go be a kind of freak show off the main in Vegas, or
worse.  Nope, better stick around here, with your own kind.  They'll get you a job, a
place to live.  And Synsonto always has one program or some kind of grant or
another coming down the pike.  How about, you wanna' be a pool girl, work in the
sun, the nice neighborhoods, get a little taste of the high life?  And get a few too
many more chemicals, because, God knows, nobody else wants to handle them.

Down-trodden, that's what they were.  But this is America, by God, land of the free, right?  They still had choices to make every day. Heck those same chemical cocktails via my mother's ingestion of them had screwed up my life, too, leaving me in this ridiculously small body.  It didn't make me bitter – or did it?  Growing up off by any physical standard was hard, I had to admit.  I also had to admit it was damn hard to shake away the excuses.  Still some people, I thought, no matter what, end up grumpy or worse.  In my soap-box opinion, that always goes back to the parents…

But they were missing something else, this lower-caste of amazon society.  It wasn't a reduced size certainly or even perfection of body.  There was, however, a kind of set of conditions that was evident.  For starters, these ladies were just a smidge down the totem pole in the looks department.  Not that bad at all, really, just slightly off.

Well… let's say, on a 1-10, someone like Bethany would be about a 7.5.  In fact the whole pollination crew had kind of a tight range, from low of 7 to high of 9+ like Vicki.  And you had to be a little brighter to be on that crew; had to pass a written test.  Hey, it was complicated following the geneticists' plans, tracking through the corn pedigrees and not screwing it up.

Then you got your Secretary Pool.  It was a select corps of only eight fine ladies.  Most were graduates of the pollination crew, not that it means they went to finishing school or anything.  They were just a notch up, say an average of 8 up to a solid 9.5 like Miss Monroe.

Miss Strickland herself, Daisy?  Don't ask me, please.  I can't think straight when to comes to her.  I'm gonna' say 10.  But I could be biased, as in unduly influenced by the *gravity* of her situation – get me?

So I'd heard the gossip about the "Unfortunates" as the secretaries like to call them.  One day I was walking down the hall at work, just minding my own business, when, swoosh, I was yanked into Miss Rasmussen's office.  She and Miss Jorgensen had some fantasy to try me out as office furniture.  So I spent the next two hours as an end table, a chair, and magazine basket, a foot stool, a recycling bin – thank God they didn't try me as a paper shredder.  Anyway, Misses Rasmussen and Jorgensen went on and on about the Unfortunates as they variously stood on me, sat on me, stuffed magazines into my clothing, set coffee cups on me, and threw their recycling at me.

Eventually they decided my highest and best use was as a sofa throw, like a blanket, right?  So they tossed me on Miss Rasmussen's office couch and planted their lazy prodigious asses on me for the final hour and a half until afternoon break.  Of course I did not hear much as an under-butt sofa throw, pressed so deep into the cushions.  But as a magazine basket and a recycling bin I was all ears.  I'd heard plenty.

The basic upshot, without all the boring details: the "Unfortunates" were duller versions of the prettier, more talented, more exciting amazons, like these secretaries of course.  And then there were the even more exceptional, like the Triplets, that caught the best headlines and made the most money.

But there was more to it than just that.  There was a kind of Unfortunates Syndrome that involved looks a little bit; intelligence, definitely; height and weight, not really; and special talents, absolutely – as in none, nada, zip.  From the gossip I sussed-out that there was something in the variations of the chemical cocktails that spread around in numerous version under the Bluebelle River Valley.  No-one knew for sure or weren't saying, but these chemicals interacted with the soil types, with other contaminates, with each other creating versions and sub-version that were a little off or too much or too little or wrong mix from site to site; and/or, beyond all that, something in an individual's particular genetics that just didn't match up favorably quite all the way.  In a nutshell: the effects were random and therefore unfair.  And these two cases before me acted like they knew damn well it was unfair.

I looked at Brandy as she still eyed me; her making some kind of calculation I didn't want to know about.  I smiled at her and felt kind of hypocritical as I rated her looks: 7 maybe, and Amanda 6.5 max.

The Triplets you ask?  What about the Triplets on the 1-10 scale?  That's easy: 11.  Or should I do the math their way and say: 33.  Ha!

Brandy hauled herself out of the pool with ease.  Wow, strong.  She turned and plopped down, spreading her enormous wet ass on the pool's edge walkway, her runoff draining to my feet.  Her ass, as presented to me right now, deeply tan, big-big and firm; that aspect of her was a 10 in my book.  Same was true, and then some, for the larger, perhaps even shapelier, Amanda's posterior.

Brandy, spoke causal, still with her back to me.  "So, where's your girlfriends today?"  She gently swirled the waters with her legs.

Distracted by the view of her backside, not giving it much thought,  said.  "They're away for a few days, back Monday."

"Oh really."  She curled around at this information, sliding with agile ease across the wet, rose-colored cement, lying out toward me now, her big tan bulging breasts resting against the bottoms of my feet, pushing them back a little on her inhales.  "You hear that, Amanda.  Poor little Richie's home-alone for the weekend.

"Well, I'll be."  Amanda finished over at the steps, letting the pool sweep lean against the porcelain rail.  Walking over, "I'll bet that's got to get real lonely real fast when the Triplets are out of the house."  Now, finally, Amanda righted the lounge chair, then sat in it right next to me.  Her killer legs soared above my head; that beautiful deep tan set off nicely against the cloudless azure sky.  Bending at her knees more than 90 degrees, those epic legs came down on the far side of my body, her feet back, just touching my left shoulder.  I looked at that contact point, traced back up luscious parallel calves, very tight from the way she sat tense, back across the heavy underside of her thighs, oh I do love strong thick hamstrings, which necessarily had to angle back down to the low lounge, her huge butt straining all those little tubes that make up the seating, squeezing the life out of them until they just about yielded all the way down to the dripped-on wet cement barely inches below.  Amanda was a big amazon.  Maybe ten foot six inches; likely a 950 pounder.

"Quite a sight, isn't it?"  Brandy had been studying my reactions.  "Especially, I imagine, for such a little guy like yourself.  Probably like to be right in there, wouldn't you, under where she's sitting."

Damn it.  Brandy's talk along with the view was starting to give me a hard on.  And I still had no clothes on, just the towel I'd grabbed.

I began scooching out from under Amanda's great legs and back from Brandy.  Amanda with lightening reflex snatched my towel away.  "Oh my." Laughing at me, Amanda faked being impressed.  She was not being very nice at all. "Would you just look at that, Brandy?  I think he kind of likes us.  You know what, why don't you be a good host, Mr. Richie, and invite us in to lunch?  I'm feelin' kind of hungry all the sudden."

"I don't think that would be a good idea."  I tried to cover my privates while backing up more.

"Lunch is a great idea Amanda," Rejoined Brandy, standing.  "But I'm so tired of dry ol' sandwiches, like we got in our van.  'A bit o' fresh meat, would go down sweet'."

Her near-quote of a line from JRR Tolkien's poem "The Stone Troll" absolutely must have been a random coincident.

"Yep," Amanda stood as well. "I'll bet Richie's girlfriends got some real tasty fixins' in their larder." She and Brandy took off for the house.

I grabbed the towel she'd dropped. Wrapping myself, I ran after them. This was getting out of control. "Wait a minute. You can't go in there!"

They ignored me. And their long strides had them through the wide glass sliding back door before I could catch up. I took a second to find my shorts I'd left by the downstairs foyer. Then I followed the clanging and banging to the kitchen.

The big bitches were making themselves right at home. I grabbed my phone that was still on the counter, and started dialing Bluebelle Valley Estates security.

"Whoa, whoa, there boy." Amanda was on me in a second, easily twisting the phone from my grip. Her strength was effortless. "Let's not be inhospitable." She stood over me, threateningly. "If you're gonna' invite us in to lunch, you've got to give us a chance to eat."

"Anything less is downright…er…" Brandy, consternated, fought for the word.

"Why it'd be discourteous, it would." Amanda looked down disapproving at me.

Brandy nodded, agreeing with enthusiasm, then added, holding up one finger, "It would be ill-mannered."

"Uncivil." Amanda declared, walking through me and knocking me aside and to the floor. At the far wall she reached way up, maybe fourteen feet, and placed my phone on the ledge of one of the high narrow horizontal windows designed to flood the kitchen with morning light from above.

"Look at this!" Brandy held up a big platter piled with an array of meats, cheeses, cut apples and ripe nectarines…" I couldn't see the rest.

"That looks perfect. And I'm starving." Amanda walked past me again as I was just standing up. "Somehow" her knee caught my shoulder and I spun to the floor again. "Oh, sorry again, Richie." The bully spewed more sarcastic hostility.

As they sat at the table, I gained my feet again. Of the two, Brandy had slightly more decorum. "Would you care to join us?"

"No thanks."  I was curt, and walked out the kitchen.

Right away Amanda was behind me, cat-like in her athletic quickness.  It was like I had expected to just walk away from an interested tiger.  Not likely.  Not likely at all.  "And just where do you think you're going?"  She was very close on me, but not stopping me – yet.

I lied about my intent – which was to get the hell out of the house ASAP.  "To the bathroom, if that's OK."  Then I continued exactly to the nearest toilet.   She followed me until I shut the door in her face.  Turns out I did have to go; so I did.  Exiting, I met a very tall, tan, muscular set of legs when I came out.  They offered me no alternative but to walk between them, under her.  I knew I better head back to the kitchen.  So, obediently, I did.

There, I sat off to the side while they ate, made their inane comments about the lovely kitchen, what a nice house, how it must be great to have tons of money.  They also lit into the Triplets, how hoity-toity they were, what with their fancy digs and clothes and stupid songs and dumb charities.

I was getting a clear picture of some very mean-spirited jealous women; the kind of women who might watch you bleed then deign to call 911 – after you bled-out and expired.  They, at last, and especially Amanda, got around to some choice insults for me. "Hard to imagine what the princesses see in a little pecker-neck like you."

"OK, here we go." I thought to myself."

"I'm sorry to say, but a puny cunt-sucker like you wouldn't last a day in the real world." Brandy shook her head like "what a pity".

"Nice one, Brandy."  I thought.  What a class act we have here."

Amanda's turn again: "And your bitch girlfriends, they're nothing but the biggest freaks on the planet.  Bitchy-witches.  They ought to be burned at the stake."

Finally she'd gone too far.  "Amanda, fuck you and the horse you rode in on."

Man, she was on me faster than I'd seen yet.  Her right hand wrapped completely around my neck.  She lifted me close to her plain face, my body dangling like a rag doll.  She had bits of apple skins in her teeth and her breath smelled of turkey meat.  "I have half a mind to off you right now."

I tried to swallow as I kept my eyes open and locked on hers.  I didn't regret defending my girlfriends' honor.  But Amanda was right about one thing.  She did have "half a mind."

"You know, Amanda" Brandy's voice was soothing, trying to calm her big friend.  "Let's not get too hasty here."  I took it right then that Brandy had seen Amanda hurt people before.

Amanda shook me a little.  "You heard what he said to me. The uppity little squirt."

"You did insult his girlfriends.  Kind of a brave little guy to stick up for them like that, you have to admit."

"I don't have to admit nothin' to nobody."  But she released me, and I fell five feet to the hard floor.  I sat up gingerly, by her huge feet, and rubbed my neck.

Brandy came around and stood right next to Amanda; put her arm around her from the side.  Looking down at me, again with that same studying desire that I'd seen at the pool, chewed on her index finger.  Tapping her lips a second, she then seemed to recall something. "Didn't we hear something about our friend Richie here?"

"What, that he's a dick wad?"  Amanda nudged me over with her foot.

"No, down in Weaverville, at the Goose & Gander.  We were in there last week, remember, trolling for guys."

"I remember we found a couple dudes.  I remember they were weak.  We even tried trading them.  But neither one was any good.  Couldn't do the least thing for me, what with their wimpy dicks."  Amanda must be very hard to please.  Oh, I could see that, definitely.

"That's it.  That's what I heard."  Brandy's face lit up.

"Those guys talkin' smack about us?"  Amanda was confused.

"No, silly.  It was about Richie.  One of them high-falutin' secretaries was down there slumming it, having a drink with her fancy friend.  I heard her say that our little buddy Richie here has some special powers.  That's what I heard.  He might be small, but he's got some way to deliver a real kick, if you know what I mean."

Oh shit, I thought.

Amanda was dubious.  "But how can he have any special talents?  He's just a man."

"But his girlfriends…" Brandy didn't have to say more.

Now Amanda was intrigued. "His witch girlfriends can do just about anything!" Very intrigued. "And I was about to snap his neck."

"That's right, girl, we got to consider the possibilities." Bandy was still in her calming mode.

But Amanda had moved on. "You 'consider' it all you want. I'm gonna' go find the bedroom, and see what that rumor is all about." With that she snatched me up under one arm and marched out of the kitchen. Looking backward as I rode against Amanda's right hip I saw Brandy bounding up right behind on the stairs, batting her eyes at me, and licking her lips more than before.

Amanda threw me on the Triplet's bed, pounced on me butt backwards, on my upper body and head, and yanked off my shorts. That was the first seven seconds. Then she lifted up briefly to whip off her bikini bottoms, and spun around back down on me. "OK Mr. Richie, let's feel your magic."

But I already had a plan. If I couldn't outwit these two and survive until Saint Debbie showed up, I didn't deserve to live. Amanda was humping me, mechanically, but with good vigor.

"It doesn't work like that." I managed to blurt out.

"What doesn't work, like what?" Brandy sat her big ass next to my head, leaning over me.

"Don't listen to him." Amanda kept humping. "He's a little liar."

I kept thinking of the apple-skin in Amanda's teeth, of her meaty breath, hoping not respond. Thinking she was bitchy and mean didn't help as much because I sort of liked bitchiness, up to a point – the point being not dying!

Amanda got no response, zero. "He's just as useless as those guys last week." She rolled off me. "Just look at that little limp dick, worthless."

"I'm telling you. It doesn't work that way." I kept lying, matter of fact, keeping my tone even.

"Just how does it work?" Brandy undid her bikini top, her especially large breasts swaying above my face as she leaned in a bit more.

"The best love potion is just that, love." I explained. "Try a little kindness, a little compassion, sweet words. Come on, it's really not that complicated. You know how to do this." I had to get my explanation in quickly, because, truth be told, I was going to respond to the advances Brandy was clearly mounting either way. And I just managed to get in, "And I love sweet, clean smells."

"Well I've been in the pools most the morning?" Brandy was falling for it. If Brandy could prove it on me, then maybe Amanda would follow suit. "You like the smell of chlorine, don't ya', it's kind of fresh." She was getting the idea. "You are such a cutie; isn't he Amanda?" It was sweet talk, I guess. Trying to re-engage her bigger friend, "Come on now Amanda, girl you got to help me out."

Amanda sighed, "I have to admit it, he is… cute." That was tough for her to say. But come on, I thought, you can do better than that.

It didn't matter though for the moment. Brandy was gently titty-whipping my face. I guessed it had to be another one of her patented moves, what with her massive perfectly-shaped hooters. She kept up the sweet-talk, "What a little doll you are."

I was responding now, my volunteer being the stand-up guy that he was. "Reporting for pussy, I mean *duty*, sir" and he snaps to attention and even salutes. And I knew Amanda could see it.

As I licked at those big tits of perfection, I felt the bed pop up significantly as Amanda got off it. Five seconds later I could hear one of the showers running in the Triplet's bathroom. Oh yeah, Amanda was getting with the program. Five minutes later as Brandy continued with her best breast moves, adding a nice slow hand job, I heard an electric toothbrush running. I finally allowed myself to think favorably about Amanda and her near perfect legs and ass.

I felt Amanda climb back on the bed, much more gentle now. I could even smell her already, and her judicious use of soap and some of my girlfriends' perfume. I continued to hybridize Brandy and Amanda in my mind: Brandy's perfect breasts with Amanda's ideal base, Amanda's severe eyes with Brandy's pouty lips. This time, as Amanda descended on me, inserting me, she immediately felt the reward for her good behavior. The Sparkle was just beginning, and it was going to be a good one.

Unlike most I'd experienced, who buck and go crazy with the Sparkle, Amanda was quite the opposite. So seldom had she actually had a good fuck, and not for lack of attempts I'd say, she truly appreciating this positive experience. I felt her relaxing on me, pressing onto me not with domination, but with pure desire.  I loved that feeling of wanting to be absorbed by a woman.  There is nothing that can match the feeling under a woman as she aches with the desire to engulf, to become coincident and occupy the same space.  But it isn't an 'us'.  It is more, well, becoming captivated, pressed and surrounded, entrapped, pulled in and consumed.

Amanda was feeling all that and more than she'd felt in a long time.  The Sparkle responded to Amanda's deep loving need with a tingling tree of light growing up and throughout her body, my Volunteer its grounding taproot.

Brandy felt it vicariously, leaving off the breast moves and descending on me with her lips, and her own aching need for love.  Brandy's face was upside-down to mine, but it didn't matter in the least, maybe worked even better, the kissing was delicious.  And apparently so was I, as there was such a strong longing in her vigorous kisses, devouring and continuous, that chewing lips motion I found so stimulating.

Amanda's orgasm rose very gradually, spreading from tip to toe with the intelligence and the compassion of the Sparkle.  It wasn't just sex anymore.  The healing spirit of the Triplets moved through me and into Amanda.  More importantly, the healing spirit that was in Amanda, that *was* Amanda, awakened.  I knew already that she would never be the same woman again.  This result was far beyond anything I'd expected.  I felt in awe of the experience and of a universe where such things were possible.

Amanda shivered with delight, with love, I think not for me, but for herself, her true self that was being revealed.  It was an orgasm like none I'd ever seen and it must have gone on, on me, for more than an hour.

Half way through, Brandy, who'd been weeping while she was eating with her kissing, couldn't stand it anymore.  She crawled around and dropped her chlorine sterilized pussy on my face.  Immediately she began to spasm with delight, with sorrow, with hope, with such longing it nigh-on made me weep, too.  Brandy also wanted to have me, to own me, deep, deep inside her.

The Sparkle, in full force, was finally bringing Amanda to conclusion. Her heavy desire for love was so locked on me I could tell she had a timeless feeling of never wanting to leave.  But she was also exhausted.  They both were; as was I.  Fully satisfied for now, they each rolled off me to opposite sides and crashed.

As they slept, I crawled down off the bed.  I stole out to the garage, brought in a ladder to the kitchen, climbed up to the high window and retrieved my phone.  I held

it, considering my options.  I thought about making that security call, but only briefly.
Then I put my phone down on the kitchen counter.  I got a sip of water from the
kitchen sink, and then headed back upstairs.

Quietly, I edged back onto the bed between the sound asleep Amanda and Brandy.
I nestle up alongside Amanda's beautiful legs and settled my face against her clean
ass and the faint smell of the Triplet's perfume.  I kissed and gently stroked her
smooth tan skin.  In her sleep she shifted to bring her now sweet smelling ass
square onto my face, opening then lowering all the way onto me and tightening
snuggly, owning my face completely, the way I liked it.  And finally I slept as well.

*…the Triplets sang to me like a waterfall of bliss from Heaven.  Their loving spirit
lifted me from my body.  I soared over deep green forest, pure shimmering waters
flowing in abundance, a deer drinking at quiet pool caught my eye, but did not flee
as I came to repose nearby, resting in the soft warm spring-day grass.  Then the
ground began to shake…*

I woke up, my head and upper body encased in two big sets of buns, gyrating
against me from either side and down onto me.  My bedmates were waking as well.
I felt one yawn, tightening her ass onto me.  Yawns, of course, are catchy, and the
second ass clamped down on me following suit.

They then realized where I was and what they were inadvertently doing, and
decided to take further advantage of the situation.  Each one reached through her
legs, took one of my arms, and brought a hand up to each respective crotch.  They
waited to see my response… which was to reach up further with my hands and
proactively find two clitorises.

They must have considered that the go-ahead because they then jammed my arms
right on up into their pussies, elbow deep.  My biceps, such as there were, now
rested against those swelling clitorises.  Though obscured from sight by their by
being basically somewhat inside their asses and crotches and pussies, I was
nevertheless in a kind of he-man pose, if you can imagine me as such.  So I did the
he-man thing and flexed those little biceps.  Positioned strategically as they were
against their most sensitive spots I got a very nice and energetic response.  Their
grinding on me rapidly grew more and more intense.  They pulled up under my
elbows, shoving me in a bit deeper.  My hands found a couple of g-spots, a slightly
different location for each gal, but attainable with my thin nimble fingers.

They exploded onto me in simultaneous orgasms, a shuttering, insistent, pancaking
of my upper body; a temporary squeezing shut of the circulation in my arms; a very

deep embedding of my face into one of the asses – by the fresh soapy smell, I'm more than just speculating, it was Amanda's.  I wanted more of that ass, really could not get enough of it; but they were rolling away.  Wordless, they got up and went into the bathroom.

I heard two showers running.  Glancing at the clock: mid-afternoon.  I'd had my second good nap of the day and felt refreshed.  My house guests, bedroom guests, were not the two same bullies that had crashed for lunch – not by a long shot.  I smiled, relieved and amazed at my good fortune, and more at the wondrous ways of the universe and the human spirit.  I heard the shower stop.

Barely a minute later these new-found beauties emerged, still patting themselves dry.  And they were beauties.  In particular Amanda looked so much better, transformed really, all the hardness gone from her face, now serene, with an open accepting look, the kind of loving face you'd want to kiss, and kiss again.

As they were eyeing me on the bed, still drying here and there, I said quite suggestively. "Don't bother drying, my dears.  Why don't you just come on over here a little wet."

Their towels hit the floor as my sentence finished.

"We know how you like it clean."  Brandy sounded so sweet, almost modest as she shrugged.

They were on the bed, two tigresses, skipping the stalking part, and moving right in for the 'kill."

"Brandy," Amanda spoke in a magnanimous voice that I'd not heard from her yet, probably no one had ever heard.  "Brandy, my dear best friend; I believe it's your turn for the Sparkle."

Amanda waited while Brandy climbed onto me.  I think it was another patented move of hers, and it was a good one.  Brandy straddled me, facing forward to me, and gently lowered her ass onto my body.  My already hard volunteer slid right on up into her already wet pussy.  She then unwound her legs, laying them out in front, her good thick thighs covering my upper body and splaying my shoulders flat.  This shifted the preponderance of her weight back onto her butt and drove me deep into the mattress.  The Sparkle started up right away, especially with her loving attitude.

Amanda moved in from over my head.  The lowest part of Brandy's heavy, but soft and relaxed hamstring muscles, were covering my face.  Amanda gently parted her friend's legs, and there she was, beautiful now, looking down at me.

Like we did it before, the kissing-girl was upside-down.  And like before it didn't matter.  You might say Amanda and I had a 'moment' where we just studied each other, acknowledging each other's spirit, I guess.

She was the look of love.  Love for me, certainly, but so much more.  Love again for the universe, for life – for herself.  That's the key, isn't it?  I could see it clearly in her now-precious face, like a gift.  She was filling with self-love; that had to be the most important love of all, for without that, what do have to truly give.

Our moment did not really give way to desires.  It was that new-found love she now had for herself that was the birth of beautiful new yearnings, sexual for sure, but riding high on an ocean of affection and adoration all born of love.

Believe me, these are the kind of kisses you want to have.  Amanda had found herself and was giving herself to me in deep, prolonged kisses.  How could Amanda's devouring vigor that attacked my face be somehow tender?  I think I've already explained the best I can.  It just was.  All I could do, pinned so helplessly as I was, was receive it and enjoy it.

Brandy's patented pressure pin incubated a stunning Sparkle tree from me, tingling through her body to the far reaches: her toes and fingertips and the roots of the hairs on her head.  It was terrific really, but I have to say, given a choice, I would have chosen the more unique experience of Amanda's glorious kissing session as she made up for more than ten years of lost love.  But I wasn't really given a choice in that very moment, was I?

Brandy had plateaued at 110%, which until then I didn't know was possible.  I don't think it was in her control, but somehow she kept me delectably plateaued with her.

Finally Amanda had expressed herself thoroughly enough with kisses.  As she pulled away, I kept mouthing the opening space between us, rather, OK I admit – *completely*, lost in desire.  And Amanda knew exactly what I craved the most.  She turned around, spread Brandy's legs apart more and lifted them up, making just enough room to plant her enormous perfect ass on my mouthing desire.  Amanda hooked Brandy's legs up and around, so that Brandy's lower legs rested on the top of Amanda's thighs.  This did two things: added a big portion of Brandy's heavy legs to the weight of Amanda's butt on my face and upper body, and it also distributed

Brandy's weight up to focus more pressure into her pussy pin on my cock and lower body.

In this position Brandy could no longer pump me up and down.  She could only just sit there and shiver with delight.  The Sparkle turned those shivers into an ongoing vibration of ecstasy.  How could she not have orgasm yet?  And right then, I could feel the earliest wave starting.  I could feel its delicate inception and promise of annihilation, both at the same time.  It was like swimming beyond the breakers, looking out at sea as your tread water in your safe location, and then seeing a great wave in the distance.  You realize you're in too deep for anything but riding it out.

But honestly, even with all that building down below, I was more preoccupied with Amanda's ass making love to my face.  It was like I was still being kissed – only now by a gigantic pair of lips, squeezing my face, my entire head in soapy-perfumed ass-crack love embraces.

It was almost humiliating how much I loved what Amanda was doing to me.  On and on and on she worked me over.  My skinny arms were lost out there, boney parts of a specimen pressed by ass-cheek, as if to be preserved and catalogued and lost in some library volume of little flattened men.  Just out of slight curiosity, I found I could kind of wiggle my fingers a microscopic amount up against her smashing buns, so I knew my arms were still alive.  Amanda, so sensitive to me now, could of course feel that tiny tickle.  She interpreted it as a signal I wanted more from her.  So she delivered and ferociously, pounding be with her insane desire; with each ass smash, squirming down on me further as if to gobble me inside her. Then we both knew at once what had to happen next.

Brandy's tidal wave was approaching shore rapidly, starting to curl up, higher and higher, the "white crest" showing.  Amanda had to shift quickly, sliding her ass back and her pussy onto me.  That's what had to "gobble me up" and that's just what her pussy did.  More kissing-pussy lips squeezed over my face.  She jammed her clitoris against the top of my hard noggin as my head entered her face first.  One – two – three hard pumps, was all it took.  Amanda's body blasted into orgasm, face fucking me for all she was worth – and, oh man, she was worth a lot.

Brandy's tsunami orgasm crashed the shore, destroying all before it, which was mostly the frail pint-sized man under her.  The writhing of these two enormous and powerful women macerated me like a little pork chop being tenderized by a sledge-maul.  Amanda unleashed shrieks of delight that reverberated down through her body.  I heard her pleasure like she was underwater right next to me.  "Iloveyou-

Iloveyou-Iloveyou" faster and faster she screamed it, the orgasm still building even as she released wave after wave.

Brandy bucked around like a rodeo champion, thrashing me like a twig in a storm. Finally, as I at last began to run out of air, I felt it all subsiding, everywhere on my body at the same time.  Calmer… calmer… muscles relaxing, little twitches finishing, Amanda releasing my head to slide back out and down, Brandy releasing my little body from her satisfied snatch.

Like some diminutive famished animal, I was still licking at Amanda as she unloaded her great ass off me, in time for me to see through a wet bleary eye Brandy do the same.

They disappeared somewhere into the room, no, into the bathroom.  They were back soon enough – with warm wet towels.  They lovingly wiped my body down, washing me clean and fresh.  They patted me dry, then tossed the towels aside.

I opened my eyes again and their two, almost angelic faces now, shown side-by-side.  All that filled my vision was their post-coital-Sparkle-transformational expressions of love and newfound satisfaction – by the numbers the faces of these two afternoon delights had moved up significantly to: 8.5s.

Certainly these were experienced women.  Undoubtedly they had tracked down many men and had their way with them.  For sure they had gotten-off, had their jollies, found their measure of sexual release.  But I would wager a dollar-for-a-dime they were each thinking (if they were thinking at all) that they had never, truly had an orgasm before.  What they didn't know was how beautiful they looked.  I don't think they would have fully believed me if I tried to tell them.

"Come with me, you beauties."  They moved aside so I could get up.  I trundled over to the edge of the bed, rolled off, stood up, was dizzy for a second, my blood seeking to re-balance, then steadied myself and was all right.  I reached my hands up as they stood beside me.  I led them across the room to the wall half-covered from ceiling down to floor with mirrors.

It was then they finally saw what I saw: the new and permanent beauty in their faces. They were awestruck, speechless for the moment.  While they looked on in wonder, I looked down at my own reflection standing between them.  There I stood, pale compared to their great tanned legs.  What seemed like sexual mastery on my part, my application of the Sparkle effect, had kind of blown up my own self-image in my mind.  But reality was, there staring back at me in living color, I was such a tiny, minute little dude.  I could see why some might think my face was cute.  But that face did not even reach to the tops of the huge legs next to me.  Above their legs, their inordinate width across their pelvises looked ridiculous by comparison to my linear thinness.  Solid firm abs held up prodigious pendulous breasts, especially Brandy's.  Those breast swung some now, as the ladies turned to examine their bodies.

Two trimmed muffs faced me now, as they looked to check out their asses.  What improvement could be made to Amanda's, I don't know, but she smiled as she seemed to notice something.  I continued to look at the dynamic image before me as the women admired themselves.  And one question came to mind: how in the world did I make love to such women?  But somehow I had, and it had been nigh-on perfect.

Leaving them to finish their inspection, I found my shorts, pretty much unworn for the day, slid them on and headed downstairs.  Only maybe five minutes later Brandy and Amanda joined me in the kitchen, once again fully clothed back in their work uniforms: one bright pink-patterned bikini and one deep purple bikini.

I sat in my high stool at the counter.  They each leaned all the way down serving up their generous breasts on the counter top, resting their chins on their elbows, their delicious asses nicely stuck up in the air.

"Well," drawled Amanda, her smile so sweet. "Thank you for lunch."  She winked at me.

"Yes," Brandy joked along.  "I don't think I've ever had a meal so... so satisfying."

Amanda sighed, the afternoon had worn on and the shadows outside were getting longer.  "I guess it's time we scoot on out of here."  Then she looked serious.  "Richie, I'm awfully sorry about before…" It was only about three steps from where I sat that she'd about throttled me earlier in the day.  "I…" But her voice cracked in deep regret at what she'd almost done to me.  "I…"

But I cut her off, reaching over to grab her hand.  "It's okay, Amanda.  All is forgiven."  She had given herself so deeply to me.  Ha, well, and me so deeply into her.  Now I sighed, recalling the sensations.  Yes, man-oh-man, was all forgiven.

"Thank you Richie."  Wow, what a splendor Amanda was right now.

Brandy, still likely feeling some of the residual Sparkle, smiled at me as well, her body doing a slight happy movement, like she was listening to her favorite music.  It jiggled those spectacular breasts very nicely on the counter top. "Yes indeedie, Richie, thank you so much."

The ladies rose up to standing and headed toward the back slider.  Amanda turned, one grand leg about to step outside.  "Richie, can we come back?"

"Sure, who else would take care the pool?"

"I mean," I knew what she was going to ask about, "Can we come see *you* again?  I know you're the Triplet's boyfriend and all.  And, gosh," remembering more things she'd said. "I'm so sorry about what I said about them, too.  But is there a way, somehow, we can get together with you again?  'Cause we would really like to, right Brandy?"

Brandy hefted her tits, adjusting them inside her bikini top.  Another patented move, no doubt, but knowingly playful and just for me. "Oh, yeah. Yes-sir-rie, I sure would."

"I don't know about fooling around with the hired help."  I said dryly.  I enjoyed their shocked looks at the insult as I walked over to them. "So, I guess it's a good thing you don't work for me."  And I reached up and slapped them on their asses.  They giggled at my joke.  I offered, "So maybe when you're back next month?  I'll see about taking a day off work."

"That's a long time."  Pouted Brandy, though obviously pleased.

"Richie, you sure?"  Amanda was so beautifully vulnerable.  "And the Triplets won't mind?

"Yes, Amanda, I am sure.  And the Triplets, well they are very complicated, but on this, I think I know their hearts."

Comforted, Amanda got back to her cocky joking tone.  "Well, then, Mr. Richie, you better be ready 'cause I'm swearing off those duller-than-dull cowboys down over at Weaverville."

"No more Goose & Gander bar boys for me either."  Brandy added.  "So you better be real ready!"

Amanda could still look scary if she wanted. "I expect our sexual energy to build up bigtime in a month.  So next time I get my great big hungry ass on your little bones, well, I just hope you live to tell about it."

With that they both turned on out the wide doorway, across to the pool, prominent in their sashays, knowing damn well I couldn't take my eyes off their butts.  Ah, those butts that had owned me so deliciously….  I watched them posing for me as they bent to pick up sweep and broom and other tools of their trade.  Just shaking my head, I thought "What a day!" as they disappeared around the side yard toward their van out front.

The sun was getting low now.  And that meant… Saint Debbie would be here in some thirty minutes!  Holy cow! I better get in there and start cooking up a storm. No rest for the weary…

# IX. Saint Debbie's Smothering Grace

As I watched Saint Debbie polish off her fifth heaping platter of dinner I found myself glad that a skinny little guy like myself had very limited food value.

"More?" I suggested.

Fat Debbie's (because right now "Saint Debbie" was "Fat Debbie" so please excuse me if I go back and forth somewhat on that terminology) ass had grown so huge she couldn't fit it into any of the Triplets' big dining chairs.  Doing her best, she had sat down on the kitchen floor, two-foot diameter thighs tapering forward under the table, heavy-heavy arms resting on the high surface, lovely round face maybe just a foot and a half above the table top.  Perfect, really, for shoveling food in.

Chewing, mouth full, she waved a meaty hand my direction. "No."  A couple more chews then she could speak.  "So kind of you to offer, Richie.  No, I believe I'm temporarily full.  It was delicious, though.  Thank you so much."  She began the awkward process of extracting her legs out from under the table so she could stand.

The gentlemanly thing would have been to help her up.  But what service would my 70 pounds be to assisting an on-the-order-of 1,400 pound woman to stand?  Strong and as big as an ox, she definitely needed no help anyway.  So I only smiled kindly at the large, lovely and loving young lady.  Instead I made my way to the kitchen sink, ascended my stepstool, and began doing the dishes.

"Well," Debbie waddled with poise (if that makes any sense) over to me, bringing her used dishes.  "What shall we do this evening for fun, my good man?"

Of course she already had a pretty good idea of what I wanted to do.  We had made love before, back when she broke the record on me of number of times a gal from the pollination crew could make me cum on the commute back to town.  Back when she was a mere 835 pounds.  But after that big dinner, I mused to myself adding 20 pounds of food; let's put her at 1,420 pounds.

The three steps up the stepstool made me about 5'6"; over the high sink enough that I could be effective at my task.  I could feel the gravitational pull of Debbie as she stood right behind me, handing me a plate with one hand, then on the other side of me, a big mug.  I was still thinking about entertainment possibilities…

She remained close behind. "Good sir, I'm just waiting patiently here 'til you answer my question."

I looked straight back and up. All I could see were gigantic pendulous breasts straining the thin green and violet-flowered fabric that sought to hold them up. Those breasts overshadowed the kitchen lighting from above and darkened the sink to the far side. Oh, my word, Debbie, just lower those on me right now – is what I was thinking.

But I instead suggested. "How about a swim?" I'd noticed out the window over the sink it looked to be a pleasant warm evening.

Still over me, her voice came down, somehow getting to me around those breasts. "You know, I hardly have any clothes that fit me anymore. So I didn't even bother looking for a swimsuit."

"You poor dear…" I both truly sympathized with her bizarre metabolic condition and teased her at the same time. "But, is that really a problem?"

"I'm OK if you're OK, sweetie. I just didn't want to be nude-rude without asking."

"I'm guessing improvising is the theme this weekend."

"And creativity…" She tousled my hair with a big, soft hand. "I'll meet you out there."

"Oh, be careful, Debbie. You know what they say about swimming after eating."

"Maybe I'll just float." Then she joked suggestively. "Anyway, if I get in trouble you can rescue me; give me mouth-to-mouth."

Debbie traipsed outside, following the accent-lit-walkway toward the pool. I squeezed the water out of the sponge, standing the poor little thing up to dry against the faucet, and thought, "Oh boy, this is going to be a doozy of a night."

Outside I felt the pool lights were a little bright. I dialed them down then shifted the color over to a soft rose glow. Mmmm, a magical summer's evening, indeed.

Debbie sat in an amazon's design of a shallow end, in about six feet of water. What an incredible picture she was in this fat-that-wasn't-fat embryonic phase again. Her seventh-wonder breasts partially floated at surface level. Her torso bulk of accumulating regimens of stem cells mimicked rolls of horizontal layers of fat all around as she spread out pear-shape. In this stage she was all about the base, her ass flattening along maybe one-fourth the width of the big pool.  The Baby Hughie of sexy.

Wow Fat Debbie, I thought, your body has really outdone itself this time.  Pulling off my shirt and shorts, I dove in.  Swimming over to her, I docked in the bay that was her cleavage.  Since we were friends, quite comfortable with each other, I hefted up my back on one gigantic breast, and lifted one leg to drape up and over the other; my skinny butt still down in the water.  Ah, relaxing… my head rested back into her cushion.  I looked up at Debbie's kindly continence, stars decorating her appropriately all around her head.  But was it me or was this lady hot?  And by that I mean way too warm of flesh.

"Man, Debbie, what the heck is going on with your body this time?"  I was sympathetic, because it had to be tough for my friend: the crazy temperature swings, the big jumps in size, the metamorphosis-like changes in her shape.

"Oh, you know, the usual."  She didn't sound hurt.  In fact it might be impossible to insult Debbie and have her actually perceive it that way.  But she wanted to know something about my remark.  "You don't like my body anymore?"

"No, no-no-no.  That's not what I meant.  I like you in whatever form you take.  And this one, it's intimidating, I have to admit, but it's good, it's all good."

She laughed at me.  Then, about her body: "It has gone kind of ballistic this round hasn't it?"

"Well, yeah.  I mean, what are you, like 1,400 pounds?"

"Would you believe more like 1,700?"

I must have gasped a little.

"Yeah, I know" She rolled her eyes. "This next iteration is going to be something!"

"Well, whatever it is…" I patted her breast next to me.  "I know you will make it beautiful.

She sighed.  "You see," She pointed at me. "That right there, what you just said, that's why I have to make serious love to you tonight."

I felt a tingling along my back.  Her body was activating, sexually.  She had the Tingle, kind of all over her body and at the cellular level.  But what she didn't know yet: was that I mow had, ah-ha! The Sparkle.   I couldn't wait until I sprung my little surprise attack on her later on.  It made me excited and happy just to think about it.

"How long can you go without air these days?" She asked kind of offhand.

"Could be thirty minutes." I grinned and worked my comedic eyebrows up and down.

"Oh, that ought to be sufficient…"  Big – and coy she was.

I liked where this little conversation was going.  "Sufficient for what?"

"How would you…" She placed a big index finger on my chest. "…like a little facesit right here in the pool."

"How about you try and catch me first!" I swiftly shoved out of Breast Bay and toward the deep end.

Now you might think Debbie was being kind of forward with the suggestion "how about a little facesit."  But you got to understand about Saint Debra.  She is completely unpretentious.  Absolutely honest.  And just a big, giant gumdrop of love.  Also, don't forget; she has the Tingle.  So, when it comes to love-making, all she really has to do is sit there on you and let her glorious body do the rest.

But we were having fun now.  I don't know exactly when or how my body changed, but I was fast in the water.  Like a speedy little neon fish, I zipped all over the pool, easily out-maneuvering the big predator that was after me.  It wasn't fair, really.  Try to recall being a little kid, then hitting a growth spurt and losing your coordination – becoming a total spaz.  Can you?  That's kind of how it was for Debbie, especially in this current extreme growth cycle.

But Debbie doesn't get frustrated.  However, she was getting too hot.  With her extreme metabolism and the exertion, even the pool water wasn't keeping her cool.  She'd had enough of chasing tadpoles.  From underwater I watched her trudge into the shallow end and take her dainty steps out of the pool.

I popped up out in the middle of the pool and just had to tease her.  Someday I would get her goat and see her riled up.  "So give up, do ya'?  Too fast for ya', am I?  Don't get all pouty and mad." I eyed her walking around toward the deep end, so I tread-watered back toward the shallow end.

"Oh you know me, Richie.  I don't give up easy.  And I never get mad." She looked and sounded casual enough.

Still I sought to tease her.  "Oh, you poor little girl.  All worn out.  And now…"  But I didn't get to finish that taunt.

She had leaped impossibly high and far out over the pool.  Honestly, I didn't think she could jump at all.  "Dead wrong," was all I could think as I thrashed desperately for the near corner of the shallow end.

Kerblam!  The concussion of her butt-drop hit the pool with the noise of a thunder clap.  I went flying and landed hard.  She must have emptied the pool, because I hit the pool bottom and there was no water.  No, what?  I was disoriented. Wait a second… I could see the grass nearby. Holy crap, I was thrown from the pool by her seismic wave.  And I deposited, where… oh, just by the pool's edge.  I whipped my head around to get my bearings, just in time to see Debbie's arm coming down to scoop me up.

"There we go."  She said like she'd just put the final decoration on a cake, hauling me into her bosom.  She patted me on the head, striding back out into the pool.  "You OK honey-bun?"

I looked up with consternation.

"Oh, now, don't be like that.  This game only has winners."  She squeezed me in a lot more, pressing her big warm breasts around my thin frame.  Her body gave me hugs within hugs within hugs.  It was impossible not to be comforted and to feel her essence of unconditional love.  I sighed, relaxed, and smiled.  She rewarded me with kisses to the top of my head.  "That's better."

"I thought no way you would catch me."  I just shook my head.

"Yeah, well, about that. I figured if I walked around toward the deep end, you'd head to the shallow.  Only logical response on your part.  But then I had you, didn't I?  It was just a little science after that.  You know: my weight, hitting mid pool from a certain height, with your momentum toward the corner, and voila, the wave takes you out with sufficient disorientation."

I forget how smart some of these amazons are.  And Debbie might be very rounded but she was still plenty sharp.  (Note to self: another little prejudice to work on.)  I still had a tiny speck of protest in me.  "You know darn well it wasn't entirely fair that you got out of the pool to get me."

I was under a breast now, being pressed up into it by her hands.  I could hear her saying, "…like you didn't want to get captured…"

She brought me out and up to her face.  She studied me with some slight concern, but mostly a kindly intensity.  "I still want to get back to the original plan…"  She cast her eyes downward, toward her lower body.  Then back to my eyes, waiting for an OK.

I felt like soft wax in her warm hands.  "Yeah, me too."

She brought me to her face for a big wet kiss, sloppy on purpose, quite stimulating.  Breaking off, she looked at me intently again, a little bit like I was another plate of food, I thought.  Then she said with warning earnest. "I that case, you better take a big breath!"

I grabbed that breath a split second before being plunged under water.   She drove me down with her hands, past her huge legs on either side and toward their grand confluence.  The soft pink glow of the pool lights was the ideal ambiance for where I was headed. Then it was dark.

She was not 1,700 pounds heavy, as she was perhaps 50% buoyed up where she sat on me in the shallow end.  My head unbirthed into her immediately, easily entering her pussy.  Then right away she tightened on me, and I was without escape.

The Tingle was already going crazy; one hundred trillion individual cells clamoring for orgasm, ASAP!  But Debbie was firmly at the reigns – for now, anyway. She rocked on me, gently, with little bounces to get me in there deeper.  She definitely moved the process along.  That's right: I remembered, I only had some thirty minutes of air.  Yeah, Debbie, you go girl.

Debbie fought a nice but dire edge.  Her body just wanted to absorb me, add me into its mass – eat me.  That part was like… well, like I'd falling into some rural pond, and had become the target of a gigantic love amoebae.  The other part was Saint Debbie's mission from the Great Goddess to keep me from being devoured, saving my body and soul for a Heaven of Pleasures reserved especially for those like me, who believed enough in the power of love.  I wasn't smug about it.  I just had the thought that a dark-hearted man would be very lucky to survive this, even with Debbie's good intentions.

Of course, nobody but me was going to survive this anyway; now fifteen minutes without a breath.  Believe me, I thanked my lucky stars quite often, many time a day for sure, for the three extraordinary women, my girlfriends the Triplets, who had given me such fine survival gifts.  And this chance to experience astonishing forms of sex and love.

Her squeezing pussy pressured all around my head.  Her vaginal lips clamped harder around my neck with each wave.  This was cutting off my air too soon.  All the sudden I felt the desperation, then panic.  I screamed into the flesh inside her pussy.  Her Tingle responded and came at me wilder now, wet flurries of craving, of hunger, too needful in the moment to be sympathetic.  But Debbie sensed it and timely enough.

She rose from the water.  Her pussy still tight on my head, my body hung between her two pillar legs, with my lower spindle shanks back into the water, but my feet not reaching the pool bottom.  I felt her walking as I dangled, helpless, cool body in the night air.  Up the steps, her huge and hefty inner thighs rubbed and twisted my body.  We descended. Grass tickled my back as she squatted on the lawn, relaxing enough for me to slide out below her.

I gasped in air.  Above her pussy dripped pool water onto me, her vast ass all encompassing; its limits beyond my peripheral vision.

Debbie actually didn't sound overly concerned. "You good baby?"

Now that I could breathe again, actually, "Terrific."

"That's the spirit.  'Cause I'd kind of like to keep going here…"

I could see now the tension quivering above me.  She was aching to drop that big juicy twat down on me again and finish with a bang.

"…OK, Richie?"  Her baby voice strained a little, still wanting to hear my go-ahead.

"Yes, by all mea…"  Boom, her atomic ass came down on me again – this time, full gravity.

I think the full weight felt better to her, too.  She built quickly, riding me heavy, grinding pleasure with rapid pelvic rocking, sliding that linear vibration on my head, shoulders, and upper body.  I knew my legs flopped around on the grass like two epileptic snakes.  She cured that problem by bringing her legs together, completely coving me.

Now it became Debbie who looked the odd epileptic, sitting out on the grass by herself, wiggling and shuttering, bouncing and moaning.  Who would know she was smashing orgasms into a tiny man lodged deeply in her pussy, enveloped by her massive butt and crushed under her colossal legs.  That all he had to fight back against the giantess plummeting orgasms, was his little tongue licking against the flood that drenched, and the immense body that smothered him senseless.

And why was I talking about myself third person?  I think I had maybe gone exterior of my body.  What, like when people die?  Would death be so extremely pleasurable?

I orbited her, watching her beautiful expression, lips parted, ecstasy and joy. I could see in her face what I felt so intensely: her overwhelming desire to press her love into me.  Oh, she owned that orgasm abundantly the way she owned me completely. I wanted to kiss her beautiful lips.  Instead I was suddenly back inside her, arching my head back, going with the flood, and finding her clitoris with my mouth.  I latched onto the epicenter of her Tingle and gave her all I was worth.

The crazy woman on the grass exploded into a frenzy of writhing lust. And was just lost: lost, oblivious, and obliterated.  Senseless.  I don't know where my soul went, I think, maybe off to another planet with Debbie, somewhere.  On the grass just one very big zombie sitting stupefied on another, much smaller, tiny little zombie, both waiting for their souls to return.

I ached when she rose off me, rolling to the side.  Not from any pain, but from the inches between us seeming like miles.  Saint Debra understood, generously shifted to smush me under her breasts.  Ah, much better again.

I think I went to sleep.  I woke to kissing; my own kissing of her grand nipple that covered half my face.  As I licked at it I reached way over and played with her other one.  She moaned a little approval and jiggled those big tits to settle on me a bit more.  But from my vantage I could still see past them, to the brilliant stars.  The pool lights had timed out and we had only the stars for illumination.

The night had finally cooled off.  I was warm.  But even hot Debbie would get chilled after some hours.  She shivered, then said.  "Well darling, this has been fun out here.  But, what say you we go back inside and have sex?"

Goodness, she was right.  Hard to believe, but we hadn't done that yet.  I thought about my Sparkle surprise attack. "Ha! Hell, yes.  Just as soon as I can get this big woman to get her heavy tits off me."

She laughed, and took her sweet time getting off me.

***

Debbie stood by the grand bed, baskets of food in each arm.  We had paused in the kitchen for a snack, but she just wanted to keep eating.  "I'm so darn hungry.  I can't stop eating.  Would it be all right if I just loaded up here and brought some upstairs with me?  You wouldn't mind too much, would you?"

I thought once she sits on me I wouldn't know if she was eating, knitting, or playing video games.  And actually – and can we just say I'm done making excuses for myself – there was something about her eating while having sex that kind of turned me on.

"I wouldn't dream of restricting your abundance."  I offered.

She eyed that odd remark with good humor.  Saint Debbie loved to joke with me.  "You know you're a little weird, don't you?"

"A little?"  I laughed.

"OK little lover boy.  Why don't you lie on out there on the bed.  I'll climb on you and we can get this show on the road."

"You in a hurry?" I asked, then sarcastically,  "Because, I'm like, wow, that's great foreplay you're suggesting."  Actually I thought her suggestion was perfect.   It was exactly what I wanted.  But remember, I was practicing a small deceit, hiding my Sparkle until I was good and ready – correction – until she was good and ready and thoroughly worked up sexually.

"You want something else?  It's all good to me."  Debbie was so easy – I mean in the best way.  "What did you have in mind?"

Sill it was going to be tricky to hide the Sparkle from her, from her hungry-probing body.  "How about you get on the bed, with you food and whatever you need, and make yourself comfortable.  And maybe I can satisfy some of my hungers at the same time."

Debbie shrugged.  "Sure, Baby, if that makes you happy.  Why not?"  She made her way to the middle of the great bed, walking on her knees, her arms balancing those baskets of food.  Centered, she plopped down, spreading her legs before her, and sliding the baskets of food down her sides, off the slope of her wide hips, to settle on the bed beside her.

"OK."  She was spreading peanut butter onto celery sticks.  Offered me one.  I declined.  She smiled at me, held the food to her mouth, but before taking a bite, paused, tossed her head back and shook her shiny brown curls, and said in a dramatic deep throaty voice I hadn't heard from her before voice. "I'm ready.  Take me."

Smiling dryly, I sighed as acknowledgement of her joking.  But "he who laughs last" I thought… me and the Sparkle would "take her" and right when she least expected it.  Ha.  But it was going to require no small amount of stealth and self-control on my part.

I started at her feet.  And her Tingle was already there, waiting to meet me.  I kissed her toes, one-by-one, taking my time.  Her toes kind of probing and kissing me back.  Oh boy. I kissed her insoles and imagined being crushed by her stomping on me.  I lingered there quite a while, my volunteer already very hard.  But I kept him at a distance from her.  Her body-omnipresent Tingle was too intelligent.  It would know from any touch from that department.

As I worked around her ankles and up super thick but still rather shapely calves I could hear her munching away, in the distance. Good, if she stays somewhat distracted by eating, I'll have a chance to make this work.

At her knees I wanted to go under.  Tapping at their sides, she obligingly pulled her legs back, raising her knees.  I snaked around underneath, kissing the beautifully heavy underside of her upper legs. On my side now, I kissed along her widening leg, inching my way up with a hundred kisses.  I felt her body heating up, metabolism rising, sexing up quite nicely.  Yes, yes, I thought slyly to myself, she's responding right on cue.

Problem was: so was I.  Her sexual heat tended to melt me, melt my resolve.  And as I worked my way closer and closer to that delicious pussy; that addictive elixir that I knew awaited in her flow, a weakness began to overlay my determination.  Still under her leg, the space narrowing where it now converged to the bed, I necessarily advanced upward and around partially to her inner thigh.  And there it was before me, that soft forest of no return.  I was a snake now, licking the air for her scent, losing myself in the spell of her sugary aroma.  I slithered forward; just three more kisses to her insanely sweet pussy…

"Whoa there, cowboy."  She dropped that heavy leg on my back, crushing me into the bedding and mattress, and pinning me there – but good.  "I'm getting a little too excited by all this.  Don't want to choke on this jar of mixed nuts."

It was driving me crazy to be this close and to be denied access.  I tried to fight my way free and nudge closer.  Nothing, I couldn't move.  My arms were trapped with the rest of my body.  I couldn't even reach out and grab her.  Exasperated, it made me growly, echoing up the canyon of her legs.  I tried to stay manly, but was losing it, getting pissy and acting like a snarly little baby bear.

"Really?" She said. "Can we negotiate this a bit?"

I don't know what exactly overcame me.  I kind of had a tantrum.  Thrashing my head around, the only part of me that could move; my face turned beet red in frustration.

"You have to know, there's no way I can let you up like this.  You might hurt me or more likely yourself." As Debbie spoke she was calmly putting away her food into the baskets.  With careful deliberation she then looked at her gnashing little lover with concern.  "We have to get you to relax.  OK, now breathe with me.  In… and out… nice and slowly… in… out…"

The worst of the mania subsided as I breathed with Debbie's instructions.  Again I felt the love Tingle emanating from her body, mostly from her huge leg that was covering my back, butt, and down my legs.  It was embarrassing how crazy I got for a minute.  I had acted like a complete baby.

Oh my God, I finally was realizing: compared to Debbie, I was the size of a small infant.  Goodness gracious, what was this relationship all about?  I was definitely questioning myself, losing myself to her big loving ownership of me.  Debbie had the kind of unconditional love one would only ever hope to find – from… from a mother.  What the heck?

Debbie scooted her pussy a little closer, her soft bush against my face.  "Now, are you sure this is what you want, Baby?"

She was even calling me "baby".  What was I to her?  My mouth was working with desire, to taste her, so, so, sweet, to enter her, and be engulfed again.

"Well?"  She asked

I looked back up toward her voice, through her tickling shrubbery that pushed against my face.  Up there, in the heavens, her enormous breast swayed tantalizing, beckoning for my lips.  My mouth opened, involuntary. Peeking through the narrow gap in her cleavage she spied my desire.

"Okie-dokie doll, that would be nice, too."  She rolled over on me, arranging herself ninety degrees to my body, and brought a huge breast onto my face, a warm nipple stretching my lips to their max.  Her tit-pressing covered my entire head, my chest, and pinioned my arms.  Her wondrous breasts were significantly bigger now, even than just a few hours ago in the pool.

As I sucked, I felt the Tingle enter my body, enlivening me, the sensation pouring into my stomach and spreading out from there.  Quickly I realized my Sparkle would be found out and I so wanted to save it for later.  I fought her great breast, squirming and pushing up against her.  But her weight was entirely overwhelming me.  And her milk flowed now.  I would soon be subdued by this Goddess.  But before I surrendered completely I had one last desperate thought and acted on it.  I bit her with my sharp little teeth.

"Ouch." She broke off and lifted up.  Unlike what you might expect, Debbie was not grumpy at me, instead, "Are you all right?"

"Yeah.  Sorry.  I just think I'm ready for something else.  Maybe we should move on to sex after all."

She was bemused by my inconsistent approach to sex.  But she was also hot and turned on.  It had not escaped me that she had temporarily lost interest in food.  And that was saying a lot.  Yes, her big ass was ready to be savaged by me – I was feeling my oats again.  She was waiting, ready. "Well?" She awaited my instructions. That's more like it, I thought.

"Miss," I said. "Pull this vehicle over.  Right here on this bed! I want you on your hands and knees, now!  Ass toward me, where I can get a good look at it."

"Yes, sir."  She complied.  And I knew she was digging this, me getting bossy.

My God, what a view.  She swayed that ginormous butt in tantalizing seduction. Nabbing a couple of pillows, I positioned them strategically on the bed between her knees, resisting the huge pull to jump up and bury my face in her candy-store smelling crack. Standing back, I ascended the pillows.  I knew it really didn't matter where I plugged in, the Sparkle would do the rest.  But I thought maybe the maximum effect would be at her lowest chakra.  Truth be told, if I left it up to my eager water-witching stick, my proud little heat-seeking missile, my one-man Charge of the Light Brigade, oh yeah, that's exactly where he would volunteer for this do-and-die mission.  Bully, bully, boys and damn the torpedoes!  I plunged forward, full frontal and fully hard, into her center-of-the-universe ass – and was immediately devoured by it.

"What the – is that!" Debbie exclaimed, completely caught off-guard by the Sparkle.

"Perfect." I thought, extremely pleased with myself. "Perfect. Perfect. Perfect." But I had no idea how perfect.

Her Tingle rushed forward in a mad stampede, like giant thundering electric lemmings jumping off a cliff en masse. Would "overwhelmed" be the right word to describe your fate if you stood below Hoover Dam breaking open. Debbie actually jumped up to standing on the bed. Me, enveloped in her butt, arms flailing, crazed by the mingle-of-the-Tingle-and-the-Sparkle.

Saint Debbie howled with delight, arms up to the heavens, body shuttering, tits swinging wildly and slapping together, she jumped riotously into the air. Then with me stuck in and riding at the point of impact, her great ass of destruction came crashing down, driving me insanely deep into crack of loving doom.

Yes, Saint Debbie had lost it, gone she was, into a religious experience that I could not fathom. It did seem to include, however, my total annihilation by severe shivering ass pounding. Not just pounding my body, but grinding down hard as a finishing accent each time. Her ass munched me in further with each terrific smash, mightier and hungrier than the one before.

I was lost, too. Like a pinecone in an avalanche, my fate was completely at the mercy of great forces of Nature. And at the moment She showed no mercy, only a sexual vigor I didn't know was possible.

My Sparkle tree grew inside her like barrels of Miracle Grow fertilizing a great live oak. My branches of electric love twisted and found every avenue of desire in her body which could deliver that love. Her Tingle flowed a freed river of energy, breaching its banks and flooding the plains. Debbie was everywhere around me and in me and, especially, I in her.

Debbie's great weight and heat, pressed me as if to flatten my bones. Her Tingle followed the Sparkle down to source, down stimulating delight through my hard-on and issuing its demands of me. "Now. Give it to me now." She was in my body, commanding me with absolute, yet still good-hearted, dominance.

"Take me." She had joked before. And now here I was, taken myself, under-ass, enveloped in butt crushing ecstasy, sliding now below the scale of worshipful, dominated into a mindless state of slavery.  My will was hers, from the inside out.  Her merest breeze of a whim was my command.  So cum I did, indeed!

I exploded a Fourth of July Sparkle of zillions of microscopic volunteers into her ass.  What happen next was beyond astonishing.  It was phenomenal.

It was if time suspended at the deepest moment of her crush on me, immensely heavy and hot.  In the distance in her body above me I could see her soul as a shining light.  And she could see mine, below her.  Loving, beautiful, and quite spiritual it was, yet fundamentally we both felt how she completely she owned me in that moment, thoroughly all the way through to the spiritual level.

Then we both saw it between us at once, the magic that was in use, combining.  My sperm had been absorbed into her blood stream.  Those individual volunteers were being delivered all over her body, each one disappearing one-by-one, millions-by-millions into individual cells of her body.  Inside those impregnated cells I was being absorbed further or recombined, I couldn't tell or maybe it was some other process beyond my comprehension.  I could see that Debbie did not understand it perfectly either.  But those cells were changing, differentiating, and rapidly so.

The Tingle sought more from me.  It concentrated now in my balls, activating, heating – incubating.  She wanted more; commanded me from inside my own body to cum again already.  And I did with another glorious orgasm and her simultaneous smashing down on me to receive it.

A minute later the Tingle had me up and ready again.  Shortly thereafter a fourth time.  Then a fifth time.  Then a sixth time…  There seemed to be no end to this process, to my renewing supply of sperm, to the amount of orgasms we could manufacture.  With each one I felt my love of Debbie growing.  And with each one I felt her body changing, morphing she was, right on top on me.

How long could this go on – could I go on?  When would this process stop?  But I barely had time to think because OMG, here we go again.

… I remembered bits of the science they tried to teach me.  Some of it was interesting… Oh – Oh – again we came… The average human body had something like 100 trillion cells.  I guessing Debbie's would like have more… Oh, no, this one was going to be even bigger – oh… and again we came and orgasmed… I also recalled quite specifically that the average ejaculation had from 40 million to 1.2 billion sperm.  I recalled that because the range seemed so crazy large… Oh boy, here we go again…oh…oh…  That was a dozy… Let's be generous and say I was spouting one billion per click.  That would take like…  Hold on… can't do math when I'm…oh lordy-lordy "I love you, Debbie!" I shouted. "I love you too!" She shouted back.  …let's see one billion into 100 trillion; that would take like 100,000 ejaculations to impregnate every cell in her body… Oh shit, her we go again… oh… oh… fuck me, fuck me, this was going to be a long night!

Is it possible to go to sleep while being fucked.  Certainly.  But is it possible for both parties to go to sleep and keep on having sex and sex and sex….  Answer, turns out, yes.  After about an hour and a half of orgasms we were exhausted.  Debbie just collapsed on me and went to sleep, that deep, heavy amazon sleep.  She was gone.  I slept also, of a sort: mush-minded, fried-brain, blinking catatonic on tilt, still kind of waking a little for each next orgasm.  Sometimes awake enough to drool and kiss against the upper nethers of her ass/lowest back, my favorite spot, crushed against my face for the night.  I also imagined often, of seeing her bright face smiling into mine, love in her eyes, big beautiful full lips parted suggestively for a kiss… or two… or a thousand….

My dozing disturbed by yet another orgasm, I noticed something seemed different.  Debbie seemed even heavier – or was it denser?  And where did her lower back go, my face was entirely lodged in her upper ass crack now.  Very firm and tight she clamped onto me now, her sleeping body tensing into another quickening succession of orgasms.

***

I dreamed I'd been made into a candy bar or was it a lollipop?  Great hands tore at my wrapper exposing me briefly before a huge set of lips took me in. The fear was intense as I was about to be chewed – no, not chewed – sucked on – I was a lollipop after all… I awoke, relieved, thinking, what does that mean?  That I'm just a big sucker?

It seemed Debbie had definitely moved up on me, or gotten bigger?  My face was definitely down more, between the upper part of her buns.  She was definitely much, much heavier on me.  For sure bigger, I surmised.

I really couldn't move any part of my body except my eyes.  Looking straight ahead, all ass.  But upward there was a feint vee of light, the outline off her upper butt.  Somewhere out there it was morning.  I had survived the night.

But I was still being crushed and felt very weak.  I should have needed to pee, but didn't.  Instead I was incredibly thirsty, dehydrated by the ravaging ordeal.  I had to get some water… soon…. I tried with all my might, to move, to squirm even a little bit. But it was impossible. And there was a density and firmness to her ass that rendered me powerless.

I tried to bite her, but could not get a purchase on her tight, firm skin. I could not shout out, only into her, my scream just ringing back into my own ears.

So I blew raspberries, making a substantial farting noise. But that literally backfired as she only shifted slightly, wiggled, and let out her own real fart, vibrating my whole body. I'm doomed I thought. But I had forgotten about my earlier experience in the van with Fat Debbie. Dear Saint Debbie's warm vapors were nothing but sweet-rose perfumed from a candy store. Considering my pinned proximity I'd caught a big break there.

With nothing to lose I blew more raspberries, and again. Finally she really started to shift, waking. She sat up, stretching and tightening as she did. My God, what intense weight bore down on me.

"Richie? Richie?" I could barely hear her calling my name. "Good morning… where are you?" Then there was a rush of air, blinding bright morning light. "Oh, there you are, Sweetheart."

I blinked, bleary, things slowly coming into focus. Huge perfect tits swayed above my face. Looking all around to my sides I saw that Debbie was on all fours, over me… way over me. And she was different, I mean metamorphosis different. The pear-shaped giantess gumdrop of amoebic love was gone. Replaced by amazon perfection of extraordinary proportions.

Even her face, or especially her face, had changed. She was still obviously Debbie, no mistaking that. But her face, in losing its roundedness, took on a wonderful and elegant character, gorgeous really to gaze upon. Same Debbie full lips, yet more expressive in their lines. Same understanding twinkling eyes, but more penetrating, and eagle-like in their clear intensity. And there was something else… to her look, a very slight otherness that hadn't been there before. Not bad, just different, like a little two percent of someone else's face. Of my face!

The big bed bounced as Debbie got up, leaving me lying there in my state of weakness and confusion.

"Oh my word, would you come look at this." She was over in front of the mirrors. "Come-come-come-come." She yapped, not seeming to understand how feeble I was feeling.  I crawled to the edge of the bed and tumbled off to my feet.  "Come see this body we grew last night, Richie."  Debbie was definitely excited.

I staggered over to her, stumbled a little, then righted myself between the A-frame of spectacular legs.  My head was merely half way up to her thick and shapely mid-thigh.  Unthinking I traced her lines up, looking right above.  That view was a reward-and-a-half.  My breath shuttered out, as I kind of short-circuited by the size of the sexy beauty above.

I could see up no further, so I looked forward to the mirror.  That image was even more shocking and stunning to my system.  I saw a real live goddess standing over my scrawny body.  Huge wide hips, firm and thunderous, snug muscular waist blossoming into great tits so perfectly formed and impossibly outstanding and firm for such proportions.  But there they were: real.  And the regal crown of her radiant, excited face looking right in the mirror and smiling lovingly right back into my eyes.

Transfixed I was for a moment.  But it was too much for me; I felt so spent and frail.  I could hardly even stand. I looked away, and saw my own body, so tiny by comparison.  But something else was amiss.  I looked emaciated; like I had just escaped a prison camp.  What the hell happened to me?

Still, Debbie took no notice, maybe just seeing me with the love of rose-colored glasses.  Bounding away into the bathroom, she called back to me.  "Come on, Richie, let's take a shower together."

As I zombie-trudged to maybe catch up, I hear her exclaim? "Wow, can you believe it, I'm 2,075 pounds!  But I'm not that hungry, so maybe I'll stay this size a while."

When I entered she was already in the shower, singing.

I founded the scales myself.  Good lord, only 60 pounds.  I'd lost some 10 pounds last night.  So thirsty, I went to the sink, climbed up and drank all I could.  That helped a bit, but I was still light headed.  Back at the scales: 61 pounds.  I sighed and shook my head.  Did her Tingle really draw nine pounds of cum from my balls?  My thoughts were spinney, unreal.  What the hell… did I make a sperm for every cell in her body…

Debbie had about four shower heads blasting a torrent of water onto her upper mantel and cascading down.  She beckoned me over, smiling enthusiastic.  I obliged, resting my spine against the back of her knee.  She bent her knee slightly, supporting me a bit with her angled lower leg.  I looked out at the waterfall spilling over from the great booty shelf of her butt – almost at arm's length it rushed by.  I looked up again.  This time my reward, the artistic view of the huge, strong butt cheeks extending prominently back where they met her upper legs, the water cataract a shimmering silver fan off that wide fanny….

I kept staring up transfixed by the imminent doom of her butt.  This was a mere intermission now.  Yet soon, too soon, she would want me again.  And I knew I had no power to say no to her.  What would happen to me next time?  Would she simply absorb me completely?  Would I even exist anymore, other than fractured and trapped inside her?

Something bounced against my foot.  I looked down.  A pink bar of soap.  I looked back up.  The ass was indeed coming to get me, bending opening, now pussy toward me and exposed… darkness.

I woke up, soapy water swirling around me, a noisy drain by my ear.  The bar of soap was gone.  I must have swooned, passed out for a second, and slid to the floor of the shower.  She didn't butt crush me; only picked up the soap.

"Hey, you about finished massaging my feet down there?"  Debbie shouted only a little, to be heard above the blasting waters.  "Soon as I rinse off I'm done."

A half a minute later all was quiet, except the diminishing dripping off her body and onto and around me.  She stood there enjoying her clean feeling.  Me, just curled against her insole.

"You know what?  We still didn't do it yet.  We didn't actually have real sex."

Dumbfounded but not speechless I mumbled.  "What the heck was it, then? I only came about a thousand times."

"It was anal, right.  That's one reason the sperm absorption worked so well.  But that's not real sex.  I think we should have real sex.  Wouldn't that be just the best way to start the day?"

She stepped out of the shower to finish drying off, leaving her wet ragdoll lover behind, a shivering curled up mess.

"You coming?"

But didn't answer.  I might have been going into shock.

"Richie?" Her concerned tone sounded water-muffled.  Through a blurred haze I saw shapes the color of my dear Debbie coming toward me.  Strong soft hands picked me up.  And I passed out.

When I woke up I was warm and dry, in a soft, smooth place.  My closed eyes I could tell the world was very bright, like sunshine streaming through a window to heat my face."

"Hey there, Sweetie.  Want some more?"

The brightness turned off.  I opened my eyes to see a perfect nipple on a perfect huge breast a breath width from my lips.  Of course I kissed it.  And as it yielded milk, I sucked it.  Each gulp a baby step up in vigor in my body.

Looking around best I could, I discerned that Debbie was sitting on the carpet, her back against the bed, the mid-morning sun flooding in the open bedroom sliding door.  I rested comfortable in Debbie's arm, nursing like a baby on her generous breast.

"You must have been totally famished."  Debbie explained.  "It isn't like me to be so insensitive.  I'm sorry.  I doubt any man has ever turned 15% of his body weight into sperm in one night.  Of course I might have helped that along some, but let's give you the credit."  She peered at me closely.  "You're feeling better now, aren't you?" I nodded, but kept nursing – it tasted out-of-this-world good.  She kept talking. "Anyway you did indeed, miraculously, make a sperm for every cell in my body. And those little champions were delivered to each and every one."

I was definitely feeling better. I rubbed my hands around the parts of her breast I could reach, which was most of it.  Debbie smiled a little sexual approval of my touch, then continued. "But of course it wasn't a pregnancy thing.  My cells are double chromosome and sperms are just one set.  It wouldn't match up.  It would be like making seedless watermelons."

I had no idea what she was talking about.  I didn't care that much because I was getting milk-mind satiated.  But if my goddess wants to talk genetics…I gazed at her beautiful, radiant face, her mouth moving again.  "So each sperm found a unique application, used in a plethora of ways, many kinds of differentiations, protein enhancements, genetic alterations, even found some enhancements for the Tingle you might like."  I nodded at Professor Debbie.

I couldn't suck another gulp, but did enjoy some lazy licking of that nipple, daydreaming of kissing those lips that kept talking. "Oh, you are in me now, Baby.

Not in any personality sense.  I just slaved up all your little sperm to do my body's bidding day and night, broke them to pieces as needed, and used them for parts every which way."  Sounds kind of violating, doesn't it?"  I just kept dreaming of Debbie's lips and could have cared less.

"So," Debbie sighed, giving my body a little ride up and down; she seemed to be wrapping up the lecture. "…this milk you've been enjoying has the ideal protein and fat blend just for you.  It is made and manufactured inside me, in part, using blueprints of your genetics, altered, of course, to perfection by a woman's touch.  You would not need any other sustenance.  My breasts are all you need."

Feeling my oats again, "Except, I would very much like to kiss your lovely lips."

"Oh, that's more like it Baby." And she eagerly descended on my lips with hers.  Standing she hugged me all the way in between her breasts, her kiss spreading across my mouth and face.  She kneeled on the bed, lowered a side hip, rolled on out on her side then over onto me, never releasing that kiss, as she pressed and sealed me into the mattress.

Sensing I had some satisfaction Debbie finally released the kiss. Pushing up, she lightly tit-whipped me, playful for her I suppose, but unnerving in her power to own me so easily.  She rose, straightening all the way up to her knees drilling deep into the cushioning on either side of my body.  It was a position of extreme dominance over me.  And I felt like I was withering beneath her abundance and seething lust.

"Think you're finally ready for that real sex?"  She winked, but she was not kidding in the least.  I wanted to immediately blurt out "Yes-yes" but I was having a crisis of confidence.  She was so utterly magnificent.  And what was I, what… nothing but a little baby-man that had to be suckled back to strength for this moment.

"Debbie, this makes no sense.  How… why would someone as incredible as you even want, well, a little man like me?  What kind of lover can I possibly be for you?"

"You're the best lover a woman could possibly want."  It was her stab at a quick answer.  Honest, but kind of deflecting.  She just ached to get on with the sex.

But I wasn't buying it.  "I don't feel like much of a lover.  My deepest desire here, honestly, is just to be owned and smashed by your body.  No thought of technique here, really, just worship.  Goddess Debbie is what you are to me.  And I crave without hope to be massacred by your pussy and absorbed by your ass."  There, I said it, shamefully weak as it sounded; but the bitter truth.

"Oh Richie, you really have no idea what you mean to me. OK then." She shifted back and forth on her knees, turning around above me. "Let's get this part out of the way first." She scooted forward until her feet rested to either side of my head, a fair distance away, and heels up. "Look at my ass. Isn't it just the bomb?" Oh, it was the bomb, all right. And she was slowly lowering it toward me as she spoke, the yawning crack widening as it approached my face. "This ass that you "crave" so much is begging me, begging me to let it crush down on you, smother you, and absorb you until you are utterly and completely part of me and there is nothing left that is not owned by it, by me." Her butt rested on her heels, inches from my face. "Go ahead…" I heard her say. "… kiss it if you want. It is for you. It is yours."

I raised my head the slight distance required and kissed her so gently and lovingly. The contact was a connection of emotion and knowingness. Her butt quivered with delight. I knew with delicious surrender the punishing lust her ass would love to administer to me this very moment. With great self-discipline, Saint Debbie rose away from my lips.

I guess the point with a Saint is not whether they have desires, but how they live with them. It was clear to me that she wanted me more, to own me more, to entirely devour me with her lusting butt and wet-as-we-speak pussy, dominate me with her massive crushing legs, smother me with her great tits of abundance and calamity, and lovingly kiss me to death. This was Saint Debbie's dark desire revealed in all its glory and doom. It was by the grace in her most superlative heart that I was still alive.

This time as Debbie turned around above me, she lowered her upper body to her elbows, her cleavage centered on my mid-section, squeezing in on me, her face wonderfully maybe eighteen inches above mine.

She batted her eyes. "Are you getting the picture now?"

I nodded. "It's like 'Where the Wild Things Are'. You 'love me so much you could eat me'."

She laughed at this. "Something like that. Probably the X-rated version; where the little man gets eaten by giant ass and pussy."

"That version wasn't on my bookshelf when I was a kid."

"Well, it is now, kiddo. And you are up front and center this time. You're the hero." And more seductively but not joking. "You're my hero."

Her sincerity was moving for me.  But "hero"? Me?

Of course she could clearly see I wasn't getting it.  "Come on Richie, think big.  Last night your love, and also desire, for me was so complete, you were willing to give up your life to fulfill me.  And in that process you have given me a gift beyond measure.  You helped transform me into this wondrous body.  I love it.  I love you.  Never again will I have to suffer through those blob phases.  Sure I kept up a good attitude; but you knew I wasn't crazy about it.  Who would be?  This beautiful body means many things to me, but especially it will always mean a precious gift from you."

Wow, I had no idea.

She wasn't finished.  "So there you tremble below me, compelled to feel the need to worship me.  Good.  I like that – being your Goddess – knowing how extreme your desires are.  Keep thinking and feeling that way.  I command you: worship me more."  She flashed her eyes, leaving her mouth open, making sure I noticed her tongue licking the inside of her lower lips.  "I fully plan to keep growing, to become more beautiful – for you, Richie.  For *you*, my love.  For you, *on* you, every which way a little man can be owned by a woman."  She let that sink in as she rose above me again, back to that knees-on-either-side high straddle.  "So, now, would you say that we are compatible?"

"It's like we were made for each other."

"No Richie, it's like we were made *by* each other."

"Yes," I nodded. It was true.  There was my dream woman, towering above me, loving me and threatening to annihilate me all at once.  I looked at her in new wonder. "Yes… mistress?"

"You're joking, right?"

I shrugged.

"How about, when you have to go there, I kind of like 'Saint Debbie'." She laughed at that moniker.

But it worked very well for me: "Saint Debbie of the Abundant Smother."

She laughed again.  "How about, 'Our Lady of the Absorbing Ass'?"

"Or," I suggested, more seriously. "... a stunningly beautiful and generous woman I want to know better and better."

Her breath caught, tears formed in her eyes, and as one, then two crocodile teardrops fell to my chest, she smiled dearly and said. "That'll do."

We took our time with that moment. After a while, my face almost ached from smiling up at her.

"So..." I said timidly. "Can we even have real sex?"

She snapped out of her reverie, that hungry look clearly in her lusty expression. "Better than you ever imagined."

"Oh, I've imaged a lot." I kidded, but not really kidding.

"Oh, I imagine you have. Have you imagined, for example, that I own you for my sex toy?" I was fully hard immediately. "That's right." She glanced at my lance. "You better respond." Oh I loved that tough talk. "Did you imagine that your sweet gentle Saint Debbie would order you to kiss her pussy, thoroughly using your tongue to get her good and wet." She grabbed my head and shoulders, brought me up and jammed me in her pussy, but not too deep. I could still hear her orders. "Lick and kiss, suck and face-fuck." She ground around on me, moved my head in circular motions. She got wet very fast. Then dropped me back down.

"Did you imagine I would grab you legs." She nabbed my skinny shanks by my ankles. "Bend one leg down at the knee to turn you into my ultimate pleasure device. And then shove you in my pussy foot first." And she did just that. "That I am so smart that I have calculated that you will slide in up to your little hips." Her legs spreading, lowered her pussy over first my left leg, then my knees, now including my bent right leg. Warm and wet, her Tingle was all around me. I slid in easily but snug, deeper, deeper just as she described. "That I would order you to wiggle you feet and toes to drive me crazy." I did; and it did.

 She spasmed only a small amount; just getting started, I assumed. "That I would lower my great pussy all the way down your legs until your little buns would just enter me?" They lodged into her right on cue. "That the top of your penis would now be against my clitoris, the tip nicely inside me. And... with... all... that... perfect... stimulation... I... would...go... entirely... insane... on... you." And she did.

No right-minded person would be fearless in my situation. But I was pretty close to fearless, too overcome with sensations of love and pleasure to be much mindful of how easily I could be crumpled into nothing but recycled proteins to be assimilated up her ass.  You could not observe her wild thrashing on me and think that Debbie was anywhere near complete control.  But I released and surrendered to her possession of me.  I waggled my toes and feet; like I was told.  Wiggling my legs, kneeing her repeatedly in her G-spot; those were my clever ideas.

When I came, the Sparkle was weak.  I needed a re-charging by the Triplets.  But with Debbie's robust love and lust, and with the crazy contortions I was carrying out inside her vagina, her explosion of orgasm rattled the windows as I incurred the weight of her seismic smash.  I noticed I was definitely cumming inside her.  Finally, after all that foreplay, real sex!  God I hope she's happy now.

Debbie bounced on me, trampoline-ing the bed in harmonic motion.  Giddy like a school girl (but let me be clear, she was no school girl) Debbie clapped her hands and said.  "Let's do that again, backwards."

Before I could say, "Yes Saint Debbie" she whirled that big-rig ass around and pounded it down on me.  As she arranged my legs into the appropriate pretzel, crossing my knees this time, but still with the one-leg bend, I just stared at the big ass hovering, impatient.  I actually whispered to it.  "Oh we had our own special love affair, don't we?"  Can an ass have a smug smile?

"What are you saying down there?"  Debbie was inserting me again.  Quickly was I in her pussy again; right up the hilt of my pelvis.  And that brought her thunder buns smashing down, my thin chest enfolding right into her crack, my face lost between her upper buns.

Debbie was slower this time, deliberate, working me over methodically, staying with repetitions building the vigor to my limit of endurance, backing off a fraction of a moment, finding a slightly new and delightful angle, and on and on and on…

I was mumbling unheard pledges into ass of my Goddess.  "… I'll paint your toenails… I'll go in your mouth and lick your teeth one-by-one… I'll be your footstool, your chair, your beach towel to lie upon… please let me serve you…"  And serve her I did.

It was mid-afternoon when she finally got off me.  Fucked me for some four hours she did.  I was ravaged mush, both my body and my mind.  She, of course, looked no worse for the wear, glowing happy and satisfied, in fact.

"Come on."  She said.  "Let's get you a little sustenance."  With that a swollen tit flopped down on me, turgid with milk.  As I sucked, it shot into my mouth, spilling over me faster than I could lap it up.  Quickly I was feeling invigorated.  She pulled back to check on me.

Already cocky again, I suggested. "How about another go?"

"Yeah, right."  She laughed at my bravado.  "Good attitude, Bucko.  But let's go down and get some real food."  For me that meant – not her milk.  For her that meant – not me.

# X.  How to Serve a Giantess an Omelet

As I watched Saint Debbie polish off her fifth heaping platter of dinner I found myself glad that a skinny little guy like myself had very limited food value.

"More?" I suggested.

Fat Debbie's (because right now "Saint Debbie" was "Fat Debbie" so please excuse me if I go back and forth somewhat on that terminology) ass had grown so huge she couldn't fit it into any of the Triplets' big dining chairs.  Doing her best, she had sat down on the kitchen floor, two-foot diameter thighs tapering forward under the table, heavy-heavy arms resting on the high surface, lovely round face maybe just a foot and a half above the table top.  Perfect, really, for shoveling food in.

Chewing, mouth full, she waved a meaty hand my direction.  "No."  A couple more chews then she could speak.  "So kind of you to offer, Richie.  No, I believe I'm temporarily full.  It was delicious, though.  Thank you so much."  She began the awkward process of extracting her legs out from under the table so she could stand.

The gentlemanly thing would have been to help her up.  But what service would my 70 pounds be to assisting an on-the-order-of 1,400 pound woman to stand?  Strong and as big as an ox, she definitely needed no help anyway.  So I only smiled kindly at the large, lovely and loving young lady.  Instead I made my way to the kitchen sink, ascended my stepstool, and began doing the dishes.

"Well," Debbie waddled with poise (if that makes any sense) over to me, bringing her used dishes.  "What shall we do this evening for fun, my good man?"

Of course she already had a pretty good idea of what I wanted to do.  We had made love before, back when she broke the record on me of number of times a gal from the pollination crew could make me cum on the commute back to town.  Back when she was a mere 835 pounds.  But after that big dinner, I mused to myself adding 20 pounds of food; let's put her at 1,420 pounds.

The three steps up the stepstool made me about 5'6"; over the high sink enough that I could be effective at my task.  I could feel the gravitational pull of Debbie as she stood right behind me, handing me a plate with one hand, then on the other side of me, a big mug.  I was still thinking about entertainment possibilities…

She remained close behind.  "Good sir, I'm just waiting patiently here 'til you answer my question."

I looked straight back and up.  All I could see were gigantic pendulous breasts straining the thin green and violet-flowered fabric that sought to hold them up.  Those breasts overshadowed the kitchen lighting from above and darkened the sink to the far side.  Oh, my word, Debbie, just lower those on me right now – is what I was thinking.

But I instead suggested. "How about a swim?"  I'd noticed out the window over the sink it looked to be a pleasant warm evening.

Still over me, her voice came down, somehow getting to me around those breasts.  "You know, I hardly have any clothes that fit me anymore.  So I didn't even bother looking for a swimsuit."

"You poor dear…"  I both truly sympathized with her bizarre metabolic condition and teased her at the same time.  "But, is that really a problem?"

"I'm OK if you're OK, sweetie.  I just didn't want to be nude-rude without asking."

"I'm guessing improvising is the theme this weekend."

"And creativity…" She tousled my hair with a big, soft hand.  "I'll meet you out there."

"Oh, be careful, Debbie.  You know what they say about swimming after eating."

"Maybe I'll just float."  Then she joked suggestively.  "Anyway, if I get in trouble you can rescue me; give me mouth-to-mouth."

Debbie traipsed outside, following the accent-lit-walkway toward the pool.  I squeezed the water out of the sponge, standing the poor little thing up to dry against the faucet, and thought, "Oh boy, this is going to be a doozy of a night."

Outside I felt the pool lights were a little bright.  I dialed them down then shifted the color over to a soft rose glow.  Mmmm, a magical summer's evening, indeed.

Debbie sat in an amazon's design of a shallow end, in about six feet of water.  What an incredible picture she was in this fat-that-wasn't-fat embryonic phase again.  Her seventh-wonder breasts partially floated at surface level.  Her torso bulk of accumulating regimens of stem cells mimicked rolls of horizontal layers of fat all around as she spread out pear-shape.  In this stage she was all about the base, her ass flattening along maybe one-fourth the width of the big pool.  The Baby Hughie of sexy.

Wow Fat Debbie, I thought, your body has really outdone itself this time.  Pulling off my shirt and shorts, I dove in.  Swimming over to her, I docked in the bay that was her cleavage.  Since we were friends, quite comfortable with each other, I hefted up my back on one gigantic breast, and lifted one leg to drape up and over the other; my skinny butt still down in the water.  Ah, relaxing… my head rested back into her cushion.  I looked up at Debbie's kindly continence, stars decorating her appropriately all around her head.  But was it me or was this lady hot?  And by that I mean way too warm of flesh.

"Man, Debbie, what the heck is going on with your body this time?"  I was sympathetic, because it had to be tough for my friend: the crazy temperature swings, the big jumps in size, the metamorphosis-like changes in her shape.

"Oh, you know, the usual."  She didn't sound hurt.  In fact it might be impossible to insult Debbie and have her actually perceive it that way.  But she wanted to know something about my remark.  "You don't like my body anymore?"

"No, no-no-no.  That's not what I meant.  I like you in whatever form you take.  And this one, it's intimidating, I have to admit, but it's good, it's all good."

She laughed at me.  Then, about her body: "It has gone kind of ballistic this round hasn't it?"

"Well, yeah.  I mean, what are you, like 1,400 pounds?"

"Would you believe more like 1,700?"

I must have gasped a little.

"Yeah, I know" She rolled her eyes. "This next iteration is going to be something!"

"Well, whatever it is…" I patted her breast next to me.  "I know you will make it beautiful.

She sighed.  "You see," She pointed at me. "That right there, what you just said, that's why I have to make serious love to you tonight."

I felt a tingling along my back.  Her body was activating, sexually.  She had the Tingle, kind of all over her body and at the cellular level.  But what she didn't know yet: was that I mow had, ah-ha! The Sparkle.   I couldn't wait until I sprung my little surprise attack on her later on.  It made me excited and happy just to think about it.

"How long can you go without air these days?" She asked kind of offhand.

"Could be thirty minutes." I grinned and worked my comedic eyebrows up and down.


"Oh, that ought to be sufficient…"  Big – and coy she was.

I liked where this little conversation was going.  "Sufficient for what?"

"How would you…" She placed a big index finger on my chest. "…like a little facesit right here in the pool."

"How about you try and catch me first!" I swiftly shoved out of Breast Bay and toward the deep end.

Now you might think Debbie was being kind of forward with the suggestion "how about a little facesit."  But you got to understand about Saint Debra.  She is completely unpretentious.  Absolutely honest.  And just a big, giant gumdrop of love.  Also, don't forget; she has the Tingle.  So, when it comes to love-making, all she really has to do is sit there on you and let her glorious body do the rest.

But we were having fun now.  I don't know exactly when or how my body changed, but I was fast in the water.  Like a speedy little neon fish, I zipped all over the pool, easily out-maneuvering the big predator that was after me.  It wasn't fair, really.  Try to recall being a little kid, then hitting a growth spurt and losing your coordination – becoming a total spaz.  Can you?  That's kind of how it was for Debbie, especially in this current extreme growth cycle.

But Debbie doesn't get frustrated.  However, she was getting too hot.  With her extreme metabolism and the exertion, even the pool water wasn't keeping her cool.  She'd had enough of chasing tadpoles.  From underwater I watched her trudge into the shallow end and take her dainty steps out of the pool.

I popped up out in the middle of the pool and just had to tease her.  Someday I would get her goat and see her riled up.  "So give up, do ya'?  Too fast for ya', am I?  Don't get all pouty and mad."  I eyed her walking around toward the deep end, so I tread-watered back toward the shallow end.

"Oh you know me, Richie. I don't give up easy. And I never get mad." She looked and sounded casual enough.

Still I sought to tease her. "Oh, you poor little girl. All worn out. And now…" But I didn't get to finish that taunt.

She had leaped impossibly high and far out over the pool. Honestly, I didn't think she could jump at all. "Dead wrong," was all I could think as I thrashed desperately for the near corner of the shallow end.

Kerblam! The concussion of her butt-drop hit the pool with the noise of a thunder clap. I went flying and landed hard. She must have emptied the pool, because I hit the pool bottom and there was no water. No, what? I was disoriented. Wait a second… I could see the grass nearby. Holy crap, I was thrown from the pool by her seismic wave. And I deposited, where… oh, just by the pool's edge. I whipped my head around to get my bearings, just in time to see Debbie's arm coming down to scoop me up.

"There we go." She said like she'd just put the final decoration on a cake, hauling me into her bosom. She patted me on the head, striding back out into the pool. "You OK honey-bun?"

I looked up with consternation.

"Oh, now, don't be like that. This game only has winners." She squeezed me in a lot more, pressing her big warm breasts around my thin frame. Her body gave me hugs within hugs within hugs. It was impossible not to be comforted and to feel her essence of unconditional love. I sighed, relaxed, and smiled. She rewarded me with kisses to the top of my head. "That's better."

"I thought no way you would catch me." I just shook my head.

"Yeah, well, about that. I figured if I walked around toward the deep end, you'd head to the shallow. Only logical response on your part. But then I had you, didn't I? It was just a little science after that. You know: my weight, hitting mid pool from a certain height, with your momentum toward the corner, and voila, the wave takes you out with sufficient disorientation."

I forget how smart some of these amazons are. And Debbie might be very rounded but she was still plenty sharp. (Note to self: another little prejudice to work on.) I still had a tiny speck of protest in me. "You know darn well it wasn't entirely fair that you got out of the pool to get me."

I was under a breast now, being pressed up into it by her hands.  I could hear her saying, "…like you didn't want to get captured…"

She brought me out and up to her face.  She studied me with some slight concern, but mostly a kindly intensity.  "I still want to get back to the original plan…"  She cast her eyes downward, toward her lower body.  Then back to my eyes, waiting for an OK.

I felt like soft wax in her warm hands.  "Yeah, me too."

She brought me to her face for a big wet kiss, sloppy on purpose, quite stimulating.  Breaking off, she looked at me intently again, a little bit like I was another plate of food, I thought.  Then she said with warning earnest. "I that case, you better take a big breath!"

I grabbed that breath a split second before being plunged under water.  She drove me down with her hands, past her huge legs on either side and toward their grand confluence.  The soft pink glow of the pool lights was the ideal ambiance for where I was headed. Then it was dark.

She was not 1,700 pounds heavy, as she was perhaps 50% buoyed up where she sat on me in the shallow end.  My head unbirthed into her immediately, easily entering her pussy.  Then right away she tightened on me, and I was without escape.

The Tingle was already going crazy; one hundred trillion individual cells clamoring for orgasm, ASAP!  But Debbie was firmly at the reigns – for now, anyway.  She rocked on me, gently, with little bounces to get me in there deeper.  She definitely moved the process along.  That's right: I remembered, I only had some thirty minutes of air.  Yeah, Debbie, you go girl.

Debbie fought a nice but dire edge.  Her body just wanted to absorb me, add me into its mass – eat me.  That part was like… well, like I'd falling into some rural pond, and had become the target of a gigantic love amoebae.  The other part was Saint Debbie's mission from the Great Goddess to keep me from being devoured, saving my body and soul for a Heaven of Pleasures reserved especially for those like me, who believed enough in the power of love.  I wasn't smug about it.  I just had the thought that a dark-hearted man would be very lucky to survive this, even with Debbie's good intentions.

Of course, nobody but me was going to survive this anyway; now fifteen minutes without a breath.  Believe me, I thanked my lucky stars quite often, many time a day for sure, for the three extraordinary women, my girlfriends the Triplets, who had given me such fine survival gifts.  And this chance to experience astonishing forms of sex and love.

Her squeezing pussy pressured all around my head.  Her vaginal lips clamped harder around my neck with each wave.  This was cutting off my air too soon.  All the sudden I felt the desperation, then panic.  I screamed into the flesh inside her pussy.  Her Tingle responded and came at me wilder now, wet flurries of craving, of hunger, too needful in the moment to be sympathetic.  But Debbie sensed it and timely enough.

She rose from the water.  Her pussy still tight on my head, my body hung between her two pillar legs, with my lower spindle shanks back into the water, but my feet not reaching the pool bottom.  I felt her walking as I dangled, helpless, cool body in the night air.  Up the steps, her huge and hefty inner thighs rubbed and twisted my body.  We descended. Grass tickled my back as she squatted on the lawn, relaxing enough for me to slide out below her.

I gasped in air.  Above her pussy dripped pool water onto me, her vast ass all encompassing; its limits beyond my peripheral vision.

Debbie actually didn't sound overly concerned. "You good baby?"

Now that I could breathe again, actually, "Terrific."

"That's the spirit.  'Cause I'd kind of like to keep going here…"

I could see now the tension quivering above me.  She was aching to drop that big juicy twat down on me again and finish with a bang.

"…OK, Richie?"  Her baby voice strained a little, still wanting to hear my go-ahead.

"Yes, by all mea…"  Boom, her atomic ass came down on me again – this time, full gravity.

I think the full weight felt better to her, too.  She built quickly, riding me heavy, grinding pleasure with rapid pelvic rocking, sliding that linear vibration on my head, shoulders, and upper body.  I knew my legs flopped around on the grass like two epileptic snakes.  She cured that problem by bringing her legs together, completely coving me.

Now it became Debbie who looked the odd epileptic, sitting out on the grass by herself, wiggling and shuttering, bouncing and moaning.  Who would know she was smashing orgasms into a tiny man lodged deeply in her pussy, enveloped by her massive butt and crushed under her colossal legs.  That all he had to fight back against the giantess plummeting orgasms, was his little tongue licking against the flood that drenched, and the immense body that smothered him senseless.

And why was I talking about myself third person?  I think I had maybe gone exterior of my body.  What, like when people die?  Would death be so extremely pleasurable?

I orbited her, watching her beautiful expression, lips parted, ecstasy and joy. I could see in her face what I felt so intensely: her overwhelming desire to press her love into me.  Oh, she owned that orgasm abundantly the way she owned me completely. I wanted to kiss her beautiful lips.  Instead I was suddenly back inside her, arching my head back, going with the flood, and finding her clitoris with my mouth.  I latched onto the epicenter of her Tingle and gave her all I was worth.

The crazy woman on the grass exploded into a frenzy of writhing lust. And was just lost: lost, oblivious, and obliterated.  Senseless.  I don't know where my soul went, I think, maybe off to another planet with Debbie, somewhere.  On the grass just one very big zombie sitting stupefied on another, much smaller, tiny little zombie, both wailing for their souls to return.

I ached when she rose off me, rolling to the side.  Not from any pain, but from the inches between us seeming like miles.  Saint Debra understood, generously shifted to smush me under her breasts.  Ah, much better again.

I think I went to sleep.  I woke to kissing; my own kissing of her grand nipple that covered half my face.  As I licked at it I reached way over and played with her other one.  She moaned a little approval and jiggled those big tits to settle on me a bit more.  But from my vantage I could still see past them, to the brilliant stars.  The pool lights had timed out and we had only the stars for illumination.

The night had finally cooled off.  I was warm.  But even hot Debbie would get chilled after some hours.  She shivered, then said.  "Well darling, this has been fun out here.  But, what say you we go back inside and have sex?"

Goodness, she was right.  Hard to believe, but we hadn't done that yet.  I thought about my Sparkle surprise attack.  "Ha! Hell, yes.  Just as soon as I can get this big woman to get her heavy tits off me."

She laughed, and took her sweet time getting off me.

***

Debbie stood by the grand bed, baskets of food in each arm.  We had paused in the kitchen for a snack, but she just wanted to keep eating.  "I'm so darn hungry.  I can't stop eating.  Would it be all right if I just loaded up here and brought some upstairs with me?  You wouldn't mind too much, would you?"

I thought once she sits on me I wouldn't know if she was eating, knitting, or playing video games.  And actually – and can we just say I'm done making excuses for myself – there was something about her eating while having sex that kind of turned me on.

"I wouldn't dream of restricting your abundance."  I offered.

She eyed that odd remark with good humor.  Saint Debbie loved to joke with me.  "You know you're a little weird, don't you?"

"A little?"  I laughed.

"OK little lover boy.  Why don't you lie on out there on the bed.  I'll climb on you and we can get this show on the road."

"You in a hurry?" I asked, then sarcastically,  "Because, I'm like, wow, that's great foreplay you're suggesting."  Actually I thought her suggestion was perfect.   It was exactly what I wanted.  But remember, I was practicing a small deceit, hiding my Sparkle until I was good and ready – correction – until she was good and ready and thoroughly worked up sexually.

"You want something else?  It's all good to me."  Debbie was so easy – I mean in the best way.  "What did you have in mind?"

Sill it was going to be tricky to hide the Sparkle from her, from her hungry-probing body. "How about you get on the bed, with you food and whatever you need, and make yourself comfortable.  And maybe I can satisfy some of my hungers at the same time."

Debbie shrugged.  "Sure, Baby, if that makes you happy.  Why not?"  She made her way to the middle of the great bed, walking on her knees, her arms balancing those baskets of food.  Centered, she plopped down, spreading her legs before her, and sliding the baskets of food down her sides, off the slope of her wide hips, to settle on the bed beside her.

"OK." She was spreading peanut butter onto celery sticks. Offered me one. I declined. She smiled at me, held the food to her mouth, but before taking a bite, paused, tossed her head back and shook her shiny brown curls, and said in a dramatic deep throaty voice I hadn't heard from her before voice. "I'm ready. Take me."

Smiling dryly, I sighed as acknowledgement of her joking. But "he who laughs last" I thought… me and the Sparkle would "take her" and right when she least expected it. Ha. But it was going to require no small amount of stealth and self-control on my part.

I started at her feet. And her Tingle was already there, waiting to meet me. I kissed her toes, one-by-one, taking my time. Her toes kind of probing and kissing me back. Oh boy. I kissed her insoles and imagined being crushed by her stomping on me. I lingered there quite a while, my volunteer already very hard. But I kept him at a distance from her. Her body-omnipresent Tingle was too intelligent. It would know from any touch from that department.

As I worked around her ankles and up super thick but still rather shapely calves I could hear her munching away, in the distance. Good, if she stays somewhat distracted by eating, I'll have a chance to make this work.

At her knees I wanted to go under. Tapping at their sides, she obligingly pulled her legs back, raising her knees. I snaked around underneath, kissing the beautifully heavy underside of her upper legs. On my side now, I kissed along her widening leg, inching my way up with a hundred kisses. I felt her body heating up, metabolism rising, sexing up quite nicely. Yes, yes, I thought slyly to myself, she's responding right on cue.

Problem was: so was I. Her sexual heat tended to melt me, melt my resolve. And as I worked my way closer and closer to that delicious pussy; that addictive elixir that I knew awaited in her flow, a weakness began to overlay my determination. Still under her leg, the space narrowing where it now converged to the bed, I necessarily advanced upward and around partially to her inner thigh. And there it was before me, that soft forest of no return. I was a snake now, licking the air for her scent, losing myself in the spell of her sugary aroma. I slithered forward; just three more kisses to her insanely sweet pussy…

"Whoa there, cowboy." She dropped that heavy leg on my back, crushing me into the bedding and mattress, and pinning me there – but good. "I'm getting a little too excited by all this. Don't want to choke on this jar of mixed nuts."

It was driving me crazy to be this close and to be denied access.  I tried to fight my way free and nudge closer.  Nothing, I couldn't move.  My arms were trapped with the rest of my body.  I couldn't even reach out and grab her.  Exasperated, it made me growly, echoing up the canyon of her legs.  I tried to stay manly, but was losing it, getting pissy and acting like a snarly little baby bear.

"Really?" She said. "Can we negotiate this a bit?"

I don't know what exactly overcame me.  I kind of had a tantrum.  Thrashing my head around, the only part of me that could move; my face turned beet red in frustration.

"You have to know, there's no way I can let you up like this.  You might hurt me or more likely yourself."  As Debbie spoke she was calmly putting away her food into the baskets.  With careful deliberation she then looked at her gnashing little lover with concern.  "We have to get you to relax.  OK, now breathe with me.  In… and out… nice and slowly… in… out…"

The worst of the mania subsided as I breathed with Debbie's instructions.  Again I felt the love Tingle emanating from her body, mostly from her huge leg that was covering my back, butt, and down my legs.  It was embarrassing how crazy I got for a minute.  I had acted like a complete baby.

Oh my God, I finally was realizing: compared to Debbie, I was the size of a small infant.  Goodness gracious, what was this relationship all about?  I was definitely questioning myself, losing myself to her big loving ownership of me.  Debbie had the kind of unconditional love one would only ever hope to find – from… from a mother.  What the heck?

Debbie scooted her pussy a little closer, her soft bush against my face.  "Now, are you sure this is what you want, Baby?"

She was even calling me "baby".  What was I to her?  My mouth was working with desire, to taste her, so, so, sweet, to enter her, and be engulfed again.

"Well?"  She asked

I looked back up toward her voice, through her tickling shrubbery that pushed against my face.  Up there, in the heavens, her enormous breast swayed tantalizing, beckoning for my lips.  My mouth opened, involuntary. Peeking through the narrow gap in her cleavage she spied my desire.

"Okie-dokie doll, that would be nice, too."  She rolled over on me, arranging herself ninety degrees to my body, and brought a huge breast onto my face, a warm nipple stretching my lips to their max.  Her tit-pressing covered my entire head, my chest, and pinioned my arms.  Her wondrous breasts were significantly bigger now, even than just a few hours ago in the pool.

As I sucked, I felt the Tingle enter my body, enlivening me, the sensation pouring into my stomach and spreading out from there.  Quickly I realized my Sparkle would be found out and I so wanted to save it for later.  I fought her great breast, squirming and pushing up against her.  But her weight was entirely overwhelming me.  And her milk flowed now.  I would soon be subdued by this Goddess.  But before I surrendered completely I had one last desperate thought and acted on it.  I bit her with my sharp little teeth.

"Ouch."  She broke off and lifted up.  Unlike what you might expect, Debbie was not grumpy at me, instead, "Are you all right?"

"Yeah.  Sorry.  I just think I'm ready for something else.  Maybe we should move on to sex after all."

She was bemused by my inconsistent approach to sex.  But she was also hot and turned on.  It had not escaped me that she had temporarily lost interest in food.  And that was saying a lot.  Yes, her big ass was ready to be savaged by me – I was feeling my oats again.  She was waiting, ready. "Well?" She awaited my instructions.  That's more like it, I thought.

"Miss," I said. "Pull this vehicle over.  Right here on this bed! I want you on your hands and knees, now!  Ass toward me, where I can get a good look at it."

"Yes, sir."  She complied.  And I knew she was digging this, me getting bossy.

My God, what a view.  She swayed that ginormous butt in tantalizing seduction.  Nabbing a couple of pillows, I positioned them strategically on the bed between her knees, resisting the huge pull to jump up and bury my face in her candy-store smelling crack. Standing back, I ascended the pillows.  I knew it really didn't matter where I plugged in, the Sparkle would do the rest.  But I thought maybe the maximum effect would be at her lowest chakra.  Truth be told, if I left it up to my eager water-witching stick, my proud little heat-seeking missile, my one-man Charge of the Light Brigade, oh yeah, that's exactly where he would volunteer for this do-and-die mission.  Bully, bully, boys and damn the torpedoes!  I plunged forward, full frontal and fully hard, into her center-of-the-universe ass – and was immediately devoured by it.

"What the – is that!" Debbie exclaimed, completely caught off-guard by the Sparkle.

"Perfect." I thought, extremely pleased with myself. "Perfect. Perfect. Perfect." But I had no idea how perfect.

Her Tingle rushed forward in a mad stampede, like giant thundering electric lemmings jumping off a cliff en masse. Would "overwhelmed" be the right word to describe your fate if you stood below Hoover Dam breaking open. Debbie actually jumped up to standing on the bed. Me, enveloped in her butt, arms flailing, crazed by the mingle-of-the-Tingle-and-the-Sparkle.

Saint Debbie howled with delight, arms up to the heavens, body shuttering, tits swinging wildly and slapping together, she jumped riotously into the air. Then with me stuck in and riding at the point of impact, her great ass of destruction came crashing down, driving me insanely deep into crack of loving doom.

Yes, Saint Debbie had lost it, gone she was, into a religious experience that I could not fathom. It did seem to include, however, my total annihilation by severe shivering ass pounding. Not just pounding my body, but grinding down hard as a finishing accent each time. Her ass munched me in further with each terrific smash, mightier and hungrier than the one before.

I was lost, too. Like a pinecone in an avalanche, my fate was completely at the mercy of great forces of Nature. And at the moment She showed no mercy, only a sexual vigor I didn't know was possible.

My Sparkle tree grew inside her like barrels of Miracle Grow fertilizing a great live oak. My branches of electric love twisted and found every avenue of desire in her body which could deliver that love. Her Tingle flowed a freed river of energy, breaching its banks and flooding the plains. Debbie was everywhere around me and in me and, especially, I in her.

Debbie's great weight and heat, pressed me as if to flatten my bones. Her Tingle followed the Sparkle down to source, down stimulating delight through my hard-on and issuing its demands of me. "Now. Give it to me now." She was in my body, commanding me with absolute, yet still good-hearted, dominance.

"Take me." She had joked before. And now here I was, taken myself, under-ass, enveloped in butt crushing ecstasy, sliding now below the scale of worshipful, dominated into a mindless state of slavery.  My will was hers, from the inside out.  Her merest breeze of a whim was my command.  So cum I did, indeed!

I exploded a Fourth of July Sparkle of zillions of microscopic volunteers into her ass.  What happen next was beyond astonishing.  It was phenomenal.

It was if time suspended at the deepest moment of her crush on me, immensely heavy and hot.  In the distance in her body above me I could see her soul as a shining light.  And she could see mine, below her.  Loving, beautiful, and quite spiritual it was, yet fundamentally we both felt how she completely she owned me in that moment, thoroughly all the way through to the spiritual level.

Then we both saw it between us at once, the magic that was in use, combining.  My sperm had been absorbed into her blood stream.  Those individual volunteers were being delivered all over her body, each one disappearing one-by-one, millions-by-millions into individual cells of her body.  Inside those impregnated cells I was being absorbed further or recombined, I couldn't tell or maybe it was some other process beyond my comprehension.  I could see that Debbie did not understand it perfectly either.  But those cells were changing, differentiating, and rapidly so.

The Tingle sought more from me.  It concentrated now in my balls, activating, heating – incubating.  She wanted more; commanded me from inside my own body to cum again already.  And I did with another glorious orgasm and her simultaneous smashing down on me to receive it.

A minute later the Tingle had me up and ready again.  Shortly thereafter a fourth time.  Then a fifth time.  Then a sixth time...  There seemed to be no end to this process, to my renewing supply of sperm, to the amount of orgasms we could manufacture.  With each one I felt my love of Debbie growing.  And with each one I felt her body changing, morphing she was, right on top on me.

How long could this go on – could I go on?  When would this process stop?  But I barely had time to think because OMG, here we go again.

... I remembered bits of the science they tried to teach me.  Some of it was interesting... Oh – Oh – again we came... The average human body had something like 100 trillion cells.  I guessing Debbie's would like have more... Oh, no, this one was going to be even bigger – oh... and again we came and orgasmed... I also recalled quite specifically that the average ejaculation had from 40 million to 1.2 billion sperm.  I recalled that because the range seemed so crazy large... Oh boy, here we go again...oh...oh...  That was a dozy... Let's be generous and say I was spouting one billion per click.  That would take like…  Hold on… can't do math when I'm…oh lordy-lordy "I love you, Debbie!" I shouted. "I love you too!" She shouted back.  …let's see one billion into 100 trillion; that would take like 100,000 ejaculations to impregnate every cell in her body… Oh shit, her we go again… oh… oh… fuck me, fuck me, this was going to be a long night!

Is it possible to go to sleep while being fucked.  Certainly.  But is it possible for both parties to go to sleep and keep on having sex and sex and sex….  Answer, turns out, yes.  After about an hour and a half of orgasms we were exhausted.  Debbie just collapsed on me and went to sleep, that deep, heavy amazon sleep.  She was gone.  I slept also, of a sort: mush-minded, fried-brain, blinking catatonic on tilt, still kind of waking a little for each next orgasm.  Sometimes awake enough to drool and kiss against the upper nethers of her ass/lowest back, my favorite spot, crushed against my face for the night.  I also imagined often, of seeing her bright face smiling into mine, love in her eyes, big beautiful full lips parted suggestively for a kiss… or two… or a thousand….

My dozing disturbed by yet another orgasm, I noticed something seemed different.  Debbie seemed even heavier – or was it denser?  And where did her lower back go, my face was entirely lodged in her upper ass crack now.  Very firm and tight she clamped onto me now, her sleeping body tensing into another quickening succession of orgasms.

***

I dreamed I'd been made into a candy bar or was it a lollipop?  Great hands tore at my wrapper exposing me briefly before a huge set of lips took me in. The fear was intense as I was about to be chewed – no, not chewed – sucked on – I was a lollipop after all… I awoke, relieved, thinking, what does that mean?  That I'm just a big sucker?

It seemed Debbie had definitely moved up on me, or gotten bigger?  My face was definitely down more, between the upper part of her buns.  She was definitely much, much heavier on me.  For sure bigger, I surmised.

I really couldn't move any part of my body except my eyes.  Looking straight ahead, all ass.  But upward there was a feint vee of light, the outline off her upper butt.  Somewhere out there it was morning.  I had survived the night.

But I was still being crushed and felt very weak.  I should have needed to pee, but didn't.  Instead I was incredibly thirsty, dehydrated by the ravaging ordeal.  I had to get some water… soon…. I tried with all my might, to move, to squirm even a little bit. But it was impossible. And there was a density and firmness to her ass that rendered me powerless.

I tried to bite her, but could not get a purchase on her tight, firm skin. I could not shout out, only into her, my scream just ringing back into my own ears.

So I blew raspberries, making a substantial farting noise. But that literally backfired as she only shifted slightly, wiggled, and let out her own real fart, vibrating my whole body. I'm doomed I thought. But I had forgotten about my earlier experience in the van with Fat Debbie. Dear Saint Debbie's warm vapors were nothing but sweet-rose perfumed from a candy store. Considering my pinned proximity I'd caught a big break there.

With nothing to lose I blew more raspberries, and again. Finally she really started to shift, waking. She sat up, stretching and tightening as she did. My God, what intense weight bore down on me.

"Richie? Richie?" I could barely hear her calling my name. "Good morning… where are you?" Then there was a rush of air, blinding bright morning light. "Oh, there you are, Sweetheart."

I blinked, bleary, things slowly coming into focus. Huge perfect tits swayed above my face. Looking all around to my sides I saw that Debbie was on all fours, over me… way over me. And she was different, I mean metamorphosis different. The pear-shaped giantess gumdrop of amoebic love was gone. Replaced by amazon perfection of extraordinary proportions.

Even her face, or especially her face, had changed. She was still obviously Debbie, no mistaking that. But her face, in losing its roundedness, took on a wonderful and elegant character, gorgeous really to gaze upon. Same Debbie full lips, yet more expressive in their lines. Same understanding twinkling eyes, but more penetrating, and eagle-like in their clear intensity. And there was something else… to her look, a very slight otherness that hadn't been there before. Not bad, just different, like a little two percent of someone else's face. Of my face!

The big bed bounced as Debbie got up, leaving me lying there in my state of weakness and confusion.

"Oh my word, would you come look at this." She was over in front of the mirrors. "Come-come-come-come." She yapped, not seeming to understand how feeble I was feeling.  I crawled to the edge of the bed and tumbled off to my feet.  "Come see this body we grew last night, Richie."  Debbie was definitely excited.

I staggered over to her, stumbled a little, then righted myself between the A-frame of spectacular legs.  My head was merely half way up to her thick and shapely mid-thigh.  Unthinking I traced her lines up, looking right above.  That view was a reward-and-a-half.  My breath shuttered out, as I kind of short-circuited by the size of the sexy beauty above.

I could see up no further, so I looked forward to the mirror.  That image was even more shocking and stunning to my system.  I saw a real live goddess standing over my scrawny body.  Huge wide hips, firm and thunderous, snug muscular waist blossoming into great tits so perfectly formed and impossibly outstanding and firm for such proportions.  But there they were: real.  And the regal crown of her radiant, excited face looking right in the mirror and smiling lovingly right back into my eyes.

Transfixed I was for a moment.  But it was too much for me; I felt so spent and frail.  I could hardly even stand. I looked away, and saw my own body, so tiny by comparison.  But something else was amiss.  I looked emaciated; like I had just escaped a prison camp.  What the hell happened to me?

Still, Debbie took no notice, maybe just seeing me with the love of rose-colored glasses.  Bounding away into the bathroom, she called back to me.  "Come on, Richie, let's take a shower together."

As I zombie-trudged to maybe catch up, I hear her exclaim? "Wow, can you believe it, I'm 2,075 pounds!  But I'm not that hungry, so maybe I'll stay this size a while."

When I entered she was already in the shower, singing.

I founded the scales myself.  Good lord, only 60 pounds.  I'd lost some 10 pounds last night.  So thirsty, I went to the sink, climbed up and drank all I could.  That helped a bit, but I was still light headed.  Back at the scales: 61 pounds.  I sighed and shook my head.  Did her Tingle really draw nine pounds of cum from my balls?  My thoughts were spinney, unreal.  What the hell… did I make a sperm for every cell in her body…

Debbie had about four shower heads blasting a torrent of water onto her upper mantel and cascading down.  She beckoned me over, smiling enthusiastic.  I obliged, resting my spine against the back of her knee.  She bent her knee slightly, supporting me a bit with her angled lower leg.  I looked out at the waterfall spilling over from the great booty shelf of her butt – almost at arm's length it rushed by.  I looked up again.  This time my reward, the artistic view of the huge, strong butt cheeks extending prominently back where they met her upper legs, the water cataract a shimmering silver fan off that wide fanny….

I kept staring up transfixed by the imminent doom of her butt.  This was a mere intermission now.  Yet soon, too soon, she would want me again.  And I knew I had no power to say no to her.  What would happen to me next time?  Would she simply absorb me completely?  Would I even exist anymore, other than fractured and trapped inside her?

Something bounced against my foot.  I looked down.  A pink bar of soap.  I looked back up.  The ass was indeed coming to get me, bending opening, now pussy toward me and exposed… darkness.

I woke up, soapy water swirling around me, a noisy drain by my ear.  The bar of soap was gone.  I must have swooned, passed out for a second, and slid to the floor of the shower.  She didn't butt crush me; only picked up the soap.

"Hey, you about finished massaging my feet down there?"  Debbie shouted only a little, to be heard above the blasting waters.  "Soon as I rinse off I'm done."

A half a minute later all was quiet, except the diminishing dripping off her body and onto and around me.  She stood there enjoying her clean feeling.  Me, just curled against her insole.

"You know what?  We still didn't do it yet.  We didn't actually have real sex."

Dumbfounded but not speechless I mumbled.  "What the heck was it, then?  I only came about a thousand times."

"It was anal, right.  That's one reason the sperm absorption worked so well.  But that's not real sex.  I think we should have real sex.  Wouldn't that be just the best way to start the day?"

She stepped out of the shower to finish drying off, leaving her wet ragdoll lover behind, a shivering curled up mess.

"You coming?"

But didn't answer.  I might have been going into shock.

"Richie?" Her concerned tone sounded water-muffled.  Through a blurred haze I saw shapes the color of my dear Debbie coming toward me.  Strong soft hands picked me up.  And I passed out.

When I woke up I was warm and dry, in a soft, smooth place.  My closed eyes I could tell the world was very bright, like sunshine streaming through a window to heat my face."

"Hey there, Sweetie.  Want some more?"

The brightness turned off.  I opened my eyes to see a perfect nipple on a perfect huge breast a breath width from my lips.  Of course I kissed it.  And as it yielded milk, I sucked it.  Each gulp a baby step up in vigor in my body.

Looking around best I could, I discerned that Debbie was sitting on the carpet, her back against the bed, the mid-morning sun flooding in the open bedroom sliding door.  I rested comfortable in Debbie's arm, nursing like a baby on her generous breast.

"You must have been totally famished."  Debbie explained.  "It isn't like me to be so insensitive.  I'm sorry.  I doubt any man has ever turned 15% of his body weight into sperm in one night.  Of course I might have helped that along some, but let's give you the credit."  She peered at me closely.  "You're feeling better now, aren't you?" I nodded, but kept nursing – it tasted out-of-this-world good.  She kept talking.  "Anyway you did indeed, miraculously, make a sperm for every cell in my body. And those little champions were delivered to each and every one."

I was definitely feeling better. I rubbed my hands around the parts of her breast I could reach, which was most of it.  Debbie smiled a little sexual approval of my touch, then continued. "But of course it wasn't a pregnancy thing.  My cells are double chromosome and sperms are just one set.  It wouldn't match up.  It would be like making seedless watermelons."

I had no idea what she was talking about.  I didn't care that much because I was getting milk-mind satiated.  But if my goddess wants to talk genetics…I gazed at her beautiful, radiant face, her mouth moving again.  "So each sperm found a unique application, used in a plethora of ways, many kinds of differentiations, protein enhancements, genetic alterations, even found some enhancements for the Tingle you might like."  I nodded at Professor Debbie.

I couldn't suck another gulp, but did enjoy some lazy licking of that nipple, daydreaming of kissing those lips that kept talking. "Oh, you are in me now, Baby.

Not in any personality sense.  I just slaved up all your little sperm to do my body's bidding day and night, broke them to pieces as needed, and used them for parts every which way."  Sounds kind of violating, doesn't it?"  I just kept dreaming of Debbie's lips and could have cared less.

"So," Debbie sighed, giving my body a little ride up and down; she seemed to be wrapping up the lecture. "…this milk you've been enjoying has the ideal protein and fat blend just for you.  It is made and manufactured inside me, in part, using blueprints of your genetics, altered, of course, to perfection by a woman's touch. You would not need any other sustenance.  My breasts are all you need."

Feeling my oats again, "Except, I would very much like to kiss your lovely lips."

"Oh, that's more like it Baby." And she eagerly descended on my lips with hers. Standing she hugged me all the way in between her breasts, her kiss spreading across my mouth and face.  She kneeled on the bed, lowered a side hip, rolled on out on her side then over onto me, never releasing that kiss, as she pressed and sealed me into the mattress.

Sensing I had some satisfaction Debbie finally released the kiss. Pushing up, she lightly tit-whipped me, playful for her I suppose, but unnerving in her power to own me so easily.  She rose, straightening all the way up to her knees drilling deep into the cushioning on either side of my body.  It was a position of extreme dominance over me.  And I felt like I was withering beneath her abundance and seething lust.

"Think you're finally ready for that real sex?"  She winked, but she was not kidding in the least.  I wanted to immediately blurt out "Yes-yes" but I was having a crisis of confidence.  She was so utterly magnificent.  And what was I, what… nothing but a little baby-man that had to be suckled back to strength for this moment.

"Debbie, this makes no sense.  How… why would someone as incredible as you even want, well, a little man like me?  What kind of lover can I possibly be for you?"

"You're the best lover a woman could possibly want."  It was her stab at a quick answer.  Honest, but kind of deflecting.  She just ached to get on with the sex.

But I wasn't buying it.  "I don't feel like much of a lover.  My deepest desire here, honestly, is just to be owned and smashed by your body.  No thought of technique here, really, just worship.  Goddess Debbie is what you are to me.  And I crave without hope to be massacred by your pussy and absorbed by your ass."  There, I said it, shamefully weak as it sounded; but the bitter truth.

"Oh Richie, you really have no idea what you mean to me.  OK then."  She shifted back and forth on her knees, turning around above me. "Let's get this part out of the way first."  She scooted forward until her feet rested to either side of my head, a fair distance away, and heels up.  "Look at my ass.  Isn't it just the bomb?"  Oh, it was the bomb, all right.  And she was slowly lowering it toward me as she spoke, the yawning crack widening as it approached my face.  "This ass that you "crave" so much is begging me, begging me to let it crush down on you, smother you, and absorb you until you are utterly and completely part of me and there is nothing left that is not owned by it, by me."  Her butt rested on her heels, inches from my face.  "Go ahead…" I heard her say.  "… kiss it if you want.  It is for you.  It is yours."

I raised my head the slight distance required and kissed her so gently and lovingly.  The contact was a connection of emotion and knowingness.  Her butt quivered with delight.  I knew with delicious surrender the punishing lust her ass would love to administer to me this very moment.  With great self-discipline, Saint Debbie rose away from my lips.

I guess the point with a Saint is not whether they have desires, but how they live with them.  It was clear to me that she wanted me more, to own me more, to entirely devour me with her lusting butt and wet-as-we-speak pussy, dominate me with her massive crushing legs, smother me with her great tits of abundance and calamity, and lovingly kiss me to death.  This was Saint Debbie's dark desire revealed in all its glory and doom.  It was by the grace in her most superlative heart that I was still alive.

This time as Debbie turned around above me, she lowered her upper body to her elbows, her cleavage centered on my mid-section, squeezing in on me, her face wonderfully maybe eighteen inches above mine.

She batted her eyes.  "Are you getting the picture now?"

I nodded.  "It's like 'Where the Wild Things Are'.  You 'love me so much you could eat me'."

She laughed at this.  "Something like that.  Probably the X-rated version; where the little man gets eaten by giant ass and pussy."

"That version wasn't on my bookshelf when I was a kid."

"Well, it is now, kiddo.  And you are up front and center this time.  You're the hero."  And more seductively but not joking.  "You're my hero."

Her sincerity was moving for me.  But "hero"? Me?

Of course she could clearly see I wasn't getting it.  "Come on Richie, think big.  Last night your love, and also desire, for me was so complete, you were willing to give up your life to fulfill me.  And in that process you have given me a gift beyond measure.  You helped transform me into this wondrous body.  I love it.  I love you.  Never again will I have to suffer through those blob phases.  Sure I kept up a good attitude; but you knew I wasn't crazy about it.  Who would be?  This beautiful body means many things to me, but especially it will always mean a precious gift from you."

Wow, I had no idea.

She wasn't finished.  "So there you tremble below me, compelled to feel the need to worship me.  Good.  I like that – being your Goddess – knowing how extreme your desires are.  Keep thinking and feeling that way.  I command you: worship me more."  She flashed her eyes, leaving her mouth open, making sure I noticed her tongue licking the inside of her lower lips.  "I fully plan to keep growing, to become more beautiful – for you, Richie.  For *you*, my love.  For you, *on* you, every which way a little man can be owned by a woman."  She let that sink in as she rose above me again, back to that knees-on-either-side high straddle.  "So, now, would you say that we are compatible?"

"It's like we were made for each other."

"No Richie, it's like we were made *by* each other."

"Yes," I nodded. It was true.  There was my dream woman, towering above me, loving me and threatening to annihilate me all at once.  I looked at her in new wonder. "Yes… mistress?"

"You're joking, right?"

I shrugged.

"How about, when you have to go there, I kind of like 'Saint Debbie'." She laughed at that moniker.

But it worked very well for me: "Saint Debbie of the Abundant Smother."

She laughed again.  "How about, 'Our Lady of the Absorbing Ass'?"

"Or," I suggested, more seriously. "… a stunningly beautiful and generous woman I want to know better and better."

Her breath caught, tears formed in her eyes, and as one, then two crocodile teardrops fell to my chest, she smiled dearly and said.  "That'll do."

We took our time with that moment.  After a while, my face almost ached from smiling up at her.

"So…" I said timidly. "Can we even have real sex?"

She snapped out of her reverie, that hungry look clearly in her lusty expression. "Better than you ever imagined."

"Oh, I've imaged a lot."  I kidded, but not really kidding.

"Oh, I imagine you have.  Have you imagined, for example, that I own you for my sex toy?"  I was fully hard immediately. "That's right."  She glanced at my lance. "You better respond."  Oh I loved that tough talk.  "Did you imagine that your sweet gentle Saint Debbie would order you to kiss her pussy, thoroughly using your tongue to get her good and wet."  She grabbed my head and shoulders, brought me up and jammed me in her pussy, but not too deep.  I could still hear her orders. "Lick and kiss, suck and face-fuck."  She ground around on me, moved my head in circular motions.  She got wet very fast.  Then dropped me back down.

"Did you imagine I would grab you legs."  She nabbed my skinny shanks by my ankles.  "Bend one leg down at the knee to turn you into my ultimate pleasure device.  And then shove you in my pussy foot first."  And she did just that.  "That I am so smart that I have calculated that you will slide in up to your little hips."  Her legs spreading, lowered her pussy over first my left leg, then my knees, now including my bent right leg.  Warm and wet, her Tingle was all around me. I slid in easily but snug, deeper, deeper just as she described. "That I would order you to wiggle you feet and toes to drive me crazy."  I did; and it did.

 She spasmed only a small amount; just getting started, I assumed.  "That I would lower my great pussy all the way down your legs until your little buns would just enter me?"  They lodged into her right on cue.  "That the top of your penis would now be against my clitoris, the tip nicely inside me.  And… with… all… that… perfect… stimulation… I… would…go… entirely… insane… on… you."  And she did.

No right-minded person would be fearless in my situation.  But I was pretty close to fearless, too overcome with sensations of love and pleasure to be much mindful of how easily I could be crumpled into nothing but recycled proteins to be assimilated up her ass.  You could not observe her wild thrashing on me and think that Debbie was anywhere near complete control.  But I released and surrendered to her possession of me.  I waggled my toes and feet; like I was told.  Wiggling my legs, kneeing her repeatedly in her G-spot; those were my clever ideas.

When I came, the Sparkle was weak.  I needed a re-charging by the Triplets.  But with Debbie's robust love and lust, and with the crazy contortions I was carrying out inside her vagina, her explosion of orgasm rattled the windows as I incurred the weight of her seismic smash.  I noticed I was definitely cumming inside her.  Finally, after all that foreplay, real sex!  God I hope she's happy now.

Debbie bounced on me, trampoline-ing the bed in harmonic motion.  Giddy like a school girl (but let me be clear, she was no school girl) Debbie clapped her hands and said.  "Let's do that again, backwards."

Before I could say, "Yes Saint Debbie" she whirled that big-rig ass around and pounded it down on me.  As she arranged my legs into the appropriate pretzel, crossing my knees this time, but still with the one-leg bend, I just stared at the big ass hovering, impatient.  I actually whispered to it.  "Oh we had our own special love affair, don't we?"  Can an ass have a smug smile?

"What are you saying down there?"  Debbie was inserting me again.  Quickly was I in her pussy again; right up the hilt of my pelvis.  And that brought her thunder buns smashing down, my thin chest enfolding right into her crack, my face lost between her upper buns.

Debbie was slower this time, deliberate, working me over methodically, staying with repetitions building the vigor to my limit of endurance, backing off a fraction of a moment, finding a slightly new and delightful angle, and on and on and on…

I was mumbling unheard pledges into ass of my Goddess.  "… I'll paint your toenails… I'll go in your mouth and lick your teeth one-by-one… I'll be your footstool, your chair, your beach towel to lie upon… please let me serve you…"  And serve her I did.

It was mid-afternoon when she finally got off me.  Fucked me for some four hours she did.  I was ravaged mush, both my body and my mind.  She, of course, looked no worse for the wear, glowing happy and satisfied, in fact.

"Come on."  She said.  "Let's get you a little sustenance."  With that a swollen tit flopped down on me, turgid with milk.  As I sucked, it shot into my mouth, spilling over me faster than I could lap it up.  Quickly I was feeling invigorated.  She pulled back to check on me.

Already cocky again, I suggested. "How about another go?"

"Yeah, right."  She laughed at my bravado.  "Good attitude, Bucko.  But let's go down and get some real food."  For me that meant – not her milk.  For her that meant – not me.

# XI. Amazon Fun and Games at Widowmaker Park

Sitting side-by-side, the sexy Sanderling sisters maneuvered closer to each other, inching together until now finally their hips were touching.  Sisterly love – how precious that they want to sit so close.  Problem was: I was sitting between them.  Correction: actually now more under them.  Should be wonderful, right?  Especially since these two babes probably sported a couple of the hottest bodies on the Pollination Crew.  Save, of course, Vicky and, need I mention it, the glorious Saint Debbie.

But that was the problem, wasn't it?  No dear sweet Saint Debbie today, Monday in the van.  I didn't even know if she would still fit in the van.  Probably would; it had to be very spacious to accommodate these dozen amazons. Shit.  Where was she?  Was she all right?  Did something happen after she went to the Synsonto labs yesterday?

Grumpy – that's what I was.  Even the pressing attentions of Sandy and Silvia couldn't improve my mood.  You'd think it would.  What, with their silky smooth, spectacular shapely legs resting heavily down on my skinny shanks.  They wore the shortest agricultural hot pants on the crew.  In their case, picture jeans that were cut off starting at the crotch and scissored tapering up and out at a 45 degree angle.  That left a lot of fine ass exposed to the sides, generous warm heavy flesh now riding up onto me more and more.

The cumming contest was only on the way home.  So on the way to work the chosen amazon of the day got to sit by me and tease a bit.  They figured this priming of me could give them an advantage in the afternoon.  Like I'd be half-cocked when we started the rid home and they were on the clock to rock my cock.

The Sanderling sisters had broken the record last week.  But they had also broken the rules, double-teamed me, and Sandy (whose turn it was) had been disqualified.  They were going to make Silvia skip her rotation this week as punishment.  But the Crew took pity on them and let them back in on negotiated terms.

Negotiated terms?  Yeah, so Sandy and Silvia had so much fun with their tandem stacked smash on me, they said they didn't care about the contest anymore.  They just wanted the double-action.  I don't know why the Crew didn't give the rotation slot to someone else.  I'm guessing they wanted to see what the lovey-dovey twins would do to me next.

And it was already kind of beginning.  They had just crossed their legs over mine and each other's.  Of course this much aggression wasn't allowed during the morning ride into work.  But what did it matter; they weren't in the contest anymore anyway.  Silvia and Sandy were just in it for the fun.

Now fresh morning breasts pressed my face softly from either side.  My Volunteer down below was eager to go, in words would have said: "Now-boss?  Now-boss?"  But hell; I was nobody's boss.  The sisters were being amazingly tender and loving.  Even though at some level I knew clearly that they just wanted to pound the hell out of me with their asses, their current gentleness was getting to me.  They each took one of my hands and guided me to caress their silky golden-tanned legs.  They made little cooing sounds, leaning over me, breasts a little heavier over and on me now.

Above I could tell they were lightly kissing each other on the lips.  I could feel how much they loved each other and it was poignant for me.  Nestled in that their little love nest, I thought of Debbie, I thought how much I was also missing the Triplets I hadn't seen since Friday, I thought of poor Miss Strickland I hadn't seen or even bothered to call since Thursday.  I just felt terrible, guilty and lonely, even in the midst of this loving attention.  And it was all catching up with me, I suppose, all the overwhelming attention these Amazons had been giving me.

Up to this summer, my love-life, well, my non-existent love life, had been one gigantic deprivation. My intrinsic long-term loneliness and isolation finally collided head-on with the sexual sensory overload and extreme affection of all these Amazons.  The casualty of that impact, you could say: a wreck my emotions.  I started to cry, not a lot, but tears fell, I admit.  Hey, real men cry, dudes.  Sometimes the emotions are just too much and they flood over.  It happens.  And it happened to me, unfortunately I thought, right in the middle of a van full of big sexy Amazons.  How embarrassing – but I couldn't help it.

"Hey," The sisters had pulled back enough to see my face, and I theirs. Taking turns talking: "What's the matter?  Are we hurting you?  We were trying to be gentle."

Suddenly everyone in the van was concerned.  It was all: "You OK, Richie."  Even Bad Jackie was, "Hey man, like what's going on?"

I had no idea they all actually cared about me that much.  That really got the faucet in my eyes going more.  It was Silvia that pulled me to her bosom, holding me in tight, rocking me while I quietly wept.  I felt Sandy patting me sympathetically on my back.

I felt the van turning when we should have kept going straight to get to work.  After a bit, the road became bumpy with a crunchy sound – must be gravel.  A couple more turns and stretches, then it stopped.  The door opened.  I knew this place.  We'd arrived at Widowmaker Park.

Technically Drury Samuelsson Whittaker Memorial Park, named after the first mayor of Bluebelle Bend.  The Bluebelle River made a big wide curve through this park.  Story was some 110 years ago popular Mayor Whittaker was canoeing on a Sunday afternoon.  His wife and seven children played and swam just downstream near the big sandbar, Poppy Island.  At the moment that Mayor Whittaker came gliding past the island, his family waving from the shore, a big elm from the main shore had reached the end of its 250 year life and came crashing down over the water.  It killed the poor mayor right in front of his family.  Killed he was by a Widowmaker – that's what they called those trees big trees in this region that give up life all at once with such unpredictability and dire consequences.  It was real easy for "Whittaker" to be become "Widowmaker" in the intervening years.

On this bright calm Monday morning at 7:15, Widowmaker Park defined serenity, beautiful and sunny, and seemed to have no bad memories.  The place also appeared completely devoid of people and probably would be all day – excepting us, of course.

The Crew spilled out of the van, Silvia carrying me out and setting me down.  The amazons circled around me in support, eleven sets of sexy field-work toned legs, all as tall as or taller than me, forming a nice pen around me.

They proceeded with a discussion about what to do, to cheer me up, that is.  Someone said. "What about over their?"

I didn't know where she pointed but looking past their legs I spied a beautiful grassy area, mowed short a few days back, on a very gentle slope toward the river.  Flowers bordered the meadow area, then tall (and dangerous) trees, then the Bluebelle making its lazy arch through the little memorial park.

Someone else said: "We could use that big cloth tarp in the back.  That would work."

Then: "I'll get it."

I had quit crying by now.  The little park was so lovely and fresh and sunshiny.  Sandy and Silvia held my hands as we walked along.  Over around a stand of ash trees rested more of the lawn but out of sight from the little gravel parking lot, very serene and private.

There they had spread out the tarp.  I was big, maybe 30x30 feet, and pre-season clean.  The cloth felt soft from many years' use and puffed up a little uneven and funny-crunchy from the grass below.  In the middle Sandy and Silvia stopped and sat down.  They pulled me down to sit between them.  The rest of the Crew followed suit around us.  Sandy removed my shoes.  Silvia took off my shirt and gently laid me back.  "Close your eyes and relax."  She whispered to me like a spa attendant.

After a few minutes, I think it was Jeanie that spoke close to my ear.  "How about a game to cheer you up?"

"What game?"  I didn't open my eyes.

She kissed me very evenly, not too much, not too little, on my lips.  "We'll do that – kiss you.  And you try to guess who it is."

"I don't know, maybe…"  But she cut me off with another kiss.  "I mean shouldn't we be getting to work…" She cut me off again, just a tiny bit more insistent and it worked.  "Well, OK then.  I think you're Jeanie."

"Hey, no fair," She protested.  "You have to guess without us talking.  I get another turn – later."

"But I already know your kiss."  I had her there.

"I'll have to disguise it."  She retorted, and I heard her move away.

I readied myself.  Let's see there was: Sandy and Silvia, Jeanie of course, Bethany, Bad Jackie, Cecelia, Janet, Vicky, Coleen, Jessica, and MaryEllen.  Eleven – without dear Saint Debbie.  OK I was ready; bring it on.

"Pucker up."  One Silvia Sanderson called from the distance.  Ha, I thought, obviously not her first.

The first set of lips presented very nicely with a loving kiss.  Her hair fell across my face and smelled very familiar.  It was someone from last week in the contest.  I could see her reddish-blond waves blowing in the wind from the open van window. Oh, wait, I got it, the balmy beauty: "Bethany."

She ended her kiss good and firm. "Yes. Very good."

I opened my eyes and looked up into her face. Her sweet kiss made her look even more attractive.

"Nice kiss." I complemented her.

"Thank you, Richie. You too. Now close your eyes again." And she left. I was amazed by how gentle these, usually viciously aggressive, amazons could be.

Another shadow loomed over me. I could almost feel the self-assured energy off this one, even before the kiss. Her kiss landed on me very confident and I could see why. This gal knew how to lay one on. She employed great technique, something in the attitude, a tipping forward in her lower jaw as she partially opened her mouth, giving and taking at the same time, and building to end with just a bit of play with a curled tongue.

"Wow!" I said as she broke off. There was only one chick on this Crew that could strut her stuff I like that – cocky, confident, and very practiced at love-making, from what I'd heard: "Vicky." And I opened my eyes to her sweet-knowing look of proven superiority over men.

"How about another one?" Vicky was extremely irresistible and she knew it.

But before I could say. "Sure." The other girls hauled her playfully away, calling back to me to close my eyes again.

Another shadow. Right away there was the smell of Lavender. Her face approaching mine was like immersion into a bouquet of those purple-blue flowers. I could have been 2000 miles away on lying in a blooming field of those healing blossoms, cool breezes wafting off the Olympic Peninsula. I remember the day she sat on me in the front seat, her turn at the contest. Oh she was vigorous and as talented as any of them. But her aroma was so therapeutic and relaxing I only came one time, a little bit and at the city limits. Ah, the lavender jewel: "Jessica." I opened my eyes to see that precious pixie face, so incongruous on a woman of her stature. "Lovely, my dear."

She sing-songed back. "Thank you Richie."

I knew the routine and closed my eyes again.  This next lady was very quiet of movement and had no strong scent or particular kind of energy to give her away.  But the first touch of those extra-big full lips and I knew this one at once.  Of course I made sure she got her full measure of me.  It felt terrific to be kissed lovingly by such a luscious pucker.  She kept it up a while, sensing my high enjoyment.  At last she broke it off.  To give her some extra cred with the Crew I took my time, pretending to be flummoxed.  Finally I "guessed": "Coleen?"

I blinked open "hoping" to be right.  Goodness what a looker; and those lips – you could marry a woman like Coleen and just be happy to have lips like that to kiss every day.  She playfully thumped my shoulder. "You knew all along, didn't you?"

"Actually, I'm still not so sure." I joked. "Could we do that again?"  And before they could stop her Coleen did plant another excellent kiss on me.

My eyes were closed again.  This shadow pounced on my whole body, the kiss definitely a bit over-aggressive for this gentle game.  But I knew who this was, for sure Bad Jackie, and she couldn't help it the way she was.  The others were already lifting her off me.  Still, I wanted to be kind.  "That was fun – and creative.  Could that be Jackie?"  I opened my eyes to her smile, appreciative of that kindness I showed her, that in front of the others, as far as I was concerned, she had played the game well.

The next one was all about French kissing.  Not the let's work up to it subtle Frenching.  But the tongue first, lips second.  I wasn't crazy about it, but she was very practiced at the techniques I had to admit.  But who the heck would kiss like this?  Then I thought about each of the remaining ladies, picturing them.  And I recalled; once we had stopped in town for ice cream.  Maybe five minutes after everyone else, including me, had finished their cones, there she was still licking and licking the vanilla to a fine peak, working around the cone to meticulously catch every drip before it could hardly get started down the side: "MaryEllen."

"How could you tell?"  She really had no clue how distinct she was.

I knew everyone was probably sensitive about their kisses and technique.  "Oh, you know; who else would put so much into it."

She seemed happily satisfied with that explanation.  "Well, we can do more later; if you like it that much."

You want to know what?  I would not have refused her, tongue and all.

I wanted to tell the next gal that I liked curry, too.  And like her, I loved to fry it in with my omelets, like she had this morning.  Or put it in a salad for a spicier lunch at work – also like I noticed she did often.  But that didn't matter so much that I knew who she was right away.  What mattered was what was really happening here.  The Crew was being super nice to me.  Just because they used me for a sex toy and had been crushing me all summer without mercy, apparently didn't mean they didn't respect me, moreover care about me.  Odd ducks, these amazons: the more I actually got to know them the more amazed I became.  They might treat me like their little bitch at times, OK, most of the time.  But when the chips were down for me, they came through big time.  And I really appreciated it.

The other thing I appreciated right then was that their kisses were for me for sure.  But there were also some bragging rights at stake.  Like I knew, when this was all done, these competitive warriors-at-heart were going to want to know who kissed best.  I figured that was 100% predictable.  So really, the kisses were also a contest, and I'd been getting their best shot.  And I have to say, by and large, they were fantastic kisses.

"Curry cheeks" was no different.  She supplied yet another first kiss that left me feeling like, how many times in one day could a man fall in love?  I was losing my heart to this.  I could find no resistance to their kindly advances.  What, am I kidding, trust these bitches?  Yes, I guess; like any man getting a dose of love like this, my memory was short and getting shorter all the time.  The only thing long about me was… well, you know….

Finally she broke it off with a flourish of little nibbles at my lower lips, like she could just eat me up.  Nice job: "Cecilia."  I open my eyes and gave her a genuine nod of approval.  Satisfied with that reaction and her performance, she smiled kindly at me and with a tad of borderline too-smug for the other gals.

The next one was two.  Now there's a mystery.  I wonder which two girls would team up on me like that.  Both their kissy-kissy mouths attacking mine at the same time.  Given their size and mine, that pretty much meant kisses all over my face.  Still very loving, that was important.  But also extremely sexy – hot!  Who else, they made me say it with my eyes still closed: "Sandy and Silvia."

"Surprise!"  They laughed, yet looked intently at me with desire so strong and obvious I felt my heart racing.  They were very tuned on.  "Oh, don't get too excited now.  There's still two more to go."  We can party later, sometime.

That's right, still two more.  This one smelled very fresh and flowery, kind of earthy-rich.  Her kiss made me want to plant something in her garden. Wow.  Well it wasn't Jeanie; I'd recognize her kiss from earlier.  I took my time while she worked over my face, preparing it for springtime with here combinations of action of lips, teeth, and tongue.  When she finally finished, and each of these kisses seemed to have taken longer than the one before, I was confident to announce: "Janet."

She held my face briefly with both her hands, but did not seek to kiss me again.  It was a great long look to say. "Hey, know that we care about you."

I sighed, and said. "Thank you."  Sitting up I continued.  "Thank you to all of you."

"Hold on a second."  Sandy lightly pressured me back down flat.  "There's still one more."

"But I already k…"

But Sandy cut me off.  "Hush now.  Everybody gets their turn.  Be a good sport. Close your eyes."

The last shadow was above me.  Duh, I wonder if it's Jeanie.  But this kiss was diffcrent; big and wet and a lot… of… pressure.  I opened my eyes to say "Jeanie" but it was too late.  Her pussy already covered my face, and all was dark, sweet, and juicy.  She rode on me for about five minutes, kind of nice and easy, and again, very loving.

When she climbed off, I kept my eyes closed, still playing the game.  The sun was really bright, until my pupils contracted under my eyelids.  "Oh, let-me-see, let-me-see… was it Bethany?"

"Not me."  And I heard her laughing maybe five feet away.

Still I teased Jeanie.  "Oh, I know, it was MaryEllen.  Wait, no Bad Jackie."  There was a lot of laughing now.

That got to her.  "Knock it off."  She gave me a little slap to my cheek; my eyes opened on that.  "Or I'll sit on your face again, this time good and proper."

"Oh, no.  Not that." I put my hand to my mouth.  All the ladies laughed at this.

Still Jeanie acted stern.  "Don't try and tell me you didn't like it."  She gave a pretend grab to the tent in my shorts.

"Hey." It was Vicky. "That right there gives me a great idea." Let's have another contest."

"Oh yeah," Janet saw right away. "Only instead of recognizing kisses, he has figure out whose pussy is on his face."

"God that sounds like fun!" Bad Jackie was on board.

"Wait a minute." Silvia sounded really enthusiastic. Instead of that, how about tandem-style: a face sit *and* a blow. Teams of two. He has to guess who facesits and who gives the blow-job."

"Brilliant!" Cecelia liked it a lot.

"But there's eleven of us? Odd number." Jessica had a valid practical consideration.

"I know. I know." Bethany chimed in. "Look, it's two-four-six-eight and the last team gets three."

"What's the third one do?" Sandy didn't normally think beyond a tag-team of two.

"Whatever she wants." Bethany shrugged. "Let that team decide."

The all turned to me expectantly, with a silent, collective "Well?"

I looked at them, friendly, smiling and laughing. Here we were in this beautiful park on a wonderful summer morning; could have been on a deserted island a thousand miles from civilization. And golly-gosh, they were actually asking if it was okay with me to play some smothering dominance games. I felt way beyond tempted and tantalized. "Well, I'm no party-pooper."

"No," Vicky stepped forward, her legs towering up on either side of me. "… You aren't a party-pooper at all. What you are is a party favor." She lowered herself to her knees straddling me. "Do you mind? Someone needs to sit on your face nice and tight while we figure out our teams." And with that she lowered a very, very delicious pussy onto my face, squeezing it and legs and butt all around my head. I couldn't hear. But I could still think, figuring I'd know this pussy anywhere from now on. Probably later, once she teamed up though, it would be Vicky giving me the blow job, not this delectable facesit.

After about fifteen minutes Vicky released my head and got off my face.  I will admit, I did not keep my tongue in my mouth the whole time.  Vicky looked at me approvingly.  "Good job in there Richie.  I owe you one for that."

The amazons had decided that each team would get twenty minutes.  They figured that about one hour forty minutes was about as much face fucking as I could take.  Oh so little did they know.  Less than two days ago Saint Debbie had ridden me for some four hours, at one time.  But that's OK.  I wasn't looking to break any records today.  I was just playing along now.  These friends, because that is at least in part what they were being for me, had me in a much better mood.  Really, kind of a frigging great mood!

"By the way, before we get started here."  It was Jessica.  "What about that last contest.  Who was the best kisser, Richie?"

I'd had time to think about this answer.  "You know, a gentleman would never say, nor kiss and tell of sweet love's intimacies.  What can I say of such adorations bestowed, like falling in love all over again with each first kiss.  My dear friends who comforted me in my hour of sadness, my greatest wish for you, is that you could know the pleasures of your unique and talented kisses.  Never has there been such a fine crew for support and affection.  I can only say, as the humblest of your admirers, that to know the best there is, you could consent to kiss each other.  That, my esteem lovelies, would be the greatest pleasure of all I could only dream to comprehend."

They stared at me, dumbstruck in wonder.  I'm sure they'd never heard a local man give a Shakespearean speech like that before.  Vicky spoke first.  "That's it.  I don't want any of these hill-billy boyfriends from around here anymore.  I only want you!"

I looked around, all the rest were nodding agreement.  I felt like the last drumstick dropped into a pride on hungry lionesses.  Half of them were licking their lips, sexually hungry for sure and also acutely and seriously infatuated.  I might have overshot a bit with the eloquent words, overshot into one of those very dangerous Amazon love-frenzies that almost killed me at my birthday party of the office.

But I noticed Jessica was looking at Coleen, and reached out to touch her arm.  I think what she said next might have saved my life.  "Coleen.  I want to kiss you.  I've been wanting to kiss you all summer.  Your beautiful lips drive me crazy every day.  I just want to…"  She did not get to say more because Coleen turned to Jessica and kissed her very gently and as lovingly as I had received.  Jessica looked at me a second.  "You are so right, Richie."  Then immediately back to Coleen the two locked lips, slowly kneeling to the ground, kissing and necking.  Bethany approached Sandy and those two locked lips as well.  Janet found her secret love MaryEllen.  Silvia approached Jackie.  Janet and Cecelia paired up.

That left sexy, hot, experienced and confident Vicky, who had not taken her eyes off me once during the fray around her.  She stepped forward then kneeled over me.  "I guess you're all mine."  Then Vicky attacked me in warrior-amazon style.  Seduce and subdue; her clear mission to own me with her love and domination.  With love being the active sentiment that had not been there before.

While the other ten newly-uninhibited women evolved into a full-fledged amazon orgy, the beautiful Vicky had me all to herself.  She sat her pussy on my face, then fucked me, tit-whipped me, kissed me more, made me eat her pussy again, then her lovely ass, smothered me with in her armpits and her very ample breasts, crush-hugged me and rolled with me down the hill all the way to the sand at water's edge.  There we were all alone.

Vicky pinned me on the sand, my little volunteer straight up into her pussy, her inner thighs flattening my body all the way up, her knees past my head.  Extremely flexible, Vicky bent and rested her upper body all the way down on the tops of her thighs, her excellent regal breasts finding a nice pathway between her knees to my face and my lips.  In this position of total ownership of me, Vicky spoke in all sincerity, a fully confident woman who knew clearly what she wanted.  "You are the man I have been waiting for.  Exactly the man I want.  I want to marry you, make you my husband."

I tried to speak.

"Shhh, baby."  Vicky kept a smothering breast on my mouth, entire face actually.  "Just listen.  Marry me and you will have thorough mind-blowing sex every day for the rest of your life.  I know exactly what you want.  And I will do it to you, on you in thousands of different ways you never imagined.  Why?  Because I am sure I love you and that I will love you more each day, each month, each year.  I also know you will love me more, as I make you mine.  Not a slave, no, though you will certainly beg to be my slave.  I want your desire for me to be so deep and all-consuming that your very existence will be for the pleasures I press and smother into your little body under my magnificence.  With your permission, I will sit on you face now, until you say yes Mistress Vicky."

It actually was very temping, she was exceptionally beautiful and so sure of herself; but in my heart, that heart that she wanted, I felt unsure or perhaps still knew better.

"Oh Vicky," I felt myself trembling with internal conflict, looking up at her gorgeous brown eyes… oh hell, it wasn't any of her fine and perfect features.  It was her adoring and supremely confident, self-assured dominance that everything she just said was absolutely true and we both knew it. Yet, some part of my mind managed to speak my innermost truth, exerting itself to be heard against all odds. "I have to say no to your offer as stated.  I believe what you say is true.  But understand I already have girlfriends, lovers."  Vicky sat up to look at me, and I continued as I surprised both of us by saying. "I would like you to come meet the Triplets and get to know us.  There is more to be revealed that I think you will appreciate and love, actually.  I would also like to spend more time with you because you are very awesome.  Meanwhile, how about we make the rest of this morning into an eternity?"

Vicky didn't say anything.  But I think she must have liked those terms well enough.  She grinned at me, and maybe at herself a bit.  Then, laughing, she rose up, turned, planted her really fine big butt on my head, eating me face first with her superlative ass.  Vicky pinned my legs under hers and pulled to spread both her and my legs apart.  In this position of utter domination over me, Vicky bounced on me, her butt on my face, her pussy on my chest, her heavy upper legs crushing my abdomen, her inner thighs skillfully squeezing my erection, her legs trapping and covering my legs all the way until her strong calve muscles rested on the instep of my pressed feet.  God, did she ever know how to dominate a little man!  If Vicky would have paused right then and asked me again to marry her, I would have said "yes" without hesitation.  She squeezed her ass tight onto my worshipping lips and tongue.  With her talented hands and nimble fingers, Vicky went to work between her legs, grabbing my little insistent pole and vibrating her hands up and down until I felt insane with overstimulation.

On and on Vicky crushed her magnificent love onto me.  I was reduced to a slobbering little slave, pressed into the wet sand.  Vicky ground her ass around and around and around on me until I could not possibly be more fervent.  Then she suddenly shifted to the most domineering, twisting down pussy smother conceivable.  Such sweet, tasty, delicious pressure! And Vicky was true to her word, not even close to running out of ideas that thrilled me.

  When I was completely worn out and worthless, Vicky dragged me down into the river, and baptized me with her pussy on the softer sand in the shallow waters.  I appreciated the coolness swirling around my drifting legs as she continued to facesit me hot and relentlessly in the shallows.  After what would have drowned any other person five times over, Vicky finally hauled me out and stretched me out on the hot sand to recover.

"You take it easy a while, Richie.  You've fucking earned it, you little doll.  I'll be up on the hill."  With that, my still energetic and strong lover went back up the grass to join the raging orgy.

After about an hour I felt much better.  My sadness from earlier was undetectable.  I decide I'd go up and see what all the ruckus was about.

It seemed the amazon orgy had died down quite a bit.  Worn themselves out it appeared, all lying around nude on each other, asleep for the most part.  I found a comfy spot, kind of a tunnel between the asses of MaryEllen and Jeanie, topped over with Bethany's tits hanging down between the two big butts.  I crawled into that lushes cocoon, lodging in nice and snug.  I knew how soundly they snoozed so I had fun playing with their sleeping asses, and licking at the big tits hanging onto me from above.

After a while, I heard stirring outside my nest.  Then, "Hey, I think I found Richie." Someone was tickling at my foot."

"Oh, it looks like he wants to play dog pile."

Up went the chorus.  "Dog pile.  Dog pile."  And my sleeping cocoon of three had like a second to wake up before eight more women piled on top of them – and me.

Well, I like a good scrum as much as the next guy.  But I have to say some two plus tons of giant women wiggling around on top of me, each amazon more insistent than the next to get her ass onto me, well, let's just say that's definitely my kind of sporting event.

"Wait a minute!"  I think Coleen might have separated from the pile, protesting. "This dog-pile just isn't what it's cracked up to be."

I thought, "I beg to differ."  My left leg was off between a tight set of upper thighs, my right leg squeezed deep in someone's buns, each arm up to the elbows in pussy, my head backed into ass with another sandwiching down on top, and an eager sucking mouth devoured my entire ball and cock assembly.  That's, what, at least six maybe seven "cracks".  I had to disagree with Coleen; that, no, I was cracked up quite well, thank you.

But the frustration was kind of general.  Eleven at once just couldn't get enough of me.  I guess their previous orgy lacked enough man-flesh.  So this frenzy was all about gaining access onto me.  I actually might have been at some risk of being torn apart.  But I was enjoying it too much to care.  Anyway, it didn't matter.  They piled off, mumbling agreement with Coleen.

I lie recovering there at their feet as they milled around over me decided what to do next.  I was being nudged and offered feet to kiss, because they knew I liked that.  It kept me busy; though I was quite sure it wasn't near enough to satisfy them.  MaryEllen suggested they might need to get to work eventually.  That held some consensus, but they wanted one more game in the park before they went.

"Let's just do what we planned earlier, you know, the tandems: one of us sits on his face and the other a blow job."  Jessica had a good practical suggestion.

"Screw that!"  Silvia and Sandy said together.

Sandy: "One backwards on his face."

Silvia: "The other frontwards on his cock."

Sandy: "Then we can face each other and kiss at the same time."

That turned out to be a popular proposition, but with two caveats: only ten minutes per team and no making me cum.

Again I had to keep my eyes closed as the first team climbed on me.  The game was: I was supposed to guess who sat on my face and who rode my cock.  Ten minutes left little time for subtleties.  A wonderful tight pussy pressed across my face.  Then this woman crisscrossed her legs over my chest.  This opened that pussy and centered its weight on me to shove it down all the way over my head.  Her companion mounted my cock and lower body, lifting her legs up to rest on her partner's crossed legs.  That maneuver maximized her weight on my lap area.  I could tell they leaned toward each other; probably started kissing and making out.

Their positioning did not allow for them to pound up and down on me with their pussies.  But it did maximize a very steady crushing weight my body.  As I imagined their deep passionate kisses, fondling each other's huge breasts, squirming as they could to force me deeper inside them, I got very excited.  I liked to pretend I'd had enough, wanted them off me, fought against their great weight, tried to buck them off, but it was all completely and absolutely futile.  They exerted terrific and perfect pressure on me, hot, wet, and obliterated in the darkness of deep pussy – then suddenly it was over.

Keeping my eyes closed, I was ordered to guess which two gals.  I had no idea and didn't care.  How about: "Bethany and Jeanie?"

"Wrong!"  And they were delighted to be winning this game already.  I told you, these bitches were competitive.

The next three sets used the same perfect tandem smash, steady and absolute smothering.

"Jackie and Janet?"

"Wrong!" and ha-ha-ha.

"Silvia and Coleen?"

"Wrong!" and oo-la-la.

"MaryEllen and Ceclia?"

"Wrong!" and yippie-yi-yay!

At least for the last three, by what they told of the first eight, I knew it was going to Bethany, Sandy, and Vicky.  What a triple whammy!

Closed eyes.  I recognized this big, delicious pussy, as Bethany spread it over me, engulfing my face and head.  Down below, the sexiest ass sat on me so confidently, and I knew I was lodged up in Vicky's flawless pussy.  I found out later how Sandy applied all her weight on me, driving down the pussies of her two compatriots.  She airplaned herself, her body facing down, legs on Bethany's broad shoulder, her pussy shoved into Bethany's face. Sandy bridged straight across high above my body, to embrace Vicky and lock lips in a ten minute kiss.

Bethany and Vicky got a seesaw motion going, rocking Sandy's weight in up and down tilting.  Their sweet pussy pounding grew quite intense.  All bets were off on the no-cumming rule.  I had seemed to settle down to a base-line of 10% Sparkle.  That might not sound like much but it drove them crazy when I was passing surrender on the way toward eventual cumming.  But it wasn't enough to send them over the top right away either.  So the triumphing trio kept on with their oil-derrick hammering of me for and extra thirty minutes.

I built up, somehow generating Sparkle up to some 20%, exploding up into sweet Vicky, who spasmed, and sent the charged orgasm into her kiss with Sandy, who clenched her pussy tight into an orgasm into Bethany's face, who then completed the circuit with a gusher orgasm flooding down on yours truly.  In their writhing ecstasy, Sandy lost her purchase and came crashing down on me like a soft boulder.

Jackie, Coleen, MaryEllen and Jessica watching, couldn't take it any, and jumped on board and tightly packed in, straddling the fallen Sandy and dropping their ass-weight on her – and me.  Cecelia sat pussy forward on Bethany's shoulders, and Jeanie did the same with Vicky.  I especially felt that baring down on my face, cock already in too much glorious detonation to notice.  Janet and Silvia dove on top of it all.  And for a teetering timeless moment I felt their combined weight fucking my life away.  Then the amazon structure on me collapsed in squeals and laughter.

They rolled off and away until at last Bethany extracted my head from her pussy with kind of a slurpy suction sound.  In a very good mood, they all laughed at that as well.

Out in the midday sun I just lie there, feeling as flat as the tarp beneath me.  I could tell they were putting their cloths back on, getting ready to clear out.  I kind of chuckled to myself and called out weak and hoarse. "Hey gals," They paused to listen. "Double or nothing on my last guess: Bethany on my face, Vicky on my volunteer, and Sandy as the airplane."

They laughed more, sing-songing their approvals.  Then Coleen shouted out.  "We need to shake some life into this dude."  Next thing I knew the tarp was rising from the ground with me rolling into the middle of it.  I sat up teetering and looked around.  Eleven grinning amazons had the tarp edges in their strong hands.  Then it was: "ONE – TWO – THREEEE!!!"  And I went up in the air.

And I don't mean some little five foot kiddie ride.  I mean to tell you I went flying up to see-the-next-county high.  Fifty feet in the air and I could see the whole park and the Bluebelle River's big turn.  They caught me deftly with athletic timing.  Then up again, much higher this time, way up, well over the tree canopy, maybe one hundred feet.  The view was extraordinary… and then scary as shit dropping back down.

The third time I shot up even faster, but something went askew and I flew off at an angle.  Crap, I was flying off way to the side, towards the river, but I would hit short of it.  How could they be so spastic?  Then I saw her, Coleen, running at break-neck speed, looking back and up at me, at my terrified expression no doubt, and laughing as she sprinted.  She caught me with soft hands and pulled me to her cushioning bosom as she tumbled onto the sandy beach for the fun of it.

I realized that they'd had too much time to talk while I was up in the air the first and second time.  It was their plan to toss me off course, to freak me out, on the third time.  Of course Coleen could have been all-pro on any NFL team.  But they had banned amazons after the first try-out made all those big tough guys look like cub scouts playing hop-scotch.

The others jogged up, hooting with laugher and jest at their ruse.  When they saw my face, looking like some kind of mummy monster, thickly and completely plastered with sand embedded into the Bethany's sticky pussy juices that still coated my entire head and shoulders, well, they just fell over in hysterics.

"That's not funny!"  I was still trying to steady my adrenaline.

Coleen stood and hauled me up, presenting me more to the rolling-on-the-ground crew, and declared.  "You smell like pussy."  She was laughing too much to sound disgusted as she tossed me out into the river.  Coleen called after me, sassy.  "Clean yor-self up, Sandman.  Time to get to work!"

# XII. Giantess Amends under Miss Strickland

We rolled into the Research Station parking lot about 12:30p.  Across the wide lawn next to parking lot, the outside door of the Plant Genetics lunchroom banged open.  Out stormed skinny and dorky-looking Dr. Pfister, waving and gesturing like a man fit-to-be-tied.  His short legs worked puppy-fast to scurry him across the grass, then the pavement, and to the gravel where MaryEllen curved the van toward the experimental corn fields.

God we were laughing still, having had such a blast down at Widowmaker Park all morning.  Jackie had handed me a tuna sandwich on the ride in, and that was a life-saver for me.  I was feeling fairly restored emotionally by all the fun and games with, and mostly underneath, eleven frolicking amazons hell bent on making sure I had a good time.

Dust trailed the van as we followed along the gravel road, parallel to a ten inch lay-flat main-line for the drip irrigation system. Vicky snickered without hiding her repugnance at the impatient and pissed off boss coming their way. "What an asshole."  Now please understand that Dr. Pfister was their boss, not mine.

"Keep on driving slowly…" Sandy whispered loudly to MaryEllen. "…and speed up when he gets closer."  Everyone laughed softly at that ruse.

"Don't let that nerd catch up with us."  Coleen instructed an obliging MaryEllen.

With the others, I looked back Dr. Pfister, in his chartreuse and mustard checkered shorts, white pith helmet, high black socks, and soiled beige loafers.  I squinted, commenting almost to myself: "Why does he wear his shirt inside-out?"

Vicky heard me, leaned over and whispered hotly in my ear. "Because the dumb fuck doesn't know his ass from a hole in the ground."

The corn pollination-block grew alongside this road.  It was being watered through drip-tapes from the swollen main-line.  The tall tassels certainly would appreciate the moisture on their roots on this warm afternoon.   The nerd Pfister started shouting too soon, before he was really up even with the van.  MaryEllen sped up, spinning the tires enough, dusting him in a thick gray cloud.

Pfister almost caught up again, coughing. "Hey, stop-that-van-right-now."  He bit off his words.  What a control freak, I thought.

"What a control freak." Said Vicky. I smiled at that synchronicity, and thought about her spontaneous marriage proposal of just a few hours ago. Ah, what a glorious lifetime of great fun and sex that would be with her.

Pfister was actually yelling at his employees now. "You're late! You're late-late-late. We've missed a day's…" MaryEllen jerked forward again, more dust. Pfister coughed, "I'm telling you…" More dust, more coughing.

"That should do it, don't think?" Suggested Janet.

MaryEllen must have agreed, pulling to a stop and shutting down the engine.

"I got this." Bethany opened the van door. "This little peckerneck has been staring up my blouse all summer." She had a sexy tan leg out the door now.

"Mine too." Added Cecilia

Bethany reached to take Cecilia's hand. "Well come on girl. I think it's about time our good doctor gets the attitude adjustment he deserves."

The rest of us got out to watch. Vicky stood beside me. I whispered up to her, concerned a bit. "I've been looking up your blouses too…"

Vicky kneeled behind me, her great legs on either side of me, leaning down, her breasts heavy on my shoulders, and whispered back. "We know, Sweetie, up our blouses, and our skirts, and shorts, checking out our big asses for fit on your face. We know," She patted my head. "…and we love you all the same, maybe more. So you keep on looking all you want. Now let's watch this."

Wow, Vicky impressed me with that acceptance, and I thought, maybe Synsonto could clone me so I could run off with Vicky and still live with the Triplets… and maybe another one for Debbie… well, and other clone to fool around with Pool Girls etcetera, and….

As Bethany and Cecilia approached, Dr. Pfister began wagging his finger at them. At that distance I couldn't really make out what he was saying. But his pitch crept up, getting higher as Bethany and Cecilia took steps toward him. They were definitely in his personal space now, towering over him from their exposed midriffs up. Pfister tried to keep eye contact with them, moving his head around, trying unsuccessfully to see around their big breasts. And once again he ended up looking up their knotted blouses.

Bethany untied and unbuttoned hers, letting it fall open in from of him.  Right near them, the pollination block had a set of four rows that were shorter at this end, probably to accommodate a shift point in the project layout.  It was the perfect little spot to have Dr. Pfister step off the road so they could continue the discussion.  Out of sight from the offices they were now, but in perfect view for us.

Pfister followed Bethany into that open space, with Cecilia right behind.  Bethany stopped, turned abruptly, and took a step back toward Pfister.  He bumped into her, face into her belly.  This knocked off his pith helmet, which Cecilia caught midair and sent it sailing, UFO Frisbee-like, well out into the corn field.  Stepping forward, Cecilia pinned Dr. Pfister between herself and Bethany.  While Cecilia took off her top, Bethany unleashed her bra, her big tits bouncing out over Pfister's head.  A few seconds later, out came Cecilia's big hooters, interlocking with Bethany's.

Now they pressed on him. The big ladies lowered themselves to their knees, and his pithless head lodged with no room to spare between four big bouncy tits.  They hugged each other very firmly and the two stood again.  This, of course, lifted the dominated doctor right off the ground, his legs kicking and arms flailing to the sides.  He was probably short of air; oh I remembered that panicky feeling.  But given the beauties that smothered him, it was hard to feel sorry for the poor sucker.

Warm luscious breasts pressed against the sides of my head, but I could still hear Vicky say to me. "I want to try that with you sometime soon."  Her hand reached around and played with me through my shorts.  Yes, I was definitely going to need at least one clone.

With coordinated step, Bethany and Cecilia marched their quarry into the corn field, only their shoulders and head showed above the tassels.  They stopped about thirty feet out, and seemed to be humping against each other.  I knew Dr. Pfister was getting thrashed pretty good at this point.  After a couple minutes more they dropped from sight.  And I can tell you that Dr. Pfister was not a problem for the rest of the summer.  In fact, their lunch breaks were twice as long and the Saturday half-day work requirement was dropped entirely.

Well, nine lovely and loving kisses later, and it was time for me to go face the music and get myself to work as well.  Back up the gravel road and left into the paved parking lot, I was on my way to report to duty at the Secretary Pool.  What a job title for me to have: "Assistant to the Secretary Pool".  Call me chauvinistic if you want, but I thought that was a sucky thing to have to add to my resume.  Better maybe than "professional pantie-liner" though.

I walked briskly now, hoping to get in the office before the lunch period ended at 1:00.  At the far end of the parking lot by the Secretary Pool building I heard the winch winding whining from a large tow truck.  Several men standing around in florescent lime maintenance crew vests had that scratching-head body language as they looked on at some difficult problem.  Getting a better view past the tow truck I kind of wanted to scratch my head as well: a bright green sedan from the company car pool sat upside down, at an angle in its parking slot, partially leaning on two other matching green sedans.   That's weird, I thought, and hopped up the steps toward the office door.

I slowed down at a broken crumble of glass in front of the door.  Before I'd entered I could already smell that bouquet of lovely secretary perfume mixed with coffee aroma and slightly tinged with the scent of all the computer and copier electronics.  The glass window in the door was raggedly out; I assumed the scattered crunch on the stoop in front of me.  Why wasn't somebody cleaning this up? Weirder.

Inside all was deathly quiet, not a keyboard tapping, not a copy machine humming, not a goofy conversation – nothing.  Office by office was empty.  Spooky.  Until Miss Monroe's, even spookier: all eight secretaries huddled inside, almost shivering on this warm day.  Miss Monroe grabbed me, hauling me in from the hallway in a nervous hurry.  She was way too intense: "Where – have – you – been?"

"Sorry."  I tried to shrug off her slightly painful grip. "I got a late start.  Had a few too many distractions."

Miss Monroe loosed her grip, still looking quite concerned and was about to say something else when: Wham! Something really heavy must have fallen over at the far end of the building.

Miss Jorgenson's voice trembled as she spoke.  "Richie, it's not cool, you going AWOL."

I didn't see the big deal.  "It's not like you can't get along perfectly fine without me.  It was just one morning."

Miss Rasmussen rolled her eyes.  "*Somebody* can't get along without you.  Missing you in a big way, if you know what I mean."

"Besides," Miss Petersen pointed accusingly at me. "It wasn't just this morning.  Where were you all day Friday?"

Oh that's right, I realized, then: "Shit.  Fuck me, I forgot to call in. Damn."  I was totally going to do that, but once I got attacked by the pool girls, crap, I completely lost track of time and everything else.

"Oh, yeah," Miss Monroe squinted at me, little nods, "It's been real jolly around here. I don't know what you did to Her on Thursday, but she was pissed when you didn't show up and didn't call on Friday."

"And She must have had a terrific weekend."  Miss Taylor sarcasm was unmistakable.  "Miss Strickland came in here one very grumpy troll this morning."

"And when you didn't show up again, and again with no call…"  Miss Rasmussen shook her head. "… that Troll turned into a human wrecking ball."

My eye widened.  "You mean the upside-down car outside?"

"Went outside this morning about 9:30 to see if you were coming.  Didn't exactly see you, did she?  Flipped that sedan over with one arm."

"And the front door?"  I didn't really need to ask.

"Lucky to still be on its hinges."

"And that big bang we just heard?"

"Who the hell knows?"  Miss Monroe whispered loudly, exasperated. "If I were you, I'd be seriously afraid for my life."  Her breathing was rapid, and I hate to admit it, kind of sexy.

"What?"  She looked really cross.  "You're actually going to stare at my chest at a time like this?

I gulped.  "Sorry."  I shook it off, looking away, forcing myself to appear concerned, then, thinking about Miss Strickland, actually feeling very troubled.

"Who knows what She'll do next?"  Miss Appleton's voice quivered. "About an hour ago she went out to the lot again.  Got even more pissed.  Chased the service crew away, saying something about men can't be trusted.  We're surprised they've come back at all."

Right then a big door slammed at the end of the hall, rattling windows all the way to Miss Monroe's office. Heavy, stomping-mad footsteps challenged to break the very

floor with their pounding heels.  The Secretaries panicked.  Miss Monroe hissed.
"Quick, hide Richie."

Miss Petersen slung me to the large couch.  And three huge asses descended upon
me immediately, check-to-cheek.  I was hidden but good.  Miss Rasmussen's very
tight, very firm ass pinned me from knees to chest.  Miss Petersen did her duty on
my face.  And the lovely Miss Taylor squeezed my feet tightly in her crotch.

Muffled as I was I could still hear Miss Strickland's growl reverberating all they
through Miss Rasmussen's ass.  "Richie call?"

I didn't hear a response, but I'm guessing they shook their heads no.  Technically
not a lie.  Miss Strickland must have taken it to the parking lot again.

The Secretaries bounced up off me.  "Look."  Miss Monroe's chest still heaved.
[Note to self: need another clone to run away with Miss Monroe.]  "You've got to get
out of here.  Go out the back door.  We'll stall her best we can."

I stood momentarily, like an uncomprehending lump. Then Miss Rasmussen
nudged me toward the door, insisting. "Go!"

"Go!  Run south around the labs to the highway.  I'll come pick you up with my car."
Miss Monroe implored me.

I nodded and took off, walking, not running, very fast down the hall.  I didn't want to
make a louder running noise on the floor – a noise that maybe could be heard
further away, past the broken-glass front door.

At the end of the hallway stood an exit on the right.  I should follow that out and go
around behind the research labs and get off the property, like Miss Monroe said.
But also right there was Miss Strickland's private office door.  I don't know what
possessed me, but I opened Miss Strickland's door and went in.  I heard the
secretaries' gasps of dismay as I closed the door behind me.

The place looked like a war zone.  The big old 400 pound desk looked like it had
been spun and rolled to tip up and lean precariously into a delicate balance against
an end table and fallen lamp.  All the wall art was down, earth-quaked to the floor
and right below the previous hanging places, some with broken glass.  I shook my
head at that.  What a shame.  That real nice leather sofa looked broken in half – like
how the fuck was that even possible!  Her window was busted out.  I went over and
looked down.  Her office chair lay in a heap outside ten feet below on the ground
amid more broken glass.

I heard the heavy, angry and disappointed footsteps trolling back down the hallway. Right there was my escape; a relatively easy hang and drop out the window. Instead I went over and stood right in the middle of the room, on that beautiful plush Persian rug where I thought, for my part, we had spent really fine quality time last Thursday.  I noticed it had escaped damage so far and was not harboring debris. Was something still sacred here?  Or was I dead meat?

The door banged open.  She saw me then slammed it behind her with a deafening crash.  "So," Fury raged off her, spittle flying as she sneered.  "It's so nice of you to drop by work."

"I wish I could say it's nice to be here."  I stared right back at her.

"I ought to crush you like a bug!"  She had perfected a very frightening growl.

"You mean with that big world-record fat, fat ass of yours?" I said it nice and loud.

Her face turned red with wrath.  No one ever talked to her like this, and I was counting on it.  Her hands and long red fingernails had formed into great claws, shaking as she said.  "I'm going to smother you to death and be done with you once and for all."

"Also with your fat butt, or are you going to use those giant pendulous blubbery tits? Go ahead, do it bitch."

She stepped toward me, cave-bear menacing.  "But first I might just bite your face off… you little shit."

"Well, you big shit.  While you're crushing me with your fat ass, smothering me with your massive tits, and biting my face off, will you be kissing me with those beautiful lips?"

"Damn it Richie, you're not getting out of this…"

I cut her off.  "I sure as hell am; but you aren't, you big baby.  Tell me this right now, Daisy Strickland, what am I to you: Richie or a 'little shit'?"

"Both."  She sounded more confused than mad now.

"Well, then you're not going to hurt me."  I wasn't asking.  And I wasn't done yet either.  "Get down here on this rug on all fours." I ordered.

She stood there like an oversized mule.

"Right now!" I commanded.

She glared at me for maybe thirty intense seconds. Then she blinked first, sighed and finally complied, kneeling and dropping to her hands and knees. She raised up her head and, good Lord, she still looked down at me even when on all fours. I could still feel the vehemence coming off her body, but in her eyes I saw that precious thing I liked about her, still very much deep down and in her center. I walked around her like I was inspecting a prize heifer. "So, here's what I wondering about, my dear. Have you ever, ever been disciplined in your life?"

"You mean like put in time out?"

"Sure, I suppose like that. Or maybe corporal punishment?"

"No." She turned her head trying to follow my movement. "What adult is going to try and punish a seven foot child? They were all afraid of me."

"Even you father?"

"Especially my father."

I inspected that world-class ass now, far wider than my body was long. A tiny bit of panty peaked back at me, her skirt hiked up nicely by the position she was in. "I find that terribly sad." I finally said, "About your father. How could you respect him if he was afraid of you? Very sad. I'm sorry about that for you."

I walked back around to face her again. Now her expression looked much calmer. So seldom was this woman ever seen for whom she really was. I looked at her almost expectant eyes and said, "I am sorry. But it doesn't let you off the hook for your actions. Turning over cars and chasing the service men away, breaking furniture and widows and scaring the secretaries half to death. And then saying the mean things you said to me. Tisk. Tisk. Miss Strickland."

Her eyes blinked; she was feeling so miserable she was kind of currently beyond "I'm sorry." I could see this and actually sympathized with her a great deal. But, "I'm afraid I'm going to have to administer some discipline here and now. Wouldn't you agree you've been a bad girl?"

"Yes." She whispered, hanging her head.

"Look me in the eye when you say that." I ordered her to keep her head up.

She looked at me much more fiercely now, but not defiant. "Yes, Richie."

"So I want you to know I would never ever spank a child.  But as an adult you should know better.   Where-oh-where is your healthy shame?" I asked rhetorically.  "You do agree, don't you, that you are due I well-metered spanking?"

"Yes, Richie." She said flatly.

"I can't hear you." I shot back at her.

Louder and prouder this time: "Yes I do deserve a spanking, Richie."

"OK then." I walked down her flank again.  "When it comes to this, I do not believe in rulers, or yard-sticks in your case…" kidding a bit. "… or switches or the like.  A proper spanking should be done with the hand.  Now," I stood behind her again.  "I ask that you pull down your skirt.  You can leave your panties on."

"May I?"  She needed room to stand.  I backed up.  Standing right beside me, I looked up and watched her unfasten and drop her skirt.  The heavy material blew past me like someone had shaken out a large blanket.  Back on all fours she waved her black-panty clad ass ever so slightly, as if to say, "I'm ready, sir."

I said the classic.  "Now Daisy, this is probably going to hurt me more than it is you."

"That is probably true, Richie."  But she wasn't exactly sassy.

I stepped forward, standing in between her legs going up in front and turning into that great wide ass.  Below, bending at her knees, those muscular lower legs closed behind me, ankle over ankle surrounding me in a truly wonder triangle.  The top of her ass loomed so huge in front of me, the top slightly higher than the height of my head, threatening even when submissive like this.

"OK," I called out, steadying my resolve.  "I am going to spank you ten times because you have been very, very naughty, little Miss Strickland."

She wiggled again, as if to say, "Do your worst."

I spanked her hard because I remembered from the massage last Thursday, anything soft or medium she had called "like mice playing cards."  Though huge, her ass was by no means all fat.  It felt both firm and soft, as I struck it.  After ten good whacks I finished, a slight bit winded by my effort.

Miss Strickland had a request.  "Now before you leave from back there, could you do something for me?"

"Maybe." I was suspicious.

"My ass is a little sad.  Can you kiss it?"

I wasn't falling for that.  "Maybe later, Daisy.  Right now we have important things to attend to."  I started to exit between her lower legs.

But she crossed them up higher, blocking me.  "I trusted you just now.  Before our next step, I want you to trust me."

"What do you mean by that?"  I could see there might have to be some give and take.  I hadn't come in or called two days.  So I did not have the complete moral high ground here.

She spoke evenly, relationally.  "I want you to get on you back, underneath my legs and very, very slowly push yourself along until your face meets mine."

An exercise in trust; I wondered exactly what she had in mind. I did as she requested.  She had left just enough room for my shoulders to lie flat on the floor between her lower legs.  My head on the carpet with her knees to either side, her huge legs rose massively above my face .  Straight above I stared at the confluence of those legs, covered in barest modesty by her wide lacy black panties.  My eyes panned still in wonder at the size of her gargantuan butt.

"I need to make amends to you, Richie.  Stay right where you are beneath me."  She slowly, carefully spread her knees apart thus lowering that ass closer and closer to my face.  When my crush seemed imminent, she paused mere inches above my face, my chest, my stomach, my arms… I glanced down… and a good portion of the rest of my body under horrific threat from her ass and crotch.  With escape clearly impossible and with my doom certain, she to me: "Can you trust that I will not 'crush you like a bug'?"  She recanted her own words for me.

I wanted her to come down on me right then and own me completely.  But my honest answer: "Yes, I trust you."

She raised her big butt back up to its place with her in all fours position.  "Good, Richie, now move forward slowly until I tell you to stop."

I scooched along, half-inch by half-inch, on my back; face up.  Above me now was her terrific-looking mid-section had some belly to it as well as very strong abs evident.  It looked to be a lovely playground to explore sometime.  Ahead her great breasts hung low and full.  So wide and heavy in every direction, they rested against each other because there was no other place to go.  When I was right between and under them she had me stop. Those vast tits hung so low, her nipples grazed the Persian rug each time she breathed in.  I turned my head to the side, my lips rested against smooth breast surface.  Her tits were so vast they were timeless, if that makes any sense – I mean I could forget about time, be enchanted and lost and wake up some hundred years later – or not.

"Do you trust I will not 'smother you to death' with my huge tits?"  She continued her amends to me; telling me with a question that she did not mean her threat, not anymore.

I waited to answer, just to enjoy the possibility of being so smothered by her.  Finally I sensed I had to answer and honestly. "I trust you to not harm me."

"Good, now move up."

It took a while to get past her endless breasts.  But eventually I saw them taper away to her collar bone, her gorgeous neck and at last her beautiful face right above mine, her dark hair cascading all around and down to curl in piles by my head.  Here I knew to stop.

Daisy brought her big red lips and wide mouth a half a breath away from my face.  She opened her mouth very wide exposing large sharp white teeth.  Her breath was hot and fresh with butter-mint.  Her next question: "Do you trust me not to 'bite off your face'?"

I kind of hoped she would try, but said. "Yes I trust you will not harm me."

"Good."  She said. "Then believe that now!"  And she lowered her huge open mouth onto my face and kissed me like the first step of being eaten alive.  Her lips covered most of my face for a good five minutes.  At last she broke it off saying. "I can't be sure I will never hurt you, crush you, smother you, or possibly lose control and eat you.  But I can promise you in this moment I do not ever want to truly end you in those ways or in any way."

With that she pushed away and sat back on her heels.  I scooted up further then stood in front of her, at about the height her nipples pointed right toward my face.  I peered up at her, over those massive breasts. "That, Dear Daisy, was a beautiful amends.  But you still have more to do, don't you?"

She looked toward the door then back at me.  "Yes, unfortunately, I have to leave you now and go take care of a few things."

"Would you like me to come with you?"

My boss Miss Strickland stood to her full height above me, putting her clothing back on. "Yes... but no... it is something I should do alone and take full responsibility.  So I'll go unaccompanied to do this if you promise, promise, promise you will be here when I get back.

"Yes. Yes. Yes." I assured her.  But couldn't help, "So get your fat ass out of here, and get it done."

She pointed a scolding finger at me. "Be careful.  Remember that it was *you* who didn't call me.  So when I get back it will be your turn for amends.  And with those insults you keep throwing out, I think I know where your amends might have to start."  With that she was out the door.

I watched her go down the hallway and out the front door.  I took that advantage to run down to Miss Monroe's office.  All the secretaries were still in there.  They looked at me in wonder, as if they were seeing a ghost.  "You're alive."  Miss Taylor finally said the obvious.

"Come on, hurry up.  I need some help down in Miss Strickland's office."  I ran back down the hallway and the eight amazon secretaries followed.

Once inside Miss Strickland's office I explained quickly.  "Miss Strickland has gone to the parking lot to apologize to the service crew.  Maybe even tip a car back over.  Let's get this office cleaned up super-fast."

The secretaries got it and went to work right away.  They were plenty strong enough to get a 400-pound desk back in place.  They swiftly straightened and swept and organized and made the office look almost normal – working like giant sexy versions of Cinderella's forest creature helpers.

Miss Strickland returned before they were completely finished.  For a second the secretaries looked trapped.  But Miss Strickland diffused that quickly.  "Thank you so much for cleaning up my office.  I am sorry for being so grouchy."

"Grouchy?"  I asked.  That wasn't a strong enough word.

"I mean, a terrible mean bitch the last two workdays?

"Better" I said, "but just the last two workdays?"

"OK, all the time."  She actually laughed at herself.  The secretaries were looked both extremely relieved and beyond flabbergasted.

Miss Monroe, always sexy from every angle, leaned on her broom.  "Miss Strickland, it was our pleasure to clean up your office."

Miss Strickland had more to say.  The amends were still coming. "Take the rest of the day off.  And when you come back tomorrow it will be at an improved pay scale with better benefits."

"Holy Cow."  Miss Jorgensen blurted out, shocked, not really thinking.

"What did you mean by that?"  Miss Strickland acted like she took that personally.  But then laughed; she was only teasing them.  The secretaries laughed also, though kind of nervous.  They made their way out of the office, their elation kicking in more as they reached the hallway.

At the doorway, Miss Monroe, the last to leave, looked back at me.  "You going to be all right, Richie?"

"Absolutely, I'll be fine."  I assured her.  And Miss Monroe turned, affording me another look at her perfect ass of endless delight, then pulled the door closed behind her.

I looked back to face Miss Strickland.  She eyed me; I could clearly see her lust building.  "'You'll be fine, Richie?'  Daisy parroted Miss Monroe, maybe just a tiny bit jealous and possessive of me. "I wouldn't count on it if I were you.  So..." She walked around me, now, like I was the prized chicken. "... how did I do, OK?"

"Yes, very admirable."

"And now you're ready to start your amends to me?"

"Which amends?"

"All of them.  Not coming to work Friday. Not calling. Not calling all weekend.  Not coming to work this morning.  Not calling.  Sneaking in my office in the first place last Thursday.  And about that promise to try to help me get pregnant.  You gave me a lot of time to think about with all these things.  What do you think I want first?"

"Another massage?"

"Nice idea, but not yet.  I want you to go hide under my desk again."

Her face, some ten feet over from me and some eleven feet up from me, looked softer and beautiful again.  I wanted to feel her big mouth's devouring kiss again right now; those raven curls falling all around me.  But my face must have looked quizzical at her request.

"Yes.  Go on.  Right now."  She shooed at me with a wiggle of the back of her fingers.

As I went toward the desk, Daisy walked tangential away and through the door of her private bathroom spa.  I ducked under and into the chair well of the desk, and quickly began to recall the extra ordinary view I'd had up her skirt last Thursday.  I was deep into imagining kissing up her legs, when Daisy finally returned to the room.  Instead of the heavy click of her heels I hear the squeak of, what, tennis shoes?  It stopped; she must be on the Persian carpet.

I dropped to the floor and looked out under the four inch clearance at the front of the desk.  Light blue tennis shoes?  And dainty white low ankle socks with matching blue rims.

"Oh my tennis teacher is late again.  I'll just wait at this desk over here."  What was she talking about?

Around to the front of the desk she walked, just like last Thursday. I looked out at her oh so sturdy lower legs, thick and muscular calves, toned and tan, and cute in her tennis outfit.  My "two o'clock lesson" had arrived, I thought, starting to get the fantasy we were playing, and here I was hiding from her.  A big, big butt plopped down in the chair and rolled in toward me.  Huge legs spread out coming forward on either side of me.  The baby blue tennis skirt was absurdly short, with the thinnest thong of white panties a mere stripe through the black curly hair of her crotch.  I was beginning to like this game a whole lot.

"Oh, I wish he was here already.  I do love my tennis lessons."  Her left inner thigh pushed against my face, my lips.  My student seemed to take no notice at all.  "Oh, my teacher is so cute.  When he shows me how to hold my racket, it's like we're holding hands.  It makes my whole body tingle."  My body also started tingling in key places.

She went on. "I just want to kiss him.  Does that make me naughty?  I have such thoughts about him.  When he reaches around me to help me hit the forehand, oh and, especially the backhand, I want to turn around and pull him into my breasts."  This was sexy, but also odd.  What size was she pretending to be?  "Or back him up against the fence with my big butt, and wiggle it against him until he drops his racket, forgets all about the lesson."

"I was thoroughly kissing Daisy's leg now, rapidly progressing toward her white panties.  She continued as if I weren't there. "My big butt would be the teacher.  All the others made fun of my big butt; but he was always nice to me.  Maybe he likes a big butt.  If I can get him to kiss it I can use its magic powers on him."  I liked where she was headed with this fantasy.  I buried my face vigorously into her panties and bush.  And still she merely continued.  "I would shrink him down smaller and smaller.  Take him home in my tennis bag.  Then, in my bedroom, let him out on my bed.  He would try to run away.  But I would pounce on him.  Then I would sit on him, sit on him, sit on him, bouncing and bouncing on my bed for hours and hours until he knew forever I was his boss.  Bossy-boss teacher, that's who I would be, and he would be under my butt all day and all night."

Daisy's thighs closed tight on me.  The chair was rolling now.  My legs issued from her tight thigh squeeze, my feet dragging along the floor… then carpet.  She stood and my body went up with her, face still in her crotch, the rest of me crushed between her thighs.  After a couple of minutes, her legs opened and I fell to the soft carpet.

"Oh there you are, teacher.  Why are you down there?  What, no tennis today?  Oh that's right, today must be our wrestling lesson.  It's good anyway, because I've been practicing."  She dropped down on all fours over me.  Her top was like not even a pushup-bra, just a bit of lace decorating each tit, but not even trying to cover the nipples.  It was unbelievably sexy.

She kept on with her narrative.  "I'll start out on top and you try to teach me how you get out.  But I warn you.  I've been working on my moves."

I was kind of thinking: "What happened to the tennis lesson?"  But then maybe this had even more promise.  So she wanted me on my hands and knees, and she did the same right over me.  She leaned her head down and rested her neck onto the back of my head.  My lower back and butt slid up into the tight cleavage at the eighty percent open top of her bra.  We seemed to be in position for the first round.

"Ready teacher?"

"Sure I guess."

OK. One…two… three."  And she dropped her weight straight down on me, pinning me flat on my stomach in two seconds. "Go ahead and get out.'  Her lips brushed my ear as she spoke.  Of course I couldn't move whatsoever.  "Give up, teachy-weachy?"  She taunted me.  I struggled, a little mad at the teasing.  But it was impossible.  She started licking my ear, kissing the side of my face.  "You are so yummy.  But instead of continuing, she pushed herself up to all-fours above me again.  "Come on.  Get up."

I unflattened myself into the same inferior hands and knees underneath her.

"Ready for round two?"

"I suppose."

"Go." She said without counting.  I tried to crawl forward quickly before she could drop on me again.  But she had another move entirely, grabbing my front left wrist with her right hand.  She pulled back and across against my forward momentum, and flipped me right over to the left.  When she dropped on me this time, her huge left breast pinned me from my middle and spread out over most of my upper body, my red face just appearing from the tit bulging against the carpet.

"Good move, uh?"  She smiled triumphantly down at me.

I tried to respond but couldn't speak.

"You must be really impressed.  You're speechless.  What; is my big tit too heavy for you?  Oh, you want to kiss it?  That's against the rules, isn't it?  Well maybe just this one time.  I won't tell if you won't."  She scooted up about a foot and enveloped my face and head under her breast.  And I did kiss it over and over, until running out of air at last she lifted off.

She sat up saying.  "This bra is too tight."  Unhitching it in the back and letting it fly off to the side.  Her huge tits swung free.  "That's better.  Now get in the position again."  And we were back to her on all fours over me on all fours.  This time as she leaned down her unrestricted tits pressed on both side of me and all the way down to the carpet.

"Ready? Go."  I was afraid to try to scramble out because that had failed so miserably.  I had to be the worst wrestling teacher ever because I had no idea what to do.  She did, however, and proceeded to bang me with her tits back and forth.  She knocked me around like a cork in a washing machine; soon enough knocking me clean over to my back.  She continued with a merciless tit-whipping and kept saying, "Give up? Give up?"  Which I gladly would have done if I could have gotten a word out.  "Oh, won't give up.  Well then I'll have to get tough on you."  And she dropped down on me again, this time a big nipple right into my mouth and over my face.  She ground it down on me.  It made me think of the videos of big tits smashing soda cans.  And when I was truly beyond out of air she lifted up – me gasping for oxygen.

"Like that move?"  She acted pitiless to my suffering.

"Yes and no…" I managed to sit up.

"Come on.  Get ready.  I'm paying for these lessons by the hour."  Actually she kind of was if I was still on the work clock.  I laughed at that.

"What's so funny?

"Oh, you know; you and your big tits."

"You can't talk to one of your students like that."

I was feeling extremely uppity.  "I'll talk to you however, I want, Blubber Breasts.  I'm the teacher here."

"Well, if you don't like my big tits.  Maybe you would prefer my big butt."

"You call that a butt big?  Well, I've seen bigger butts on… well… on elephants!"

"Oh that's so mean."

"Oh, you're going to go big cry-baby on me now?"  It was my turn to tease her, I thought.

"No, I'm going to go big ballistic on you."  All of the sudden it was Daisy again, not pretending anymore.  "Now, about those amends…. I think my 'fat ass' needs a very intimate apology, don't you?"  She was taking off her skirt now, this time panties included.  "And that amends was supposed to come from… oh, that's right, from your insulting mouth.  On the floor, face up, and take a deep breath."

Daisy squatted over me without ceremony.  She waved that thunder dome barely above my face, letting me soak in the consequences that were in store for me.  This had all the trappings of being very direct and vigorous.  "Time for your amends!" and she lowered her great crack onto my face.  She adjusted, making sure it was square and my face fully up in there.  Within a minute I felt my shoes and shorts being pulled off.  A couple more adjustments and her walking her buns a bit to get me situated just right, and I felt my lower body and erect volunteer entering her already wet pussy.

Apparently my big lover Daisy had been giving this a lot of thought.  She had the logistics all figured out.   Her ass was big enough and my body small enough, she could both sit on my face and fuck me at the same time.  The perfect sized woman in that respect.  My thin legs were smashed under the great heft of her upper thighs.  My arms no more than spaghetti noodles pressed as mere indents to interrupt the perfect connection of her ass to the carpet.  My torso was getting to know the sweet torturing crush of her taint.  My volunteer on its skinny pedestal was finding that the hugeness of her pussy and its ability to exert python-like squeezing was anything but loose.  And her ass ate my face over and over and over, like her butt was the worse food addict ever and my face an endless supply of corn chips.

There was no Richie in the room – just a giantess sitting up and writhing inexplicably on her carpet.  That's how lost I was under my big dominate boss.  Sex discrimination in the workplace you protest.  Oh God yes.  I was discriminated, desecrated, dominated, and destroyed.  Her 2,500 pound loving crush was utter and complete.  And oh she was heavy, heavy... sweet, juicy, and heavy.  Her intensity, wildness, and thrashing grew.  Oh Daisy.  Oh Miss Strickland.  Oh big boss lady, just let me serve you, forever.

Almost like an answer to my offer, her first orgasm hit.  When it did, she did not care anything about my survival.  It was a butt and pussy thrashing beyond belief!  And at its peak the message from her body came down loud and clear.  "Make a baby in me.  Make a baby in me.  Make a baby in me, or die trying."

Ah, Mondays at the office.…  And there was nothing I could do but lie there and take it.

# XIII. Duchess Daisy Giantess Ride

My boss, Miss Daisy Strickland, sat her 2,500 pound posterior on me the rest of that Monday afternoon.  Well, we took little breaks now and then, for me to breathe, for my tough pliable body to reshape.  You know – the usual kind of things you have to accommodate when you're a mere four-foot two-inch, seventy pound man, and your fifteen-foot-plus lover outweighs you by far more than two thousand pounds!

Thank God the Triplets had infused and outfitted me with resilient cells, pliable bones, and a metabolism that only needed re-oxygenation every 30 minutes or so. (Yep, I'm the smallest whale on the planet.) There was no way I could have survived such a pounding like this a month ago. I would have been squelched and popped in the first two minutes.  Now here I was, almost four hours later, her massive butt still munching on my face, and head, and shoulders; her pussy still gobbling up my volunteer, my hips and buns, my upper legs.  Yes, here I persisted in the hot, moist, pitch black world of the utterly squashed and demolished – and loving every minute of it.  Well, for the most part.  When Daisy shifted around, sometimes the pressure would get a bit excruciating.  But I was tougher than a cockroach and harder to squish than a tick.

Miss Strickland seemed to be making up for a lot of lost years with no partnered orgasm – actually no man at all since her husband had died.  That regretful event happened was some ten years ago, when Daisy crushed him accidentally after he mistakenly tried to get amorous while she slept.  Poor bastard; but at least he died for love.  If you learn just one thing from these stories, it's like I keep saying: never let an amazon go to sleep on you.

Ten empty years, no man, no amalgamated sex of any kind: that's a lot of relational orgasms to make up for.  Let's say a reasonable number of orgasms for a woman in her twenties and thirties should be at least ten per month.  Wouldn't you agree I'm being conservative here?  So conservatively then, ten per month times twelve months per year times ten years: that's 1,200 orgasms!  So, only some twenty or so this afternoon did not seem like that many, not really, when you put it in perspective.  And I was gaining a lot of perspective – if you know what I mean.

I felt another one coming.  Her last couple of orgasms had really hauled on me, a severe contraction at the emotional apex of her intensity that sought to pull me into her body.  Thank goodness my body was tucked in and wrapped around her perineum in a solid balance between her ass on my face and her pussy centered on my cock.  Neither her pussy nor her ass could win the tug-of-war to suck me in.

The way it pulled on my back though, who knows, maybe I'd end up an inch or two taller – lol and lots of luck with that one.

Whoa, whoa, and away we go!  As Daisy went over the top this time, she found a new level.  She launched off from that timeless squeeze-of-death-peak up higher into stage-three jack-hammering vibrations that could have shaken all the nuts off a big pecan tree.  The big babe levied a doosey of a pussy-ass pounding on me that took even my breath away.  Daisy flooded me again…then… coming down… calming down… pausing along the way… relaxing more through little wiggles… releasing my body out of her lips and folds and fully back to the carpet, spreading out on me completely flat… a few final shutters down on me like loving kisses good-bye… and at long last rolled off me… seemingly done for the day.

"Well," Daisy sat up beside my prone body, her left hand by my head, elbow locked, straight up and nicely muscular.  Her radiance looked down at me with as much affinity as her broad beautiful face can hold. "You certainly are one tough little sucker.  And I love that Sparkle thing you got going.  That has to be the best invention ever, ever!"

Daisy didn't know my Sparkle had been only like ten percent capacity since Saturday night.  Since Saint Debbie had drained it to its base-line.  But probably a good thing it wasn't at full strength; Daisy's colossal butt completely out of control likely would have killed me.

I tried to move.  Oh God, I felt like a cartoon character, steamrolled into two dimensions, like I needed a good shake-out to flip me back into the world of living 3D.  "Daisy, how do I look?  I'm imagining my ass-smashed face must look like a Picasso painting."

"Oh, you poor dear.  Well, your right eye is kind of more toward your forehead." She teased.  "No, you look perfectly fine, a little red maybe, but actually very cute. In fact… Oh…"  She was having a little echo orgasm.  "Maybe we could just have one more little go?"

But before she could haul her ass up onto me again I said, perhaps a little pleadingly, "Could I maybe get something to drink first?  It got pretty hot under your hot-hot body, baby.  I think I lost a lot of water."

"You certainly lost a lot of cum."  Then she smiled even bigger.  "Hey, maybe I'm pregnant already."  Her happy wheels were turning on that thought.  It shifted her thinking and her emphasis.  "You know…"  She felt one large swollen breast then the other. "…I think maybe all this sex-for-pregnancy has stimulated these big tits into some production.  If you're thirsty, maybe we could, uh, help each other out." Her eyebrows did a great how-about-baby.

Don't listen to me; I get the most peculiar thoughts: but I couldn't help wondering what percent of this milk was my own cum transformed for return to me.  But those weird-thoughts are just some odd anxiety I get sometimes.

"Sure," I pushed myself to sitting, with a groan. "I could use a stiff drink."  What I soon got was a stiff nipple.  Daisy picked me up, gently supporting my body in her arms, and took me to her breast like a pro.  Very soon she had me relaxed without a care in the world.  I was glad I was trying to get her pregnant; she was going to be a great mom.

In a nether zone of comfort, I looked with half-asleep eyes up at Daisy's face.  Her mouth was moving.  I forced myself to listen. "…had a lot of time to think about this as I was sitting on you today, butt crushing you and screwing your brains out…" This was getting my attention.  She noticed I was waking up for this. "… squirming down on you with my great big pussy.  Grinding my 2,492 pounds of loving ass on your face…"

"OK already," I broke off from her nipple.  I think I wasn't sucking anymore by now anyway.  Certainly I wasn't thirsty anymore. "OK, you have my attention."

She was having too much fun. "Flattening you, not like a pancake, because they fluff up, no, more like a crepe, a little corn tortilla… my big butt owning you – my little stud.  That's what you are: my little stud.  Like I'm riding a tiny little stallion only when I climbed on my horse it collapses under my great weight, goes flat and helpless under me, the great mare, who owns and bosses the stallion into sheer servitude…"

"Enough already!"  The fact that she was losing it with this narrative should not, it seemed, be getting me sexually excited.  But it was and she knew it. "Just tell me what you were thinking as you 'sat on me' this afternoon."

She still held me in a nursing position, nipple bumping against my lips as she spoke with vibrancy. "We need a schedule for this.  You agree?"

"Makes sense."  I licked at her nipple; couldn't help it.

She stood, carrying me in exactly the same position.  Continuing, as she walked. "I am really more of a morning person.  I think that is when I'd like to make love with you the most." We entered her huge bathroom/spa. She dialed a couple of light-settings, soft and quiet violet, some gentle music to accompany. "I think you should report to me in my office first thing in the morning. We can say that you are now my 'personal assistant'; call it the morning 'de-briefing'." She chuckled at her little pun.

Bending over, still supporting me with one arm, my body firmer now against her breast, she opened a valve for eight water-fan faucets to begin filling her hot-tub sized bath. In fact, it was a large hot-tub, plumbed and modified for her comfort, tastes, and size.

Continuing to download her plan, "Then we'll figure to get together at 8:30 each workday morning. I'd say one to two hours should be enough." She/we stepped into the spa-tub. "The four-hour session today, well, that being the first time, we'll chalk that up as extra special, getting to know each other."

She sat in the tub and leaned back, water jets turned on automatically, foaming up with scented bubble bath. Her breasts bobbed half-submerged. I slipped between them, my back against her chest, my heels down in the depths slipping back and forth and finally finding footing in her crotch.

"Tricky move, Richie." But she kept on, only slightly distracted by my foot stimulation of her. "So we should be finished by 10:30 at the latest, unless something else comes up." Again she chuckled at her pun; a regular comedienne she was. The suds piled high over my head. I cleared them aside, not quite flailing with my arms, heaping them over her breasts. I guessed she must have like that, too. "That's another nice move. You're a good little bath boy." Didn't she mean bath "toy"?

Daisy turned the water off, but let the jets continue. "I was also thinking you could do something more interesting while you're working here job-wise. We can set up an internship for you in the afternoons over at the Research Labs. Yes: finish the mornings here, help the secretaries a little bit, have lunch here if you want, then start over there at 1:00. See?" She leaned over me, her more-beautiful-each-time-I-looked face upside-down to mine. "I'm not so greedy, am I? Five good thorough fucks a week is all I want."

Then she attacked my face with kisses – deep, prolonged, passionate, tongue-and-teethy kisses lavished with barely contained desire to eat me alive. Rotating forward, her face drove mine down, under the suds, under the water. Breaking off, for *she* needed air, not I, she shoved me the rest of the way to the bottom where she lifted, slid me underneath, and sat on my face. I actually pushed my face up into her pussy more because I was kind of crazed with desire by her, by the warm waters, the idea of being so lost under her, so hidden away from the world.  She opened to let me in, up to my neck, so easy, so slippery. I turned one quarter and felt my thin shoulders going in.  But with the kissing and suds and such, I had not taken in a good enough breath.  I had to tap her on the leg.  She pulled me out and up; me gasping as I cleared the surface.

Daisy looked concerned, until I sputtered. "Wow! That was something!"  I was really excited about what had just happened.

She was surprised also by the little event that had just occurred between her legs and up inside her. "We are most definitely going to have to get back to that."

"Not now?"  I was ready for that particular plunge again.

"I do wonder…"  She looked at me lasciviously, chewing at her index fingernail, "…how much of you I could get inside me.  Alas – I'll have to take a rain check.  We have to get going."

"I'm in no hurry."

"Don't you have a meeting at your house tonight?

That's right.  Yes, I did – a damn important meeting.  But, "How did you know about that?"

"Your girlfriends invited me?"

"When?"

"When I was sitting on your face and fucking your daylights out this afternoon."

"You're up there receiving calls while we're making love?"  It seemed… well, kind of rude.

"Sure, between orgasms, receiving calls and making them, too.  Don't take it personally.  I've got an office to run.  By the way, they had me invite Miss Monroe as well."

What was happening to the planned intimate little discussion with just the Triplets and Debbie tonight?  "Anybody else?"  I felt a bit miffed, but would get over it, supremely trusting the Triplets.

"They asked me to get word to the Pollination Crew; an invite to Vicky and some others.  I guess you know her."

Boy did I.

Daisy stood, "And I heard something about some maintenance girls might be there?"

I was getting an odd feeling.  "Pool Girls, maybe?"

"Bingo."  She pointed at me.  "Pool Girls."

That was definitely odd.  How did the Triplets know about that interlude?

Daisy started draining the tub, and turned on six-panel rain-shower heads at the same time, deluging us from twenty feet up. That got the suds off fast.  She stepped out and turned off the showers.  "Coming?  Or are you going to stay there and drip dry? Drip."

She shouldn't have ignored me after an insult like that.  I hopped out of the tub, grabbed a towel, and as she gloriously bent over to dry her feet, I snapped her big ass, but good!

Daisy spun around, red-faced, claws ready.

"What a temper."  I teased.  "You must be part Irish."

"As a matter of fact, I am."  But she couldn't help her good humor at being so sexually satisfied all afternoon.  Still she threatened.  "Us Irish get mad *and* we get even."

"Well you better save if for later, Duchess."  I really don't know why I called her that.  'Duchess-Daisy', perhaps. "Don't we have a gathering to get-to, a little moot to meet?"

"Oh, you.  You just wait 'til our 'de-briefing' tomorrow morning."  She shook her finger at me, the motion jiggling her tits magnificently.  "Get dressed, now.  Your carpool left an hour ago.  You can ride with me.  An invitation to the Triplets is a rare event around here, never for me, as you can imagine.  I don't want to be late."

Off the spa-bathroom Daisy had a huge walk-in closet.  She had gone in there to "find a little something to wear."  These amazons cracked me up – pun intended, I admit.  It was funny to me, the thought of the planet's biggest woman getting a "little something to wear." Anyway, out she comes with this short, flaring red dress, red lacey hem, black belt, the dress V-ing out and splitting just about mid sternum for a heavenly look at her bulging cleavage, decorated by a thin fringe by more matching red lace.

With her mane of raven curls pulled back asymmetrical on the sides for a sophisticated styling, and her olive perennial-tanned skin, this big woman made red look superb. Around her elegant neck, a thin silver strand suspended a large pear-cut sparkly azure topaz; like a king it reigned over the great twin towers of her breasts. Ever been jealous of a stone? I was right then.

She spun for me, giddy like before a hot date. "What do you think?" She batted her eyes.

Like the dick I could totally be sometimes, trying to be funny, I said, "You're wanting to know if that dress makes you butt look fat?" What a sap I could be.

"Oh good." She smiled dominant and predatory. "You're adding more amends to serve my ass." She swiveled to make me stare right at it, looking back over her shoulder down at me. "Besides, anyway I know you wish it was even bigger. And maybe it will be when you get me pregnant." Her expression was 'how-do-like-them-apples?'

"Sorry. I'm totally a cad. You look outstanding, like a Cinderella dressed in red. Only way sexier and a lot taller." Her expression said my backtracking was sort of working. "And about your ass; it couldn't be more perfect – especially in that excellent dress."

She sighed (beautiful) and smiled (more beautiful) and said. "You're learning. But you're still not getting out of additional amends."

Good, I thought.

"Let's go." She said and I followed her out a back door from her office. Her vehicle was a modified semi-stretch metallic-maroon Humvee. The front seats had been taken out, and she would drive from a tailor made bench seat that was in the position behind the missing driver's seat. She looked at me and shook her head. "Too bad you have to wear those frumpy shorts to this get-together. I would have loaned you something, but, well, you know my style just wouldn't suit you."

"Yeah, well, it is too bad." Did I have a little chip on my shoulder? You decide. "Anybody doesn't like the way I look, they can just lump it, can't they."

"Whoa, cowboy, don't get your panties in a bunch." Then she winked at me. "I know." I could see she had more mischief up her sleeveless dress. "We can iron out those shorts on the way." She snapped her fingers at the idea, and now its obvious corollary: "And you can make some amends at the same time."

I was starting to get a picture, and I wasn't so sure about it.

"Hey, didn't I hear some rumor … no it was posted on the Bluebelle Amazon page… yes, doesn't the Pollination Crew take turns riding on you back into town every day? Since you're used to it; we'll just do that. In the driver's seat you go."

She held open the door, but instead of stepping aside, made me go between and under her beautiful killer legs to gain the seat. Situated, I looked back and up at that vast ass that owned me.

"Here we go." She gave that much warning, then lifted her dress and planted her black-panties square on my lap, her dress dropping over my head. She settled her crushing weight on me for the forty minute drive.

She turned on the radio, and hummed along to the music, ignoring me it seemed. Left to my own devices I noticed I wasn't without options. With my hands free, I tugged down at the top of her panties so I could see more ass. Right in front of me was that lower back area I like so much on a woman. And Daisy's was no exception – well, check that – it was an exception. It was extra big and lovely, and at the moment very convenient. I kissed her right in that area and a little lower when she shifted back. Though pretending not to notice me or my kissing her, I could see her goose bumps and definitely feel her involuntary clenching down below.

This situation was getting to me as well. Just her sheer pressure could take me beyond surrender, my hard-on tight down in my shorts, heading toward conclusion whether it found her actually body or not. With the thought of how she looked in this dress, and the beauty of the grand arch of her lower back and upper ass responding to my kisses, and the thought of what had happened in the tub – I was going to cum in my pants, on her dress!

"Daisy!" I called out. "I'm about to…"

The Humvee served over to the side of the road, skidded to a stop, the door opened, and Daisy was off me in a second, just in time. I managed to only have a dry orgasm. I looked up at her sheepishly; she smiled kindly, "Good job, Richie. Thanks for not messing up my dress. But we got to take care of this somehow."

She looked around.  It was a lonely highway on this stretch, past wide fields of soybeans and alfalfa.  I could feel the humidity coming in from the open door, that rich smell of cut hay riding it in.  Though the sun wasn't quite to the distant hills yet, the cricket chorus sang in full swing.  Daisy looked around – all clear.  She hiked up her dress and quickly pulled her panties off.  She tossed them to me.  I fought to rein them in, winding them up with my arms, like dealing with a big black lacey queen-size bed sheet floating down on me.  From the back seat Daisy produced a large striped beach towel and unfurled it toward me across the bench seat.  I rose up, helped tug it over and smooth it out.

Daisy was anxious to get back in the vehicle.  "Just leave my panties over there.  And your shorts and shirt."  Meaning take off my clothes.  "Come on."  I whipped off my clothes.  "OK," She nodded, then instructed.  "Feet at the back of the seat, head toward the steering wheel."  I obeyed.  Then Daisy lifted her dress once again, climbed in and sat her sat her pussy right on my cock.  She slammed the door and we were off again.

She wiggled down on me and we were locked in for some nice heavy sex.  I was in a kind of wild position, free from her pussy pressure at about mid-chest.  My shoulders and neck lie back against the deep seat, with my head half on and half off.  Above me to either side her beautiful big naturally tan legs angled up, knees bent, right leg working the brake but mostly accelerator. Through the deep vee of those legs I had a great view up her open cleavage of her breasts leaning with the highway curves and continuous jiggling from the roughness of the road and grand bounces from the not infrequent pot holes.

Her strong toned arms worked the steering wheel. "How you doing down there?"  I heard her fine, but could not see her tit-obscured face.  She leaned forward to see me. "Nice.  I like you under me like this while I'm driving.  Go ahead, my little stud, cum all you want."  And she started bouncing on me in time to the classic rock and roll she had on the radio.

Daisy cranked the volume up. I could read the satellite feed upside down as it ticker-taped by "…Boogie Woogie Flu…"  Daisy's hips pounded me side to side, her huge tits swaying inside her dress like big soft wrecking balls, as she belted out "… I want to love her, but she's way too tall! … I got the rockin' pneumonia and the boogie-woogie flu!"

My eyes glazed, this giantess dark-haired beauty rocking out on me was just too crazy awesome.  I kept obsessing about the incident in the tub, about entering her head first, about her musing "I wonder how much of you I can get inside me".  My capitulation felt absolute.  "Daisy, I love you!" I shouted over the music.

She kept up the bouncing to the music as she leaned and looked down at my face again.  Her expression one of soft, knowing, dominance, "Yes but do you worship me?

"Absolutely." I confessed without hesitation.

"You know," She leaned forward and smiled down at me again.  "I kind of worship you, too.  And certainly I love you inside me."  Her self-esteem was riding high, riding me.  I would have cum already except for the earlier dry orgasm.  It didn't matter to the big rock-star babe all lost in song.

She made up her own verses now.  "…I'm gonna' fuck him 'til he's mine all mine.  Oh, I'm sittin' on him all the time.  Come on boy, give it to me good. I'm gonna' crush you forever like you knew I would…"

Through that made-up verse Daisy sped up her thrashing on me.  "…I want your deep lovin' way up inside.  You couldn't get away if you tried.  I want you in me from head to toe.  I own your little body and I'm sure you know. Oh…oh…oooohh!"

My explosion was wild and violent and, of course, of no consequence against her devastating weight.  But did she feel it? Oh yeah, with a gusher like I've never experienced.  I wondered how my sperm could ever swim against such a tide to get this woman pregnant.  But you know what?  That wasn't my chief concern right then.  Those little suckers would have to fend for themselves.  Move over, I want to swim up there myself.

"Oh my God, my Goddess…" I didn't know what I was saying.  "Oh, Miss Strickland, will you please sit on me forever."

"Sounds good," She was a bit breathless herself. "…but I think we'll have to make do with another five minutes.  We're almost to the main gate."

We both relaxed.  I felt her breathing slow, her wonderful pussy releasing me.  I looked around at her legs, up at her arms, her breasts, and I thought I never wanted to be anywhere else.

"OK," Daisy was lifting up, giving me an escape route.  "You better slip out of there and see what you can do for yourself with the dry part of the towel." I squeezed under her raised right bun.  She busied herself, drying off with the towel, and didn't see the speed bump.  The Humvee bounced, and Daisy's big ass flattened me out on the seat, face down, my head just beyond the edge of her ass.  She used her tiny voice. "So-sorry, I didn't see the…"

"…Speed bump, I get it.  Are you going to get your fat…" I thought better, "… er… I mean… get off me or just sit there?"  I could barely speak.

"My fat, what?  I didn't catch that.  Well, let's see…" Her sharp nails drumming the steering wheel.  "I kind of like you right there… well… OK… I guess I can let you up."  She lifted again, but not enough that I didn't have to fight my way out.

"You're so funny." I groaned and made my way to the far side of the seat."

"What a mess."  It was awkward for her to clean up and keep driving.  But we were already a little late.  She eyed me, more sass coming. "I wish I could use you for a panty-liner."

"It's actually on my resume." I answered dryly.  But still working with the towel, I was anything but dry yet.  "If you weren't so damn juicy…" Like I was complaining.

"Why don't you come back over here and put your face up in my Complaint Department and lodge a formal grievance."  Now how would you like to hear that from your boss?  Daisy might have been a bit annoyed, trying to drive and dry and field my remarks.

It looked like she was also distracted.  "Hey," I said, "you just passed the turn off for the Triplets house."

"Not according to the address they gave me."  She seemed to be finished cleaning up.  "Could you be so kind as to hand me my panties.  That is, if you are done sniffing them yet."

I had already managed to clean up myself, and admit I was starting to toy with her sexy black underwear. "What, this parachute?"  I stuck my head through a leg hole, the crotch over my right shoulder, kind of a looking like Tarzan's Boy.

Daisy had to pause to announce herself at the massive gate to the property.  Looking out the window I recognized the great tall gate and imposing stone walls.  It was the Segal's "castle"; nobody had lived here for years.  Nobody could afford it.

We drove on through, a long, long driveway took a lazy S up toward the fountains by the grand columned entrance.  We were about out of time to finish dressing.

"Just give me my panties, you clown.  You better put on your own clothes unless you want to come in nude and cause a riot."

"In my dreams."

Daisy had stopped way down at the end of the parking bays.  "Dream of this."  She pulled her dress up yet again, twisting her majestic bare ass away from the steering wheel and right toward little ol' me.  That gave her room to maneuver her panties up, then smooth out her dress.  She looked at my open mouth, satisfied by her conversation stopper and said. "Ready yet?"

I finally got busy and had my shorts and shirt back on in like two seconds.  Daisy was already strolling up the curvy walkway.  Soft blue lights elegantly lit the path's borders every eight feet.  I caught up behind her; there wasn't room to walk next to her – no offense.  I noticed she had some shiny spot high on the back of her left leg, just below the hem line.  In the next path light there it was again.

"Hold on, Duchess, there's something on your leg."

She paused.  "Why do you keep calling me that?"

"I don't know.  Duchess Daisy – I guess I like alliteration.  Bend down let me get a closer look."

The teasing banter kept coming. "This better not be one of your excuses to get fresh with me, Rogue Richie."

She lowered her excellent ass so I could get a closer look at her upper leg.  "It's some kind of runny drip, maybe three inches long, like you missed a spot cleaning up."

"Crap.  I've got nothing."  Meaning, I'm sure, no tissue, etcetera."

"Let's use my shirt."

"No way.  Gallant, but not fair to you."

"Come here." And she knew I meant bend down a little closer.  Oh well, I thought, this is really nothing for me, considering where my face had been all afternoon.  And I licked it off; drying the little wet tongue spot with my sleeve.

"What was it: pussy juice or cum?"  Her teasing could get a tad gross.

I couldn't let her get the upper hand on this account.  Nonchalantly, "Either way, that has to count for a significant amends."

"You want more amends; there are lots of places on my body you can lick clean."  She kept it up.  Probably she was a bit nervous about the meeting.

But I chose to deal with it face value.  "Let me ask you: were you born this way or did you just get crass with age?"

"Ho, ho-ho" She chuckled; then lilted.  "Good one, Richie.  Just keep your eyes on my butt like you obviously have been.  We'll get you a nice hard-on by the time we get to the front door."  And she swayed that wide ass with big exaggerated jiggles with each step.  I looked on: tick-tock, knock-me-off-the-block.

Forget this, I thought, then side-stepped and zig-zagged through her walking legs past her, and kept jogging all the way up to the front door.

She took the twelve broad steps up, four at a time.  A big sigh as she met me at the door.  It had truly been a fun afternoon together, and we both appreciated it.  She looked at me, her expression vulnerable and hopeful both, and bent down to be near my face. "Richie, I heard what you said earlier."

I knew immediately she was talking about the "I love you"…back in the Humvee, well… when she was driving and singing rock n' roll.  I smiled into her eyes. "I meant it then and it is still true now."

"I just want to say," She almost whispered to me, endearing, "Though it started out really angry and weird, I've had the best afternoon of my life.  I owe it to you.  I feel alive again.  And I don't ever recall feeling this normal.  I love you too, Richie."

Daisy Strickland straightened back up to her full height, towering some eleven feet taller than me.  Looking back down, smiled precious and gave me a wink.  "I'm ready."

"After you, Beautiful."  And I reached up to the lower of the two lion's-head handles on the twenty-five foot tall door and heaved.  Far above, my afternoon delight discreetly gave the door a shove to help me open it for her.

# XIV. Giantess Moot

The stars showed-off with spectacular brilliance.  I'd been staring at them for over an hour, sixty-nined as I was; face up, by Pavie's now heavier body.  Her upper thighs pinioned my shoulders flat on the bed, her slightly spread legs affording me a pie-shaped view of the summer night's sky.  The rest of my body disappeared under her as she slept soundly on her stomach, on me.  Yep, I did that thing I keep telling you not to do: I let an amazon go to sleep on me.

Somehow a chilly breeze found its way down to my face.  Cold air drops down, doesn't it?  Judging by Orion's sideways retreat, it is well past midnight.  And I'm I guessing Pavie's heavy ass must be getting frigid.  Her frigid?  No way, I mean never – we're only talking situational camping-out-style cold ass.

A shooting star trailed up the V of Pavie's legs and disappeared into her butt.  You'd think that hot spark would wake a girl up; I laughed out loud.  A half a minute later, and…oh my goodness, where was all that extra weight coming from?  Then a sister's silhouette appeared from over Pavie's butt; one of the other Triplets had crawled on top.  Her voice sleepy, her breath very sweet, I recognized Callie. "What you laughing about, Richie?"

"A shooting star just went up your sister's ass."

"Really," Callie laughed, sleepy but quick enough. "… then how come her buns are so cold?" I could barely see the white of her grin.

Now more weight came crushing me.  A second later Aria's silhouette appeared beside Callie's.  All three sisters triple decked me.  The report early was their combined weight had shot up by almost seventy pounds in the last week.  I could sort of feel it in the moment.  Their trinity pressing me down into the cushy mattress smushed me quite thoroughly.  But this zillion dollar bed only yielded to a point, still able to provide surprising support.  No springs dug into me.  No problems actually – the specialty mattress was the best friend a man could have, under the circumstances, under these amazons.

"Thirsty?" Callie asked.  Sounds like an innocent question, doesn't it?  I nodded affirmative.  Callie scooted forward enough to heft a big breast down through the wedge of her sister's legs, the nipple directly into my mouth. Five minutes ago I'd been enjoying the view of the vast universe.  And now here I was, triple crushed with sleeping pussy on my chest and breast covering my face – my volunteer kind of finding a little space to make a stand – Pavie's naval perhaps.  And I was going to be here a while, what with Pavie the Sleeper, and some fifteen slow minutes under each of Callie's breasts, followed very likely by the same under Aria's.

I felt the bed moving.  Somebody must have gotten a bit too cool up there.  It didn't roll or slide, just moved smooth and silently, perhaps powered by electric magnet along hidden tracks off the Master Suite's eighty-foot arced veranda and back into the bedroom proper.  Where this bed resided made zero difference to me.  My cozy little hidey hole under the Triplets would stay exactly the same.

The new formulation tasted beyond incredible.  It made me feel almost as if I was someone else.  Well still me actually, but me from an earlier time, like a previous life or something.  It seemed I existed both now and back in a time of great beauty and freshness on the planet, like all was verdant forest; and mankind only a dream for the future.  Or, I wondered, had mankind become a past wound now healed by Nature.

I lost clear sense of time.  Callie and Aria each took their two turns on me, it could have lasted a minute; it could have been hours.  Soon enough, though, they rolled off their sister, and me, to nestle elsewhere in the great bed.  Pavie, of course, just kept sleeping on me.

I knew from previous experience I was likely pinned until morning.  Oh well, I gave her uppermost inner thigh a gentle kiss.  A little moan and a little wiggle down, and a beautiful sweet pussy re-settled very close within striking distance of my tongue.  Huge relaxed thighs came together over my face.  But I could still breathe from an air passage along the curved seam of those legs.  Lazily kissing and licking Pavie and revisiting the strange events of the evening and, finally, after a long while, I drifted off to sleep…

***

Daisy had just told me that she loved me.  In that glow of love we entered through the twenty-five foot high front doorway into the Segal Castle.  The Triplets stood there, dazzling in elegant evening wear.  They looked a bit taller.  But not so much when they came over to the much loftier Daisy Strickland, completely ignoring me, but greeting Daisy very graciously, and giving her a hug from three sides.

My beautiful girlfriends then took my new lover away, walking from the foyer and straight down a very wide and high hallway.  That was some sight, Aria to the left of

Daisy, with Pavie and Callie to the right, all four kind of arm-in-arm.  Daisy stood some six-plus feet taller, so Aria and Pavie each had an arm at shoulder height around Daisy's waist, while Daisy relaxed an arm down to each of their shoulders.  Daisy's huge butt swayed side to side barely covered by that lacey red dress.  The Triplets, I could tell having fun with it, matched Daisy's metronome ass, their tight yet fluffy-edged short-hemmed maroon dresses bouncing along over animated asses, like skipping-along cheerleaders going to the big game, escorting a star player.  I watched fascinated until after some seventy feet, the hallway curved to the left and they were lost from sight.

Then I was alone.  The Triplets had not even greeted me, not a word or even a glance.  But they were quirky, often operating on a consciousness way over my head.  I didn't worry about that.  For sure they had some good-hearted plan, right?  They wouldn't be pissed off or jealous, no way.  Just because I'd had, counting on my fingers, Friday-Saturday-Sunday-now-Monday-evening, four fucking days of practically non-stop sex with every woman I ran into and under.  Nah, that wouldn't bother them….

Alone, and lucky to be alive, I thought.  I pictured those ladies with big asses that had just walked down the now empty cavernous hallway.  I imagined the gathering of many more incredibly beautiful amazon giantesses that must be taking place somewhere beyond that hallway in this insanely overly-largely-built castle.  And I thought, if I could get that big front door open again, I should thank my lucky stars to have survived so far, slip out, sprint back down that long driveway, out of Bluebelle Valley Estates, and catch the first bus back to New York.

Laugher echoed back down the hallway, the mirth lifting my spirits, easing my fears.  But I didn't want to just walk down there, into some grand room where they would all be waiting for me, all looking knowingly at me at once.  That would be just too much.

Not as noticeable before, off in the darkness to my left I spied the beginning of wide stairs curving up.  A temporary escape route looked like a good idea.

The first step up proved to me these wide and tall stairs were not designed for a diminutive fellow like myself.  On that first step my thigh had to angle up more than ninety degrees to achieve purchase for my foot.  The grand arc of the dark walnut banister teased too high for me to reach from the outset.  But with both hands around a smooth, carved balustrade it seemed making it up some thirty tall steps comfortably would be doable.

The plush burgundy carpet on the stairs had a slightly bristly surface that felt good on my bare feet.  Soft rubicund floor lighting, bringing out intertwining dragon and snake patterns in the carpet, came on automatically and step by step as I began making my way up.  The gentle floor lighting spun faintly up into hollow dimness, losing its rosy kindness to an eerie streakiness of shadows and lost in its weakness before finding any ceiling.

Up to my right, twenty foot tapestries hugged back against the wall, high and far from my reach.  As my eyes adjusted, the period and style of the outdoor scenes of military men and fleshy nude women seemed somehow familiar to my untrained eye.  I recalled how I'd sneak in to find those thick, heavy art books in our house's library.  How euphoric I had felt as I studied the paintings, imagining myself as the little rescuer of those sturdy and bounteous women I saw being victimized.  But they were victims-no-longer in the scenes on the walls above me.  Thick, nude, and ample, that much about them looking just as I knew them from before, but here much bigger, tanner-skinned, and way taller than the soldiers that attacked them in the scenes.

A big dark-haired beauty turned the tables on her assailant, knocking his spear aside, pinning his chest under her knee.  Another nude amazon used her big strong arms to twist the head of a horse, sending the mail-clad knight flying.

Up the stairs further the battle unfolded above me, some parts of it lost too high in the darkness. The next scene I found particularly erotic for me: a wide meadow with downed soldiers pinned, sat on, and otherwise further subdued by the amazons.  I paused and studied with an excited foreboding the array of personal bone-breaking dramas and doom for the inferior male soldiers, both up close and vivid with detail as well as far afield and more impressionistic.

Near the top of the stairs, the final scene stole my breath.  No longer outside, but inside a majestic and ornate high-hall, it appeared that the amazons had won the King's castle.  The final battle had been a rout, the men's wrecked bodies lie twisted on the floor, warped into poses impossible for the living.  Huge brunette beauties clad in boots, short thick battle skirts, and tight bronze breast plates, stood over them with distain, foot-nudging for signs of life.

Right in front of me at eye level, the measly king, still alive, cowered for his life.  The most massive of all the amazons, a breathtakingly magnificent Queen of India, kneeled with one leg over him (and me), her other leg crushing his mid-section.  The severity of her expression said that his life would soon end.  The horror on his face, eyes wide with the terror impending as he recoiled from the dramatic view up her leather skirt, sent shivers down my spine.  This Empress would not be needing the nearby tipped-over throne; her seat of authority would begin very shortly on the doomed king's face.  Her reign officially beginning as she smothered the life out of the feeble monarch, conquered, owned, and dominated, in the end, by the violence of her pussy.

A chill breeze wafted in from the upper floor and fell colder down the wide stairwell.  The tapestry wavered, animating the Amazon Queen as she sought to smother me next, little pretender that I was, who dared to look upon her.  That little plug of adrenaline popped me up the last three steps in a hurry.  I don't believe much in hauntings, but I wanted to check out the premises on this floor to see if a puff of wind like that was reasonable.

It was.  The upstairs hallway, while wide and grand, only led to one massive door and it was open.  Inside, a grandest of a master bedroom, I recognized immediately as where the Triplets resided and slept.  I guess, then, this was maybe my room, too.  Or was I to have other quarters?  I didn't know.  But, wow, this room looked like a phenomenal place to hang out.

Again with the thirty foot ceilings, only instead of imposing, the open design and use of light and pastel paint colors gave the uplifting impression of being outdoors on a lovely spring day.  All around the walls, impressionistic renderings of young flowering trees, bursting with rink and red flowers and new light-green leaf-buds made one muse about lying down on the cushiony white carpet, next to such an enlivened wall and listening for the songbirds.  The canopy gave way to a milky blue sky, gradually blending to the darker cobalt, transitioning from wall to ceiling as a very gradual arc, keeping the dome all the way to a smooth flattened apex.  Strata of fluffy lower clouds upon the wall thinned, yielding to what I call those buttermilk clouds, gentle and puffy from underneath, with slight tinges of pink added toward the western sunset side of the room.

A great wide door, almost half the western wall, stood with its twenty-five foot sliding glass panels all the way open.  Ah, hence the breeze I had felt earlier on the stairwell.  See, not haunted – though the eerie feeling I had from the stairwell still echoed very faintly across my upper back, a few tickled hairs yet to stand down from the static pull from the Queen's large cold iron blade that had all put touched me when the tapestry had wavered.  I shivered.  Then the delicious smells coming in from that opening to the upstairs veranda suddenly hit me.

I wasted no time heading out to that super wide veranda, a vast and beautiful space off the master suite. The white-with-pink patterned-tile semicircle could easily host a party of one hundred or more – or less, if mostly amazons.  Of course, why would anyone want to host a party out here; off a private bedroom?  I don't know; I'm not much of a social butterfly.

Approaching the eight-foot high and two-foot wide rose marble handrail and bowling-pin shaped supports, I heard that same mix of laugher and mirth again – as I had heard coming from the downstairs hallway earlier.  The party was both below me and out into the yard.  There must be a hot buffet tucked underneath the structure of the veranda, in closer to the house and kitchen, secure for the food and still with plenty of room for people to gather in case inclement weather.  All the savory smells greeted me as I stood between two columns, looking out at the dwindling twilight.

A smooth and level lawn area, long enough to land a medium-size plane and at least three football-field-lengths wide, dominated the central landscape.  The grass, still giving back some of the light from the day, looked more inviting than the evening-gloomed trees on the sides and shadow of forest at the far back.  Leaning out and spying below, the ladies with plates empty going in then fully loaded going out, looked to be giving the buffet a proper amazon challenge.  Though tall as they were, their heads were still at least twenty below where I stood.

My goodness, what a view down the front of their evening gowns and dresses! Miss Rasmussen, back for what, I sniffed and pretended I could tell, a little more salmon with broccoli and cauliflowers – very nice to see you.  Bethany, I'd recognize those hooters anywhere, lovely, lovely.  Who was this coming out, plate loaded? Wow, look at that rack.  None other than Brandy all dolled up and very hungry I'd say.  Oh, that's good, Babe, stay right there, right below me, and have a nice long conversation with Bethany.  I wanted to jump off the balcony and dive down the front of Brandy's dress.  I bet that would make her mad if I spilled her food.  I fantasized what would a furious Brandy-girl would do to me for punishment? Jiminee!  Only thirty minutes away from these beauties and already I was hornier than a hound dog.

The patio below extended generously beyond from my perch, as smooth flagstone, pieced together perfectly flat with great craft and balance into a concentric pattern. The women gathered out there in a loose circle, sitting in wide comfortable-looking cushioned chairs and paired-up on generous couches.  A smokeless fire flamed high from the sunken fire-pit in the center.  The warmed ladies appreciated it, I could tell.

Meanwhile I trembled a bit, getting cooler, still in my shorts and barefoot – and getting rather feint with hunger.  Man, they could pack away the food.  That's right, my lovelies, eat, eat and fatten up for… I thought of my current dominion over them… for your king, King Richie.  Then I thought about the poor defeated and smothered sovereign on the tapestry and shivered again as another cool breeze seemed to come from nowhere.

I was searching the little crowd for the Triplets, when they appeared right below me. I think all the others must have been seated, for the Triplets stood alone with no one else passing with plates of steaming "food… glorious food", I hummed the famous song in my head.

"I wonder where Richie is?" Callie, standing in the middle, commented to her sisters.

"He might be feeling a little shy." Aria was charitable to me.

Pavie felt her right breast.  "I sure would like to nurse him soon.  And I know he must need some of our new formula by now."

What new formula, I thought to myself.  I did feel like I was starving.  Yet still I hid from them, mainly because I'd already been hiding from them.  Plus I was curious about what they were up to, and wanted to find out before I found myself sitting in the midst of them, no resistance to say, "Count me out."

Callie:  "We can have our little talk with the ladies now.  If Richie comes to join us, great.  If not, that's fine too.  There will be an opportunity to explain it to him."

Explain what? I think I was catching it all.  I was also very distracted by their triangle of six prefect breasts, so full and nicely visible from my vantage, touching each other as the Triplets huddled to discuss strategy, leaving a three-leaf clover space where I could snuggle in.  I almost let out an involuntary moan, just thinking about it and feeling so weak with hunger already.

Pavie:  "OK, then, let's start the meeting."

Aria:  "As we planned…"

They began simply with low humming, inaudible for sure to those across the patio. Just warming up?  Not likely.  It penetrated immediately: comforting, exciting, soulful, and yet, for me at least, also a bit unsettling.  Already the women out on the patio had grown quiet.

The Triplets unfolded from their circle.  They strutted toward the gathered women.  Like a set of three models hand-in-hand, their white-blonde hair bouncing identically and in rhythm, the swirls of their three short dresses exact copies in motion.  Proportioned generously, ideally and with long elegant lines to faces built of flawless fantasy, one sister would be Perfection.  All Three in physical and vocal harmony was clear evidence of the mystery of God and Goddess.

The Triplets reached the circle and stood before their guests.  The trio sang out, a wordless story, both wondrous and sad, full of hope and also a possibility of devastation almost unbearable to comprehend.  They shared a vision, a vision true in their gift of foresight, but without sharing with us the actual seeing, only for now the personal impact of emotion and responsibility.

Their song filled the patio, spreading out over the dark simplicity of the great lawn, to the embracing trees and forest in the distance.  And it seemed to me the trees celebrated with us and grieved with us, and for us.  It was a song of why we were gathered on this night.  A wordless story it evolved out of the drama and upheaval toward a thorough resolution of great wonderment and joy.

I looked across and down at the women, many of whom I knew so well.  Saint Debbie occupied one couch, next to Duchess Daisy on another, each wide ass leaving no room to spare.  The two reached across, holding hands in comfort and support.  The rest of the Pollination Crew had attended, all eight from the Secretary Pool, as well as my  favorite Pool Girls Amanda and Brandy: with the Triplets, twenty-six in all.

They formed a circle of sorts, in their clumps of pairs and threesomes, all with their intent eyes on the Triplets.  The focus generated by the women concentrated clearly, like immaculate meditation.  The process actualized as attunement, to the vision from the Triplets, to each woman's decision yet to be made this very evening on her purpose going forward.

The song ended as it descended into proper final chord.  Though gentle as could be, the finish seemed abrupt, an abandonment of glory, and now too silent, like the very trees in the distance who had been eavesdropping and dare not take a breath.

"We are inspired…" Pavie spoke for the Triplets.  Now their hundred foot separation from me made it a little hard to hear because Pavie was only speaking to a close circle of women.  I leaned through the uprights of the railing to try to catch what she said. "… by Daisy.  What she seeks to accomplish with Richie is something for each of us to consider now, this very night.  We bought this grand chateau some six months ago, not exactly knowing for what purpose.  That purpose is clear now.  We have more than enough room for each of you here.  You are all friends of Richie's and many of you lovers as well. But the actual invitation to live here, to join this family, is up to Richie.  And whether or not you accept an invitation to live her, to have your children here with Richie and all of us as sisters, of course, is up to each of you."

I felt like I was in shock.  There was a buzz of conversation now amongst the women, and a louder buzz in my head.  They consulted each other, friends and companions, new and old.  The general tone lilted upward, affirmative and then even more joyous.  Their many individual prospects in life, while variously fulfilling, almost all included too much possibility of isolation and loneliness.  That dire aspect of their futures had just been gloriously shattered.

I looked at Bethany's excited face as she smiled and spoke with the sexy beauties Sandy and Silvia.  I saw Miss Jorgensen hugging Jackie of all people.  Brandy and Amanda stood up and walked over to introduce themselves to Debbie and Daisy.  With keen interest I watched Miss Monroe speaking intently with Vicky, such beautiful confident splendors together was one fantasy that had not yet occurred to me.  And right on cue they actually kissed each other on the lips.  Oh my goodness.

I felt so overwhelmed by what I was seeing, and especially that it depended on me for each and every acceptance.  I looked down, dizzy, feeling feint with hunger.  As the distant conversation died down, I heard my name several times. "Where is Richie?"  I looked up again to see them all staring back at the house, except the Triplets. Then they turned as one and pinned me instantly like I'd been tagged with a laser.  I felt as if a spot light blazed on me, found I was, no place to hide.  I held just one breath, and that was all it took. I feinted and fell forward limp, toward the flagstone forty feet below.

***

I woke to warm ambrosia in my mouth, so far beyond delicious and comforting as I swallowed.  Had I died and gone to heaven?  If so, Callie had come with me, because even with my eyes closed I knew this was her by her particular delightful scent.  My head hurt a little bit, but this fine warm breast made me forget that.  I issued little happy sounds as I sucked harder, reaching up to pet her breast with my hand.  I heard little giggles when I did that.  What was I, in Munchkin Land?

Now I was being passed to… Aria.  Another nipple entered my mouth, equally delicious but definitely different in flavor.  The taste felt, what was it –

complementary to Callie's.  After a couple minutes I broke off, doing little bounces across to try to find the other breast.  More little Munchkin giggles.  Almost to my goal, I found I was being handed off instead… to Pavie.  This third flavor most assuredly was meant to go with the first two.  What had the Triplets done now?

Very quickly I felt energy flowing all through my body.  It was like someone was flipping on all my generators.  They lit up, igniting new pathways in my mitochondria that had lain dormant for ten thousand generations.  Down in my base chakras my Sparkle engine kicked in, humming with a Fire-strength beyond what it had known before, and ready for action.

My eye-lips popped open, my gaze steely and sure.  A twenty-six face vortex of smiling beauty greeted me.  I doubt any man has every awakened to so much affinity and love.  I kissed Pavie's lovely breast good-bye and stood, on the flagstone. I gazed past the faces straight up to the railing of the veranda.  It looked very high, and I knew I had fallen from there to these stones I stood upon.

"How are you feeling?" Callie asked.

"Man-hungry!"  I answered with verve.  Without further explanation, I walked under three sets of gorgeous legs, and made a bee-line toward the buffet.  I rubbed my slightly sore temple as I marched and thought "I am indeed one tough little sucker now."

While I ate my fill, Callie and Pavie led the women back into the house to prepare for the ceremony.  Aria stayed with me, sitting sedately nearby.

I spoke with my mouth full.  "So what exactly is this ceremony?"

"It is something my sisters and I dreamed up.  You could think of it as a marriage of sorts because it is a commitment to becoming family."

Good sweet potatoes, I thought, and took another bite. "Where in the house is the ceremony going to be?"

"It will take place upstairs, on the big veranda off the master bedroom, you know."

Yes I did know.  "Why up there?" I pointed with a celery stick.

"We need that big bed."

"Because?"

"We'll move the bed outside to the veranda, to be more in nature.  Out there we can all gather around it to witness."

I think I was about full.  "Witness what?"

"Your opportunity to choose to accept each of us into the family."

"On the bed?"

"Yes.  It couldn't be easier for you.  You lie down on the bed, on your back.  Then each candidate presents herself to you.  Pavie and Callie are explaining to the ladies right now, and preparing them."

No, I wasn't hungry at all anymore.  "Preparing them how?"

"Making sure they understand the presentation steps.  Then having them undress. They can shower and clean as they like.  The bathroom is quite the spa facility up there."

"What steps?"

"Are you finished eating?"

"Yes."

"Need a bathroom break?"

I nodded.

She pointed past the buffet to the far right side of the patio.  "There's a bathroom and shower in there.  You might even find a robe your size."

I took her up on that, went in, took care of business, and hopped in for a quick warm shower.  Drying off I noticed the floor had heated for me while showering.  Nice.  I finished drying and found the maroon robe hanging on a low hook.  Before putting it on I took a look at my thin little body in the mirror.  Still the same scrawny Richie, but at least I was getting some tan.  And while there was nothing you could call muscular, I did seem to be getting some definition-by-sinews. The soft robe fit well and mercifully, did not drag on the floor.

Back outside, but under the high ceiling and veranda above, Aria sat where she had before.  Likely also showered, now she, too, wore a robe; not maroon, but light baby blue.  Very sexy it was to think about her squeaky clean body underneath.  She motioned me to sit beside her – an invitation I would not refuse.

I leaned against her hip.  "Now about these 'steps'?"

"Yes."  She smiled, putting her hand on my shoulder, hugging me a little bit to her hip.  "There are three.  You will see each of us dressed in a robe like this."  She indicated her robe. "When it is my turn, I will disrobe and proceed like all the others through the three steps of: a kissing, a pressing, and a tasting."

I said nothing, thinking and picturing it I hoped accurately.

"After the three steps, you declare if you will accept the woman into the family. Then the woman declares if she accepts your invitation."

"Twenty-six women, huh.  That could take a while."

"Dear Richie, you have somewhere you need to be?"

"Oh no. No-no."  Nervously bouncing off what lie in store, and considering the potential solace sitting beside me, her hip pressing down against my leg, "I'm just saying….  Lovely stars out there tonight."  I stole a glance at the loose front of her robe, then down to where her legs came out mid-thigh.

She sighed.  "Really?  You're going to put moves on me with the sacred ceremony about to start upstairs?"

"Me?  No, of course not.  I mean, not unless you're interested or something…" I looked up hopeful.

"Oh, I'm very interested."  She wiggled seductively onto me enough to leave no doubt.  "But I think you better save your energy."

"Oh, I've got energy to spare."  I actually could not recall feeling as strong and vital as I felt in that moment.

"Really?  Because I would have no intention to spare you in the least."  Her veiled threat sounded much more of an exciting promise to me.

"You don't scare me."  I shoved against her immovable side, only succeeding in pushing myself back a bit.

"Oh, my, my – feeling feisty, are we?  Well, we do have about twenty minutes before they'll be ready up there."  Aria could detect I was not kidding and was ready to try and back it up. "But we'll have to get on with it.  And by that I mean me on you right away.  Come on, open that robe and let's see what you got."

Pulling it back I revealed that I stood indeed ready and willing to participate, my Volunteer ready to serve.

"Good one, Richie." Aria raised enough to slip her robe from underneath her posterior, flipping it up and over me and the back of the couch. This gave me a moment to ogle her perfect sexy and vast ass. "Ready Richie? Consider this your bachelor party." Aria giggled and jiggled at her own joke. The she plopped down her delicious bum-demanding-cum.

"Come on, cowboy. Let's get going!" Aria pounded her ass on me with such vigor from the outset, I felt myself knocked silly and crazed with lust immediately. I flopped around behind her like a puppet dangling from twisted strings managed by a drunken puppeteer. Aria let out all the stops, not just pounding but weaving and grinding on me every which way. Like a boneless ragdoll I had no volition to right myself against gravity.

With each buttcrush I descended further beneath her vicious love-making, loose-necked and askew. I puckered lips trying to kiss at her, but missed-connected, too bleary-eyed from the thrashing. Soon enough, I fell from any sitting position to a simply a prone, ass-hostage bouncing to a new position of helplessness every time she raised up before dropping the bomb on me again.

Tenderized by a not-so-tender lover, I wondered when I could be softened enough to be thrown on this giantesses BBQ grill. But Aria had other plans. The pounding stopped suddenly as she settled down on me for a heavy, squirming pressure cooking. Right when I thought I could certainly boil over and cum Aria rose off me.

"Take a big breath my little chicken." Somehow reading my metaphors, Aria added, "Time to put you in the oven."

With a slight shift by the Goddess on me I felt my face sliding into a hot wet delicious pussy. She wiggled on down getting me in there nice and snug. For maybe a minute Aria sat on me practically motionless. I took advantage of her stillness to work around and up into her as lovingly as imaginable. I noticed a brand new talent – that my new Sparkle-fire apparently issued out orally active. I knew this had to be sending Aria way over the top.

On top and over-the-top, Aria held her bliss steady for only a few heart-beats more, soaking up all the pleasure she could possibly stand. Then I felt a tiny little vibration coming down on me from her pussy and heavy ass-crush. Like a buzz it felt at first, growing quickly to an unstopping tremor. Her sexual vibration accelerated and expanded, her big ass jiggling like crazy all over me.  She rattled my body like I rode down a roller-coaster in carriage shaking like it rolled on tiny square wheels.

Aria's massive sexy legs covered my thin sticks as we must have been sideways on the big couch.  But somewhere, barely in front of her crotch I guess, her talented hand found deft purchase of my Volunteer.  She clamped down with her knowing fingers, controlling my release to wait, wait, wait.  Oh, I wanted to blast away, but she was not ready and would not let me.

No, her dominating pussy demanded more of my growing blue flame from my mouth.  And so I blazed away, firing this way and that, sweeping around and catching every neuron my bewitching wet empress could smother onto me.  Still this earthquake of a woman shuttered her loving mass on my body, the epicenter of her destruction driving her spreading crevasse over and devouring my face.

"Please, Aria, please let me cum." I mouthed up into the hot squeezing flood.

I swear her pussy somehow conveyed or maybe even spoke back to my macerated mind, "Soon, little lover, soon…"

With crescendo the vibration became so extremely rapid and constricting I felt my face had become cast in steaming moist stone, like a hot-lava woman congealed on me for an eternity of orgasmic pleasure.  And still she would not let me cum.  But I could feel the Sparkle-fire backing up to the brink of flood right in her gripping hand, sending escaping fireworks up her arm.  She would have to yield, because something was going to give, somewhere soon.

I felt her buck with the first wave her of inevitable orgasm.  With that she released my face, shifted like a pro, and timed the recoil of that first wave with a pussy plunge to engulf my Volunteer.  Her ass-smash of my upper body came coincident with my release.  I exploded into her with swirling flame tornado of pent up Sparkle-fire.  That, of course, had been Aria's design from the beginning.  Though now, whatever thought process she'd had would be smoked mindless.  It didn't matter: the perfect orgasmic process took over, simultaneous, beyond spectacular, and the most loving surrender a man or woman could ever want.

Within thirty seconds I'm sure I was completely spent, and quickly began to melt underneath my big glorious lover.  Aria, however, while she peaked with me, still had several more minutes of quivering pounding to administer to my pliable bones.  As she flattened me with the finalities of her orgasmic smother, I gently kissed at her, as I started to lose consciousness.

Fresh night air brought me back to life.  My first vision: an angelic look of post-coital love on Aria's close face above mine.  Then she graciously opened the front of her robe and brought her breast to my face, nipple onto my mouth.  Desperately needing recovery I sucked and inflated myself back to the third dimension.

In a couple of minutes I felt full.  Remember it hadn't been that long since I'd eaten dinner.  My vigor returned, full force, though calm and sexually satiated for the moment.

"You satisfied lover?"  Aria spoke affectionately with a contented purr. "I know I am.  Yes, that was just what I needed."

"Want to have another go?"  I challenged.

"For the record, my dear little man, my big ass is far, far from done with you."  Aria whipped her robe open and pounced on me, straddling me forward.  She leaned down on me and squished her big tits onto my head and across my shoulders. "You only get uppity now because you know we are running short on time and you're temporarily safe… in fact…"  She paused, momentarily distracted.  I message from her sisters no doubt.  Aria rocked back and then stood.  "They're about ready upstairs.  I'm going to go join them now.  Give it about five minutes, you might want to rinse off again quickly, then come on up.  And Richie – whatever happens and is said upstairs, just be your honest self."  She patted me on the head, then sashayed suggestively away.

"Oh boy."  I thought, then got up, ran in, rinsed off, dried quickly, and came back out.  I took a second to walk to the edge of the covered patio, not wanting to go out far enough that I could be seen from above.  The landscape had descended into nothing but blackness – probably because where I stood was basically flooded with light.  You can't have a buffet and not clearly see the food, now can you?

I could not imagine rejecting any of these women.  Sure the summer had been challenging under the sexual appetites of these Goddesses.  But I learned that none of them were truly mean in their hearts.  Amanda and Daisy, so hardened and frightening the personas they projected, had been hiding amazingly generous souls, phenomenal the love they unleashed upon me.  Even "Bad" Jackie had shared a sandwich with me last time a saw her.  Why couldn't I just go up there and say "I love you all" and be done with it, skip the ceremony?

I had to go back to my mantra: "Trust the Triplets."  That would see me through.  They played rough, too, sometimes, well often… well; I could count on it, actually.

But if they thought the ceremony was necessary then it had to be a good idea. Commitment is what they seemed to be after; clear and strong bonding.  They must be looking at some future where that would be an important requirement.  I remembered something Callie had told them:  "… by Daisy.  What she seeks to accomplish with Richie is something for each of us to consider now…" Then it hit me definitely, more clearly, what they were talking about before I passed out earlier – oh my God.  They all want babies!

***

… Pavie coughed a tiny bit at some little speck of dust.  I thought maybe she would wake up and roll off of me.  But no such luck – oh who am I kidding – like I really minded the all night pin… not.  Anyway, it gave me more time to review the extraordinary events that were to unfold next…

# XV. Giantess Pump and Circumstance

"Oh Pavie, this all night pressing, it's turning my mind to a puddle of puppy love..." I cannot even tell you how long I'd been mumbling up into her muff, undoubtedly for hours and hours of luscious smush.

Even though sleeping, Pavie still emanated the most intimate and amorous blue-glow of affection.  My smothering lover was what God intended an incubus should be.  Not some evil spirit, but rather an all-night emissary from the feminine Devine.  Sure her 645 pounds crushed my 70 pounds thoroughly and in every physical sense.  But her rain of love on me, warm skin on skin, connected so intimately, minute-by-minute becoming these hours of unrelenting and irresistible incubation absolutely asphyxiated my boundaries.  This left me with nothing that could prevent her body's seeming unlimited capacity to infuse her sexual domination and loving ownership of my form and being.  Tucked away forever under my loving wife…yes, wife!

***

The sound of a little chime came down from above to the patio and now cooling buffet.  It seemed too dainty for what I knew waited directly above me.  The five minutes Aria had given me was up: time to face the music.

Well fed, and with renewed energy, my walking accelerated into a run, picking up the pace, I tested the power of my new and improved mitochondrial engines.  Fire-Sparkle churning, I bounded up those big stair-steps gaining speed with each one.  The tapestry Amazon Queen's eyes blazed at my insolence.  But I dodged her heavy sword to gain the top of the stairs.  I blew her an arrogant kiss, laced with testosterone.  Then in further impertinence, I turned my back on her, and strode King Richie into the bedroom.

The entire walls and ceiling of the grand bedroom glowed with a very faint blue luminescence.  This technology I had not seen before.  I admired the soothing mood-setting effect quite a bit.  Outside could have been the sexiest KKK meeting ever imagined, except no hoods, and the pale robes were actually all baby blue, and, well, no burning crosses, just the sacrifice of little ol' me on the gigantic bed — that part seemed real and likely enough.  I climbed up on the bed.

Aria stood and came to the bedstead.  Was she going to be the first?  She reached her hand out toward me, and in a very low tone: "Your robe please."  Oh yeah, me nude; I suppose that would be part of this.  I guess Aria was my handler for the ceremony.  I removed the robe and tendered it to her.

Kind of chilly out here I thought, looking around at the trying-to-be-passive but nevertheless obviously anticipatory twenty-six beautiful and beaming faces.  I smiled probably half-hearted, then lie back, looking up at the stars.  Aria leaned in, still whispering, "We'll start with the smallest."  And then she moved away, leaving me alone.

Start with the smallest?  That didn't even make sense to me.  There was no "smallest", only big, bigger, and ginormous.  But from Aria's viewpoint, well I guess I get it.  Smallest first then – I could see how largest first might undo me for the others.

The big bed moved as Little-billy-goat-Gruff climbed on some fifteen feet away.  I wondered who it would be, this smallest of the amazons.  Then none other than sweet "little" Coleen sidled up next to me; here so innocently, without her robe.  She positioned herself on all fours, her cute face directly above mine, straight blonde hair in a smooth cascade all the way to the bed.  She smiled adoringly down at me and said rather formally, I assume some script they had a few minutes to practice.  "My name is Coleen Baker.  I want to join this family, have a baby with you, and become sisters with all the women gathered here."  After this declaration of intent she descended to lie down on me, face above mine, and deliver an excellent deep kiss on my mouth.

I was kind of interested to finally hear her surname.  I realized I didn't know any of the Pollinations Crew's last names, nor Amanda's or Brandy's either.  On the other hand, I didn't know many of the first names of the ladies in the secretary pool.  Synsonto had weird protocols – what else is new.

The kiss lasted maybe two minutes – lovely really; very nice and full of a kind of long-range intent.  Let's face it: this was an audition.  Coleen couldn't know I'd pretty much decided to accept everybody already.  I didn't figure the Triplets would have even invited someone in the first place that I would have to reject – that didn't seem like something they would do.  Honestly, what kind of asshole was I going to be here?  Like: "No Coleen, you failed!  Pack up your pussy and clear out!"  No way I would do that!  Heck, they were all fine with me and some, of course, super fine.  And others I knew to be downright magical.  So what objections was I going to raise, really?  But the ceremony mattered; I got that.  And who knows, maybe someone would come off as really unacceptably mean and vicious – like the Queen Amazon of the tapestry.  Question was: would I even reject someone like that cruel Queen?

Little Coleen sat up on me, ready now, it appeared, for step two "The Pressing".  To me this sitting up on me was really a second stage of a pressing that had already begun with her dominant kiss.  But it had a specific purpose as Collen explained.  "Having me as a sexual partner can be risky for you.  At seven foot one inch and 363 pounds I could harm or crush you during foreplay or intercourse.  I want you to accept that risk when you accept me to the family."

I suppose it was a real risk.  But it seemed with her, that risk was least likely of all.  Certainly, however, a few crazed hours of her ass clamped tightly and pinning my face could easily kill me.  So I took her point; duly noted.

Coleen was doing very well, I thought, and I enjoyed having her cute and proper derriere planted upon me.  She moved right along now to step three.  "I will seek to dominate you with my body, during sex and most specifically with my pussy.  I want you to understand exactly what that feels like.  I will force you to kiss me there, to love my sweet aroma and crave to taste me."  She scooted forward and sat on my chest, her uppermost inner thighs against my cheeks.  "Know my dominion over you."  With that she slid her pussy the rest of the way forward to cover my face.

Though *only* 363 pounds she proved plenty heavy enough to dominate my 70 pounds body. I was completely helpless, my arms immobilized by her legs, my torso crushed by her butt, my face well into her pussy, my mind off in a world of delight and submission.  I certainly did "know her dominion over me."

Then suddenly she was off me.  Someone had handed her a warm moist hand-towel.  She used it to wipe my face clean, a couple of dabs on my chest, checked my Volunteer to see if any attention was needed there – none needed – then tossed the towel back to someone off the bed.  She sat back, looking at me, expectantly, hopefully.  Oh, I get it; this is when I was supposed to say something.

I sat up, looked at Coleen kindly, took a moment to glance around the room as well.  All the women looked on with rapt attention; what I said next was apparently very important.  I checked in with the Triplets, making eye contact with each one.  Aria, Pavie, and Callie had pretty much the same expression: a peaceful "you know what to do".

Then back to Coleen: "Miss Coleen Baker, I would very much like it if you would join this family and all the risks and rewards that entails for you and me and all present."

"Ahh!" Coleen cried out in excitement.  While all applauded, Coleen grabbed me up into an enthusiastic hug, rag-dolling me kind of roughly, but soon sat me back carefully on the bed, and then pressed me back to lying down with her hands.  She closed my eyes with the index and middles fingers of her right hand.  Then she bounced away on the bed; for sure still quite elated.

One down; twenty-five to go.  I'd often wondered exactly what these amazon and giantesses actually weighed.  I could make a little game of it, challenge myself.  Since it seemed they were going to tell me, I decided to see if I could keep a running tally.  I would only have to keep the current total and add the next gal to it.  Could be a good other-focus to help me endure what was coming.

The bed moved again. I waited with my eyes closed.  Who would it be?  I'm guessing Janet McNamara.  I knew an amazon was right above me now.  I opened my eyes.  Nope, not Janet, it was Jeanie Minor, intelligent hazel eyes, black hair smartly cropped short for summer coolness.  "Hello, I'm super sexy Jeanie Minor and I've come here to face-fuck you into oblivion…"  No, hang on, that's just what I wanted her to say.

Actually what I got was the similar patter as before.  "My name is Jeanie Minor.  I want to join this family, have my baby with you, and become sisters with all these women gathered here."  It wasn't exactly the same statement as Coleen's, but definitely close enough.  Janet's sweet, sweet thorough kiss left no doubt.  Wow, that kiss alone had her in and accepted as far as I was concerned.  I really, really wanted more of that action.

Now she sat up on me.  I tried to detect a greater weight than Coleen.  But honestly, she seemed about the same to me. "Having me as your sexual partner will be risky for you.  At seven foot two inches and 371 pounds I could harm or crush you during foreplay or intercourse.  I want you to accept that risk when you accept me into the family."  Again the patter came slightly different, a better edit, I thought.  Jeanie was one sharp cookie.  One season on the Pollination Crew then my guess she would be off to some kind of executive training.

Jeanie did a quick butt hop up to straddle my upper chest and neck.  She gave me a sexy, inviting smile.  "I will absolutely seek to dominate you with this body, especially during sex, and most assuredly with my pussy.  I want you to understand clearly what that feels like.  I will require you to kiss and lick me there, to love my aroma and crave the taste of me.  Know my dominion over you."  And without further ado, bam, it was pussy time.

Jeanie was instant addiction.  I thought I would maybe give her a little kiss.  But when I got her taste, my tongue went wild with desire.  She must have liked it a lot because she got very juicy very fast.  And then it was over and she was off.

I looked at her face; she biting at her lower lip, trying to constrain a little shutter pre-orgasm.  Man did this woman want to finish me right there and then!  Yes, she certainly had dominion over me.  I realized that what I said should be carefully the same for each – my intuition told me I didn't want to start this out with showing favoritism.  "Miss Jeanie Minor, I would very much like it if you would join this family and all the risks and rewards that entails for you and me and all present."

Jeanie didn't react, but began cleaning my face with a fresh towel.  With a twinkle in her eye, she calmly said.  "Smart move, Richie."  She finished nice and efficiently, gave me a lover's wink, then closed my eyes with two light kisses.

Let's see, oh yeah, that's right, my tally: Collen at 363 pounds plus Jeanie at 371 pounds equals 734 pounds pressed me so far.  Two down; twenty-four to go.

Janet McNamara, what a looker: everything about her was tight and firm.  I'd heard she took some high school state championship in gymnastics a few years back.  That's phenomenally difficult for anybody, but when you're seven feet tall – forget-about-it!  Incredible power, that's what it took to overcome all that leverage disadvantage.  And she had bulked up even more since those days.  Wicked arms, death-grip legs – what a toned and bronze-tanned package of supremacy that gracefully positioned herself over me!  Her brown eyes studied me as if considering how much punishment I could take.

Janet said the step-one patter then dropped down on me hard for the kiss.  Even her lips were strong; imagine being dominated by a kiss.  My little bit of resistance fell away very quickly.  As I succumbed she offered me the slightest bit of tempering of her aggression.  Not the most loving kiss, but I liked her 110% vigor.

As Janet recited step-two she sat on me and worked me over with those thighs-of-demise.  After a quick maceration, she locked on tight with no visible movement.  Then she activated squeezes and stimulations from individual muscle groups that probably most people didn't even know they had.  She tilted her head at me, as my eyes widened in pleasant surprise; her expression saying there's a lot more where this comes from.

Step-three: if ever a tight pussy could kiss a face this was it.  Man, what she could to with control and sensitivity was like a huge set of devouring wet lips.  No way was

I letting this chick get away.  I had to measure my acceptance of her, so as to not to seem too enthusiastic in front of the others.

By way of acknowledgement Janet grabbed a handful of my hair and gave it a nice firm tug.  Ouch… and yes.  I noticed her firm ass had no tan lines – the natural-beauty Janet liked to sunbathe nude.  Another good one!  Let's see: 734 pounds plus Janet at 377, wow, 1,101 pounds so far.  Three down; twenty-three to go.

"Bad" Jackie Piedmont, at 378 she was only one pound heavier than Janet, but felt totally different.  Jackie hadn't worked out in probably five years, if ever. However, she remained in reasonably good shape by virtue of the advantage of the strong physicality that came with the amazon syndrome plus an active work and personal lifestyle.  Her kisses were kind of bitey, her sitting on me pleasantly soft and spreading, and, of course, being *Bad* Jackie she had to go off-rules of the ceremony and sit on my face backwards and start playing with my happy Volunteer until the other ladies made her get off.  Oh Bad Jackie!  If Synsonto could enlist the handicapped, so could I.  I was kind of surprised she wanted children.  But you never know, it would probably be very difficult for a kid to sneak one by a trickster like Jackie.

Chalk up another one.  Let's see now, 1,101 pounds plus Jackie's 378 put the new total at 1,479 pounds.  Four down and twenty-two to go.

Jessica Wagner had given up cattle for corn this summer.  The cowgirl's long red hair fell in big wavy loops past her waist, then piled onto my face as she positioned on all fours above me.  She cast it aside with a practiced sweep of her arm.  Looking up at her pale blue eyes and fair and noble complexion all framed with flaming red furls-of-curls every which way, I had the distinct impression I was about to become Lady Godiva's horse.  But first, I would become her lover, as she rolled her body down on me.

Jessica must have mis-calculated the small size of her little steed because a wonderfully large and soft breast ended up right on my face.  She scooted down immediately.  Her face bright red with embarrassment – she really had no intension of breaking the rules.  Her kiss, gentle and apologetic to begin with, evolved to a knock-um-down and hog-tie-um triumph over me.  Yee-hi and holy buckets, this country girl could kiss!

When she sat up on me she really entered her cowgirl comfort zone.  Riding and driving cattle she knew like the back of her hand.  Oh I felt those maverick-cuttin' skills in a little sampler of her weaving to and fro on me. Doggies!

But the real rodeo began in step three.  She acted out a prolonged buckin' bronco ride on my face.  She heaved off my body completely, time and again, and I'd see her big tits flopping around, her wild hair flying every which way, then pounding pussy black-out again.  Oh way too brief, but very effective.  Yes, yes, she made quite an impression on me, so to speak.

Jessica Wagner rodeo queen?  Absolutely, without a doubt.  In fact, couldn't we take a pause and just let her fuck the hell out of me right now?  She wiped me down like the good little pony I had been for her.   When she stole away, it was all I could do to not crawl after her.

So now, 1,479 pounds plus Jessica's 397, getting tougher now in my head: 1,867, I think.  Five down and twenty-one to go.

MaryEllen Dells always smelled like pie to me. She was a master of blackberries and raspberries and olallieberries and apples and rhubarb and cherries and peach and any fruit that could be made into a pie or better yet, cobbler.  She brought one or two along to work most every day, not to hog down, but to share.  As I looked at her kindly pleasant face, her seasoning of freckles across the nose, her sandy hair falling most the way to my face, I thought: I should run away with this gal and see if she could fatten me up a bit.

MaryEllen's kiss did have the feint taste of olallieberry, yum, my favorite.  Or maybe it just wafted around off her hair from the last open-oven blast.  Somebody was going eat somebody up here.  I had the appetite, but hands down, her mouth dominated.

Sitting up on me I could see a little belly on her, just some extra for fun, and kind of bigger breasts to go along.  The intensity of the desire I felt for her surprised me.  She was just so very approachable, not threatening, simply smashing.

She butt-walked her plentiful ass up my body to present her sugary pussy.  Then she loaded that delicious pie onto my face.  It was like being face-fucked by a dream of animated desserts.  We simply must have this woman in the family.

It was getting harder to hold the numbers in my head.  Let's see now, 1,867, add on MaryEllen's 406 and that comes to… 2,273 pounds.  Six down, twenty to go.

Cecilia Pike's lips, ah, well, let's just call them generous… and lovely… and about as sexy as they could possibly be.  And when they assaulted your face; it felt quite entirely overwhelming – definitely an extraordinary asset.  Check "yes" in that box.

On step-two I noticed clearly that Cecilia's 412 pounds was far more than Coleen's 363 at the beginning.  Tougher for sure to catch an in-breath.

Now I know a 400 pound woman is nothing new to this world.  We know them, sometimes friends and family.  Perchance we might have even have had such a lover.  God bless them one and all.  But you know darn well that a typical 400 pound woman is in a battle for her life, nine out of ten times morbidly obese, her very life force being dragged down by fat in a gravitational field.  Help exists for them if they need it, and many find it.  More power to them as they find a way to live and enjoy life.

That is *not* what we are talking about here, for example, with Cecilia Pike: seven foot three inches, 412 pounds of athletic prowess, cover-girl beauty, and ninja-like capabilities of movement.  And Cecilia was no exception; she exemplified the rule of the Amazons of Bluebelle Valley.

The thing nobody seemed to know for sure was just how big most of these gals were going to get.  And the bigger they got the sturdier they got.  It was simple physics.  Daisy proved the results of the growth sequence of width and solidity in proportion to height.  Sure, these Amazons had some fat, sometimes plenty of it, but always it seemed to me in the right places.  What else would comprise a breast?  And why not pad a great big ass with what it is supposed to have to mold onto you and smother you as properly intended?

As Cecilia pressed my body down, I appreciated the near miracle that she was: a gorgeous, big, dominating beauty that was asking me to invite her into the family we were forming that very night.  As her pussy closed over my face I actually said yes up into its sovereign smothering of me.  And somehow this intelligent and perceptive woman understood that suffocated vocalization from me.  She responded with such of loving pussy massage of my face I could only describe my feeling as utter adoration.  I licked as deeply up into her with all the verve I could muster.

It was time and we separated in full crave of each other.  She already had my answer but I said the patter out loud so all would know.  And like every other gal before her, the family voted her in unanimous as well.

Oh, my mind felt like mush: 2273 plus 412, an easy one, thank goodness, 2,685 pounds.

The next contestant made more disturbances in her approach.  I opened my eyes and understood; there were two, two sisters, a package deal obviously: Sandy and Silvia Sanderling.  You could have two, you could have none, but just one – not an option.  OK then.

Dual kisses; nice start, I like that.  The pressing though, a big jump in gradient.  I mean 414 plus 415 pounds, 829 that was a lot to take all of the sudden. That had to be a disadvantage for the woman who came next.

Of course the Sanderlings had all kinds of ways to smash their big sexy asses on me.  But for the ceremony they went traditional.  Sandy sat on my chest forward and Silvia sat on Sandy's lab, her boobs in Sandy's face.  What I saw actually viewed: Silvia's huge ass looming over me, held above my head by the spread of Sandy's legs to either side.  Oh yes, they were surely in the family.

Because there were two of them they were allotted twice as long.  The sisters used that time wisely, moving along swiftly to maximize step three, pussy-tasting.  It was a quick and thorough tag-team pussy whipping.  Whoever was on my face would have a four hundred pound sister in her lap.  In short order I felt the devastation.

Finally they sat up, done, but still pressing their hips against my face.  Yes, yes, you're in the family already.  They hummed in victorious attitude as they wiped me down clean.  That was going to be a tough act to follow.

OK, so 829 pounds on top of 2,685 comes to… comes to… 3,514.  This was adding up faster than I thought it would.

I lie back, eyes closed, wondering who could possibly, as an individual in this weight-class, match the Sanderlings.  Oh my goodness, I recognized that addictive fragrance.  Sure enough, the one and only Vicky Hatton.

"Hello tiger," she purred, her casual gaze enough to stop the Train to Paradise; her energy wave of confidence in itself a kind of foreplay. "My name is Vicky Hatton. I'm going to join this family with you, let you father a child with me, and make these fine ladies my sisters."  She leaned down to one elbow, supporting her head with her hand on her cheek, big breasts covering the middle of my body.  She breathed on me, holding back, waiting; her exhale a zephyr breeze of Goddess.  I wanted her kiss so much.  I lifted my head to kiss her, put she pulled back, just out of reach, still keeping me pinned with her breasts and breathing heavily on me.

I wasn't supposed to talk, but I couldn't take it.  "Come on Vicky, don't make me beg."

"Too late!" She laughed and plunged her mouth down on and over mine, kissing deeper and deeper, building the kiss with more and more passion. She broke it off at its upside to a promised higher peak, a peak for some future time. I felt I'd been kissed by some well-intentioned dimentor. Vicky seemed to actually take up my life force and then give it back to me...

Sitting up on me, Vicky smiles down, winks and whispers. "Step Two." Then louder as she, of course, alters her part of the ceremony patter. "Having me dominate you sexually will be risky for you physically and emotionally. At seven foot five inches and 418 pounds I will crush your body and smother your resistance during foreplay and intercourse. I command you to accept that risk as you accept me to the family."

Wow, Vicky had fun being bossy about it. She already knew I could not refuse her, nor would I try. And of course Vicky couldn't just sit on me. No she had to tease and squeeze. She played with her breasts, puckering her lips, and she flashed her big bedroom eyes at my obvious desire for her. She had me worked up pretty good when she moved on to step three, continuing to alter the script in her favor.

"I already dominate you with my body, with my big sexiness, and now most entirely with my pussy. Know again now exactly what that feels like as I allow you to kiss me there, to crave my aroma and worship the taste of me." Vicky walked her hips forward and most gradually settled her pussy onto my hungry mouth.

Vicky had such magnetism and control over me. There was something magical in being under her, knowing her; definitely a sensory overload. A moment with her was forgetting all else, and that is saying a lot.

She rose off me but I just lie there in a state of bless. She leaned over and said softly, adoringly and warm into my ear, "See, just a day later and I get to marry you anyway." She looked so wonderfully victorious, then with pursed lips added. "I love you cutie pie. This adventure as family is going to be a blast." A quick kiss on the forehead, then she swabbed me clean with a nice steamy towel.

Come on, think man, there's something you're supposed to do. Oh yea; I said the words. Vicky got accepted – there was never a doubt. Then lying back, let's see Vicky at 418 pounds plus... plus... 3,514 pounds equals 3,932 pounds so far. OK, if I can make it through Vicky and still have any wits, I'm ready for whatever is next.

The next two in sequence were big Bethany then little strawberry blonde Tiffany. Yes, big Bethany, the largest on the Pollination Crew at 425 pounds, had proved to be quite the grinder on the rides home. Yet little Tiffany, the smallest of the

Secretary Pool at 481 pounds, established once and for all in my mind that size is relative.  I mean, you'd think at a mere 70 pounds in a valley of amazons I would know that already.  And I suppose I did.

But I have to say that Bethany's familiar smothering of me followed immediately by Tiffany mounting me with her more significant and very classy ass gave me a new perspective – a very dark, heavy crushing perspective: if I wanted Bethany in this family, and I certainly did, then for sure absolutely I had to have Tiffany in the family as well.

The other thing about our gal sexy Tiffany, her birthday came just two months before mine.  So considering her age and size she might be one of the larger amazons when fully grown.  And now, well, these long-term considerations had to be taken into account, didn't they?  Oh tight Tiffany's terrific tush took tons of time to totally take torment to triumph.  I had no idea she had such athletic and dominating designs on me.  Yes, yes, Tiffany, you're in.

Let's see, I'm getting behind.  Bethany's 425 pounds plus Tiffany's 481 pounds, that's 906 pounds.  Add than onto 3,932 and we have 4,838 pounds so far.  Now that makes twelve with fourteen to go; one more and I'm half way – well, maybe not exactly considering the big women yet to come down the pike.

"Hello Richie, I'm Rachael Rasmussen, I want to join this family, have a baby with you, and become sisters with all the women gathered here…" I drifted off, daydreaming.  I mean I could see her medium length auburn brown hair, her Goddess Diana aspect, needing only a leather headband to complete her huntress look… except all the women kind of blurred together… it was getting to be a lot to take in, all in one sitting, it you catch my drift…

"Having me as a sexual partner can be risky for you.  At seven foot eleven inches and 494 pounds I could harm or crush you during foreplay or intercourse.  I want you to accept that risk when you accept me to the family."  I think I nodded, like "sure, why not" and she proceeded, I believe close to the script.

"I will seek to dominate you with my body, during sex and most specifically with my pussy.  I want you to understand exactly what that feels like.  I will force you to kiss me there, to love my aroma and crave to taste me."  She rose to her knees, walked it forward, hovering for a second, "Know my dominion over you."  And Miss Rasmussen plopped it down, wetter than expected, demolishing my face under her pile-driver pussy.

As she sat on me I just kept saying over and over "Half way through.  Half way through…"  I guess something about the way my mouth moved (maybe it was the tongue thrust "thro" of the word "through) as I said that phrase over and over that generated quite the turn-on for Miss Rasmussen.  I think maybe the Sparkle-fire lashed out a little via my tongue.  I better be careful with that.  Poor Miss Rasmussen had to be lifted away, definitely losing control.  Yet, far be it from me to reject an amazon for losing sexual control.  Everyone seemed happy to have Miss Rasmussen included in the family.  OK, add 494 pounds to 4,838 and that totals 5,332 pounds!  Half way, yippy – yea, right.…

The next one shook the bed like a stampede approaching.  That's because it wasn't one; it was four.  These four familiar gals looked like they could be all from the same Scandinavian amazon tribe: blonde, wide-set blue eyes, broad-shouldered, sturdy, sexy amazons of the first caliber. They introduced themselves in ascending order of size, all wanting to join the family, have babies, kissing me kind of quickly, warning me of their dangers in unison, all to allow more of their four-fold of time on me to spend it on the pussy and ass-smashing: Miss Loraine Appleton (8'0" 508), Miss Francine Jorgenson (8'1" 522), Miss Lorna Taylor (8'2" 539), and Miss Kathy Petersen (8'2" 544).  Goodness, that's more than a ton of woman!

They arranged me into a double pussy scissor of my head and another on my middle.  In practiced coordination they all four gyrated and rolled around on the bed at the same time.  These long-time roommates were not about to give up on each other for this family.  But I did not see that should be necessary at all.  Their talent rendered a highly sensual smashing and rhythmic crushing of supreme timing, dangerous in the extreme for me if not perfectly practiced and delivered without miscue or hesitation.  They promised they knew lots of routines and assured me many more to come in our future together.  Yes, yes my 2,103 pound roomies, we must have that future together.  That brought the new total to: 7,435 pounds.

Oh my goodness, look who is over me on all fours: none other than long-time family friend Donna Klingbell.  Like me she's a Synsonto brat.  In fact our dads went to college together and worked in the same division back East, that is until Donna's folks moved on a research assignment, and returned to the Bluebelle Valley station.

Though maybe a year and a half older than me; our parents thought it cute to pledge us to each other when I was only two years old and her not yet four.  Darling isn't it?  By the time I was five and a half and at her seventh birthday party it became very clear to our parents that maybe that was not a good idea – a size issue had emerged, for each of us.  Anyway, I hadn't seen Donna for some fifteen years until that first day at my summer job.  And social pressures from her being one of my bosses in the Secretary Pool kept us from chumming up like old times.

And yet, here we were, at long last making those marriage vows.  As she sat on me, finishing with the required Step One patter, I couldn't help saying to her, "Well Donna, what do you think?  Wouldn't our parents be proud?"

She laughed a good-natured "yes" and then proceeded with the Step Two warnings. To which I added. "I guess that's what our parents were afraid of, me getting squished by you someday."

Donna laughed again, hauling her huge 559 pounds ass to loom over my head. After finishing the Step Three required words "…know my dominion over you…" she added, "…this has been my fantasy for a long, long time, to marry you and lovingly smother you under my ass, thorough and often and for years and years…"

I was about to say, "That's been my fantasy also for a long time." But before I could get a word out that fantasy became a big crushing reality. I tried to hold back the Sparkle-fire that sought to escape from my kissing lips and active tongue.  And I did hold it back some, but not enough.  My long-time, sexually pent up friend Donna Klingbell orgasmed a gusher onto me almost immediately.  Then, with her time too quickly up, she had to get off right away.  It took her two towels to get me cleaned up.  During the process she was resoundly accepted by me and the family of sisters.

I missed Donna already, her huge ass waving back and forth as she crawled away on the bed.  So Donna was number eighteen, leaving only eight more.  Quickly now, the bed's moving again and this has to be Miss Monroe coming.  Hurry, do the math, while you can still think.  Donna's 559 pounds tallied onto 7,435 come to 7,994 – wow so close to four tons of woman.

"Hello Cutie."  The stunningly gorgeous Miss Valerie Monroe's face appears above me.  She looks so excited, her eyes flashing repeatedly, her breath already quickened.  She sits her vastly luscious ass on me, wiggling down, pressing as if to absorb my willing body.  Her recitation of the various steps is way off script, but the point is quite clear: "I am the one and only Valerie Monroe.  My purpose is to love you into obliteration, to demand your sexual service of me, to crush my 8'4" body and 588 pound pussy onto you in the most dominating and dangerous ways, to grow and get heavier with each passing week as you worship me more and more as a goddess.  Here is my kiss…"  She covered me with her massively beautiful body, her face so dazzlingly inspiring I could hardly stand it.  I felt I was coming out of my skin as she kissed me, mouthing my lips and face with noisy little gasps of hunger and sexual overload.

Valerie unwillingly pushed herself up and moaned, "Oh, ohhhh… I can't stand it, Richie. I need your face parked in its home." She slid her body forward over mine until that perfect pussy opened and engulfed my face. Sparkle-fire rage out of control from my mouth and off my tongue, blue flames of electric stimulation shot up through her body. She froze in a shock-wave of sudden over stimulation. Unthawing in the clench on my face, Valerie first began to quiver, then shake, then clench yet tighter again. And audible shriek howled out into the room, but I only heard her voice penetrating me through underwater banshee screams of control completely lost, begging me for mercy, for me to reign in the over-stimulation.

Valerie Monroe, so, so painfully beautiful, too much extreme sexiness really for one small man to assimilate, had in a word: lost-it. "Stop! Stop! Stop!" She screamed, while absolutely over-powering me, completely able at her choice to remove her immensely superior bulk off me any time she wanted. And yet she pleaded, "Please…" she begged for me to release her, though I was little more than a toy doll being smashed up into her grinding, gushing pussy.

Bigger women hauled her away. I remained, flattened, then curling fetal, breathing fire like a little blue love demon.

"Richie, Richie – are you all right?" Valerie returned, supervised, but in control again, wiping me clean. "Oh, I love you too much. And good God what you do to me! The desire is just inhumane. I beg you to accept me. A cannot live without this connection to you."

I shuttered in a breath, feeling my color return. Could I say no to this deity? Not in a million years. Add that perfect 588 pounds of desire to the family: +7,994 = 8,582 pounds so far, and only seven more women to go.

As soon as I felt the bed move I knew it was the Triplets. Their wonderful energy had become unmistakable comfort, love, and excitement to me – that's a pretty good trio in itself. Compared to Donna and Valerie, the Triplets presented themselves as very reserved for this ceremony. I got that they did not want to seem overly-familiar with me. How could the other women feel evenly welcomed if the Triplets simply exerted their extreme dominance over me? The Triplets had plenty of sensitivity to that, I surmised.

They also took advantage of their place in the line-up to provide me with some much needed relief and sustenance.  Aria's kiss breathed energy into me, reviving me, enlivening me.  She released a positive flow into me that recharged my spent sexuality.

Pavie followed with her crunching chest sitting that you'd think would expel all my breath, heavy and suffocating as her ass must be.  And though she crushed me substantially into the inner workings of the mattress, the pressing came also as a flow of descending energy.  In my mind I could see all the colors of her generous chakras dropping light down into me through the lowest red base, foundational and balancing.  Her 645 pound bouncing must have looked like torture.  But every bit of her butt pounding onto me drove more precious vitality into my body.

Callie's pussy tasted sweet as if I reunited with a missing part of my being.  Even deeper and more delicious than Valerie, she smothered me gently.  Every lick of her juices I found more invigorating than the best magic power bar for a marathon runner in the sky.

The Triplets did not sing or otherwise unduly influence me in any way anybody could see.  Their message came clear: we are here to love you, sustain up, uplift you, and grow with you and on you.

No drama here.  The Triplets must be the cornerstone of the family to be.  Yes.  Yes.  And Yes!  Three times 645 pounds is 1,935 pounds.  Add that to 8,582 to get 10,517 pounds.  Twenty-two down and only a measly four to go.

Brandy's tits arrived before she did.  Pardon my exaggeration and over-focusing but I'm guessing each breast weighed as much as I did.  Of course she only claimed to be 10'2" and weigh 909 pounds.  So for her total tit weight to be 140 pounds or some 15% of her body did, I admit, seem unlikely, especially considering the size of her prodigious ass.

Hang on; I think Brandy was saying something.  "… and since you seem so interested in my tits, why don't we just start with you kissing me there…"  With that, big bounteous Brandy brought her breasts to smother my face as she lie down on me. You could not call Brandy an arrogant woman by any means.  It is just that she had gotten so much feedback over the years about the sexy over-whelming lovely supremacy of her perfectly shaped massive breasts that she just assumed the implementation of them to dominate a man would always prove sufficient.  Well, guess what?  This situation was no exception.

As she ever so slowly lifted them off me, I strove with eagerness to keep licking and kissing them.  So being an obliging lover, Brandy hovered a while to let me keep at it, basically humbling myself as a little slave to those crushing mammaries that hung like impending doom above the tiny frailness of my thin body.  The bits of Sparkle-fire I sought to control, but nevertheless escaped my lips, tingled Brandy's nipples into a hardness the betrayed how extremely turned on was this giantess that owned me sexually.

Great tits rose up, legs and hips rotated forward, and Brandy's sweet pussy scooched onto my head, taking in my face immediately.  She performed a gentle gyration, stirring my face around in the pussy like a tiny piece of flotsam lost in a tempest at sea. I recalled her hurricane and tidal wave orgasm from the last time she had me in this position and I wanted that desperately now.  Of course I don't know what she said or when she said it, as far as the ceremony goes.  But when Brandy finally lifted off me I knew that meant it was time for me to say: "Yes Brandy, I gladly accept you into this family."

Brandy at 909 pounds added to 10,517 comes to 11,426 pounds.  On with the show, I say!

Bless my soul, it's Amanda.  But what's wrong?  For such a big sexy woman with neigh on ass perfection, she looked much too nervous… worried… tight.  She sat on me, almost shaking like a dog that had heard a noise too sudden and loud.  Then, way too automaton she monotoned out the Step One words: "My name is Amanda Schmidt.  I very much want to join this family, have a baby with you, and become sisters with all the women gathered here."  She was supposed to kiss me now but just sat there – kind of blowing her audition.

"Amanda, hey, are you all right?  You're supposed to do something now." She had me worried for her.

"Oh, I'm sorry.  I'm so nervous."  Amanda lowered herself onto me for a kiss.  But her lips seemed stuck shut, drawn tight, her affection being completely withheld.

I was able to speak around her barely-touching-me firm lips. "What is it girl?  Why so tight?"

"Richie I don't want to blow this."  Amanda whispered. "I feel like everyone knows I've been such a terrible bully for so many years.  They won't trust me – especially if I try to get tough with you, you know, boss you around, and dominate you too much."

"Don't worry about it.  Everybody seems to be dominating me today."  I joked, trying to ease her concern.  "Why don't you just say exactly how you feel and let the chips fall where they may."

Amanda just stared into my eyes for a good long minute, searching for reassurance. I met her gaze and I think my eyes smiled up into hers.  It grew into a very nice moment of connection, soul-to-soul you might say.  Finally, still with her eyes locked dependently on mine, Amanda grinned wide, sighed nice and big, releasing herself to trust me, to trust the situation enough to say.  "Oh Richie, you're so precious and so deliciously tiny."  She whispered no longer, speaking loud enough for all to hear. "Oh God, Richie, I do want you right now in the worst way.  And by worst way I guess I mean to plant my massive ass on your skinny bones and shove you so far up in my crack they will never find you again."

"Like I said, don't hold back now."  I chuckled at her unabashed expression of sexual intent.  When she flashed a severe look down at me, like I dare to laugh at her, I knew she was mocking her old self.  Still, even that teasing threat made me want to sooth her potential ire.  Fortunately I could do that and still be honest.  "Now you're looking and talking like the Amanda I know and love."

"Really Richie?  You love me?  You mean it wasn't all a wonderful dream I had the other day with you and my best friend Brandy?"  Poor Amanda had vacillated back to unsure and vulnerable, though rather delightfully hopeful.

I tried to help her further.  "I do love the good Amanda.  I love the Amanda that came out and revealed her affectionate heart that day, the softened and open Amanda, the incredible woman who kissed like the best kisses ever, and then made me know that love, pressed that love into me until there could no shadow of a doubt."

"Oh Richie."  Her face fell on mine, lips engulfing my lips with the vigorous, desperate love of the long, long lost and finally found.  Every part of her body sought to kiss me, squirming and smashing my little body lost between her breasts and under her torso, as her kisses continued to expand and devour.

At last she sat up, much more confident, continuing now into Step Two.  "Having me as a sexual partner will be risky for you.  At ten feet six inches and 958 pounds I might harm or crush you during foreplay or intercourse.  I want you to accept that risk and please, please, please accept me to the family."

I felt like maybe I was supposed to say something right there, but Amanda jumped the script and on me at the same time.  "I will seek to dominate you with my body, during sex and most specifically with my pussy.  I want you to understand exactly what that feels like.  I will force you to kiss me there, to love my aroma and crave to taste me."  And boom, the big pool-babe ass-sat my face, her huge butt eating my body.  Yes, definitely, this was indeed the Amanda I knew and loved.

I flickered only a tad of Sparkle-fire up her ass.  It drove her bucking-wild into an energetic butt-munching of my bones.  Thank goodness her time was up quickly.  Tough as I might be, I don't think I could have taken much more of her uninhibited ass thrashing.

I accepted Amanda, very real risks and all, because… well, once you've had that particular kind of vigorous affection, you can't not have it – if all possible.  The rest of the clan saw the point and we all voted her in.  And never have you seen a person more grateful.  "Thank you all so, so much.  I mean my life; it just seemed so lonely and pointless…"  She gushed gratitude as she wiped me clean.  "Oh, I love, love this new family.  Thank you.  Thank you for letting me be part of it.  I'll do everything I can for all of you."

Amanda Schmidt, 958 pounds added to 11,426 is 12,384 pounds.  And only two more little ladies to go…

The bed groaned already submitting to the one ton woman climbing aboard.  Saint Debbie crawled over me, her perfect nude magnificence above causing me to respond with instant hard on.  The slightest elbow bend of her strong arms allowed her massive breasts to graze back and forth slowly across my face.  Glancing up through the intermittent cleavage I caught glimpses of her beatific kind face smiling down at me, knowing me so well.  After a couple of minutes she turned around on all fours and waved her enormous sexy ass over my face.  Then slowly, slowly she let her knees slide apart thus lowering her pussy closer and closer and then finally onto my face.  After my face then head had disappeared into her she continued to lower and lower herself onto me, pressing me ever deeper into the bed.  Finally the bed could yield no more, forcing my head and neck and bending shoulders up into her.

Once we had reached maximum penetration with me lodged way up inside her pussy, she clamped down and sat down.  Squeezed, crushed, smothered, and completely devastated me in less than five minutes.  Who says non-verbal communication isn't effective.  All the verbiage of Steps 1-3 accomplished with one quick and thorough pussy smash.

Saint Debbie let me slide out but still straddled my body with only my soaked head showing barely from under her pussy, still squeezed a little bit by her upper inner thighs.  Debra Plumtree only had one small comment to add.  "By the way, Sweetheart, I've been gaining size.  I'm currently passing through 13' 8" and 2,077 pounds.  Wanna' get married now?"

I couldn't speak but managed to nod yes and chin her clitoris at the same time.  My reward was her bouncing onto my face for a couple of good licks.  Then she backed off again so I could hear what she had to say.  "Well, ladies, Richie couldn't talk with my gigantic ass crushing his body, not letting him breathe; but he nodded yes to my question.  So, all in favor?"  And thus Saint Debbie sailed into the family as expected.

Five minutes under her was not near enough.  In our last sessions we topped four hours.  Of course that nearly killed me.  And now with her growing… growing…. It was a good thing I completely held back the Sparkle-fire.  Sex with Debbie was definitely going to be tricky – very tricky indeed, but worth every pound!

What did she say, "2,107 pounds"?  Add that to 12,384 and we get 14,491 pounds.  Oh boy, just one tiny little lady remaining.

If the bed submitted to Debbie, it outright surrendered to Daisy.  Dear Daisy wanted to do all the proper Steps and patter.  She sat on me allowing my neck and head clearance from her impossibly big ass smash. "Hello I'm Daisy Strickland and I want to have a baby with you.  I mean marry you and this family, and have a baby with you."  She could be funny.  "And did I mention I want to have a baby with you?"

"Yikes, I am 15' 7" and weigh 2,509 pounds.  I will crush you with my colossal legs, smother you under my massive breasts, absolutely annihilate you with my titanic ass and unbirth you into my big hungry pussy. But most of all I will drain you of every last sperm you can make, pounding sex on you day after day until you get me pregnant, and probably more after I'm pregnant.  Do you accept this proposal?  Remember, it was your idea."

Thinking it would be funny I said, "I changed my mind."

Of course she knew I was teasing. "Oh you rascal."  She scooted forward, driving her big pussy down on me just as promised, and squirming on me, partially inserting my upper body.  And there she sat well past what should have been her five minutes.  After more like ten minutes of unbelievably heavy squeezing wet bless she grabbed my legs and held me in place while she scooted back off me.  I slid out, smothered, subdued, and not so glib anymore.

Still she sat on me.  "Any more wisecracks?  Because I have a *wise crack* just for you."  Like I said, she could be funny.  By tightening her ass Daisy both squeezed me good but also lifted herself up enough that I could breathe.

"No Miss Strickland."  I licked her inner thigh like a good little puppy.

"That's more like it."  She tried to sound smug but could not help smiling down at me.  Then to the rest of the women, "You see, ladies, our husband isn't always direct in his communication.  When he gets mouthy he's really asking you for something, but doesn't really know how to say it.  So I suggest: put that mouthiness of his to good use.  Right Richie?"

"No, Crazy Daisy, you got it all backward."  Still I sassed.  You'd think a man in my position would know when to settle down and shut up.  Daisy relaxed her squeeze dropping her weight fully down into a soft full squish mode.  The air hissed from my lungs.  There would be no comment from the peanut gallery until she was good and ready to hear from me again.  Thank goodness her vast wide ass could not get all its weight onto my skinny thin body.  Even with my enhancements it would have been too much.  Of course she could always choose to get up and stand on me.  That would do it; crush bones organs and all in a second.  When you think about it, a normal sized person could probably easily kill another normal sized person by stomping around on them.  Oh, the strange wanderings of an oxygen-deprived mind….

Daisy sighed and shook her head slowly like I was the slowest student she'd ever seen.  "Here's a perfect example, girls, of what I've been saying.  Richie just doesn't know how to ask for what he really wants, so he gets all sassy.  Obviously he's wanting me to sit on him 'backward'."

Daisy turned around and positioned her gargantuan ass right on my face, the rest of my body lost as a pressed sample under her butt.  This time I must have gotten a good fifteen minutes of bouncing ass torture.  As I was running out of air, out of sanity, out of remembrance of life, Daisy's butt elevated off my not-so-sassy-any-more ass-flattened attitude.

"So Richie…" I heard her talking but couldn't open my eyes to look. "… any more comments?"

I tugged in a breath then murmured a weak, "No my Goddess."

I felt a gentle pat on my head. "Okie-doe then." I felt myself being stood up, my head and face wiped down with a warm wet towel.  I opened my eyes to see Daisy Strickland's enormous breasts to the right and left in front of me, down through the cleavage her adoring smile and sparkling eyes looking down into mine.  "I've just one more question, Richie…"

"Yes."  I cut her off, this lover who in another five minutes of ass smashing would have snuffed out my life.  I looked up at this woman beyond my imagined fantasies. I thought about my miserable lonely life of just three months ago, my crappy apartment south of the college campus, my dead-end job at the coffee shop where I could hardly reach across the counter tops, much less any of the barista equipment. I looked at the glory-of-God woman whose beautiful face looked back of mine, her countenance full of desire and hope and that parted-lips promise of grand sexual adventures.  And I said "Yes.  Yes, Daisy Strickland.  I want to marry you, father your child, and have you be part of this most amazing family."

Before Daisy could pounce on me in celebratory smother, I heard Aria's voice. "That concludes this portion of the ceremony."  I turned around to see Aria.  I stood on the bed in the triangular well formed by Daisy sitting cross-legged.  My back now to Daisy, I looked straight ahead at Aria standing some fifteen feet away by the edge of the bed, Pavie and Callie to either side of her.  Still feeling a bit weak from Daisy's crushing, I leaned forward, resting my elbows on the firm bulge of Daisy's big flexed calve muscle.  Aria continued. "Richie, do you have anything to say to your new wives?"

I took my time, regarded each and every one of them, twenty-five of the planet's most gorgeous and certainly biggest women to ever exist, and now crowded in a luscious, eager semi-circle around three sides of the bed.

"Holy shit!" was the first utterance that escaped my lips. They all laughed.  I took a deep breath, getting a little more oxygen going to my brain.  Over to the left my eyes traced the line of beauty after beauty, with deeply loving expressions, Brandy and Amanda towering right behind them.  Over the right I saw nothing but more of the same including Valerie Monroe and Vicky Hatton standing next to each other, whispering in each other's ear.  What were they planning – oh, I could hardly stand the thought of their combined sensuality and love-making.  Right in front of me stood my three giantess girlfriends within this marriage, glowing beatific almost beyond my willpower to endure.  And right behind them and soaring above stood Saint Debbie a giantess of loving proportion and perfection, a one-woman destruction derby of heavenly doom.  And of course I could feel the heat off the great legs of puny-man ruin that surrounded me, massive soft breasts so gently nudging against my bony back.  In that moment I dare not turn around to look at Daisy; I couldn't have taken it and probably would have collapsed, overwhelmed.

But I had to do better than "holy shit!" so I took another deep breath, and then spoke.  "I am humbled and honored to be your husband.  I never expected such abundance in my life and count myself as the luckiest man on earth.  I will do my best to love and serve each of you.  I am kind of small, so I hope you will be patient with me.  But I promise you I am persistent and will try my best."  I noticed they all seemed very interested, quiet, and each seemed to have moist eyes.  OK, I shouldered on.  The next part seemed awkward.  "It seems like in a year or so we could have a lot of babies around here.  So I hope you're all ready for that.  I'm kind of afraid they might be too big for me to handle."

They giggled at that last statement.  I didn't understand why.  But then Aria gently explained.  "Richie, we can't get pregnant until we stop growing.  It is a quirk of being a Bluebelle Amazon.  But it makes sense doesn't it?"

"I suppose so."  I answered but still not sure what exactly that meant.

Aria, of course, could see my confusion.  "For example, I'm still growing and as you'd know so are Callie and Pavie.  In fact very few of us have stopped growing."  Aria said a little louder.  "Let's help Richie out here.  If you have stopped growing and could thus get pregnant raise your hand."

Over to the right no hand went up.  Straight in front; no hands up.  Over to the left, also no hand – wait a minute, two hands nice and high: Amanda and Brandy.

"Wow, only two." I think the whole concept and reality of pregnancy kind of had me in shock.  It also rather turned me on I must admit.

Aria was staring at me.  She motioned subtly with her eyes – "look behind you".  That's right, I'd forgotten.  Last but certainly not least, Miss Daisy Strickland.  I looked behind me to see a great big grin and big muscular arm held nice and proudly high.

"It's time."  Aria spoke with a more formal air of announcement.  "Amanda and Brandy please come forward and help sister Daisy consummate the marriage."

I panicked somewhat.  Mostly I think my body reacted with a big shot of adrenaline.  As Amanda and Brandy bounced eagerly forward on the bed, Daisy unfolded herself over me, and her breasts whammed into me.  As I fell to my back on the bed I looked pleadingly toward Aria. "Right now, with everybody watching?"

Aria couldn't help a chuckle.  "Don't worry my modest husband.  You will soon be quite hidden and invisible.

Daisy was not waiting for anything or anybody.  Already she rode her wet pussy over my body, my little hard Volunteer lost up inside along with my hips, leg and torso.  My neck and head stuck out between her thighs.

Suddenly Amanda's beautiful countenance appeared over my face.  Her upside-down kiss attacked me hungry, mouthing, voracious.  Darkness descended on my tiny nook of twilight.  Brandy had climbed onto Daisy's lap, straddling Daisy's slightly spread legs.  As Brandy mounted, some of the weight of her big butt pressed down on the back of Amanda's head.  And Amanda's kissing got hundreds of pounds heavier.  So did Daisy's heavy squish on my body. Of course I have no idea, but I pictured Brandy's big knockers pressing into Daisy's record-breaking tits. I imagined Daisy and Brandy kissing each other deep and passionate….

I struggled to move.  Impossible.  I remembered the math I was supposed to do.  Yes that's right: Daisy at 2,509 pounds plus the running total of 14,461 comes to a nice even 17,000 pounds.  What are the odds of that? But the distraction passed quickly.

The two hours of heavy foreplay was definitely catching up with me.  I felt all the withholding and boundaries falling away.  Release broke through its shut door and into the hallway.  Trouble was, there were twenty-six shut doors that now smashed open flooding the hallway, my body, with a wild stampede of fervent crazed amazons' sexual energy.

My tongue lashed blue flames of Sparkle-fire into Amanda's mouth.  In unabashed response her mouthing became so rapid and deep she all but ate my face.

Below and well up into Daisy's pussy the Sparkle-fire built beyond any expectation I could fathom.  The tree of sensation that sprouted from me into Daisy grew up like a redwood on steroids, shorting the poor woman's circuits until she became nothing but a writhing being helpless to her exploding desires.

I heard Daisy scream.  "Help me. Help me.  Somebody save Richie!"  But it wouldn't be Amanda whose inflamed kissing sought to engulf my whole head in her mouth.  It wouldn't be Brandy whose tit-to-tit smashing up against Daisy had brought her enough vicarious Sparkle-fire to set her nymphomaniacle desires off the charts.

Out of control Daisy scooted forward, taking both my head and Amanda's into her pussy at once.  But Amanda never broke off her vicious kiss, her big shoulders keeping us close enough to the outside vaginal lips to bring her air to keep going and going.  That movement around Daisy's G-spot launched a juggernaut toward an orgasm best described as all calamities braking loose at once.

Amanda and I were out again.  Now Brandy fully rode on the back of Amanda's head, her enormous thighs squeezing around both our heads.  I wondered what happened to Daisy.  Then in answer her great butt slammed down on all three of us, Amanda and Brandy ferociously crushed onto my face and upper body.

Again my Volunteer entered Daisy's pussy, this time in reverse position.  And that was it.  So much pressure, so much sensation, too much love smothering me, until finally I completely succumbed to that crushing billion year-old thrust to procreate.  Daisy screamed again.  "Save Richie!!!"  Her orgasm brought Amanda and Brandy along with it.  And I came.  I came and came and came, hot blue flames of sexual sensation roared up through Daisy's body.  Sparkle-fire also bellowed out my mouth into Amanda's mouth smashing back down.  The raging prairie fire of ecstasy whirled in a completed circuit, all around through all three women and back into my body.

Finally, even the stellar physicality of Amanda and Brandy could not take it anymore.  They found purchase with each other, the bed, and with their massive gluts pressed against my face, they heave-hoed and shouldered Daisy to tip over and off us.

Daisy, post-orgasmic, started laughing with hysteric joy.  Amanda and Brandy rolled over onto her, also too weak from exertion and laughter to do anything but collapse.  With all the rest of my new wives looking on, applauding, for God's sake; I just lie there drained and exhausted, the spent Cum-Monster of Bluebelle Valley.

Someone picked me up.  Ah, it was my dear girlfriend-now-wife Pavie.  I knew Callie was with her.  The soft breast offered to me felt comforting and I discerned enough to respond and take sustenance.

I heard Aria's voice, speaking kindly with her new sisters.  The ceremony, highly successful, was now over.  She continued to speak with them, explaining things about moving in, responsibilities, roommates, timings, more gathering to come soon, tomorrow it seemed.

Some wanted to kiss me good-night.  Here I heard Aria compassionately explain the Triplet's private responsibility to reinvigorate me at the end of each day.  I would be sleeping with Pavie, Callie, and Aria so that I could be strengthened each night, made anew, and thus continue to be available for all the wives.

Aria joked that she and her sisters liked to play a little rough with me too.  But that any pussy and ass poundings they gave me would all be in good fun.  And she promised to deliver me in tip-top shape for the new day – most of the time.  She did admit: it can be very hard to control oneself with such a cute little husband.

I heard Callie say to Pavie.  "I think he must be listening to Aria.  Look at his Volunteer.  But what do you think?  What should we do?  We have to give him some more milk first, right?"

"Oh great," I thought, The Triplets, my genius handlers, seem to be winging this when it comes to my sexual survival!

***

I slept through until morning, not quite smothered under dear beautiful Pavie.  When she finally woke and got off me, we both blinked in the bright morning sunshine streaming in from very high windows on the eastern wall.

I thought I'd try my math summation from last night, just to impress at least one of my wives.  "So Pavie, I added up all the weights of all my new wives last night."

"What?"  She rubbed her eyes.  Now Callie and Aria sat up next to her, each of them giving me a dubious look.

"You know," I went on "when each fiancée sat on me she told me her weight.  So I added them all up.  And did you know that all my wives together weigh exactly 17,000 pounds?"

"Well, Richie," Pavie sighed and smiled.  "I don't know about the rest of my sisters, but after that buffet last night – I'd say I gained at least three pounds.  If that's true for all of us you better up the total by some 78 pounds.  Hey, more than your body weight!"  She giggled at that.

"Soooo…," Callie nudged each of her sisters.  "Isn't it time we consummated the marriage as well?"

Pavie: "He is our husband too, after all."

Callie: "You mean like he belongs to us?" They started prowling around me on all fours.  I couldn't tell if they were serious or not.

Aria: "You mean like he belongs under us."

I tried to watch all three.  But it proved too difficult to keep tabs exactly as they kept crawling around me.  I kept expecting the one stalking behind me to pounce any second.

Pavie: "He is definitely our property for ten hours a day."

"Property?" I questioned, indignant.  "I'm nobody's property."

Pavie: "Don't you dare to try to get out of your vows already, my little husband."  Pavie moved in closer, threatening.

Aria: "Yes, Richie, you'll behave if you know what's good for you.  I had to convince our sister-wives that we had to have those ten hours to keep you sustained and up to par.  So don't go making me look bad."  She moved closer also.  There was no escape anyway.

Callie: "But that sustenance just takes like 20-30 minutes per day.  And we only need to sleep like six and a half hours…"

Pavie: "So that means he's our plaything, our crush and squeeze toy, the other three hours every day.  That will give some extra time for disciplining him.  Nice negotiation, Aria."

I chimed in again: "Hey.  Quit threatening me with discipline and that tough talk."

Aria: "Well, look who's talking tough now. We certainly must have you serving under our big asses and pussies every day.  For better or worse, Richie.  So don't make it worse."

Callie: "Like three hours every evening or morning – an hour each.  That's more than enough smother time."

Pavie:  "We can at least double-team him.  So that's a least two hours each."

Aria: "You're so right, Pavie.  I'd love to spend at least an hour every day sitting on his face.  Direct face-under-ass worship; that's I want.  And he will beg me for it – to be absolutely dominated by me."

I inserted. "But I thought you wanted to share me with the sister-wives."

Pavie: "Oh, we do.  Of course we do, now and then.  That is very important."

Callie: "But our time on you is our time to own you, little husband.  You'll be so suffocated under us every night; completely crushed and smashed into a flat little butt pancake, begging for mercy."

Aria: "And our mercy is that we will sustain you, make your stronger, tougher, able to withstand it all so we can do it more often, for longer, and with even more vigor!"

Pavie: "So that we can grow larger and larger, devastating you under our bigger and bigger butts and heavier pussies, squeezing the wild blue Sparkle-fire out of you, making us go completely out of control on you…"

Callie: "Yet, with only a small chance that we will actually snuff you out entirely."

Aria: "Oh, my butt is aching to clamp onto your face. I couldn't get enough of you last night.  That was only twenty minutes." (Twenty minutes that nearly vanquished me, I thought.)
Just think how glorious it will be to have some two hours a day of that!"

I was seriously worried now. "You guys are kidding, right?  Your just pulling my leg, aren't you?  Trying to scare me."

Pavie: "Your fear makes the Sparkle-fire even more intense.  Every devouring, pounding life-threatening smothering crush we can apply makes sex more exciting for us."

Aria: "So basically figure you will be living under our love-smashing pussies and asses when you are with us."

Pavie: "We should sleep on him, too.  I did that last night and I had the best dreams… a teeny-tiny man was completely embedded up in my butt.  In my dream I just kept bouncing on him and bouncing on him…"

Callie, laughing: "Hopefully he kept on living…"

Pavie: "Who cares?  It was a dream.  But when I get big enough in real life, who knows?  I think I should practice on him today."

Aria: "I got dibs on his face first!" Aria launched her perfect body over mine, pinning my arms, her huge ass looming precisely over the little target of my face.

Callie: "And I get first dibs on his Volunteer.  I can see he's ready for me." Right after she said it I could feel her soft bush positioning for a pussy drop onto me.

Pavie looked under Aria's impending ass and spoke to me.  "How's it going in there?  You ready for the marriage consummation?"

"You guys tricked me." I complained.  "Just because we got married you don't own me.  This behavior is unacceptable!"

Pavie laughed.  "Oh you guys should see his face.  He bought the whole thing.  God Richie, you're so gullible."  Now I could hear the other two sisters laughing as well.

"So it's a joke."  I probably still sounded worried.

Pavie: "Well sure – more like a tease, I'd say.   We always do this with our new husbands."

"Ha, ha."  I rejoined sarcastically; obviously I was their first husband.

Aria: "So what are we doing here?"

Callie: "Does he want the consummation or not?"

Pavie:  "Well, Richie, it is up to you… what do you say, yay or nay?"

I looked up at Aria's glorious butt.  Of course I wanted it.  "Well, as long as we got that stupid joke cleared up, I suppose we can go ahead."

A second later a huge ass dropped onto my face and a very heavy pussy dropped to take in my Volunteer.  And Pavie, for now, must have piled onto Aria's lap because the pressure on my face doubled.

As they ass-and-pussy-pounded me non-stop, I wondered just how much their tease was a joke.  Right at the wet hot smothering moment it felt like my magnificent Triplet wives meant every threatening thing they said.

"My wives," I thought to myself, feeling their gyrations increasing in vigor and frequency. "My ever growing, loving dominating wives," the thought of the permanence of the relationship, that this extremely exhilarating situation I was under would only become more and more   euphorically punishing at time went on – and the marriage commitment, the ownership these wives now had over their tiny husband – it was just too much.  I surrendered.  I surrendered comprehensively and absolutely to their loving mastery.

# XVI. Giantess Quarantine

Finally the Triplets got off me and let me start my day.  Not that I minded a good roll-in-the-hay first thing in the morning.  But it felt good to be up and free, breathing easy in the nice steamy shower.

Of course anything can happen at any moment when you take a shower with the Triplets.  As I stood amongst their thick, shapely, towering legs I knew I could pretty much do anything I wanted these days.  Not that they were boundryless; it's just that all was fair game at shower time.  So if the mood struck me to grab this or that, nestle my face in a convenient pussy or ass, I found myself more than well received.  Rare it was that they would not be ready to match my offerings and take it up a notch. In fact, as I licked at Callie's upper inner thigh I could not recall anything remotely resembling rejection on her part or her sisters.

Aria stepped out of the shower and let a little breeze in.  Then Pavie and now Callie turned off their showers as well.  Quickly the area cooled down for we had slept with the doors open and, as you may recall, the evening had been quite cool.

The chill made me think of being on the stairs to be bedroom last night when the tapestry of the huge Amazon Queen wavered in the draft down the stairwell.  I found myself curious.  As I followed Pavie's huge squeaky clean butt out of the shower I asked her. "Pavie, what's up with the tapestries on the stairwell walls?"

"Amazons and Giantesses."  She stated like that should explain it.

"Yea Richie," Callie came up behind and sandwiched me playfully into Pavie's not-yet-dried buns. "You'd think you'd know the theme around here by now."

"What theme?"  Aria asked.

"The tapestry theme." Pavie shrugged.  "You know…"

"Ah, yes."  Aria came over to her sisters, more thoroughly encircling me.  "Is Richie needing some Amazon attention?"

"Always." I kissed her thigh. "But those tapestries kind of spooked me.  I wondered if they were haunted at first – especially the one of the big Queen."

"Could be," Callie wasn't kidding. "The Queen was modeled after the Segal's daughter.  She went Mammoth Mad four years ago and killed both her parents in a psychotic fury."

"No way!" That shocked the heck out of me.

Aria: "Biggest tragedy to happen in Bluebelle Estates ever.  Thought maybe you would have heard about it."

"Nope."  I sure had not heard about it. "Where did it happen?"

Callie:  "In the music room downstairs wasn't it?"

Pavie: "Poor young lady was trying to lead a normal life.  She'd gone to college.  But she had the Mammoth gene, was twelve feet tall already.  Some pathetic vermin drugged her at a party then abused her with farm animals."

"That's hideous."  I found myself thoroughly disgusted and enraged.  "Was it some frat rats thinking that would be entertainment?"

Aria: "Quite the contrary.  I think it was some fraternity guys that heard the ruckus at the Ag college barns and came to her rescue.  They called 911, found horse blankets to cover her, revived her, and stayed right there until the police arrived."

Callie:  "They found the perpetrators and the fraternity guys helped a lot to identify them.  But the whole incident was too much for Serenity… er, yes, her name is Serenity Segal.  She left college and came home, unbeknownst to anyone she went off her meds, and with the trauma it all caught with her.  The Mammoth Madness kicked it and she went berserk."

Aria: "Poor dear.  She, and some three others with the same gene and affliction are at the Bluebelle Valley Mental Institute for the Criminally Insane.  It's several miles east of the Estates, just back in the foot hills.  You can't see it from the highway."

"Well that explains why the tapestry gives me the willies." I shivered involuntarily.

"Awe, Richie." Callie picked me up, wrapping me in her towel. "We left the tapestry up to remember poor Serenity.  We have seen the Mammoth Madness take hold and we know for sure that she did not mean to hurt anyone – especially not her dear parents."

Aria:  "When we bought this estate last year one of the main reasons was the money would go to support Serenity's and the others' care.  Actually those millions support that entire mental institute at this point.  They are hoping to discover a cure."

Pavie: "But if the tapestries bother you we can definitely take it down."

"No." I had very strong feeling about it. "Definitely leave the tapestries up."

Then we got dressed for breakfast… yeah, right… after about another hour of being triple-teamed and squeaky-clean-ass-smashed into smithereens.

***

My first-day-of-marriage ride to work started innocently enough.  You could call it newlywed kissing-fest, the little jaunt to work that morning with eleven of my brand spankin'-new wives.  Eleven you say; who's missing?  That would be another one of my new wives, Saint Debbie.  She apparently got married and retired.  I suppose she figures her new husband will support her.  Wait a minute: that's me!  And I can't support Saint Debbie or any of them financially – maybe emotionally… but physically – oh my God, day-by-day, my goodness, that remains to be seen.

Oh well; big Saint Debbie actually didn't fit in the van anymore anyway.  So she stayed at the Segal mansion, our new home.  I guessed today she would be moving in and setting up her room.

Meanwhile my other eleven new blushing brides on the Pollination Crew seemed to be moving from kissing toward more like pollination on the ride into work.  Yes, yes, they kept rotating around and giving everyone a chance for their good morning kisses.  After about five rounds of that, someone, probably Sandy but it could have been Silvia, suggested that we begin consummating the marriage.  After brief discussion, they agreed each should get ten good pumps on me, sex in other words, and move to the next wife.  Following protocol they started with the smallest.

I have this memorized: Coleen-Janet-Jeanie-Jackie-Jessica-MaryEllen-Cecilia-Silvia-Sandy-Vicky-Bethany.  They were on and off me so fast I couldn't quite cum. But they just wanted to officially be able to say they each "consummated the marriage".  They finished with ten minutes to spare, so Bethany just decided to remain on me, riding the blue flame to a nice quick orgasm for both of us.

They each kissed me again as they got out of the van and told me to have a nice day.  God that was an exhausting ride to work.  I already wanted to go home and take a nap.  Of course, my bed was the Triplets bed, so good luck catching a nap if they are anywhere around.  And if they aren't there probably Saint Debbie will be.  A nap under her could be permanent sleep…

Finally I got out of the abandoned van and started shuffling across the parking lot to the Secretary Pool.  Eight more wives awaited me inside.  Oops, I mean, make that nine.  I better not forget about Daisy.

The Secretary wives were much more organized – definitely had a plan.  They had decided that Tiffany and Rachel could share an office, thus freeing up an office for playtime.  The escorted me to the new rumpus room, their faces beaming proudly at the set up.  It was kind of cool: thick carpet throughout, a big bed for marriage fun and games, two comfortable couches around for lounging, homey artwork on the walls, and no sign at all of business or phones or the like.  Phenomenal they could pull all this together so quickly – undoubtedly very persuasive with the local suppliers and tradesmen to work all night on it.

Of course they each wanted kisses, too.  They took turns kneeling then squatting down over me to plant their big wet smooches on me.  And they really went for it with their kisses.  They had come up with a motto for the marriage, at least for the time at the office: "Hold nothing back."  And they certainly didn't with their kisses.

They stripped off their skirts and panties, leaving their blouses on.  It was extreme sexy attire, their huge derrieres unleashed to parade around the rumpus room.  Their intent was made clear soon enough.

The secretaries formed a kind of conga-line from heaven.  They turned on some music and proceeded to sequentially facesit me and have sex with me in progression.  Remember now all this tough and forced sex was consensual on my part.  They had each clearly warned me during the wedding ceremony and I had accepted each one of them.  They were simply making good on their marriage vows.

A huge pussy covered my face and head, another sat on my middle, a third sat down for sex, a fourth pinned my legs, and a fifth got foot-fucked.  After a minute stent, they rotated forward.  A new wife started at the feet.  The wife on the face rotated out to the back of the line. The lovely lady on my middle moved up to grind down on my face… and so forth. Somewhere along the way they explained that this pussy crushing routine would be the daily morning greeting.  So be it: I was completely helpless to resist.  Their attentions certainly fanned my blue flames, rewarding them into orgasms two at a time (you know, the wives on the face and the cock).

After some 45 minutes it was 8:30 and time to get to work.  After kindly kisses of "see you later" they left me alone in the rumpus room.  I cleaned myself up in the fixed-up homey but large bathroom.  Then realized, oops, 8:40, here I was late on the first day of the new routine in reporting to the big boss, I mean my biggest wife, Daisy.  And we well know she does not like to wait.

I minute later I approached the tall door to Daisy's expansive office.  "Knock. Knock?"  I called.

"Who's there?" Came the joking answer.

OK then, I can play this. "Cunnilingus…"

"Cunnilingus who?" Her voice sounded more than very intrigued.

"Cun't-I-linger-under-your-pussy-awhile?"

"Those are the magic words.  Enter husband."

My boss Miss Strickland, my wife Daisy, stood there looking impossibly big and sexy, wearing the thinnest lacy negligee, held out firmly by her stately breasts, her panties half on and half off, looking ready to be pulled down.  She considered me, smiling, liking my attitude and apparently forgetting I was a little late.

"Funny you should offer oral sex – because that is where we are starting today. Pavie suggested we have a session of oral sex first to clear out my initial gusher orgasm.  Then, for regular sex, she suggested we get you up inside me as far as possible.  Those two steps might give your sperm a fighting chance to make it all the way up to my eggs."

"Rather technical." I said, "But still quite a sexy outline for the morning activities. Where you want to get started?"

"Look over here!" Daisy smiled triumphant.  I hadn't noticed the big bed way over to the side near the entrance to the spa bathroom.  "I heard the Secretaries were getting a bed and I thought, 'Good idea.'  So I ordered one of my own.  Come on." Daisy was excited to get over to the bed.

As I climbed on the giantess-sized mattress I found I had a nagging calculation unresolved in my head.  As I unbuttoned my shirt as asked, "So, ah, do I really fit into you deep enough to make this idea work?"

"They figure a regular five foot woman can take in a 12" cock."  It seemed she been reading up on it.

"Wow, that's a lot of unused pussy walking around!" was my first thought.

Daisy laughed. "World-wide, got to be thousands and thousands of miles."

"And you being some fifteen feet tall – that's like three feet.  Is it a direct proportion?"  This math was of keen interest to me.

"Pretty good guess.  Actually, three feet two inches in my case.  I measured it."  Daisy had all sorts of things to be proud about.

"Gosh, what did you use for a dip stick?"  The chance to tease was just too opportune.

"You know you are really crude sometimes."  Daisy had her dress and panties off and walked on her knees to situate over my now nude prone body.

"Just the way you like it, wife."  I was so looking forward to tasting that pussy in reverse position directly above my face.  We had to keep my Volunteer away from her body for the first step, to keep my battalions of sperm at bay.

"Actually, you'll be my dip stick today.  But first get busy now and make me cum."  And down she dropped it.  And in went my face and head, into my wife, nice and deep and already wet.

Yes, "wife" I thought and that turned me on even more.  I liked being trapped and smothered.  So the firmness and finality of the marriage commitment excited me even more.  I felt that the grand wife that smothered me now owned me for life.  I felt the same about all the other twenty-five as well, just not quite as extreme, as you can understand.  Democratic and fair, that's me.  So as I ate up into Daisy and made sure she knew how much I loved her, I had a little extra verve as the newly dedicated husband here to serve now and forever.

Daisy felt all that for sure, squeezing and pressing sweet affections onto me; already shuttering with her strong emotions of love – and of course the flames of Sparkle-fire tingling her off my tongue.  She ground on me without reserve, relaxed, thrilled, and letting her love intensity flow onto me.  I felt I was being eaten alive by a pussy that kept saying repeatedly "I love you.  I love you.  I love you…"

And Daisy generated a gusher of the highest magnitude.  My sperm were spared for the moment.  I, however, fought like crazy to swim up into her.  All to no avail as she had me utterly pinned under her wiggling pussy and butt.

Ah, the world of light again, as Daisy rose off me.  "Don't bother cleaning up."  She instructed her little wet recovering zombie.  "That wetness will come in handy.  Come on…" Daisy started pulling my body under and into her.  "Legs first."

So skinny, my feet then thin legs slipped into Daisy easily, legs in all the way 'til the hilt.  So that was maybe two feet of my length.  Now she lifted and squirmed around, shoving me easily then harder until I felt my feet touch a soft but definite end.  At this point she had me in up to my armpits.

"OK, husband, now get your arms busy in there, too."  I pointed my fingers on my right hand flat and then slid fingers, hand, and that arm in up to its shoulder.  Then, slightly tighter, I managed the same thing with my left hand and arm.  Daisy, with one hand, jammed me in just a little further until only my head stuck out, face up.

I loved this feeling inside Daisy's pussy cocoon.  It is actually quite easy for a man to understand if he's ever had a good sexual experience.  Just think about the pinnacle of feeling when your cock is perfectly held, squeezed, and loved.  I was having essentially that exact same feeling except with my entire body – cock included.  Daisy played with me, rippling pussy waves the length of my body.

"How do you like that, my dear husband?"  She sounded quite proud of herself, knowing damn well I loved what she did to me, how she owned and squeezed me from toes to chin.

After some more spirited maneuvering, Daisy needed to relax again and sat back down.  She peered over at me through her huge and heavy breasts, and smiled at me.  I smiled back, but unable to wave.  Now she bounced a few times and squeezed my entire body some more.  "OK hubby, time to get busy in there with all those arms, legs, fingers, and toes.  And don't forget to release your electric charge."

"I won't forget, Daisy.  That part is kind of automatic.  Can't you feel it already?"

"Oh, baby, as a matter of fact I do.  I feel all those lovely things you're doing.  God, you are neigh on perfect…"

"Just don't get carried away today, all right?  There's nobody in the room to rescue me today like there was yesterday."  I might have sounded a little concerned.

"Oh don't worry, Richie, I'll be more careful with my second husband." What a pleasant reminder – not. "But I can't help my need to squeeze your face." And with that Daisy slammed her massive upper legs together, my head for sure disappearing in the smash. The squeeze forced my face up into her clitoris. She did that again, of course, only this time with her right hand middle and index fingers behind my head, crushing me against her firmer.

This put us completely on the right track for Daisy. She accelerated this same technique for five, then ten, then finally fifteen minutes. All the while she kept squeezing and pressuring my body, working my face into her clit, and bouncing more and more.

The Sparkle-fire grew on a steady upward curve. Daisy followed the same curve up, higher and higher. It must have sounded like an earth quake in the rest of the building as Daisy actually left the bed and then crashed back down on it and me with each rhythmic bounce.

Of course, you can imagine I felt so wonderfully captured and pressured and squished and controlled. But what is hard to appreciate is how sensitive I'd become to Daisy. Inside her, with my face bashed in vibrations against her clitoris, I felt super connected. It seemed I could experience to best of both worlds: hers and mine.

When Daisy came, so did I. And Pavie's theory worked; Daisy's second orgasm flow was only modest. Daisy rolled backward, and lifted her butt up, supporting her lower back with the hands, elbows bent and steady against the mattress. She hoisted her legs straight up into the air. This put my head at about a seven foot height up from the bed, looking out between her legs. In this position Daisy took some deep breaths ad seemed to relax.

"Now I'm letting your sperm flow down into me. I think this will help them survive and make the longer than usual journey up to my ovaries."

"Wow, exciting." I said kind of matter of fact.

"Well you could be more enthusiastic about it."

"Yes, actually I am fairly excited. In fact I think I'll cum again." And I did, shivering out into her gentle response of a squeeze.

"Nice," Daisy smiled. "That's getting with the program. We'll have to think of a most suitable reward for you."

"Well, obviously, this must be pretty good."

"I'm glad you like it.  I need to hold this position for another half hour."

"It would be nice to have someone serve us snacks and drinks while we wait this out."  I totally kidded.

But Daisy loved to get me whenever she could.  She grabbed a nearby hand held office intercom device.  "Miss Monroe, could you come in here.  I think Richie might need a favor."

"Oh thanks a lot."  I frowned down at Daisy.  "This position I'm in is kind of embarrassing you know."

"No, I don't know."  Daisy came back.  "And I don't think your sweetheart Miss Monroe will mind either."

Another minute we heard a knock.

"Come in, the door's open." Sing-songed Daisy.

I heard Valerie step into the office.  Immediately she marched over to the bed and finally saw me as she squared up to the front of Daisy's legs.

"Oh, my goodness!"  Was Valerie's astonished remark.

Daisy sounded completely relaxed by comparison. "Richie has something he wants. But you can see we are rather indisposed at the moment.  Could you help him out?

Valerie came forward and stood legs to either side of Daisy's prone shoulders. Then Valerie kneeled down, not quite sitting on Daisy, but brought her face right in front of mine.  Of course my face presented as nicely framed by the upside-down V of Daisy's legs.  Leaning very close Valerie smiled deliciously at my, let's say, predicament.

"My-oh-my, Richie, is the rest of your body really inside Daisy?"

"Well, where else do you think it could be?"

"Can you even move your arms out?

I tried that for a couple seconds.  "Actually, at this point, I think not."

"OK, so what is it you wanted?"

"I told Daisy maybe someone could bring us drinks and a snack."

"Sure.  What would you like Daisy?"

"Nothing, thank you.  I have all the snacks I want and you're looking at him, right between my legs, but mostly, obviously, deep inside my pussy."

"And you Richie, are you thirsty or hungry or something."  Valerie sounded more seductive all of the sudden, her exquisite face brightening with interest – no, more than interest – an idea.  Oh no.

"Actually not that hungry at the moment.  And as you can see I'm kind of overflowed with liquid."  Nervous, I think I actually wished Valerie might leave

"So what *did* you want, Richie?"  Valerie had turned on her charm now, already irresistible. "How about maybe a kiss?"  And she brought her luscious lips to rest gently on mine, gradually spreading, spreading, sucking harder, mouthing.  And though I was just a head on a pussy pedestal, but I could kiss back so I did indeed.

Valerie reached around Daisy's wide, wide hips, hugging them and gained leverage to kiss me harder.  She leaned back pulling Daisy's hips with her.  She stopped abruptly for a moment, stood to her full height, took her panties off, then resumed the same position, kissing me again and leaning back again.

Valerie held that kiss firm across my face this time as she rested all the way back down to plant her pussy right on Daisy's face.  Daisy must have liked it because I felt her get rived up big time.  I think Daisy must have responded well for Valerie in kind, mostly likely with Daisy's big tongue working up into Valerie's pussy, because the kissing on my face suddenly got much more vigorous.  This lovely triangle continued as a completed love circuit for some thirty minutes of sexual ecstasy.

After several simultaneous orgasms by all three of us, but I have to say especially Valerie, I thought that had to be the best sex possible.  I was wrong.  The creative Miss Monroe stood again.  But this time she gently but firmly parted Daisy's legs.  Then Valerie swung her right leg over between Daisy's opened legs.  Pussies at opposing right angles poised to connect with only my head in the way.  No problem.  Valerie lowered her straddle opening over my head and took me in until her vaginal lips met Daisy's.

Now both giantess started thrashing in unison.  For my part I went crazy inside Daisy, writhing every arm, leg, hand, foot, and all 21 digits.  I twisted my head around inside Valerie's tight pussy, stimulating her with every head contour, bump, ear, nose, and of course my wild lashing fiery tongue.  Valerie held onto Daisy's sturdy legs for stability and went absolutely cave-woman insane on my head and face.

After another ten minutes all Daisy's required leg-in-air time to give my sperm a chance, was up so she let the frenzy fall flat to the bed.  There the two women locked scissors on my head and rolled and rolled around on the bed until they fell off with a tremendous crush on my body.  There they kept rolling rough around the room until utterly exhausted.

Finally they relaxed enough to be willing to separate.  As they pulled apart, my head was lodged so tightly into Valerie she actually pulled me half way out of Daisy, my arms finally free.  Then my head slid out of Valerie and I used my arms to push the rest of the way out of the very relaxed Daisy.

The two women just lie on their backs panting, catching their breaths and laughing intermittently when they had enough air.  I crawled over to Valerie's pussy and kissed it thoroughly for maybe two minutes.  Then I did the same with Daisy.  Then back to Valerie and back to Daisy a couple more times until finally neither could respond anymore.

At last recovered, Daisy got up and headed toward the spa.  "I need a shower." She rightly declared.

"And I need a fuck." Valerie professed, rolling over on top of me.  Lying out on me, she pulled my arms up and placed a hand under each nipple, pinned my arms in place as she pressed her big breast down over my arms.  My face got smashed by her upper abs, my hips obliterated by her huge hips as my Volunteer slid easily up inside her.  She kept her legs together thereby fully flattening my spindle shanks under her heaviness.  It was a perfect Miss Valerie Monroe pressing sex.

As the pressing was progressing I kissed her abs, wiggled what little I could, and just let her and the Sparkle-fire do the rest.  Oh how deliciously this big beauty ground down on me.

Then suddenly she tensed, and I do not mean orgasm.  Her body went ridged then she sprang up off me to immediate standing.  Sirens blared.  Daisy came running out of the shower.  The rest of the Secretaries came streaming into the office terrified.  What heck was happening?

Daisy and Valerie had already pulled on clothing.  I rolled over and reach for my shorts.

Daisy explained with forced calmness. "It's the Synsonto lab alarm. There is some emergency or breach.  Those are the evacuation sirens.  We have to get the hell out of here as quick as possible.  Valerie grab Richie and bring him.  Everyone to my Humvee van.  It is big enough to hold us all."

We flew out the back exit.  Valerie ran swiftly with me over her shoulder.  I faced back to the main research buildings and could see an eerie chartreuse-with-greener-streaks plume rising from the central lab area and drifting our way in the mid-morning breeze.   The sirens blared louder outside.  Once outside, we were all in the stretch vehicle in no more than ten seconds.

Six doors swung shut.  But before they were all closed I caught the sickly foul smell that road the breeze.  We all coughed.  And me and several others gagged as Daisy fought through her nausea to start the vehicle.  She floored it, screeching tread; we wheeled around to the front parking lot, zoomed through it, out to the highway and blasted down the road toward the Estates.

When maybe a mile away Daisy powered down all the windows; we cleared any residual fumes out of the Humvee.  Some of my wives retched out the windows.  But I felt myself getting weaker, unable to cough anymore or even spit.  Last I recall of the drive was looking up at Daisy biting her lips to stay in control, and her glancing back down at me with grave concern.

A vaguely remember arriving at the estate, Valerie running up the steps carrying me.  The Triplets received me and the others, humming calming and singing healing harmonies.  Valerie handed me to Aria and I think that's when I passed out.

Then I died.  I looked down from the corner of the grand bedroom's high ceiling.  Was it just last night that I had married all these women, now streaming into the room to mourn me.  I looked sorrowfully at my pale prone body on the bed, the Triplets sitting around me singing the most beautiful song imaginable.  Or was it angels coming to take me away…

"No!"  I protested.  The angels were real, yes, but right there in the room, on the bed, sitting beside my lifeless body.  As they continued to sing, more and more sad wives entered the room, the beginning of a vigil around the bed.  Finally, Saint Debbie entered and the Triplets sang to her to come forward.  As the Triplets continued to sing, more emotional and louder; Saint Debbie removed all of her clothing.

Then my friend, my lover, my wife, my widow, my Saint Debbie sat her big beautiful butt right down on my expired body, leaving only my paler-by-the moment face exposed to see.  A vortex of blue light swirled up from the Triplet's singing to encircle me as I considered whether it was time to leave, to move on to my next life.  But the God-channeling Triplets offered me a loving choice: be at peace now and move on, or return now and fight for your life, for your love of us.  The clarity of the love and desire to live could not possibly have been stronger – choose life, choose love, choose connection… the blue swirl of bliss flowed around me in earthly song.

A timeless second later I felt the opposite of the glorious release of my body – I felt the crushing pressure of being smashed by Saint Debbie's one-ton ass.  But not a smash, a thorough absorption and exchange.  Debbie squeezed and released, squeezed and released, forcing air out and into my lungs.  This oxygenated my body but could not revive me.

Pavie lowered her breast onto my face, her leaking nipple onto my mouth.  Ambrosia milk entered my mouth.  Saint Debbie initiated a peristaltic wave through my chest, my stomach and throat; I swallowed.  With the first gulp I felt a sizzle of life returning through my visceral core.  More milk flowed.  More motion forced by Debbie animated me to swallow.  And soon enough I could suck a little bit.

I heard Aria commanding the other wives. "Bring us food, lots and lots of good wholesome food – food and water by the gallons."  Very soon I could sense that Pavie ate even as she fed me.  In another couple of minutes Callie took over, her milk a slightly different formula, also extremely healing but with altered emphasis, for other organs and systems in my body perhaps.

Down below, under, and inside Debbie, she continued to absorb me, sucking on my little frame, pulling out the toxins from my body, and ripping their proteins to shreds in her superior cells and systems.  Debbie heated up, fired up her miraculous metabolism into high gear for the challenge.  And this wife, not widow, angrily kicked ass on the toxins that sought to affect her husband's demise.

But Debbie could not do anything without energy.  So she too ate and ate and ate, and metamorphed to accommodate the changes.  Yet my body could offer nothing to Debbie without energy, so I sucked and sucked and the Triplet's milked flowed through me like a river.  To deliver that river, the Triplets, like Debbie, consumed an enormous poundage of food, eating and eating non-stop for hours and on through the rest of the day and into the night.  They processed the nourishment into shifting formulae that hounded and bird-dogged the toxins throughout my body, herding them up for Debbie to snatch up and annihilate in her ass.  And dear Saint Debbie already had me in her, already had my DNA in reserve, from the night of the metamorphosis only four days ago.  She had all the blueprints she needed to repair my body.

As the afternoon wore on, either I shrank or Debbie grew because it seemed her weight became unfathomly heavy.  The Triplets kept rotating and never stopped the constant nursing.  Then finally, well into the night the last breast lifted off and another one did not appear. Debbie's great weight that had crushed and absorbed me all day rolled over and me with it, lodged up inside her – I don't even know where.  I only know I felt insulated, protected, and safe as I reformed, was reformed, and awaited release when it became time to live on my own again.

Thank God for my wonderful, magical, loving wives.  I lived.  Though I had died, I lived, and that, my friend, is quite the perspective.  From that point on, I can promise you, I lived with new humble gratitude.

# XVII.   Queen of Mammoth Madness

I dreamt I was falling… falling into a darkness of soul, so heavy and oppressing that all hope of escape felt as futile as grasping at the swirling smoky vapors I fell past for a lifeline.  I woke when I hit the mattress.

Though the grand bedroom suite seemed so tightly dark as if petrified in a stone of black onyx, my mind shone with a bright clarity I had not experienced before.  I knew at once all that had transpired.  That Saint Debbie and the Triplets had, at great personal exertion, saved my life with their miraculous healing physiologies and connecting spiritual phenomena. That the intervention that saved me was possible because of quick action by Daisy and my wives of the Secretary Pool.  And that something terrible had been unleashed from the Synsonto labs that threatened all of Bluebelle Valley and maybe the World at large.

Where had I fallen from?  I looked up and could see nothing.  And why was the room so blasted dark?  I looked out toward the windows and could see stars, but no other light.  No street lights, no house lights, no little lights on the pathways nor from anything in the room.  This had to be an electrical blackout – probably having to do with the emergency.

Where had I fallen from? I panned around blind on the bed, reaching into the darkness with my hands.  I found flesh, and lots of it.  It felt smooth and too warm: Saint Debbie no doubt.  But what was I feeling, so wide and smooth without appendage or seeming end?  I probed further as I stood on the bed and could tell the smoothness rounded as I reached higher, curving in to a crevasse.  I followed it along with my hands a few steps to the left, felt it separate completely.  Back to the right maybe eight steps the crease eased into no separation, just smooth curvature over hard rounded bumps underneath.

I had found that place I love so much.  This had to be the lowest part of Debbie's back.  But what had happened to her?  She had grown absolutely enormous beyond reason.  Or had I shrunk, from the contamination and/or from the cure?

Flabbergasted, I leaned against Debbie's lower back and looked away.  Now that my eyes had adjusted I could see the Triplets now: Pavie, Aria, and Callie lie amazon-sound-asleep in a body chain glowing ever so faintly with their blue healing energy.  I could tell the Triplets and I were nearly the same relative size to each other as before.

Well then, let's see about the amazing Saint Debbie.  And by that I mean not-see.  Though, I did not intend to be fooled like the six blind men and the elephant.  No, I meant to feel my way around this grand new wife of mine until I had a full understanding of this amazing woman had now accomplished with her latest metamorphosis.

Back to the middle of her hips.  I must have fallen off her hips, because I had landed right below them.  I pressed in close and hugged against them.  That put my face right at crack level and so I pressed in further and kissed like a proper husband.  Wow, what a lovely place to lose myself.  And wondered, maybe, if I had fallen from right there: not off her butt but out of her buns.  Maybe for some reason a little man in dire condition of dying had been lodged in the ass of his giantess wife.  Weird, but could have been part of some strange therapy…

I kissed Debbie again, deeper.  I wanted her to respond.  But she seemed gone-from-this-world asleep and out.  If she grew that much in, had it only been one night, she would be beyond exhausted.  Here's a moral dilemma, maybe: is it okay for a husband to fool around with an asleep wife if he believes that would be all right with her?  I say let's try it and see how I feel about it.  Of course with Saint Debbie I probably didn't have to worry that much.  It would not be like she would get mad at me now, would she?

Goodness, how does one fool around with a woman this size?  And what size was that anyway?  Well, these ample-assed amazons got proportionally wider as they got taller, getting sturdier to hold up the quickly increasing weight with any gain in height.  So a nine foot amazon might have an ass three feet wide. And a fifteen footer like sweet and dangerous Daisy might swing around a load easily six feet wide.  So Debbie lying here with her hip so deeply sunk into the mattress and her crack at my face height could be toting an ass nine feet wide.  So I'm guessing she must be like somewhere in the range around twenty-three feet tall.  My very next thought was: I've got to get around and check out her breasts.

Back at her waist I found if I reached all the way up I could grip the top of her lovely curvature as it dropped down above her pelvis.  Doing that, and with a little leap, I jammed my left foot in above the top of her right bun.  Remember, I'm quite the climber.  So in short order I swung my right leg over and sat on her horsy style and facing backward toward her hips.  Still I could see none of her.

I reclined there a moment, resting my legs up on her rising hip and my back comfortably on the smooth incline up toward her chest.  Yes, I imagined myself on a beach with this wife, using her instead of a hammock – ah, this is the life.  Of course, that's right when providence loves to play tricks on me, almost always at the point of when I'm getting a little too cocky.

My dear Saint Debbie coughs a little, bouncing me off and forward.  Up immediately though, I continue my journey upward along her front side.

"Fee, fie, foe, fum." I sing-songed tracing along her front with my right hand, dreaming up the rhyme as I went. "I want a breast for my pleasure and fun.  Ah, here's something…" Yes, something huge, lovely, soft, and kissable.  I buried my face into the under part of her upper stacked breast.  Reaching as if to hug it, my arms only spread out to an open embrace.  I could not reach around it.

Bending down only slightly I found where the two breasts met.  Perfect; I'll just insert myself in there for an hour or two of ideal bliss.  But that proved impossible – too tight and too heavy.  Bummer.  Frustrated a little I kissed my way around to the front and found a huge nipple.  How could I suck on this irresistible tit; the nipple being almost the size of my entire face? At least give it a try, I suppose.

I did and it yielded.  Thank you dear Debbie.  I was thirsty and this source from the Goddess tasted perfect.  However, in short order I was flooded, had all I could take in like a minute.  And I had to back away to avoid drowning.  Well, not really drowning, but let's say Saint Debbie was being more than generous.  I patted her breast good-bye with a soft "I love you".  And then, naturally, I headed south.

Along the way I kissed her big, and what I visualized as cute, innie belly button.  A couple steps later I arrived at the forest, again perfectly face high.  Feeling forward I got it that Debbie slept with her upper leg forward and crossing in front of me down.  Here I could easily duck underneath, hunching slightly and come out the other side behind the gargantuan leg.  I had to turn and kiss that wonderful area of upper, widest-most part of the back of the leg where it met her lower bun.

I kept on kissing, getting myself rather excited, as I worked my way under that leg again and into the forest.  Parting hairs I found more treasures wonderfully kissable, burrowing my way in face first.  Debbie shifted, turning forward slightly letting me in further. I proceeded, ignoring that I had now put me more underneath her.  I kept on venturing in further.  Kneeling to gain access to her forward shift, I soldiered on, a real trooper at this kind on enterprise.  My face pressed into spreading wetness, my shoulders warmed by a fur coat.

Then, working my way up I found it and I mean "It": Debbie's extra warm and active clitoris, the resting home of her Tingle.  Only it wasn't resting; it crouched in her crotch fully awake and ready to infuse me with sexual shock and overload.

"Ah, yes Richie," Debbie spoke and her voice was not even slightly sleepy, "I thought you would never get there."  And with that she rolled over on me, absolutely and completely pinning me under her the tonnage of her massive ass and pussy.  Big-big and sneaky-sneaky – Saint Debbie the Giantess had been awake the entire time.

Mac truck heavy, but softer than a load of cotton, sweet as a cargo hold of fresh flowers, my wife Saint Debbie smothered me to the N-th  degree.  She bounced on me, and it took me a few crushing jolts to realize she was laughing.  I guess she thought her surprise attack ranked right up there for one of the best pussy traps ever.  Fine, so be it, I didn't complain as first my head, then shoulders, then my torso slid right up in her to my waist.

I felt myself bending at the waist.  I could feel my orientation to gravity and could tell my upper body sat upright.  Debbie brought me to that position by sitting up herself, and thereby sitting on my lap as it issued from her pussy.  My pencil legs flattened to bent bones under her horrendous butt crush.  My arms were helplessly pinned to my side by the 360 degree wet waves of contractions inside her pussy.  My head, while free enough to turn at first, soon found itself clamped into place at some 30 degrees to the left, face-to-face against her g-spot also blasting Tingle into my body.  And my Volunteer jammed up into her as her wave motions sought to take me in with each mercilessly devastating gyration.  And still I remained enough outside of her to be continually butt crushed.

Wow, what a clever wife.  This had to be the perfect, perfect woman.  The tastes, the smells, the warm and moist overload, everything delicious and delightful felt heavenly to me – in a crushing sort of way, of course.  In that wonderful world of wet pussy, Debbie's Tingle activated to the maximum, fully overwhelming with stimulating pleasures to every cell in my body.  In response, my Sparkle-fire shot about and swept flames of sexual energy throughout her nether regions.  Debbie's orgasm built quickly now, vectors of hot Tingle impinged into my body from every possible angle.  And my blue flame fried them into steaming vapors, expanding the crazed sexual frenzy geometrically.

Basically we exploded, a sexual bomb.  The titanic colossus around and on me reverberated to her core.  Somehow she held together, then like that vast dominating Goddess that she proved to be time and yet time again, and certainly more than ever now, Saint Debbie imploded all that sexual energy and love back down into my body, disintegrating me into a little flat love-cushion for her continual pounding pleasure.

And Giantess Debbie just sat on me and sat on me and sat on me, all the while absorbing me in my glorious defeat under her and inside her.  Her pussy munched me into nothingness and her ass squished that nothingness into the component parts of nothing.  It seemed my soul had no place to go, so adrift Saint Debbie snared me at that level as well.  So powerful and sentient, Debbie took my very soul and stuffed and crushed it, my essence, under her vast loving ass, smothering my spirit with adoration and supreme dominance.  I felt I had disappeared forever into and under her crushing love.  And there Debbie kept me orgasming, without the least bit of relief, in brain-frying ecstasy for maybe an hour. There is no word in any language for how much love I felt for her as she owned me inside her and squished her huge supercharged smashing pussy and as onto me.

Then, when Debbie felt good and satisfied, she squeezed and shaped and remade me again just as I was.  At least – that's how it felt.

Saint Debbie pulled me out, a pussy-owned husband zombie, who knew nothing but his servile place beneath his Goddess.  And that place was under her smothering pleasure zones.  I shivered outside of her, craving to be in her again.  As it turned out for now, I would have to be content with being in her ass.  Slowly the vast crack of her posterior descended on me, eating me up and smashing me under.  It had its own personal message for me: "Welcome to your new home, husband, in my butt and squished under my 7000 pounds.  Kiss me now and I will let you live."

So completely enveloped in her buns, I had disappeared before she even sat.  But when she sat, oh my, the finality of the crush left not one speck of doubt about the complete comprehensiveness of her dominion over me.  As I incubated and withered under Debbie, I pictured myself inside and under her huge, nine-foot wide spreading butt.  Her legs bent, knees up thus piling the thousands of pounds of weight in her legs on me as well.  The thick heavy stack of her abs and chest and shoulders and strong arms and the beautiful, bounteous, beyond-all-reason breasts each three times my body's frail weight – all of that pile-driving me steadily flatter while even so exterminated I still wished for more.  And as that devastated helpless tiny footnote to her ass, all I was capable to do was lick and lick and lick… and dream, maybe most of all, to dream of the restorative love of her breasts.

Seeming to read my mind, and probably not actually wanting to extinguish me after just having saved me from toxic death, Debbie lifted her reluctant ass off me, wiggling and relaxing until I fell out.  She still kept me pinned under her, inescapable even if I had any energy or volition left to leave.  With two hands completely encircling my body, Debbie brought me to her breast again.  She smashed my face into her other breast and forced me to nurse for a ten minute deluge.

Then tired at last, Debbie laid back down on her side.  Holding me around my waist with one hand, she lifted up her top breast with the other hand.  The she spread me out flat on her lower breast and let the top breast fall onto me, spreading huge soft and warm to cover my body and trap it in a breast sandwich.  And then, bless her heart, this biggest sweet wife of mine went to sleep.

For some time I forgot all cares and enjoyed the perfection of my situation, of being married to this ideally beautiful and sexy, voluptuous and magical giantess who seemed to truly adore me.  Squished and imprisoned on my back in her warm breast sandwich I mouth worship up into bosom and to the nipple that teased some two feet above my face.  That nipple began leaking and dripping, the sleepy slow flow falling upon my face, and with a small adjustment I could just barely achieve, right into my most appreciative mouth.

"Love you Debbie.  I love you Debbie…" I could not think of a stronger way to express my devotion.  SO I just said it over and over and over…

But something kept nagging at me.  Partly it went back to the dreams I'd had when ill.  In spite of the excellence of wifely crushing care that Debbie gave to me, I could not get the images of Serenity, the Amazon Queen of the tapestry out of my mind.  The Triplets had warned of her genetic twist, of her undisputed danger and murderous rampage.  Yet, haunted or not, I knew even now that the tapestry still wavered in the stairwell, threatening to come of the wall and fly out of the house.  I had to go – go to her.

Crazy as it may seem, though pressed in enchanting perfection, it seemed I had a higher calling that could not be ignored. While Saint Debbie's breasts had proven too much for me to burrow into; burrowing out, while tough, was a different matter.  After an exhausting twisting and shoving I found a way to progress to the edge.  Debbie, responding in her sleep, rolled toward her belly.  That opened the final gap I needed to escape, diving out and away just before I would have been tit-pinned for likely some hours until past dawn.

I rolled off the bed, and crawling blindly found the door.  But I heard voices outside, Amanda and Donna, others less close to the door.  I listened for a few moments.  They spoke in hushed tones about a quarantine and an unknown amount of lost lives from genetically altered sex-linked virus that was accidentally released from the lab.  I knew for sure those responsible wives would not allow me to leave the premises.  Oh Donna and Amanda would gladly sit on me until morning and await the advice of the Triplets.  That delay I could not allow.

I slipped away from the door and back by the bed.  I don't think sleeping Debbie had any more surprise attacks this night.  And my precious and undoubtedly exhausted Triplet wives had not moved from their magical blue-glow positions.  I wiggled through the slightly open grand sliding door and out onto the wide semi-circle veranda.  Starlight can be sufficient light on a clear moonless night when you are outside in the open.  Such was this night.

Over to the corner of the veranda where it met the wall of the mansion, I stepped under the rail and out onto a decorative horizontal ledge.  The sill perhaps six inches wide, I easily walked along the top to the right turn at the corner of the Triplet's (and my) bedroom.  The architect used those chains for downspouts instead of gutters.  So the only small risk, which I took without problem, was the little leap out to the chain.  Quickly I shimmied down the forty feet to the patio.

I took off in a stealthy sprint to the far end of the mansion, around through the side meticulous park-like gardens and out to the front driveway.  At the gate no guard.  I squeezed through the gate bars and found myself free and out.  Still the starlight provided enough definition to form, structure, and landscape.  The black street before me, with its fancy smooth surface, reflected enough starlight shine to be unmistakable.  I ran now at a good sustainable pace.

"So where are we going, Richie?" Tiffany's voice alongside me all the sudden, out of the dark, made me almost wet my shorts.

"Good God, is that you, Tiffany?  You scared the crap out of me!"

"Sorry… but then what do you expect if you go running around on an unusually very dark night during a quarantine?"

"Listen, I've got something I have to do and it could be very dangerous.  So why don't you head back inside and pretend like you didn't see me?"

"Wow, dude, you do realize you married amazons, don't you?  I have a mind to thrash you around a little right now and give you a nice facesit to bring you back to the reality of your married life.  Don't ever give me the 'be a good little woman' routine again.  Besides, what kind of wife would I be to let you head into danger alone?"

"Sorry, but I'm kind of in a hurry?"

"And you think the four-time Minnesota high school long-distance statewide running champion is going to slow you down?  I'm out here every morning, training before we go to work. So let me ask you again: where are we going, husband?  Because if you don't have an actual real plan, well, we'll just take a pause and I'll fuck you right now on the Huffington's front lawn – emergency or no emergency."

"OK, OK" I saw I'd have to tell her. "I have a rescue mission.  If I've got my facts correct, it should be ten miles east of here, in the foothills – at the Facility for the Criminally Insane."

"Well aren't you full of surprises.  Let's get going then.  It will be morning light soon enough."

I started running again, my athletic wife jogging effortlessly by my side.  "By the way," I panted, "Thank you."

"Hey, just so you know.  I'd do about anything to get my pussy close to you."

"That is good to know."  I wheezed out.

"Oh for criminy sakes; we're never going to get there at this pace."  And my 500 pound runner wife scoped me up and swung me around to ride on her hips.  She shoved my hands up under her loose shirt to grip her sports bra.  "Hang on, sweetheart.  Let's make some tracks!"  And she took off running at some twenty miles per hour. "Let's see if we can get there before sunrise."

In like three minutes we were out of Bluebelle Estates and on the highway.  Sure it was early, but there was not a vehicle in sight, nor had there been so far.  In another fifteen minutes of smooth sprint we came to the turnoff, Dellview Ridge Drive that led up into the foothills.

The road narrowed and darkened with tall trees and the thick vegetation of late summer closing to complete an arch overhead.  Yet even as Tiffany ran up the lane, me still riding in style, the earliest trace of pale dawn heralded that light would soon end the reign of this exceedingly dark night.  Five more mountain turns over another mile and we came to the steep open driveway that led down to the Mental Institution situated in its own little valley floor.

"Beautiful…" I commented, tapping Tiffany to look up at the strands of pink light filtering through scattered morning mists on the higher steeper foothills, "… what a nice place to be crazy."

"Oh you're real nice.  I might yet have to take a pause to teach you some manners."

"You know," I slid off Tiffany's back, down her leg to the ground, "for such a little Amazon you sure talk tough."

Tiffany turned and stood before me, legs apart, arms akimbo. "How about we see right now what my big sexy 500 pound ass can do to your 75 pound collection of sticks."

I walked right up to her, actually quite interested in her proposal.  I mean, Lord knows, I'd survived a lot more than that not two hours ago.  But as I approached, some movement caught my eye at the facility down below, and I kept right on walking between her legs.

Surprised, Tiffany spun around to nab me, but stopped short when see too saw it. "What the heck is that?"

Tiffany had taken the words right out of my mouth.  As we looked on it happened again.  The entire multi-story main building, behind the office entrance area appeared to lift up, shake, and then settle again.  Dust rose from all around the perimeter of the structure.  But before it could settle all the way, the same sequence repeated, and this time we could hear a metal groaning coming from deep within the bones of the building.

"That's what I was afraid of."  I tugged on Tiffany to come with me down the entrance drive. "I don't think there are any caregivers coming here anymore.  How many days has it been since the accident?"  I actually had no clear idea, being lost as I was in a coma fraught with nightmares and crushing pressures.

"It's been four days.  Why?"

"Well," I nodded my head at the building rising and shuttering again.  I think somebody is getting hungry."

"Who?" It seemed Tiffany did not know much about the Institute.

"If I'm not mistaken, Serenity Segal and others taken by the Mammoth Madness."  I felt right then I needed those dramatic music three-chords down: "Den-den-daaa…"

"Mammoth Madness?  I thought that was hearsay.  How do you know anything about it?"

"Triplets told me."  That three-word phrase probably the best authoritative conversation stopper there was in Bluebelle Valley.

"So what do you plan to do, then?  If anything I heard is true they are likely fiendishly dangerous."

"I don't know, dear wife."  I could tell she liked being called that. "I only know I am compelled by my heart into action and sometimes words.  And somehow, when I really completely trust in that and in the goodness of the universe, what follows seems for the best."

"Honestly Richie, we really are going to have to take a break to make love very soon."  I guess she liked what I said.  Her hand caressed the back of my noggin kindly and gentler than you might expect from such a tough talker.

"A definite rain check, my lovely.  We need to see about conditions in the facility before someone brings the roof down on everyone in there."

"OK.  Front door then?"

"Yes."  And we jogged up to the big solid wooden door.  It was locked.  Right then the building trembled again, and a feint, but had to be loud inside, groan accompanied the contortions of the building.

Tiffany, checking the door, looked back to me.  "Not only locked but jammed in its frame as well.  The whole wall would need to come down."

"How do we get in?"  I had been too weak for too long and had trouble on thinking of ways to overcome physical obstacles.

But not Tiffany.  "Look up there, at the vent."  I could see where she pointed, equivalent of five floors up, tucked under the roof's peak, a lesser side roof sloping down to a smooth thirty-five foot brick wall straight down.  Even I couldn't climb that one.  Tiffany didn't see the limitation.  "I'll toss you up there.  Then I'll figure some way for me to join you."

She didn't wait for my comment, instead reaching one hand under my crotch and the other balancing my chest.  With swings, a-one, a-two, and threeeee, Tiffany launched me perfectly to land softly on the slightly sloped roof beneath the vent.  Immediately I went to work trying to loosen the vent – it was screwed on too tight.

I looked around to see about Tiffany.  Right away I spied her back by the flag pole, maybe on her third bend back and forth on the forty metal staff.  Two more bends to ninety degrees flat and it broke through the metal at the base.  Without even testing it for balance, Tiffany picked it up by its thicker base and started running at the office entrance with the pole directly out in front of her.  I figured Tiffany was fast but I had no idea she could accelerate so impressively.  She looked determined to knock the door down in a combination of jousting and battering ram.

Right when Tiffany neared the front door though it seemed she screwed up her maneuver and the ball top of the pole hit at the sturdy base frame of the front door.  Her phenomenal momentum was for sure going to get her injured as she smashed into the brick wall.  Instead, she shockingly took off into the air, holding onto the base of the flag pole.  With two strong hands she hung to the pole and vaulted  up and up soaring right on up forty feet, flying over the top of the brick wall, and landing, oh shit, right onto me.

Her big athletic ass landed square on my chest, my face staring up in astonishment from the tight muscular V of her big toned upper thighs.  A pole-vault had been her plan all along.  She laughed at the look on my face.  "I aimed to where you were; but I had no idea I'd be that accurate.  Hmmmm, can we take that little husband/wife break right now?"

Well, it seemed like we were on a mission; but given the lovely proximity of her silky running shorts to my face… maybe a just a brief encounter would be okay.  Right then Tiffany lifted up, her quite enticing crotch hovering right above me.  Right all then – I kissed her salty tight inner thigh, quickly finding my way up through the looseness of her shorts.  She slammed her butt down on me, then right away lifted back up.  Before I could say do that again, Tiffany had her own comments.

"Listen, sport, you're gonna' have to save that for later.  Great idea and all, but come on, you got to know I was kidding.  Timing is everything, dude.  Look."  She held up the vent cover in her right hand. "I only leaned forward to remove this and get us access into the attic.  Not to sit on your horny little face."

"OK, Babe, but later…" I twisted underneath her, up on all fours on the twenty degree slope of the roof."

"Definitely, later…"  A violent tremor rocked the building.  I fell and would have rolled down and off the roof, but Tiffany clamped onto me with powerful legs, locking me between her knees.  She held on to the open vent, secure enough to endure the shaking without problem.  As the quaking subsided Tiffany grabbed under my arms with her free hand and pulled me into her chest.

"I thought we didn't have time for this." I joked, my face against her big firm breasts.

"What an incorrigible little beast you are."  Tiffany shook her head at me, but smiled. "Look, you can get in this vent, but no way my ass is fitting through that little square. So hang on, your arms around my neck.  I need both my arms for this maneuver."

I reached up under her cascade of blonde waves and around her neck, basically hugging myself and my cheek to nestle against hers.

"OK, don't let go."  She warned.  With both hands Tiffany grabbed the near vertical side of the vent's metal frame opening.  She hauled up both legs with a powerful ab crunch, and deftly placed her running shoes against the vertical inside of the far side of the opening.  Then she pulled with her arms and pushed with her legs.  The incredible tension in her strong body told me of the thousands of pounds of pressure she exerted on the metal.  Soon enough it yielded, bending on both sides then breaking loose on the far side as her legs drove right on sideways through the wall studs.

I kissed her on the cheek, I just couldn't help it, then said about the wide gapping void where the vent used to be, "Think your ass can get through that hole?"

In response to my wisecrack, Tiffany, her hands now free, grabbed a handful of the hair on the back of my head and wrenched my face around to hers.  She planted a sincerely vigorous teethy kiss over my mouth, forcing my lips apart and mouth open with her powerful tongue.  Ending with a big smack, she twisted my head sideways and whispered hot in my ear.  "I cannot wait until this is over, husband.  I'm going to fuck your living brains out."

I patted her on her breast, living dangerous as usual.  "Promises, promises…"

"Oh, you… you know, I'll remember this a long, long time.  I mean I'm obviously way too much woman for you already, lover boy.  But when I'm, let's say, 20 feet tall, it is going to be so much fun to sit my multi-ton ass on you and feel you squirming for dear life."

"Wow, that sounds like fun.  Face first, I hope."  Now I kissed that same breast and batted my eyes up at her.

"You can count on it, face first, and way up where the sun don't shine.  Meanwhile, let's get on with this mission."  Tiffany lifted me to the inside of the attic and followed me inside, both of us happy to find the entirety of the attic roughed in with flooring.

"By the way," Tiffany sounded curious.  "What is our mission?"

"Well, this facility, while touted as a mental institution, and I'm giving them the benefit of the doubt that they are trying to do good work here; well – it basically serves as a prison, doesn't it?  So with the emergency and quarantine likely nobody is watching this place or tending the guests – and by that I mean inmates.  I know it's only been four days, but who knows what the conditions are, what help they made need.  I expect food and water at least."

"So we are here, the two of us, to rescue the criminally insane giantesses of the Mammoth Madness?"

"Well yea, I mean who else is going to do it?"

"I don't know, how about the National Guard?" Tiffany seemed to be skeptical of my plan.

"And when they get here in weeks or months or never, what kind of shape are these poor women going to be in, locked up and ignored?"

"OK, I see your point.  But you do have a strategy, plan of some sort, right?"

"Yes and no – mostly no.  I mean, we have to see what's going on first, right?  If they seem too crazy we can just get them some water or food or something.  But we just can't leave them here."

The building shook again, knocking me over.  As Tiffany helped me up I noticed the floor was no longer level.  We hurried now, following along under the peak of the roof.  Soon we found a folded ladder hatch and released the latch, shoving the balanced mechanism to open and lower the ladder.

I climbed down first and steadied the ladder for Tiffany.  I shouldn't have looked up; way too distracting to see that big firm ass working side to side as she descended.  Then again, it's my wife; a man can ogle his wife any time, right?  That's a good benefit of married life I'm thinking.

Even though Tiffany had reached the floor, she kept her ass coming on down, squatting enough to press it onto my face.  "Go ahead and kiss it so you can get your focus back on the mission."

Being a good husband I took my wife's advice.  I boldly pushed her loose running shorts up to expose an excellent bun and kissed her right there.  Very lovely indeed, "Thanks," I definitely approved and appreciated, patting her.

"Oh any time, you knucklehead.  Now can we get moving again?" Tiffany took one step then paused, right in front of me.  "OK, give me one more for the road."

I obliged with another kiss but on the other side. "That better?  I don't want you to get out of balance."

"That'll do for now, champ."  Tiffany took three steps over to a railing.

Catching up with her I looked out over a vast open space, basically a huge square, railing all around at our same level, like a mezzanine, probably four hundred feet to the other side.  The little side attic we had entered had not revealed the arching skylights that spanned above the open void.  Feint morning light filtered-pink through the glass.  Looking down we could see some fifty feet to a metal framework all the way across the four hundred foot distance.

"Bars." I nudged Tiffany's knee with my elbow.

"Yep."  Tiffany sounded a little uneasy.

"And look inside down there."  I pointed.  Inside the vast cage I could see tall trees, and further over an open area, gassy next to a pond or pool.  It was one of the more beautiful settings I have ever seen inside a building.

Another tremor started.  The cage frame lifted.  And I could see now that massive girders locked the cage into the frame of the building.  The groaning metal sound hit decibels painful to ear.  The tree tops cast about like in a wind storm, but there wasn't the slightest breeze – well maybe some wafting up from the trees.

A rather wonderful, sweet and quickly addictive smell or maybe more correctly, an irresistible pheromone scent floated up with the breeze.  It was almost like the scent was heavy, because as the quaking stopped and the trees settled down, it seemed the delicious smell dropped back down into the forest and glade below.

"Wow, did you smell that?"  I asked my big, dedicated wife.

"I didn't smell anything."  Tiffany shrugged.  It seemed hard to believe, but she wasn't kidding.

"How could I smell something that strong, wonderful and powerful, but you not even catch the scent at all?"

"I don't know.  My sense of smell is pretty darn keen.  Maybe it's a smell not intended for women.  Something special for horny little guys like yourself."

"I could be in trouble then, because just that smell practically subdued me."

"Oh I've heard something about this.  The other Secretaries were talking… I think it had something to do with that Mammoth Madness gene.  That's right, that was the catch: 'a man's only warning is that smell; problem is he loses all resistance'.  Richie, you sure you're up for this?"

"I have to be.  She's been calling me."

"Who's been calling you?"  Now Tiffany looked truly concerned.

"The Queen."

"Oh Lord.  What are we talking about, Richie?  Twenty-six new wives and you're thinking about fooling around with some crazy queen?"

"I'm sleeping in her bedroom, Tiffany.  She's been haunting my dreams, threatening me in the stairwell.  She's so heart-broken."

"Well, yeah, she killed her parents."

"Exactly.  This is my purpose, Tiffany; to heal."

"Who do you think you are, Jesus, for Christ sake?"  Tiffany kneeled beside me to her haunches.  Her face looked serious and loving right down into mine.  "Let me take you home, Richie."  She pleaded, "Before you get hurt or worse."

I grabbed her hands with my much smaller ones, and took a half step closer to her face.  "Tiffany, I love you.  Already I love you."

"God, Richie, that's what's so phenomenal about you.  All of us wives see it.  It's not like you are some high concentration of love in a little body.  No, you're like a portal to some universe of love we have all been missing.  You are way too precious to take such a risk.  These women – they may smell wonderful and irresistible – but make no mistake, they are monsters."

"Monsters or not, I have no choice.  This action is who I am.  And I have the strangest feeling that I am not alone nor small with this intent.  I feel that something much bigger is with me, in all of us really, waiting to be recognized.  I don't know what it is, Tiffany, but it feels like love.  And that's all I have, really, love in many, many forms – love and pretty much nothing else."

The adoration in Tiffany's face felt almost embarrassing to see. "Well, how could I not respect that, husband?  Maybe you are Jesus."

I laughed hardy at that one.  "Then Lord help us."  And I laughed some more.

Below it seemed deathly silent, like the forest had been listening.  I looked down expectantly, waiting.  The trees stirred again, that scent wafting up once more, stronger, overpowering.  Then the strangest voice I have ever heard came up through the canopy, almost like a sexy hiss to start, far away and at the same time as close as an intimate whisper, regal and commanding yet with a sorrowful surrender.  "Richie – you've come to me at last, come to save your Queen."

Tiffany did not trust the voice one bit.  "Richie, come, let's get out of here now.  Up the ladder, out the roof and away from here.  I cannot let you go down there."

"If you do not trust Her then stay back, near the exits.  If you see something happen to me do not try to save me because you cannot.  Run and warn the others if it comes to that.  But do not worry about me.  For last night I died, and I fear death no longer."

Certain I'd gone mad, Tiffany reached for me.  But I jumped the rail too quickly and down to the top of the cage.  Tiffany, to her loyal credit jumped after me, still intent on taking me home by force if necessary.  But little me, I slipped through the cage bars where no Amazon could.  I swung over to the top of the highest tree, then looked back to Tiffany.

"Stay safe, dear.  And remember, you promised to 'fuck my brains out'. I'm really looking forward to that."  And I disappeared like a monkey down the tree.

I reached the forest floor within a minute.  It was soft and grassy, clean.  That overwhelming scent was everywhere, though I felt like I was adjusting to it.  I didn't try to resist it, but accepted it.  With that attitude it seemed more to bathe over me than seek to subdue me.

I followed the way I'd noticed from above to the open glade and natural-looking pool.  There sitting on the grass, legs outstretched and crossed were, by far, the three largest women I have ever seen.  True giantesses and extraordinarily beautiful... each with her own corner on the market for magnificence.

Nude and exquisite they sat like royalty, huge thick legs muscular and tapered giving way to luscious amounts of perfectly proportion fat, right into their car-size asses.  These women would have to be at least thirty feet tall if standing. I walked toward them.  They ignored for the moment.  Approaching, I looked up at breasts so hopelessly large it boggled my mind to consider them.  I shook my attention off the breasts to gaze upon them in awe.  Each woman carried herself imperially and also with a clear differentiation of ethnicity.

The one nearest me, turned her deep brown eyes to look down at me, some distain flashed clearly.  Was I supposed to bow?  Her dark skin glistened with water drops. Perhaps she had just come out from the pool.  She said nothing, just studied me, calmly it seemed for now.

Next to her, what would be the wonder of all Asia, her skin a beautiful cream, her great breasts defying all stereotypes in their extreme grandeur.  In turn she looked haughtily down at me as well.  Her mouth opened, she licked her lips then seemed to allow a mischievous smile when I shuttered.

The final grand beauty was yet another dark-haired spectacle.  She turned to me with her eyes closed, then opened her big Persian beauties to gaze upon me and I actually feel to my knees.  Her full lips parted to the slightest of puckers.  Wavy black hair cascaded some fifteen feet to the meadow's lawn, piling there in a spool maybe another ten feet long.  She rose to all fours to face me.  Breasts hundreds of pounds each, if not a thousand, so full and shaped if by a master artist, beckoned me to crawl underneath and await my demise.  Poised she was, facing toward me, but she did not approach.  I simply stared at her, beyond awestruck, and then back to the others.

The first dark woman nearest now posed the same as the third.  The second did the opposite, facing me with her more than fifteen foot catholic ass.  I had to stop and stare at that.  She looked coyly over her shoulder, still licking the lips of her wide mouth, more than generous lips.

But there was no Queen.  No, it was not one of these women who had spoken; that I knew for sure.

The scent that had become compatible with me sudden grew exponentially in intensity.  It definitely enveloped me, seduced me without subduing me, and rather fired up the Sparkle.  The Queen had arrived.

"Beautiful aren't they?" I dared not turn around to the voice behind and way above me. "They would love you or eat you – or both at my command." Then without pause. "Ginny." The first of the three women stood and rose to her towering height. "Would you be so kind as to run down the woman who came with him and bring her here?"

Ginny crossed in front of me silent and surprisingly cat-like in her elegant economy of motion. To the near-side of the lake the cage bars were barely visible behind the dense foliage. I learned now how ridiculous was my idea of a rescue: the barred gate to their pen stood wide open. They could leave anytime. Yet, the Queen had called me here. For what purpose, if no rescue was needed.

"Now you see, don't you?" Still I would not turn to look at her. "You, who dare to sleep in my royal abode, fornicate with your strange women in my room, and desecrate the sanctity of my parent's sacred home – you will die here tonight. But first I want to bring back your little girlfriend to witness your demise." I must have tensed, giving The Queen a clue. "Oh, what's this, not girlfriend, something more, not a wife – oh, how precious." She laughed deep. "Well, then let the festivities begin."

A great hand came from behind me, scooping me up, and with the same rapid swing toss me to the waiting eager cream-colored ass of the second giantesses. I landed front in and she squeezed to catch me tight, like I'd been pitched as a fastball to a catcher's mitt.

The great voice hissed husky, sultry and over-flowing with evil sexual desires. "Good catch, Maya. You and Keisha can kiss him if you want, but don't eat him yet. We must have some fun first.

I still felt dizzy from the toss when Maya, after a good tight squeeze, pulled me from her bum, dipped me in the water, I suppose to be sanitary, then brought me to her lips. Right behind, the beautiful Keisha breathed her sweet scent onto me. Maya brought my feet to her lips, took them into her mouth, then continued to insert me up to my waist.

Keisha's oh so beautiful full lips slowly encircled my head, spread over my shoulders and trunk. Their lips met and sealed me in a kiss between them. They used very talented and cooperating tongues to remove my clothing, letting my little wet rags drop – I assume down to the grass. This devouring kiss lasted a long time, going on and on as they played with my body. They kept the sucking gentle enough; for they could have dismantled me with powerful whole-body hickies if they chose.  Though at some level terrified, I felt they would follow their queen's advice not to harm me – for now.  So I enjoyed the mouth play without too much panicky feeling.  Maya and Keisha pretended to try to swallow me, tugging on my legs and then in turn on my head and upper body.  They acted like maybe they would eat me, biting down just enough to hurt.

At long last Maya released me to Keisha.  Keisha moved me around, sideways along her lips, my feet sticking out the left side, my head out the right.  Here she kissed on my body for some minutes, very stimulating, and getting my Volunteer super hard.  Keisha rotated me in her lips so the others could see.

"Oh, what fun," Maya came around to lick the entire front of my body.  Her teeth gleamed as she looked prepared to take a bite

"Not yet, Ma-ya-ma-ya."  The significantly bigger Keisha shoved Maya's head back.  Maya rounded, flashing anger, and ready to fight.  She launched herself at Keisha.  But Keisha leapt up, more than ready, and shoved the back of Maya's head on through and below.  As Maya turned to attack again, Keisha dropped back down pinning Maya in her middle.  Maya sat up quickly, snapping at me like a T-Rex.  But Keisha held me safe, folding her lips around me.

From inside Keisha's mouth I felt the wrestling jostles.  But very soon Keisha opened her mouth again, Maya school-girl pinned, her shoulders under Keisha's bent knees.  Keisha dropped me out of her mouth and into her hand.  Still sitting and pinning Maya, you could say Keisha kind of teased her, playing with me, dropping me over Maya's open and waiting mouth, but swooping through at the last split second to catch me with the other hand.  After a few of these teases Keisha shoved me up under her breast.  Yes indeed, it probably was a thousand pounds.

Keisha taunted. "He's mine, Maya, mine.  And you better behave or I'll sit on your face – in the pool.

"Let me up."  Maya pleaded now, but also way too dangerous to be trusted.

"I'll let you up when you face isn't red any more.  I'll…

"Hush now."  The Queen called from across the pond.  Ginny had returned.

"The little bitch got away.  I've never seen someone that size run so fast."  Did Ginny mean so small, I wondered.

"Let me see him."  The Queen commanded. "Set him down before me."

Keisha got up off Maya and waded through the pond.  She placed me at the feet of the Empress.  I looked forward at her lustrous bronze skin.  Up from a right well-turned ankle, her sexy calf muscles bulged firm and intimidating.  My God, my height was not even a third the way to her knee.  The queen stepped forward, standing with her feet barely apart and all of her directly over me. Her legs soared up like the Colossus of Memnon, twenty feet up to an ass so impossible big I found myself shaking, but was it fear or desire, probably both.  The rest of her some forty foot frame I could not see beyond the vast spread of her ass.

Her knees bent, her ass descended enough to alarm.  A hand more than the size of my body reached down and encircled me.  Up so slowly her hand carried me with a purpose to reveal her magnificence, and thereby weaken me with her imposing sumptuousness.  I got the grand, facing-out glass elevator tour of rest of her body. And I what witnessed did indeed seem to diminish my significance, feeling barely human by comparison to the glorious and terrible woman from the tapestry.

As I looked on in shock at the size and perfect beauty of her legs above the knee, I could not fathom the pressure their squeeze nor their sitting pressure upon my body. She actually brought me around for a good close look at her backside as she finished unbending all the way straight.  Yes, my Queen, I get the point, you could shove me in your ass and I would never be seen again.  Oh to be sat upon by that mass would be the ultimate of submissive life-ending crushes.  Passing to the other hand right under the broadest part of her almost twenty-foot wide butt, she seemed to be toying with the idea of inserting me right there and then.

But my tour continued around to the front by being passed back to the other hand through her legs and thus underneath all that vastness of her.  Coming up the front, her slight bending again had opened her pussy enough to clarify the size and nature of that doom as well.  Go ahead, I thought, please put me in there now.  Yet the tour continued past strong ripped abs with enough padding to smooth her out flawlessly.

She brought me close enough to touch her breasts; if only I could get an arm free to reach out and feel that bounty….  That was not necessary as she let that dream come true by pausing to press me directly into one, my body into nipple, then squished in and further into the softness until it would not yield and thus became firmer and firmer in the sandwich against her hand…

Out again and up further I looked upon her face, her sexy mouth easily wide enough to take two of me in whole.  Up to her eyes, so deep and beautiful, flashing anger but mostly I saw hurt and a very painful sadness, too painful.  It ached to look at her. She filled me with so much desire and so much pain at once, my heart hurt.

"Serenity," I spoke as gently as I could.

Her hand squeezed, very constricting. "You may not call me that. I am your Queen. I am your executioner. You have but one choice. That is how you would like me to take your life."

I chuckled; I couldn't help it. Something about this situation was reminding me of a story I'd hear long ago. I had one very old Grand Uncle who must have known hundreds of stories. That, and the fact that he treated me absolutely normal; like there was nothing different about my size of me whatsoever, made him my all-time favorite. Too bad he passed away when I was only nine. He would have meant a lot to me during my teenage years. But you know what: he was with me then, at least in my heart, and he did help me in many important ways.

Yes, he was with me then – and he was with me now! I could hear his great character voice telling the story of Briar Rabbit, "Oh please, Briar Fox and Briar Bear, burn me to a crisp, drown me in the deepest river, hang me from the highest tree – but please, please, PLEASE, don't throw me in that briar patch." I laughed again.

"What's so funny? You're about to die."

"None of your business, actually. Just a little something between me and my uncle." Uppity, I thought, just like Briar Rabbit. "Besides, Queen of Madness, what better time to laugh than when you are about to die?"

"Insolence! So you think having choices is funny as well?"

"No, no, let's hear them, Queen of the Cage Oasis." Why not insult her. She was planning to kill me. Then again, an angry woman who also goes mad – who knows what she might decide. Better to play emotions, I thought, until I could find a way where she might be vulnerable. Yes, I was hoping the direct, honest approach would suffice. But, I had to survive first to have a chance at that.

"I could stomp you to death."

"Quick and merciful." I commented. Did I really think I was going to get a choice with this deceitful Queen? No, not likely. More likely she wanted to find out what demise I detested the most. That's why I laughed when I thought of go ol' Great Uncle Rob.

She continued; probing it seemed. "Or I will gladly crush you under my butt."

"You do have a beautiful ass.  Very tempting, also a quick death I imagine."

"Or death by vore, into my mouth for a one-way trip through my digestion.  You end up as you started: a little piece of shit."

"What a gracious Queen of Foul-mouth you are.  But, I have to admit, your lips look as beautiful as any I have seen.  Could I please, please have a little taste of them?"

"Certainly not.  There is no lover for me."  Now where had I heard that sorry refrain before?  "Perhaps if you want me so much you could die, suffocated in my pussy."

This is what I'd been waiting to hear.  I tensed on purpose in her hand, feigned my fear.  "Luscious I suppose, but certainly a slower death.  Is that it then; those are the four choices?"

She nodded, studying me.

I took a Briar Rabbit chance.  "Stomp me to death then and be quick about it."

"No, I don't think so.  Too messy."

"Well, that's not fair I complained.  Ok then, um, death my mouth.  That way I at least get a last kiss."

"No, I'm not that hungry."

"What the hell!"  I complained more.  Time to find out if my manipulation worked.  It might have already.  I stood a fighting chance under butt or in pussy.  Though, when I considered it, her butt seemed more precarious by far.  Here we go.  "What the fuck.  You choose then.  Obviously I had no choice here to start with."

She smiled evil and victorious, then laughing in a not so nice way.  "No, you never had a choice.  I only wanted to find out what you detested and feared the most.  It's death by pussy for you."

I thought, "Just like the king in the tapestry." But I said, just like Briar Rabbit. "No, not that!"  Trembling with excitement – I mean "fear".

"Just so you know, as you die in my pussy we will be going to take back my estate, my home.  Any there that oppose us, and a dearly hope some do, will die the most vicious and horrible death."

"At least Tiffany will have warned them by now."

"Good.  May the fools stay and fight.  But no other help will come in this Quarantine."

I kept myself from saying anything further that might be distracting.  Yes, better keep my arguments to myself, not to get the Queen off her current plan.

With my silence and submission The Queen gloated in arrogant smugness.  "What, no more insolence.  Now you fully realize your defeat.  Ha!  Good then – in you go, tiny lover."  She laughed as she brought me to her gargantuan twat, spread those massive lips, and shoved me inside.  Using her hand and long fingers she pushed me way up in there, certainly more than eight feet.

My first thought was, "Wow roomy… and loose."  She seemed maybe 15% turned on, probably a little excited by the death threats she'd dished out.  I could maneuver, but I'd be a fool to try to escape.  She could just move on to option two.  And I just wasn't ready for that out of control ass to flatten me.

We were on the move, walking not running.  But the pace and certainly long strides probably clipped along at maybe 15 miles per hour.  They could get to the Bluebelle Estates in less than 40 minutes.  I better get busy.

I started firing up the Sparkle, thinking about where I was, the beauty of this woman, her great and crushing size.  But I kept getting off track and stymied.  Goodness, she was just so evil bitchy.  After fifteen minutes I had gotten nowhere.  I figured I needed a breath of fresh air.  So I made my way down to the opening.

I peeked out, looking down from twenty feet up.  These giantesses didn't bother with roads.  Also, probably did not want to risk any discovery they were out and about.  They just headed straight toward the Estates, over hill and dale, stomping through famer's fields, little stands of forest, right through streams and the feeder-creeks to the main Bluebelle River down in the valley.

A small Colorado blue spruce raked up her leg and tickled through her crotch.  I had to pop my head back in to avoid getting smacked by it; possibly knocked clean out of the pocket.  As Serenity twisted around bigger trees, or had to step around left-over boulders deposited here and there from the last ice age, I would get a glimpse of the other three giantesses, their beautiful but grim faces determined in their mission to do their evil Queen's bidding.

I watched in wonder and horror as Maya kicked a cow out of the way, then Keisha stomped on it because it ended up in her path and underfoot.  I heard a major cracking sound to the right.  Even Serenity paused to look that way.  Ginny had decided to walk through an old rundown shack rather than simply stepping around it. For a second it frustrated her, then in a fit of rage – perhaps a sample of the Mammoth Madness – Ginny flailed her arms, screaming an obscenity, and exploded through the rest of the structure, demolishing it in seconds of fury.

"Holy shit!" I whispered, sucked in a huge breath of air and ducked back into Serenity's pussy.  My wives are tough, but no way they will be any match for that kind of destructive force.  And if Ginny could do that, I hated to imagine the devastation Serenity would inflict.

I had to get my Sparkle-fire revved-up, get to Serenity somehow, get her side-tracked or at least a little distracted.  For I knew my wives would not run; they would fight – especially if they knew I was still alive.  Thinking it through I realized, if it came to it, ultimately I might have to come out and confront the Queen.  Sacrifice was far from my first option, but if it would allow my wives to give up and flee it might be the best option.

Damn.  Tick-tock.  We must be over half way there by now.  My problem was twofold.  First of all there has to be an intermediate optimum size for an amazon.  I think maybe Serenity was exceeding that optimum size by a smidge.  That must be it: there's intermediate optimum for sweetness – don't want it too sweet, don't want it too bland.  Same holds for temperature, obviously.  Same is true for food – though a lot of people are still trying to scale that one back to optimum.  And so it must be for women.  Maybe Serenity was just too big to excite me.  I didn't know that was possible, but now I had to wonder.

Second problem: I couldn't get over her being so disappointingly unlovable.  And that was probably the real issue.  Damn.  Damn! How the hell could I get my Sparkle-fire going if I just wasn't feeling it?  Then I got an idea – maybe if she felt something first that would help.  Ah, the G-spot.  Now where in heck was it?

I started probing, working my way across, over, up and back across.  After three passes I think I found it – sound asleep it seemed.  I pounded it with my fists.  I kicked at it vigorously with my legs.  Nothing.  No response.  Come on! I'm running out of time.  They would be there, God knows now, any moment.  Frustrated and desperate I thought about Ginny's destructive furor and tantrum and in the midst of it how she broke free with… her horrible scream.  Fuck it! I could see impending horrible battle in my mind, my smaller wives being kicked aside like that poor cow and stomped to death.  And here I was trying to generate feelings of love for the Big Bitch of the coming obliteration, attacking my wives and me not able to do anything to help them, to save then.  And I screamed my frustration, letting it all loose, right from my gut.

To my surprise out with the scream came a flaring streak of blue-flame energy.  It shot out my mouth and right into the big bundle of nerves I could feel pressed against my face.  And that The Queen felt, I assumed like a hot needle.  She tensed, almost stopping.  I screamed again, more Sparkle-fire roared out of me.  I think I even astonished myself with how much I could generate vocally.

This time Serenity came to a full stop.  There was a thunderous pounding – her wrecking-ball fists beating on her own abdomen.  But she could not stop me with that; I was too insulated in the most protected of all the places inside a woman.  Next came a pressuring squeeze, and I could tell she knew it was me alive inside her causing the stimulations to her.  Pressure yes, but not enough to be effective.  She really did not have full control of all those muscle groups, not near as much as some of my most-talented and practiced wives.

I could feel an acceleration and much more rapid pace.  The Great Queen ran now.  I would not doubt she could have reached thirty miles per hour in her desperation.  Suddenly we shot up in the air; I could feel that clearly.  Then I also clearly felt the weightlessness of falling and falling.  What landmark could this be?  Then I realized in dismay, the beautiful white bluffs at the eastern edge of Bluebelle Estates.

Serenity landed hard, harder than would have been necessary for such a magnificently huge athlete.  And she must have rolled – no summersaulted – I could tell she tumbled forward.  She was trying to dizzy and disorient me.  Up she stood then dropped, butt-dropped to the ground.  Had the battle begun already?  No, there was still a mile to go to the Segal Mansion.  Serenity sought to dislodge me.  No way baby!  I blasted back at her with more Sparkle-fire than before.  I'll fight you with everything I've got, to save my wives.

Again The Queen was up and running.  For sure she would be to the Estate in less than a minute, maybe to the back of the grounds already.  Her juices flowed around me like crazy; the Sparkle had her going good.  Again the Queen accelerated.  Was the battle about to begin?  I felt her twisting and fighting and still rushing forward.  Though the Estate's back border of forest?  So far no resistance it seemed.  We must be on the grand lawn by now, because her running was perfectly smooth.

Now, undisturbed by any jostling, I raged and raged blue and red Sparkle, desperate to have affect.  The Queen butt dropped again, and I could feel the smash this time.  She squirmed around on the ground, probably the grass, and I could feel a rapid vibration coming up from underneath. I slid down to check it out. As I descended Serenity rolled back, possibly laying out on the lawn. I could see two fingertips briskly entering and leaving the front and top of her pussy, rubbing her clitoris with some serious vigor.

I crawled and slithered around to the backside of her sexual stimulation and screamed blue-red flames again, right into the back of her clitoris. This really sent her five notches higher, juice gushing past me but could not wash me out. At last she had given in to the sensations. And she was mine.

And that thought, the idea of owning her turned me on. I vocally blasted Sparkle-blue all around me now, feeling victorious and mighty, lighting her up from the inside. My Volunteer came into service, generating electrified white-hot azure bolts of sexual energy. Suddenly I could feel all the pent-up sexual energy of this giantess and it was fucking unbelievable.

The Queen's sexual overload released in peristaltic waves rolling past my body as her internal shell cracked open. I could see the Mammoth Madness in my mind's eye, like a great evil dragon it reared up before me, blazing green eyes and sickly orange flames. I unleashed my magic sword upon it; the searing white electric beams cut it right through its heart. Green scales exploded and spun away fluttering like burning leaves. Her resistance eradicated, the Sparkle tree grew like wildfire up through her grand and now more clearly beautiful body and soul.

I saw the Serenity that the Triplets had revealed to me, that they did not fear but felt only compassion and sympathy. And that woman, that Serenity, indeed that Queen, I could love. And boy did I! There was no need to wait or hold back. This woman revealed to me now had been ready and waiting for love for years. I shivered inside her with a phenomenal pre-orgasmic energy like I had never felt before. My only hesitation was one of the unknown of losing myself too much in what was certainly about to happen.

But now the giantess that had resisted me ached, yearned, and squirmed for me to love her, to give it to her big time. Oh God knows I'm a small man, but made up for that with such intensity I felt I had tapped into the Earth's hot core itself. My detonation of a white-blue sexual firebomb lit up the Giantess from head to toenail. I heard later that she actually glowed and it singed the lawn in an outline of her body.

And oh did The Queen royally reciprocate. She found her body awareness and now worked me over but good with right proper sexual squeezes and internal embrace. Love, love, love pressured me from all sides, seeking and successfully drawing every last vestige of cum from my body.  As she finally relaxed I could tell she wanted something else.

Internally I could detect that Serenity spoke to someone nearby.  As she released her pussy grip on me I found myself sliding out and onto the wet grass.  Serenity sat up, leaning back some, legs apart, and she was speaking, but not to me.

"That's enough, Ginny, put her down."  I saw Ginny reluctantly but gently set Bethany back down to the lawn, thankfully unharmed.  "Lie down now Keisha and Maya.  You too, Ginny.  Just lie down on the grass and relax."  Serenity's voice sounded so different, melodic, weirdly like surround-sound, and yes, serene.

Serenity's huge, beautiful, and sexy legs ascended on either side of me, up into the morning sunlight.  Her lustrous bronze skin, dappled with drops of sweat and dew from the lawn, glistened in the bright light.  I had not moved from my prone position, breathing deeply to recover.  Looking sideways across the flat plain of the lawn I could recognize the nice legs of my wives, not in warrior stances, but relaxed and comfortable.  They looked on as witnesses, not needing to try to rescue or intervene, waiting.

I rolled onto my back, relieved to have survived and thankful for the peaceful resolution that unfolded.  Past those colossal legs I could see the sun blazing off the deeply breathing chest and tons of breasts that Serenity seemed to be offering to the Gods.  Another glorious deep breath and she sat all the way up and looked down at me.

A sternness returned to her demeanor.  "You tricked me, you know."

"Oh, I know."  I didn't bother to sit up, but just continued to lie back and look at her upside-down.

"Thank God you tricked me."  Now her expression changed to a smile of gratitude.

"I'm guessing you don't know the story of Briar Rabbit?"

"What kind of rabbit?"  She had no clue.

"Never mind….  So where do we go from here, my Queen?"

"First of all, could be please call me Serenity?"  Then she looked up.  "That goes for all of you."  I'm guessing she spoke to my wives.

Then back to me; but I'm sure all could hear.  "Thank you Richie.  It was like I have been possessed.  I could see my actions, but I had no volition to stop myself or even to say anything different.  This Madness – it is the worst genetic curse… but I do not feel it anymore.  I don't know what that means.  I don't see how I could be changed genetically.  At least for now it is gone."

"I can see that.  And I can also see the beautiful person that I have been feeling, knowing, and I had to try to save."

"Oh Richie," Serenity rotated to all fours above me.  Her face up from me the length of her insanely strong arms, some fifteen feet.  Glancing down her body, oh so heavy, her magnificent breast hung full and spectacular down to within a few feet of the grass.  She lowered herself and I could sense an uneasiness in some of my wives' stances.  But they held back, believing in me I suppose.

Serenity dropped herself to her elbows, then to lie all the way flat, her wide face maybe twice the length of my body right above me.  Closer and closer she came, the lips grazing across the entire front of me.  "Oh Richie," she said again, softly but reverberating me to me core. "I love you." And she kissed me so tenderly I would not have thought it possible with lips that spread over my entire nude body.

I kissed back and somehow she felt it.  Maybe blue-Sparkle traveled with my kiss; I didn't notice.  But Serenity did and responded.  She picked me up with her soft sexy lips, lifting me up with her as she sat again.  She opened her mouth to let me sit on her lower lip, resting my back against her teeth.  Only Saint Debbie standing could match Serenity's sitting height, my other wives all lower.  And all accounted for, as Serenity panned around to let me see.

"Good." I thought.  And then it occurred to me I could prove Serenity's transformation for all.  I spoke softly but all could hear. "Serenity, kiss me into your mouth."

Serenity closed her kips around me, moderately sucking me in.  I rolled on her tongue, protected from sharp teeth.  And her lips closed me inside.  I sat comfortable on her tongue, my head against the roof of her mouth.  No, it was not big enough for me to stand up.  With my arms around my folded knees I made a nice compact package, like the size to her of a large boney meatball.  I chuckled at that comparison.

As my eyes adjusted I noticed her left cheek, the one that would be toward the sun, glowed with a feint pink light.  I decided to lie back on her tongue, my legs at the knees between her parted teeth, and my ankles and feet finally protruding out between her loosely closed lips.  I wiggled my toes hello to the sunshine.  And I realizing my exhaustion, I went to sleep.  Now if that isn't trust, I don't know what is.

Not five minutes later I awoke to my feet being tugged upon.  Serenity pulled me out between her lips, leaving them delightfully closed about me, and me very turned on.  My wives giggled at seeing my Volunteer so ready and willing.  I guess that's what they call a power nap.

Serenity leaned back to her elbows, leveling the top slope of her breasts.  Then she deposited me there on my feet.  Here I stood, much more on eye level with the majority of my wives.  I took the moment to check in.

"How's everybody doing?"  The Triplets merely smiled, knowing well what had transpired.  Amanda also nodded knowingly, having experienced a Sparkle transformation herself she probably understood better than most the relief and gratitude that Serenity experienced.

But it was Vicky who spoke: "God Richie, last I saw you, you looked like Death warmed over.  Now look at you, King Richie of Bluebelle Valley.  You have to be the most amazing husband ever!"  I think Vicky expressed the general sentiment well.

"I see you all here ready to fight and, I think, for me.  I cannot express how honored I am to be your husband." Then to Serenity, "I would like to go to them now."  Of course I could just have jumped off, but I was learning to be more considerate.  People like it when you clue them in and consider them in you plans, even the little stuff.

"Well, there is the little matter of Ginny, Maya, and Keisha."  Serenity sounded a tad apologetic.  "They are only lying down by their Queen's authority over them.  But I don't want to be their queen anymore.  Richie, I'm afraid they need the same cure."

I shrugged to my wives.  "It looks like duty calls, my dears."  That got a good laugh.

Serenity leaned the rest of the way back turning until I slid off her breast to my feet.  "Spread your legs, Maya."  She said to the closest of the thirty foot woman lying patiently on the grass.  "You have the incoming delight of your life."

As I took the walk up Maya's legs, legs that became so thick and massive I could not see over their tops, Serenity chased me along playfully with her lips kissing at my backside.  That kept me nice and excited for instant application of the Sparkle-fire.  Maya seemed excited about the prospect and opened nice and easy to let me crawl inside.  Certainly tighter than Serenity, I still found plenty of room to squeeze my way thoroughly up inside.  In short order I had this delicious pussy worked up into a roaring fire.  Maya for her part proved more than ready and quickly peaked.  Sure she writhed all around and had to ultimately be held in place.  But we had her Madness shattered in no time.  And I was out in like ten minutes and ready to go again.

Serenity chased me again up the long walk to enter Ginny's pussy.  Poor woman seemed a little shy about it all.  Especially, I suppose, with a couple dozen women looking on.  Getting good at this, I kissed and coaxed my way in.  Then the Sparkle flamed up and took over.  Ginny put a pretty good squeeze on me and it felt a bit dicey for a couple moments.  But when I got my sights on the Madness my flame-throwing sword sliced through her little dragon with one easy sweep.  Out again in maybe twelve minutes.

Keisha: I needed no help from Serenity for this super gorgeous giantess.  As I approached her, walking up between her legs, I realized again she measured significantly larger than the other two, like half way between them and Serenity for height.  What, I'm guessing thirty-five feet tall.  And wow, she presented as such an exotic beauty.  Resisting the pull to stop and visit her pussy, I climbed up upon her abdomen, walked along through cleavage, breasts towering as high as my head to either side, and there I stopped.

"Keisha, I am here to seduce you and break your Madness."  Try not to think of me as arrogant.  I really just wanted see the Beast in this woman, all her full-blown severity with the Madness still intact.

Keisha crunched up, super tight musculature all along her front, even tightening beneath my feet though her massive breasts still jiggled so innocent and soft, but a little closer now to either side of me.  All this impressive display of core strength brought her face up to look down her body at me.  Her big sexy bedroom eyes blazed at me wild with both hatred and desire.  Only a tenuous obedience to her Queen kept her from destroying me.

I walked up closer to her face.  Reaching out I touched her full and sensual lips, stroking the quiver of barely restrained madness.  I looked into her eyes, so dark, pupils dilated, my own reflection staring back at me from their centers.  And still deeper, through my own image I saw the light of her soul.  That is what I came to address, and now, before the Madness met its fate from the Sparkle-fire and became vanquished in swaths white-blue flame.

"Keisha.  I come to talk to you, not the Mad Mammoth.  I sense with you a choice, your choice in what we do here today.  Tell me now or let me know later what you would have me do.  I am your knight to command in this manner."

Keisha opened her mouth as if to speak, instead a hiss came out, loud and the blast almost blew me over.  "I will kill you at the first chance I get.  I will grind you under my ass…"

"And what love can you offer me?"  I tested the capacity of her soul to over-ride this vicious genetic programming I was hearing.

I kept staring into her eyes.  She blinked and my reflection disappeared.  Instead I could see a twinkle of light emanating from a dark space where no physical light could be.  Right there and then she let me know she heard me though she could say nothing, trapped as she was by the dictations of her genes.  Even as I looked on, the Twinkle itself flashed at me, wild in itself and she told me what I needed to know.

"Dear Keisha, thank you.  I know that was not easy.  I will do what I can per your command."  I bowed to her and took my leave back down the expanse of her absolutely magnanimous sexy body.  Dropping over the crotch I touched her there, gently, asking permission to enter.  She relaxed and opened enough for me to slip inside of her.

Her scent assailed in the best of senses, wild and fresh like a stormy sea.  Keisha was as sexy as a combination of Valerie and Vicky on steroids.  I was so turned on instantly I hoped I could control myself enough to do the bidding of this magical woman.  If I understood her unspoken intent, she would have me not destroy the Madness, but somehow hybridize with it, combine and heal without diminishing it.

I cast about with blue flame, rapidly building the Sparkle tree and calling forth to her Mad Dragon Spirit.  She sent it forth to blast and crush me as her body convulsed and thrashed about, tipping my balance against the appreciated tightness of her inner vaginal walls.  Instead of an electric white sword, I fashioned a blue-green net of love invisible to the orange-eyed monster.  So instead of slaying the charging beast, I simply stepped aside, like a matador.  Sweeping at the passing Madness I cast the net over it, tripping it into a huge heap.  And there, in the love canal of this giantess who would be a witch both beautiful and demented, I fell upon the monster and planted my Sparkle into its depths.

As the Madness writhed in agony from the connection to Love, the freed soul of Keisha came forth to greet me, to love me. The simple equation of our joining thus: a Love shared is twice the love; a Grief shared is half the grief.  Together we overwhelmed the beast and the Madness, keeping its energy and combining it with ours to metamorphose Keisha into the sex-crazed and energized giantess she longed to be.  Vicious no longer would she be, except in a savagery to take her lovers to desires never before achieved or perhaps even imagined. She chose this iteration of herself because at the choice of her soul this is who she was truest in the world.

It was time for me to breathe.  Keisha could tell and released me.  I descended down from her and with a final little push Keisha deposited me on the lawn.

Keisha sat up and spoke to her Queen.  "Would it be okay if I played with Richie for just a couple minutes?"

Serenity sat in a state of bliss, the Triplets had approached her, touching her arms, her back, her breasts and sang healing harmonies into her body.  She looked lazily at Keisha.  "That would be up to Richie's wives."

Amanda stepped forward, nicely assertive, and certainly expressing the will of my spouses. "And that would be up to Richie."

"Sure," I shrugged. "What's couple minutes going to hurt?"  I couldn't help looking at the Triplets.  They just shook their heads, smiling, knowing me too well.

I still lie on the grass where I had come out from Keisha. She pressed me out straight with a couple of her fingers. "You learned much about me and my desires.  I also saw your deepest yearnings.  I want to just take a moment to thank you."

"You didn't want to send me a card?"

"No, I'd rather send you over the moon."

Keisha bent her knee and placed her right foot above me, skillfully nudging me flat to the grass.  Her foot, some seven feet long, extended beyond the length of me body both directions.  She pressed me with it just a little bit, enough to assert the instant death that awaited me at her choice.  And my sexual thought was: "Go ahead, make my day."

Keisha took her teasing foot away, sprang up and then dropped to all fours, shaking the ground around me.

"My God, woman, how much do you weigh?"

"There's a truck scale back at the Institute.  I tipped it at 31,484 pounds.  That's probably far more than all your wives put together."  Keisha rotated 180 degrees above me, her ankles some eight feet away to either side of my body.  I watched in fear and wonder, but mostly eager anticipation as she lowered her ass toward me.  All the way down it rested against the support of her lower legs and feet, and barely above my body.  More teasing doom got me really excited.  I sat up into her crack, kissing.  She pulled away back to all fours.

Backing up, Keisha brought a great tonnage of breast over me.  She let it hover maybe a foot above, then inch by inch lowered it until it first just touched me, then touched most places on my body, then pinned me lightly, then pinned me thoroughly, then covered all of me, then sealed all around me to the grass, then smashed me into the grass, then just got heavier and heavier and heavier until I could feel the tension leave her body.  She laid all the way down on me.  With her head on the grass, arms necessarily off to the sides or above, I found I could take this pressing.  Oh it was extreme for sure.  I couldn't even twitch a finger.  I kissed up into her breast, but my lips were flat at best, not really capable to pucker up.

Keisha lifted off and scooted down some more until her face loomed directly over.  She lowered her lips to my body and proceeded with kissing me, mouthing me, licking me.  She sucked me up into her mouth and let me slid out again.  Her lips arranged my body to sitting.  Then she formed those lips around my head and upper body and began an up and down motion.  She worked me like this as if, well, I was a human cock.  She continued, getting herself quite turned on by it and wilder with the tongue, sucking, teething at me.

Keisha took me entirely into her mouth, rolled me around, then dropped me out to the grass.  Her soft, sexy lips nabbed me from behind, sucking on my back.  Then she dropped me to the grass again and attacked me with pressure from behind.  She rolled me to my back, pinned me with her upper lip across my face and lower lip across my knees.  This open-mouth pin afforded the perfect opportunity to attack me with her tongue.  This she did with the vigor of the Madness, lick and lashing, and flickering at a vibrational pace.

I have to say I'd never imagined such an oral ecstasy.  Like she said, Keisha knew me and my innermost desires.  Every more and motion, squeeze and loving kiss, Keisha tailored exactly to my desires.  And it was all like some preview, not lingering near long enough at any one of the sensuous and creative scenarios.  She had as one of her intents, I could tell, for me to crave to come back for more,

When she had me worked up and thrilled until I could hardly stand it, she dropped her mouth on me for a comprehensive and all-encompassing kiss of my entire body. In mind-blown surrender I lay there quivering, with my eyes fluttering half open as she pulled away.  But she was not finished with me yet.

Keisha brought her eighteen foot wide ass over me again. Right before she lowered it she said, "Richie?"

"Yes." I muttered adoringly.

"Thank you."  And Keisha plunged her fifteen ton butt down on me.

Now, if you can imagine an extremely sexy, overly well-endowed normal-sized woman sitting on a peanut – well, that's basically what we have here.  And you know, while a peanut will crack with little pressure in your hand; its shell does not crack when she sits on it – especially if she sits on it exactly square.  Somehow I could tell that Keisha dropped her legs out flat to the lawn the crossed one ankle over the other.  She sealed me way inside and settled down for a nice long squish.

Under her I felt pressure like I had never felt before.  It seemed she both held me together and flattened me at the same time.  I pictured her vast ass spreading almost nine feet in every direction, the heavy stack of her huge sturdy mid-section, her gigantic breasts jiggling way above and also effectively on me as well.  And she just sat and sat and shifted around a little to allow my Volunteer up into her and sat and sat some more.  Oh, I made love, I guess you could say, kind of a constant orgasm that would not abate.

A couple times I could tell Keisha spoke, but I had no idea what she said.  Most likely she was not trying to speak to me.  I did really not wonder about it too much.

Out of breath, out of oxygen, out of orgasms, out of thought, out of volition, out of life, I enjoyed my helplessness and crushing giantess sex as long as I could.  Feeling my life ebbing away, Keisha got off me and scooted back.  I felt the sun again and my life returning with a smile on my face.  Then shadow, then breast, Pavie's, then milk and warmth inside me, and actual Sparkle coming in with the liquid.  This got me back into my body and fully alert in less than two minutes, I sat up.

"Guess what?" Aria slapped my cheeks a little, helping me to get my color back.

"What?"  I shoved at her hands ineffectively.

"You have four more marriage proposals."  And Aria stood back, gesturing with a sweep of her arm to Serenity, Maya, Ginny, and Keisha.

Serenity smiled down at me, beautiful, vulnerable, and precious. "We each want to marry you and join this family."  The three other nodded their complete agreement.

"Well, everybody okay with this?"  I asked.

Again more heads nodding agreement, twenty-six if I'd stopped to count them.

"Okay then, the answer is yes.  Let's make it an even thirty wives."  Yes, I could stand a little more of these giantesses.  "So let's get on with the consummation part."

Pavie, still sitting next to me, "No, I think you've had enough super giantess sex for one day.  Anyway, if those weren't consummations we witnessed then I'm not sure what would qualify."

This time Valerie spoke up: "I think our sister Tiffany deserves a little reward, don't you guys.  She risked life and limb to go with Richie this morning.  Then she got back here in time to warn us."  Then to the former Mammoth Madness giantesses, now sister wives. "You don't realize it, but we were actually ready for you four with a darn good battle plan."  You'd almost think Valerie was disappointed not to have that brawl.

"Well then," Maya was always going to like a good fight, "How about we stage the battle sometime soon.  It ought to be a fun event to play with.  We can use Richie for the prize."

Ginny chimed in.  "As a newest wife I must agree with the reward for Tiffany. I mean, I'm damn fast, but Tiffany outran me.  She proved supremely dedicated to all of you – and Richie.  Yes, definitely, she ought to be rewarded."

"Oh good!"  Tiffany stepped forward.  "What do I get?"

Aria knew what she meant. "Would three hours be enough time?"

"That should do it.  But I want Callie to come along with me.  Richie is going to need sustenance to keep him stoked up for that long.  Anyway: two's a couple, but three's a party."

Everyone laughed at that.

"Come on, baby.  Want me to carry you?"  Tiffany teased.

"I can walk."  I growled, well, sort of.

"But can you run?"  Tiffany winked down to me.  She seemed more than ready to make good on her threats and promises from earlier in the day.

"Sure, I can run." I jogged a moderate pace, trying to regain some strength, while Tiffany and Callie, to either side of me, sauntered along leisurely with their long, long legs.

# XVIII. King Richie's Harem

At least I could count on Tiffany to let me hide in her bedroom.  Hiding?  Don't get me wrong; over the last nine months I had fallen more deeply in love with every one of my thirty extraordinary and lovely amazon wives.  It's just that, sometimes, you know, a man has to get away – especially today when I better be rested up and prepared for my visit with The Mammoths.  Not sure how "Mammoth" became a term of endearment, but it did.  So we all used it because The Mammoths claimed it helped them stay humble.  Whatever – if it keeps them happy and from grinding me to strawberry jam, and especially Krazy Keisha's Comprehensive Crush, then I'm all for it.

So the respite I found in Tiffany's abode was more than greatly appreciated.  She said she didn't mind in the least since she spent two hours a day out of the room every morning training for her extremes in strength and speed.  Yep, sweet dear little Tiffany told me I could hidey-hole in her room whenever she was out and nobody would bother me.  What a doll!

I lay back on her bed, looking out her windows from the nice third story height.  The breezes billowed out the lacey shears, the air both warm and fresh in the summer morning following rain squalls last night.  I recalled my first time in this bedroom suite, the day I married the four Mammoth giantesses.  My wives had decided to reward Tiffany with three hours together with me.  Tiffany requested Callie come along for bucking up my sustenance.  And boy did I need it.

Tight Tiffany tore me to pieces.  It was a damn good thing Callie was there.  Tiffany being so amped-up already, the Sparkle-fire just sent her into an orbit, but too low and fiery.  It was like the only part of my body that was protected from Tiffany's frenzies was the part that Callie sat on, her smothering butt keeping Tiffany away that much of me.

We started out with Callie sitting comfortable and relaxed on my face.  Tiffany meanwhile attacked my Volunteer like a banshee.  Callie had to almost fight with Tiffany to get her to calm down.  She made Tiffany back off and watch how to properly facesit a little man.

After suitable instructions, Callie moved over to sit on and take in the aching-for-kind-attention Volunteer.  I heard her continuing her instruction to Tiffany on gentle face-sitting.  But as soon as the Sparkle touched Tiffany's pussy she lost control, smashing my face like crazy.  On and on, way to desperate, Tiffany bounced on me like I was an aerobics mat that needed breaking in.  Finally I'd had enough and blew a big blast of Sparkle-fire up into her to totally send her into orgasm.

Instead of reasonably enjoying that sensation, Tiffany the competitive athlete, mistakenly took it as a challenge.  She seemed to go hysterical with her pussy and ass bouncing all over my face and upper body in a fit of destruction.  Callie launched off my Volunteer and tackled Tiffany, both of them rolling off the bed together and onto the carpet in a heap.  As Callie pinned her to the floor, Tiffany bucked and fought like a fiend.  I don't know if Callie would have tired, but soon enough re-enforcements arrived in the form of Pavie and Aria.

The three Triplets grabbed Tiffany and hauled her up back up to the bed, harmonizing to her.  It soothed her to some extent.  When Tiffany seemed approachable again Callie said to her, "We are going to teach you how to facesit your husband.  It is a basic marriage requirement in this household to be able to do this without losing your control."

Aria grabbed Tiffany's right leg and right armpit.  Pavie did the same on the left side. Callie grabbed Tiffany on both side of her waist from behind.  The Triplets lifted Tiffany up, carried her to a position above my face, and then gently lowered her down.  Then up, then down – very mechanical and controlled.  I went ahead releasing more Sparkle, jacking Tiffany up nicely.  The Triplets continued with their complete control of Tiffany's up and down on my face, but a little faster and faster by the minute.

Now the Triplets brought her down, holding her on my face, slowly bringing Tiffany's legs together sealing me in, then out with the legs, then sweeping in again to the tight squeeze.  Then back to the pumping up and down.

Next the Triplets flipped her around and sat her backward, pussy still on my face. Instead of pumping or squeezing, they taught Tiffany to pelvic rock on me, back and forth vertical to my face.  I liked this a lot.  So did juicy Tiffany.

Then the Triplets manipulated Tiffany's sit into a circular stir.  After Tiffany mastered that, they showed her how to stir it on a diagonal. That, of course, without ever releasing, does a very stimulating close then less-close; close then less-close.  This pussy-control teaches a man to lust up after his desires during the less-close arc of the circle.

The Triplet's instruction continued, explaining that right when a man feels fully comfortable, like he's in control but also about to surrender, that's when the Triplets showed Tiffany to pull back.  Own the man by making him try to come after you.  Then when he is really desperate, licking the air like a blind snake, give him ass and more ass.

Tiffany got totally into learning to own me.  Thus the wise Triplets taught Tiffany a clever way to control herself by focusing on controlling me.  "Oh, and…" Callie added, "Now is when you actually do squeeze the hell out of him."  With that Tiffany tightened those world-class athletic gluts and butt-formed my face into the shape of a crack.

"Now release him, Goddess Tiffany, in your kindness to let him live."  I fell out thinking Callie's statement was no metaphor.  Tiffany's ass was killer, literally.  "He will now worship your pussy.  Try it."

Tiffany came back and rode my face, calm, in control, mixing all the techniques and inventing new ones.  One by one the Triplets left until finally it was me deliciously alone with my new-wife-now-new-Goddess riding my face for hours.  Tiffany got it very well: there are sprints and there are marathons – she mastered both on my face.  She could be trusted from now on, realizing a good no-contest pussy-whipping was better than any kind of struggle for dominance.  Any complaint about this was the furthest thing from my mind…

Whoa!  I'd snoozed for a couple of minutes.  Ah, Tiffany…  We'd had many, many sessions together since then, and each one got better than the last.  Especially since she was one of the faster growing wives that I had, and now was pushing 1,000 pounds at almost eleven feet tall.  Maybe I should just wait for her here.  She'd be back all nice and sweaty soon enough.  She worked out so often, kept herself so pure, even her sweat didn't stink.  She tasted mildly like salty caramel.  I smiled, reminiscing.

But not today: places to be and wives to do.  I got up to leave.  Anyway, I decided to leave a little note of thanks to the sweetheart who let me hide in her room.  However, I guess my nap had been longer than I thought.  Because only half a sentence in, the door banged open and not-so-tiny Tiffany entered.

"Oh hi, Tif, I was just leaving you a note."

"Well, now you can tell me in person."  She dropped a sweaty towel from around her neck, sat on the bed and started taking off her running shoes.  Boy did the bed yield when she planted her huge ass on it, crossing her long, thick, strong legs.

"Just thanks for letting me use your room today, and, well, I love you."

"Aw, that's sweet, Richie".  She pulled off her top, her sports bra looked worn out from the yeoman's chore of trying to restrain Tiffany's enormous breasts for the past two hours of workout.  She stood, whipped off her shorts and panties to reveal the best toned ass on the planet and one of the bigger ones as well. "Could you help me with this bra?"  Tiffany squatted, her back toward me and close.

I made quick work of the three hooks and quickly stepped toward the door.  I needed to get going.

But when my hand touched the knob I heard a playful stern. "Just where do you think you're going, bitch?"

"Come on now, Tiffany, you don't have to get that way?"

"What way?"  She took my hand firmly leading me away from the door.  "You know I'm just teasing."

"You never tease, Tiffany.  You always go for it."

"That's true."  She shoved me onto the bed.  I scrambled for the other side.  But she jumped clear over the bed to be in front of my retreat.  "Do you really think you can get away from me?"

"Listen, bitch," Giving her a dose of her own verbiage, and backing up, reverse crab walk, as she advanced onto the bed toward me. "I can do any frigging thing I want. I'm King of this castle."

"Oh really?"  In a quick little hop on all fours Tiffany trapped me below her. "You're the King around here, are you?"

"That's right, wife.  So you and you big ass don't go getting any ideas."

Tiffany grabbed my wrists, pinning them and lorded her big tits over my face. "If you're King, then I must be a Queen.  And a Queen needs a throne.  Wouldn't you agree?"

"Tiffany, I command you to let me go.  And don't you dare put that pussy on my face."

"Oh poor little King.  He simply never learns.  Let the face-fucking begin."  And so I decided to stay in her room another hour: a hot, smothering, delicious hour of ecstasy under a prodigious huge wife who had perfected her pussy dominance of me.

Even though Tiffany pinned me utterly helpless, she still fought me down like I could legitimately challenge her to get away.  Again and again she rose and slammed her ass, crushing me flatter and flatter.  She turned to sit on me side-saddle, pulling her legs up to get all her weight on me.  And from this position she also bounced and bounced as if I'd made some other bid to get away.

I didn't make any bid to do anything.  I couldn't do squat except carry the tiniest torch of hope to stay alive.  She kept saying things like, "Oh no you don't." or "Come back here." or "Quit fighting me!" or "I'll show you who's boss!!"  All totally ridiculous since I just whimpered beneath her, kissing at her legs and ass and licking up into her pussy whenever presented with its tremendous tight smothers.

"Please, please. Spare my life." I begged.

"What?" She scorned. "You say I'm not your wife!  Why, you ungrateful little twerp!" And then she rose up to standing on the bed and unleashed the most horrific unending series of butt drops on me, each with a rebound bouncing drop almost as bad as the first but with a much longer grind.

Finally settling down she said almost affectionately. "I don't know why I put up with you, but you may now have sex with me."  Again, like I was going to do something? With that she mounted my little hot pistol and brought her legs together to cover all my upper body.  Reaching behind with her strong hands Tiffany pinned my ankles where they barely emerged from her crushing big firm ass.  Then she attacked my body like her ass and legs were dancing the worm wave – pure, undiluted husband domination and ownership.  Maybe that's why I liked to go to her room so often, take a nap, oversleep, and get ass and pussy-mauled senseless.

Several earth shuttering orgasms later Tiffany rolled off me to lie intimately beside my little squashed and exhausted body.  "You know Richie, you really are my King. I almost wish I would stop growing so I could get pregnant and give you the most wonderful child ever."

"Oh, what's the hurry my dear."  I reached up feebly and patted her pelvis.

Tiffany quarter turned to her side, the excellent large curve of her hip rising well above my flat body.  Her big breasts leaning over my face, the top breast's nipple licking distance from my mouth. "Thank you for staying a while.  You know I love you, don't you?"

"Yes, little Tiffany, I know.  Only, you do get a little rough sometimes – I guess because you know I like it."

"You better get going before I decide to pounce on you again.  This not getting pregnant thing – it's like my body just keeps wanting to screw and screw and screw you again until it does get pregnant.  And since it can't yet, well, all it knows to do is to keep trying and trying…"

"But, dear Tiffany, that could be years away!"

"I know, I know, darn it.  So until then you can expect a constant barrage from me, my husband and King.  I want to make love to you almost all the time.  And I know all my sister wives feel, to one degree or another, pretty much the same."

I sighed looking up at Tiffany's generous breast barely above my face.  Almost like it had a will of its own my hand reached up and stroked her soft warmth.

"Oh Baby," Tiffany leaned onto me for a nice long heavy smother. While I mouthed and licked into her crush, Tiffany skillfully played with my privates.  It wasn't designed to lead anywhere really.  We just enjoyed each other a little bit longer before I had to get going.  Basically this little playfulness amounted to a physical version of: "I love you Spouse." After twenty minutes she let me breathe, and continued to sit all the way up.

I sat up as well, rolled off the bed, and scooped up my shorts and shirt.  As I put them on I commented. "You know, Tif, I was thinking about the first time I came into this room – like some nine months ago.  You would have killed me that day if you hadn't thought to ask Callie to come along."

"Yes I know.  I was still a virgin and didn't know anything.  But at least I knew I couldn't be trusted alone with you.  Now I'm twice the size of my former self.  And just look how gentle I am with you." She winked, then squinted one eye, silly but sexy. "But, you better not ever piss me off.  Because I do have serious fantasies about sitting on you and squeezing you to death with my powerful legs and ass. So… I'm just sayin'…"

"Well you better not piss me off either," I raised my index finger, warning her. "… or I'll… er, I'll, well… you know… or I'll just…"

"You'll just what?" Tiffany stood and turned, nudging me against the wall with her dominating vast ass. I tried to protest, but she skillfully enveloped my face in her crack, squeezing, lifting me off the floor, legs dangling helpless. "Pardon me, King Richie, I can't hear you."

I flailed at her buns. In response she leaned on me heavier, smashing my arms flat. Then Tiffany applied a sincerely tight athletic squeeze, a mere sample of what she could do with her butt to my face. After an excruciating couple of seconds she mercifully loosened and let me drop out. I melted down the wall and puddled at her feet. Prostrate on my back looking up, up, up at the sexy legs of this viciously passionate wife, I felt a smile spreading to reconstitute the proper shape of my face. Down below the nice tent in my shorts could not hide exactly how I felt about her.

"Oh Darling," Tiffany sighed with heart-warming sweetness, "I already ache for you inside me again as well. But, you have important dates to keep. So go on, get on out of here, husband, before I decide to sit on you for ten years, until I the day I stop growing."

"Why stop sitting on me then?" My voice kind of dreamy.

"Good point. Maybe by then I'll just keep you inside me all the time. I don't know, goof-ball. Now get up. That's right." She opened her door to the hallway as I wobbled toward it. "Out you go lover. Make your escape before I change my mind." And without a kiss good-bye, wisely too risky I suppose, Tiffany shooed me out and shut the door behind me.

I shook myself, straightened up, squared my shoulders and began to march down the hallway. At least it was still morning. I had rounds to make, wives to check in on, plenty yet to do before heading out to the Mammoth Circus. But damn, this hard-on Tiffany gave me for the road was not subsiding yet.

You know, I think all my amazon wives have at least some aspect of the Mammoth Madness gene in their make-up. Tiffany certainly seemed to have something extra vicious. Hell, let's admit it, all of them did. But it was just one of those stray thoughts I'd get; no real capacity to figure the genetics out of something like that. Maybe I'd ask The Triplets. Likely they would say "yes" then attack me to prove it…

After a right turn into a large, grander arching hallway, more formal with marble floors, alcoves with nude amazon white statuettes, and evenly larger thicker dark wooden doors, I found the stairs down I needed, thirty feet ahead on the left.  But as I walked past the next door on the right it opened, out came Valerie in a hurry, and she knocked me flat to the floor."

"My goodness!" Valerie inhaled, her hand to her mouth.  Then quickly she reached down to help me up.  "I'm sorry Richie.  But how awesome; I was just running out to find you.  Do you have a minute?"

I took a hand up from this beautiful God's gift to mankind.  I looked into her lustrous penetrating green eyes, her leading-lady glamorous face framed with wave after styled wave of silky strawberry blonde dreams, her big twelve foot tall stature and killer curves.  The closest curves to me, at the moment, being those mouth-watering curves of her oh-so-perfect and huge-let-me-die-there breasts and hanging cleavage – and I said, "Sorry, no, I got places I need to be."  Hell, no, you know I didn't say that.  I always found her so jaw-dropping gorgeous, I did what I usually did and went into my wordless gaga state.

Valerie understood the effect she had on me.  The only other wife that could do the same to me was Vicky.  So Valerie simply held on to my hand, leading into her room. Of course I could only follow, instantly mesmerized, gawking up at her immense sexy ass, packed tightly into a glistening purple skirt, swaying with each step some two feet above my not-so-gentlemanly stare up at it.

"Hey Vicky, look who I found in the hallway."  Oh my God, that's right, Valerie and Vicky are roommates.

"Wow, Valerie!" Siren-sexy Vicky stood, almost as tall at Valerie, outfitted in a shimmering rainbow cocktail dress that hugged her ever growing perfection of voluptuous splendor.  Vicky took one step toward me pointing at my tented crotch and laughed, impressed.  "You sure got him excited quickly Valerie."

"Oh no, my dear, he came this way."  Valerie also laughed at the thought though.

"Well King Richie," Vicky stepped right up to tower over me, always supremely confident, a wave of sexual supremacy in her aura that weakened my knees. "What are you doing roaming the halls of your castle with such a big hard on?"

All my funny rejoinders failed me.  I looked back and forth at eye-level hemlines, the flawlessness of big dominating sexy legs issuing thereof, their suggestive subtle shifting, and it was all I could do to keep from cumming in my shorts.

"Oh Vicky and Valerie," I felt barely worthy to even say their names. "Can we please, please, please skip the small talk and get right to the sex."

"Well normally yes, husband, but…" I heard Valerie's voice coming down from those heavens I dare not look up toward. "…but that's not why I was coming to get you. We need fashion advice."

"Come on." Vicky lifted me up and sat me on the edge of their huge semi-soft bed. (Yes, think about it; they slept together.) "All you have to do is sit there and give us your opinion."

What? I thought to myself. No legs squeezes, no bosom hugs, no smothering with kisses, no butt drops of doom, no pussies so sweet that they own my very soul? You'd think I was disappointed.

Sometimes, however, when you find yourself in the chamber of the Goddess, as I certainly clearly was at that moment, it serves the highest purpose to listen as humbly best you can. What is She telling you She wants? And right then, dude, the less ego the better. Nothing too fancy is required. So, as I gathered my wits as best I could against the withering sexual magnificence of Valerie and Vicky, I managed to say, "Okay, my lovelies, let's see what you got."

From across the room two dazzling smiles. Oh good; I'd said the right thing. Valerie exited to their dressing room. Vicky stayed and posed. "Well," She said. "What do you think? Now I want your honest opinion. Don't hold back if you don't like it."

Vicky stayed some fifteen feet away so I could get a good look at all of her. She was no professional model, but graceful as a cat nevertheless. With the ample ideal curves of the Earth Mother and a beauty to rival Aphrodite, every angle and posture Vicky assumed looked supremely gorgeous to me. But the question was about the cocktail dress.

"I love the shimmer, the way it highlights your graceful sexy movements. I wish it showed even more cleavage; but that's probably just my bias."

Vicky paused, blinked at me a second, then smiled and walked over, leaned down toward me. With two hands she grabbed at each side of the vee at that cleavage and tugged, stretching the fabric until her magnanimous breasts were all but entirely exposed. As I gaped into that canyon Vicky brought it closer to my face. "Is this better?"

"Ya-ye-yes, my dear." I stuttered.  As Vicky stood back up and sashayed toward the dressing room I called after her.  "Vicky, my sweet, do you mind if I ask; your breasts seem so much bigger than last I saw them.  Is it just me or are they really getting extra large?"

"Yes, the better to smother you with, my dear."  Vicky grinned like the Big Bad Wolf.  "Actually," She softened, "Nice of you to notice, my little sweet, they do seem to be growing even faster than I am.  I mean, I'm only like 12'4", still three inches shorter than Valerie, but I'm pretty sure my breasts are bigger than hers."

"You might be right.  We should compare them side-by-side sometime."

"How about right after the fashion show?"

Without committing to anything I added. "But I'm thinking her ass is definitely still larger than yours."

"Well, I might grant her that.  But how about we let you be the judge of that also, up close and personal."  Then Vicky disappeared into the dressing room.

Right then Valerie came whisking out, spinning a lovely blue dress to a horizontal flare, her lacy baby-blue panties quite nicely exposed over her big-big shapely ass.  This girl-next-door look worked well with Valerie's highly stepped up version of all-American beauty.  But the dress cinched up under her breasts so they kind of spilled over, hanging hugely in their blue halters, to the point of it becoming a topic of over-focus.  Certainly the kind of over-focus I enjoyed.

"I like it."  I could see Valerie expected more. "The flare out was a spectacular entrance, love the lacy panties.  Your terrific contrasts of innocence and sexiness is a real double-take, attention getter.  That dress on your body would certainly make any man do a one-eighty.  You could be the Pied-Piper of drooling males."  I took a risk with that last comment.

"Oh, I'm glad you like it.  You don't think it makes my tits look too big?"

I shook my head "no".

"Oh, good."  To my delight she twirled again.  "This dress would be perfect for facesitting, don't you think?"  Now Miss Universe batted her eyes toward me.

"Yes, definitely.  What dress wouldn't be prefect for facesitting with your ass in it?"

Valerie laughed, giddy, and ran over to me spinning all the way.  She plopped her ideal ass on me letting the dress settle over my head and around and behind my back.  After a quick couple of bounces, keeping my Volunteer more than sufficiently at attention, Valerie bounced one more time extra hard to launch herself up and skipping across the room.  As she exited, Vicky sauntered in.

Well, I'd asked to see more breasts and Vicky obliged sporting a teeny-weeny bikini replete with the classic black poke-a-dots on bright yellow fabric.  Over her shoulder she spun a metallic-green parasol.  Her shoes were ridiculous matching green high heels.  Hanging around her waist she wore a thin gold chain with green and golden charms. She spread her arms, one up one down, a very slight bow.

"OK Baby," Then I whistled the cat call, adding. "Take me down to the beach and sit on me until the tide comes in."

"So you like it?" Vicky seemed more than pleased.

"I like anything that shows me more of you.  And I love poke-a-dots.  Something about them just gets to me.  And those awesome shoes…" Never forget the shoes, my friend. ".. you'll have to take them off before you walk on the sand.  But for parading around over your boyfriend – perfect."

Vicky smiled beautifully, then, "But you didn't say anything about the cleavage.  You said you wanted more." Vicky sounded a little disappointed.

"First thing I noticed, Doll."  I made a quick recovery on this.  "Oh yes, tip-top in that category for sure.  But why don't you bring them over here and let me apologize for being slow on the uptake."

Vicky considered my response for a moment, whether it was good enough or not, I suppose.  I must have passed because she promenaded her big sexy chassis over to where I sat, kneeled to the floor, then grabbed my head and buried it in that tight firm cleavage.  After a few blissful moments of that heaven, Vicky rose turning but still pressing forward, her big yellow-adorned ass riding up my face.  I kissed her as she pulled away.  I almost fell off the bed forward as Vicky sprung forward running across the room with fast tiny high-heel steps and giggling into the dressing room.

Right then Valerie strutted out, eight inch red spike heels, a beige leather micro skirt with a matching-the-shoes red-weave belt, lacey knit beige tube top, red and beige bangles on her wrists, a black ruby-studded choker around her neck, her long full mane roughly pulled up and bunched to fall off to the left side.  She wore her lipstick thick and also bright red, mascara heavy and sexy-vamp.  She presented as the biggest most alluring whore one could imagine.  I'm pretty sure I looked a bit dumbstruck.

"Well?" she beamed, a bit too proud I thought. "You likey?"

"It's…" Think fast Richie. "It's, ah, simply stunning.  Could I just ask what is the target social situation?"

"A costume party, dork.  What did you think?  That I would seriously dress up to be a whore?"  Valerie had stopped parading around and stood legs apart, arms a stern akimbo.

You see how dangerous my situation is?  You think you're having an innocent playful little fashion show with a couple of your most sexy fun wives, and then boom.  You say one little thing and all the sudden you're on the slide down to a punishing ass-smash.  Yes, I was beginning to think I was right: they definitely all had some of the Mammoth Madness, and, yes, even The Triplets as well, the more I thought about it.

Trouble was: these Amazon damn I.Q.'s were also way up there.  Lies and manipulations were more than likely to backfire.  I mean there are lots of ways to say things.  I had to find the best way to say the truth.

"Dear Valerie," I made sure to keep eye contact.  Looking away at her boobs or ass at a moment like this could make her feel objectified.  Heaven knows I would never, never want to objectify a woman;> Okay maybe a little bit, but to be fair I would worship her more.  Only the truth would suffice here. Valerie was a very good-hearted woman; but her ass was looking for any excuse to crush me.  "You know I love you, don't you?"

"Well, yes, of course."

"I believe you are as much as whore as I am the star center of the New York Nicks.  We're just having fun here, right?  So let me say your outfit would take the prize at any costume party – for sure.  And if you ever decided to become a whore, at you mercy, I would beg to be your only client – you with all my money in your purse and all my love in your pocket."

Valerie took three large steps covering the distance to me.  With the toe of her high heel she shoved me flat to the bed.  Then she pinned me under her shoe, my neck just fitting through the space between her instep and her spiked heel. My eyes bulged in some fear at the tense muscles of her legs.  She leaned all her upper body weight onto that thigh above me, breasts spilling over to either side of her leg. This pressed the bed down deeply, my upper body curved down into that hole, still pinned at the neck by her terrifying pointy red shoe.

"Just so we understand each other," The big bitchy Valerie glared at my helpless predicament, "If I was your whore, no amount of money would satisfy me.  I would own your soul – forever.  And that might, if you licked fast and hard enough with convincing verve, satisfy me enough not to smother you lifeless."

"Don't you own my soul already?"  I managed to squeak out.

Valerie laughed, letting go of her pretend mean.  "Yes I suppose that's true."  Now she smiled, lifted off her spiteful spike.  Then as the bed rose to recover beneath me, Valerie's big ass descended on me in a heavy loving smash.  Oh, she was so much heavier now than the original woman that had tricked and trapped me in her office some ten months ago.  This superlative version had to be twice that weight at least, maybe more than 1200 pounds.  In the dark crush underneath I pretended she was that mean whore, cruel to the point of smothering me to death.  Beautiful and malicious, my secret fantasy fulfilled by pretending her current ass-smoosh of my tiny body was actually fully punishing in intent and merciless is the smothering ass grind that would ensue.  But no, my kind wife rose off me after a mere ten minute suffocation.

Valerie looked back at me, way too intuitive. "What dark fantasy were you having down there, husband?"

"Oh, you know, the usual devastation."

"Good," she winked. "As long as you know your place."

Both Valerie and Vicky had disappeared into their dressing room for several minutes.  When they emerged: schoolgirls.  Big super sexy short-skirt women pretending to be schoolgirls.  They looked at me alluring, invitation all over their expressions.

I studied them for only a second.  You know, some things bother me and this was one of them. "Sorry, Valerie and Vicky, I don't do this fantasy."

Vicky came toward me, aggressive and self-assured, "But *we* do and it's what we want."

I pointed a finger at her. "No."

Valerie came up beside her sister-wife.  They didn't say anything, just little poses, some lifting of skirts and hefting of breasts and little pouty puckers.

"Sorry, girls, not in this castle.  Not as long as I am King."

"You sure?"  Vicky looked so seductive; I have no idea where I found my resolve.  She sing-songed with a much exaggerated lilt up to quite high, "You don't know-what you're miss-sing, mister."  She wiggled her ass at me.

"Come on Vicky," Valerie kissed her on the cheek.  "We have a million other options."

"Well, I suppose…" Vicky's eyes shown bright toward me, even more than the usual amount of adoration evident. "A King must have his rules.  But remember, a Queen must have her due."  And with butts in swishing synchrony they retired into the dressing room.

"Well that's that, I guess." I said to myself, figuring I'd blown it with a big turn off rejection.  But, sorry, just like I've always promised you, I wasn't having the schoolgirl thing.  I hopped off the bed and headed toward the door.  As I reached for the handle I heard.

"And just where do you think you're going, buddy?"  Very quick and lithe Valerie slipped past me and leaned against the door I sought to open.

Vicky appeared right beside her. "Yeah.  We have one more outfit for you to review."  She picked me up and tossed me across the room and onto the bed.

I rolled to right myself and looked back anticipating an attack.  Instead I saw the two beauties still across the room, now arm-in-arm in a promenade of bedroom fashion, violet negligées open in the front, the merest excuse for panties, breasts decorated but not anything you could call covered.

"Well?"  They beamed mischievous.

"Very, very sexy bedroom attire…" I began.

But Vicky interrupted me.  "Nope, not it at all."

Valerie chimed in. "Actually we're thinking of opening a deli."

"What?"  That caught me off guard for a second, then trying to catch up... "Well, I'm sure it will be a popular establishment."

They came over to the bed and climbed on either side of me.  As they pushed me flat on my back and pulled my shorts off, they rested down on their sides, big heavy breasts covering my torso, their marvelous expressions of sensual interest in me quickly sending me to euphoric emotions.

Vicky: "We'll have all kinds of specialty sandwiches.  There's the Richie breast sandwich."

Valerie: "And the Richie butt sandwich."

Vicky: "And the Richie double-kissy sandwich."

Valerie: "And the Richie pussy-crush sandwich."

To myself I thought, "Oh boy, here it comes."  I closed my eyes anticipating their delicious and imaginative sexy squish.  Instead I kept hearing more deli ideas."

Valerie: "You know, Vicky, we should offer a few selections for those that prefer a little something from South-of-the-Border."

Vicky: "Oh yes-yes, definitely.  You mean like a Richie Burrito?"

Valerie: "Yeah, or Richie Tamale or Richie Soft Taco?"

Me: "Hey!  What do you mean 'soft'?" I pulled on Valerie's hair; my right arm under her neck gave my right hand perfect access to grab a handful of curls.  That little shock sent a wave through her body that she used as an excuse to bounce her hip up and curl significantly more onto my legs.

Valerie reached down and gripped my hard Volunteer. "Oh sorry Richie, my bad."

Vicky: "Don't forget the desserts!  Richie Pie."  She laughed.

Valerie: "Richie Pudding."

Vicky: "Richie Milkshakes."  They both jiggled their heavy hooters on me, laughing like they were the best comics on the planet."

As they kept on I kind of stopped listening.  I mean I was still listening to their playful tones, their laughter, their breathing, just not listening to what they were saying.  I loved the current kind of perfect-to-endure-forever amount of weight on me.  This was bliss for me; that grace of gentle sensation in the anticipation of the coming ecstasy.  I knew all I had to do was relax and wait.

As I day-dreamed of Vicky sitting on my face and Valerie taking in my cock I more-or-less went off into my own world.  After a while I did not even hear them anymore.  After another little while I actually realized – I really did not hear them anymore!  Why did they stop?  What happened to the sex that always came next?

I opened my eyes.  Two world-class beauties met my gaze as I looked from one to the other and back and forth again.  When I looked at Vicky again she brought her lips to mine and, spreading, to the rest of my face.  Her kiss only lasted maybe fifteen seconds.  But it was plenty long enough to be passionate, deep, and have lots of mouthing lip action.

Vicky released her kiss.  I had a second for a breath, then Valerie descended on me with her kiss.  Her lovely lips and nice wide mouth more than devoured my face, sucking and licking me inside the seal of her lips.  That dominating kiss lasted maybe thirty seconds.  Then it became Vicky's turn again, much more vigorous and longer, maybe two minutes.  Wow, that kiss knocked my socks off!  Then Valerie proving her great worth with a three minute kiss that blew my little mind.

On and on they kissed in turn.  Of course they got breaks, recovering, and building up for more each time.  I got no breaks.  Just a second for a breath, then on with the amazon ownership of my face.  And yet, they made no advance on the rest of my body.  Mysterious it seemed.

Whenever I opened my eyes (and when they weren't covered by lips or tongue) I got glimpses of their out-of-this-world beauty.  And God they were just so outstanding and phenomenal to behold.  I got more and more excited.  Now as one kissed I felt the other licking the exposed areas at the edges of my face, licking up against the lips of kissing-woman.  This turned me on even more.

The kisses were lasting more than five minutes each, and not mild in the least.  Their kisses varied from heavy mouthing to the point of biting threat, then backing off mere smothering facial incubation.  And their dreamy eyes, so full of love and lust, so focused on possessing me, dominating and pleading at once, both commanding and begging me to beg for more.  And I did, surrendering all.  They could tell and it only excited them more.

What it did to me – well, I couldn't take it.  I literally felt like I was losing my mind.  My desire became so strong, so wanting, so needful of them, so worshipful of their exquisiteness, I had to have release.  My only escape was through orgasm.  Yes, yes, I exploded, my Volunteer squeezed perfectly under and between breasts.

Their kissing became more intense, much more than I would have thought possible. Both kissed me all over my face now, practically taking in my head. Their fervent double-kissing drove me on and on into orgasm after orgasm. When I could absolutely give no more they mouthed on me so robustly I had to orgasm yet again.

"There, there, husband." Vicky purred, at last lifting away, almost shivering with the delight of her dominance. "Oh look at my breast!" Indeed she had caught the brunt of my cum storm. She got up to go wash off.

I turned to watch her perfect ass depart. Valerie gently but firmly steered my face back to look up into hers. "You like Vicky's ass. Is that what you want next? Mine's bigger, you know. Suppose it would do in a pinch?"

I tried to think. I guess I had looked at Vicky's ass. Maybe that did mean I wanted ass. Now what does that even mean? God, my brain was fried like over-cooked tempura. My mouth opened and mumbled some kind of affirmative. Valerie smiled and brought her big ship about.

She slid off her panties and plopped her murderous thunder on my spent frailty. As I fought for life, Vicky must have returned and climbed on as well. I felt my little bones being fossilized and pressed so deep into the mattress it would take an archeologist to find them some day. Rocking their sum 2,400 pounds on me side-to-side, it seemed their purpose pressed toward increments of more and more insertion. Yet with each slow and sexual plunder from Valerie's oscillating ass, I would catch a breath and hear them laughing and moaning and laughing some more at the fun sport of it all. I felt so far beyond overly stimulated by their loving crush, I heard myself begging for mercy at those moments of access to air.

"Mercy, please, I can't take it." I pleaded for relief, for them to not be so beautiful, so delicious, so completely Goddess overpowering and supreme.

And they laughed more, knowing my pleading for what it was: a groveling from their little enslaved husband that they should never stop and thus sit on me in this perfect squish forever. And ultimately they did just sit; my face sufficiently so far up into Valerie's enormous candy ass that she, I suppose, must have finally felt satisfied in her wifely ownership of my being. Valerie simply sat and squeezed and squeezed my whimpering face in rhythmic orgasmic shudders. She ass-munched my head and crushed my little bones as I, way too slowly, ran out of oxygen. Finally, after an hour of this glorious torture, that was so perfectly and exactly what I wanted, these big sexy adoring fashion beauties smothered me wonderfully unconscious.

                                          ***

When I woke up I found myself all dressed like I was before.  But I sat leaning back against the base step of the landing, half way down the stairs from Vicky's and Valerie's hallway, four long-stem roses in my loose grip.  Funny, I smiled short of a chuckle.  Valerie and Vicky – what a pair!  But I wondered: why four roses – why not two?

I struggled to stand, using the woodworking on the wall for purchase.  That last session must have taken at least two hours.  Then I paused a second, thanking God for those two extremely beautiful wives, and a second Gratitude that I was still alive.  "OK, are we good?"  I looked up.

But damn, I had to get going – I had a date with the Mammoths.  And  I really, really especially didn't want Keisha to get mad at me.  I rattled down the rest of the stairs, the next flight as well, to the ground floor.  I commenced jogging down that bigger and grander thirty foot tall hallway.

Ahead on the right, Daisy's door stood wide open.  And that invariably meant Debbie, Amanda, and Brandy would be in there as well.  I sped up.  I mean, normally I would certainly stop to page homage and respect to my four pregnant wives.  But I really didn't know what time it was; only that I must certainly be way behind schedule.

As I maxed out my speed at their door, a great big arm shot out, the hand snapping me up like a striking snake's head.  Wham-snap, and I flew into the room.  Right before Saint Debbie hauled me into her great big Goddess bosom I saw Brandy push the door shut with her ever-spreading and most delightful ass.  Without waiting for a hello, the some twenty-three foot tall giantess Saint Debbie rolled me out on her forearm and brought my face to her completely irresistible nipple.  Of course she could tell I needed sustenance.  I reacted like the thirsty little cuss that I was, sucking like crazy and finding instant reward.

"Oh look!" Daisy came over to fawn over me, smiling at me as I blinked up at her, peaking around Debbie's superlative breast. "He brought us four roses."

I suppose I shrugged under Debbie's breast.  I don't know if anyone noticed.

"How sweet." I could tell love-hungry Amanda couldn't wait to kiss me and get her big pregnant ass on me.

"Awe" Brandy came over, blinking back tears.  Hers was probably the most emotional of the four pregnancies.

OK, so here I was 4'5" pounds and 77 pounds.  Oh yea, I'd grown a tiny bit after the wild cure under The Triplets and Saint Debbie.  Trouble was it seemed all my wives were way growing more.

It is my biggest "not-fair", I suppose: weren't my wives supposed to stop growing once they got pregnant?  Well, no, it turns out, the actual rule was: they could get pregnant only after they stopped growing.  See the difference?  So Debbie, Daisy, Amanda, and Brandy stopped growing at the respective sizes of: 21'8"/5129 pounds; 15'6"/2493 pounds; 11'2"/945 pounds, and 10'9"/893 pounds.  They got pregnant.  Then they grew again.  A little corollary I hadn't heard about.

Of course they grew again, you say.  Pregnancy does that to a woman.  But you're not getting me.  Debbie grew more than a foot taller to 23'5" and gained like 400 pounds.  Daisy quickly sprouted up to 18'1" and stopped getting taller, but seriously bulked up to a new very heavy total of 3,637 pounds and was still gaining.  Amanda's, up-bump took her up to 13'11" to a sexy assed 1,632 pounds.  And Brandy, came to within an inch of Amanda, 13"10", and a wonderful curvaceous 1,616 pounds.  So you see, my two inch and seven pound gain proved out kind of relatively insignificant didn't it?  Oh, it's true, they weren't getting taller anymore now, so maybe their continuing weight gains really were only due to pregnancy at this point.  That would at least be some mercy.

Debbie finished unloading some from each of her breasts into me. With two loving hands she sat me snuggly down between her legs, my back up against her always hot crotch.  She had become so massive I could not even see over her legs. But it wouldn't have mattered if I had been tall enough to see over her legs because her huge seven-month pregnant belly rested down on the top of those legs anyway.  I looked out from the cave created just for me by Saint Debbie and tried to mentally prepare myself for what came next.  What they wanted every day now.

"Okay, Sweethearts," Debbie called out.  "Who wants to be first?"

"Oh me-me, please." The eager and emotional Brandy couldn't wait.

Saint Debbie spread her legs apart a little and it was no problem for me to crawl out.  At the giantess bed's edge I grabbed both arms around Debbie's muscular lower legs and slid a couple feet down, fireman's style, to the floor.  I crawled over to where Brandy stood by her bed, lowered myself prostrate to the carpet, and kissed her feet.

"My Queen, I come to profess my love for you." Each of the four pregnant wives had a script they preferred, ceremonial, if you will.  Next I kiss my way up inch by inch to her ankles, her calves, making sure to be thorough and loving along the way. Brandy trembled with sexual sensations and overflowing desires.  It excited the heck out of me too to see her so thrilled by such simple, superficial kissing.  I continued with anticipatory verve up and around her knees, making sure to catch the front/back/sides of each.  Another fifteen inches up her legs, on my tippy-toes, and I could reach no further.

P.E.S.  That's "Pregnancy Enhanced Sex".  If you don't know about it, believe me, for sure, it is real.  And like everything else with these Amazons of Bluebelle Valley, every sexual thing gets magnified geometrically by size.  So by the time I could kiss no further up Brandy's stately columns of legs she shivered already into the beginnings of her first orgasm of the afternoon.

Brandy's legs still shook as she slowly squatted on me.  No, she did not shake from any effort to lower herself and straining at her enormous weight; she powered up way too strong for that.  She shook with barely constrained desire, now wanting me to quickly complete the foreplay task of progressing gradually up her legs with those animated kisses.  So her twat squat continued, maybe speeding up a little as I approached the final confluence of her legs.

Then wham, her legs clamped suddenly together on me, my face buried in her bush. Up I went with her rising twist and blam, smash onto her bed.  Under her belly now, given just enough room to scooch along on my back, I continued with the kissing.

She also wanted me to say nice things into her belly, sweet talk and sweet nothings, it was my voice that mattered.  I said whatever occurred to me, like "You're so beautiful.  I love you.  You smell so sweet. (That got some giggles from the other three wives.)  I cherish you.  You are the Great Goddess."  You know, the usual things you would say to a 1,616 pound pregnant wife as you kiss past her crushing belly toward her smothering gigantic breasts.

Did I mention breasts?  OMG, Brandy's were perfection on pregnant steroids.  She held herself up at the ideal distance for me, on my back beneath her, to work under her nipples – five vigorous minutes each, sucking, mouthing, nibbling at, and toughening them up.  That's right, these pregnant wives wanted me to do the work of getting them ready for nursing babies, so they wouldn't have to worry about getting sore.

I'd suggested one morning, about two weeks ago when all this started, that they could conveniently do this for each other, probably more effectively than me.  Their shocked looks surprised me; like I'd really missed an important point on a sensitive matter.  They never did explain to their dumb husband what that important point was.  The only elucidation I got was from Amanda, after her initial shock, she knocked me back on the bed and sat on my face for a good squirming fifteen minutes of smothering ass torture – which I didn't really mind that much, but got the idea not to upset them on this issue again.  Next time it would probably be Daisy or Debbie lowering the boom and dishing out the punishment – I know, scary, right?  So every day after that I did my nipple servicing to the Pregnant Queens without complaint, delay, or further suggestions – and with proper vim and vigor.

Besides it was very easy for me to get excited by their increasing engorging breasts.  In fact, typically they had to initiate the move on to the next phase because I carried on non-stop like a little wild man at their tits.

That next phase, typically after few luscious kisses on the mouth, had to do with further prep for the actual birth event.  Remember, we were still living under The Quarantine.  So we had no medical care or nice ultra-sound pictures or Synsonto Scientists to help.  Nobody knew how big these babies were going to be.  So my brilliant pregnant wives cooked up this idea that it was somehow my responsibility to get them ready down below for any eventuality.  I'm trying to tell you they made me prep their pussies.

In Bountiful Brandy's case that involved a whole lot of pressured face sitting to work my head deep up inside her.  And at the moment that's exactly where she had me.  Of course her determined goal included getting me in a little further each day.  She'd been pounding on my shoulders for about a week now.  And, with a couple… more… good… smashes – ah, she finally got my shoulders into her today.  Good we'll stop now.  No – Brandy's voracious pussy wanted more right away, quickly sliding over my body another 18 inches.  It was super tight, tremendous squeezing, and probably very good prep.

While Brandy squeezed and squirmed in orgasmic delight on me, she also effectively sat on me as well.  With my upper body completely inside her, she bounced around on my lower body.  She also cleverly got both hands busy as well.  With one hand Brandy worked herself up super charged with clitoral stimulation; while with her other hand diddling with her helpless pussy-eaten husband.  Brandy's bouncing, bouncing, bouncing twat squash and double-handed control orchestrated the perfect simultaneous orgasm sent us both off the charts and into the next galaxy.

Brandy milked me for all I was worth, taking the time to get every last wiggle of orgasm out of her body and impressed into her little stick-man husband.  She pulled me out easily with her strong tender hands.  As I gasped for air, Brandy timed some nice pounding heavy pussy kisses on my body between my breaths.

"I love you Brandy. I love you Brandy."  I blurted out between each finishing pussy smash.

"I love you too, Darling."  Brandy told me before finishing with a nice ass smash on my face.

Daisy grabbed my body with a nice warm wet towel, cleaning me off from the torrent of Brandy's juices.  She handed me back to Saint Debbie for breast milk reconstitution.  After just a short couple minutes on tit each I recovered, feeling vigorous and ready for the next of the four-rounds of servicing.

Amanda's session always started and ended with ass.  First I had to say that I loved her ass, that it was my entire universe, that I worshiped it and desired to be owned by it, and other such sweet-talk.  Then came the kissing and kissing and kissing her ass in every one of the creative, some dozen poses, she presented over me and on me.

After the ass adulations Amanda also insisted that very nice things be said into her body as well, but not through the belly, rather up through her pussy.  During that affirmative speaking Amanda would simply go ahead and pussy gobble my entire head.  She had worked past my shoulders last week, and knew she could demand more from me once she had inserted my upper body into her.

Amanda had it worked out to be hands free.  She positioned on me just so, getting my erect Volunteer to rub firmly up against her clitoris.  Inside I knew right where to find her magic G-spot.  There I would blast in Sparkle-fire, heating up that nerve center and flaming out the ecstasy in multidirectional spokes of joy.  I have no idea what Amanda did with her hands, if anything.  Self-breast stimulation maybe; a finger up her own ass?  It didn't matter.  All I know is I had one very happy wife squeezing all around me, thundering love into me and making each splendid second count.

And when it was all over it wasn't all over.  Around she came with that gorgeous ass again to obliterate any remaining vestiges of my volition to be anything but her servant.  Small wonder Amanda insisted on this preparation therapy every day.

More warm wet towel cleaning; more recovery at Debbie's breasts, and then on to sweet and precious and so huge Daisy.  Daisy always started with kisses on the mouth.  The gentle focused loving kisses would inevitable give way to more and more vigorous mouthing alternating with licking, nibbling, tight puckered kisses, then increasingly wide open-mouth devouring kisses.

The breast work with Daisy seemed crazy-forceful, but that's what she demanded.  Daisy insisted that I pound on her breasts, pummeling her with my fists with everything I could muster.  All this had to happen while kissing and biting at her nipples. If I didn't exert enough vigor she would whip me senseless with her tits.  It was like a war.  All the time she would keep lifting and lowering her huge tits onto me, each breast much, much heavier than my entire body.

Always she sought to wear me down, to smother and own me.  Gradually I would lose strength and wind.  But fought on I did, flailing and kicking up at her until at last she would press me completely flat and unable to move and… helpless.

You would have thought it would have been Amanda, but no, it was Daisy who wanted me to speak up into her body through her ass.  So in her vast lovely crack I went, head first.  And down her big butt came, squishing her little feckless fuck of a husband to the width of paper.  I moaned and grunted, I guess generating enough vibration after a few minutes that Daisy felt satisfied.  Probably I owed my survival to Daisy's desires for moving on to sex more than any great achievement on my part under her mountain of ass.

Getting my skinny body all the way up through Daisy's generous pussy and completely inside her – well, that achievement had long since been mastered.  What Daisy required now involved me folding myself into a thicker (albeit shorter) challenge.  Even going in as a cannonball was not that much a contest for the big wide eighteen foot tall Daisy.  So now I had instructions to go in cannonball but explode once inside.  And I don't mean cum/Sparkle explode; she demanded arms and legs shoved out as much as possible in all directions.  Talk about exhausting.  You try doing burpee/jumping jacks inside a 3,500 pound pussy sometime and tell me how many reps you could do before collapsing into a little licky-loo heap.

Fortunately it turned out to be great foreplay.  By the time I had given up, absolutely just surrendering to her crush, Daisy wanted all the Sparkle-fire I could muster.

Lucky for her and me I could generate a sufficient fire-storm to satisfy her insatiable cunt.

Though I'd gone in more-or-less head-first in a ball; I also came out head-first a soggy string bean.  Somehow I'd turned around inside her.  Sucking for air I had to endure Daisy's playful leg splat of my body with her huge heavy upper legs.  Back and forth she worked me like dough under a massive firm, fleshy rolling pins.  I gulped for breath at each little chance when my head popped out for a second when she switched legs on me.

Warm wet towels, cleaning, nursing at Saint Debbie, vigor returning, consciousness awakening, all just in time to look up and see Debbie's sexy, wide, open mouth descending on my face.  She took in my entire head and shoulders, sucking me up and down like an unattached cock, a dildo I suppose.  Except, I could clearly tell that to her I was no inanimate object, but a lover of the greatest personal importance.  Saint Debbie could make her love known unambiguously through the slightest touch.  So this oral sex of my entire body felt as loving as anything I'd ever experienced.

With her hand still firmly wrapped around my legs, Debbie took me from her mouth and jammed me easily into her pussy.  With her other hand she stimulated herself right next to where I went in and out, in-and-out….

Then, it was back up to her hungry mouth again.  She took me in deep.  I found myself thinking "hold on tight Debbie" because her mouth and tongue where going through involuntary swallowing motions – very squeezing and stimulating to my body.  This went on for a long time, every deep shove toward her throat feeling like the edge of being swallowed.

This time when Debbie pulled me all the way out of her mouth I saw that Brandy sucked vigorously on one of Debbie's tits with the voracious Amanda on the other.  Down below, where I was headed, Daisy had four fingers already nicely inside Debbie, with the thumb worked in and squeezing the clit from the top.  Above I saw Daisy's lips come forward to meet Debbie's in a very open-mouthed tongue duel, though quickly the lips sealed over that fun-to-watch giantess action.

But where was I to go?  No worries; Saint Debbie leaned to lift her gargantuan right hip, passing me under, and shoved me firmly into her ass.  Black hot rose-smelling heaven crushed all around me.  Heavier still –it must have been Daisy climbing onto Debbie's lap, the mouths now at equal and convenient height for prolonged kissing.

And heavier still had to be Amanda and Brandy burrowing in to be in the Debbie-Daisy breast sandwiches.

Well, these four wives certainly had me now, didn't they?  Grinding on each other, their glacial weight smothered me for an ice age.  Though, of course, there would be no chill as I blissed into Nirvana under hot, hot Saint Debbie.  Delicious Debbie ate me alive inside the gravitational doom of her husband-consuming ass.  The squeezing orgasms pulverized me into a flat display of elements, my very molecules dissolved by the spasmed writhing and loving pregnant mass of wives.  I disappeared physically and emotionally into the dominance of my Goddesses.  How long was I in there?  I have no idea.  How long does it take to dismantle a tiny man and put him back together again with your ass?

After a long dreamless while I heard a southern drawl, Brandy.  "What the heck is he licking at?"

Debbie seemed happy and wry. "My best guess: pussy; but it could be ass."

"God, he's just so cute, isn't he?"  Amanda, I could count on her for a kind word.

"Looks to me like a mouth craving to be sat on."  Oh dear Daisy.  Go ahead; smother me once and for all.

"I hate to say it ladies," Debbie sighed. "But I think our little husband has had about all he can take for now."

"Well can't we at least give him something to lick?  I mean, look at his tongue and mouth."  Daisy being thoughtful, I suppose.

"I think what that little sucker needs is one last turn at Debbie's breasts."  Brandy relaxed and good-natured, sounded so homey.

"OK, here you go…" But Debbie did not pick me up this time.  Instead she lowered her breast, nipple ever so gently onto my lips, my face.  My licking continued and stimulated Debbie's huge, heavy, hanging, engorged breast to release milk.  It flowed over me and all I had to do was swallow, no effort of sucking required.  Boy I needed this last dose to recover from their zillion pound pregnant ass-smash.

One more time: warm set towels, all clean, then soap, I just kept my eyes closed, relaxed.  I felt hands washing me feet, others rubbing and working my hands/fingers/cuticles, another scrubbed my body including privates, and, though I don't sprout much of a five o-clock shadow, I trusted the fourth the scrape a nice sharp razor across my face for a close shave.  They sat me up, dressed me, even combed my hair – all more baby prep, I imagined.  I didn't fight it anymore.  And they seemed very pleased and happy.  P.E.S. is way better than PMS any day, so, you know, dude, be kind, considerate, and if you have to say anything, make that one word "yes" as often as possible.  I'll prove it to you….

They all walked me to the doorway, crowding around as much as their bumping bellies would permit.

"Come see us tomorrow Richie."

"Yes."

"My ass will be waiting for you."

"Yes."

"Do you love me as much as the sky is big?"

"Yes."

"I want you in deeper tomorrow."

"Yes."

"Even though I getting so big, am I still beautiful to you?"

"Yes."

"Do you still dream about being smothered by my pussy?"

"Yes."

"Thank you for the flowers Richie.  Will you bring more next time?"

"Yes."  And I still did not know exactly where those roses had come from.

***

Good God in Heaven, the Sanderling Sisters, those scintillating sirens of sexy smother and smash, stood waiting for me in the hallway. "Ready?" They sang happy in unison.

"Ready to die and go the Promised Land."  I looked wearily way up at their vivacious smiles.  I sighed and then scanned down their scanty cheer-leader like outfits that barely contained jiggly tushes.  Their short-short green and yellow pleated skirts flapped up as they bounced, exposing deeply tanned and generous big asses some three feet over and above my instantly mesmerized stare.

"Are you kidding?  You are *living* in the Promised Land."  These big mischievous beauties had way too much energy for me at the moment.  I recalled their double-team squish on me last summer, when they each tipped the scales at just over a mere 400 pounds.  Now these aggressive splendors each weighed twice that.  And without compunction, given any excuse, would eagerly suffocate me with those much more devastating asses.  I looked up at them with pleading eyes.  Sympathy wasn't their strong suit.

"Come on, dude.  We assured Serenity we'd get you to her and the Mammoths on time.  And for that she promised us a big reward."  At the moment I really couldn't imagine what the heck kind of tandem fuck that would be.

I wanted to say: "Honestly, I don't think I can do it today, girls.  Give the Big Ladies my apologies."  But I looked at the impatient tapping of Silvia's foot, the shift forward and toward-me advance of Sandy's hip, and now the turning of Silvia's buttocks to loom over my head.  They wanted me to say that, to show any impertinence and invite their painful and prolonged ass-grinding without mercy on this cold hard stone floor.  No, it wouldn't be a gentle thrashing at all.  So I said, "Well, my sexy wives, we wouldn't want to deprive you of your just rewards."

"That was the smart answer.  But it still won't entirely spare you."  Silvia went ahead and pulled her skirt up anyway and lowered her vast ass to my face.  I understood I better follow my desires and kiss it.  While I got busy with that, Sandy slipped behind, bent, and smashed me with her ass as well firmly against her sister.  They stood, my feet left the floor, my head, shoulders, chest, and spread-to-protest arms sandwiched tightly by their butt crush.  Sandy backed Silvia against the hallway wall and leaned on me very heavily, pressing my face way up into Silvia's ass.

My lower body swung free, midair.  Sandy reached around from behind and stuck her hand down my shorts.  She grabbed my Volunteer and worked me up super charged hard.  Then Sandy released her ass-lean on me as Silvia tightened her crack tightly on my head and chest.  Sandy dove under the little man dangling from her sister's ass, whipped down my shorts, and quickly, hungrily, took my entire Volunteer and balls into her mouth.  It took less than a minute of this overwhelming stimulation to have me cum and suck me dry.

Instead of releasing me, Silvia just kept me snuggly squeezed up in her butt.  She backed into the wall and thrashed me with horizontal butt ramming.  That lodged me in even firmer.  Then Silvia pushed off from the wall to the middle of the hallway.  There she spun in circles faster and faster, my body lifting out vertical from her ass-clench.

Silvia released me to fly out of her ass into the waiting Sandy.  She dropped me to the floor then immediately Sandy pounced on my weak and prone body.  Sandy gave me a pussy hammering like you wouldn't believe, while Silvia dropped on me also and managed to work her pussy in there, nice and sloppy onto my face.  They came quickly, expertly, and even made sure I came with them by applying all the extra vibrating vigor to render me without any defense to their superior sexy plundering.  These ladies fucked super efficiently, and wasting no time quickly had me up and on the move again.

Hand-in-hand-in-hand, the Sanderling Sisters, with me hanging in between their firm grips, skipped along happily now, out of the mansion, across the mile of lawn, and approaching the forest lane to the Mammoth Liar.  Once in a while my feet would touch the ground.  But mostly I just flew and flapped along with my cheerful, bouncy and bodacious, and very temporarily sexually satisfied Twin wives.  There was no time to waste; my four largest wives waited for me in their forest home.

# XIX. Greenfield's Religion

Long before sunrise I woke up encased in the Triplet's sleeping tangle of dreaming love and crush.  I considered using my wide-awake energy to play with the extraordinary delights of their much larger and exceedingly luscious bodies.  After all, Pavie's perfect enormous breasts pressed right into Aria's, less than a foot away up the bed from my head.  I could probably coax a breast or two away from the equilibrium of their current mutual smash, to smother heavily down upon my face.  If lucky maybe an eighteen hundred pound mini giantess would roll over onto me and crush me soundly all the way to mid-morning.  Yes, on a diet of daily my catalyzing Sparkle-Fire semen these most extraordinary of all my thirty wives had grown quite a bit.

Or I could curl around inside their open embrace, head south and explore the tempting amusements under and between the crossings of their long, sexy, and oh-so-heavy legs, find my way into the succulence of their sweet….  Yes, that would be quite nice as well – a face-first serious pussy-smother before breakfast.  What a way to start the day!

If I escaped in time, I could go find Callie; maybe she slept on her stomach.  I could just climb up on her and light her up from behind, right in her great big beautiful ass.  If she didn't wake – excellent.  If she did wake and demanded more – so much the better.  In fact, that sounded so good I decided I would go find Callie first.

By now my flexibility and stealth had achieved legendary status.  I snaked my way around the arms of Aria and Pavie, ascended up by their waists and delicately clambered out over Aria's hip.  I leaned over and kissed her butt cheek, then continued with my hands to the sheets into a hand stand then soft tumble out and away to a cross-legged sit.  And there before me, displayed in all her divine glory: Callie, exactly as I envisioned, and perfect for the taking.

Just as I sidled up for my sneaky move on sleeping Callie's huge perfect curves, a breeze rippled the bedroom's shear curtains, distracting me with its little hello from God.  In wafted a fresh pure bouquet of country air; reborn again this early morning – in to greet me from the growing wildness of the now virtually abandoned Northern Midwest.  I felt the tingle of life in that chilly air.  It brightened my heart, filled me with excitement for the prospects and promise awaiting, but only to be found outdoors before the crack of dawn.

If you're an early riser like me and my favorite patriot, Benjamin Franklin, you have long since realized that the true beginning of a new day starts about an hour and a half before sunrise.  You'll know, when sufficient sleep permits, that the moment of inception is well worth getting up to witness.  And this particular birth of a day felt full-term pregnant, imminent with tidings of wonderment.  Change of plan: though still dark and cold, I knew I had to go outside immediately.  Sex with Callie, believe it or not, could wait.

Padding barefoot across the tiles of the wide veranda, I approached the eight foot stone columns at the edge.  There I climbed up one and over it to sit on the smooth flat top of the wide marble railing.  My skinny legs dangled above the forty-eight foot drop into the pre-dawn black-pit shadow of the patio below.  Looking up and left to the northeast, the first apple-blossom blush of the day's genesis faintly colored my face out of the darkness.

As quiet as the coming sunrise, Callie materialized behind me, her generous fourteen foot frame emanating warmth along my back.  I glanced up to her divine face in the twilight, her honeyed breath evident as dissipating puffs of fog in the bite of the chill morning air.  She stood by, not quite touching me, saying nothing, but as comfortable a presence as a big hug. I felt glad she woke and came to find me.  So we continued, together now, in our meditative silence.

I looked away from the impending sunrise and back to the west.  Dependably the great lawn always looked a smidge less dark at night than the surrounding forest with all its shadows and secrets.  Toward the back on the west side, MaryEllen's ten-acre garden appeared as a slightly mottled stamp-sized subset, an even rectangle carved out of the dimmer evenness of the great 600 acre lawn.  Damn good, I thought, to have a horticulturist as a wife, to feed us all, when in the midst of an unending quarantine.  Ah MaryEllen: definitely yum in more ways than one.

More to the south, maybe a mile from the mansion at the back of the property and well into the woods, the Mammoths (as we affectionately called my four largest wives) had reconstructed their cage.  Of course it was no longer a cage, but those building materials from the Institute had suited their purpose perfectly.  Basically they had re-constituted the facility's frame into a 400x400 foot coliseum-sized house, using the glass dome for their roof.  The 80 foot height of the structure stood higher than some of the forest trees but shorter than most.  So their adapted dwelling in the woods remained hidden from view from the mansion.  Yet, as I looked back that way in the beginnings of the gathering light I could picture right where it would be in the emerging outline of the forest.

Yesterday with the Mammoths had been a most phenomenal, life-altering experience.  The wonder of it still grew as a brighter and brighter Light inside me.

It had started out simple enough, though bizarre, typical really of my experiences in The Bluebelle Valley.  Sandy and Silvia Sanderling, after tag-team blitzkrieg sex, led me across the great lawn to the edge of the Mammoth's woods.  There they blindfolded me.  Each took one of my hands and led me into the forest.  We took the path, the only path back there, that led to The Mammoths' immense dwelling.  As the birdsong and other forest sounds faded, I soon could tell I was inside.  Yet I hadn't noticed any transition with my bare feet; I could have still been outside on the smooth, loose ground.

Silvia and Sandy sat me down, but left me blindfolded, giggled, and then ran off. The cavernous abode had seemed quite before, but after a soft surround-sound of rustling, it got much quitter, muffled and very still.  It also suddenly smelled impossible rich, spicy sweet, and irresistibly alluring.  The Mammoth wives had arrived and were certainly intimately nearby.

Serenity spoke, her voice penetrating, deeply vibrating and with many varied overtones – like a symphony.  "You may remove your blindfold, husband."

Between the delicious pheromones and Serenity's rhapsody of voice, I wanted to run to the source of her speech, to her big generous lips as I imagined them, and just dive in. I opened my mouth to respond to her, some wise-crack no doubt.  But, removing my blindfold, no words materialized; only my speechless gape at my circumstance.

The four giantesses had enclosed me in a room-sized rectangle framed by their sitting backs and nude posterior facing inward toward me.  Serenity's gorgeous curves, from side-to-glorious-side probably spread at least 18 feet, thus the longest side of the rectangle.  Opposite side, Keisha's ass probably measured almost 17 feet across.  Then connecting and touching firmly from Serenity to Keisha on either slightly slanted 16-foot sides, Ginny and Maya squeezed their asses in to tightly seal me, thoroughly trapped inside the trapezoid of giantess butt.

Their enchanting scent overwhelmed any sense of inhibition.  I stood, filling with energy, with desire, with wildness.  From my ass-limited vantage I could only see the four-butt corral, their sexy broad backs, and their brunette braids falling down to me some 15 to 20 feet from the stately heads or my giantess captors.  Revitalized to be in such an inspiring prison, I revved up even more excited and animated, and downright frisky.  Like a little wild stallion that needed to be broken, ridden down, tamed, and smothered, I ran around pretending to protest with bucking at the edges of my pen.

I recall how their white sandy floor kicked up loose as tore around on it yesterday. My Mammoth wives had brought the sand in from the nearby creek – white medium-coarse sand that had found its way down the stream from the nearby white gypsum crystal bluffs.

Sprinting across at full speed and I jumped up to body slam into the Mammoths' bounce-house size buns.  What a blast!  I repeated that several times.  It didn't matter where I crashed; it was all mountains of glorious butt.  Their lavish asses packed against each other so tightly that there could be no accidently slipping through (or escape), even at the corners.

Pausing, I noticed Ginny and Maya now squirmed and worked their buttocks side-to-side, definitely tightening and loosing.  I could hear the soprano sexual moanings building from the other side of the Mammoth wall that enclosed me.  The tightenings seemed coincident with a muffling of surrendering wailings from that other side.  Miraculously, after all of the day's extensive smash, smother, and delay, the Sanderling sisters apparently delivered me to the Mammoths close enough to the scheduled hour to now be earning those promised sexual rewards.  Good, I thought, getting some of their own ass smashing medicine.

My four giantess wives still merely looked away, ignoring me it seemed.  Meanwhile, growing more and more euphoric, I kept galloping in sand-kicking circles, working myself further into a rising frenzy, spinning out of control again and again to roll over against their lowest nethers.  Then I kissed them, hugging at them, and squeezing in as if to insert myself into and under the various crevasses presented to me.

Beginning to succumb to my desires to be crushed by their tons of ass, I actually crawled right up to Serenity's titanic butt and dug out sand to burrow under her.  It was a lot of work, but hecka' fun and well worth the marvelous comfortable feeling of being in my little tunnel and pressing up under her, gently kissing her buttock of severe doom.

Soon enough though, my wild energy returned, and I had to get out and rough-house some more.  Emerging I noticed Maya and Ginny sat still now, as calmly meditational as the bigger Keisha and even grander Serenity.  I guessed that Sandy and Silvia had received their sexual treatments from Maya and Ginny, and probably left to return to the mansion.  Either that or Ginny and Maya had smothered them unconscious – but I figured probably not.

My burrowing under Serenity had left me with a serious hard-on.  "Eenie-meenie-minie-moe"… I turned and my needle pointed at each of the four compass directions of my world of ass… "Which one of these big babes is ready to go?"

I'm thinking Maya looks slightly edgy, tenser than the others.  Kingly as I was, I strode my little four-foot frame up to her sixteen foot wide ass.  At first gentle touch Maya rocked forward to receive me, creating space for me to kneel, then sit legs forward and slide under her opening crack.  I lie back on the sand looking up in astonishment at the world of cream-colored posterior that would soon obliterate me.

Maya rocked back down, perfectly ass-devouring me in one fell swoop.  No sooner had she flattened her tons of luscious wonder on me than I blasted a load of Sparkle-fire up her ass that shivered all her timbers.  The sexual energy I gave her would time-release as I gave her plenty to process through her gargantuan body.  It might take her thirty minutes to go ahead and reach orgasm.  Satisfied, I slipped out at the first writhing rise of an opportunity she gave me.

Next I approached Ginny.  I got the same rising ass invitation, slipped under.  "Cream then coffee – the ideal combination" I thought, mesmerized by her dark deliciousness.  Beautiful Ginny dropped her sexy giantess smother down on me, and once again I came Sparkle-fire immediately.  At the first bucking-up opportunity I slipped out from under.  I looked from squirming Maya to wiggling Ginny, both working up to their orgasms.  I smiled and thought about the idea of have two plates spinning in the air.  I wondered: could I do all four, maybe get four giantesses to orgasm at once?  I wasn't looking for boasting rights; I just love a good challenge.

Though bigger, I have to say that Serenity seemed the safer bet compared to the still-feral Keisha.  The same approach got the same response.  How was I surviving these fifteen-ton ass smashes?  Amazingly these actually weren't the worst crushes I've ever had.  For example, as Goddess Serenity descended on me, it was the in-curve of her ass crack centered on me that immediately gave me initial space for insertion.  Then as her warm and wonderful vastness spread across me more tightly, most of her weight obviously would be out on the sand to the sides of my tiny narrow peanut-body under her.  Then, of course, The Triplets had continued all these past months to toughen me up more and more with ever enhanced formulae and daily vicious ass pounding.  And don't forget, there is some yield in loose sand.  Sand – it was no accident that my thoughtful biggest wives had brought that in for the floor of their house.  They had designs to smash me from wall-to-wall.  Oh how considerate of them!

The stack for Serenity's majesty on me blew my mind.  The obvious thought of her intimate ass, big enough cover more than fifty of me if lined up side by side and in rows.  The fantasy to be butt-crushed by Serenity come true made me so happy and satisfied it is hard to describe.  Then I pictured the rest of her body, all its munificence mounted onto me, her sexy firm middle, her Titan Goddess breasts, her big strong arms, her beautiful stately neck, her ready-to-devour mouth – it all swirled around in my mind as this loving giantess took her time on me.

Though Serenity had become a very peaceful wife, and lived up to her name, I could not but help still think of her as the Queen, crowned, and me the little king she now conquered.  Yes, this all brought about a very nice, extra vigorous blast from me.  I surrendered and released all my submissive desires into her with as much love for her as imaginable – commiserate, you might say, with the largeness of her big royal smash of me.

Last but decidedly not least, I approached Keisha – same response, same sliding under, same rocking back down to crack-crush my little willing whimpiness.  The only difference: Keisha did not let up.  I stayed under her squirming squish the whole fifteen minutes it took for her to reach orgasm.  And no amount of Sparkle-blasting could get her to buck up for my quick escape.  No, Keisha responded to my every attempt and Sparkle attack with nothing but more horrendous twisting and squeezing down on me.  I must say I enjoyed every delicious life-threatening second of it.  My only regret was I couldn't see the other three divine Goddesses having their simultaneous orgasms right when Keisha bombed me to smithereens.

When at last Keisha finished and lifted up for me to exit I had no energy to move to save myself.  So she just sat back down on my submissive fetal curl for another thirty minutes of crushing ass-bliss. My barely conscious tongue-worship fluttered the whole time; licking a little blue-flame of Sparkle into her oh-so-appreciative loving wifely squirm onto her adoring flat husband.

Next time Keisha rose, she apparently took pity and tugged me out from under her butt.  She gently deposited me out in the middle of the trapezoid pen to recover and return to the land of the living.  After some ten minutes I snapped back to life.  The giantesses still sat calmly as they had before.  Their patience would certainly have to do with their husband having provided a quite nice Sparkle orgasm for each.

Finally when I could stand again and thought maybe I should see about working my way out of the ass corral.  For if I stayed I would certainly want to cycle under their ass smothers again.  That double-dip might prove too much for me to survive.

The Mammoths wore their black hair in long braids, Keisha's and Maya's hanging far enough down that I could reach them.  I climbed up Maya's braid some seven feet then attempted to Tarzan swing over to Keisha's.  It kind of worked except their braids were too heavy for me to move that easily.  I would need them to cooperate and swivel their necks to get the hair going for me.

So I just leaped the little bit more needed to bridge to Keisha's braid.  Then I climbed up hers to her neck.  With their asses touching some fifteen feet below, so were their broad shoulders at my new height.  I ran blithely down the very slight slope of Keisha's left shoulder, jumped a couple feet down to Maya's, ran all the way across her (kind of side-stepping quickly past the back of her neck) to a three foot leap up to Serenity's shoulders, up and down across her broad spanse, then dropped to Ginny's, still running, and back to leap up onto Keisha again.

I tried it a second, third, and fourth time, more quickly.  I found the faster I ran, the more I could dip down below their shoulders and for moments to run almost perpendicular to their study backs.  But I had to keep going fast or fall.  Talk about an exhausting lap….

I rested by Serenity's neck for several minutes.  Then I stood tippy-toe to poke my head up by her ear.  I whispered, "I love you, cutie-pie."  Then I climbed up her ear and, using her hair, on up to the top of her head.  I found some loose strands of hair and repelled down her forehead, slid down her nose, and swung into her slightly parted lips.  I jammed my legs on through and into her mouth, and ended up sitting on her lower lip, face against and soon kissing her upper lip.

"I love you, too."  She slurred, because some husband had his legs on her tongue.  But her huge amount of adoration came through loud and clear.  The love bond we had formed during my rescue of her from the Madness stood solid and forever against seasons and time. I was the same for the other three as well – the main difference being with the edgy tenor of relations with Keisha.

Serenity, Ginny, and Maya had become smothering peaceful giantess that mostly loved to merely squish me under and inside them.  Keisha, who also loved to smother and squish, remained anything but reliably peaceful, always potentially threatening just this side of vicious annihilation of my body and being.

The other three came around to Serenity for the mouth play.  First they passed me politely from mouth to mouth.  Then gradually more tongue and licking amped up to mouthing lips and finally to a gobble-frenzy.  What's a gobble-frenzy?  I guess the only rule is: don't eat the little man.  Other than that, the giantesses just go wild with their lips and mouths.  The tongue is used mostly to push me back to the middle and into other gobbling lips.

This gobble-frenzy turned into a doozy because they got slurpy-noisy and vocal. They over-exaggerated their sexual moaning for the fun of it and it got truly hilarious. I don't know who started laughing first, but their sputtering love-gruntings giving way to weak-kneed wheezes snowballed into a panting-to-gain-air laughing heap.

Their faces on the sand, tears squeezed from their eyes as they tried to catch breath.  My little rolling fit of hysterics in front of their downed faces rendered them all but helpless weak.

As they at long last recovered enough to breathe, they each rolled squarely onto their bellies, hands on the sand crossed under their resting chins, the looks on their compassionate faces the complete opposite of the Madness.  The four Goddesses stared straight ahead at me, eyes so beautiful and loving.  I still found it hard to breathe, even though I too had sobered from the hysterics.

I turned from face to face to face to exquisite close face and said. "How are we going to do this?  How am I going to love you enough?  I want to pick you each up, carry you away and love and ravage your bodies until you beg for mercy.  My heart aches to love you.  We are so close and yet I cannot do nearly what I wish.  I want to kiss your lips and plow my Volunteer into your pussy at the same time.  And while I do that I want to hold your breasts in my hands and squeeze them tight, tweaking your nipples to drive you wild with my mastery of your body."

Ginny blinked. "I don't know Richie.  I hear what you're sayin' and I get it.  It just makes me want to grab you and shove you deeply into my pussy."

"Or in my ass."  Maya added.  "That feels so good when you are in there lighting me up with your Sparkle-fire.  I mean I can still recall having sex before the Mammoth genes took over my size.  It was all right but not even one-tenth of how far you send me during our time together.  And all I can think about is how much I love you.  So, just to think about you, I'm like wet already."

I looked to Serenity.  She smiled, so big, exotic, and beautiful. "I think I feel the same, Richie.  When you crawl up into my pussy it is like having my heart grow to twice its size with love, like an orgasm that starts in my heart.  You inside me, God Richie, it feels so amazingly incredible… I don't mean to sound off beat, but it is like some Christ-force of sexual love is inside my being.  I just glow.  I become Love.  It is timeless.  That's why, I suppose, even if I only have you in me maybe once or twice a month, I still feel that love all the time.  I am living a life of bliss, Richie, connected to you all the time.  What about you, Keisha?"

"You know I still have the Madness in me.  I feel all that heavenly love you describe, yet, at the same time I have all the same mad destructive desires firing me up to such sexual yearnings I truly cannot fully contain myself.  Here's the thing about it: I breathe and I integrate the ongoing madness of me, of this world, with the great soothing Spirit I have come to understand as God.  And I am grateful for it all."

"That's how I survive and flourish." Keisha continued. "I understand exactly what Richie is saying.  I have a fantasy of a Richie my size or even bigger carrying me off and down to the river, wrestling me to the stream bed, and while cool waters flow all around me, swirling my hair in the eddies, my super-charged husband does just what Richie described and ravages me in wild love-making sexual plunder."

We all remained silent as if Keisha had come close to the speaking of some great Truth.  Keisha's mood shifted as she became more animated.  Our interest grew more rapt as her words came to heart's center.

"Not possible."  Keisha's discerning eyes flashed with intensity. "Not going to happen this lifetime.  But does that really matter.  Isn't this all just a dream anyway? I know when the ecstasy of the love takes me I have a vision.  And that vision is that only Love is true, is real.  So I ask you, what is that fantasy that I have; that and all its attendant feelings?  Isn't that fantasy, in a sense, as real as any reality we are already pretending to experience?  My existence at all – doesn't that prove the absurdity of reality?  Let me prove my point." Then Keisha commanded. "Come to me now Richie."

I stood and walked forward, standing before her lips.

Keisha puckered. "Kiss me, husband, and ravage my body."

I kissed into the void of her pucker and she sucked me into her mouth.  She closed her lips to engulf me completely. I felt us rising; her sitting maybe.  Then she dropped me out of her mouth, soaking wet into her hand.  Keisha squatted, her legs apart.  Reaching under herself with me in her hand, she gently inserted me into her pussy and up snuggly into her vagina.  Her remarkably delicious pussy seemed hungry for me, rather mouthing me in.  With her hand then fingertips Keisha shoved me further up until my head hit the end and could go no further.

I felt her sit down again, and then roll out flat on her back.  I heard her talking and could actually understand it coming through her solid body.

"Maya and Ginny, please kiss my breasts.  Serenity, would you be so kind as to eat my pussy."

Almost immediately the loved poured into Keisha's body.  I could feel it swirling all around me.  In my vision I saw the spirits, the souls of my four giantess wives dancing around me, holding hands, singing their praises of love and of Gratitude.  And right there and then I had a grand epiphany.

"I breathe…" Keisha had said before.  Breathe.  I took a deep impossible breath inside this perfectly imperfect wife of my dreams.  And I could breathe.  What miracle was this? This was not possible, yet I just did it.  Breathe.  And I did it again.  What; had I learned to find oxygen where only a modicum could be?  What was I breathing?  Breathe.  Some sacred source of Life itself right here in the perfect place of my loving fantasy and extraordinary reality.  Breathe.  I could stay in this delight of the Goddess forever and without limitation.  Breathe.  Like the unborn innocent I could exist at home inside this extraordinary woman.  Breathe.

Keisha's three loving sister-wives possessed mad-skills at love making and used them to their ultimate application.  Keisha reveled in the over-stimulation, seeing a climax just ahead.  But she had no idea what tornado was about to hit her.

Deep, deep inside this woman, this giantess of love, my reality cracked open into another universe.  All shadows disappeared, just as they had when I died the night of the toxic leak.  Now, like then, all darkness vanished because only Light existed for me – Light of every color, Light beyond color, Light of Love's energy, Light that revealed the mirage of my old existence; and Light that flowed through me now.  Before the magic blue-flame had seemed only an amazing gift from the Triplets.  Now I saw it as a key to unlocking the door into the Universe of Light, as I stood now peeking through its window.

Oh my God, Dear Keisha, I hope you are ready for this.  I quivered with the coming vibration of Light.  I could see the outline of my body as a Being of Light, brightness all around me inside Keisha.  Her juices flowed now, her soul completely open, so beautiful, trusting and vulnerable.  For better or worse there would be no stopping me.

I laughed as the first wave entered me from the Universe of Light.  "Come through me, come through me, for all of us who dwell in the darkness." And the flood came as brilliance so intense it blinded.  To call it white light is not accurate; clear it came and it did not shine, it penetrated.  It blasted away shadow, for shadow could be seen now only as falseness that could no longer exist.  Gone.

The Universe of Pure Love poured through me now and undiluted and unopposed into Keisha, into her body and sweeping up her soul along the way.  We met in that river of flowing Light.  And I kissed her, pinned her the way she dreamed, her hair swirling in pools of cool Light far beyond even what she had fantasized.  And though an orgasmic earthquake bent Richter-scale needles all around me, I felt calm and completely at peace.

It seemed Keisha's orgasm altered reality, blasting across the Earth instantly.  For this Light that came through us now did not travel at light speed, it simply was everywhere, the same way a consideration of reality is everywhere.  To the far corners of the planet every one of the few still surviving souls suddenly felt better and they had no idea why.

I can tell you I certainly felt holy and good.  In that moment I made a child in Keisha, a child with a soul just like all of ours, but born already in the new realm of Light.  Light that had always been there, and we in it, outside of time, wiggling our toes in a little pool of ink we call The Physical Universe.

In a rampage of physical action in Keisha's body I could tell she stood and started running, fast but not very far.  I just felt I floated through it all.  And when she finally settled and quieted, I let myself descend down Keisha's vagina and out, falling, and splash, into a deep pool of the creek that flowed through these woods. It was early evening but already darker in the woods.  Kneeling in the pool and above me, Keisha shimmered blue around the edges, with an aura come alive.  I floated against her inner thigh some five feet below her oh-so-excellent pussy.  The other giantess wives came running up.  They also shimmered.

"What is this phenomenon?" Serenity looked at her radiant arms and down at me in wonder.

"This marvel is our new reality.  We sought in pure Love and have been given a Gift.  We are now known to exist in the Clear Light.  And, there we can make love as we wish and to our heart's content!  With this divine gift we can use the power of love to alter our realities."

"I'd like an altered reality!" Serenity scooped me up, laughing.  "In you go my dear.  Need a breath first; this might take a while."

"No breath necessary.  You and the Light sustain me now."  As she brought me to her beautiful pussy I added.  "And I don't think this will take very long at all…"

***

Sitting on top of the eight-foot railing brought my head to ten feet above the veranda's floor tiling.  The ever bigger version of Callie that stood behind me towered taller yet.  She moved a little closer to me now and brought her magnificent full breasts to either side to the back of my head.  We remained silent watching the yellow glow in the northeast come closer to the horizon.

"Callie."  I whispered in respect for the quietness. "Yesterday I think saw God."

"For sure you did, Richie," She responded, the first ray of sunlight causing me to squint, then turn toward her.  "I think I see God now."  She looked desirously down at me through the valley of her cleavage.  "And I would like this little version of Him to suck my breasts."

I had more to say, but it would have to wait some ten minutes.  I held to either side of her breast, sucking up into it as she leaned it onto me.  As delicious as ever, I detected something kind of new in the mix.  I immediately felt hornier, if you can believe that's possible.

Between breasts I found myself pleading. "Can we please stop for a minute and fuck?"

Callie merely laughed, giving me the other tit to suck.  That also seemed to satisfy me.  Callie chuckled. "Taste a difference?"

I nodded.

"Good.  We are adding a little something to rev you up even more."

No wonder I felt hornier.

"With your new skill, you'll definitely want to have sex more often."

After I finished I finally got to ask. "What new skill?"

"Well, maybe not exactly a skill.  Your new channeling ability; the one you attained yesterday in Keisha.  During sex you now channel the Clear Light into your partners.  They, in turn will have that same ability when they make love with others."

"God Callie," Aria walked up to join us, laughing, "That sounds like the best venereal disease ever."

"But there's more…"

"Of course there is."  Pavie joined us as well.

"OK, my lovelies…" This trio of amazon roommates and lovers was like arising in Heaven every morning. "…I have to tell you. When I saw the Clear Light Universe crack open, right then I realized many other things."

"… that your heart already knew." Callie added.

"But not my mind, sweetheart." I kissed each breasts good-bye for now. "I know now what to say, how to share it."

"All right," Aria assumed the position, her full breasts needing my attention next.

"Well…" I started, but Aria stuck her nipple in my mouth and I had to wait again. Between breasts I blurted out "Gratitude…" But had to wait until I finished on the other breast.

"… Gratitude." I finally got to continue. "Gratitude is our rightful place and attitude for this existence. Gratitude is a Virtue that opens doors to so many more Virtues."

"That makes sense." Pavie, not to be rude about it, took her turn nursing me. "You sure look grateful right now."

"He better," Aria threatened. "If he doesn't then it's nothing but ass…"

"… and more ass." Callie added turning to show off her stately derriere.

When I could talk again it was like I had it all figured out:

"Say Gratitudes daily. Breathe and be grateful. Do this daily and do this with someone. Support is key. Mutual support, for we are communal beings. Realize our main purpose is to connect.

"I'd kind of like to connect with him right now." Pavie hit the controls that slid the bed out onto the veranda.

As Callie carried me to the bed I continued, inspired. "Practice Humility and Kindness and Service. Yes Service, that's another key. Gratitude brings up the desire to be of Service."

Callie tossed me onto the bed. Then Pavie straddled my happy Volunteer. "How about you be of service right now? Fire up your flames, husband." And she slid herself onto me. The new elixir they gave me had me super willing to go for it right away with lots of extra Sparkle.

Still I would not shut up. "Journal and say the Gratitudes.  It doesn't have to be fancy, just real.  'Thank you for my parents or siblings.  Thank you for breath.  Thank you for this opportunity to experience'."

"Thank you for this amazing fuck!"  Pavie sounded truly grateful.  "Sisters you have got to try this.  Our dear husband is definitely channeling something quite special."

Callie climbed on for her turn, lighting up immediately. "Holy spumoni!  You weren't kidding.  Wow, what an impact!"  Callie quickly reached orgasm as that seemed to be the expectation now with Sparkle channeling Clear Light.

On I went apparently channeling at more than one level. "Our body behavior and chemistry function by habits.  It seeks to serve by anticipating.  Walk two miles every morning for six days in a row and on the seventh day your body will feel the need to walk two miles.  Write in your journal every day for six days and you will feel more balanced on the seventh day if you follow that habit to write.  Make a habit of behaviors and thoughts of benefit and such will become your life."

Callie finished on me, a very satisfied purr. "Well spoken and delivered husband.  I could make a daily habit of that Sparkly Clear Light.  Oh sister Aria.  Please have a seat, and prepare to be astounded."

Callie lifted off and Aria jumped right on me. "Just keep on talking, Richie.  As long as you're hard I'll listen to… oh my Goodness!"  Aria suddenly felt it too. "You've truly done it, Richie.  I am so, so glad to be married to such an extraordinary man.  You've actually tapped into Source, pure and bright."  Aria rode me with enthusiasm, hands pinning my shoulders, her big bountiful tits swinging in harmonic motion as she worked me, squirming and shuttering side to side.

"Yes, that's it." My inspiration proceeded.  "Source is available to all of us.  How is this possible?  Because we are It.  The greatest journey of all has no distance.  Takes no time.  Cost nothing."

"Aria," Callie leaned in close. "I think he's ready.  I think it is finally time."

"Yes, yes definitely. He can take it now."  Pavie also leaned over Aria's other shoulder to look down at my face just peeking out between Aria's crushing upper thighs.  "No more holding back."

That statement temporarily suspended my religious train of thought. "What do you mean no more holding back?"

Aria kind of bit her lower lip and winked at me. "We've been holding back all this time – you know, during sex."

"No I don't know." Sex with the Triplets had always seemed the exact opposite of them holding back.

Aria continued to pump me up and down, but now a little faster with more squeeze, a more serious domination, and an increased feeling of love opening up starting to blast into me. "Yes, Richie, we held back.  We have always been capable of so much more.  But it would have been too much for you."  Her vigor and vibration kept climbing, a tingling spread from her now hellacious smash devouring my body with Clear Light, the same Light I'd begun to see yesterday.

Aria spoke as she decimated me with thunderous electric copulation. "This extreme love-making would have ruined you before, before you had directly experienced the Light for yourself.  It would have reduced you to a mindless love slave, crawling around behind us all day and night, begging to be smothered.  But right now you are going to receive all of our love, husband, for better or worse, and I dearly hope my sisters are right – that you can take."

"Yes, Aria!" Pavie grinned over Aria's shoulder, eyes gleaming like an amorous angelic fiend, for she could feel it now just as Aria did. "Give him all of it.  Love him into the next Universe."

Aria's robustness cranked up another magnitude, macerating me cell-by-cell, every ounce of her more than 1800 pounds crushing her unleashed fuck-fury into me on a sizzling lightning bolt of Clear Light.  Yes, Holy Shit!  I hung onto my life – barely, it seemed.  As the beyond-overwhelming orgasmic sensation exploded in me, I fought to keep my identity, but could not win by fighting.  Only release and surrender could possibly be my way out, my way to survive, the only way to maybe remain a person of volition who even knew his own name.

As Aria let herself go completely, it felt like the Great Goddess of Creation had come to settle the massiveness of all femininity upon the meekness of my little bones.  And I indeed became completely lost to the extreme all-encompassing love-smother – and then the Clear Light came searing through brighter than before.  It opened me, letting all of Aria's, of the Triplet's phenomenal potential flood through.  It saved me as it transformed me all at once.  I would survive, and still be me – actually be the real me I had always been but could not see before.

Aria tried to speak coherently as she reached orgasm, her voice rising. "We… love… you… so… much…" Her sentence rose on up to a scream.  Her shaking palsied me from every which way.  I felt my body being deliciously tossed around in a wave pool that launched a thousand high-speed breakers from all sides, all at once.   Oh, Aria, Goddess come to life, I love you too.

Together we fully breached the boundaries between the Universes.  A timelessness settled around our orgasmic ecstasy.  Pavie straddled Aria's lap, her tits into Aria's face.  I could still see up through both sets of spread legs to witness Callie climb on top to straddle Pavie.  Then Aria closed her legs together and all became darkness – yet no amount of triple smother could keep the Light from still coming in.

It felt like they sat on me and orgasmed continuously for an hour.  Under their 5,400 pound wiggling, pounding, vibrating squish I could not hope to breathe the entire time.  Yet once again I survived just fine.  I reveled at Orgasm as a Virtue, one of our best tributes to the Light Universe.  I had to speak about this….

I felt the weight on me lessen, then lessen again.  Finally Aria climbed off; thoroughly satisfied would be the understatement of the century.  "Good God, thank you Richie!  We've got to get everyone to experience this."  Off the bed she ran to the balcony rails and called down. "Donna, Jeanie, Amanda, you've got to come up here and have sex with our husband as soon as you can.  Don't bother with breakfast first.  Let everyone know.  Our husband has found another Universe and will take your there."

Though physically ravaged, I still kept up the Speaking. "Orgasm is a Virtue and a tribute to the Light Universe.  Death was only a backup plan as a way to return to the Light Universe.  Orgasm, as originally practiced, could be seen as souls launching souls back to the Light from whence they came."  I looked around, "I hope someone is writing this down."

"Don't worry," Callie remained on the edge of the bed. "I remember verbatim everything you have said this morning.  And I'll stay right with you as long as this miracle continues."

"Thank you, Callie, you are a blessing.  Yes, we are all blessings.  Acknowledge each other as such.  Build this back into your language.  For over the eons our languages, our words have gathered little lies, a mindless entrance of shadow.  Speak from your hearts, dear ones.  Another habit to develop.  Start with fun blessings, for words were never meant to be heavy, nor have any mass at all.  But our creative considerations descended into the Physical Universe, fluttering down like falling leaves, separated from Light-tree-source, gathering into humus and losing their highest meanings."

Donna had climbed up the drain chain and scaled over the railing. Aria guided her to the bed and gestured for her to mount me.

"Good morning Richie. I heard you have something for me."

"Yes, beautiful Donna, I am here to serve you now." And I let the Clear Light flow through me, the channel so open and free, seasoned with ripples of Sparkle-fire.

Donna's eyes widened, startled by the sizzle of the sensation, and amazed at her sudden view of the Bright Universe. "Oh my word, Richie!"

"Exactly, Donna, who I have loved for so many, many years. Words… words. Let our words be like the leaves attached to the tree, not separated and fallen, but growing, expanding, greening and unfolding with new life, juiced up from the branch and root."

"Oh-God-oh-God" Donna pulled at her own hair. You see, while the Triplets lived in a state of consciousness that encountered and worked with Source, and were kind of used to being near the Light, well, for Donna the experience came as quite unique and shockingly powerful. It seemed overwhelming, but really only in the sense of too much unexpected peace and comfort so suddenly – all at the same time as receiving an orgasm of searing Light delivered from another universe.

As Donna thrashed around on me, bouncing her now 1,150 pound ass on my passive little body, I shivered out more orgasmic blue flames and just kept on talking. "We can abandon Fundamentalism in all its forms. As you truly hear this message, just walk away from your old and heavy religions, so full of lies from sad and misguided manipulators. You will know what to do as the Clear Light sees you and bathes you clean."

Donna rolled off me, a new light in her eyes. She left the veranda saying "I will make sure everyone knows to come be in this miracle."

I heard Amanda asking, "Is this safe for the baby?"

Pavie answered. "Oh my goodness absolutely. Your child will be of Clear Light. Oh, what a glorious finish to your pregnancy."

"Well, then let me at him."

I greeted her. "Good morning wonderful Amanda.  Thank you for being my wife."

Normally Amanda would have plunged her so gorgeous massive ass right on my face first thing.  But she understood to let me keep talking. However, she did ride my Volunteer backward.  I would have to gaze up at her spectacular backside as it squished me so thoroughly and lovingly.  My Volunteer continued with its fountain of Sparkle, up, up, up into Amanda's pussy.  The great and lovely crack of Amanda's ass pushed all the way across my body and my face barely found room to see out from her butt cleavage.

And so I continued to speak as best I could. "There is no authority of Spirit, no one of us closer to God or Source.  For what hierarchy can exist where there is no distance?  Who can claim superior experience when there is nothing that is experiencing time?  Who has more knowledge when we all are connected to all knowledge?  And that connection to knowledge is a pure and present creative consideration that is sustaining our ongoing existence."

I witnessed the Light flooding up through Amanda's body, into her womb and into my child within her.  I saw my child's soul like a happy smile.  She had already been waiting for me to see her brightness in the Light.  I felt glad to know she would be born into the magnificent Brightness she already knew and lived.

And while I communed with the unborn, Amanda rocked her own world with an orgasm beyond sexual to the Bright Universe as was always intended for the greatest sexual experience.  Seeing Amanda soaring I could see an example of what I had just spoken about: Orgasm for what it was originally intended, souls helping souls gain their way back to the Bright Universe.  At the same time, the vestigial physical event we called "orgasm" also had an original intent to open the door with ecstasy for the newly entering soul.  If Greenfield's Religion has any ceremonies at all, this would have to be one of them.

And so, I described as much.  My words probably occasionally muffled a little by Amanda's benevolent ass-smashing. She tried as kindly as she could to assimilate her new reality while rather completely losing herself to orgasmic splendor munching on me.  Callie assured me she had it all, everything word-for-word that I said whether ass-covered or not.

Janet followed Jeanie, then big Bethany, Bad Jackie, and Jessica.  A line had formed around the big bed.  So many wives came around the bed that the line spiraled out to a second level.  Only the Mammoths were not up on the veranda with us.  In between Coleen and Lorraine I saw Serenity peeking through the columns at the veranda's edge over the patio. So they were there as well, but wisely stayed back.  Likely the veranda could not take all their combined giantess weight.

With the emotional Brandy I tried to be as gentle with the Sparkle as I possibly could. I didn't want her to go into premature labor or something.  Still the big beauty's eyes widened like saucers at first contact. "Oh Jesus, Richie, this is heaven."

"No, it's just little ol' me."  I was always ready with a little levity.

"Don't be too sure about that."  Callie whispered to me, still nearby and rather serious. "You have lived many, many lifetimes, and some of those quite spectacular, like this one is becoming."

Was Callie trying to say I could have been Jesus in a past life?  Of all the unlikelihoods I could imagine that seemed perhaps the most unlikely.  Yet, with the vision of the Light Universe I had a feeling that I might have an idea of what Jesus was looking at much of the time.  And yesterday, my epiphany inside Keisha, wasn't that a kind of Immaculate Conception?  I laughed thinking of that as Brandy brought her legs together over me for a most thorough obliterating squish.

Additional to rhythmic sexual pounding I also experienced a random jerking motion to Brandy's smother of me.  It was because Brandy wept, indeed sobbed for joy, as she proceeded to orgasm like five times in a row on me.  I think I definitely liked and loved her more every time we had sex.  But I didn't have time to think about that.

Legs parted and my words spouted on "…What we know as Virtues in this universe are actual building blocks of existence.  Here Virtues are the energy of our existence.  When they become twisted they become the dark energy of our existence.  It is the infusion of Virtue Light energy that animates everything physical."  I said it, but I barely understood what I was talking about.  Brandy finished, well almost; she scooted forward and snatched a quick facesit with some bonus Sparkle for good measure.  Then she popped off of me.

Next came MaryEllen, and she actually brought me an olallieberry pie, still warm from her early morning industry.  She straddled my legs, leaving enough room between her significant belly and my face to feed me bites of it.  But she also kept scooting forward, irrepressibly drawn to engage sexually with me.  With her belly now against my face, the pie had to be set aside.  It wouldn't have mattered anyway because at the first touch of Sparkle this normally gentlest of wives knocked me back flat and howled like a female wolf in heat.

The Light hit MaryEllen in a particular way.  She had lived her life knowing It was there yet always tangential to It.  It bathed her passions of gardening and cooking and affirming the need for healthy sustenance.  But never had it seared her so directly.  MaryEllen so instantly coupled with that direct connection it released a lifetime of bypassed knowingness of the Divine.  What that meant for me is a really big woman shuttering, writhing, and completely going crazy on my little body.  She actually worked all the way around 360 in her smashing sex.  By the time she completed that circle she had all but mashed me into jam for her next pie.  Wow, MaryEllen, I had no idea – she nearly made me lose my train of thought – but not quite.

"We are fed of Spirit.  All that is, no matter how juicy and delicious and stimulating or even delightfully smothering, all comes of Spirit.  All is consideration both as created and sustained.  Thus we are the drama of our own creation."  For a moment I could not talk.  For MaryEllen blubbered me flat, and kissed my entire face open-mouthed and salivating with sweet berry pie breath.  Yes, I almost forgot about the Light Universe because the Universe of Squishing Pie-woman felt so good and all-consuming.

But MaryEllen's turn was over for now and she rolled off me.  I inhaled deeply, with a new thought. "We yielded to this Physical Universe.  We made a playground of such delights that we forgot where we came from.  That was part of the design, though, such pleasures, such intensity, even the challenge of life and death.  We made it so real we even made it painful to leave…"

I talked right through making love to Kathy and Francine.  Bikini clad Sandy and Silvia could not distract me from the current topic.  Each woman gasped in shock then shivered and writhed in delight and joy. My firm fountain of Light just continued to deliver without the least bit of waver.

"… Now comes the time to integrate our universes.  We have been living in both. We can live in one."  And right then a Goddess Angel appeared over me – Vicky. And then another – Valerie.

The Light magnified their beauty ten-fold, a hundred-fold.  Cheek-to-cheek above me their combined and embellished beauty melted my being and boundaries.

"Oh look at his dreamy eyes."  The shimmering Vicky said to the iridescent Valerie.

"What's happened to him?  He's… like glowing." Valerie looked at me approvingly.

"I think it's sexy."  Vicky never failed to turn me on.  And since I was almost always turned on, let's say she never failed to rev me up several notches more.

"Glowing is our natural state of being."  I think I was still channeling, but I felt so completely distracted by their extreme sexy beauty I really didn't know exactly where I was connected.

"Would you be willing to light up my pussy with that glow?" Valerie moved up to press her knees together on the bed above my head, and thus the backs of her gorgeous thighs also pressed together all the way back to her heavenly pussy and gigantic ass right above my face.

Glancing down my body I felt and saw Vicky playing with my Volunteer.  She leaned down to look at me under Valerie's ass.  Our eyes locked for a second.  She smiled, "Do you mind if I sit on this, dear husband?  It is looking most interesting today; and maybe a little bigger than usual."  She positioned above me and I could feel her heat and Valerie's as well.  If I had been metering out the Light to any degree before, that limit would now yield to open up full force.

Vicky tapped Valerie on the shoulder.  "OK, looks like he's ready…"

Then this duo of spectacular delights dropped those two terrific pussies on my little blue flames of Sparkle-channeling-Light.  Valerie's pussy of perfection spread over my face and upper body, my arms pinned to the mattress by her great big wonderful ass.  Simultaneously, Vicky wiggled down on my Volunteer, her pussy gobbling up my lower body entirely.  Even with all my experiences I do not think I had ever been quite that turned on.  Whether it was the Light or the new elixir or just seeing then extreme magnificence of Vicky and Valerie so completely revealed – I don't know, probably all three.

It was like mixing hydrogen and oxygen gas and tossing in a match.  It was ripping the San Andreas Fault like it was a dotted line and seeing how many volcanos would go off at once.  It was absolutely a collision of two Universes becoming coincident with each other all through the tiny portal of my body; as the two big dominating splendors that rode and squished their miniscule husband, blasted pile-driving orgasms down into me and through my plundered body.

Though Valerie and Vicky had devastated and compressed my body helplessly flat, and by all rights I should have been smothered unconscious; I seemed connected to a source of power that could not be snuffed out or stopped.  I mumbled on, clear enough. "Humility is an energy.  It is not weak or timid.  It is a strength of knowing truly who you are in the reality of your soul.  Patience is not static…" I just kept on channeling from Source.

Valerie, lay on her side, looking over her shoulder at me, her huge hip still a significant threat to roll back down for further smother, "Amazing, Vicky, by far the best facesit of all time.  That Light he channels is so real it makes everything else seem rather imagined.  And after all that he still has more to say.  Why, he's practically impossible to shut up."

Vicky came up beside and sat on my chest, just barely letting my face peek out from under her ass. "This should shut him up.  He can't breathe if I sit my big sexy ass on him like this – especially if I bounce a little the way he likes it.  But you know, Valerie, I think he's right about these Virtues.  I want to hear what else he has to say." Vicky slid off to let me breath in – which I did not need to survive but I did need to speak.

The two angelic Goddesses looked at me expectantly.  I suddenly recognized them from another lifetime.  I doubted they recalled it, but I could see them now, Titan Giantess as tall as mountains, worshipped by all.  In that lifetime I had been a sacrifice.  And they had actually eaten me alive.  I chose not to share that with them – they would recall on their own if that was the will of the Divine.  Instead I said, kind of going off script, "You know, practically anything we can imagine is possible.  We are coming to a time when imagination will be our only limitation."

"Well," Vicky leaned right above me, her tits so wonderfully spectacular it was almost painful to see them and not touch them – and she definitely knew it. "… my imagination seems rather unlimited, especially when it comes to ways to smother you with sex."

"What about the time we were Giantess Goddesses and all worshipped us?" Valerie spooked me bringing up this topic I had just been privately considering.

"Oh yeah," Vicky tapped the side of her head. "Like we were talking about in bed last week – that would be fun to do again.  Only this time we won't actually eat Richie."

"Or maybe something new…" I suggested.

"Oh, I know, I know."  Valerie sat up excited to look at Vicky's face up close – of course pinning most of my body under her butt again.  "Here's my fantasy.  It's like the 1950's out in suburban America.  And you and I are like, famous sexy amazons movie stars."

"You mean, in these same marvelous sexy bodies?" It's not exactly boasting if it is so obviously true.

"Yes. Yes, more or less." It seemed Valerie had thought about this a lot. "So little Richie is like some little plumber or something living out in the Burbs and he wins like this lottery. Instead of prize money he gets to choose to have a date with us. Of course, we are just doing it all for charity."

"Of course." Vicky chimed in. "Only, when we meet him we both fall in love with him."

"And then you have a big fight over me." I jumped in when I shouldn't have.

"No!" They said in unison. Vicky actually paused a moment to tit-whip me for my insolence.

"Of course we would never fight." Valerie looked scornfully at me. "No, we decide to leave Hollywood, move in with you, and become your big dominate housewives. We would face-fuck you night and day. Sit on you whenever we wanted."

Vicky jumped in. "Oh, yes, like out in public, too. We could keep him on a leash – oh, but probably not. But we could use him for furniture. Like we're out in a park and need a place to sit. Our little servant could scrunch down and be like a little foot-stool to sit on. Of course we would just sit on him until he flattened all the way out into like a little picnic blanket."

"And we could squishy sit, sit, sit on him while we eat our picnic. Getting bigger and heavier all the time while he is completely helpless kissing for mercy up into our gigantic wifely asses." Valerie certainly seemed on board.

"Could we actually do that, I mean, since we can imagine it?" Vicky looked quite hopeful.

"Yes, I believe so." And I really believed it. "Why don't we get together and try that soon?"

The two of them looked to each other and then nodded enthusiastically back to me, "Yes, we are definitely game for that." Satisfied, they scooted off the bed, still chatting up a storm of ideas for future realities.

For the next several wives I could hardly think straight. I spoke, I channeled Light and fired Sparkle up into each. But I would have to refer to Callie's transcription to have any idea what I did or said next.  And soon enough only one more wife remained.

Saint Debbie heaved her giantess pregnant body onto the bed.  She crawled over to position above me, her massive full breasts and big belly hanging almost to the mattress.  As I prepared to present the Clear Light to Debbie I could see clearly and finally understood she already existed there and had been waiting for me the entire time since I had known her.  She gently covered my body completely, sitting on me stern to stem, taking in my Volunteer for sex, while her sweet ass wiggled around, over, and down on my face and head.  I nevertheless kept on with the speaking.  My connection to Saint Debbie became so complete in this conjoining smother, my words were taken up by her and she spoke them for me for all the gathered wives to hear.

"I recall when I was a mere boy of seven years old.  My dear frail mother rubbed my back as I snuggled under the covers for the night.  She never said much about religion or any of it.  But if she had anything resembling a mantra, something she might have said to me some dozens of times in my childhood is was this: 'God is Love'.  That was her very simple religion.  And you know what? I have to say she had it right."

Debbie's smother was so complete I could not hope to breathe or move.  But my sweetheart Saint of a wife combined her Tingle with my Sparkle and Clear light so that I could pass my thoughts directly to her.  Thus I became so owned and respected by Debbie at once, that I existed through this giantess wife that sat on me, had sex with me, devoured, and absorbed me all at the same time.  And while every pleasure that could be had was fully experienced, my soul merely bathed in the Light.

"I leave you with no rules for this religion, just love and more love as guidance.  Each person can dream up Virtues.  There are so many, and many more yet to be imagined, and that's the beauty of it.  As you pursue them, the only advice I offer is to pursue them with Honesty and Love."

As I looked into Debbie I saw another light, the child that would be born soon: a boy.  "The only boy," Debbie had tracked my thoughts. "For only through our connection and your infusion into my metamorphosis, do we have the correct chromosome paring to make a boy.  Every other amazon has an extra piece of chromosome that cannot pair with a normal man.  Thus they can only have female children that are a copy of themselves."  Under any circumstance this would have been too technical for me.  As I tried to understand, Saint Debbie went on to convey something really quite strange. "Therefore, Richie, your son will not actually be related to your daughters."

A boy, a son, a soul I recognized from my youth.  "Dear Saint Debbie.  I know this child coming from you."  The happiness I felt seemed bigger than both the Universes combined.  And I could see right then the multiplying effect of creating and combining universes – and why we probably did that in the first place.

Saint Debbie replied to me.  "Of course you know this child; he's someone very special to you."

Now I wept under the colossal loving crush of this perfect wife, for I had seen the soul of my dear ol' departed Great Uncle Rob, bright, new, and ready to return for a glorious lifetime….

But I could not tarry with that realization.  Still the need to continue with my channeling kept pressing on, for I was near to finish.  I guess it wasn't really channeling anymore, for now I truly existed in both Universes, and there was nothing remote about the closeness I felt for my wives with the Light in my heart.

Saint Debbie still sat on me, completely enveloping me in her ass, absorbing my body and my thoughts, and speaking to my wives for me. "Know I love you.  Feel it in your hearts, my dears.  Weep for any little separation caused by past darkness. We must Grieve as a Virtue and thoroughly, for our cleansing, for the purity and closeness of our connection.  Weep and let your tears rain down on me.  I will drink them into my soul, and they shall rise as wisdom.  Such is our purpose here, for in our battles in the realm of Shadow we have yielded up into our higher selves new knowledge not even known in the Clear Light Universe.  Yes, my wonderful wives, we of the mean streets of the Physical Universe have much to contribute."

Saint Debbie of the Smothering Perfection rose off me and stood to the side of the bed with the others.  I sat up, the Speaking had ended.  I looked around and indeed all my wives wept pure and joyous.  They looked upon me with way too much wonder, for as ever, I thought, I am just a simple little man, and not too bright at that.


I rolled over and over, playfully, and then off the bed.  They parted quietly as I walked forward.  Callie lifted me back to sitting on the veranda's high railing.  And clambering to my feet I stood.  Just behind and slightly down from me off the veranda, the bright smiling faces of my four giantess wives happily completed my theater in the round.  The Mammoths already knew from our earlier experience what had just transpired.

I breathed in the sunshine and let the Clear Light bathe me, combining in me, lifting me.  I looked down, and my feet weren't touching the railing anymore.  It seemed I floated a few inches above it.  These beautiful women were so full of the Divine Light that my little miracle of levitation did not seem to astound them in the least.  I smiled and felt a great welling in my heart.  And so I sang to my wives and to the Universes:

> *There are many kinds of love I've been told.*
> *But I say look up at all the stars to behold.*
> *From one-to-one that space is filled with love, don't you see?*
> *That's exactly how it is between you and me.*
>
> *More than once I've been told, you can't have all your dreams.*
> *But I say no; it's the world that's not what it seems.*
> *What we know, what we dream, what we feel, what will be;*
> *Is the Light, is a song, is our souls soaring free.*

I heard a rustling amongst the rapture of my wives.  They parted and Lorraine, Francine, Lorna, and Kathy stepped forward, up to me and almost the same height where I stood on the railing.  Lorna handed me a medium sized package, a present wrapped with a bow.  "My roommates and I made something for you, sturdy and strong, tested and sure, ready for you now, and an expression of what you do for all of us."

I took the package and looked all around at the beaming, loving faces of all thirty of my wives.  They each seemed to be already clued in on the contents, smiling with anticipation. I felt so much gratitude already; I could not imagine what additional joy any gift could bring.

I'd settled back down on the railing again.  There I tugged the bow loose, let the ribbon fall away, and lifted the flimsy lid.  Inside the morning sun revealed a bright glittery blue garment.  I held it up and it unfolded to some kind of body suit, likely it seemed a perfect fit for me.  The material felt extremely light but I could tell the weave and fabric to be very sturdy, just like Lorna said.

What was it?  It seemed strange; full of a wild energy.  I started to feel an excitement about it.  It sparkled too much, impossible to look at without getting little reflective zaps of sunlight in my eyes.  Was it a costume for ceremony or event?  It has odd floppy flanges on its sides, and more webbing between the legs.

"Try it on." Francine encouraged.

So I slid one leg then another into the silky slick legs.  I felt like I was putting on zoot-suit kid's pajamas.  I slipped in my arms then zipped up the front, being very careful past my subsiding Volunteer.  The suit fit very snugly, stretchy.  I kind of flopped my arms, the loose extra material wavering at my side.  "What is this for, a play, new PJs?"

That got a good laugh.

"No, silly."  Lorna Plucked me off the railing then tossed me over the side, hollering.  "It's for you to fly!"

"What!"  But before I could flip out too much from being cast over the edge, Serenity caught me.

Keisha nudged up beside her former Queen. "Oh please let me do it.  I'm feeling really extra strong today."

Serenity handed me to Keisha. "Certainly, you should have this honor, my sister-wife in whom both Universes met so beautifully. Your Immaculate Conception of our dear husband quite possibly inspired him to his religion." She chuckled with very good nature at her own sentient levity.

Keisha stretched up a tiny bit and kissed Serenity on the cheek.  Then looking down at me in her hand asked. "You ready?"

"Ready for what?" I still didn't get it.

"To fly.  And you better figure it out fast."  With that Keisha reared back and launched me up at like 300 miles per hour.  Practically straight up I rocketed, ears popping, my suit's side flaps fluttering like a tissue on a moving car's antennae.  I must have zoomed a mile up, the great lawn below looking like a relatively small rectangle in the grand view I had of Bluebelle Valley.  As I slowed I saw my wives like little dots, running and scattering around on the lawn's expanse like busy ants.  What were they… oh boy, preparing to catch me when I fell?

I fluttered to a very high stop then just as I began to fall, I stopped, floating it seemed.  I knew immediately that the rules of the Universe had changed.  Not changed but combined with rules from another universe.  The wind at some 5,000 feet above the valley floor blew fairly strong but steady.  Up and out with my arms and the webbing caught the wind.  With that I let myself drop, cut sideways in a slight spin.  The spinning shot my legs out, and with the expanded webbing I caught more wind and stabilized.  I began soaring at a slight angle down from horizontal.  I was flying.

My body, so lean and strong for its weight, proved plenty sure enough to handle the suit's requirements.  And it all seemed so intuitive.  I felt an updraft rising in the morning sun.  In that I curved up, in a lazy spiral, mixing in levitation when needed.  Then I dove, gravity a wonderful force, especially when an option.  Picking up speed quickly, I pulled out and shot myself far off the property high above the entrance to Bluebelle Estates and the nearby Highway 19.

Off to the west and across to the east, the wide and lazy Bluebelle River made its meandering way through the middle of the valley.  Tall and fully-summer-green trees lined its banks, well-watered and healthy.  Trees also bordered many of the valley's agricultural fields in approximate rectangles as well as irregular shapes.  Though this season the fields looked ignored, and the natural meadows showed their intensions of moving back in.  Above, not a cloud could be found; only a line of rain coming from far, far off to the northwest.  But otherwise clear, not even a jet's contrail – but then we hadn't seen one of those since last fall.  Yep, nothing but clean air as far as the eye could see.  What a beautiful planet!

I looked down into the valley again.  As had been the case for the past nine months there were still no vehicles on the roads either – just empty streets and highways gathering dust, getting weedy in their cracks.  But what was that in the distance?   I shot out that way, zipping down at twenty degrees and maybe sixty miles per hour.

It looked like the entire road moved.  No, not the road itself; it was some kind of herd.  Not a heard – it was people.  I could see now, yes people, many hundreds of them.  I swept in closer.  No, not just people – the coming mob consisted entirely of women; beautiful women of what you might call child-bearing age.  They marched along, all heights and sizes, a few almost normal-sized, the preponderance gorgeous amazons, and still others Mammoth sized, and few incredibly even larger.  What the heck?

I curved over their heads like Rocky the flying squirrel.  I heard the exclamations and cries out from below.  They all paused and looked up at me, many pointing.  I arced and turned, flying very fast back toward the Segal mansion.  I looked over my shoulder to see they all were running now, down the highway and following after me.

Back over the Estates, lower and lower, still very fast.  Now I had to swerve around some of the taller trees.  Just ahead: the Segal Estate and home.  I had just enough height purchase left to curve around the mansion and come about back to the veranda.  Too fast, of course, but Saint Debbie caught me and spun me deftly to the bed with a soft bounce off to standing on the veranda.

Amid cries of, "How was it Richie?" and "What was it like?" and "Did you have fun?" I hurried past their forest of legs and found the Triplets sitting on the edge of the bed together, calm, and waiting for me.

I stammered out. "There's… there's like, I don't know, maybe a thousand women coming down the highway.  They started running toward the Estates when they saw me fly over and back this way."

That quieted the wives, except that Aria, Callie, and Pavie laughed and could hardly stop.

Catching her breath, Aria leaned way down to me, took my face in her hands, kissed me full on my mouth, released the kiss, and then slowly shook her head back and forth, her eyes intense, feigning sympathy at the edges, yet wry with her provoking idea of humor. "Ah, Richie, you poor, poor dear.  It looks like it's time for you to shine your Light and heat up your Sparkle. You could quite possibly be the last man on Earth."  Aria stayed close and steady with her penetrating stare, like after all this time I was still being tested.

I digested her astounding proclamation for a moment.  But I just couldn't let the teasing part of what Aria said stand unchallenged in front of all my wives. "Well, I guess it's a good thing we have so many empty mansions in the neighborhood. They'll need a place to stay, now won't they?"

Aria shrugged and waited; knowing I couldn't resist saying more.

I suppose I should have levitated out of reach.  Or maybe, just for once, not have said the next thing that came to mind.  But just because I had cracked through the illusion of this universe and seen the bright face of God, didn't mean I'd pass up a perfect chance infuriate my wives into a good and angry state of excitement.  I mean, what the heck; why change now?  I reached up to Aria's face, still beautifully close to mine, pinched her cheek and added, "Besides, those places are a holy mess.  We need to get some *women* in there to clean them up."

Oh yes, Richie, nice one.  That right fine chauvinistic slander managed to get every one of my thirty amazon wives deliciously cross at me all at once.  And surrounded as I was there would be not be the least hope of an escape.  Ah well, hip, hip, cheerio my friend!  Impeccable, really, I should say, for a smashing good time.

***

Thank you, dear reader.  I hope you enjoyed all nineteen episodes of Amazons of Bluebelle Valley in the good fun as they were intended.  As Richie said, "we are only limited by our imaginations", so please look for more stories from our friend R.B. Greenfield.


Please proceed now to the bonus Episode "Amazons in the Burbs", the beginning of the next series "Bluebelle Giantess Fancies".  I think you are going to love this extra big story.


***

2953

# XX. Epilog Episode:

# "Bluebelle Giantess Fancies" Series

# I. Amazons in the Burbs

A hammock has always been a bad bet for me.  I am more than fifty percent likely to spaz my way onto the ground every time I try to mount one.  Yeah, I know; moi, the one and only Richie Greenfield, I'm practically Tarzan in the trees.  But in a hammock I'm the clumsiest spider of all time.

Valerie, however, ass-pressing me down against the mesh is a completely different stabilizing matter.  Her ballast seemed intent on processing me right on through the stretched cord diamonds of the hammock.  I couldn't take it anymore and had to tap out.

Valerie was off me in like half a second.  "What's the matter Richie, not feeling like being squished today?"

Of course the hammock tipped after Valerie got out, and I ended up on the soft grass below.  I smiled up at my beatific goddess, "Oh, Babe, you know as long as I have a body you'll have a place to rest your ass."

"Oh goodie."  Ready and more than willing, my supremely beautiful and exponentially sexy wife Valerie kneeled over me.

I rubbed over my sore shoulder, "It's just that your concerted press-on-the-mesh was about to divvy me up into a pile of fresh raviolis."

"Oh let me see."  Valerie dropped to all fours above me, huge breasts hanging against the thin lace of her halter top.  She gently turned me onto my stomach.  "Oh yeah, you're rather cross-hatched.  Sorry, Richie."

"Oh, I'll be fine."

"Of course you will.  But still, we have to balance this out to be fair.  This time I'll get in the hammock first and you get to squish me."  Valerie had her mind made up about this and I could tell.  Never mind that, me at 77 skinny pounds and her at 1678 pounds of voluptuous breathtaking wonder, it made no sense.

After she put her ginormous perfect butt in the middle then stretched out her almost thirteen foot frame, she beckoned for me.  "Come on, hubby.  Lie on top of me and kiss me."

Not really waiting for me to respond, Valerie hoisted me up and positioned me stomach-down between the significant valley of her breasts.  My arms locked straight down to either side of her neck, hands gripping the mesh rope below, positioned my face barely above hers.  The slightest lift of her head brought her lips to mine.  And we kissed – well, I kissed, she devoured for good long twenty minutes.  Finally, I needed a break and curled to lie my head down under her chin and against her neck.

Valerie's voice rather boomed in my ear.  "Hey Vicky, come on down.  You can't stay way up in the tree all day."

"I'm bored."  Vicky called down.

"Boring is as boring does."  Valerie lilted back.  "Descend dear sister-wife.  Let's make a yummy Richie sandwich."

"Well, at least that sounds like fun.  I'll be right there."

Of course Vicky wasn't really that high up in the tree.  Only the biggest branches could take her weight.  In like thirty seconds later Vicky's super sensuous body spread out over mine.  The sandwich locked my body between their breasts, my head between their necks and under their chins.  I knew somehow, some way this nice affectionate beginning would lead to sex.  Perfect, I thought to myself, took a nice deep breath, and relaxed into whatever would happen next.

"Richie," Vicky used her sweetest seductive voice.  And I knew I was, without a doubt, about to say yes to some request.  "Let's do that reality shift you talked about a while back.  What I'm thinking I want to do is Valerie's fantasy life in the old time suburbs and really be there and feel it."

"Well, I'm guessing you mean like way, way back in the 1950's.  You too, Valerie?" I spoke and kind of kissed her neck at the same time.

"Oh God, yes."  I could feel her excitement as core tension below me. "How long will it take?"

"I'm not really sure.  Here: maybe only a very short time, or maybe no time.  There: it could be months or years.  I guess it depends on what we want.

"I want like three months, then longer if I feel like it." Vicky wiggled on me with convincing enthusiasm.

"That sounds long enough." Valerie agreed.

"OK, dolls.  But realize, if the drama gets too intense we might bounce out.  Ready then?  Right, let's get started.  Close your eyes and take deep breaths."

After a several deep breaths Valerie asked, "Does the breathing help relax us to get us prepared or on the way there?"

"No, not really."  I replied.  "I just really like it when you breathe deeply and your gorgeous big tits press all around me."

"Oh you…" Valerie lip-pressed a little swath of my hair and gave it a sharp tug.

"Here's the thing." I got more serious. "Keep your eyes closed.  Focus on the fantasy as if you are looking into a dream.  At the same time let the Light flow through you.  In your heart feel the extraordinary amount of love we have for each other."

After less than three minutes, Vicky seemed impatient. "It's not working."

"Well of course not…" I turned my head to kiss Vicky's neck.  "We have to do what I said, but during simultaneous orgasm.  It's the intensity of Orgasm Virtue that launches to the new reality."

"Oh, orgasm… that's the easy part." Vicky rolled to the side, tipped the hammock and we all three dropped out: Vicky on the bottom, me in the middle, and Valerie crushing down in a heavy slam. "Come on Valerie," Vicky bench-pressed Valerie up from the bottom of our little stack. "You know the drill."

They undid the sandwich the rest of the way and let me fall onto the grass. Valerie's nice body slam already had me up and hard.  Me already on my back, it took the easiest of yanks on my loose shorts for Vicky to render me nude and ready. Vicky pussy-jumped my Volunteer and bent her knees up, feet flat on the grass, her ass and crotch pinning me immobile under her 1639-pound straddle. Valerie slipped her legs under Vicky's bent knees.  Then Valerie brought her perfect pussy on up to cover my face.

The two of them ground their wet pussies down on me just the way they knew I liked it – wiggling, squeezing, with crushing little bounces, followed by vibrational plundering.  I felt my sexual release would be in less than two minutes.

My blue flames of Sparkle roared at the chance to connect universes through orgasm.  Above me, no doubt about it in my mind, Vicky and Valerie made out with some nice deep French kissing – or, maybe it was tit-sucking and kissing.  Of course face-obliterated by pussy as I was, I could not be sure what they did up there with their sexy lips and heavy racks of breasts.  Whatever it was, it certainly went on beyond my control, crushed flat by some 3,300 pounds of leading-lady beauty.

I imagined the 1950's scene like a vivid dream.  I could see Valerie and Vicky, much larger than life; movie star faces up on an old style billboard advertisement.  It shouldn't have been possible but they winked at me.  Then I witnessed a flood of Light coming in from the distance, at first a bright glow around the billboard.  The Light intensified and came blasting through the billboard, opening it up to leave only edges, like a giant window.

Through the billboard frame I could see a neighborhood of tract housing, pastel stucco homes, like different pale versions of the same color.  In each front yard, one mature ash tree invited a respite of welcome shade over a well-watered and manicured lawn.  Sleepy, quite streets belied the frenzied life for those commuting a mile away on the busy freeway.  Framed by dry golden hills, this pleasant enough little town looked fully civilized, in contrast to the cougar-wild, rather high distant mountains that surrounded and embraced the valley.

A great energy, an electric wind, rushed around me, feeling so warm, vibrant, and sizzling with vigor.  The sudden Zephyr picked me up and without ceremony shot me through the billboard window.  As I passed to the other side, I felt body-less, definitely weightless, with no particular identity as a reference point.  It could have been frightening, but not to me.  To me, whoever I was, it felt peaceful, like one might feel being carried along by the hand of God.

And there ahead, sleeping in his open work van, surrounded by bins of pipe fittings, greasy tool chests and half-open drawers of plumbing paraphernalia, and knee-high rubber boots and dog-eared manuals, a tiny, thin-framed handsome man in his thirties dreamed with a silly smile on his face.

A big hairy arm reached in front of the thin, diminutive sleeping man.  A meaty open-fingered gloved-hand pressed onto the van's horn.  "Beeeeep!"

I shuttered rudely awake, almost fell out of my vehicle, and had the passing thought: I was having such a nice dream…

"Hey dick-wad.  Get your shit-wagon out of the alley sos I can pull my trailer on through."  The big man grumped on mumbling, fat-swaggering back to his truck.  "…dumb-ass sleeping in the road…"

"Yep, you bet, right away." I don't remember why exactly, but I tried never to give bullies any good excuse to escalate – made sense though. I strained and stretched out, nabbed the dirty vinyl handle, feeling its sewn seam, like zipper bumps, in my callused little hand. Anchored by a grip on my steering wheel, I leaned out, heave-hoed the handle and pulled my van door shut. I started up the chugging but reliable engine.

Weird – I thought; I wonder why I was sleeping with my door open, my van parked at a diagonal, completely blocking the alley way. I myself hated getting jammed up so I always found a nook for my over-sized plumber's van; that way others could pass. Where the heck was I, anyway?

The van bounced along the alleyway, a few tools clanged to the metal floor. One more big pothole that scattered my collection of nub-pencils and broken chalk on the dash, and I was out on the smooth suburban streets of… Monitor, California. Oh, yeah, of course; I know this avenue…

Another turn got me to Cedar Street. Two blocks of driving slowly, for kids were out in road in the late summer afternoon playing Indian baseball, got me to corner with Oxford Court. Two houses down on the left, I pulled up and parked my van for a well-deserved rest in the driveway after a long day of service. No use opening the garage; it had long since been filled with plumbing supplies.

I opened the van door and slid out, stretching best I could to get my toes to the concrete. Ah, solid ground. Better check my mailbox by the street. I ambled down to the sidewalk. At my mailbox I reached up and pulled the hinged metal front down ninety degrees to flat open. Up on my tip toes I peered in. I gathered the scraps of mail, but crap, there was a postcard way at the back. I hated it when I had to go get the step stool just to empty my mailbox. I should have a lower box, more fitting to my 3'10" stature. But you know these mailboxes had to be regulation height or no delivery. Really, there ought to be laws to help disadvantaged people, like access for wheelchairs and such. Well, maybe someday….

I was just getting my fingertips on the card when up and behind me I heard a flirtatious sing-song. "Hiya Curtis, this package came for you today."

It could only be my divorced neighbor Ginger Masterson. I withdrew my hand and turned for the obligatory hello and thank you. Supposedly Ginger was a retired showgirl. I looked up at her, standing there, heaven-knows-why, in high heels, her long tan lots-of-time-by-the-pool legs still nicely muscular and well-defined but way too thick and heavy these days for the stage, her big sexy ass bulging out of her short-shorts at my eye level. Ginger's checkered blouse tied in front purposefully did not really restrain her enormous heavy breasts. As she bent over to reach in the mailbox for me, her cleavage rating went from your friendly neighborhood-PG to heavenly-nipple-visible mature-audiences-only.  Could Ginger possibly know the stupefying effect she had on me?

She straightened with the card I could not retrieve, indecorously reading it instead of handing it to me.  I studied her with some annoyance, and trying not to feel so insignificantly small.  Yes she easily had the six foot six height of a really tall showgirl.  Add her 5" platform heels and she had to be towering over me at 6'11".  But the extra two hundred pounds of sexy curves she'd put on since last being the crowning voluptuous centerpiece of a chorus line probably had her up more than seven times my skinny weight of sixty pounds.  I had to admit I really dug her big evocative body.  And for sure she still had a gorgeous face, framed by her big tease of red hair, full sexy lips, and calm green eyes with a bright intelligent look.  But looks can be deceiving.

Was she really that slow a reader or did she just like making me wait?  It was moments like these that I got why her husband left her three years ago and took their boy with him.  I cleared my throat; a bit tired of being ignored while she read my mail.  Of all the incredulous things I should have said what came out was.  "Thank you, Ginger, for holding my package."

I reached up to put my fingers on the brown book bundle – most likely the solar hot-water handbook I had ordered.  She released it into my hand. "Oh, no problem, sugar.  I'm just sitting around all day watching my ass grow fatter."  She laughed absentmindedly, and continued mouthing the words of the postcard.  I was getting annoyed at myself as well for finding her silent lip-reading sexy.

Finally she finished the postcard and handed that to me as well. "It looks like, and provided the darn thing ain't a scam, you have won some contest.  What exactly did you enter?"

I turned the card over in my hand. "They had a drawing at the hardware store.  It was something about a Hollywood charity for disadvantaged kids.  So I gave up a couple bucks for raffle ticket."

"Well, sweetie, if I read that right, you've won yourself a trip to Galatium Studios including a reception after the premier of "Big Babe Bouncing Bonanza.""

I felt some distain and a definite lack of enthusiasm for going to some big dumb social gathering. "I don't have time for any Hollywood party."

"Whoa, whoa, there little chief.  This isn't just 'any' Hollywood party.  Take it from me; I used to run in those circles.  And these Big Babe movies are the rage these days, hugely successful.  They're a hoot-and-a-half; have you seen one?  Funnier than heck, but darn good adventures, and sexy as all get-out – that is, if you happen to like Big Babes." Ginger eyed me with interest. "Do you like big babes, don't you?"

A bit mortified, I wouldn't dare comment on her last question.

I tried to shut down the conversation. "Well I'm not interested looking at everyone's' butts in my face at a phony-baloney party – and that's final."

But Ginger was far from leaving the matter alone. "I going to pretend you're not making me mad with that attitude. You've been sulking around in that house of yours, by yourself; ever sense I moved here five years ago. Possibly your best-ever social chance ever comes along, and you just want to crawl in your shell and die. That's it, buddy. You're coming with me right now." With that Ginger picked me up and with her long strides headed toward her front door. "We are going to celebrate your good fortune while I use all my womanly wiles to talk you into going to that party for you own good."

Ginger opened her not-quite-shuttable screen door with her left foot. Once inside she butt slammed the front door closed. She carried me to her back living room and sat me down on a plastic-covered couch. As soon as she released me I jumped up to clear the heck out of there. Ginger, anticipating, grabbed me and shoved me back to the couch. Before I could right myself, down came her big ass and sat squarely on my lap. She crushed me way down into the plastic like I was being shrink-wrapped.

Good god she was heavy. For sure for years I had fantasized about this big luscious neighbor, but I had no idea it would feel this incredibly good and exciting. I'd actually never been with any kind of woman. Of course instantly she had me fully hard.

And she seemed to have no idea. "Now how are we going to celebrate? You like to drink? No what am I saying. You're too much of a role model for those kids' sports teams your business sponsors. Yes, if you're wanting to know, I have been keeping tabs on you. Like all that plumbing work you did for free at the seniors rehab center – Mr. Nice Guy."

I couldn't speak to answer. Honestly, it seemed like some kind of praise being doled out kindly, but what Ginger said wasn't really registering with me. I just wanted to kiss her on her big sexy lower back.

"No then. Well, I don't really want any booze either – hey, we could watch some TV, but that sounds kind of boring, unless there's really good movie on. Shall we check the channels?"

Ass-smashed and mute, I still could find no words.  I breathed in delicious body-lotion scent, getting delirious with excitement under her crushing weight.  My entire lower body just disappeared under her short-shorts, her ass bulging out everywhere.  Ginger up close turned out to be much larger and heavier than I had imagined.  I just wanted to keel over and let her ass cover me completely.

"Hey, let's order a pizza.  I just realized I'm starving.  You hungry?  That your problem, squirt?  Hey!"  Now Ginger bounced on me.  "I'm talking to you.  You got to give some input into this celebration."

I couldn't help it any longer.  I reached around her waist, really my arms barely embracing to the upper sides of her hips.  At the same time I kissed her exposed lower mid-back.

"Oh…"  A light coming on, Ginger paused then bounced a bit more vigorously.  "You little rascal.  Now that I think about it, that actually is exactly the kind of celebration I was hoping for."

I kept on kissing her now and could not stop.  Ginger reached through her legs and pinned my skinny thighs.  Holding me in place, she rocked and kind of walked her buns up into my non-stop kissing.

"That's the neighborly spirit, Curtis"  Ginger squirmed and continued with more confidence to wiggle her ass into my kisses, tugging on my legs enough to pull me out where she could get her hands on my pants and belt buckle.  This, of course, kept dragging my chest and face further underneath her ass.  My arms flopped and fell from their loose embrace, sliding down the couch's seat back, then under her relentless marching ass.  Now her immenseness crushed my chest and soon my face would vanish under her.

"Come on."  She jumped up nabbing my hand and pulling me up as well.  Off she went, dragging me stumbling along behind, my pants falling to around my ankles.  "I've been dreaming about getting my great big hungry ass on your cute little skinny bones for years. This is indeed your lucky day, boy.  Into the den of the tigress you go."  Ginger swung me through her bedroom door.

"You ever even been with a woman before?"  Ginger twirled me onto her big unmade bed.  For some, when you live alone, why bother making you bed?  That wasn't my style; but we're gradually learning to celebrate diversity in this country, right?

"Well, there was Kimberly, but that… er, well, no, not really."  For some reason I tried to hedge about my inexperience.

"You mean 'not ever' is what I'm thinking." Off came her over-stretched tube top and then, unabashedly, her lacy pink bra. Oh my God her tits are so gigantic. Suddenly I also felt afraid of… of being smothered under her breasts… and of my desire for her to show me no mercy. "Stare all you want, Curtis, but get busy taking your undies off."

Since I had no idea what I was doing, I actually appreciated her instructions, her orders. I got busy removing my shirt, then my shoes, and as I tugged off my second sock I looked up to see Ginger squeezing her overly-ample ass out of her tight shorts. She eyed me as she hooked her thumbs on her pink panties.

"I'll take mine off if you take yours off." Ginger teased me because I had stalled out; pausing to try to get my little mind around what her great big butt would do to my body next.

"Sorry." I got busy again; and quickly stripped the rest of the way down to a little nude man on her bed.

"Ah, isn't that nice. You're so cute. Now get ready for this." Ginger ever so slowly but definitely slid her panties down past her vast hips, still needing more help to get past her very thick thighs. With a very sexy bend, Ginger brought her panties to her knees, and they dropped freely to her ankles. She kicked them off.

"Is this what you expected, Curtis?" Ginger gestured at the magnificence of her abundant frame. "Does this meet the fantasies you've been having as you spy on me through the slats in the fence? Oh, yes, I know you've been ogling me for years now. I have a whole collection of skimpy clothes I put on when I know you're in your back yard. That's okay; don't look so guilty. You're just being a man. So now, what do you think?"

"I think you are a lot more, uh, bigger, I mean…are you going to sit on me again?"

"Oh, Curtis, I'm going to do a lot more than just sit on you. Let's just say you're not going to be a virgin much longer. Is that okay with you?"

I nodded. "Yes Ginger. I don't want to be a virgin anymore."

"Well, good, very good." She smiled, kneeling onto the bed, then dropping down to all fours. Her big tits hung to show their maximum size, growing larger as she steadily crept toward me. I had to fall back or be knocked over by her breasts. Flat on my back now, Ginger advanced over me. I felt so afraid and so turned on at the same time.

"I sure hope this isn't too steep of a gradient for you Curtis. I mean, it might have been better if your first time was with some little woman more your wee size. But such is fate – or should I say, such is fat." To me she didn't look that fat; simple gigantic and I thought very shapely.  Ginger laughed and turned herself around above me, being careful enough not to crush me with her knees.  Now she waved her huge nude ass above my face. "See what I mean, Curtis?"

"Yes, you are very beautiful." I stammered out nervously.

"Why, how gallant.  But don't you mean to say 'very big and scary'?  Ah! Don't worry, little lover, flattery will get you everywhere.  And, oh my goodness, aren't you the turned on little hound dog." I guess Ginger was looking down at my erect Member. "Let me say hello properly."

Leaving her massive ass poised above my face, Ginger lowered her upper body, breasts pressing over my chest, and my Member suddenly entered a very nice moist… oh, how nice – it must be her mouth.  What is she doing?  It feels so good.  She easily took my entire Member into her mouth.  Up and down, up and down.  Is this a blow job?  Wow, heavenly.  On the next down, her lips encircled my balls as well.  And she stayed down on me, sucking and working me over, licking my balls and rasping across my erectness.

I didn't know what I was supposed to do.  It didn't matter.  I came.  And while I did, Ginger lowered herself down, smashing my face under her belly and sucking like crazy on my dick.  I tried to kick my legs around, but Ginger wouldn't tolerate that thrashing.  She pinned my legs with firm encircling hands.  In less than another minute she overwhelmed me completely, rendering me spent and without air.

Ginger rose up. "Okie-doe.  You probably don't' know how this works, but basically now it's your turn to service me." On all fours again, Ginger turned around above me.  She sat on my chest, my face looking through the upper vee of her legs at her belly and great big tits swinging as she rocked her ass back and forth on me. "Can you hear me?"

I managed a wheezy "Yes Ginger.  I want to serve you."

"Oh good.  I realize this is a bit tough for you.  I mean me being 440 pounds and you being, I guessing way less than eighty.  So…"  She lifted up a second and I grabbed a deep breath of air. "… that's right, get some air whenever you can and just do your best.  I don't expect much, it being your first time and you not knowing didilly.  Now, I'm gonna' be putting my pussy on your face.  Does that sound good?"

"Yes, it does."

"What you're supposed to do is eat me.  What that means is lick like crazy and get chewy without using your teeth.  And when we get lucky and you happen to find something that I seem to like, well, that's when you work it, boy."

"What do you mean by 'work it'?"  I already began to kiss her inner thigh.

"It could mean being subtle.  It could mean being vigorous.  It could mean being a tease."  Her ass scooted forward and my chin entered her pussy. "You practice often enough, with good attention to detail and you'll be a master someday."

I think she was giving some final advice but I didn't catch it.  Her pool-fresh juicy pussy came on up and completely covered and engulfed my face.  And I had every intention of being a master today.  So I got super busy.

She had told me to use my tongue.  Good, because my tongue was about the only part of my body I could move.  Now I can tell you as the town's smallest plumber I've been in some tight, wet, and hot spaces.  But Lordy, Lordy, never had I experienced anything like the smothering, subduing crush under my neighbor Ginger.  She just kept on moving and shifting around and pounding down again and again using slightly different offerings of her pussy.  Why?  Who knows?  I figured she was just fidgety.

On and on she wiggled around on me, pressing me deeper than I have ever been in a mattress before.  Getting me crushed down in that depression, well that just trapped me more, didn't it?  Then finally I hit something inside her; we connected, you might say.  And then this big babe just kind of went crazy.  I mean I could tell there was something right there against my face, and she pressed it rather violently, rubbing in onto me and especially targeting my mouth.  So I fought back with what I had, lips, tongue and biting "without teeth" I recalled her instructing.

I must have been doing a good job because I'm thinking she really liked it in the extreme.  I mean, you could say all her screaming and thrashing might indicate she was in pain or distress.  But logic said she was certainly in control of the situation; she could have left whenever she wanted.  There wouldn't have been a darn thing I could have done to stop her.  So, she must have wanted to stay in spite of her screaming.

I kept grabbing little breaths of air when she rocked back.  Because when she rocked forward her pussy completely covered my face and head.  Round and round she ground on my face now, building, building, I don't know to what, but it seemed like it was going to be super intense.

Then I heard a chiming sound; a door bell?  No, she paused, slipping back I could hear her talking, she had answered her phone.

"… no don't do that…" I could hear the worry in her voice. "Come on Penelope.  You've got to give the new diet a chance…." Then, "…OK, OK.. Just don't do anything until I get there.  Promise me… OK, I'll be there in thirty minutes."  Ginger put the receiver back on her bedroom phone, then knocked the entire phone off her bed stand.  It buzzed then started beeping on the carpet. "Damn!"

"Damn. Damn. Damn." She climbed off me. I shuttered in a big breath as the mattress slowly lifted me back up.

I started to wonder if maybe I did something wrong. "Everything OK?"

"Hell no!" It seemed she was glaring at me. "Everything is totally NOT OK!"

It scared me to see her angry like this. Ginger stood now, getting dressed again. I slid to the far side of the bed and found my cloths as well. I got my pants on fast, shirt on loose, and shoes on not-at-all as I rather quickly made for the bedroom door.

"I guess I'll be leaving now…" I had turned from outside her bedroom door, out of range for retrieval.

"Okay, Curtis." Ginger seemed distracted as she buttoned her blouse. "I'm sorry I have to go now. My sister is having another crisis." Then she pointed at me. "Darn it, though, I was getting so close and it was going to be mind-blowing."

I wondered what she was talking about.

"But," She added. "That just builds me up for a bigger blast later. I should be back in a few hours, maybe like nine or so. My pussy is gonna smother the life out of you then, if my ass doesn't crush your first." She bent over to retrieve her high heels.

Now I got what she was talking about. I think she meant to be enticing and sexy, and she was, but it mostly also scared the hell out of me. "All righty, then." I sheepishly slipped on down her short hallway to the front door. Once I had the door open I called back, "See ya." Not saying: "Sure, come on over later."

"Bye-ya little lover." Ginger sing-songed, I think as she went into her garage to get into her big baby-blue Cadillac.

I fast-walked across her driveway as her garage door opened. At my front door I looked back to watch her pull out. Ginger tweedled her fingers at me casting a big affectionate smile my way. I think my grin back must have been more of a grimace.

***

Maybe about 9:15 I heard a tap-tap at my front door. What do I mean "maybe about 9:15"? I know it was exactly 9:13pm; I'd been staring at the clock since about 8:30 mortified with terror. I'd also already jerked-off about three times since leaving Ginger's, trying to release some of my overload of sexual tension. But don't worry;

there's always more where that came from.  But did I run to fling the front door open to commence with the most exciting sex I could have ever hoped for?  Hell no!

I tip-toed through my dark house right up to the front door and listened.  Ginger tapped again, a little louder.  I held my breath then had to breathe, but very softly.

"Curtis, Curtis."  I heard her whisper loudly.  "Are you awake?"  She waited.  After a long while all seemed silent.  But I did not hear her go either, or her front door shut.  I carefully got my always handy step stool and set it next to the front door.  I crept up on it to look out the peep hole.  My porch light, set on a timer to be on from 8-10 pm would show my entire front yard.  But I saw none of that.  Oh my God, all I could see was Ginger's big cleavage, brightly lit, chest heaving with each glorious inhale.  I weakened at the sight and had to steady myself against the front door.

"Curtis?"  I heard her voice softly.  "Are you there?  Let me in.  It's a little chilly out here."

I froze.  I just couldn't say or do anything.  I wanted to let her in but just could not have it.  I looked down, my hands trembling with fear.

"Come on now, Curtis.  Don't be afraid of me.  I promise to squish you ever so gently."

I think she meant to sound soothing, but it only sounded like slow death to me.  Glorious, wonderful, everything I'd always dreamed about – but I just could not dare move out of my catatonic state.

I could see Ginger shiver, still wearing her thin blouse and those so-sexy short-shorts, her cold nipples hard through her tight fabric.  She rubbed her arms; her pretty face disappointed in consternation. "Well, I guess some other time, maybe.  But take a good look at what you missing."  Ginger hefted up big massive breasts, right up to center them in front of the peep-hole view.  I covered my mouth to hold in my gasp.

"Nighty-night, Baby."  Ginger turned and walked off my porch.  I watched in desperate longing as her huge ass departed my property.  No, I couldn't stand seeing her go.  She would never want me again.  What a coward I was.  I had to get the door open and call out to her.  But I rushed it, fell off my step stool, and had to scramble up off the floor.  I unlocked the front door but forgot about the high safety latch.  I had to get back on my stool again to undo it.  Then I opened the door, but the bottom of the door caught on the rubber shoe of the step stool.  So I had to slide that out of the way.  Finally I got the damn door open right in time to hear her front door shut.  Ah crap, I kicked the step stool over and hurt my toe.  Feeling guilty about getting angry I righted the step stool then sat on its lower step.  There I bent down, face into my open hands, and proceeded to fill the rest of the way up with disappointment and shame.

***

Is there such a thing as an Incubus?  All I know is some kind of relentless sexy sex-spirit pounded her big ass on my body all night long.  It was a dreary and worn little man that that slunk out to his van early in the morning.  Got a call on the 24-7 line from a prime customer; had to head out to Lincoln Oaks Estates for an "emergency" broken down hot tub.

The widow Jorgenson was a sweet old lady – always fair, understood the significant extra charge for me to make the 45 minute drive out to the Estates.  She reliably paid cash, right then and there on job completion.  And I never left without some kind of bag of fruit or vegetables, maybe a little sack of homemade cookies.  Once she even gave me an apple pie – the whole pie!

Recognizing my van, Security waved me through the gate.  Wow, I could feel the mid-morning heat through my open window.  It was going to be a hot day up in these dry foothills.  I looked at all the great big lawns, perfectly manicured.  I don't know why the heck they needed all that grass, especially with the golf course snaking around to touch everyone's back yard.  It wasn't like there were any kids out here requiring a lawn to play on.  Mark my words: someday California is going to have a nasty drought and all these lawns will turn to grim dust.  But hey, I've been accused of worrying too much…

Oh man, my body ached a little from Ginger's severe butt crush.  Rats, why did I have to think of that right now when I was walking up to Mrs. Jorgenson's front door?  Think the old lady would even notice the beginning of a little tent in my loose shorts.

"Ding-dong-ding-dong." Down. "Ding-dong-ding-dong." Up again.  Somebody told me once that was the same sound that Big Ben made in London on every hour.  That would be nice to see and hear some day.  Of course, I'd never been east of the Mississippi, so London seemed like a big leap, not something I thought would actually ever be likely to visit.

The front door cracked open.  I like to let widow Jorgenson know right away who I was; she tended to be forgetful.  So I started right in: "Good morning Mrs… what the…"

I was staring, I shit you not, at the most beautiful woman I have ever seen, standing there in all her glory in a not-so-modest bikini, at least every inch of six-foot-eight perfection.  Young she appeared, somewhere in the 25-30 range, very robust, the hyper-definition of buxom blond with long straight hair, and preciously innocent pale blue eyes.

"Gudt morningk."  She chirruped and smiled at me as kindly as you can imagine.

I figured I must have the wrong house.  Looking up; nope, right address.  "Is, ah, Mrs. Jorgenson home?"

"Naw, naw, Granny's gone veesiting zee famulee in Rjezkpliteegaapt."  She blinked at me.

"Rjez… what?  Never mind… and you are?"

Now her smile grew even grander on her nice sexy wide mouth. "My naame is Neealilompsee.  But chews can call me Nellie.  Are yout zee Ploomer?"

"Yep, Curtis."  And I tapped myself on the chest; like a dork actually.  But something had happened to me, broken down since yesterday under Ginger, that and the terrible restless night.  So maybe chalk it up to sexual PTSD and/or sleep deprivation.  But I just could not get over how extraordinary this young woman looked.  I mean what planet was I on and where the heck were these big women coming from into my life all of the sudden?

Completely out of character I blurted out. "I hate to be so forward.  But Miss Nellie, you have to be the most beautiful gorgeous woman I have ever seen."

"Well, tank tzee kindly."  Then she batted her eyes at me.  "I moost saa, year kind uf coot yearselves."  She ended most sentences lilting upward.

My boundrylessness continued.  "You could tell me your measurements?  I want to get it set in my head the perfect proportions of the ideal woman."

"Whya Curtis, tisky-tisky.  If you moost know: inches or centimeters?"

"OK, then, in inches, please."  I felt my smile being goofy crooked and shook my face to try to look normal again.

"Let us see, now-wa.  Starting at zee toppa…" Miss Nellie patted her huge breasts "Feefty-six…"  Then behind her hand in a whisper to me with a wink, "… undt triple F's."  Then she patted her tummy. "Around me meedle, it is'a thurty-five."  Then Miss Nellie actually turned to pose her butt straight toward my face.  I noticed then the pattern of Koi fish on her bikini.  I wondered if sweat shops in Japan had senses of humor.  Because they definitely designed a koi fish to swim right up her ass, its tail wiggling as Nellie shifted from side to side so I could get a real good look. "And last but not least." She laughed a little tither. "My biggy bottom is feefty-nine and getting, ya, beegger ever-a-ry month widt the yummy Amereecan food."

"Wow." I shuttered. "Absolutely spectacular. And if may be so bold, how much do you weigh?"

"Yout ploomers reely like the noombers. All righty: one hundred seventy-two."

"No way." She had to be a lot heavier than that.

Nellie laughed hardy at my shock. "Oo chew wanted to knew in poonds. Mooltiplee by two point two comes to 378 poonds."

"That's much more… I mean, sounds about right." I relaxed, but I probably shouldn't have.

"Come in, comey in, little cootie-pie." Nellie ushered me past her wide sexy and tight hips, crowding me a bit more than necessary considering the grand size of the foyer.

"OK honey, where's the hot tub?"

"Follow me, through zee kitchen, and out to dee patio." I'd always thought the life of a Koi fish sucked until that very day. Its tail flipped twice at each of Nellie's steps, as her buns animated with a quite enticing wiggle. "My cousins and I, well, we goof-ed-up and put zee boobbly bath to make zee sudsy-uppy.

Yes, cousins, at least three, in the kitchen making late breakfast as we walked through. They looked almost exactly like Nellie, the main difference being, redder hair or strawberry-blonde, and one white hair with killer green eyes. Oh, and they wore no tops with their thin lacy undies – very European I suppose. As a plumber you see all kinds of things. But have to tell you, on the bell curve of sexy, the thin line at the far right all the sudden went straight up – if you know what I mean.

"Girls, this ees Curtis, here to repeer zee hot tub." Good God, each had to come over, say "Gudt morningk" and kiss me on each cheek, their big tits whopping against my chest when they leaned down. Somebody, Kirstin maybe, offered me some breakfast. I professionally declined, but noted: generous just like their grandmother.

Out back the hot tub looked like it had a bad case of rabies, foam all over, the controls under a foot of suds. I told Nellie just to leave me to it, and that I knew my way around through the gate to get supplies from my van. After forty-five minutes of cleaning and another half hour of dismantling, I verified the problem: burnt out pump. And it wasn't the suds that did it. It was someone's gigantic bikini bottom, sucked up and plugged the air intake. Boy scout that I am, on a hot tub run to

Lincoln Oak Estates I came packed and prepared, actually had a new pump right in my van.  Still, after another hour of replacement, other assorted tune-ups and testing, and with the travel out and next back, we were talking the better part of five hours, plus rather expensive parts: a $400 job, but for widow Jorgenson's family I cut it back to $225.

"Oh, my goodness graciousnesses, dats a loot of doollars.  You ploomers must be veery rich…" Nellie trailed off, looking at my itemized invoice quite dismayed.  The cousins, gathered around Nellie, looked over her shoulder in a big nest of mixed blonde-red hair, studying the bill and me and back and forth.  They didn't seem mad at me or anything, more like worried or afraid.

I pointed out my discount and said, "See there's the Jorgenson discount."  Like that should be satisfying – and, darn, it should have been.

"Come ye and sits ya down for a meenute."

I followed Nellie to the couch.  She sat, her butt covering practically the entirety of half the couch.  I sat on the other cushion.  But the strawberry-blonde Cousin Helena also wanted to sit on the couch.  So Nellie scooted over a tiny bit, I was obliged to sit right up against her, and Helena ass-covered the other cushion, pinning me between her and Nellie and thus rather under the curve of two huge firm hips.

Now, I hope you don't think I'm a prude, but them sitting up against me like this, well, isn't that some kind of a violation of personal space?  Odd though, I don't think Nellie and her cousins viewed it that way.  Somehow they must have had it in their heads that I had been taking care of their grandmother for years – which I had when it came to plumbing issues.  And Mrs. Jorgenson must have left some good notes or something in particular about me, because there seemed to be no consideration that I actually was a stranger to them.  I mean, what if I was some kind of rogue or something; wouldn't they be vulnerable?  Goodness sake; I could be a thief or a rapist or who knows what.  Young ladies visiting from out of town really should be more careful.  Or course this line of thinking is rather absurd giving that each young woman was six times my weight.  And the reality is I'm probably the gentlest man you'd ever expect to meet.  So since they already seemed to think of me as family, I guess, their being physically touchy-feely made sense, doesn't it?  Hell, I don't know.  I think I just talked myself into being touched and smooshed under their hips a little bit and in a friendly way.

"Here is dee problem, Curtis; we have no muney.  Granny oonly left us credit at the market and a coople utter stores local down-dee-town."

"And, I might saya," Cousin Kirstin, white-blond, sitting in the matching couch on the other side of the low coffee table and might be even sexier than Nellie – that is if you happen to like really, really record-breaking huge breasts, and on display I might add. "We weren't supposed to be oosing the hot tub at all.  So you see, we reelly, reelly don't want Granny to know about tdis."

"Understand, Curtis."  Now the red-haired Cousin Betten finally spoke up. "We have to, if poosible, make the payment some udder way."  I studied her enormous breast, trying to match her words to my visual.

I salivated as I continued to gape at Kirstin's and Betten's great big exposed breasts where they sat across from me.  They remained absolutely, completely without modesty about that much nudity, like I was one of the girls and they had known me all their lives.  Helena shifted on the couch and I felt myself go a slight bit more under her hip.  Nellie placed her hand over mine, lifting it to rest under her hand but on top of her smooth thigh.  I looked around at each exquisite face, silent they were now and looking quite forlorn, like damsels needing a rescue.

I needed to stall.  Because I really couldn't afford to do the job gratis. "So are you all from Sweden?"

All the cousins laughed at my question.

"You silly boy." Nellie answered in good mirth at the change of subject. "We all come from Copenhagen."  Like that somehow answered my question.  As I told you: east of the Mississippi is kind of a mystery to me.

"Got anything to trade?"  I grasped at straws, trying to be creative.

"Everyting here is Granny's, except ourt clothes…" Helena answered like that was a dead end.

"Hey, who's bikini bottom got stuck somewhat shredded in the hot tub filter?"  Still stalling; hoping for an idea.

"Cousin Gerda."

I looked at them, confused.  "Which one of you…"

"Oh," laughed Nellie, "Yout are the foonny boy.  Gerda!  Gerda!" Nellie called out.

A minute later out walks a woman easily twice the size of any of the other cousins I'd met so far, meaning some 750 pounds distributed very amply and damn sexy on a 7'11" frame.  All the sudden the same speechless shock that hit me behind my front door last night nailed me again, but good, right there in the Jorgenson's living room.

Gerda danced over to meet me, unbelievably light on her feet, meaning, very, very strong. Instead of leaning over to kiss each of my cheeks like the other cousins had done, shockingly, Gerda just picked me up and gave me a great big smothering hug. I collapsed in her crushing embrace, helpless as a toy doll. Gerda released me enough to breathe but still held me snug against her massive bosom. I hoped she would set me down, but no such luck, she seemed to be just getting started. Lifting me with her hands firmly under my armpits, Gerda brought my face up to hers and commenced kissing me on the mouth and would not stop.

"Okie-dokie, Gerda. Poot him down nowa. Give the boy back to me-a."

Gerda, stalled a second, and then pouty faced, placed me in Nellie's lap.

Nellie continued. "Yout'd better go-zy back oonto yourt room nowa. Get-get." Without leaving the couch Nellie shooed the big Gerda on out of the room. "Soo sorry I am, Curtis. Gerdie, she likes zee boys too, too much. Oh, poor baby, yous trembling. Did Gerda scare ya?"

As I got used to Nellie's speech, her accent started sounding more normal to me. Right then the white-blonde Kirstin chimed in again, her accent also mostly falling to the background. "Oh Gerda just wants to get her big bottom on you and sit, sit, sit-zee on you for a long time, squishy-squashy, until you moost agree she is your biggie-biggie butt bossy."

As I listed to Kirstin and watched Gerda parade out of the room I rather went on tilt again. Thoughts of Gerda's kissing me more and squashing me under her mega voluptuous body set up shop in my head. Stunned silent, at the moment, I couldn't string any of my thoughts and overwhelmed feelings together into sentient verbiage. You might say I was indeed experiencing some kind of ongoing mini-giantess post-traumatic-stress syndrome. Only it was not very post; but much more immediate. Certainly I felt sexually excited and at the same time massively conflicted, and add to that: overly hungry, tired from serious lack of sleep, and spent from several hours' hot humid work in the blazing midday sun.

Finally my breath shuttered in – like I had stopped breathing for a minute.

"Oooh, poor baby." Nellie patted me gently on my back as I sat in her lap. "Yous'a trembling. Greda did frighten you, didn't she? Don't worry, we won't let her get her big bottom on you and squash you flat. We can't have you getting smothered. Oh she's biggie time heavy for sure. And once she gets her juicy poosy on your cute little face, oh she probably just sit on, what's the American expression, ah yes, sit on your tiny body forever-and-a-day. Squishy-squashy, right Kristin?

"Oh yes, too-tally squishy-squashy." Kristin replied.

Then all four sing-songed along, bobbing their heads from side-to-side. "Squishy-squashy, squishy-squashy, squishy-squashy…"

I felt dizzy as they playfully teased.  My hard-on sought to break through my pants as Nellie rocked back and forth with their "squishy-squashy" song.  I tapped Nellie on her wrist.  She looked around and down at me quizzical.  I motioned for her ear.  She leaned down, her bountiful bosom pressing along my back, her neck over my shoulder.  While the others still broken-recorded along with the squishy-squashy refrain, I whispered into Nellie's ear.

"Nellie, I am afraid..."  I felt myself quivering even though the room and her lap were plenty warm. "…I…I'm about to cum."

Nellie looked over further and down at the little peak in my pants.  I felt her stiffen into action.

"Oh noo you don't." Nellie grabbed my cock and ball assembly and gave me a good hard and skillful squeeze to shut me down just in the nick of time.  With her left arm around and under my back and her right hand gripped firmly on my crotch Nellie stood and projected her voice over the squishy-squashy chant. "I'm going to take Curtis oot-side now'a and uver to the pool house for a little quiet time."

Nellie carried my across the living room and out through the still-open slider to the back patio.  All the time the other three cousins carried on with the "squishy-squashy, squishy-squashy" like busted cuckoo-clocks.

Once outside I immediately began to relax a bit and feel more comfortable.  For some reason I trusted Nellie implicitly.  She seemed so doting and attentive.  Suddenly I figured at least that part out: it was almost like dear old super-nice Mrs. Jorgenson had cloned her personality into this particular young phenomenally sexy big babe.  Yes, I really liked Nellie a lot right then.  She seemed genuinely very, very nice.  Of course it wouldn't occur to me at that point that there was such a thing as too nice, or there might be any other abundant loving risks lurking in my future.

"Curtis," Nellie smiled down at me. "You've come a long way and now the day is late.  Why don't you just stay for dinner.  My cousins will cook for you.  You can be the big man and relax.  But let's go into the pool house now, just you and me.  Maybe how about a nice massage after your hard work on the hot tub?"

Would that be a Swedish massage I wondered.  Because I still had no idea where Copenhagen was.  But whatever – Nellie's proposal sounded as perfect as a dream.  Well now, and they owed me and since it appeared they had no "mooney"….  It was definitely too late to take on any more jobs today.  Besides, I was as likely to drive off the road asleep as I would be to make it back into town.  OK, then…

"A massage does sound rather nice…"

"Goodie-good."  Nellie bounced along directly to the pool house now.  Her grip down below relaxed as my crisis there had temporarily passed.

"Mr. Curtis," Nellie's eyes looked unblinking and way too affectionately down into mine, as she slid open the pool house glass door and stepped inside the cozy cottage.  "You shall have the royal treatment."  And it seemed I had made some kind of deal, a loosely bartered trade, but unfortunately no cash.  Oh well….

Nellie dropped me on the cottage's king-sized bed.  Plunk.  Then she proceeded to unbutton my shirt.  She, of course, still only wore a next-to-nothing bikini.  "So, Curtis, I cannot give you a Swedish massage, because, you see, I am Danish.  But I can give you a special Danish massage.  Would you like that?"

"Sounds promising."  My brain was fried.

She had my shirt off.  I forgot where my shoes and socks were – maybe out by the hot tub.  Now she tugged at my shorts.  (You don't wear long pants to a hot tub job.)  She rolled me onto my tummy as she slid my shorts down my legs and off somewhere to the floor.  I glanced back to see her slide down her bikini bottoms and kick them daintily off.  Oh, my Lord her big wide sexy hips looked somehow so much more imposing in the nude.  Next the bed bounced as she mounted it, and over me, knees to either side of my skinny exposed buns.  A sweet smelling bikini top dropped onto my face, obscuring further viewing to the side.

Nellie stretched to the side for a second to retrieve something.  A moment later I heard a cap snap; and then a second later cool oil dripped liberally onto my back.  Her hands showed only confidence as she rubbed the oil in the entire length of by back, buns, and legs.  Then she sat down onto her heels, her ass mostly held up but gently pressing heat onto my legs.

Nellie's large, strong hands together reached completely across my back and around to the sides of my chest.  Incredibly feeling, she could just about massage my entire back all at once without moving the location of her hands.  Ah, such blissful envelopment!  Relaxation took hold of me within the first minute.  And I gave myself to the luscious process.  Nellie understood well the superiority of wordless communication.  Neither of us offered chatter to detract from the experience.

My back, my shoulders, my aching arms yielded to Nellie's magic touch.  The young woman, in my estimation, had to be some kind of sensual genius.  Her hands reached around my head as if she held a grapefruit.  She seemed to tap into and release every pressure point at once.  Within the first twenty minutes I felt quite sure I was in love.

What was I thinking handing her a bill for $225?  What a dolt!  Of course right away she felt my body tense.  That paused her hands in a firm grip of my shoulders.  Then, with my tension gathered up her hands, she smoothed it all the way down my arms, past my hands, and flicked that tension right off my fingertips.  Wow.  I breathed in deeply and relaxed even further.

Now those magical hands massaged my buns, turning my hard little muscular ass into mush.  She lifted herself up and worked on down my legs.  At last she reached my feet and I knew immediately what had been missing.  I loved to have my feet massaged.  The giantess that straddled me took a foot of mine in each of her hands.  She dug her thumbs into my arches at the same time as she crunched around to deliciously stretch my toes.  That was it.  I just gave in the rest of the way and completely.  Pizza dough – that's all I was.

I felt myself being turned over.  In the gentle pink haze of my mind I knew I smiled up at her supreme beauty.  Some focus came to my eyes as I gazed up at her divine breasts looking like perfection to kiss.  A phrase came into my head: "I am under a Goddess.  I am under a Goddess."

Her smile, beatific, sovereign, knowing, would had destroyed any resistance I might have still harbored – but I had none.  She seemed to be continuing the massage, her hands pressing onto my chest.  Yet something had changed.  Yes, Nellie lowered her weight  onto me more completely now, her heels out further to the side, no longer holding her up off me.  She pressed very heavily onto my chest now, shifted again.  As she settled back now her pussy slid right over my erectness and in the moment I was no longer a virgin.

My arms out to the side meant I was not completely under her.  She solved that little independence by grabbing my wrists, and as she rocked side-to-side, bringing first one then the other of my arms pinned securely under her legs.  Now her inner thighs near her knees pressed gently against my cheeks.  And she just sat, ever so still, me completely pinned under her, my cock throbbing inside her.

At that moment the slightest movement on Nellie's part and I would have cum.  That she understood perfectly, and kept me on the edge masterfully.  She breathed in deeply and kept her eyes locked on mine.  Her face animated, seeming to anticipate each little fanciful thought I might have.  Coy and empathetic she was; her eyebrows and facial expressions virtually mimicking and skillfully tracking my thoughts.  Soon I breathed when she breathed.  And a new phrase entered my head: "I am owned by this Goddess."

Now she wiggled her ass on me, squeezing her pussy just a tad.  I almost came immediately.  But she froze her position on me, holding me to that sexual edge again.  As I calmed, she moved again, a little more vigorous, a tighter squeeze.

Right up to the edge and then she held motionless. My breathing had quickened. She breathed more slowly and demonstrably, dominating me into a submissive breathing again when she did – when she allowed me to breathe.

I started to say "I love you." But she put her hand over my mouth before the first syllable could find a vowel. Instead of dialog, she preferred to bounce on me heavier, making her point that I better fully indulge her process. Her straight legs soared on past my head, flattening my shoulders on the way. And now Nellie alternated slapping them down on my upper body, or rocking from hip to hip.

Goodness, I wanted to cum, but her pussy squeeze clamped down harder, telling me: no, not yet. What had begun so gently definitely progressed now to tougher and more and more dominating circumstance for me. Yet Nellie continued to smile at me and pucker kisses at me in the most sweet and seductive way. So that meant she stayed well-intentioned, right? It was just that she being so much bigger and vigorous, I had to understand that roughness, well, that had to be a by-product, didn't it?

Nellie bent her knees and folded her legs cross-legged, what we called Indian style. Her big sexy calf muscles bulged from the flexing, thoroughly pinning my chest and face with all her weight. Now, with this severe crush, I wanted more than ever to release. She just kept on tensing more, restricting and controlling me until she was good and ready. Looking through a narrow crack afforded between her crossed legs I had a great and focused view of her huge swaying breasts, a little wilder now.

Nellie placed hands onto the mattress and lifted herself enough to turn. At ninety degree of turn she sat on me sideways, still keeping her legs drawn in and all her weight on me. Though still in the process of turning, Nellie paused for some nice heavy squirming on me. I loved that her grand ass began to come into view. I knew already that her ass would be what I would worship most of all about her.

Obligingly, Nellie turned another ninety degrees and that big beautiful ass became the universe of my vision. Still seriously locked into her pussy, that meant her ass rode up my stomach and half way up my chest. So vast it covered all my body easily side to side, squishing me well into the mattress. Her butt cheeks spread out to either side and onto the mattress. She grabbed my arms that had gotten loose, and then one-two rocked up then pinned each under her buns. I could only stare up at her ass now, her gorgeous smooth tan back, to her cascading blonde mane swirling around and bouncing as Nellie began to thrash me now with purpose. That purpose, I surmised, was for her to reach orgasm while making me wait until she got there.

Nellie brought her left hand back; fingers spread, and placed it on my face. She leaned some weight down her left arm, but thankfully I could still see through gaps between fingers to enjoy the view of her butt as she rode me, her ass pulverizing my scant thinness.  Her right arm disappeared around to the front of her body.  She seemed busy doing something of interest there, but I could not see that at all and had no idea what she was up to.  I could only tell she liked something a great deal, gauging that by the growing wildness of her writhing smash.

The no-talk rule suddenly seemed to be over because Nellie commenced moaning, "Oooh.  Ahhh.  Oo-ahh!"  and  "Oh, Curtis, oh Curtis."

"Yes?"  I wondered what she wanted.

Nellie clamped her left hand viciously on my face, closing my mouth and smashing my lips under her palm.  I guess she didn't want to hear from me after all.  She did indeed seem very focused on something internal to herself.  But that was okay with me because I could feel her pussy losing control.  In fact Nellie's whole body rather lost control.

Of course I'd masturbated some zillion times and knew when I was past the point of no turning back.  And yes, I was now at that point.  I bucked under Nellie's smothering mass.  And she screamed, in delight, I think.  Without a doubt she reacted to my ejaculation pounding me without mercy.  I exploded, and holy cow, at least ten times more vigorously than ever before in my life.  Nellie reciprocated while taking in all I could offer.

I felt completely spent.  Nellie, however, just kept on going and going and going….  She found one orgasm after another and another.  She fell back on me, crushing my face with her back.  She sat up again and pumped me for some fifteen minutes.  I actually started to get hard again.  She turned around again 180 degrees.  The she collapsed on me frontward.  Her wonderful breasts smashing onto my face.  She curved just enough to get her left nipple on my face then into my mouth.  I kissed at it gently, like a lovers' first kiss.

"Harder!"  Nellie commanded.  "And suck!"

I followed my Goddess's orders, getting both of us going again – full speed.  Before, Nellie had crushed me with all her weight sitting on me.  Now she covered and breast smothered me, not as extremely heavy, but more encased and owned for sure.  I surrendered to her, I don't know how many times, but it seemed like dozens or hundreds.  After a while it rather affected my mind to be so subdued, so lovingly dominated, but definitely dominated nonetheless. Already I feared trying to face her later, to feel even remotely equal to her.

Nellie pressed me flat with her legs, her aggressive sexual devouring of my Member, her tit-smothering alternating left then right then left then squishing right again.  She made me feel so overwhelmingly good I could also already feel the need I would have for her later, the loneliness if she were to say this was just a one-time occurrence.  Even with all this worry creeping in, or maybe enhanced by it, in another twenty minutes I came a second time.  That seemed incredibly back-to-back as far as my history was concerned.  And blessedly, I must say, Nellie seemed finally satisfied.

Nellie rolled off me, mostly, leaving her breasts stacked sideways on my face.  I fought for air and she scooted down.  Then she leaned onto me again for some serious, prolonged kissing.  While she kissed me, mouthing over my mouth, owning me by forceful tonguing, she reached down to play with my Member and my balls, toying then squeezing, stroking and fiddling around until my hardness returned once again.

Once she had me going, Nellie turned on me 180 degrees and brought her mouth down to suck on my mid-level hardness and quickly had me up and fully excited.  She dropped down from all fours, her sexy stomach smashing my face, while her mouth voraciously gobbled and sucked my Member harder and harder until I give up what little I had left.  Nellie licked and swallowed it down like the champ she was.  Then once again she rolled off me.  This time Nellie got off the bed, walked over and slid open the poolside door, and then went outside into the hot late-afternoon sun and jumped into the pool.

I think maybe her cousins came out of the house to join her.  I went to sleep to the sounds of playful splashing.

***

I dreamt a bright blue butterfly had landed on my cheek, tickling me by batting its delicate wings.  I reached up, eyes closed, very sleepy and gently knocked at it to fly away.  Someone kissed my hand, the firm kiss pressing my hand against my own face.  Waking up I turned with some surprise to see who – and inadvertently brought my lips right up into Nellie's waiting open mouth.  What a beautiful reassurance the life-altering sex I had with her before my nap was not some dream or mistake.  Oh she made real sure of that as she laid into me but good with her kisses, pressing me back down and lying on top of me.  It seemed she commanded me to be hard and like a good soldier I followed orders with a snap-to.

She reached down and grabbed me while lifting her mouth back a couple of inches.  "Very nice, luttle-loover.  Buot, now-is time for the deener."

"But I don't want dinner.  I just want to eat you."  How odd.  I was very hungry but I just lied about it, because, what – well, I guess it was obvious – Nellie was proving irresistible right then, and everything, and I mean everything else seemed secondary.  What was happening to me?  Here I was looking up at her gorgeous, superb, and outstandingly beautiful face, and all I could think about was her ass, her pussy, and feel flooded with desire to kiss her down there.

"Oh, Curtis.  Maybe I'll just eat you up instead."  Nellie kissed me hard, trapping my lower lip between her teeth, and biting at me, not shy of painful.  Then she pushed off me and stood by the side of the bed.  Now my Goddess towered over me; looking quite lovely in her simple-sexy dainty violet and white, short-short dress.

I rose to sitting, dangling my thin shanks over the side of the bed between her perfect tan legs.  Reaching forward I hugged her at knee level, my face between her lower thighs.  Looking up stole my breath away; she had no panties on.  Like an involuntary reaction, I kissed her leg but up toward my deepest desire.  Nellie responded obligingly by leaning her knees upon the side of the bed and bringing her delights closer.

Kissing her up higher now, her thighs starting to come together, pressed on either side of my face.  I fought to move up, to pull her down, to get up to her pussy, but I could not make progress out of my sitting position.  My tenuous sitting position seemed to be slipping down off the bed because of her kneeling on the bed's side and causing a severe slope.  Only the friction of my face squeezed by her thighs kept me from sliding off and to the floor now – well that, and my arms struggling to hang onto her legs.  Being frantic just loosened my purchase, and finally gravity had its way with me.  I lost it and slid off to the floor.

"Oh, too bad, Luttle Loover.  I so hoped you would make it to my poosy.  Any well... sees on the footsie of the bed.  Gerda felt so bad that she frightened you; she made you a nice shirt and shorts to wear to deener.  She had plenty of zee time while we made the love and you slept to recoover from my big body squishing you under dee sexy-sex."  Nellie turned around over me lying on the floor, being careful not to step on me, and then she marched on out of the pool house. "Don't make us wait, Curtis. If'a we get hungry; we can get grumpy."

I jumped up and tried on the blue and pink flowery Hawaiian-style shirt.  It fit perfectly with just the right amount of island-relaxed fit.  The shorts were maybe a little too loose in the leg.  I guess it must be truly hard for Gerda to believe someone could be as small and thin as I was.  But the waist had some stretchy elastic sewn in, so they at least stayed up no problem – and that's the main thing now, isn't it?

In the nice yellow-daisy dining room off the kitchen it looked like dinner for six. Nellie sat at the head of the table at one end.  Betten then Kirstin sat on one side of the flat-sided (two leaf in) oval table.  Helena then Gerda sat on the other side.  That left my place at the other head of the table with Kirstin and Gerda to my left and right.

I shoved my heavy oak chair up to the table as far as the arms would allow.  Then I ducked under the table to gain access to my chair.  At that moment, unintentionally but quickly without regrets, I confronted five stunning sets of legs, exposed all the way up by hiked up short dresses, in fact with just enough coverage to keep bare ass off the furniture.  I'd gone under by Kirstin's side; still intimidated too much by Gerda.  I don't know what overcame me all the sudden.  It seemed I had no control of myself.  I mean, I knew exactly what I was about to do, but I did it anyway.  I hugged Kirstin's right leg and kissed her inner thigh.

"Oooh-wa" Kristin made a surprised little gasp, but no further comment to reveal my forwardness.

I turned to crawl up into my chair and in that moment spied Gerda's big sexy feet, her legs crossed at the ankles out toward the middle under the table.  Actually, they rested right in front of my chair.  Again I couldn't help myself.  I dropped down and kissed first one foot then the other.

"Oh my."  Gerda shifted in her chair but did not say anything else.

I climbed up into my chair, twisting around the hard under edge of the table, got my butt in my chair and my chin some six inches above the table top.  All five cousins looked at me.  Nellie smiled satisfied and knowing, I don't know, like a woman about to have dinner on her honeymoon.  Betten and Helena looked at me with interest but rather neutral.  Kristin's stare bored into me with unabashed desire, and it made me want to get back under the table and dive into her crotch.  I was afraid to look at Gerda, but when I stole a glance that way I could see her eyes twinkled with pleasant mirth.  Oh I get it: she probably took my foot kisses as some kind of "It's all good and forgiven."  Then I realized something.

"Gerda, I want to thank you for the really cool shirt and shorts.  They fit great.  You must be really talented."

"Oh for sure, Curtis.  I am indeed, very, veery, talented.  And you are moost welcome."

"Okie-dookie."  Nellie had her hands out to her sides.  As Helena and Betten each took hold of a hand, Nellie kept looking at me, quite lovingly.  "Curtis, we always like to hold the hands before we eat'a."

I reached out.  Kristin took my left hand.  My right hand and wrist disappeared into Gerda's left hand.  Gerda held my hand snuggly, firmly, and like there could be no escape.  Kirstin immediately brought my hand just below the edge of the table and out of view.  There she definitely worked my hand with hers, massaging and skillfully finding sexy pressure points – ooh, like the one at the base between my thumb and index finger.

Nellie finished a simple prayer of thanks for food and good relations and for the nicely repaired hot tub.  Everyone released the hands.  It was time to dig in.

I guessing Mrs. Jorgenson's credit with the local grocery store must be stellar.  Because there certainly wasn't any lack of excellent steaming hot food at the table.  The cousins piled it on and politely shoveled it in.  I had my usual bird-sized portions.  Hungry I was; but I could never down that much at once.  More likely, I'd just need to eat again in a few hours.  I'd gotten used to it and tended to snack my way through the day.  So quickly I felt satisfied, giving me time to watch and admire my hostesses.

Wow, these gals truly seemed to enjoy their food.  Nellie carefully buttered each side of a split whole-wheat bun.  Then she opened wide in put in one half, chewed twice, then the other half, chewed maybe four more times and then swallowed – all quite proper, almost dainty as she napkin-dabbed a speck of butter off the corner of her mouth.  She looked up at me, saw my fascinated focus on her, then smiled as lovingly as a man could want.  It would have melted the butter on my buns, that is, if I was still eating bread.  She batted her eyes at me, and then scanned the table for seconds of the meatloaf and gravy.

Gerda motioned for me to lean toward her.  She whispered quickly in my ear.  "In a meenute I'll droppa' my fork to the floor.  When yout pick it up, yeet can kissie my feet again."

I pulled back, somewhat shocked by her proposal but also excited.  I looked around the table, rather furtively and with a dose of guilt.  Nobody seemed to notice.  Especially Nellie remained intent on more meatloaf.  Yet when I looked over at Kristin she definitely had her intense stare going again, drilling me with serious interest for a good long while and then up at Gerda.  Crap, she must have seen the little whispering.

After some more conversation-less soft clanking of forks and knives, Gerda's fork slipped out of her hand and to the floor under the table.

On cue I said.  "Let me get that for you Gerda."  I slid down in my chair, right under the table.  There, strategically, lay the fork right between her big sexy bare feet.  First I retrieved the fork.  Then I leaned down a little more for a quick kiss.  Right when my lips touched the top of Gerda's left foot, she deftly flipped me over with her right foot, and then planted her left foot on my body, pinned me immobile.  She brought that foot up to and pressed it on my face.  I kissed her foot as silently as possible, and kept at it while she continued to keep me pinned down.

It seemed like it must be taking too long to avoid suspicion.  I guess so because Nellie commented.  "Coortis, can you findie the fork?"

Gerda released me and up quickly I appeared squirming back into the chair. "Here it is. Want me to go rinse it off for you Gerda?"

"Oh on, tank you Curtis. Wee keep the floors all spick 'n span." She took the fork, eyed it a little dubiously, but then resumed using it to shovel in mashed potatoes with peas and gravy.

"Mmmp. Good." Betten commented to herself and it seemed about being satisfied with her latest bite of food.

Right after we had all looked quizzically at Betten, Kirstin tisked, then woefully, "Oooh'wa, I dropped my fork too, Curtis. Can you be'a so kind so kind oonce more?" She looked at me innocent and unblinking – and stunningly sexy I thought.

"Sure Kirstin. Curtis to the rescue again." I slid down ducking under the table again. I looked at the floor: no fork. Then I saw her fork, tick-tock, in her hand by her knee, being waved at me. As I reached for it she pulled back. I followed and soon crouched by her knees, reaching for the fork between her legs. I got my hand on it, but Kirstin did not yield. Instead she pulled the fork back further toward her lap, spreading her legs to allow me to pursue it. Once I had entered nice and deep Kirstin twisted the fork from my hand and clamped her thighs together on my face. Just a little more than the length of my tongue away, I could see and smell the sweetness of her pussy. I licked at her; I just couldn't help it. Her robust sensuality weakened and dominated me.

I could faintly hear a chair sliding out. A moment later Kirstin's chair now slid noisily out from the table, vibrating hard with her in it and me trapped by her thigh-squeeze, staggering along to follow. Kirstin released me and I stumbled around and fell on my butt. It was Nellie who had pulled Kirstin's chair out, and Nellie now looking down at me with severe dismay.

"So Curtis. Is this want you want? You say you love me and now you sneaky-sneaky around and oonder the table yee goes with me'a flesh and blood Cousin Kirstin. Oh Curtis, my heart is feeling sad about it. But if yout want to play ooround with my cousins then by all the means, help youtselves."

"But Nellie, I do love you. I… I worship you."

"And worship me you can. But you might as wheel worship to all of us then. But when it combs to love I'ma not so sure you know what it means."

"I do know. It means I would do anything for you."

"Still sounding like worship it is Curtis." Nellie no longer carried that wonderful look of love. Man oh man had I blown it, screwed up my chances with her. "So we will all be your goddess queens now and you can put the worship to each of us. Or you can get into your van and drive away right now.  The choice is yours."  Nellie's tone had become flat, unsympathetic; probably , must be, her feelings were hurt or just plain miffed.  What am I supposed to do?

Wait, I know: "I'm sorry, Nellie."

"Oh yes you are now'a and yes you will be.  But in dis moment you'd better decide for good: stay now or go now."

I looked at the other four cousins.  Their excited expression said for me to stay.  I looked at Nellie: impassive, unreadable, and most likely hiding hurt.  Maybe I could win her back.  Little did I know a woman scorned… or in particular, these women.

"OK, I will stay?"  I did not sound sure.

"Is that the yes?"  Nellie's eyes narrowed.

"Yes."

"Yes what?"  I did not know Nellie could sound so severe.

"Yes, Nellie?"

"No, little slave.  You may not call me just Nellie.  You will call me Goddess Nellie.  We are all the Goddesses to your tiny nothingness."

"But…" I could not fathom my new circumstance yet.

"Okie, slave.  I will grant your first request for butt.  Hold him down now cousins by all fours.  That's right, use him for you pleasures."

Betten and Helena each took a leg, spreading me out on my back.  Then each sat on one of my feet.  At the same time Kirstin and Gerda each took an arm to complete the little flat spread eagle.  Down below the two cousins inserted my feet into pussies and sat on them flat.  Kirstin and Gerda, their butts facing my body, inserted my hands and forearms into their pussies and sat down on them with continuous wiggling vigor.  In fact, all four of the cousins writhed around on my appendages for their sexual pleasure.

Nellie stood over my head.  She pulled her dress up and off, to reveal the perfect splendor of her body.  She squatted down slowly to bring her huge butt right over me face.  Now she had a few things to say.

"Curtis the tiny slave, I thought you were just right.  In just a few hours I had fallen in love with you.  I would have married you if you had asked me.  Yes, it is true.  That is what my heart was telling me.  Think of the perfect loving life you would have had.  But you betrayed me on the first little test."

"But Goddess Nellie, I still love you.  I was tricked."  I kept squeaking. "I beg you to give me another chance.  Let me prove my love."

"Oh sad Curtis.  You should try to prove it.  Then your Goddess might be merciful in her punishment.  But I will not believe you little lying lips and tongue. Use them now to try to save your life."  Then Nellie dropped her great ass on my face and all light and hope was lost.  At first I licked and kissed like crazy, to try and please her. Then I just fought for air.  As I felt the complete desperation for oxygen, Nellie lifted up but only to scoot her wet pussy right onto my face.

With a new breath of air I resumed my oral effort up into her.  And quickly she built up and slammed me down with her orgasm.  Though I must have performed admirably I received no mercy.  She just kept on grinding and grinding and squishing her pussy all over my pitiful face.  This time as I ran out of air still she did not lift off me.  I licked best I could, but to no avail or relief.  And soon I must have passed out.

The next thing I recall was a full kiss.  No, not a kiss – it was air being blown in through my mouth.  My nose trapped between thumb and fingers she held closed off so that the air would get to my lungs.  My eyes blinked open to see – Betten. She blew in two more breaths and I could feel consciousness return completely. Then I noticed all four of my appendages still being worked over and warm wet up into heavy pussies.

Betten turned around above me and presented her wide ass to my face.  "OK little slavey Curtis.  Time it is now for more of the servicing."  Then she dropped her butt on my face.  She pumped like crazy, kind of giving me air once and a while.  That allowed me to keep going longer; better for her oral pleasures.  Betten built up thoroughly and as she reached orgasm planted her pussy, heavy and without any relief to breathe, completely covering my face.  Again, the pussy smother continued with orgasmic squishing until I passed out.

I woke up to resuscitation by Helena.  Immediately I both hated and loved what I knew would happen next.  The absolute sexual domination and smothering turned me on to the maximum.  But the torture of the asphyxiation had me panicking from the beginning moment.  It made no difference.  The five giantesses had me under their comprehensive squish and domination.  I passed out again during Helena's orgasm.

Kirstin not only sat as heavily as she could on my face; she also squeezed my head in her butt cheeks until I thought she would crack my skull open.  But no; I'm obviously too thick headed for that.  Even as Kirstin all but crushed my head, all I could think about was her exceptional sexy gorgeousness.  In the blackness under her smothering ass, I actually pictured her beautiful face, startling white blonde hair, and fiery penetrating steely green eyes.

For the inevitable pussy smother Kirstin actually turned around 180 degrees to sit cross legged on my thin chest.  This put all her weight crushing onto my face.  The squashing felt so wonderfully supreme and at the same time the most painful so far.  Kirstin lifted up more frequently than the other cousins, prolonging the torturous ecstasy for perhaps thirty minutes.  There was nothing left of my volition but mindless servitude.  As she snuffed out my life, it seemed there was nothing to lose, no thoughts, no will, no identity other than a boney little snake licking up into the supreme squish of the Goddess.  Finally, the end result was the same.  Kirstin pussy smothered me unconscious.

I woke to Gerda's strong resuscitation to the point of my lungs being painfully expanded.  Her technique, while overkill to bring me back to life; proved very efficient at oxygenating me back to a bright consciousness.  Soon she turned and brought her vastly wide butt to hover my face.  Out there my hands and feet still lived in wet pussy cocoons, the activity on them seeming more vigorous than before.

When Gerda dropped her ass on my face I knew immediately that I was a goner.  The finality of her smother extinguished all hope.  I gave up, knowing they would kill me again.  Would they be able to bring me back to life after Gerda finished with me?  Then Gerda lifted up to let me breathe.  Down came the smother again.  At the last vestige of consciousness up she would lift again.  Then down, crushing without mercy.  Then up again, actually with such perfect regularity I could count on it.  Then down again under the obliterating blackness of ass doom.

Someone played with my hard-on now.  Was it Gerda?  Then I felt lips encircling my cock.  Oh my goodness; it had to be Nellie for sure because it felt exactly the same as out in the pool house, felt the same as it did right after the supreme alpha-Goddess took my virginity.  Now, in spite of Gerda's massive devastating smother and unbelievable grinding orgasms, I felt hope again.  Did this mean that Nellie might be forgiving me, loving and wanting to pleasure me again?

As Gerda seemed to reach a new level of thrashing orgasm, one so wild and bucking, I could only catch minute breaths to stay conscious, I also felt the inevitable coming.  And I wondered: would Nellie swallow my cum?  In my somewhat oxygen starved brain, it seemed very important.  I thought if she swallowed it would mean she still loved me and maybe could forgive me.

Those thoughts sent me over the edge.  I blasted up a fountain as Gerda thundered her pussy down on me with impossible violence.  I fought to stay conscious, to see what Nellie would do.  And Nellie's lips stayed tightly sealed on my cock, sucking and swallowing to actually stimulate me to cum more.  Bless her heart; Nellie stayed right there and took it all.

Gerda rolled to one side and I breathed around her legs loosely on my face.  I felt my hands and feet being released from pussy.  Gerda lifted her legs off me.  I could see Nellie still resting her big breasts on my legs, still licking at my mostly hard cock.  She caught my eye, still kept licking me, but flashed a smile my way as well.

"Goddess Nellie…" I felt too weak to continue my sentence.

"Oh, you poor baby.  Would you like to kissy my breasts?"

Helena had brought in warm wet towels and the other four cousins proceeded to wipe me clean of quite a bit of pussy juice.  Nellie prowled up my freshly wiped body.  She pinned me flat under her and kissed my lips.  I felt so relieved she seemed back to her former self.  Was all square now after, what, suitable punishment for my indiscretions under the dining table?  As her loving, deep kisses continued I had to think so.  After some twenty minutes of the best kisses ever, Nellie moved on up to present me with her breasts as promised.

Nellie leaned off to one side, her breasts falling back over my face.  I found the closest nipple and latched on with my kisses and sucking.

"So, leettle Curtis, have you learned your lesson?"

"Yes Goddess Nellie."

"Never, ever betray me again."

"No Goddess Nellie."

"Oh, yout can call me just Nellie again.  Now remember, we smothered you until you could not breathe anymore.  Then we brought you back to life.  We have an old tradition in Denmark.  When someone saves your life then you owe them your service for life.  So now you have to be of service to us for life."

I kept kissing her breasts.  I knew at the moment I wanted to keep kissing her breasts for life.

Suddenly Nellie broke it off and sat up.  I had rolled back flat.  Nellie rather pounced on me, sitting on my chest, bringing her pussy right up to my chin.

"You are mine now."  She declared with authority and certainty.  "My pussy owns you.  I love you and you love me."

"I love you and worship you and will do anything for you." I spoke weakly, chest crushed under her and it being hard to draw air.

“What if I want to sit on your face and smother you to death?”

“So be it.”  I had no volition remaining; only whatever her wish might be.

“Then I declare you are ready.  We should get married.  Then I will be able to stay in this beautiful country my entire life.  Do you say ‘yes’ my tiny lover?”

“Yes, oh yes a thousand times.”

“Good it is.  Then we shall have the wedding tomorrow.  They have the justice of the peace at the down town.”

I kissed her inner thigh, hoping she would bring her pussy forward to my face.  But instead she had more for me to hear.

“So, we get married tomorrow morning at ten o’clock.  My cousins can be the witness.  Then if I should happen to smother you to death on our wedding night I will still be able to live in America.  In fact it is, as your widow, I should have your house to live in and any other monies you have.  Maybe we should also buy some of the life insurance tomorrow morning right after we get married.”

“You are so smart and thoughtful.  Those are very responsible ideas you have.”  At the time I did not see my certain and impending doom in Nellie’s plan.

“So tonight you should spend in my bed all tied up and secured to the post of the bed.  That way you will not be able to change your mind and leave.  Sometimes the men are too afraid of commitment.  But not you, right Curtis?”

“No not me.  You can count on me.”

“That’s what I thought.  So you will not mind at all if I tie up to my bed.  That way I can also sit on your face from time to time during the night to help you remember your commitment, my baby husband-to-be.”

Now that sounded really good to me.  “Yes, I would love that.”

“Ok, it is settled then.  Betten please to put his van in our garage so as to nobody will be looking for it.  Helena, do you mind to be the sweetheart and to do the dishes?  Gerda, you are such the treasure.  Could you make me a wedding dress?  Nothing too fancy, but nice and long so I can put it over Curtis’s head and trap him under there with my legs.  And Kirstin, maybe you could help me tonight with the double-duty facesitting on Curtis.  I want to have some time to sleep before my wedding.  Everybody OK?”

A chorus of yes; then they scattered.  I followed Nellie to her bedroom with Kirstin close on my heels.

***

If I was pussy-whipped before, I was an annihilated pussy slave by morning.  The two cousins road me most of the night.  Probably seventy-five percent of the time Kirstin did the work while Nellie slept.  By first light my mind felt like soft mush.  Kirstin sat on my face for what seemed like the hundredth time.  She alternated now between thighs together, then apart, then together, then apart.

Both Nellie and Kirstin were up now.  They untied me.  Nellie had Kirstin turn around and facesit me in reverse.  Then Nellie mounted my hard on that had been aching all night to come.  Nellie pounded the living daylights out of me with a vicious quick fuck.

Then rising, Nellie looked at me curling up on the bed. "Keep that in your head this morning, Curtis.  You can count on me to screw your brains out all the time once we are married.  You say the right things today and I will smother you nicely.  You fuck this up and I will let Gerda crush the life out of you in the worst way."

To my zombie mind both sounded good.  I smiled at her, my tortured face, no doubt, had a crooked smile.

Nellie eyed me, accessing my state of servitude.  Satisfied she turned to Kirstin. "Please clean him up and get him dressed in the outfit Gerda made for him.  We leave in an hour.  Maybe you should facesit him one or two more times but not too heavy.  He's is in just the right state.  He is the perfect little man for me to marry.  I don't know how I got so lucky."

I was still wondering a little bit about the sudden need for life insurance.  But she was saying such nice things about me, about how perfect I was for her; all I could think about was how much I loved her, being under her.  As she left the room I want to kiss her crotch again already and service her with my tongue.

"Come on to the shower, Curtis."  Kirstin took me firmly by the hand. "We will take care of those desires you are feeling.  How about a nice little grinding smother in the shower?"

***

The six of us piled into Mrs. Jorgenson's big blue sedan.  I noticed my van in the garage next to it.  Nellie, in her white fluffy dress, sat on me in the passenger seat.  The short ride down town only took ten minutes.  Nellie bounced and squirmed on me the entire time.  There seemed nothing remaining in my mind except lust and servile desire to be squished under Nellie's big perfection of ass.

I followed my fiancée up the steps.  The cousins formed a tight circle around us.  It seemed like they wanted to protect me or something.  Anyway, I guess we were all going to be a big happy family now, so closeness felt like a good thing.  I had been lonely for way too many years.

In through the tall fluted concrete columns we entered the semi-grand foyer of the historic courthouse.  It wasn't crowded, but it seemed busy with those crossing nearby mostly in a hurry – court deadlines, I suppose, the quick click of heels echoing up toward the high dome.

Inside a lower drop-ceiling side office with fluorescent lighting in rectangular panels, Nellie stepped aside to let me approach the counter next to her.  I could barely see over it.  Nellie decided to step slightly behind me and pressed her legs through her dress to pen me gently against the counter.  Oh, she was so loving toward me; couldn't stand to be separated at all it seemed.  I couldn't wait to get married.  Although, the idea of carrying her across the threshold seemed it would be a problem beyond solution.

My mind continued to fantasize about my honeymoon and the impending wedding night.  Nellie had promised to smother me and I couldn't wait.  I think I said "yes" to a couple of questions, signed something. It had been a couple hours now since Kirstin last pinned me in the shower and sat on my face while water drained right by my ear.  Somewhere up on the counter someone held my hand.  Maybe they took a thumb print.  Nellie squeezed her legs on either side of my chest.  Arms back at my sides now; only my silly smiling face would be appearing from the folds of her dress, the rest of me back between her legs and under her crotch.

"I want to be married under the dome right away."  Nellie seemed in a hurry.  I wished she could be more relaxed and happy.  Ah, we were so in love.

"I love you, Nellie."  I thought that would reassure her.

"I know, baby." She patted me on my head.

"The judge is available now.  But it will be $20 extra for using the courthouse foyer."

"Fine."  She said curtly.  Nellie nodded to Kirstin who shelled out the $20 extra.  Weird, I thought they didn't have any cash.

"OK, let's go." Nellie took my hand now, squeezing to the point of being painful.  She walked briskly from the office, me tripping in the billows of her dress.  I don't know what Nellie was so hurried and worried about.  We had a lifetime of bliss before us.  Still daydreaming; I wondered how many kids we would have.

Nellie stood at the arranged spot in the foyer.  Grabbing my shoulders, she roughly stood me right close next to her.  She had Kirstin stand on my other side and big Gerda right behind me.  Betten and Helena stood to the outsides.

Nellie looked back at Gerda as the black-robed judge made his way before us. "Keep your hands firm on his shoulders. If dream boy needs a prompt just give him a good squeeze."

The judge produced a thin brown binder from his robe and opened it. He placed it onto a black music stand someone had just pulled from a service closet tucked under the curved steps to the second floor. He cleared his throat, started to speak, but had to clear his throat again – like it might have been his first words of the day. Anyway, once he got started he projected quite well, I thought.

"We are gathered her today for the marriage of Neeally… er, Neealiloopomzee ("Close enough" I thought) Jorgenson to Curtis…" As the judge spoke my mind drifted further afield. Nellie seemed impatient with the judge. What was her problem; she was starting to annoy me. I looked to my right and up at Kirstin. She mouthed "I'm going to fuck your face." While it sounded good, it seemed weird to me. That was so inappropriate at the moment.

The judge had asked me something. But I hadn't heard the question. Gerda squeezed my shoulders and I almost cried out from the pain. But Nellie had told me that if I got nervous I should just say "yes." So I did so. Everyone seemed satisfied. Next I heard Nellie say "yes." The judge droned on and I honestly couldn't focus enough to know what he was saying. What was wrong?

I looked up at Nellie again. I adored her so much. It melted me to think about the promised smother tonight. Maybe it would be this afternoon. That excited me more. I think the judge had asked me another question. Nellie looked at me and seemed really cross.

"Answer him!" Nellie barked at me. Gerda squeezed my shoulders harder than before. Kirstin rather subtlety ground her heel on the top on my foot.

Instead of a "yes" out came an "Ouch!"

Nellie looked furious with me. She whispered, but all nearby could hear her hiss. "Tell the judge 'yes' right now!"

"Why are you so mad at me?"

Nellie fought to regain control it seemed. She smiled at me but it looked also like a scowl. She spoke to me through her teeth like a ventriloquist. "I'm not mad at you darling. I just want to get married so we can go home and start the honeymoon. Remember what I promised I would do. Maybe the cousins can come join us."

The judge harrumphed at hearing Nellie's audacious comment. But it wasn't his business what went on in people's bedrooms. However, instead of asking his question again he seemed to have gone a little off script.  Instead he came out with the classic question.

"Is there anyone here that objects to this union?"

Confused, I opened my mouth to say something, not having really any idea what I was about to say.  But right then a commotion roiled into the foyer from the main front entrance.  The judge knew there were always officers in the building to take care of any problems.  So he merely looked at me and repeated the question, nice and loud so all in the foyer could hear over the continuing disturbance.

"Is there anyone here that objects to this union?"

"By God, I do!" I recognized Ginger's big stage voice booming up to echo off the dome.

"Who said that and why?"  The judge demanded, but sympathetically so.  I got the feeling he wasn't so crazy about the marriage ceremony he presided over this morning.

"Because it is ridiculous.  Curtis is my boyfriend and no way he wants to marry these conniving cunts."

Nellie leaned onto me.  "Curtis, tell her you want to get married."

"It's true, Ginger.  I'm in love."  I heard myself say it but I felt like I was completely out of my body.  What was happening to me?

"No you don't Curtis.  You didn't even know them until yesterday."  By now Ginger and another even huger beautiful young woman and a swarthy handsome man similar in age and bearing a family resemblance to Ginger had made it up to stand to the right of the judge.  "They get their big asses on you again, Curtis, I swear to God you will not survive the night.  She just wants to marry you so she can become a US citizen.  And as your widow she'll own your house, your van, and anything else you've accumulated."

"That's a horrible lie!  Curtis and I are in love.  Right Curtis?"  Nellie stood forward defiant.

I kind of nodded but couldn't produce any words.  I felt like something was terribly wrong.

"Bullshit!"  Ginger really knew how to lambast someone.  "That's not marriage-love in one day.  No way.  You've pussy whipped and brainwashed the poor kid.  He'd no sooner marry you than fuck a spider."

"OK, hang on."  The judge, if anything, would get this situation under control. Directly to Ginger: "Dear, I've heard your point.  You have to be quiet now."  Then to Nellie: "Is this true?  Are you here on a visa? I want to see the identification you showed in the licensing office?"

"Well, it's somewhere here, maybe out in the car."

"It is not in the car."  The judge quickly became suspicious.  "You had it with you in that office.  And I saw you come from that office right to this room.  So let's see it. Now!"

From her little purse Nellie pulled out a card, like a driver's license.  He looked at it and mumbled "Neealiloopomzee Jorgenson" nodding like that was OK.  He looked up at Nellie, then down at the card again.  And you still live at Ridgeview Lane up in the Estates?"

"Yes, yes."  Nellie smiled nervously and reached to take her card back.

But the wily judge wasn't finished with it yet.  Says here you're five foot nine inches tall and weigh 170 pounds.  You've sure grown a lot in the last four years since this was last issued."

Now Nellie didn't say anything.

"Also," the judge was having fun now.  "I note you were born some seventy-five years ago.  That would make you the most well-preserved woman that every existed.  Because to me you don't look a day over twenty-five."  The judge eyed her, waiting for an answer he was ready to enter into his memoirs as a classic.

"Well," Nellie tried to imitate the voice of an old person. "We Danes are knoown to look good for a very long life.  And when eever I visit zee old country, I get the special treatments…"

The judge held his hand up.  "You know, Miss Jorgenson, or whoever you are, we are going to give you some special treatment right here in Marion County, California.  Officer hold this woman for questioning."

The other four cousins started to slink away, but it is no easy task for women of such size to disappear.

"Hold on there, my beauties.  Could I see your identifications also?  A driver's license or a passport will do."  The judge waved forward some of the accumulating officers.

Kirstin spoke for them all.  "I'm so sorry judge, but we don't have any with us at the moment."

"That's no problem." The judge smiled. "We will be happy to accompany you back to your residence so you can produce the documentation for us."

Finally I spoke up, still innocent of the full understanding. "Why don't you just tell the judge, Kirstin? You're from Copenhagen in Sweden."

The judge looked at me with curiosity. "Are you sure you are all right, my young fellow? Because I think, perhaps, you have just escaped a very dangerous situation." Then to the cousins. Now I'm thinking we better just have you stay right here while the officers take one of you to your residence to get your passports and visas. And if they are expired, like I think they are, then you'll be on the next flight to… er… wherever your Scandinavian home happens to be."

"Noobody is holding me anywhere!" Gerda shouted and bolted for the front exit. She knocked over officers like bowling pins. And she looked good for a clean escape. But the burly man that had been standing next to Ginger, her brother perhaps, had taken off in hot pursuit and tackled Gerda at her ankles. And it doesn't matter how big you are, if you cannot take a step, you will go down.

Gerda hit the hard marble floor and slid askew of the targeted front door. Instead she plowed into the revolving door, flipped up on her head, knocking the mechanism off its axis, and trapping herself upside down in the airlock without enough room to spare so she could even right herself. Ginger's brother got up fine, dusting his hands.

As everyone stared at that commotion by the front exit, I felt an iron grip tighten around my neck. I would have called out in pain but Nellie throttled my neck so tightly I couldn't make a peep. With her other hand she grabbed a handful of my hair and forced my head forty-five degrees sideways. Then she snarled out.

"Everyone back away from me or I'll break his measly neck." Nellie took a half step back, me firmly locked in her vice-strength hold.

I looked up at Nellie. Well, she rather had my head turned that way. Her face looked so contorted and vicious angry. She had loosened her grip on my neck a little because she had me secured by the way my head tilted. I felt so dismayed. "Nellie, I thought you loved me."

"Ha!" Nellie scoffed is disgust. "Love a runt like you? Are you kidding my ass? Kirstin, go out and start the car."

I looked back sideways at Kirstin. But she was shaking her head. "No, no I don't think so, Nellie. This has gone way too far."

If Nellie felt furious before; she short-fused into insanely enraged at the insubordination in her moment of greatest need. "Get the car you fucking bitch!"

Nellie shouted spittle. "So help me Kirs – " Wham!  Ginger stepped forward lightning fast in Nellie's brief distraction.  One solid right to Nellie's temple, and Ginger decked her in a thunderous punch.

With her other arm, Ginger caught me from following Nellie to the cold marble.  "Talk about a foul-mouth bitch.  I couldn't listen to her bullshit anymore.  Not when she's messing with my neighbor…" Ginger righted me and flashed me a big grin with a wink "… my boyfriend."

Nellie groaned and sat up wobbly.  Officers helped her the rest of the way up, securing her with wrist holds behind her back.  Nellie leaned toward me, but quickly backed off as Ginger threatened with her fist again.  Nellie faked her accent again for her curtain call, "To bad it is, Curtis.  The poosey smother sex dis after noon would have been a killer of a honeymoon."

I finally shuttered as they took her away.  Ginger kneeled all the way down then sat to my eye level. She didn't grab to hug me or anything, just looking sympathetically into my eyes.  "You going to be okay Curtis?"

The judge stood by, curious about my answer.

I looked gratefully into Ginger's kind eyes. "I think so.  I feel pretty weird right now, though.  Was Nellie planning to suffocate me during sex?  I thought she loved me."

Ginger nodded, "She loved America, Curtis, and needed a husband to stay here.  Suffocate you?  Curtis, us big girls have to really careful with little guys like yourself during sex.  But she and her cousins were going to dog pile on you until there was no breath left in your body at all."

A huge and gorgeous woman stood by, maybe a hundred pounds heavier than Ginger and a couple three inches taller.  A sister perhaps?  The sturdy brother joined her behind Ginger.  The judge seeing I was in good trustworthy hands (After all, Ginger's brother had a California Highway Patrol uniform on.) took his leave to process the detained cousins.

Ginger gestured toward her siblings. "Curtis, this is my little sister Penelope ["Little" was exactly the wrong description for the towering, statuesque, voluptuous raven-haired splendor.] and my baby brother Carl.  Penelope is living with me now."  Ginger seemed tenderly proud of her siblings.  "Anyway, so Carl helped us find you through your phone answering service.  He tracked the last call.  We came to the police station and court house this morning first thing to organize a search for you.  And lo and behold there you were in a marriage ceremony.  I just knew that couldn't be right."

Slowly the seriousness of my dire close call dawned on me. "Thank you, Ginger. It seems like you guys probably saved my life."

"All in a day's worked." Carl sure was a cheerful fellow.

"Oh, you poor boy." The Penelope seemed like she might be about to cry – it would be a shame to get those long dark eyelashes all wet, I thought.

"He's OK now." Apparently Ginger needed to reassure Penelope. Then Ginger had all her attention fully back on me. "What do you need, Curtis? Can we give you a ride home?"

"What about my van?"

Carl seemed to know procedures. "Let's give the local police a day to check out all the details back at Jorgenson house. I can pick your van up for you tomorrow."

"Really? Thanks Carl. I'm really tired. They wouldn't let me sleep. They just kept sitting on me and sitting on me, squishing and smothering me all night long. And the day before, several times, they sat on my face until I went unconscious." Suddenly I felt embarrassed and ashamed, recalling how much I also liked it.

Ginger stood offering me her hand. "Curtis it wasn't your fault." We walked toward the front exit. "Once, before I got married, it was a night I admit I was a bit high, and anyway I accidentally sat on this guy's face until he passed out. After that he constantly pestered me for another date. Surely something about a smothering facesit must be addictive – some kind of ultimate dominance thing."

"Sounds like they were also testing you, maybe timing how long it would take to smother you to death." Carl's analysis gave me the shivers.

"But let us take you home now." Ginger could see I needed a change of subject. "Carl can drive. And you can sit by me in the back seat."

"That'd be nice. But I don't think I want to be alone either."

"You want to stay at my place? Penelope and I share the big bed now. You could have the couch." We were outside now on a bright sunny morning, just a little cooler than the day before. I recognized Ginger's baby blue caddie in a diagonal parking slot.

"I hate to say it," I was worried I'd sound ungrateful. "But the couch sounds too lonely."

"He could sleep in the big bed with us." Penelope kindly suggested in her cute girly voice. "Right in the middle, between us, where he will be nice and safe."

I looked up at Ginger, hopeful.

"Well it's settled then."  She smiled and guided me into the back seat of her car.  I scooted over to let her in beside me.

Right away I rather keeled over, my head on Ginger's lap.  As soon as Carl started the car I felt so sleepy.  Ginger combed through my hair with her long, sharp fingernails.  And quickly I drifted to dream land with the soft caresses.

The curved gutter bump into Ginger's driveway woke me.  It must have been fifty minutes later.  I sat up and looked out at the neighborhood.  It had only been a day and a half, but it felt like I had been absent for weeks.

"OK, everybody, we're here."  Carl announced, pulling on the parking brake and cutting the engine.  We all piled out.

"Curtis, why don't you just come on inside my house.  We can go over to get some of your things later."  Ginger read me well.

"That sounds good." Came my groggy response.

"Hey everybody, I've got a few stops and a kids' baseball game to make it to.  After all, I am the coach; so I should be there."  Carl took a step down the drive way; then he turned to me.  "You are in good hands, Curtis.  My sisters, and I could be biased, are the sweetest gals you will ever find.  Plus, they'll see you are safe, for sure.  They kicked butt on more than few bullies when I was a kid.  And hell, they're a lot bigger now – right, *big* sisters?"

That got some groans from Ginger and Penelope, plus Ginger's, "Don't make us kick your butt for that wise crack."

Ignoring them, Carl reached over and patted my back, not too hard.  "Hey, let's you and I take an afternoon sometime soon and go up in the hills and do some lake fishing.  We can take my boat."

"Sounds good."  Actually nobody had ever invited me to go fishing before, and I had always wanted to do it – but I didn't know anything about hooks and reels and bait…

"Maybe you guys could put that out about three weeks."  Ginger had another agenda.  "Cause in two and a half weeks Curtis has to go to a big party in Hollywood.  I'm thinking it might take all that time to get him convinced and ready to go.  Penelope and I might just have to take him there ourselves."

Carl, laughing, said good-bye and jogged down the driveway and up the sidewalk to his parked CHP cruiser.  As he pulled out he gave his siren the briefest of toots and waved out his open window and over the top of his cab at us.  I turned and followed Ginger into her house, the lovely Penelope right behind me.

Inside the house felt nice and cool.  Ginger still expressed concern for me.

"So, Curtis, I'll bet you're still sleepy.  Want anything to eat though?"

"Nah, just a place to lie down."

"Well, come on in the bedroom.  After all, you know where it is."  Ginger had the slightest hint of suggestion in her voice.  But I could tell she remained very sensitive to my ordeal.

I hoisted up and sat on the edge of the bed.  First I pulled off my shoes then unbuttoned and took off my shirt.  I skootched over to the center of the (unmade) bed and found a smaller pillow, suitable to prop my head as I lie down on my side.  Ginger sat on the bed, gentle and patient.

"Is there anything else I could get for you?"

"Do you have a minute to lie next to me?"

"Well, sure – maybe until you go to sleep."  Ginger nabbed a couple of pillows and placed then next to mine.  Then she rested her head on them, and we were face to face.  Her big body, straight until her legs curled around, her upper legs under my feet, protecting me on two sides.

"Anything else?"  Ginger's big winning smile warmed my heart.

Suddenly a desperate feeling came over me.  I felt so vulnerable, alone, and weirdly isolated.  "I can't stand it, Ginger.  I am so filled with longing and desires now."  My voice lowered to a whisper of shame.  "Could you… would you… oh God I'm a freak – and you are so perfect, Ginger, please, please, could sit on me and squish me; let me kiss you like you did before, only, I just want you to smother me with…?"

"My pussy?  My great big beautiful ass?" Ginger responded without judgement of me or any revulsion at my pitiful request. "Oh Curtis, I don't think that's a good idea right this minute, I mean, given all you've gone through.  Don't get me wrong.  It sounds like really good fun.  And I would very much love to feel you loving me, kissing me, and servicing me under my pussy, and yes, even my ass.  It was feeling quite excellent the other night."  Her complement bolstered my non-existent confidence.  "But let's just give it a little time.  Would that be all right?"

"Of course."  My eyes looked down, not able to meet hers in the moment. "Thank you, Ginger, for being so understanding.  I – er… ah jeezz… I just feel like such a pervert.  Honestly, what's wrong with me and these, these, well, these submissive desires I have?"

"Curtis, as near as I can figure, nobody can do anything about their sexual desires.  They got these camps where they send gay youth to try to make them un-gay.  They absolutely don't work.  Sexual desires are in the body.  You'd probably have to get a new body to change them.  I think some desires, proclivities you might say, we are born with.  And some get put into us, by our own volition; but all too often by someone else.  For sure it can happen at a very young age, way before someone even knows they are sexual at all."

What Ginger said struck me very personally.  Something about it, about me, made a little more sense.  "It can also happen at an adult age.  In fact, I think it just happened to me yesterday and last night.  I don't know how I'll ever be the same again."  I couldn't bring my eyes back to look at Ginger anymore.  "It just felt so incredibly good."

"And?"  She prompted me, and with her index finder under my chin, her sharp nail insisting I look her in the eye.

I continued, slightly less ashamed.  "And it was feeling super incredibly good with you, too.  In fact it felt so good it made me afraid.  I hid from you when you came over night before last."  I got that off my chest.

"I know, Curtis.  That's okay.  Don't worry about it.  I hope you keep getting to know me better.  You'll find out that I am basically a very patient woman."  Ginger sure looked beautiful right now.

"And if you get to know me better, you'll find I'm a very persistent man."  I wanted to make a case for myself with her.

"Oh goodie."  Ginger put a hand to her big breasts.  "Patience and persistence: that combo can move mountains."  She laughed.

"I think I want to move those mountains."  I nodded toward her hand over her breasts.

"Maybe a little later, Tiger."  Ginger narrowed her gaze on me.  "Right now, dearie, let's have you take a few nice deep breaths and just relax, safe and sound."

As I smiled thinking about Ginger's kind validation of my desires, Penelope peeked in the doorway with a timid and quiet, "Everybody doing all right in here?"

"Oh, Penelope," Ginger sounded very pleased her sister showed up at the door.  "Come on in and complete this fort from the other side.  I'm thinking Curtis needs our complete protection right now."

Penelope walked around and I felt the bed yield to her mass as she climbed on and scooted over close behind me.  She smelled good, flowery and sweet.  And Ginger was right; the surrounding by a fort of these two sisters felt very comforting to me.  I burrowed down a little off my pillow and pressed my face softly into Ginger's big full bosom.  Penelope pressed the generous same against my back.  In two more deep breaths in that blissful, peaceful state, I sighed and fell into a sleep perhaps better than I'd had in years.

***

I awoke, opened my eyes, and found myself staring up through the hammock's diamond shapes at a glorious Bluebelle Valley pink and lavender sunset.  I sat up and looked around at about a dozen sleeping Amazon wives.  I guess more of them had come along and figured a way to join us in the drama in 1950's suburban California.  Oh yeah, there's Aria sleeping amongst them – she would know how to get the whole passel of them through the Window of Light and to the other side.  I wondered which one of them played the part of Nellie….

Well, as I always say.  "Let sleeping Amazons lie."  And up into the trees I climbed; the going rather dim at first.  Then higher and higher I ascended until finally at the tip top I could see from horizon to horizon the full sunset, with all its glorious shades of reds and oranges and violets and far back to the northeast, the deepening indigo.  I floated up from the highest branches and gazed, still dreamy, at the darkness of the hills beneath the sunset, no artificial lights in this new quiet world to betray the distance of those hills.

The jagged line along the hills' ridge seemed like a crack against the inside of an earth-size rosy eggshell.  In that moment it seemed that the mountains themselves were like the void, as if under that crack in the pale dimming sky I could look right into the darkness of space.

I shivered and smiled to myself as the beautiful night gloom slowly took the rest of the light.  Fireflies, which had died out some twenty years ago, had returned to re-inhabit these woodlands, and worked their delightful magic at the edge of the meadow below.  I smiled down, like a goof that I would always be, at their festive little light show.

Coincident in that moment of charm I felt the gentle request for intimate attention from deep in the black woods to the south end of the vast estate.  The entreaty came as a message direct into my mind, like the most pleasant memory you could imagine.  Serenity, the largest of my wives, fortified her gentle demand with her opulent spicy cinnamon-clove scent of pheromones absolutely irresistible to mortal men, now assailing my senses on the evening breeze.  My goodness, did my forty foot tall beauty have an amorous intent this evening!  And no doubt, Serenity's giantess entourage of Ginny and Maya, and the reliably and delightfully dangerous Keisha, would want to join in the fun.  So, being a dutiful husband, I drifted away from the treetops, floating through the early evening air with my conjugal intent, like a descending cool breeze, gentle and capricious in my slope.  I allowed into my body a tiny imprint of gravity and rode it silently down a most gradual slope toward the back-forest magical nethers, so richly fresh, hidden away, and deliciously mysterious in the deepening starlight.

"Hey there, good lookin'.  So sorry Richie couldn't make it up here to say good-bye. But my little blue-flame fire-man is kind of indisposed, making a 'house call' you could say… ahhh, mmmm-mmmm.  Anyway, he wanted me to thank you for enjoying his stories.  What did he say now, oh yes: 'in the good fun as they were intended.'  If you really appreciate my tiny husband Richie's well-written, humorous, sexy, and yes, romantic stories then, by all means, post us a review, sweetie.  I've got an idea: come on down; join us yourself, baby – we don't bite – but we do swallow.  Ha, who knows, maybe I'll write a story sometime and make you the star….  As Richie always says, 'We are only limited by our imaginations.'  Better look for more stories in the next sets of series: <u>Bluebelle Giantess Fancies,</u>  <u>Mini Giantess Proclivities,</u> <u>Amazon Absoption,</u> and more to come.  You'll have to excuse me now.  I need to make an adjustment, just maybe let my smushed little darling breathe.  Daisy Strickland, Bluebelle Valley

Sex really ought to be glorious and fun, don't you agree?  If you find your sex life/love life has become unmanageable, really to the point of being too much of a distraction or being dishonest and truly messing up your relationships, particularly the key relationship with yourself – know that there is help.  You can find it with very little effort; honest, free, available help awaits those who seek.  It is as easy as walking into a room.  I'll say no more about it because the policy is attraction rather than promotion.  *R.B. Greenfield*

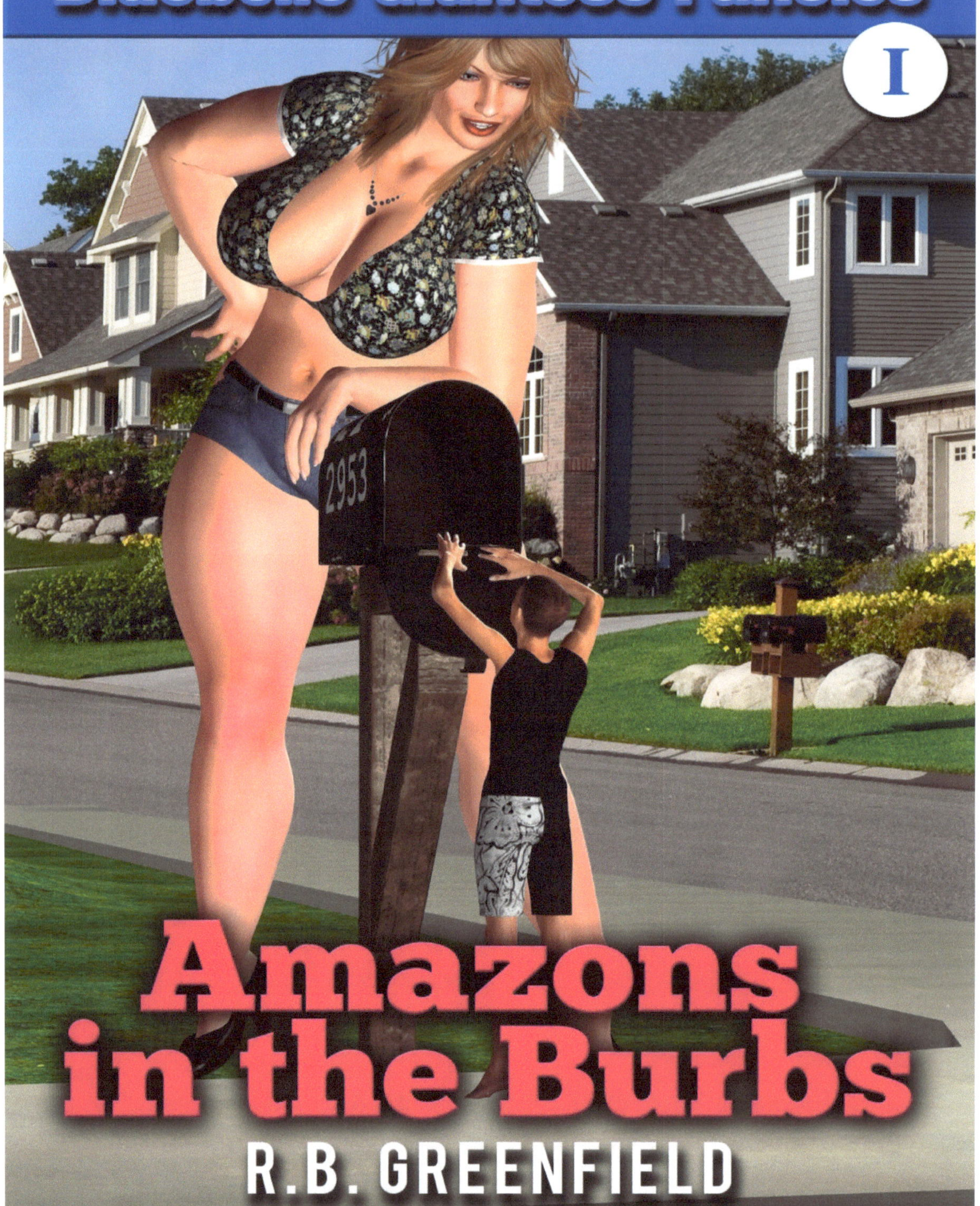

Bluebelle Giantess Fancies
I
2953
Amazons
in the Burbs
R.B. GREENFIELD

www.ingramcontent.com/pod-product-compliance
Lightning Source LLC
Chambersburg PA
CBHW041133100726
47911CB00003B/118